*She Corr* ◁ SO-CAZ-890

*Who Touched Her*

There was Rodney Schneider, the sardonic young blood who seduced Fanny, then debased her, and lived to feel her vengeance . . . Norma, the society girl whom Fanny allowed to give her pleasure, and repaid in torment . . . Beau Dan, the most celebrated pimp in Storyville, who thought to add Fanny to his stable, only to be reduced to being her paid stud and her hopeless slave . . . Oliver Prescott, the superbly virile planter who made the mistake of conquering Fanny physically, the one sin she could not forgive. . . .

And above all, there was the proud and handsome French Creole aristocrat, Philippe Sompayac, the one man whom Fanny could not help loving . . . the man she had to have, even if it meant destroying them both. . . .

"Yerby knows and writes about sex better than any living writer. . . . With *The Girl from Storyville*, I nominate Frank Yerby for the Pulitzer Prize in first-class, original American fiction. And to the best seller list." —*Cleveland Press*

# The Girl from Storyville

*A Victorian Novel*

# Frank Yerby

A DELL BOOK

Published by
DELL PUBLISHING CO., INC.
1 Dag Hammarskjold Plaza
New York, New York 10017

Printed in Canada

First Dell printing—February 1975

This work is dedicated
—and fondly—
to all the literary Whores With Hearts of Gold,
from de Maupassant's Boule de Suif,
and Dostoevsky's Sonia to the present,
since they prove that the retention of
a pure and childlike innocence is sometimes possible
in even the greatest minds

BE IT ORDAINED, by the Common Council of the City of New Orleans, That Section 1, of Ordinance 13,032 C.S., Be, and the same is hereby amended as follows: From and after the First of October, 1897, it shall be unlawful for any prostitute or woman notoriously abandoned to lewdness, to occupy, inhabit, live, or sleep, in any house, room, or closet, situated without the following limits, viz:

From the South side of Customhouse Street to the North side of St. Louis Street, and from the lower or wood side of North Basin Street to the lower or wood side of Robertson Street;

2nd:—And from the upper side of Perdido Street to the lower side of Gravier Street, and from the river side of Franklin Street to the lower, or wood side of Locust Street, provided that nothing herein shall be construed as to authorize any lewd woman to occupy a house, room, or closet in any portion of the city.

The above is the final form of the ordinance introduced in the New Orleans City Council by Alderman Sidney Story, on July 6, 1897, thereby—to his great disgust—giving his name to Storyville, the biggest Red Light district in the history of the United States of North America, if not in the entire world, for it consisted of thirty-eight solid blocks in which *every* house was a brothel, a house of assignation, a cancan saloon, a pretty waiter girl bar, or a dance hall offering hostesses paid by the dance. Lest the reader be deceived—or relieved—by the inclusion of the last three categories, be it noted that all their female employees (and some of the males) were part-time prostitutes.

To those readers unfamiliar with New Orleans, it should be pointed out that all the streets in the second paragraph of Alderman Story's ordinance are, or were, in the French Quarter; for neither Customhouse, nor Basin—the late, great Louis Armstrong's immortal "Basin Street Blues" to the contrary—now exist; while all those in the third paragraph are, or were, in the American Section.

# A Word to the Reader

The writer, for what seem to him several plausible, if not completely justifiable reasons, has subtitled this work a "Victorian" novel. The first, and most obvious reason is that the events it depicts took place mainly between 1895 and 1903, which were the final six years of Victoria's reign, and the first two of the post-Victorian epoch. During these years, the influence of Her Gracious Majesty upon manners, morals, habits of thought, continued to be, throughout the English-speaking portions of the world, at least as strong as it had been in the previous half century, which is to say, to all extents and purposes, overwhelming.

The second is that its subject, the "fallen" woman, and her—in those days—inevitable descent into prostitution, used here, your writer confesses, to carry the rather more profound theme which really interests him, is peculiarly Victorian. In a world where no woman ever "falls" anymore (largely because with all our excruciatingly joyless Pre/Extra/Post-Marital and/or Group Sex, she hasn't even time to get up; and falling from a prone position appears to this weary and bemused old writer quite a trick indeed) the very conception strikes us as quaint; but to a maiden of the epoch, letting her heart (read certain little mindless and hyperactive glands) get ahead of her head was a one-way ticket from tragedy to disaster, with stops at every local station in between. In any event, to the question of subject matter as opposed to theme, he will return a little later on.

Actually, however, among the more seductive reasons for writing a "Victorian" novel so long after the epoch, are certain techniques, now sadly—and foolishly—abandoned, that were the virtual hallmarks of the great Victorians, and which, besides being marvelously appropriate to both subject matter and theme, have the additional appeal of allowing the writer to keep a degree of control over his material which is simply not possible in any other way.

For the Victorian novelist enjoyed certain and most enviable privileges: he was omniscient (and also omnipotent, which doesn't concern us here); he didn't bother to play games with himself under the guise of artistic discipline, such as pretending that he doesn't know what his characters are going to do next, what they think, and what their ultimate destinies will be. Because, strictly speaking, if you aren't omniscient, you can only write in the first person, or eliminate the interior monologue altogether. "I thought," is perfectly legitimate even to your modern, self-limiting novelist; but "he thought" is cheating. You *never* know what he thought unless he tells you, and nine times out of ten he's lying, bragging, editing his thought for public consumption, or concealing the all-too-frequent fact that he is woefully incapable of cerebration anyhow. But the elimination of the interior monologue plays havoc with literary economy, forcing the novelist into all sorts of circumlocution, and more or less dishonest substitutions for it, using pages to do, less effectively, what "he thought" can do in a line. Which is why the Victorian novelists' calmly assumed omniscience is such a blessed relief.

Another advantage enjoyed by the Victorian novelist was his perfect willingness to speak in his own voice, to explain, clarify, predict, comment, thus saving his readers pages and pages of weary plodding through set piece scenes designed to do the same thing, but oh so subtly, oh so cleverly that they set all this incurably irreverent writer's built-in detectors of the deadly vapors emanating from bovine or equine excretia to ringing at the same time.

The greatest single privilege granted the Victorian novelist (and during the murderous labor of writing this work, it became increasingly clear just how great a privilege it was) is the only one that this writer has *not* availed himself of, by which he means the great Victorians' flat refusal to write any detail, action, or event that might offend their own or their readers' sensibilities, keeping on hand a red plush Curtain of Charity (that most marvelous, and unjustly outlawed literary device!) to draw, as they quaintly put it, over the ensuing scene. For,

if the initials of "For Unlawful Carnal Knowledge"* with
that gerundive "ing" added spell out what is admittedly a
fine and pleasant activity when indulged in properly, i.e.,
with respect for your partner, some degree of tenderness,
love; the act, itself, however described, despite whatever
skill at imagery, command of language, purity of style the
writer may possess, by its very nature seems always to
move out of context in the literary sense, taking on an
emphasis (unintentional, even unwarranted though it be)
that inevitably halts the flow of the narrative, making of
the scene in question an end instead of a means. That,
against his own (sturdily mid-Victorian) inclinations, this
writer has not employed his forebears' charmingly archaic
curtain, nor any other evasion of hairy, naked, sweaty or
otherwise malodorous and unlovely truth is due to the
simple fact that after many, many attempts (the rejected
pages from this novel weighed eight kilos, seven hundred
and fifty grams) none of the alternate methods he devised
to substitute for his reluctant inclusion of the sexual
manifestations of his female protagonist's wounded mind,
her crippled spirit, her maimed self-respect, proved convincing enough to illuminate the depths, and the horror,
of her increasingly irreversible psychosis with the almost
brutal clarity they had to in order to render believeable a
theme of this profundity, or a novel of this quality.

To the legions of dear, sweet ladies who without fail
write him every time he publishes a new work (for Victorianism and Puritanism are both alive and well in the
U.S.A. even at this late, late date) taking him to task for
his use of "obscene" language, and demanding that he return to their beloved (and wholly mythical) antebellum
South for his themes, this writer offers his most humble
apologies. If he could have done this aspect of his novel
another way, he would have. Truthfully, he would be far
happier if the aforementioned ladies—whom he genuinely
admires and respects, for his own mother, his aunts, and
his sister, while they lived, were numbered among them

---

*This is the phrase that the Medieval English bailiffs used when
booking the local daughters of commercial joy. And the trouble
started, not when they got tired of writing the whole thing out,
but rather when, with really excessive sloth, they left out the
periods after the initials as well, thus coining the twentieth
century's favorite word.

—wouldn't read this novel at all. But sad experience has taught him that short of using a pseudonym there is no way of preventing readers addicted to his lighter, more pleasant efforts from diving into a work in many ways beyond their intellectual and spiritual depths; it is very hard for the comparatively sheltered, who have not experienced it, to accept, or even believe in, hell. To them, he can only say he is sorry; but it would be too great a concession to the limitations of public taste for him to issue over a nom de plume a novel of which, in sober fact, he has legitimate reasons to be proud.

Yet, despite this, he hopes to find readers sufficiently thoughtful to realize that nowhere in this work are Fanny's sexual activities employed to titillate, or shock, or even as a commercial device, but simply as symbolic markers pointing out the steepness of the incline at each crucial point along her private road to damnation.

Enough! To bring this perhaps too technical discussion to a close, this writer confesses that he has, with joy, with delight, availed himself of all he could manage of the above-mentioned literary devices which were some of the reasons that the Victorians wrote great novels, and their descendants largely haven't.

All the other reasons for his choice were philosophical, and these were the most potent of all. The Victorians believed in Man. In this Age of Aquarius (which should be named, more justly, the Age of the Lemmings, since to abdict from rationality, responsibility, thought, is ultimately suicidal; not to mention that to substitute revolution for evolution, and to import political systems that are demonstrably miserable failures in their countries of origin is more immediately so) one reads novel after novel in which the protagonist is ineffectual, idiotic, cowardly, comical—and a lousy lover. The Victorians (except, probably, for that last, because they learned sex from whores which was like training one's taste for music at a rock festival, and for food at a hamburger stand) were none of these. They had, very truly, dignity, authority, responsibility, and the power to think. Even their taste wasn't as bad as we like to think it was. The world will one day discover that many of their objets d'art were rather charming. Hence they make marvelous subjects for the novelist. He can respect them, and, because he does, write of them with dignity, with love.

And, finally, philosophically, the Victorians were not afraid of the big, meaningful themes. This writer hereby takes his oath, and solemnly swears that the theme of this Victorian novel is Evil, with a capital E; and that he has carefully developed the right questions about said theme, whose answers, of course, he doesn't even pretend to know, through the character of a damned soul. A female damned soul. A woman.

Herein, he hopes, instead of the usual writer's wish— fulfillment psychosis dream of fair women, or even its opposite, your emotional castrate's hysterical shriek of vengeance against those women, (his mother/his wife) who gave him what he jolly well had coming to him for being what he was—you will find a woman. A poor, tortured, tormented, vengeful, vile, tender, loving, good, evil, vicious, terrible, pitiful woman. Even a lovable one, if your love includes the elements of compassion, charity. As inconsistent, as contradictory, as life. He hopes, too, that you will love and hate her simultaneously, as men do women who are persons, and therefore, real.

And now, at long, long last to return to the subject matter, as opposed to the theme, i.e., Prostitution as a vehicle to carry the real theme of Evil, of man's sickening inhumanity to man, your writer is sure that you, Reader—Post, Neo, or Anti-Victorian, will find herein, even in this, the exercise of understanding and pity, for all the humiliated, the offended, and the damned, by which he means those who pretend to purvey, as well as those who delude themselves into believing that they purchase what essentially can never be bought or sold.

November 27, 1971


*A Word to the Critics*
This is a novel; not an entertainment.

# Chapter One

On the morning after her birthday—she had got to be eight years old yesterday; "A real big girl," Poppa said—Fanny felt the warm wetness and woke up. Then she started to cry, but not very loud, because she didn't want Martha to hear her. She knew that if Martha heard her crying, she'd come into the room, yank all the covers off, and bend down to see if Fanny had wet the bed again. And Fanny had.

Of course Martha—"I won't call her Mummy! I won't!" Fanny said under her breath, tasting the bad, salty taste of crying—would find it out later anyhow, and tell Poppa when he came home, and Poppa would take Fanny across his knees face down and paddle her bottom with the hairbrush.

That hurt. It hurt something awful and in two ways: Not only did it make her bottom so red and sore that she couldn't sit down, even on a pillow, to eat her supper, but it also broke her heart, because it proved to her—again—that her Poppa didn't love her anymore.

Lying there in the sopping wet bed, Fanny tried to figure out just when it was that Poppa had stopped loving her. She reckoned it must have been the day after he'd had that terrible fight with Mummy, both of them yelling and throwing things and calling each other names. Because when the next morning Poppa had told her that Mummy wasn't going to live with them anymore, Fanny had asked him some things that she hadn't ought to, and made him almost as mad as Mummy had the night before. Of course, she'd been only five years old then, but Poppa didn't even stop to think of that.

"Poppa, where's Mummy gone?" she'd asked him first. And he'd looked out the window and said real quiet-like, "To hell."

"Where's hell, Poppa?" Fanny said.

"Oh, skip it, Babydoll," Poppa said.

Fanny liked for him to call her Babydoll. It showed he loved her. Poppa was very tall and strong. He had green eyes and red hair. People were afraid of Poppa because he was a policeman. Only he didn't dress like a policeman; he dressed just like everybody else. The reason he dressed like everybody else was because he was a detective. A lieutenant detective in the Shreveport Police Force. Of course, when she was only five years old, Fanny hadn't known exactly what a detective was, and to tell the truth, she still didn't know, although she was now a big girl eight years old; but if her Poppa was a detective, then a detective was a mighty fine thing to be, because her Poppa was just about the sweetest and prettiest man in the whole wide world. But once, when she'd told him that, he'd said:

"Men aren't pretty, Babydoll. Girls are pretty. You're pretty, 'n so is Mummy. But I'm as homely as snakebit hounddog baying the moon down by Bitter Creek."

Fanny hadn't understood any of that, but she'd liked the way Poppa's voice had sounded saying it. Only that was before he 'n Mummy had had that fight and Mummy had gone away.

But maybe it had been then that he'd stopped loving her, because that was the first time he'd hit her, Fanny, in her whole life. And all because she'd said a bad word. Only she didn't know it was a bad word, then. It had stuck in her head because Poppa had called Mummy that two dozen times while they'd been fighting. So she asked him:

"Poppa, what's a 'hore?"

Then Poppa slapped her so hard it made her see stars, and caught her by the shoulders and shook her 'til her teeth rattled, and clenched his own teeth together and hissed at her:

"Don't you *ever* say that word again!"

And she hadn't, even though she still didn't know what a 'hore was. Except once. Except the time she called Martha that.

But, later on, Poppa had stopped being mad at her. In fact, he'd tried every way he could to make up to her for not having a Mummy anymore. Every time he came home he brought her candy and toys, and took her on his knees and squeezed her and tickled her and kissed her until she was squiriming and squealing from how good loving Poppa made her feel.

"I do declare, Mister Bill," said Eliza, the old nigger woman who took care of Fanny when Poppa wasn't home—which was most of the time, since whatever it was that detectives did kept him away all day and most of the night—"you's purely spoiling that child rotten, I do declare you is!"

Then he had to go and ruin everything. Part of ruining it had to do with something Fanny heard Eliza say to Poppa outside in the hall. It was very late, and Fanny should have been asleep, but she wasn't.

"When you catch 'em, Mister Bill," Eliza said, "don't you go and shoot, sir! Fool trashy woman like that 'un ain't worth goin' to jail over. You git yourself some witnesses and then you marches down to the Co'thouse and ax the Judge for a bill of divorcement. That's the smart way to do it, sir . . ."

"Reckon," Poppa said in the voice he used when he was making like he was mad, but really wasn't, "that there's no way on earth to keep a nigger housemaid from poking her flat nose into her whitefolks' business, is there, Eliza?"

"Nosir!" Eliza laughed. "Not no way a'tall, Mister Bill! 'Sides I got my baby's interest at heart. You git shut of that poor white trash you never oughten to even looked at, let alone git yourself married to, and you can marry yourself a good-family young white lady—real quality for a fact!"

"In the first place," Poppa said, "Maebelle isn't hill trash, Eliza. She's English. Comes from Liverpool."

"Then just let me ax you one thing, Mister Bill," Eliza said. "Whoever told you they don't breed no poor white trash over there?"

"Reckon you've got a point at that, Eliza," Poppa said. "Still—"

"Still my baby needs herself a Ma! I does all I can, sir; but I'm a old woman, and I ain't white. 'Sides I'm too ignorant to teach that child all the things a young lady in her position is got to learn. Never did work for no 'ristocratic folks—afore you, sir, that is—"

"I'm not an aristocrat, Eliza," Poppa said. "Who the

hell ever heard of an aristocratic policeman?"

"You ain't no policeman, Mister Bill; you's a detective. That's different. And you talks and dresses like quality. But anyhow, like I said, I ain't never worked for them rich high class folks downstate, so I ain't never had no chance to learn all the highfalutin' airs houseniggers in their houses gits to know. I can't teach my baby right. I plumb downright can't."

Poppa had laughed a little then, as if he'd kind of liked what Eliza was saying.

"All right, 'Liza," he said, "I just might take your advice at that . . ."

"You do that, sir, and you won't be sorry," Eliza said.

It wasn't long after that that Poppa came home with a big piece of yellow-white paper in his hands. It had writing all over it, and a mashed flat piece of red wax that stuck a red ribbon to it. Poppa showed it to Eliza, for all that Eliza couldn't read, and said:

"This is it, 'Liza. The judge got himself mixed up with ol' Abe Lincoln 'n set this poor child free!"

"Praise the Lord!" Eliza said.

"Funny thing. Mae didn't even contest custody of Fanny. Reckon she thought the kid would be a hold-back—or else she didn't dare, seeing as how I had three witnesses with me, and a search warrant to make it legal, when we broke into that place and caught 'em in flagrante—"

"What's 'in flagrante," Mister Bill?" Eliza said.

"It's Latin," Poppa said, "and I don't even need to tell you what it means. An evil-minded old witch like you can figure that out for herself!"

"Hmmmmn," Eliza said, "then I reckon hit means mother-nekkid 'n making bedspring music, don't hit, Mister Bill?"

"Yes," Poppa said, and his voice changed all of a sudden, went cold and—and like he was feeling sick, Fanny decided—"that's it, 'Liza, damn her wicked soul to hell!"

But after that it was all right, for a good long time. Then it stopped being all right, and Fanny lay there in a pool of her own pee-pee that was getting cold now, and felt awful, and thought that it would never get to be all right again.

Because the next thing that had happened was that Poppa went all the way up to New York City and stayed there for a whole month and when he finally came back he was leading Martha by the hand. About four or five years after that, Eliza told Fanny that Poppa had known Martha before he'd even met Mummy, while he was in law school in New York, and that he'd been engaged to marry her, "When your Ma come along 'n broke 'em up, and even made poor Mister Bill quit law school, so that he had to come back down here 'n pound a beat like his Pa afore him, 'stead o' gittin' to be a rich, respectable law-yerman. Mighty wicked li'l ol' gal, your Ma, child!"

But on that bad, awful day she'd never forget as long as she lived, Poppa stood there holding Martha by the hand, and grinning at Fanny as though he was sorta 'shamed of himself.

"This is your new Mummy, Babydoll," he said.

Fanny didn't say anything. She stood there looking at Martha. Martha was little and slim and pretty. She had black hair instead of yellow the way Mummy's had been. She was dressed nice, too, and she smelled real good. But none of that made any difference to Fanny.

Martha put out her arms to her.

"Come here, Fanny, and kiss me," she said.

Fanny put both of her fat little arms behind her back.

"No," she said, "I won't!"

"Why not, child?" Martha said.

"'Cause you're not my Mummy and—and I hate you!" Fanny said and ran out of the room.

"Fanny!" Poppa said, very loud, and started after her. But then she heard Martha saying real soft and sweet-like:

"No, Bill—let her go. If you punish her now, I'll never win her over. She's still a baby—a little over six years old, isn't she, darling? And—and her reaction's natural, I guess. Let me do it my way. . . ."

"All right, honey," Poppa said, but he still sounded mad. "All the same that blamed kid's got no right—"

"On the contrary, she has every right, dearest. It was her home first," Martha said.

That night, Poppa and Eliza, between them, moved

Fanny's bed out of Poppa's bedroom. She had slept there, next to his big bed, ever since Mama had gone away. When Fanny saw that, she threw herself down on the floor and kicked and screamed and acted like a very bad little girl indeed. But when Poppa started to grab her by the arm, Martha stopped him again.

"No, darling; we must be patient," she said.

And they had been—Martha more than Poppa—for a long time. Two or three months, maybe. But nothing could change Fanny's mind; she wasn't even fixing to start to like Martha, let alone call her Mummy. 'Cause Martha wasn't her Mummy, and she could never be.

For one thing, she could be mean. She stopped Poppa from bringing Fanny candy, saying it would ruin her teeth. And she made Fanny bathe all over every day instead of only on Saturday night the way Mummy had. Of course Fanny kicked and screamed—"Like a jenny," Poppa said—every time Martha started to bathe her, and the soap got in her eyes and up her nose and nearly choked her to death. But Martha wouldn't quit it.

"You can't have a girl child smelling of sweat and urine, Bill!" she said. "You simply can't!"

Afterwards, when Fanny asked Eliza what a jenny was and Eliza laughed and said it was a lady donkey, Fanny hated Martha more than ever for making her Poppa call her that.

It wasn't long after that that Fanny started to wake up in the middle of the night. The first two or three times she didn't know what it was that had waked her up, so she went right back to sleep again. But the next time she waked all the way up and knew that even in her sleep she'd heard a noise. It had bumping in it, and squeaking, and a sound like the one that Spot—the speckled dog who had followed Fanny home one day and whom Martha wouldn't let her keep—had made because it was very hot that day, with his tongue hanging down and dripping spit and his breath coming out of his mouth real fast.

Then Fanny heard her stepmama's voice. Martha was —well moaning and groaning like the niggers did in that nigger church Eliza had taken her to one Sunday when Poppa had shouted, "For God sakes, 'Liza, get that child out of my sight!"—only not so loud. Real soft like as if

something was hurting her, but not too bad. Then she started to say Poppa's name with O in front of it, running
the O's and the name all together so it sounded like
"OBillOBillOBillO!"

That was when Fanny got out of bed. She wasn't
scared. She didn't even know what it meant to be scared
because having a Poppa like hers, she'd never had reason
to be. She wasn't even scared of that filthy old Mister
Jacob Fields that all the girls ran from when he came
down the street they were playing in. Besides Mister
Fields was nice in spite of being old and whiskery and
filthy dirty and smelling something awful. He gave Fanny
candy. And he told Fanny he would give her lots more if
she would come to his house. Only his house was too far.
Fanny and Poppa and Martha and Eliza lived on Fannin
Street and Mister Fields lived way out on Market Street
almost to Greenwood Cemetery, so Fanny wouldn't go because it would take her too long to get back home again,
and Martha would fuss at her.

So now she went out in the dark hall and stopped in
front of Poppa's door. Martha was still saying OBillOBill-
OBillO but louder now, and all the noises were louder
too, especially the dogbreathing noise. Then Fanny
pushed open the door and saw them. They were wrestling,
and Poppa was winning 'cause he was on top. Only Fanny
had never seen people take off all their clothes to wrestle
before, and that made it even more interesting, so she
stood there and watched them a long time until Poppa
slammed himself down on Martha and she made a very
loud noise like she was dying. Then Fanny clapped her
hands and said:

"That's right, Poppa! Kill her! Bust her all to pieces!
She ain't nothing but a 'hore!"

Then they both turned their faces toward the door and
lay there all tangled up with each other and stared at
Fanny with their mouths and eyes opened wide, and then
Martha started to cry.

"I told you, Bill!" she said with her voice all broken up
and breathy. "I told you! She's not normal! She's not!
She's a little monster!"

Then Poppa untangled himself from Martha and came
toward Fanny and Fanny saw that he was pinkish white
and hairy all over and that he was made different from

the way little girls were. She thought that was the most interesting thing of all, but by then Poppa had got to her and caught her by the shoulder and shoved her out into the hall.

"I'll attend to you in the morning, young lady!" he said and slammed the door.

Inside Fanny could hear Martha crying and begging Poppa:

"Don't whip her, Bill! Please don't! It'll only fix this in her mind! Don't you see, darling, she'll forget otherwise; she's so young, so young . . ."

"She's her mother's own child," Poppa said, sounding madder than ever, "and I'll get that taint out of her, or beat her to death trying!"

"Please don't, Bill," Martha was saying; but Fanny ran back in her own room and shut the door, and got into her bed and stuck her head under the pillow so she couldn't hear anything anymore and cried herself to sleep.

And that next morning, for the first time in her life, her Poppa spanked her with the hairbrush. He spanked her a long time and very hard. And it turned out that Martha was right. Fanny never did forget.

It was after that that Martha stopped even trying to be nice to Fanny. She never spanked her, but she'd save up all the bad things Fanny had done all day long to tell Poppa when he came home, so there was a time that Fanny got spanked every night for more than two weeks and the soreness never had time to wear off before the hairbrush or Poppa's belt or even his razor strop came whistling down again.

What stopped that was that Martha got sick. She'd wake Fanny up every morning with the noise she made vomiting into the basin on the washstand in Poppa's room. And Poppa was being extra nice to Martha, all the time acting like he'd forgot Fanny was even there. It didn't take Fanny long to decide that it was better to have Poppa mad at her than this way, so she started being naughtier than ever.

Only it didn't do any good. Papa would simply yell for Eliza to "Get this bratty kid th' hell out of here!" and Fanny found herself walking all over Shreveport with Eliza, or playing with the colored kids of Eliza's friends.

Playing with them was fun at first, but it wasn't like being Poppa's big girl so she got tired of that, too.

By then, she began to notice that Martha was getting fat. But the funny part about it was that Martha only got fat in one place, her tummy, while the rest of her stayed as skinny as ever. By the time she'd got so she looked like she'd swallowed a watermelon whole, Fanny decided that she wasn't really getting fat but was only swelling up like a balloon. And that made Fanny feel real good, because she reckoned that when her stepmother got big enough, she'd burst just like a balloon and maybe die.

But it didn't happen like that. What happened was that one night Martha started crying very loud, and Poppa got up and ran down the stairs only half dressed and yelling back over his shoulder to Eliza to put some water on to boil. Then he ran out Fannin, the street they lived on, 'til he got to Pierre Avenue, and down that 'till he got to Milam Street and out Milam Street 'til he got to the house Dr. Thomas Mitchell lived in, so far out on Milam that it was practically in the country.

The funny part about it was that the livery stable where he kept his horse 'n buggy was on Travis Street only one block from home, so he didn't need to do all that running. But with Martha yelling like that he got so excited he forgot. Anyhow, Doctor Tom, as Eliza called Dr. Mitchell, brought Poppa back home in his own buggy, and even then they needn't have hurried 'cause Martha kept yelling all night long.

But just before morning she quit screeching "like two alley cats with their tails tied together and throwed over a clothesline to fight"—and another thing that Eliza always said—and Fanny sat up in bed and thought out loud: "She's dead. Her tummy's busted open and she's dead!" Then folding her hands together, Fanny looked up towards the ceiling and said a prayer:

"Oh Lord, please let Martha be dead so I can have my Poppa back!"

But even at seven and a half years old she realized that was a mighty wicked prayer, so she wasn't surprised when the Lord didn't answer it, although she kept on hoping He would until the next day when her Poppa took her into his room and pointed toward where Martha sat up in bed.

"Go meet your baby brother, Fanny," he said.

Fanny went up to the bed so slow that she was almost creeping. Then she saw what Martha had in her arms. It was a little red wrinkled thing that looked just like a monkey. It had black hair all over its head and its eyes were shut so tight Fanny couldn't see them. And the worst part about it was that Martha had slipped her nightgown down off her shoulder, and let a big fat white part of herself that was all streaked and crisscrossed with blue lines like spider webs hang out and the little monkey was biting it.

"Don't it hurt?" Fanny said.

"Not don't—doesn't," Martha said. "No, it doesn't. You see, Fanny, Billy hasn't any teeth yet."

"Well, Babydoll," Poppa said, "how d'you like your baby brother?"

"I hate him," Fanny said.

"Now just you look here, Missy!" Poppa started to say, but Martha looked at him and shook her head real slow-like.

Somehow or other, that made Fanny mad.

"I hate him!" she yelled. "I hate him! He's little 'n ugly 'n looks just like a monkey 'n—'n he bites!"

" 'Liza!" Poppa called out, and his voice sounded tired; "Will you come and take this unholy brat the hell out of here?"

And after that, it only got worse. Because Billy didn't keep on looking like a monkey. He got to be fat and happy and pretty and his eyes were open now so that Fanny could see they were green just like Poppa's even though Billy had black hair. What made it worse was that even Eliza forgot Fanny now. Poppa and Martha and Eliza and all Poppa's policemen and firemen friends and their wives all oohed and ahhed over little Billy and told Poppa that he'd done himself proud. " 'Course fillies is all right," one of the policemen said, "but a man's just nacherly got to have hisself a son, 'pears to me, Bill. Yessir, mighty fine thing to know the family's going to go on . . ."

"But a daughter's children are family, too," his wife said.

"Yep, reckon so. But they don't bear your *name*," the policeman said, "and that makes a mighty big difference. 'Sides, I just nacherly cotton to boys. Girl children now, you're always worried for fear some fast talking sport's going to put in a crop afore building a fence, and—"

"Why, Henry! How you do talk!" his wife said.

Everybody loved Billy, and nobody loved her, Fanny decided. The funny part about it was they went right on loving him even if he yelled himself blue in the face, burped up his milk, made pee-pee in his cradle and big stinky in his diapers. And there wasn't a thing Fanny could do about it, not a thing.

But it was then that she started doing what she hadn't done since she was three years old: she started wetting the bed. Only she didn't do it on purpose. It just happened. She'd sit on her potty for the longest time before going to bed, and the pee-pee just wouldn't come. But once she was in bed and fast asleep, it would just pour out of her all over everything. And the more Martha scolded her and the more Poppa spanked her, the worse it got. Eliza thought she knew why. And one night, outside in the hall, right in front of Fanny's door, she even argued with Poppa about it, a little. Of course they both thought Fanny was asleep. Only she wasn't.

"Mister Bill," Eliza said, "that there po' child is fair starvin' for a little affection. If you was to fuss over her 'n pet her like you used to do, she'd quit peeing in the bed. Don'cha see, sir, hit's her way o' tryin' to make you pay her some 'tention?"

Then Poppa said it, very quiet and slow and cold so that hearing his voice Fanny got goosebumps all over.

"I know that, 'Liza; but I can't. She reminds me too much of her Ma. Every day she gets to look more like Maebelle—and, much as I hate to admit it, that gets on my nerves. The truth is I can't stand the sight of her!"

And it had been only last night that he'd said that, after Fanny had been good all day long, and had eaten her ice cream and cake without making a mess or spilling a drop on her party dress and had taken the baby doll Poppa had given her for her birthday present and had kissed Martha on the cheek almost without feeling like she was going to throw up and had gone off to bed without anybody making her, not even Eliza.

So it wasn't any good. Nothing was. And it wasn't fair! It wasn't! Nobody ever spanked Billy no matter how bad he was. And now her bottom and the backs of her legs were stinging and getting chapped from the strong pee-pee she was lying in, and that reminded her that tonight she was going to get another spanking as sure as shooting, and it was all Billy's fault anyhow.

So then it came to her what to do. She got out of bed and tiptoed out into the hall. She pushed open the door to Poppa's room just a little, but enough to see Martha wasn't in it. Poppa wasn't either, but she'd known he wouldn't be, 'cause he had to go down to Headquarters every morning before she even woke up. So now Fanny pushed the door all the way open and went into the room. Then she started looking for Martha's sewing basket; but she couldn't find it, because Martha was sitting in the kitchen talking to Eliza and mending things at the same time. So Fanny didn't have anything to do what she wanted to with. But then she saw Martha's little manicure set and opened it. First she took out Martha's fingernail file, but when she touched it she decided it was too dull. So she took out the little bent scissors that Martha used to cut her fingernails before she filed them, and felt the two curving little blades. They were plenty sharp. Only they were so little! Still, since she couldn't find anything else, they would have to do.

Then she tiptoed over to the cradle where Billy lay laughing and gurgling to himself and stuck him in the stomach with the scissors as hard as she could.

Billy quit laughing and started to scream and the blood came out of him and ran down on the sheet. Then Fanny got scared. It was the first time in her life she'd been really scared; but was scared enough now to make up for all the other times she ought to have been and hadn't had sense enough to be. 'Cause if Poppa beat her that hard just for making pee-pee in bed, what would he do to her now that she'd killed Billy?

So she ducked out of the bedroom and ran down the front stairs and out into the street, barefooted and in her nightgown and it sopping wet at that. She could still hear Billy screaming even from out in the street so she ran away from there very fast until she got to the little booth on Texas Street where old Mister Fields sold gumdrops and peppermint canes and licorice sticks to the kids.

She stood in front of his stall and yelled at him:

"Mister Fields! Mister Fields! Take me home with you! Hide me!"

Then old Jacob Fields who everybody said wasn't in his right mind because he liked little girls—What was wrong with that? Fanny wondered; She'd sure Lord be mighty glad if her own Poppa liked her a little, 'stead of hating her and paddling her bottom so hard he almost killed her most every night—came out of the candy booth and looked at her real hard. After that he took her by the hand and the two of them started walking. But maybe the old man wasn't all that crazy because he took her out of town by back streets that Fanny had never even heard of before, passing by a passel of nigger shacks, and some poor white people's houses that were just as dirty. Fanny didn't know any of the white people they passed and what's more she didn't know the niggers either because they were too lowdown and no'count to be friends of Eliza's. Eliza's friends all went to the First African Baptist Church of the Lord, and were clean and neat and worked for good whitefolks just like Eliza did.

But by then, they were all the way out by the cemetery and Fanny saw Mr. Field's house. It wasn't nothing but a shack, either, dirtier and more rickety than even the lowdown niggers' cabins. She went inside with him anyhow, because there wasn't anything else to do since she had killed her baby brother and had to hide.

Once they were inside, they didn't even talk. Mister Fields brought out bags and bags of all kinds of candy and gave them to Fanny. She sat there and stuffed herself like a pig. It was the first time in her whole life she'd had all the candy she could eat, because even before Martha came Poppa wouldn't let her eat this much. So she went right on digging into the sacks and pushing the candy into her mouth with both hands until she forgot all about Billy, and she was too full to eat anymore, and so sleepy she couldn't keep her eyes open.

Seeing how sleepy she was, old Mister Fields picked her up and put her on his bed. She was fast asleep before her head hit his filthy, greasy black pillow.

She didn't know how long she'd slept when she felt something scratching her middle and that woke her up. She opened her eyes and saw it was old Mister Fields's whiskers. He was kneeling by the bed and kissing her belly-button and he'd rolled her nightgown almost up to her neck. Then he started to kiss her further down on her stomach and even on the part of her she made pee-pee out of.

So then she knew he was crazy and she really got scared. She hit him with both her fists on top of his head and screamed so loud that he opened his quavery old mouth and said: "Now honey, now honey, don't take on. Didn't I give you candy? Didn't I always treat you good? I won't hurt you. I won't so much as—"

But Fanny twisted out of his arms like a wild thing and ran out the door, not even stopping to think how lucky she was that it hadn't even a lock or a bolt on it and was hanging down crazy like on one hinge, anyhow.

And the minute she got outside she saw Poppa coming up Market Street in his buggy and there was a crowd of men following him and they all had guns in their hands. Fanny was so scared that she forgot she'd wet the bed last night and killed her baby brother this morning and that Poppa was sure to beat her something awful for doing such terrible things. She ran down the road towards the buggy, screaming:

"Pop-paaa! Old Mister Fields! He was bad! He done something to me! Don't let him catch me! Don't let him catch me, please!"

Then Poppa jumped down from the buggy and took her in his arms. But he didn't keep her there for even a second. He passed her over to another policeman, and looking at him, Fanny forgot to cry or even to breathe. His eyes had turned to green ice. He went running toward where old Mister Fields was standing in front of his shack and blinking at all those men out of his watery blue eyes. And when Poppa was close enough, he pulled his pistol out from under his coat and shot old Mister Fields in the face.

Old Mister Fields fell down without saying anything and Poppa stood over him and shot him five more times as he lay there on the ground. Then Poppa came back to the policeman who was holding Fanny, and held the pistol out to him, backwards.

"I give myself up," he said. "You better put me under arrest, Hank."

"Why th' hell you say! Don't talk no sich goddamn foolishness," the policeman named Hank said. "That there dirty ol' degenerate bastid's had that coming to him a long time. Put your gun up, Bill. I'll take this po' li'l baby over to Doc Mitchell's—"

"Doc Mitchell's?" Poppa said like he really didn't understand.

"Yep. Little as she is—only eight years old, ain't she?—reckon he must of tore her all up down there." Then Hank pulled up her nightgown in front of all those men and looked at her and said: "Don't appear to be bleeding none, but you never can tell . . . You git on down to Headquarters on your own recognition and give yourself up to the Chief, Bill. And I got twenty bucks agin' a plugged lead nickel what says you don't spend not even an hour in jail!"

Hank was right. Poppa didn't. The Chief of Police wouldn't even accept his resignation from the force at first. But after Doctor Mitchell told the Justice of the Magistrate's Court that old Mister Fields really hadn't done anything to Fanny, the Chief did accept it, although the Magistrate's Court found no true bill and ordered Poppa freed on the grounds that he'd been driven out of his mind by what he'd thought had happened. So the Chief let Poppa quit the force, and gave him a letter of recommendation to the Chief of Police down in New Orleans.

So they went down there, all of them: Martha and Poppa and Eliza and Fanny and Billy. Because Billy wasn't dead after all. He only had a little cut in the belly that healed up in a week.

But they had to go. Martha cried and screamed that they were disgraced forever in Shreveport by this eight-year-old she-monster who went around trying to kill babies and getting innocent old men murdered with her filthy lies.

"She'll come to no good end, Bill!" she yelled at Poppa. "Mark my words, she'll end up bad!"

Years later, when she was a grown woman and could think about her life, it came to Fanny that Martha had been right. But, by then, it was too late, even though she more than halfway understood the things that had shaped her into what she was:

A whore.

"A born one," Martha said.

# Chapter Two

"Fanny——" Martha said.

"Yes, ma'am?" Fanny said. That was as close to Mom, Mama, Mother as she ever got. She stood there waiting, and her eyes were cold and still. They were a blue so pale that it seemed to Martha that there was something unnatural about them. And, to make it worse, Fanny had a way of looking at people without blinking at all, so dead level, unmoving, expressionless that, as always, Martha found it hard to go on with what she had to say.

"Where have you been?" Martha said, hearing with disgust the quaver that had got into her own voice.

"Out walking," Fanny said.

"Out walking—where?" Martha said.

"Just out walking," Fanny said; "no place in particular . . ."

"With——whom?" Martha said.

Fanny looked at her.

'I won't lower my eyes!' Martha raged; 'I won't! I won't!'

But she did. Then, with an effort of will, she faced Fanny again. 'It's shameful to let oneself be cowed by a fifteen year old girl!' she thought; 'I simply cannot permit her to do this to me!'

"I asked you a question, Fanny!" she said.

"All by myself," Fanny said; then: "Who'd go walking with *me*?"

"Fanny," Martha said, trying to force her voice to sound at least a little less harsh, a trifle kinder, thinking: 'Why can't I even feel sorry for her? She deserves pity. I guess that if I—or anyone—could get to her, it might save her.' She said:

"Sit down, Fanny."

Fanny sat. She went on looking at Martha, her ice blue eyes unwavering.

'Basilisk's eyes,' Martha found herself thinking. 'Gorgon's head. Face of Medusa—'

"Mrs. Farley came to see me today," she said.

Nothing. No change. Those eyes went right on laying out those ruler-straight parallel lines of light on the naked air. 'Is there a mind behind them?' Martha thought. 'Is there anything behind them at all?'

"She—she said you haven't been to school since Monday. Might I ask why?"

"I hate school," Fanny said; but there was neither anger nor passion in her voice. It was flat, toneless, dull. "You hadn't ought to waste Papa's money sending me. I can't learn. I'm stupid. Didn't Mrs. Farley tell you that?"

"No," Martha said.

"That's what she always says to me," Fanny said, "and right in front of all the other girls, too . . ."

Hearing the slow, quiet misery in the girl's voice, a crippling blade of pity stabbed into Martha. 'Poor thing!' she thought. 'Poor dull, ugly, shapeless thing!' But at once she revised her thought as being, at least in part, unjust. Fanny had a pretty face, a very pretty face. In the future, it might even get to be beautiful when it was no longer covered with clusters of pimples, each of them crowned with its yellow peak of pus. 'No,' Martha thought uneasily, 'not even then. Because her expression will go on ruining it, that look of . . . of sullenness, of dull misery, half-suppressed anger. Besides, it's her gluttony that's made her keep her adolescent acne so long. All her schoolmates' skins have cleared up . . .'

Martha realized suddenly that she had started to form the phrase "girl friends" and had amended it instantly almost without conscious thought. For Fanny had no girl friends. Nor male companions, either. At an age when her classmates were learning to flirt and pass notes, and to make the best of whatever attractive features they might have—not always subtly—by wearing a belted skirt, say, to show off a tiny waist, a tight blouse to call attention to budding breasts, combing their hair in artful ways, even—some of them, anyhow—daring to use red lip salve, and rice powder to improve muddy complexions, Fanny, as a girl, was an unmitigated disaster.

'She must be,' Martha thought, 'at least forty pounds overweight. And still she eats as though her life depended upon it. She looks like a haystack walking. And she's so . . . untidy.' Again Martha's northern trained exactitude of mind caused her to amend her thought: 'Just plain dirty is what she is, really. Sluttishly dirty. She—she's with her monthlies right now. A normal enough female function that I shouldn't even be aware of in another woman, except for the fact—the utterly appalling fact— that I can smell her. From over there. From across the room.'

"Fanny," she said desparingly; "What on earth am I to do with you? I don't want to tell your father about this, but . . ."

Fanny looked at her, said:

"Tell him. Maybe he'll beat me to death this time."

"Fanny!" Martha said.

"What have I got to live for?" Fanny went on in the same dull, dogged tone. "Nobody likes me. They call me Fatso Fanny. At least they used to. Now they've got a new one. You see, one day last week, I wasn't, well, feeling so good, and I . . . broke wind in class. So now they call me Fanny Fartbuster. That's howcome I stayed outa school."

"Oh dear!" Martha said.

"Don't blame them. Why should anybody care about me? I'm fat and ugly and I've got bad skin, and on top of all that, I'm stupid. Never can think of bright, clever things to say, like June can. Or Rose. Sometimes I wish I'd never been born. Then I wouldn't feel anything, would I? Or know anything either. Like that everybody hates me."

"*I* don't hate you, Fanny," Martha said.

"No," Fanny said slowly, "you don't. Eliza neither. But you both feel sorry for me—and that's maybe worse. Ain't I something, though? When a old nigger woman sixty years old has got th' right to feel sorry for me?"

"Fanny," Martha said slowly, choosing her words with care, "in a way, it's your own fault. You have a very pretty face. And you'd be the prettiest girl in Mrs. Far-ley's school if you'd stop stuffing yourself like a pig. I'm sure your skin would clear up if you'd eat a few less sweets and . . ."

Fanny looked at her with eyes that were hoarfrost: misery's own pristine self.

"I know," she muttered. "But I haven't got any will-power either. Besides, even if I was to quit eating and got to be slim and pretty, would that make Papa stop despising me? Would it, Martha—I mean, ma'am?"

"You may call me Martha," her stepmother said. "I don't mind. Now look, Fanny, about your father—"

"Nothing will change what he thinks," Fanny went on slowly. "I look just like my mother—who did him dirt with another man. And then cheated on that fellow, too. So now she's out west in San Francisco. In a whorehouse."

"Fanny!" Martha gasped. She was shocked almost speechless. In the early 1890s, it was unthinkable for a girl to know, not to mention say, that word.

"Well, she is. Even like that, she's got it all over me. I couldn't so much as get a job in a whorehouse—except maybe at scrubbing floors. But they've got niggers for that, haven't they?"

"Fanny, who on earth ever told you all these horrible things?"

"Eliza. Papa confides in her. 'Cause he can't talk about things like that to Billy. Not fitten for a boy seven years old to hear, don'cha see? And as far as he's concerned, I don't even exist. And he can't say 'em to you—'cause he—he loves you and don't—doesn't want to hurt your feelings, I reckon. He found it out by accident, anyhow. Arrested that fellow she left him for, for being drunk 'n disorderly. And the darn fool talked his head off. Drowning his sorrows, I guess. Told Papa she'd left him too, run off taking nearly every cent he had, and how'd he had the Pinkerton Agency tailing her until they traced her out to California."

Martha sat there. What was there, really, to be said?

"So Papa thinks I'm bound to turn out bad. I can't. I wish I could. But to be bad, that way, you've got to be attractive. And I'm not."

"Fanny," Martha said slowly, "when I was your age, I didn't know what a—a house of prostitution was. Nor—"

"Where babies come from. Well I do—both. Never had a mother to—to shelter me from all the ugly things in the world . . ."

"You had me," Martha said.

"Yes. Only, I wouldn't—no, couldn't—let you. Mother me, I mean. Don't know why. Reckon I was just born poison-mean."

"No, you weren't," Martha said. "I think your mother's

and your father's . . . separation affected you and—"

"Made me stick a scissors in Billy's belly? And, after that, get a poor old crazy man killed by telling lies? No, Martha, I'm just no good, that's all."

Martha bowed her head. 'That's one more thing—no, two—' she thought, 'that had it been left up to me, you'd have never been told. Or at least allowed to forget. Bill's conceptions of—of discipline, of rectitude, are excessive. One day, I'll ask him whether they stop short of—vengeance. Or who it was that actually pumped six bullets into a defenseless old man. Or even if the poor old lunatic had actually accomplished what he set out to do—a physical impossibility, anyhow, in a girl child eight years old—whether the crime could be equated with his life.' She looked up again, her dark eyes bleak.

Fanny hadn't moved. She sat there, grotesquely fat, pimply, frowning. Then she said, very low, almost whispering the name:

"Martha—"

"Yes, Fanny?"

"Did they—did they have dances when you were in school?"

"Yes. Why yes, of course! Why?"

"You—you know how to dance, don't you?"

"Fairly well. I'm badly out of practice, but—"

"Oh, Martha, will you teach me how? It's only a couple of months off and—"

"*What's* only a couple of months off, child?"

"School closing. Mrs. Farley lets the boys from Mr. Bromley's come over that night and dance with us. It's—it's real respectable, Martha! All the girls' parents are there, and the boys', too. You'll have to come, anyhow, if I go. And Papa—"

She stopped short and Martha saw her eyes glitter too bright, suddenly; but she shook her head angrily to clear them.

"Papa'll be out arresting drunks and burglars and fighting those guineas in the Mafia as usual, I reckon. But you'll come with me, won't you, Martha?"

"Yes, of course, Fanny; and I'll be happy to teach you the little I know about dancing, only—"

"Only what, Martha?"

"What'll we do for music?"

"Don't know. Hum, I reckon. Or—say, that's an idea!—get that nigger who plays the organ in the church Eliza goes to, to play the piano for us. He plays real *good!*"

"Well . . . " Martha said doubtfully. Then she thought: 'I mustn't fail her now! I mustn't! Maybe this is the way to reach her!' She said: "Well, all right, if Eliza will vouch for him. But, Fanny—"

"Yes, Martha?"

"I'm not going to teach you to dance gratis. You'll have to pay me."

Fanny sat there, her moon-shaped face settling into its habitual expression of anger and suspicion.

"Pay you—with what?" she muttered. "You know what kind of an allowance, Papa—"

"Not with money. By trying to be . . . nicer. By eating a great deal less—especially sweets. Going to school and doing the best you can. And, above all, by being more . . . fastidious, say. Boys don't like dowdy girls. And no one, absolutely no one, Fanny, can abide . . . a female who . . . smells!"

Fanny sat there. She bent her head so that her long, blonde hair fell down about her face.

'Why, her hair is lovely!' Martha thought. "Will you try, child?" she said.

Fanny raised her head, faced her stepmother. There was a new look in her pale eyes—as though something were struggling to be born behind them, fighting free of the womb of fear, distrust, self-loathing that had held it imprisoned so long. And the name of that thing was—hope.

"Yes 'm," she muttered. "Yes, Martha—I'll try . . ."

'And she has tried,' Martha thought sadly, as she sat in the kitchen with Eliza, both of them busily engaged in putting the finishing touches on Fanny's party dress. 'Lord, how she has tried! But will it be enough? She's lost five whole pounds—out of the thirty she needs to lose. And her skin's almost completely clear, thanks to Eliza's Draconian measures—'

She shuddered a little, thinking of that. Eliza had simply caught Fanny by the back of her neck and plunged her face into a basin of water so hot it was almost scalding. Then when the girl's face had turned tomato-red, the old woman had calmly squeezed the pimples out, one by one—a dreadfully painful business that Fanny had submitted to without a whimper. After that, Eliza had coated her face with baking soda, and made her go to bed like that. In less than a week, the pimples were almost all gone.

"But," Eliza said sternly, "you stuff your gut with candy 'n cake 'n suchlike and they'll come right back. You hear me, chile?"

"Yes, Eliza," Fanny said, "I hear you. Now leave me alone, will you, huh—please?"

But she actually did stop eating sweets. And she picked up her books to such good effect that she didn't fail her classes, after all, squeaking through with a barely passing grade. And, wonder of wonders, Eliza told Martha that she had taken to bathing and changing her underwear daily.

"First time I ever seen that chile's drawers when they wasn't so stiff with dirt that they couldn't stand up by theyselves," Eliza said. "Now I can pick 'em up 'n put 'em in the washtub without putting a clothespin on my nose to hold it shut. Don't know what you's done to her, Miz Martha, but it's sure Lord working, for a fact! Now tell me, ma'am, how's them dancing lessons coming along?"

"Just fine," Martha said. "You'd never believe it, Eliza; but she's as light as a feather on her feet. Strange, isn't it?"

"No, it ain't. Lots of big fat gals is good dancers. Hit's knowing how to carry your weight what counts . . ."

'Oh, dear!' Martha thought, appalled at the image that Eliza's words called up, 'she's still . . . immense . . . Oh, if I only had a little more time!'

But she hadn't. And that night, when she tried Fanny's party dress on her, she had all she could do to keep from crying.

The dress was a lovely combination of various shades of blue that did wonders for Fanny's complexion and her eyes. And, as the latest mode demanded, it was cut in the popular "princess" style, of pale blue satin, with huge puffed sleeves of dark blue lace net over the same material. Above Fanny's voluminous breasts there was a smart little bib of the same dark blue lace net, from both sides of which, two immense ribbons of blue velvet trailed down to the hem of the flared satin skirt, which was embroidered with darker blue threads.

Around her neck, Fanny wore a collar-ruff made of blue velvet ribbons, totally independent of the dress; in her pale hair, a pair of bluebirds' wings nestled. She wore white suede gloves on her big, red hands. In them she carried a painted silk fan with amber sticks forming its framework. The whole ensemble, in that year, 1895, was absolutely le dernier cri.

The only trouble with it was that on Fanny, it looked awful.

'On her,' Martha thought despairingly, 'it's simply . . . grotesque!' Then, looking up, she saw Fanny's eyes. They were aglow, soft and beaming with real happiness.

"Oh, Martha!" she breathed, "I do look so nice!"

And bending down, she kissed her stepmother willingly, meaning it with all her poor, forlorn heart, for the first time in her life.

After that, Martha was lost. She couldn't force herself even to hint to Fanny how horrible that dress was on a girl who weighted slightly over one hundred sixty pounds, and who would have been quite pleasingly plump even at one hundred twenty. 'One hundred—one hundred five is more than enough for a child as short as she is,' Martha thought. 'But I'll need six months to get her down to anywhere near that—and that darned dance is day after tomorrow!'

There was nothing she could do. In the whole history of fashion nobody has ever succeeded in inventing a style becoming to the grossly fat. And Martha candidly admitted to herself that she was nobody's designer. So all she could do was wait and hope. But how vain her hopes were, she could not, did not know, for in her sheltered childhood she had never been exposed to an aspect of life, so seldom mentioned, so carefully subjected to the auto-censure by which the human mind blinds itself to what it does not want to, can not bear to see, that most people forget it even exists, not to mention what an actual commonplace it is: the savage, unthinking, utterly bottomless cruelty of the young.

So when she walked with her stepdaughter into the gaily decorated gymnasium of Mrs. Farley's School for

Young Ladies, on Poydras Street, she was unprepared for what was going to happen. Totally unprepared.

But Fanny wasn't. She more than half expected it. Her pale eyes darted from face to face, exactly as a trapped beast's do, as with that final desperate courage born of the loss of all hope, it turns to face the encircling pack.

It was then that Martha became aware of the silence. By a sort of purely casual additional cruelty, no one's fault, really, the orchestra had not yet begun to play, so that the silence was absolute. Martha's dark eyes followed helplessly the light-locked pointing of Fanny's gaze as it swept from face to face, brilliant, expressionless, still, neither begging mercy, nor entreating grace. There was something admirable about the girl's self-control as she surveyed the mocking grins widening on idiotic adolescent faces, girls nudging each other and rolling their eyes ceilingward like black-faced comedians in a minstrel show, two of them, whom Martha recognized as classmates of Fanny's unwilling, or unable to bear the burden of their mirth any longer, collapsing finally into each other's arms, rent and shaken with hysterical laughter; but Martha, being unprepared for any of these manifestations of those young, undomesticated ape-mutants' demonstration of how little they were of the genus homo, and sapiens not at all, felt the tears of purest rage sting her eyes. And then a boy's uncertain voice, near soprano, actually, soaring over the rising tide of giggles, said loudly, clearly:

"My, my! Didya ever see such a big blue gasbag on such a low tether before?"

And the giggles became a roar, beast-voiced, merciless.

Then dark, tall, much-too-handsome Rod Schneider—who, Martha had already discovered, was the object of all poor Fanny's half-articulated dreams—drawled:

"What d' you say, fellows? Let's go dance with Fanny. All five of us—at the same time, naturally. You, Tim, take the left quarter. Phil, you 'n Hank will have to share the middle; while me 'n old Joe, here, will rally round the rest . . ."

And it was only then that, head down and sobbing, Fanny fled out into the night.

To Martha's pleased surprise, despite the catastrophe of her first dance, Fanny didn't relapse into her formerly

slatternly ways; nor did she retreat into the infantile plea-
sures of gluttony. She simply stopped talking, beyond the
barest monosyllables, to anyone at all. So withdrawn did
she become that finally even her father noticed it.

"What the hell's got into that child, Martha?" he demanded.

"Just . . . growing pains, Bill," Martha said gently.
"You leave her be, will you?"

"Papa!" Billy called out then, "can I have a gun? A
twenty-two? Fred Walton's father bought him one, and
he's two months younger than me!"

"But you have a gun, Billy," Martha said.

"A li'l ol' baby BB gun!" Billy complained. "That ain't
no real gun at all, Mama! Don't even make no noise,
and—"

"Billy, your grammar is atrocious!" Martha said. "And,
as far as a gun is concerned, it seems to me—"

Bill senior reached out and sat Bill junior on his knee.
Then he winked at his son.

"We'll discuss it tomorrow, Billy Boy," he said, "when
there're a few less womenfolks around—"

Fanny got up then, without a word, and left the sitting
room.

"Now what on earth did I say or do—?" her father began.

"Nothing, Mister William Pelham Turner, I.D.," Martha said.

"I.D.?" Billy piped. "You got it wrong, Ma! It's D. S.,
Detective Sergeant. Ain't that right, Pa?"

"Well, maybe we'd better ask your Mama what *she*
means," Bill Turner said. "With female critters, you never
can tell. I'll bite, Martha; what does I. D. mean?"

"Insensitive Dolt," Martha said sweetly, "and it's what
you *don't* say or do that's driving your daughter away
from you. Now, if you big, hairy-chested, gun-shooting
he-men will excuse me, I'll go see after Fanny—"

Fanny was lying on her back in her bed, staring up at
the ceiling. She wasn't crying. Her eyes were as expressionless as ever. But something about her, the intensity of
her stillness, perhaps, reached out and caught Martha by
the throat like a clutching hand.

"Fanny!" she said.

Fanny turned her head ever so slightly. Her gaze flickered like clear water over her stepmother's face.

"I'm all right, Martha," she said.

But she wasn't. Later that same night, after she was sure that everyone in the household was asleep, she rolled her nightgown up around her waist, and began to touch herself down there, slowly, rhythmically, steadily, while shaping Rod Schneider's dark, sardonic face in her mind. She did that every night, now, burying her face in her pillow at the end of it to stifle the cry that was invariably torn from her. Then she'd lie there face down and cry herself to sleep.

'Folks say,' she thought miserably, 'that people who—who do *this*—go crazy. So—so all right! What's so bad about being crazy? Lots of crazy folks laugh all the time—'n sing. Maybe they're . . . happy. And Lord knows I'm not! 'Sides—I—I can't help it. Took after my mother, I reckon. Born bad. Or else why would I even want to—to do this? Oh Lord, here I go again! Make me stop it, Jesus! Make me stop it, please! Only—I can't—I can't—Rod, my Rod, oh my darling—Ohhhhh Lord!'

"Miz Martha," Eliza said; "That chile done quit eatin' altogether. Swear to Gawd what she put in her stummick wouldn't keep a jaybird alive!"

"I know, Eliza," Martha said. "I'm watching her. I suspect that the shock of having her ill-bred, brattish schoolmates laugh at her at that dance was maybe good for her, after all. Now she's really determined to get thin, isn't she? But we'd better let her alone. It'll turn out all right. At least I hope so, anyhow . . ."

Or, all wrong.

On August 17, 1895, Fanny went for a walk—alone, as usual. From an upper window of her father's house, standing each of them so that they were hidden by the curtains, Martha and Eliza watched her set out.

"My, my!" Eliza said, "but my baby sho' do look sweet! That she do!"

"Yes," Martha said soberly, seeing the flare of the white chambray walking skirt with its blue pin stripes; the short jacket of the same material with enormous, gathered leg-o'-mutton sleeves swaying above the skirt; and, as Fanny turned and looked back at the house, the snowy sheen of her "lingerie" shirtwaist, "she does, doesn't she? Know what she weighs now, Eliza?"

"One twenty-two!" Eliza said triumphantly. "Just about right, Miz Martha!"

"Well," Martha conceded, "you could at least call it pleasingly plump, anyhow . . ."

"Look at that figger!" Eliza laughed, "laced into that corset so tight she can't rightly breathe. Real hourglass shape my baby's got now!"

"Eliza—" Martha said, seeing the graceful gesture Fanny made, opening her frilly white parasol above her head to protect her milk-white complexion from the August sun, "do you think she's—well—meeting a boy?"

"No 'm," Eliza said. "Only boy she's got a eye for is that there fast Schneider boy. 'N he don't pay her no 'tention. Good thing—that there boy is plumb too wild for my baby. Got one awful reputation, he is. Know what he done? His pa bought him a new trap, with a seat in the back for his nigger man, Tobias. First day he had it, young Mister Rod drives it down to the buggy works 'n had that li'l back seat cut right off'n it. 'Lowed as how he wasn't gonna have no fool nigger breathing down the back of his neck whilest he was out having fun . . ."

"What," Martha said faintly, "does he call having fun?"

"Fast hosses 'n faster wimmenfolks. Folks call him th' King of Customhouse Street. Swear to Gawd if he don't plumb nigh support all them parlor houses down there all by his lonesome. 'Specially Mrs. Frankie Belmont's. There's a light nigger gal there—passin' for white; me, I knows her folks tha's how come I knows she ain't what she's pretending to be—that he's fair wild over . . ."

"Oh, dear!" Martha said. "Then I hope he *never* pays any attention to Fanny!"

"Me, too, ma'am," Eliza said.

Does the pious wish invite the contrary fact? For it was on that very day, for the first time since the disastrous dance, that Rodney Schneider saw Fanny.

He came sweeping past her in his yellow woven rattan trap, driving a really splendid Morgan trotter. The moment Fanny saw him, her heart stood still; then it began to beat so hard she could see it move her shirtwaist.

'Fool!' she told herself. 'Damn stupid fool! Only time

he ever noticed you was alive was to poke fun at you!
And now here you go, lookin' at him like—'

Then she saw that Rod had yanked the Morgan to a
stop and was sitting there waiting for her to come up to
him.

'Turn around!' she told herself fiercely. 'Go back the
other way! Ain't you got no shame? Or no sense either?'

'No,' her heart told her, 'not neither one. Far as *he's*
concerned, not none at all . . .'

So she couldn't go back. She simply couldn't. Step by
slow step, like a wound-up mechanical toy, she went
toward that smart, spanking-new little rig, towards what
was perhaps inevitable, inescapable, even then. Who, in
this world of sin, can say?

Rod sat there on the seat of the little yellow trap, its
curves singingly graceful above its bright red wheels. He
kept a tight rein on his spirited horse, and grinned at
Fanny. He had on a white linen summer suit, under which
he wore a white silk shirt with a high stiff collar and a
dotted silk bow tie. A hard-brimmed straw boater was
perched jauntily atop his head. He was smoking a long,
thick, fragrant Havana. To Fanny he looked like something she had no words for. Rose, or June, or Maud, her
schoolmates, would have said: "Just like a Greek god!"
But Fanny couldn't put it that way. Through her sullen,
defiant refusal to study, she lacked even such elemental
culture. To her, there was only one God, a stern, white-
bearded old Father God, who was going to send her
screaming down to hell for what she'd been doing every
night for the last two weeks while dreaming of this face.
All she was aware of at the moment was that Rod Schneider was smiling at her. At her! Lord God!

"Fan!" he said. "Who'd have ever believed it!"

"Who'd have believed what?" Fanny said sullenly.

"You. D'you know you're deuced pretty now? No, I
take that back. You're—beautiful!"

Fanny stood there. 'I'm going to cry,' she thought. 'I'm
going to cry—and I mustn't. Please God, don't let me cry.
Kill me first. Let me drop down dead right now, while
I'm—happy.'

She averted her face, muttered:

"Don't make fun of me, Rod."

"I'm not! Cross my heart and hope to die! C'mon, Fan! Take a little spin with me?"

Fanny stood there, frozen despite the heat of the day. To be seen in that smart little rig—with Rod Schneider! All the other girls would purely curl up and die from envy! Only—it was too good to be true. There must be a catch in it someplace; there must be!

"C'mon, Fan; be a sport!" Rod said.

In her confusion, and to her own vast surprise, Fanny took refuge in anger.

"Ain't you scared it'll break?" she said venomously. "Puny li'l cart like that? And don'cha need a whole brewery wagon team to pull my weight? An' all four of your smart-aleck friends to help you lift me up into it?"

Rod threw back his head and laughed aloud. Then, throwing his cigar away with the most dashing gesture Fanny had ever seen, he jumped down from the seat, put one arm around Fanny's now fashionably slim waist and the other behind her knees, sweeping her up into the air as though she were weightless.

But then he stopped, holding her like that, peering into her face, and making his voice go husky with the utterly insincere art of long practice, whispered:

"Fan, I—I'm going to kiss you. You can slap me if you like; but I just can't help it!"

Fanny looked at him. 'This is wrong—wrong!' her mind told her. 'You mustn't, Fanny Turner! Not that a little old kiss is all that much; but are you real sure he'll stop there? Or that *you'll* stop him if he don't, stupid girl? You mustn't, mustn't, mustn't . . .'

But by then Rod Schneider had his mouth on hers, and she couldn't hear her mind for the beating of her heart.

When Fanny finally did get home that night, creeping up the backstairs with her white walking oxfords in her hand, and imploring deaf heaven to let her father still be out putting the fear of justice, the law, and even the Almighty into malefactors—which, fortunately for her, he was—she did a strange thing.

Going into the kitchen, she peered into the huge black iron range, to see if the fire was entirely out. It wasn't. Eliza often left it banked like this, to keep the water at least warm until morning.

For that big stove was the very latest model: two big pipes came down from the immense water tank above it and were connected at opposite ends of a coil of copper tubing suspended above the grate. So when a fire was laid in the firebox, it automatically heated enough water for the whole family to have baths, and for Eliza's washing, too.

Fanny opened the drafts, and poured more coal into the firebox. The coal caught easily, and blazed. Then she went into her bedroom and got her nightgown, slippers, and her bathrobe. She came back into the bathroom, and took off her clothes. She sat on the edge of the big tub and waited. When she knew the water was hot enough, she opened the tap. The water gushed out of the faucet into the tub. It was almost boiling.

She didn't run any cold water into the tub at all. She simply stepped into that all-but-scalding water. As she stood there in the tub with her feet and legs turning lobster-red, she caught sight of her face in the mirror.

'Yes,' she thought miserably, 'anybody could tell. All they've got to do is look in my eyes and—'

Then, very slowly, she eased herself down into the tub and began to scrub herself all over. She kept it up for almost an hour, until she realized finally it wasn't going to do any good. This particular filth lay too deep to reach. It was, maybe, on her soul.

Then Fanny bent her head and cried. She kept it up a long time, helplessly, hopelessly, her teardrops dripping into the soapy water.

But that didn't do any good, either. Nothing could, or would, now, ever.

She knew that very well.


## Chapter Three


"Martha," Fanny said, "do people *like*—making love? Womenfolks, I mean? Even . . . ladies?"

Martha dropped her sewing into her lap and stared at her stepdaughter. She searched that plump, pleasant face, smoothly oval now instead of moon-shaped, a pretty face, a really pretty face, except for those eyes. Those too-pale, wild woodthing's eyes, that always, even in the most subdued light, seemed to . . . glitter. 'As mirrors glitter,' Martha thought, 'or bright pieces of tin. Brilliant, opaque, throwing back the light—never letting anything through, never letting you see behind them . . .'

"Fanny," she got out, forcing her voice through her shock-constricted throat so that it sounded, high, reedy, dry, "have you been—well—experimenting? I mean, have you been doing—something you shouldn't?"

Fanny bowed her head, threw a wild prayer ceilingward: 'Let me lie *good*, O Lord! Keep my face straight! Let it come out like it was the truth! Not for my sake, Jesus, but for hers! She'd be so hurt—so hurt—after all she's done for me—if she found out that—that I'm bad—'

She raised her face, looked Martha straight in the eyes, said: "No 'm. No, Martha." Then: "Reckon I shouldn't ought to ask things like that, should I?"

Martha clasped her two hands together so tight that her knuckles whitened from the strain. Then she said, very gently:

"I don't know whether you should or not, Fanny. Most people, even today, believe that the best way to keep young people from getting into trouble is not to tell them—anything. I—I'm not sure I agree. I wish *my* mother had told me a great deal more than she did. That I hadn't entered into a marriage—late in life, after having resigned myself to spinsterhood—on the basis of the sort of wildly distorted misinformation that schoolgirls whisper to one another . . ."

"You married so late—almost thirty wasn't—weren't you?—because you didn't want nobody else but Papa, right?"

"If," Martha said, with a smile, "you'll change that 'didn't want *nobody* else' to 'didn't want *anybody* else,' I'll have to agree with you. I suppose the idea that there's only one man in the world for any given woman is nonsense, but I believed it. I still believe it. But then, I was lucky. Your father is . . . an exceptional man, Fanny."

"I know that," Fanny said, "He's—brave 'n handsome 'n—'n good. Only he—he doesn't care very much—for me."

Martha thought before answering that, told herself: 'Lying's ridiculous under the circumstances. The child's no fool.' She said: "That will change. That *is* changing, Fanny. And I think the—well—distance between you and your father will . . . disappear the day he finally realizes that you aren't . . . your mother. That you aren't even anything like her."

She was totally unprepared for what happened next: Fanny's eyes suddenly exploded into tears. There was no other way to describe it. There was no sequence of welling up, slow brimming, spill. Instead, in one half heartbeat that wild glitter was twenty times as bright; and the plump, rosy cheeks were awash with liquid silver, no mere tear streaks, but a flood.

Martha jumped up at once and took her stepdaughter in her arms.

"Fanny!" she said. "Oh, I'm so sorry! I—I didn't mean to hurt your feelings, child!"

"You d-d-d-didn't!" Fanny wailed. "It's only th-th-that—I'm *j-j-just* like her, Martha! I—I have—b-b-bad thoughts! And sometimes I—I want—oh, Martha!—to go out and kiss every g-g-good-looking boy I see! Even let 'em do—whatever it is boys do to g-g-g-girls!"

"Fanny," Martha said, thinking: 'The truth, Martha! Only the truth will serve!' "Listen to me, daughter. That—that's perfectly normal. Oh, I know that people insist that women—decent women, anyhow—shouldn't have that particular kind of emotions. But we do. All of us. Every daughter of Eve that God let be born into this world . . ."

Fanny had lifted her face and was staring up at her stepmother. The flood of tears slowed; but it didn't stop, not entirely. She thought: 'If only I could tell her! If only I could! But I can't! I can't! She'd be so disappointed 'n hurt 'n—'

"How do you think the Lord would keep the world populated if that weren't so? Having a baby is burdensome, and terrifying—and dreadfully painful, child. If we didn't have this . . . overwhelming—well—let's say it straight out, shall we?—physical desire—for the men we love, we'd *never* let it happen to us. Certainly not after the first time!"

Fanny looked up at her accusingly.

"You—you only had *one*," she said. " 'Course Billy is a pain in the—the neck, but—"

"That, Fanny," Martha laughed, "is one of those things you have to blame—if on anybody—upon the Good Lord. For that we have only one child is most certainly not because your father and I haven't tried!"

Fanny straightened up. She stared at Martha.

"Martha," she whispered, "tell me the truth—I—I won't ask you no—any—more after this: You—you *like* making love?"

Martha's face went a dusky rose that, in itself, was answer enough. But she had the courage of her convictions; she believed that truth was the highest of all virtues.

"Yes, Fanny, I do," she said. "Of course, I can't speak for other women, not being married to *their* husbands; but for me—love—all kinds of love, including—physical—has been the supreme joy of my life . . ."

She stopped, seeing that Fanny was pushing—gently enough—free of her encircling arms.

"What's wrong, child?" she said.

"Nothin'—I—I just don't feel so good, tha's all. Reckon—guess—I'll go lie down. My head aches somethin' awful . . ."

Martha smiled at her.

"Wrong time of the month, Fanny?" she said.

"Yes 'm," Fanny said and went to the door. In it she turned, looked at Martha a little defiantly, said:

"Rose Clifford told me that her mother says that no *decent* woman enjoys making love. That it's a—a—re—re—pug—"

"Repugnant?" Martha suggested.

"Yes 'm, that's it. That it's a repugnant duty a woman owes her husband—and—and to have babies. But if she's *decent*, Mrs. Clifford says, she should just—just lie there 'n turn her mind to pious thoughts 'n put up with it 'til her husband gets through. Men can't help their animal natures, she says—at least Rose says she says that—'but a woman's a higher development of the Lord's, more spiritual-like, so—' What do you think of that, Martha?"

"That Mrs. Clifford is a hypocrite or a liar or a fool, or maybe all three. No, very probably all three," Martha said cheerfully. "Not that you're going to mention to Rose that I said that, child. And if that's what she calls decency—

always within the bounds of holy wedlock, of course, Fanny—long live indecency, say I!"

Fanny smiled at her stepmother, a little sadly.

"Thanks, Martha. Reckon you're just about the best—mother—a girl ever had . . ."

Lying there on the bed, Fanny tried to keep the thoughts from going through her head. But she couldn't. There wasn't any way to.

"There *is* something wrong with me! I *knew* there was! 'Cause I—I *hate* it! I—I don't have no—any—fun at all. Not that I don't want—Rod. I do! Oh, I do! I love him, so! But—*that's* no good. It's—dry—'n it hurts—'n it's—over with in a minute—at least for *him*—before I can even get started good. That's one thing. Another thing is —ugh!—*this!* Every month, right on time, regular as clockwork. So I mustn't be made right. Something's wrong with my insides. Every novel I ever read, girl who does what I do with Rod finds out she's gonna have a baby before the end of the second chapter!

'But me—nothing. And I *want* to have a baby. *His* baby. A little him all over again to hold 'n nurse 'n keep 'n love. 'Sides, that's sure Lord the *only* way I'll ever get Rod for keeps. Every time I even mention us getting married he either laughs, or gets mad. But if *that* happened, he'd marry me, sure. After all, he *is* a gentleman. The Schneiders are quality. Rich, too. Of course they're Lutherans instead of Methodists like us. But that doesn't make any real difference. Not like they was Catholics, say . . .'

She lay there, staring up at the ceiling.

'Over-whelm-ing physical desire—that's what Martha said. Well—I feel *that,* all right. Only, what good does it do me? With Rod I—I get so steamed up that I have to come home'n—'n do the—other. What folks say will drive you crazy. Well, I'm not looney, yet. Part of it's *his* fault, anyhow! 'Cause if he don't—doesn't—learn a little about how—how to treat a girl—how girls really work— or anyhow how *I* work—soft-like 'n sweet 'n gentle 'n slow—instead of pounding me to pieces in half a minute, then look out bughouse, here I come!'

Fanny grinned suddenly.

'That old vinegary Mrs. Clifford! I knew she was lying! Nobody'd have *that* many brats without getting *something* out of it! She's lying, lying, lying! And lying is—'

Fanny straightened up, her eyes very wide and bright.

"A sin!" she whispered, and got up, very quietly. Then, step by slow step, she walked over to her mirror, and stood there, staring into the reflected image of her face.

"Lying is a sin," she whispered to her image.

Her image didn't answer her. It stared back at her, its pale blue eyes alight.

"But," Fanny murmured, "what about when you're already sinning? Sinning *real* bad? Taking a chance every time on—on Papa's finding out 'n breaking every bone in my body? He would, too! Or throw me out in the street. And then I'd end up . . . like . . . Mama—goods for sale to be bought by any dirty old man who's got himself ten dollars!

"I—I've got to marry Rod! I've got to! Not only 'cause—'cause I love him, but to keep from—from breaking Martha's heart. 'N Eliza's too. 'N Papa's. Wouldn't even a lie—a little old white lie—or a great big black one for that matter!—be better than that?"

She stared at her reflection. Her reflection stared back at her solemnly.

'Only . . . he'd be . . . so awful mad . . . when he found out it—it wasn't so. That—that I'd lied to him. Maybe he—he'd even hate me! And I couldn't stand that! I couldn't!'

She turned away from the mirror.

"O Lord!" she prayed, "tell me what to do!"

She went back to the bed, lay down, let her fingers stray over her clothes, feeling all that maddeningly uncomfortable bulk, all those pins and harness she'd have to wear for another four or five days now.

'When *this* is over,' she told herself, 'I'll go see him. I'll tell him that either he—he makes a honest woman outa me—or it's quits! That's what I'll tell him!'

But immediately that pitilessly lucid part of her mind that she could never entirely silence answered her:

'And you know what he'll say to that, Fanny Turner? "All right, Fan; have it your own way. It's quits, then. No hard feelings; none at all. It's been fun, y'know. Well then, bye-bye Babydoll!"'

She turned over, face down on the bed, and lay there crying.

About two hours later, she heard Eliza calling, outside in the hall:

"Miz Martha! Miz Martha! Mister Bill's home! Real early for a change!"

Fanny got up at once and started to go into the sitting room to greet her father. Then she realized that her sanitary protection needed changing. That delayed her for a considerable time. So, when she finally did get to the door of the sitting room, she heard her father's voice, deep, and—and sad, she decided, weighted down with sorrow and anger both, saying:

"Fool girl let this bounder take her into Tilly Hendrick's place—one of the most notorious assignation houses in the city—"

Fanny hung there, frozen. How many times had she been in that place now—with Rod? And he'd sworn it was safe. That nobody knew about it, but him! And now here was Papa, saying:

"Of course he'd got her drunk first. Anyhow, when the girl came to her senses and realized she'd been ruined, she tried to kill herself. Cut both wrists with a pair of scissors she stole out of Tilly's sewing basket. Of course she didn't really mean it. Just a way to keep her Pa from beating her to death, I guess . . ."

"How do you know she didn't, Bill?" Martha said. "It seems to me that—"

"Listen, honey, people who seriously mean to kill themselves don't cut their wrists. Too slow. That takes hours, which makes it a lead-pipe cinch that somebody's going to get there in time to save them. If that poor little bitch—'scuse me, honey! That slipped—had really wanted to leave this old world of sin 'n sorrow, she'd have slammed the points of those scissors into her left breast. Or the base of her throat or—"

"Bill, please!" Martha said.

"I wish to God they'd shut those places up! They're worse than whorehouses. At least the women in whorehouses have been ruined already. But harpies like Tilly make it easy for smooth-talking sports to lead poor little stupid wenches like that one astray. Anyhow, I took her home, and spent two hours persuading her old man not to throw her out into the street—to give her another chance. 'This way,' I told him, 'the girl's got an opportunity to reform; and nobody knows about it but the bounder.' And he won't talk; he can't, seeing as how I booked him on a statutory rape charge, the poor filly being a little over seventeen years old—a hell of a long ways from the age of consent even in this benighted state . . ."

'And me—fifteen!' Fanny wailed silently. 'And my birthday's not until month after next!'

"So this old party calmed down finally and agreed to let the girl off with a good beating—later on, when she was able to take it. That was my mistake. He was a rough old customer. Anyhow when the girl heard that she sort of crept out of the room. About five minutes later—I had to sample the old boy's rotgut and a piece of tarred rope he called a cigar, and listen to him being grateful out loud that it was me, a plainclothes man, who'd brought her home and not a harness bull, so the neighbors would never know—we heard his old woman yelling her head off.

"This time the kid had done it right: his razor, the jugular vein. Not a damned thing we could do. The poor little thing bled to death in a shade under one minute flat. And that goddamned Tilly's got the politicians paid off, so I can't even shut her dive up! I swear to God, I'd like to soak that joint in kerosene, tie Tilly down in the middle of it, and throw a match! And believe you me I could sit back and listen to her screech her way to hell and grin!"

"Bill,"—Martha's voice had an edge to it—"are you sure that that sentiment isn't . . . personal? That you're not harboring a grudge . . . after all these years? Because I have a *good* memory, dear. I remember that that's the same place where you—"

"Caught Maebelle with her fancy man. It is. But you mustn't think, honey—Oh, Martha, for God's sake! You don't believe that I—"

"Still love her?" Fanny could hear the tears moving through her stepmother's voice. "I don't know, Bill. I truly don't know. But I hope . . . you . . . don't. Because in that event, you just might . . . have another of tonight's cases on your hands. For I'm sure I—I'd be too hurt to live . . ."

"Goddamnit, Martha!" Fanny heard her father's voice rasping; and what was in it was—terror. "Don't you say that! Don't—you—ever—say a thing like that—again!"

Fanny turned then, and fled back to her room. Her
mind was made up now. She couldn't hurt Martha and
Eliza and Billy and—Papa, by turning out like her
mother. She couldn't! What she had to do to avoid that,
she'd do.

"Look at him!" Tim Waters said, "sitting there with his
face hanging down to his knees—a-drowning all his sorrows! Whazzamatta, Rod, old boy, old boy? Little Fanny
throw you over?"

"More likely Frankie Belmont won't give him cut rates
at her cathouse anymore," Phil Sompayac said. "Come
on, Rod, let us onto the secret: What are you looking so
down in the mouth about?"

"No!" Hank Phelps laughed. "My guess is that Fanny's
papa has had a medium sized flea put into his ear, like,
say how a certain party is playing round with his daughter! Boy, is he *mean!* Even cute as Fan's got to be now,
since old Roddy's sweated all that lard off her, I wouldn't
take a chance with Plainclothesman Turner!"

"Will you shut up, all of you?" Rod Schneider said.

"Say—this is *serious!*" Joe Downey said. "Come on,
Rod—'fess up. Tell a fellow what's all that wrong?"

Rodney Schneider looked from face to face of his
friends. His eyes were very bleak. Then he said, slowly:

"There's going to be a wedding. Mine. Complete with
the traditional irate Papa, brandishing a scattergun. Wonder if I can get him to paint it white so as not to clash
with the decorations?"

"Jesus!" Tim said.

"Good Lord!" Hank and Joe chorused.

"Holy Mother of God!" Phil whispered.

"Sit down, all of you," Rod said. "Get drunk with me.
Least you could do, don't you think? I'm buying. After
all, this is *my* funeral, isn't it?"

There was a silence that lasted through half a bottle of
bourbon. But it was Philippe Sompayac, who had drunk
nothing at all, who broke it.

"Rod," he said, "is she—is Fan—"

"In the family way? Yep. Hung my pants on that particular bedpost one time too many."

"And she's told her Pa?" Joe said.

"Not yet. Wants us to elope before all and sundry start

counting on their fingers. Says she won't tell him unless I
make her. Says she'd rather not. All I've got to do is to be
a perfect little ass, and go trotting up to stick my head
into the offside collar of that double harness . . ."

"Now look, Rod," Phil said, "little Fanny's not all that
bad. Truthfully, if you hadn't been a friend of mine, cute
as she is now—"

"You'd have cut yourself in for a due portion thereof? I
knew that a long time ago. Fan's as good as gold. Pretty.
Sweet. Only—"

"Only what?" Tim Waters said.

"I'm not the marrying kind. Why should I make one
poor little girl miserable when I can make thousands of
them happy?"

"Then—whatcha gonna do?" Joe Downey said.

"Don't know. Marry her, I guess. You see any way out
of it?"

"You could leave town," Joe said.

"Yep. And starve to death. My old man would cut me
off without a red copper. Upright old character, my loved
and respected pain-in-the-ass of a father."

Hank Phelps lifted a brimming glass, downed it a gulp.

"Jesus!" he said; "and to think I was half planning to
cheat on you, to get into those lacy little drawers,
myself!"

Rodney Schneider put his glass down, stared at Hank.

"Say that again!" he said, very quietly.

"Now look Rodney, old boy, old boy," Hank said with
drunken gravity. "You can't hold what he was only thinking against a fellow. That way you'd have to go gunning
for half the town. Starting with old Phil, here. The way
old Froglegs looked every time li'l Fan went by on your
arm was a criminal offense! So don't take my head off
over it!"

"I'm not," Rod said. "In fact, I thank you."

"You—you thank me?" Hank said.

"Yes. You've just given me one beaut of an idea. How
to get out of this, I mean. Say, are you fellows *really*
friends of mine?"

They looked at him, studying his face, until comprehen-
sion began to penetrate even the whiskey fog in their
heads.

"You mean you wants us to—" Philippe Sompayac whispered.

"Yep. I want you all to stand up in court and declare that you've individually and collectively enjoyed Fanny's plump and delectable little—anatomy. Or one small portion thereof, anyhow. Located a little south of her navel. That she can't possibly name the guilty party with any degree of certainty, because his name is legion. So that even that bruiser of a Pa of hers, rough as he indisputably is—"

"Oh, no you don't! Let me out of here!" Hank said. "I'm not startin' to tangle with Detective Sergeant William P. Turner, and 'specially not for something I didn't do!"

"Me neither!" Joe said. "Boy is he ever *mean!* Remember those two dagos?"

"What two dagos?" Tim said.

"That's right, you were out of town last summer, weren't you?" Joe said. "Well these two guinea bastards, black-hand boys sure as hell, decided to rob the New Orleans Citizen State Bank. They were coming out the front door with th' loot when Mr. Turner surprised them. Dropped the first one in his tracks, and the second one exactly one yard further on. Used *two* bullets; just two. Same place for both those wops; right between the eyes. They didn't even kick!"

"He can't," Rod said, "shoot all of us . . ."

"Us!" Tim squealed. "Listen to him! You heard what the man said? Us! Now let me tell you one little old thing, Rodney Schneider: I'm not going to get daylight let into me on account of a piece I ain't never laid a finger on! I'll be an usher at your weddin', but tha's aaallll, boy!"

"Now, fellows," Rodney said. "I'm not asking you to take the risk for nothing. What would you say if I were to arrange a little champagne supper—for all five of us—with Fan—as the pièce de résistance?"

They looked at one another. A smile started at the corner of Hank's mouth, spread slowly into a grin of pure, unalloyed lechery.

"Now that's what I call a real gentlemanlike idea!" he said. "Noble, ain't he, fellows?"

"You, Tim?" Rodney said.

"All I can say that that's the stinkingest, lowest down, filthiest trick that I ever cut myself in for a piece of!" Tim said.

"You, Joe? Phil?"

"Well," Joe said, "at least this way I'll die happy!"

Philippe Sompayac stood up.

"Good-bye, fellows," he said.

Rodney's brows crashed together over the bridge of his nose.

"You mean that you won't—that you don't want to—"

"Sleep—merde alors!—stay awake with little Fan? I'd be delighted to, Rod—if *she* wanted me to. And even then she'd have to be cold sober and mean it with all her poor, deluded little heart. Caring at least a little for me. For me—a person. The way she cares for you. But you wouldn't understand that, would you? Anyhow, thanks—",

"Thanks for what, Phil?" Rodney said.

"For proving to me that neither my boundership nor my cadhood are complete. That I'm finicky, say—or fastidious. I don't, for your information, Rod, go poking mine into any female hole, awash with the muck of all my friends. My ex-friends, I suppose I should say, now. No, don't get up. Good-bye, all; I've enjoyed our little gatherings—up 'til now; that is."

Rodney lurched to his feet.

"You're calling me—cad," he grated, "and a bounder, Phil?"

Philippe stood there, studying him. Then he said, very quietly:

"No. But only because they don't fit you. For you, Rodney Schneider, I'd have to invent a new word."

Then calmly, smoothly, he turned on his heel, and left them there.

"Catholics!" Hank sneered. "Got to have Holy Water sprinkled on it afore they'll even—"

"He'll ruin it, Rod!" Tim said. "He'll tell Fan—or her Pa—or—"

"No, he won't," Rodney said. "He doesn't have even a nodding acquaintance with anybody in that house. Damned Creole prig! What he might do is to send his nigger with a note. But since we all know his nigger by sight, we can put a stop to that."

Could and did.

For when, the same night, Henri, Philippe's manservant, came up the street toward the Turners' house, quite suddenly he found himself staring into the muzzles of a double-barreled derringer, held in a rock-steady hand. The Creole mulatto stopped there under the street lamp, his smooth dark-brown face graying with fear.

"Hand that note over, boy," Rod Schneider said. "Hand it over, right now, this minute!"

Henri stared from one face to another of the four young white men who had stepped out of the darkness. Their faces were grim, unsmiling. Of course Henri recognized them. He had seen them many times before as invited guests at the Sompayacs' town house.

"We," Rodney said, "don't like niggers, nohow. And 'specially not niggers what go poking their cotton-picking noses into what don't rightly concern 'em. Give me that note, boy! Or do I have to let some daylight through your black hide?"

Tremblingly, Henri passed the envelope over.

"Now git!" Rod said. "No, wait! When you get home, you tell Monsieur Philippe that you delivered his billet-doux to the party it was intended for. You hear me, boy?"

"Yessir, I hears you, me!" Henri said.

"And don't think you can lie to us, compris? You try it and what we'll do to your black carcass won't leave enough meat on your bones for the buzzards to eat! You hear me, boy?"

"Yessir, M'sieu Rod, I hears you, me!" Henri said. "And I won't say nothing, not atall me, sir! Pas un 'tit mot! Not wan leetle word!"

"Then get going!" Rod said. And catching Henri by the shoulder, he whirled him around, and sent him sprawling with a well-aimed kick to the seat of his pants. The little mulatto got up and scurried away from there, running as if all the devils out of hell were after him.

"That's that!" Rod said mockingly. "Now let's sample a bit of deah Philippe's lit'ry style!"

He read:

> Dear Miss Turner:
> You will doubtless find it strange to receive this missive from one unknown to you. But believe that he who writes it is one who secretly admires you, and has your best interest at heart.
> I beg of you, therefore, that you do not accept an

invitation to dine, or to a party, or anything of the like this week, or, for that matter, any time soon, even if such an invitation comes from a person—or persons—whom you trust. He, and they, mean you no good. Believe me, you will bitterly regret it if you do.

I write in the sad certitude of their monstrous intent, for I had the information from the very lips of those who plan to work you irreparable harm.

Trust me and believe I write the truth.

> Regretfully,
> A Friend

"Ha! Touching, isn't it?" Rodney said. "Got a match, Joe? I feel a little pyromania coming on. I like to burn things, don'cha know? Especially tender little missives like—this!"

"Where's you going, Miss Fanny?" Eliza said. "Lawd but you sho looks happy! C'mon, tell ol 'Liza! What's you's up to, chile?"

"It's a secret!" Fanny laughed. "All right—I'll tell you this much: I'm going to a party. A suprise party—for me. I'm not supposed to know; but my—my friend let slip. Tell you all about it when I come home tonight. Who was there 'n all. And 'Liza—"

"Yes, Chile?"

"Don't worry—if I'm late. If—if Martha asks too many questions, tell her what I just told you. But no more than that, please, huh? It's going to be a very nice party—to celebrate the happiest day of my life. And, of course, it's real respectable. I won't get into any mischief, that I promise you!"

Then, her eyes alight with tenderness, she bent and kissed Eliza's withered cheek.

"Don't want no more cham-pagne!" Fanny said. "It— tickles! Tickles my nose! 'N my head's spinning round 'n round 'n round! I see ten—of you. No, five of you with two heads a—apiece . . ."

"Yep," Tim said. "Just what I want—a piece. How's about it, Fan?"

"You—you're wicked, Tim! Say, what was that you

said, Rod, dar-r-r-rling—'bout why th' fellows didn't—didn't—didn't what?"

"Give two hoots up a hollow stump?" Joe suggested, helpfully.

"No, Jo-o-o-oseph! Now, I remem-m-m-mber! Why th' fellows didn't bring their girls? Why didn't they, dearrrest? I know you told me but I've forgot-t-t-t!"

"I asked them not to, baby," Rod said. "Girls talk too goddamn much. Be all over town before we get halfway to the Justice of Peace. Rather confront your old man with a fait accompli, if you don't mind, sweetheart . . ."

"What's a fait accom—accom—accom—what, sweetie-pie? No—don't tell me. Don't care. Just—kiss me. Tha's all I want . . ."

"*All*, Baby?" Rod said, in his best, deepest, most theatrically tender tone of voice.

"Now, Rod!" Fanny giggled. "Don't be a n-n-naughty boy! We can't! You know we can't, Lover! We've got gue-e-e-ests . . ."

"They can wait," Rodney said, and picking her up, walked through the doorway with her into the dark.

She was sick. She'd been sick four times in the hansom cab, coming home. Rod had called the hack and put her in it. But now she was sick in a different way, because there wasn't anything left in her stomach to throw up. The way she was sick now was the kind of sickness people died of. Or ought to be able to die of—if there was any—mercy—in the world.

Only there—wasn't. She knew that in a little while her head was going to come all the way clear, and she was going to—to remember. And she mustn't remember! She mustn't!

'If I do—if I do,' she thought, 'I'll go crazy sure! Go stark raving crazy 'n—'n curse th' Lord 'n die!'

But then there it was, and there wasn't any stopping it. How she'd opened her eyes in an effort to make the bedroom's ceiling quit swinging round and round and round and saw that the face above hers wasn't Rod's. It was—Hank's. Then she felt somebody pulling at them—at Hank anyhow, and she closed her eyes and opened them and it was Joe's face now and then it was Tim's, then Hank's again, and then Joe's . . .

And it was then that she'd thrown up the first time, which cleared her head a little, enough for her to realize what they were doing to her, but not enough for her to be able to stop them from doing it.

And then Rod was there, standing by the bed saying:

"Give it to her, Tim! Filthy li'l whore. Does it for anybody, doesn't she? So now she'll have a great tale to tell that cheap gumshoe of a pa of hers. Explain to him how there're four fellows now who can take their Bible oaths she can't pick out who the father of her li'l bastard is. Too many candidates for that honor, eh boys? That's it, Timmy me bye, ram it up her! I wouldn't spit on this cheap little no-good tart now!"

She came creeping up the backstairs, dragging herself, a curdog bitchthing, belly down, groveling.

'No good,' she thought. 'They had me—all of 'em. Four fellows did it to me. Made a—a whore outa me. Made—ha! I was born one. Got my mother's blood in me, haven't I? I was drunk. So drunk. No excuse. I'm just no good—no good—'

She staggered into the kitchen. Looked into the range. The fire was out. No matter. What good would bathing do now? She sat down on a chair. She hurt all over, inside and out. She smelled of vomit. The inside of her legs—were sticky. Then she realized what they were sticky with, and put down her head to cry. But the tears wouldn't come. It was an awful feeling to sit there and not be able to even cry, knowing she'd never be clean again.

'Served me—right,' she told herself, more conditioned now than any Pavlovian dog to the automatic reflex of self-loathing. 'I lied to Rod. Told him I was going to have—a baby. His baby. Well, I'm not. And even if I was—'

She sat bolt upright, her pale eyes flaring.

'I could be now,' she thought miserably. 'None of them even bothered—to use—a thing. And if I am—if I am—he's right. I wouldn't know who—which one—I wouldn't know! Oh God, I wouldn't know!'

She bent her head again. But tears still wouldn't come. She was beyond crying now. She heard a noise, lifted her head, knew what it was: Eliza's tired old footsteps, coming on. She sat there, forming in her mind words that almost made sense:

'She—loves me. She ain't nothing but an old black nigger woman, but she loves—me. I can't face her, Lord! I can't look even *her* in the face. And—and Martha! Who's so tender-hearted she wanted to—to die—'cause she thought Papa was—was still grieving over—over Mama—

'Over that filthy whore!

'Martha—good, kind, sweet Martha—wanted to *die*— over that—over that—and I—and I'm still sitting here— like a lump of thick slops and—

'What am I still here for? To ruin—everything—for everybody—shame Martha—disgrace Papa—have the kids poke fun at Billy 'cause—goddamn you! You little bitch whore's daughter—move! That's it. That's it. This one. The longest, sharpest one. Now. Now Fanny! You see, Papa? Not—my wrists. This is for real—for real—I don't play games!'

Eliza came through the door and stood there. Said: "Jesus." Like that, very quietly. Then she said it again, louder: "Oh, Jesus!" Then she was screaming it, making the windows shake, slamming the Holy Name like slivers of broken glass into even Fanny's ears down there on the floor where she lay, hurting now, hurting bad, so bad:

"Oh, Jesus! Oh, Jesus! Oh-h-h-h, Je-e-e-sus! My Baby! My po' li'l baby! Oh, Miz Martha, come here quick! Oh please Miz Martha come here! I can't stand this I can't! Oh please Miz Martha—please—"

## Chapter Four

"I've sent Billy over to Mary Etta Collins'—to stay for the duration," Martha said.

"Good," Bill Turner said. "You did right, honey. That was smart. How long has that sawbones been in there now?"

"Half an hour—no, nearer three quarters," Martha said.

"My baby! My po', po' baby!" Eliza moaned.

"Will you please for Christ's sake shut up, 'Liza!" Bill Turner said.

"Bill—" Martha said, "please. She—she found Fanny.

She's almost out of her mind. The—the shock, you understand—"

Bill got up and put his arm around Eliza's shoulders.

"Sorry, 'Liza," he said. "Reckon I'm upset, too. Didn't mean to take your head off that way . . ."

The door of the bedroom opened, and Doctor Lucien Terrebonne came out. The Terrebonnes had been physicians and surgeons in New Orleans from the time of Sieur Bienville. Which is not to say they had all been doctors; the family over the years had produced many types of men: duelists, gamblers, lechers, drunkards, soldiers, statesmen, priests. But in every generation, there had been at least one dedicated, high-minded practitioner of medicine among them. As doctors, they were the best Louisiana had to offer. Everyone knew that.

Dr. Terrebonne stood in the doorway of the sitting room, and looked at the three faces, two white and one black, but each of them arrested, halted in the same expression of—of acute anguish, he decided, except that the man's had a different quality about it, was not unalloyed. 'Because there's so much—anger in it,' the doctor thought. 'He's going to give me a hard row to hoe. Sometimes I wish I were a plumber or a carpenter or any goddamned thing except a doctor. Like now.'

"Well," he said, "there's some comfort in the fact she missed her heart. By a hair. But that knife went into the left lung, and there the damage is—major, I'm afraid. I'll have to operate. Open chest surgery, which she may, or may not, be in a condition to take. Even if she survives that—and, frankly, I shouldn't bet a plugged-lead picayune on her chances—she'll be at least a semi-invalid. Any cold she catches within the foreseeable future could kill her."

"Oh God!" Martha said. "Oh dear God!"

"I'm sorry, Mrs. Turner," the doctor said; "but in thirty years of practice, I've learned it's—kinder—not to raise false hopes."

"Kinder!" Eliza sobbed. "Oh sweet baby Jesus!"

"I've sent for the ambulance," Dr. Terrebonne said. "It should be here within half an hour, say. In the meantime, if there's anything else you'd like to know, except, of course, the kind of questions that only the good God could answer now, I'll tell you what's so, and what's not, within, of course, the limits of my poor knowledge . . ."

Bill Turner got up and took the doctor's arm. "Come over here with me a minute, Doc," he said.

Doctor Terrebonne glanced quickly at the two women; then he allowed himself to be led across the room.

"Doc—" Bill Turner said, in a hoarse whisper, "is my daughter—pregnant?"

The Doctor stared at the detective. He thought: 'The stern father. One of the two types whose daughters always get in trouble. And the other is his opposite, the weak-kneed, spineless fool whose woman wears the trousers in his house . . .'

He said, evenly: "I don't know. If she is, the pregnancy is so recent that it would be practically impossible for any doctor to be sure. Besides, I shouldn't worry about that, if I were you, Mr. Turner. If she is, in her present condition, she'll probably miscarry. Or I'll cause her to abort, if necessary. To allow her to come to full term, even in the unlikely event of the operation's being successful, would be a sight too close to willful murder to suit me . . ."

"But I thought you Catholics—" Bill Turner muttered.

"Call me—a Christian," Dr. Terrebonne said. "There are a good many things the Mother Church and I no longer see eye to eye about . . ."

"I see," Bill Turner said; then: "But it is possible to tell if a girl's been—raped, isn't it, Doctor?"

"Sometimes. And sometimes not. If the violation were her first experience, and the victim brought to us soon enough thereafter, we can usually tell. If not, it's difficult—extremely so . . ."

"Doctor, my daughter's fifteen years old!"

"So?" Dr. Terrebonne said. "As a detective, Mr. Turner, you should know it's not unknown to find girls that age—and below—in some of our better parlor houses."

"God!" Bill Turner said. "All right, I do know that. But my daughter's had good upbringing. She's been sheltered, protected. And if anything like that took place, it happened *last* night. Or else why did she stab herself?"

"Young girls often do exceedingly foolish things for motives they, themselves, would laugh at, once they're older and wiser. Quite recently I reached the home of one of New Orleans' most distinguished Creole families just in time to pump what would surely have been a lethal dose of vernol out of the stomach of a sixteen-year old girl whose seventeen-year-old beau had committed the unpardonable offense of kissing another girl at a public dance . . ."

He stopped, looked at Bill Turner, gave an eloquently Gallic shrug.

"But to tell the truth, I didn't examine your daughter's genitalia. There was no reason for me to. I can have a look now, if you want me to. Do you?"

"Damned right I do! If some bastard's been abusing my girl, I'll—"

"I should think you have more serious matters to worry about, now, Mr. Turner," Doctor Terrebonne said quietly, "such as whether you'll still have a daughter this time tomorrow. Mais, chacun à son goût! If you'll excuse me, sir!"

When he came out again, Bill Turner was sitting beside his wife.

"Doctor—" Martha said, "is she—is she—"

"She seems to be holding her own," Dr. Terrebonne said; then: "Mr. Turner, if your wife will excuse you, I'd like a word with you in private."

"No," Martha said quietly, "I won't excuse him. Anything about—our daughter—concerns me, too. I have a right to hear it."

"Mrs. Turner," the doctor said, "it seems to me you're sufficiently upset now and—"

"You mean," Martha whispered, "you mean that— Fanny did that—tried to kill herself—because—because she's with child!"

"No," Doctor Terrebonne said, "I don't mean that, madame. There's simply a—a technical question that Mr. Turner raised that I'm prepared to answer now. But I should much prefer to give that answer to him alone—"

"No!" Martha flared. "I must know, too!"

"My wife is not my daughter's mother," Bill Turner said tiredly. "I was married before, Doctor. That marriage was ended by—divorce. Martha, here, knew my first wife, knew what she was like. So anything you say, she'll—or at least she should be able to—understand . . ."

"Very well," Doctor Terrebonne said. "As I told you before, I cannot tell if your daughter is pregnant or not at this stage. All I can say is that she—could be. There are evidences of recent—and probably multiple—sexual intercourse. And since your daughter is not—virgin, and probably hasn't been for quite some time—"

"Jesus!" Bill Turner said.

"The question of violation by force, rape, if you will, is difficult to determine. I'd say her amatory experiences of last night were—voluntary, Mr. Turner. There're no bruises, nail marks, or erosions of any kind. Her underwear has not been ripped or torn. But to judge from the quantity of semen on her thighs and in her vagina, I'd say that—several young men participated. I'm sorry; but you asked me, sir!"

Bill Turner stood up. His eyes glittered like green glass.

"Then—those several young men," he whispered, "had better give their souls to the Lord, because—"

"Bill—" Martha's voice was very soft; but listening to it was, the doctor decided, the most nearly unendurable thing he'd done in all his life. "You mean to—to shoot someone else—*again*? Over—this?"

"You're goddamned right I do!" Bill Turner said. "Why the dirty bastards! I'll—"

Then he saw Martha's eyes. What was in them then stopped even him.

"You can't, Bill," she whispered. "Don't you see you can't? Aside from the fact that in this case the crime would have to include suicide, because the one person on earth ultimately responsible for Fanny's lying there like that is you, you simply can't. You owe Fanny too much—"

"I owe Fanny—" Bill Turner said.

"Yes. You owe her—time. Patience. Understanding. Little enough to make up for all you've robbed her of. Hasn't it occurred to you even yet what she's really dying of? A knife wound? That's too easy, Bill. Too simple. Let me have a try at defining it for you. Shall I call it—hunger? No. Starvation's better. More—exact."

"Martha, either I'm crazy, or you are! You mean to stand there and tell me that Fanny's—"

"Dying of starvation? Yes, Bill. For the love *you* never gave her. For one fatherly kiss, one little caress, one kindly word—all these years—from you. And you wonder that she got in trouble! Who wouldn't have? The starving have no defenses, Bill. What she didn't get from you, she tried to find elsewhere, was willing, as any woman under heaven is, to pay any price whatsoever—virtue, reputation, life itself—for a little—love."

"Martha," Bill groaned, "I—"

"So you can't. You've done too much to her now. Denied her, rejected her, starved her of your affection. Heaped her worthless mother's sins upon her poor, defenseless head. But whose fault was it that she had such a mother, Bill? I hardly think the choice was hers!"

"There you've got a point," Bill Turner said, sadly. "I've never denied I was a fool that time, Martha. Only—"

Dr. Terrebonne looked at the big man in a new way, then. With the beginning of—respect. And that respect was real. Then Martha's voice came over to him again, saying slowly, thoughtfully:

"Only it's time you stopped being one, don't you think, Bill? Learned the essence of decency, which is that the innocent must *never* be punished for what other people do? You've made Fanny a—a scapegoat—for Maebelle's sins—and for your own. For your private sin of vengeance, of not being able, not being big enough, to either forget—or forgive. One of which is always necessary to make life even bearable. Both—to make it civilized. But that's too much to ask down here, isn't it?"

"You're saying that *I* kind of crowded her into—"

"The arms of those lecherous young swine? Yes, Bill; I *am* saying that. And, what's more, I'm saying it isn't even important now. That the past never is. It's the future that counts, my dear. So will you please, please, please stop trying to reduce every problem, every trouble in this world, to a question of marksmanship? Life just isn't that simple, darling. In fact, I doubt that anything of importance in all of history has ever truly been settled with a gun . . ."

"Nor ever will be," Lucien Terrebonne said.

"Thank you, Doctor!" Martha said. "So—let's forget your hurt pride, Bill Turner! Let's consider—your daughter. Her life, her future—if God grant her either. For her sake, I'm asking Detective Sergeant William Pelham Turner to put his profession aside long enough to function as a human being. I—I'm asking—no, begging him to—to promise me one thing—"

"Promise you—what, Martha?"

"That—if Fanny lives, or even if she dies—you'll do absolutely nothing at all about this. Oh yes, I agree those young swine deserve any punishment at all, that killing's too good for them; but you can't. This way, no one will know *why* our daughter tried to kill herself. She'll have a chance—with our help, Bill; yours and mine—to remake her life, a point of view even you understand, because it's the same one you used to convince the father of that girl who—"

"Did this, too," Bill Turner said. "Cut her throat, anyhow. Martha! You know what I think? That Fanny must have *heard* me talking about that! I gave her the idea, Martha! Oh, Jesus, I—"

"It doesn't matter," Martha said. "What does matter is that you can't hang a scandal around her neck that will sink her forever. At the expense of letting Rod Schneider and his gang—"

She stopped short, seeing those green eyes flare. Then she went on, firmly:

"Get away with near—or actual—murder, you can't. You owe that much to Fanny if she lives—and to her memory, if she dies. Promise me, Bill?"

The way Bill Turner was trembling then was enough, Doctor Terrebonne thought, 'To send a chill of fear through a stone statue. If he doesn't master the rage in him, that instinct and capacity for violence, sometime soon he'll have a stroke. I'll bet my professional reputation on that!'

"My baby ain't a gonna die," Eliza said suddenly. "I done talked to the good Lawd, 'n he done promised me!"

"And I promise *you*, Martha," Bill Turner said. "It'll damn near kill me, but I promise."

Then they heard the clang of bells, the clatter of hooves outside in the street. Doctor Terrebonne sighed with pure relief.

'Emotional people unman me,' he thought. He said: "The ambulance is here. Now, if you will be so kind, my friends, as to clear the way, I have work to do . . ."

The operation took three and one-half hours. And

Fanny's strong young body survived it at least reasonably well. But the damage done to her mind, her heart, by then, was, of course, another thing . . .

Before the operation was even over, young Philippe Sompayac had heard the story by the fastest means of news-transmission known to Southern men, the Negro servants' grapevine. Now Philippe knew very well that this method of telecommunication, while unmatched for speed, left much to be desired as far as accuracy was concerned, for the simple reason that its operators, members of one of the most artistically gifted races on the face of the earth, would never transmit dull truth or sober fact when an exciting exaggeration, a dramatic distortion, or some romantic substitute could be found. But, in this peculiarly tragic instance, he was inclined to believe what he heard because his acute and painful knowledge of the events leading up to it forced him to. And because he not only believed it, but what was worse, acted upon that belief, nothing for him was ever the same again.

Philippe, on that afternoon that was to change his life, wrenching it out of its normal context, making it alien to all he had previously known and loved, sat at his books. For, although he had reached and passed his twenty-second birthday only a week before, he was already the possessor of a Bachelor of Science degree, earned, *summa cum laude*, at Princeton that very spring. The books he was studying—in a rather desultory fasion, to tell the truth about it—were all medical books, lent him by Dr. Lucien Terrebonne, to whom he had expressed his interest in medicine as a possible career. But, to be even more truthful, it must be admitted that the young Creole's interest in the science and/or art of healing was so slight as to be almost nonexistent. He *was* curious about the profession, but that was about as far as his interest went. What the idle show he was making served for, really, was to ir- ritate his father, a pastime appealing to any son with blood in his veins, and to delay his being dispatched abroad upon an extended grand tour which, to Philippe, had the serious drawback that he'd be forced to call upon the heads of all the European firms with whom Sompayac et Fils did business, thus robbing his Continental tour of most of its charm.

But, for all that, his love for scholarship was real, a fact he was a little ashamed of since it ran counter to all the mores of his society and his region. But by then he was beginning quite seriously to question Southern customs, a process notably accelerated by the disgust Rodney Schneider and his friends had waked in him. So it was not without annoyance that he heard the knocking on the door of his study.

"Qui est?" he growled. At home, all the Sompayacs, including the servants, spoke French, a custom that Jean-Paul Sompayac, Philippe's father, insisted upon, lest they forget their native tongue, as so many Creole families by that late date had already done.

"C'est moi, maître—Henri," his manservant said.

"Entrez donc," Philippe said. He was genuinely fond of Henri, although he never called him anything more affectionate than "vieux âne"—"old jackass"—to his face.

Henri came into the study. The moment Philippe saw the mulatto's face he knew something was wrong. And judging from the way Henri's underlip quivered, seriously wrong at that.

"Qu'est-ce que c'est que vous avez fait, maintenant?" he demanded. "What have you done now?"

"Moi, rien," Henri quavered. "Me, nothing, master. I have done nothing at all! C'est cette jeune fille, cette Mam'selle Turner. Elle s'est suicidée, ce matin . . ."

With one bound, Philippe had Henri by the throat, and was shaking him as a terrier shakes a rat.

"That note!" he said. "That note I sent her! You told me you'd given it to her!"

"I—I tried to, sir! But them fellows, Mr. Schneider, him, and his friends, they put a pistol in my face and swore they'd burn my brains if I didn't give it to 'em, me! And after that, they told me they'd kill me, them, if I told you the truth! Oh, maître, j'ai eu si peur—"

Philippe opened his hand, turned Henri loose.

"It's all right, vieux âne," he said. "It was my fault. I should have thought of that . . ."

Philippe dressed slowly and with great care. There was no need for haste, now. He even knew where to find Rodney Schneider and his friends. For if they weren't at the Real Thing, a cabaret on Rampart Street, they'd be at

The Arlington, a little farther down the same street, or the Stag, on Gravier. All these saloons belonged to the same man, Thomas C. Anderson, who also had an interest in half the better bawdy houses in town. It was Rodney's proud boast that Tom Anderson was a friend of his.

That boast, Philippe knew, was, if not a complete lie, at least a gross exaggeration. Tom Anderson had no need for the friendship of a band of young wastrels, most of them barely into their twenties. He did, however, tolerate them for two reasons: first, because they were free spenders, and could be depended upon to become even more so in the future as they entered into, or inherited, their fathers' businesses; and, second, their endless indiscretions might well provide him with a lever one fine day to pry needed concessions out of their socially prominent and politically powerful familes. But if these two reasons for tolerating Rod Schneider and his friends hadn't existed, Philippe was sure that Tom Anderson would have kicked them out of his establishments with the greatest pleasure.

He found them at the Stag. And he saw at once, from the expressions on their faces, leering at him contemptuously, that he was in luck: they had not been informed.

"Now do tell!" Tim Waters said, as he walked in. "If it ain't old chastity 'n purity, himself!"

"The one-man Reform League," Joe Downey chuckled. "When this boy gets through, won't be a piece to be had 'twixt here 'n Lapland—'n tha's a natural fact!"

"Howdy, Phil ol' boy, ol' boy," Hank Phelps gibed. "Been gettin' any lately?"

But Rodney, who was far shrewder than any of his friends, sat there, studying Philippe's face.

"Come to bury the hatchet, Phil?" he said. "No hard feelings, boy. Sit down—I'll buy you a drink."

"I," Philippe said, "still don't drink with—swine. But I did come here looking for you—gentlemen. You knightly, chivalrous Southern gentlemen. I came to extend you an invitation on Fanny's behalf, since she's unable to extend it, herself. To—her funeral. You see, she killed herself this morning. And it occurred to me somehow that you four sweet innocent lambs might just possibly want to know . . ."

He stood there, looking at them for that rarely awful dead-stopped little eternity it took them to recover. To draw enough breath back into their lungs to talk, anyhow.

"Phil," Rod said, "if this is your idea of a joke, I—"

Philippe looked at him a long, slow, ice-cold time, without bothering to open his mouth.

"No," Rod whispered, "you're not joking. Oh, Jesus!"

"Phil—" Hank passed a tonguetip over bone-dry lips before he could get the rest of it out. "Does—does he—does Mr. Turner—"

"Know who the parties responsible for his daughter's suicide are? No. Fanny didn't tell him. She didn't even leave a note. Just slammed a kitchen knife into her left breast so hard it came out her back. Quite a girl, Fanny. Gallant, I'd say . . ."

He could see their eyes. 'So it's occurred to you,' he thought. 'The only thing you need to do to save your hides—your miserable, mangy, cowards' hides—is to kill me. Or hire it done. Only, you haven't the guts, have you? Anything beyond taking turns at a helpless, dead-drunk girl is beyond you.'

He smiled then, slowly.

"Don't work up a sweat," he said. "I don't mean to tell him, either. Prefer to leave poor Fanny's memory—unsmeared with public filth, shall we say? Besides, I don't want you fellows—dead. I'd much rather that you lived, and strangled on your own puke every morning when you look into your shaving mirrors. Now, if you'll excuse me?"

"Phil—" Joe Downey got out then, "where're you going?"

"To the Turners', of course. To extend my condolences. Want me to convey—yours? To tell them how sorry you all are, that you—murdered—their daughter?"

"Phil, for God's sake!" Tim Waters all but wept.

Philippe looked at him.

"No, Tim," he said softly. "Not for God's sake. For Fan's. You see—I'd got quite fond of her. Of her—a person. Or at least of the person she would surely have got to be if certain dear friends and gentle acquaintances of hers had given her even the chance of a nigger at a Klan meeting. Her, herself—her personality, say—entities, gentlemen, quite distinct from the useful female parts she had in common with half of humanity. There was something—gallant—about her. But I said that before, didn't I?

Even her curious ability to love with all her heart—misplaced as that love was; pearls before a boarhog, Rodney!—seems to me, in retrospect anyhow, kind of fine . . .”

They stood there, staring at him. He wondered if along with the ugly, naked fear for their own precious hides he saw in their eyes, there were the slightest degree of—remorse.

‘I doubt it,’ he thought. ‘That calls for imagination. And if you’ve got that, you don’t sink this far.’ He said:

“So now, good-bye. I hardly think you’ll be seeing me again. More comfortable that way, for all of us. I don’t want to be reminded of all the lowdown, stinking, rotten things I’ve done in your benighted company, all under the general heading of what you—and I, maxima culpa mea!—called fun. And I damned sure don’t mean to spend the rest of my life serving the four of you as a substitute for the consciences you haven’t got. I’ll say a prayer for you all besides Fan’s bier. It’ll probably go up like a lead balloon; but, anyhow, I’ll say it.”

Then he turned and left them there, far farther behind him than he—or they—then knew.

“Yessir?” Eliza said. “Who I’m gonna say is callin’?” Then her old eyes hardened in her gray-black face. “Young Mr. Sompayac, ain’t you? Mr. Philippe Sompayac. Well, Mr. Phil, lemme tell you one thing, right now. Just you step back from this here door ’n go down them stairs real quiet-like. ’Cause if you ain’t the biggest fool on two left feet, you oughta know you ain’t welcome in this house.”

“I do know that—” Philippe paused until the name he had got from Henri came to him “—Eliza; but I came anyhow. I had to come. Couldn’t have lived with myself if I hadn’t. Will you tell your mistress that I’d like a word with her?”

“I’ll do nothin’ o’ th’ kind!” Eliza flared. “ ’N what’s more, I ain’t even fixin’ to! Now lemme tell you, Mister Phil—”

But Martha had come out of the sitting room and was standing there.

“Who is this—gentleman, Eliza?” she said.

“That there gentleman business you can plumb downright skip, Miz Martha," Eliza said. "But this here young feller's Mister Phil Sompayac. And him and that Mister Rod Schneider is—frens. Fact it, they's thicker than thieves at a lawyer's funeral. So if it was left up to me . . ."

"But it isn't, Eliza. Will you come in, young man?" Martha said.

Wordlessly, Philippe bowed. He had been prepared to find many things in that household, but never anything like this woman. 'This is where Fan got her dignity from,' he thought. Then he remembered Rodney's once saying that Mrs. Turner was only Fanny's stepmother, attributing the information to Fanny, herself. So, therefore, whatever traits the two of them had in common, could not have been a matter of heredity, after all. 'But—influence, surely,' he thought. 'The natural desire to copy so remarkable an example of womanhood as this . . .'

He followed her silently, this slim, straight little woman with only a strand or two of white in her dark hair, into the sitting room, took, a little awkwardly, the Morris chair that she indicated with a curiously regal gesture of her hand. Then he saw that she was still standing, and bounced to his feet.

"Oh, I say, Mrs. Turner!" he said.

"All right," she said, and sat down upon a straight-backed chair, her back rod-rigid. "My standing was only to remind you to be brief, Mr. Sompayac. But first, may I say that you had your nerve, coming here?"

He shook his head sadly, said:

"No, Mrs. Turner; you're wrong. For me, that didn't take nerve. What would have taken nerve on my part would have been—to stay away."

Martha stared at him, and, all unbidden, the words, 'An aristocrat, and a gentleman,' formed themselves in her mind. But then she remembered Fanny lying there in New Orleans General with drainage tubes and catheters and God knew what else coming out of her poor self-mutilated carcass, and hardened her heart against him.

"I suppose you're going to tell me that you weren't in-volved in—the incident—no, the crime—that caused Fanny—"

He lifted his head and his eyes were naked. Martha was sure she had never seen more pain in a human face.

"Would you believe me if I did tell you that?" he said.

Martha looked at him. When she spoke finally, she was very sure.

"Yes," she said; "I *would* believe you, Mr. Sompayac. Aside from the fact that you're here, and none of the others is, which in itself is an indication of a certain quality, say—there's something—straight about you. Something that convinces me you wouldn't lie."

"Say, rather, couldn't—to you," Philippe said. "All right, Mrs. Turner, I *was* involved in it; but only to the extent that I knew about it beforehand, knew what they were planning, and failed to prevent it from happening. And even that, I tried. I sent my colored man, Henri, here to your house with a note, warning Fanny what my friends—my ex-friends now, madame!—were up to, what they'd invited me to take part in. They intercepted my man, took my note from him by force, and scared him so with their threats that he dared not tell me he hadn't so much as delivered it. I have never been sorrier for, or more ashamed of, anything in my life than this: the fact that by associating with those swine, participating—oh no, I shan't spare myself, madame!—in their unsavory activities, I'd so demeaned myself that I had no right to resent the insult of their believing that I'd leap at the chance to join them in the—well—call it mass abuse of a helpless girl. I say this to you, madame, offer you my humblest, most abject apologies, even though I, personally, wasn't even there when that abominable affair took place, and honestly believed I'd put a stop to it . . ."

Martha sat there, studying his face.

"What proof have I that you're telling me the truth—at least the *whole* truth—now?" she said.

"None," Philippe said. "Except my word. The word of a Sompayac meant something in New Orleans once, Mrs. Turner. My grandfather killed the only three men in all his long life who dared to doubt it. But times have changed, haven't they? I wonder if it still does—if *I* haven't debased the metal of that particular coinage too much by now? But I should like to be permitted to do something, that to a lady—to the very great lady I see before me—should serve as a kind of proof: I'd like to be allowed to—to attend Fanny's funeral. To lay some flowers on her grave. Even say a prayer—for her, and for my sins, though they were only of omission, and not commission, against that dignity of hers. I ask that, Mrs. Turner, because I'm sure you know enough about people to realize I shouldn't dare to offer what would be an unpardonable affront to your grief, and to her memory, if I, personally, had ever so much as touched her hand."

Martha stared at him. Her face went white. She put up her hand and let her slim fingers lie along the curve of her own throat. Then, very quietly, she said.

"I'll grant you that, freely: Only, Mr. Sompayac, what makes you so sure—so dreadfully sure—my Fanny's going to die?"

Philippe was on his feet then, towering above her.

"But I thought," he got out, "no, I was told that she—that she—"

"That she—what?" Martha said.

"That she was already dead! My man Henri told me—that she'd committed suicide this morning!"

"Sit back down," Martha said. She studied him a long, slow time. Then she said, choosing her words with care: "Your man got it—almost right. That is, he should have said 'attempted' instead of 'committed.' But even that is—conditional. Fanny stabbed herself before dawn, this morning. The wound was not—or at least not immediately—fatal. At any moment now, a message from the hospital might well convert your Henri's probably quite honest error into truth. Dr. Terrebonne says she has a slim, fighting chance to live. And that's just the rub: Will she fight? Would any girl, any woman, so humiliated, offended, shamed—have any desire to live—left?"

Philippe bowed his head, looked up again, said: "I don't know. Not being a woman, how could I know?"

"No, you can't, can you?" Martha said; then: "Fanny's not a brilliant girl, Mr. Sompayac. A career is—has always been—beyond her reach. All she could have looked forward to was the joy of making some man a good wife, and his children an excellent mother. Now even that ambition—simple and modest enough, God knows!—has been denied her. Or to put it more accurately, she's been robbed of it—of the remotest possibility of ever attaining even so normal a thing. For what man among your aristocratic set, or even among our far humbler one, would take as a bride a girl who has been publicly reduced—even thought it were in no way her fault—to, well, shall we call it shopworn goods?"

Philippe stood up again.

"Mrs. Turner, your husband's down at Headquarters now, isn't he?" he said.

"He may be," Martha said, "though with his peculiar—and peculiarly unhappy—profession, one can never be sure where he's going to be at any given moment. Not even he, himself. It's quite likely that he is at Police Headquarters; he's usually there at this time of day. But, if he isn't, you'll find him pacing up and down the hospital waiting room like a caged lion. In any event, Mr. Sompayac, if I were you, I shouldn't call on him. He knows that the—the crime—no less a crime even if Fanny were tricked or induced—"

"Neither," Philippe said. "You don't know your stepdaughter, do you, Mrs. Turner? Say, rather—violated, if I may use so offensive a word in a lady's presence. They got her drunk—gave her too much champagne, knowing that she was unaccustomed to even a glass of wine . . ."

"I—I thank you for that," Martha whispered. "And I suppose it's true. Then the word 'crime' is even more fitting, isn't it? I started to say that my husband knows that the crime was the work of Rodney Schneider and his friends. By now, being the past master of his profession that he is, Mr. Turner knows the name of every individual with whom Rod Schneider has exchanged a civil time of day since infancy. And upon the list of the gallant Mr. Schneider's more recent companions, your name figures prominently, Mr. Sompayac."

She stopped, looked Philippe full in the face. Then she went on, soberly:

"I have my husband's promise that he will not take action against—any of you. Oh, not for your sakes, but for Fanny's. If she lives, the less the citizens of this city of the ever-wagging tongues know about that unsavory mess, the better, say I. And Mr. Turner agrees. But he is—a violent man. Whether he can contain his wrath—his so very just wrath, Mr. Sompayac!—when confronted by one of Rodney Schneider's cronies in the flesh—is something I, who know him best, wouldn't wager even a picayune on. In your place, young man, in spite of the fact that you've convinced me of your personal innocence in the matter, I shouldn't call on Mr. Turner. An innocent dead man is just as dead as a guilty one, it seems to me."

"And rots just as fast," Philippe said wryly. "Then what do you suggest I do, Mrs. Turner?"

"I'd suggest you do nothing at all—at least until we *know* Fanny's out of danger. In fact, considering your rather admirable behavior in the whole matter, I neither see why you should run the quite terrible risk of trying to talk to my husband while he's in the emotional state he's in right now, nor can I imagine what you could possibly want to say to him. Wait! I'm not prying, Mr. Sompayac. You may tell me or not, as you like. But—quite apart from a certain irreducible minimum of curiosity that you must allow me, as a woman—I might be able to help, to intercede on your behalf, if that's what you want, though, in your case, I fail to see why any intercession is, or even should be, necessary."

Philippe smiled. He had a good smile. It did pleasant things to his already not unhandsome face.

"I was going to ask him if he'd do me the honor—the very great honor—of granting me his daughter's hand in marriage—once she's sufficiently recovered, of course," he said.

Martha sat there. Her face paled, perceptibly. But she said nothing. Nothing at all.

'She's surprised,' Philippe thought. 'No, astonished. As astonished as I am, almost. Now how the devil did *this* happen? What circumstance or whole chain of them, or plain damned attack of insanity made me say that? A thing it wasn't in the back part of my addled head to say? Not ever in this world!'

"My daughter," Martha said quietly, "will probably never be sufficiently recovered. Even if she lives—and that, according to Dr. Terrebonne, is still more than doubtful—the best we can expect is that she'll be an invalid, Mr. Sompayac."

Philippe heard his own voice saying clearly, firmly, and with easy confidence:

"Doesn't matter. I'm beginning the study of medicine any day, now. As a doctor, I'll be prepared to take very good care of Fan. And, as her husband, I—"

He stopped short, confused at having said still another

thing that he'd never dreamed of saying, but even more so at the surprisingly real possiblity that he meant it. 'But why?' his conscious mind demanded. 'You've never more than toyed with the idea of studying medicine before! And, what's more, you don't love Fanny! As a wife for a Sompayac, she'd be absolutely dreadful! She's ignorant and gauche and more than a little stupid and—'

But he had said it. There it was.

Then Martha's face came clear. She was crying very quietly, but she was smiling at the same time, so that her tears danced on the trembling, upturned corners of her mouth.

"Oh, you fool!" she said softly. "You sweet, dear, kind, sentimental fool! I said no man would have her now, and you must prove me wrong. Prove that absolute nobility of soul exists, and that, as always it's absolutely idiotic! Still, I'm very touched, young Mr. Sompayac—oh, so *very* young Mr. Sompayac—"

"I'm twenty-two," Philippe said stiffly.

"I know. That's not what I meant. I'm afraid you men never really do grow up, do you? At least not entirely. My husband is in his late forties, and he's still playing Policemen and Robbers, and you—the White Knight Come to Rescue the Demoiselle in Distress! Oh, please! Don't look so hurt! I'm not trying to mock you! I'm very touched, and very honored—but, even so, you'll permit me to refuse? On my husband's behalf, on my own—even on Fanny's—"

"I don't see—" Philippe began.

"I know you don't—and that's just the point. You want to undo a wrong, a wrong you had no part in, by the very noble process of taking upon yourself the consequences of other people's sins. You'd marry a very badly damaged girl—oh, I'm not talking about her physical injuries, nor even her lost virginity—Oh, dear! Now I have shocked you, haven't I?"

"A little," Philippe said ruefully; "but please do go on, Mrs. Turner!"

"All right. I must try to remember that you're a Southern gentleman, and that my beliefs—my ardently feminist, bluestocking beliefs—had best be kept under control, shall we say?"

"No!" Philippe laughed. "Please don't control them,

Mrs. Turner! I find you—enchanting—so please say what you will!"

"Again, all right. Put it this way: I've been married a good many years to a difficult, choleric, utterly impossible man—whom I love with all my heart. There have been times when I've wanted to shoot him. There will be such times again; but I never will, because, you see, I love him. Wait! Please don't interrupt! You'd take upon yourself his daughter who all her life has been even more difficult than her father: moody, sullen, often terribly irascible, uncommunicative—in short, in her own way, impossible, too—"

"But I *know* Fanny!" Philippe said. "She's brave and gallant and gay! And she—she has enormous dignity, which *you've* taught her surely, if not by precept, then by example, and—"

"Once more, I thank you," Martha said. "Everything you've said, is, to some degree, true. She has many fine and winning traits. And I love her as though she were my own. You—you knew she—isn't, didn't you?"

"Yes," Philippe said.

"Good. But she, like her father, also has all those quite opposite, negative traits I mentioned. And those are the ones you'd have to live with, Philippe—Oh, I am sorry!"

"And I—delighted. Please do call me Philippe, Mrs. Turner! Since like it or not, believe it or not, you're going to be my mother-in-law—ugh! How horribly you Anglo-Saxons put it! Say rather, ma belle-mére—my beautiful, beautiful little mother, whom I'll always respect, cherish—and love, what else could you call your son?"

Martha smiled at him, sadly.

"You *are* a dear," she said. "And if I were the kind of woman I despise, I'd leap at this chance to save my stepdaughter from the terrible situation she's in. I'd acknowledge that marrying Fanny off to a Sompayac would be what most middle-class American housewives would call a godsend. But I won't let you, Philippe Sompayac, wreck your life. Neither nobility nor self-sacrifice—and especially not when they're based upon a sudden impulse towards pity, say—are enough to sustain a marriage. There has to be love, my boy—the kind of love that passeth understanding, or the close confinement of two beings as essentially different as any man and any woman are, in the same house, even in the same bed, for a life-

time, would be the closest approximation of hell ever
dreamed of, a torture beside which Dante's *Inferno* becomes as innocuous as a children's playground."

She stopped, and smiled, seeing how white, how
shocked his face had become. She thought: 'He's a true
romantic, and romantics endure truth with even less grace
than other people do. Still, I can't afford—mercy, now.
Besides, the word's wrong. It's hardly merciful to keep a
man locked—or trapped—in childhood. For I suspect that
maturity's reached the day we don't need to be lied to
about anything, when we can accept, or at least endure,
truth's atrociously appalling ugliness!'

She said: "Marriage often is just that still, even when
the people involved love one another. But then, there are
compensations: minutes, hours, rarely even days that—
that blaze with joy. That's precisely what I'm afraid of, in
your case. I'm sure that you and Fanny would be separated, even divorced, before three years were out. That is,
unless you're prepared to say a thing I'm sure you're not:
that you love Fanny. You said you couldn't lie to me. So
now let's give that statement rough proof. Do you love my
daughter, Mr. Sompayac?"

Philippe bent his head.

"No," he said miserably.

Martha got up, smiled, put out her hand to him.

"Then this interview is over. Continuing it is rather
fruitless, don't you think? I—I've enjoyed your company.
And you're welcome to call whenever you like—"

"Mrs. Turner!" Philippe got out. "I'm neither a child
nor a fool! I—I wouldn't *let* myself love Fanny before,
because I—I thought she was Rod's fiancée, sort of—
and—"

"You mean," Martha said tartly, "that you *knew* she
was his mistress, don't you?"

Philippe hung there.

"Yes," he said finally, "I did know that, Mrs. Turner,
and hated it with all my soul! You see, I was powerfully
attracted to her from the first, and—"

Martha reached up and patted his cheek. The gesture
was oddly maternal, strangely comforting.

"It's all right, Philippe," she said. "That particular
snare: the lure of common carnality, has kept the race
alive all these millions of years. I don't despise it. I, as a

woman, ask only that it be accompanied by other things: friendship, liking, love—the meeting of minds, of spirits, even. For if it isn't, Darwin's wrong: we remain un-evolved—and apes."

Philippe bent then, took her hand, raised it to his lips.

"Oh why didn't *I* see you first!" he wailed.

"Probably because you weren't even born when my wild man came along and swept me off my feet," Martha laughed. Then she added, softly. "Thank you for the com-pliment, dear boy. I assure you that I appreciate it. Any woman in her forties would!"

He stood there. Then he said.

"Will you give me a chance? If, within a year or two, I can demonstrate to you that I love Fanny enough to—"

"Forget her past?" Martha said wryly. "Refrain from throwing her sins into her teeth every time you quarrel? Remember I know men, Philippe. What you propose ap-pears to me so very difficult as to be practically impos-sible. But—there's something about you—a rare quality, it seems to me . . . Oh, very well, if you insist, you have your chance! Call upon us day after tomorrow. Sunday night. By then, Dr. Terrebonne assures us that he will be able to tell for certain if—Fanny is going to live—or not. So I can't tell you now whether you'll be joining a cel-ebration—or a wake. But, in either event, please do come . . ."

So it was that young Philippe Sompayac took his leave filled with a wild determination to embark upon a public career and a private way of life he hadn't so much as dreamed of before that very hour. What was worse, he was far from sure he wanted either; and was achingly aware he'd been a fool, not realizing that folly is man-kind's normal state, and only one of the many penalties imposed upon every man of woman born for the mortal sin of being young. And that he, like every son of Adam—or of Grandfather Ape—upon the face of earth would go on paying the penalties of the bending, burden-some, corroding years until the sin itself had been expi-ated.

But, by then, it wouldn't matter.

## Chapter Five

As it turned out, Martha's predicition was wrong: that evening at the Turner's proved to be neither a celebration nor a wake; but something poised delicately between the two. For if the family could rejoice over Dr. Lucien Terrebonne's assurance that Fanny would live, they had to mourn his equal certainty that she would never be well again.

"That lung's a mess," he said gruffly. "The amount of scar tissue it's going to have in it when it heals will play the very devil with its normal elasticity. If I dared, I'd extirpate it entirely. She'd be better off without it—"

"Then why can't you, Doc?" Bill Turner said.

"Because she'd die on the operating table before I was halfway through," Dr. Terrebonne said. "This way, she'll live. With care she might even live out her normal life span. The point is, Mrs. Turner—and I address you deliberately instead of your husband, because it's going to be largely up to you—she'll need a great deal of care. No violent exercise—ever. No lawn tennis, bicycling, swimming. She might manage a little croquet from time to time—in fact, mild exercise like walking, for instance, should be good for her. Never let her go out on even a slightly cloudy day. For, if she catches a cold and it settles on her chest—don't call me! Call your priest—sorry! I mean your pastor—and the undertaker—"

"Oh dear!" Martha said.

"I know I'm being rough," the doctor said, "but it's better to be in cases like this. She'll be particularly susceptible to pulmonary and respiratory diseases. If we can get her through the next two years without her catching pneumonia or tuberculosis, we can count the battle nearly won. Any infection that makes her cough could tear that scar tissue loose and she'd hemorrhage so massively that she'd be dead before I could get here, before any doctor could, for that matter, even if he lived across the street . . ."

"Jesus!" Bill Turner said.

"Doctor—" Martha said, "what if—if he lived in the same house with her?"

Dr. Terrebonne stared at Martha. He tried briefly to explore the ramifications of her question, but he could not. 'Woman!' he thought. 'So now she's dreaming up a captive pillpusher, chained to the doorpost for all emergencies!' He said:

"If he were good—very, very good, Mrs. Turner—in that case, he might save her. The chances are remote, but he might."

"Doctor—" Martha said then, "can she—can she—ever marry?"

"A doctor, you mean?" Dr. Terrebonne said, getting the picture now, seeing it clear. "Do you have such a candidate in mind, Mrs. Turner?"

"Well—" Martha said, "say—a medical student, so far. But he impresses me as being exceptionally bright and—"

"Does he know about—*this?*" Dr. Terrebonne said grimly.

"Yes," Martha said, "and has already expressed his willingness to take on Fanny's case on a permanent basis—"

"Martha!" Bill Turner said. "Who the devil—"

"Later, Bill," Martha said. "Well Doctor?"

"Then he's very noble—and a fool. But the words are usually synonyms, aren't they? I'd have to give a very qualified answer to that, madame. You're a married woman; and you've had a child. Have I your—and yours, too, sir!—permission to speak frankly?"

"Of course!" Martha said.

"Martha's a dadblamed blue stocking, Doc!" Bill Turner said. "You *can't* shock her."

"All right. Sexual relations would have to be very limited—at least at first—although I shouldn't rule them out altogether—"

"Why not, Doctor?" Martha said.

"Now that's truly a woman's question!" Dr. Terrebonne laughed. "One, Mrs. Turner, because I assume, having married him, your daughter would like to keep her husband. And, despite my religious background, I assure you that celibacy is an offense against nature for men and women, both! It's unhealthy, mentally and morally dangerous, and destructive to the personality of anyone who tries it. And to make myself entirely clear, for the woman, marital relations provide a calming, soothing effect, quite apart from their procreative uses—"

"Not to mention," Martha said mischievously, "that they're an awful lot of fun!"

"Martha!" Bill Turner roared.

"Ha!" Dr. Terrebonne said. "You've got yourself a treasure, Mr. Turner! D'you know, half my female patients would be cured miraculously overnight if I could get them to admit the simple fact that physical love is *not* a one-way street. But since that fat, idiotic woman came to the throne of England and drowned all the world in her absolutely abnormal if not actually deranged concepts of morality, every day I'm called in by more and more women who're nervously sick because they're trying to forget, or deny, one basic fact: that while homo sapiens may be the highest of the animals, he is, none the less, an animal, and that goes for his mate, too! So this outrageously idiotic attack upon nature's laws—great, strapping women trying to change themselves into delicate, swooning flowers, instead of healthy, normal females, to leave the animal for the vegetable kingdom, as it were!—is foredoomed to failure. For—damn it all!—the female has to *like* loving and being loved, and I do mean in the fleshly sense—or this old world would grind to a halt in one generation . . ."

"Sore subject with you, isn't it, Doctor?" Martha said with a smile.

"It is. Causes me tons of unnecessary work. Where was I? Oh yes: The question of your daughter's eventually marrying. Offhand, I'd say a tender, considerate husband—very considerate, of course—whether he were a doctor or not, might well prolong Fanny's life—"

"And if he *were* a doctor?" Martha said.

"That would be a help," Dr. Terrebonne said dryly, "especially if he were also a millionaire, and doesn't need to practice his profession. Except at home, of course!"

"Oh, dear!" Martha said. "I never thought of that!"

"Well, think of it now," the doctor said. "What would your daughter do, if she started to hemorrhage while her husband was on the other side of town delivering a baby? I know of no other profession whose members are so seldom at home . . ."

"Mine," Bill Turner said grimly.

"Well, perhaps—yes. I can see how that could be," the doctor said.

"It's so, Doc," Bill said. "I have to be so busy watching over other folks' children that I have no time for my own. What happened to Fanny couldn't have happened to—a lawyer's daughter, say—or an engineer's or—"

"Bill," Martha said sadly, "don't blame yourself. Blame—me. I had both the time and the opportunity to watch over Fanny, and I—I didn't. I didn't because I mistook my theories—my so very advanced theories—for facts. I thought that too much supervision would—harm her. I thought that by loving her, trusting her, she'd—"

"Honey, all you forgot was that she isn't *yours*," Bill said, "that she's got her mother's blood in her. A daughter of yours and mine wouldn't have needed watching. But Maebelle's child damned sure did. Forget it. Water under the bridge now. So, Doc, you think it might not be a bad idea for my girl to get hitched to whatever young sprig it is that Martha's dug out from under a rock?"

"I didn't say that," Dr. Terrebonne said, "I should have to know the young man, too, before I could judge. I merely said that I shouldn't rule out marriage for Fanny—in three, four, or five years from now. If she survives to reach nineteen or twenty, her health might even get to be reasonably good. But her husband would have to give up the idea of becoming a father. A pregnancy would kill her surely. They could adopt an infant or two, of course; bringing up a child might even be a joy and a distraction. But giving birth to her own would be suicide . . ."

"I see," Martha said softly.

"One other thing, Mrs. Turner," Dr. Terrebonne said. "Watch her weight. Oh, I know that in this benighted region we associate plumpness with health; but it isn't so. Fat's unhealthy. Taxes the heart, the lungs, the circulatory system—everything. She'll have to be somewhat idle; so she'll gain back the pounds she's lost since her—accident—much too easily. You must convince her of the necessity of maintaining a really spartan diet, which, of course, I'll write out for you. And now, by your leave, I must go. I have a good many patients to see . . ."

"Doc," Bill Turner said, "when d'you think we can bring her home?"

"Say—three weeks. A month. Mid-November. Make sure her room's warm, well ventilated, but with no drafts. Good night, friends; I'll drop in again from time to time . . ."

"You do that, Doc," Bill Turner said.

But if that evening was for Bill and Martha Turner neither truly joyous nor truly sad, for young Philippe Sompayac, who arrived dutifully at the stroke of eight, half an hour after the doctor had gone, it proved an ordeal in the primitive sense of the word—that is, a trial by combat and by pain.

Before he could even ring the doorbell to summon Eliza to open the door for him, he could hear Detective Sergeant William P. Turner roaring:

"Young Sompayac! One of the gang! By God, Martha, a body'd think you'd taken leave of your senses! I'll see Fanny dead and in hell before I'll—"

"Bill," Martha said, "he had nothing to do with it. He wasn't even there. What's more, he tried to warn Fanny and—"

There was a silence; then Bill Turner said in a quieter tone of voice that fairly dripped skepticism, Philippe thought:

"Just you tell me one thing, honey: how the devil do you know all that?"

"He told me so, himself," Martha said.

"*He* told you!" Bill Turner bellowed. "Ye gods and little fishes! There's nothing like a woman! The bastard tells her and she—"

"Believed him. Yes, I did, Bill. You can't deny that I'm an excellent judge of character. So I believed Philippe Sompayac; I still do. Just as I believed you when you came back to New York and asked me—for the second time—to marry you. I had no proof that you were over that really dreadful creature either, then—except your word. I don't think you've ever deliberately lied to me about anything serious—in part because you know I'd see through you in a minute. Well, this boy is like that. Straight. He doesn't lie—"

"So, on the basis of your feminine intuition, I'm supposed to—"

"Believe him, too? No. Let me give you some circumstantial evidence, Sergeant Turner! He came *here* to this house, believing Fanny was dead, to offer me his apologies for having failed to save her. I had to restrain him from seeking you out to offer them to you. Even knowing that you'd probably shoot him first, and ask questions later, he wanted to do the right thing. I like him, Bill. I quite honestly think he'd make Fanny a wonderful husband. My only hesitation is based upon my equally honest belief that she'd make him an awful wife—"

"There you may be right," Bill Turner said sadly. "But all the same—say! Isn't that the doorbell?"

"Yes," Martha said. "Which means the subject of our discussion has arrived. I told him he could come tonight. Bill, I ask you, I beg you—"

"To mind my manners? All right, honey. I believe in fair play; and, except for that once in Shreveport, I've never condemned anybody without a trial . . ."

Eliza opened the door.

"Come in, Mister Phil," she said.

Crossing that room to offer Mr. Turner his hand was a re-acting of the Biblical tale—or myth—of Daniel in the lion's den, except that there was nothing legendary or mythological about it now. The glare in Bill Turner's green eyes was that of the great predatory beasts, to whom the act of killing was mere instinct, a reflex, really, and who didn't even know the meaning of fear. Worst of all, Bill Turner kept his hand firmly at his side.

But, seeing that, all the hot blood, high valor of his ancestors, duelists par excellence, rushed to Philippe's head.

"I offered you my hand, sir!" he said, his voice a whipcrack.

"Bill, please!" Martha said.

"No, Mrs. Turner," Philippe said, "I fight my own battles. Mr. Turner, do you honestly believe I'd be here now, that I'd risk your known temper and expert marksmanship, if I were—in any way guilty of the—offense against your daughter?"

Slowly the stiffness went out of Bill Turner's big body.

"You might think I couldn't prove it one way or another," he said, "but, anyhow, I like your nerve, young fellow—and here's my hand on *that*."

Philippe took his hand, said, evenly, quietly:

"Mr. Turner, when I left the hospital an hour ago, your

daughter was both alive and fully conscious. They wouldn't let me see her, of course, since I'm not—or at least not yet—kin. But when you visit her, sir, don't ask her who her assailants were; she probably wouldn't tell you, for fear of what you might do to them. Instead, please do ask her specifically one question: Whether *I* was among them. Surely, in your profession, you've learned to know when a person is telling the truth. And even more so, as a father, you ought to be certain when your own daughter is—"

"I," Bill said ruefully, "wouldn't bet on that last one, son. Wait until you have a daughter, and you won't be all that sure, either. But I am a good judge of men—and now I'm inclined to believe you, too. Damned if I'm not! I see what Martha means. You're a sterling article, aren't you, young Sompayac? Say! Come to think of it, I may have some proof—at least some mighty fine evidence—at that. Were you, or weren't you in the Stag day before yesterday—with Rodney Schneider and his gang of junior rapists?"

"Bill—" Martha said.

"It's all right, Mrs. Turner," Philippe said; then, to her husband: "I can't answer that with a yes or no, sir. I was in the Stag day before yesterday; but I was not with Rodney Schneider and his friends. I came there looking for them; that's true enough. You see, I had something to say to them. I came, said it, and left. Didn't your informant tell you that?"

"Yep," Bill chuckled, "and also that you gave 'em merry Ned! He'd already put his hand on his gun next to the cash drawer in case one of those young fools started shooting. I'm talking about Mike, the bartender, of course. The funny part about it is that he didn't know who you were, and that's downright strange, seeing as how he knows all the rest . . ."

"I'm not much of a drinker, sir," Philippe said. "I've run with that pack at the racetracks and—" He stopped, his face gone scarlet.

"The sort of houses that young men frequent not only at the risk of their own health, but that of their brides, and even of their unborn children," Martha said; and the fact that her voice was gentle didn't lessen its severity one iota, Philippe realized. "And that I want your promise that you won't, again—if you and I are to remain friends, Philippe. Do I have it?"

"Yes, madame," Philippe said without hesitation. "In fact, I made that same promise to my father confessor, Père Du Bois, day before yesterday, after leaving here. I'm sorry, Mr. Turner; but I seem to have forgot what I started to say—"

"Martha confuses even me," Bill Turner laughed. "You were saying, I think, that you're not much of an elbow-bender . . ."

"I'm not. I don't claim excessive virtue, sir; it's just that I don't even like the taste of the stuff. That's why the bartender at the Stag didn't know me."

"Bill," Martha said tartly, "is the inquisition over? If so, I should like to ask Mr. Sompayac to sit down—and offer his a small glass of light wine before dinner. You do drink wine, don't you, Philippe?"

"Yes, Mrs. Turner, but nothing stronger," Philippe said.

"Sit down, young fellow," Bill Turner said. "Reckon I'll sample the juice of the vine, too. Martha was telling me you want to marry my girl. Is that so?"

"Yes, sir, it is," Philippe said.

"In spite of all you know about her by now?" Bill Turner said.

"The Book we read in our churches," Philippe said evenly, "says: 'Let he who is without sin cast the first stone.' Don't Protestant Bibles say the same thing?"

"They do," Bill Turner said, "but practicing that commandment is a lot rougher than preaching it, son. Believe me, I know . . ."

"Bill," Martha said; "must you discuss this now? It will be years before Fanny's well enough to marry—if she ever is. And Philippe has to finish his studies, both pre-medical and medical. Why don't we leave the whole thing up to time? Philippe *thinks* he wants to marry Fanny. And, even disregarding youth's natural bent towards romantic folly, the probabilities are that he'll meet some nice, sweet girl, entirely sound of body, who—"

"Never!" Philippe said. "Wait, Mrs. Turner; let me explain: I don't mean I might not meet one or a dozen attractive girls, but that it will make no difference. I intend to marry Fanny, and that's that."

"You mean," Martha said with a smile, "if her father, and I, and even Fanny herself haven't any objections, don't you, young man?"

Philippe turned, stared at her, and his eyes were appalled, suddenly. Martha felt a wild, almost irresistible desire to laugh aloud. 'He looks just like Billy,' she thought, 'when I've taken some dangerous or—or filthy object from him, a thing he doesn't really want, has practically no interest in; but *because* it has been denied him, suddenly it becomes an article of supreme value in his eyes. Men! Why do we even use the word when you all remain boys 'til the day you die at age eighty?'

"Well, don't you, Philippe?" she said.

Philippe laughed then, wryly, said:

"Y'know, I never thought of that! I'd figured that Mr. Turner might object rather violently; but I was—and am!—confident I could win him over once he saw my intentions were entirely honorable. And you, madame—I was sure you'd eventually see that Fanny's best interests would be served by such a marriage. But that Fanny, herself, might object never occurred to me! And yet—you're right. I—I should almost surely remind her—too much of—of an episode in her life she'd much prefer to forget and—"

"Dinner's served!" Eliza called out.

Philippe looked up at the old woman with a rueful smile.

"And you, Eliza? You haven't put any poison in my soup, have you?" he said.

"Nawsuh!" Eliza laughed, "just a mite o' gris-gris. Love powders, making sho' you gits your heart's desire. You see, Mister Phil, I'm on your side, now. You'll make my baby a mighty fine husband, 'deed you will!"

The supper was pleasant enough. All through it, Mr. Turner asked Philippe questions about his studies, his family, his background, the sort of questions any father might well ask a prospective son-in-law. Seeing that he asked them with no intention to offend, even kindly Martha didn't interrupt him. Besides, one of the things Bill Turner's profession had taught him was what the right questions to gain the maximum information were, and also how to ask them without betraying his own motives or angering or alarming the suspect too far ahead of time—though he could do both when the occasion seemed to warrant it.

Yet his need to ask them was not motivated by the religious and racial differences between him and his young guest. By that October day in 1895, the social distinctions between the original French Creole settlers of Louisiana and the Americans who had taken over after Jefferson had bought the territory from Bonaparte had broken down almost completely. The reason that William Turner knew so little about the Sompayacs was not because they were Creoles, or even because they were Roman Catholics, but because they were aristocrats, a class forever closed to policemen. In fact, he knew no more about the Schneiders, the Waterses, the Phelpses, and the Downeys, who, though Americans and Protestants, belonged, if not to any real aristocracy, at least to a plutocracy, and hence were on terms of easy intimacy with the wealthier French families. On that level, he knew from the society pages of the newspapers, intermarriage was becoming a commonplace. But a wedding involving a Sompayac and the daughter of—as he himself put it—"an ordinary gumshoe," was anything but a commonplace. Hence his feeling of being beyond his depths, his need to acquire enough solid information to be able to estimate accurately what both the possibilities and the dangers were.

He found out that Jean-Paul Sompayac, Philippe's father, was in the import-export business, dealing largely in luxury articles from Europe, with those from France predominating: perfumes, fine textiles, Breton laces, the wines of Bordeaux, Burgundy, and Provence, the best champagnes, Limoges china, and the like. He also discovered, to his astonishment, that the Sompayacs were a little ashamed of the source of their considerable wealth.

"We *were* planters," Philippe said ruefully. "We still own Les Granges; but only because Papa's a sentimentalist. Doesn't pay. It's—cane, you see; and there's no money in sugar these days . . ."

"Cotton doesn't either," Bill Turner said. "Had me a place, I'd grow livestock and garden produce: vegetables, fruits, and a few grains. Though Louisiana's too wet for grains, mostly . . ."

Philippe looked at the big man with surprise, hearing

the note of longing that had got into his voice.

"That—that's your dream, isn't it, sir?" he said softly.

"Touché!" Martha laughed. "It is, indeed, and mine, too. To leave this miserable police business and retire to a farm. Country living is ever so much more gracious . . ."

Philippe looked at her, then turned back to her husband.

"Mr. Turner, may I ask *you* something?" he said. "Frankly I'm curious: how'd you happen to meet Mrs. Turner? You seem so—so different and—"

"Meaning Martha's a lady, and I'm a rough, vulgar old flatfoot? Right. Damned right. Well, I had ambitions once, son. I worked as a law clerk in her father's offices in New York. He was going to take me into the firm as soon as I finished my studies and passed the bar. For Martha's sake, you understand. Since she persisted in being fool enough to care for me, the old party meant to raise me up to their high level, or try to anyhow—"

"Bill, please!" Martha said.

"God's truth. They're real Northern aristocrats, Martha's folks, as you can tell by the tricks she can do with the Queen's English—"

"She does talk—beautifully!" Philippe said. And there was warmth and fervor in his voice.

"Wish I could get Fanny to copy her way of talking, and blamed near everything else," Bill Turner sighed. "Anyhow, son, to make a long story short, I got in trouble. Oh, nothing dishonest—it was woman trouble. Even married the filly—"

"And broke my heart," Martha said softly.

"And mine," Bill said grimly. "The result of that—mistake—was Fanny. And maybe my punishment for making it, too—"

"Why, Bill!" Martha said.

"Aren't you being—a little harsh now, sir?" Philippe said.

"Maybe," Bill Turner said, "and maybe not. Depends on a lot of things: whether I—we—can figure out a workable way of saving my poor child. Not that I'm throwing out your idea, young fellow. But that's still such a long way off. You've got your studies to finish and—"

"Which reminds me," Martha said crisply. "School opens in September. It's mid-October now, and you're still here. May I ask why, Philippe?"

"Well—" Philippe said, a dark flush of embarrassment spreading over his handsome young face, "I was—a trifle late in getting my application in . . . The truth is, I haven't heard from the Dean of Harvard's Medical School yet. I'm afraid I won't be able to matriculate before mid-term, now. But I'm sure they'll take me. My grades at Princeton were plenty good enough . . ."

"So, in the meantime," Martha said with a smile, "you indulge in sweet idleness, go on wasting time?"

"Not exactly. I'm reading every medical book I can get my hands on—Dr. Terrebonne lends them to me. Swears he's going to tutor me a bit, if he ever finds a minute free; but since he never will, I'll have to forego that privilege, I suppose . . ."

"All of which indicates," Martha said dryly, "that your decision to study medicine was rather sudden, wasn't it, young man? And I wonder if your motives for making it would stand close inspection, as it were? Tell me, Philippe—"

"Martha, for God's sake!" Bill Turner cut her off. "Who's grilling the suspect, now? Leave the young fellow in peace, will you?"

"Why thank you, sir!" Philippe quipped. "I was shaking in my boots, to tell the truth!"

Bill Turner took his watch out of his vest pocket, looked at it, said:

"Lord, it's late! I'll have to be going. Got a job to do, tonight—"

At once Philippe was on his feet.

"Then I'll be going, too," he said.

"Have I frightened you that much?" Martha laughed. "Please don't go yet, Philippe! I promise not to—to 'grill' you anymore. And while Bill is rather an ogre, he really doesn't mind your staying and chatting with me a while. Do you, darling?"

"Not at all," Bill Turner said. "But before I start out on my job—this doggoned, dirty, rotten, miserable job that somebody's got to do—"

"Oh, I should think being a detective must be very exciting," Philippe said.

"It's not," Bill Turner said tiredly. "Don't believe what they write in the penny dreadfuls, son. Usually all it adds up to is being cold and wet and sleepy and bored stiff waiting for things to happen that generally don't, at all . . ."

"Like those two bank robbers last summer, sir?" Philippe said.

"I was lucky, and they weren't," Bill Turner said. "Incidentally, that kind of thing's a sore spot with Martha, here. She doesn't believe in shooting folks for any reason whatsoever. Reckon if she had her way, we'd go around kissing crooks!"

"If you put her on the force, sir, I'm sure they'd all surrender if offered *that* inducement!" Philippe said.

"Young fellow, I'm beginning to wonder if it's my daughter you're planning to court, or my wife," Bill Turner said. "Anyhow, what I meant to ask you before I got kind of sidetracked is: Say this business of you and my Fanny getting hitched gets somewhere, how're you going to get around *your* folks? Don't tell me they aren't going to raise holy Ned at the idea of your marrying a filly who's both a Protestant and the daughter of an ordinary plainclothes policeman to boot?"

Philippe knew better than to lie. "That will take some doing, I admit," he said. "But my father's a very honorable man, Mr. Turner. I'll tell him I'm—well, obligated to marry Fanny. That I'm in a way responsible for—her present condition. As I am. I didn't try hard enough to prevent it. I should have come to you, to Mrs. Turner, or to Fanny herself, instead of merely sending a note . . ."

"Forget it. Water under the bridge now," Bill Turner said. "Well, good night, son. Don't keep my missus up too late. For all that she doesn't look it, she's getting along in years, herself . . ."

"Why, Bill, darling," Martha laughed; "what an *extremely* gallant thing to say!"

A week from that day, Philippe came striding through the waiting room of the hospital with a huge bouquet of red roses in his arms. They had his visiting card attached to them. On the card was written: "Get well soon, for my sake—Philippe."

'My penance for the sin of folly,' he thought, 'my offering before the altar of the patron saint of fools!'

He had brought Fanny a fresh bouquet every day that

week. 'And,' he told himself with wry amusement, 'I'm going to go right on bringing them until they let me see her. Another two weeks, Dr. Terrebonne says. This business of not letting her have visitors at all—not even, bondieu! Martha—doesn't sound too good. Says she's very weak. A slight relapse. Tonnerre! I wonder what he means by slight?'

He had almost reached the reception desk—in fact the old battle-ax guarding it was already smiling at him, having fallen easy victim to his much too practiced charm, when that feeling hit him—again.

'I'm being—watched,' he told himself. 'I'm sure of it, now. Every time I've come here, I've sensed it. And whoever's doing it is very good at it; very expert. Because I *never* catch him . . . Which means—somebody sent by—Bill Turner.'

He stopped in midstride; stood there, frowning.

'That hurts,' he admitted to himself. 'That hurts like hell. I was letting myself actually start to like the horny-handed old cuss. Always so affable with me, now. It's "son" this, and "son" that; and "Let me tell you, Phil-boy, I—" A fraud! Suspicion's second nature to him, I guess. And haven't I been running into him a damned sight too frequently here of late?'

He stared at the visitors in the waiting room, one by one, carefully. If Bill Turner had "hung a tail" on him, as the big detective called it, he had chosen his operator very well indeed. Every man in the waiting room was so ordinary, so normal, each face so set in the expected lines of worry and concern proper to a man visiting a sick relative or friend, that if one of them were a paid informer, Philippe decided, he'd missed his calling, for an actor of that caliber could have made a fortune upon the legitimate stage.

He looked them over again, even more carefully. 'No, damn it all!' he thought. 'I must be crazy! Not a single one of these types could possibly be—'

Then he stopped. Did Bill Turner's operator have to be a *man?* Wouldn't it be subtler, and all the more effective for being unexpected, for the detective to have set a woman on his tail?

'He could quite easily,' Philippe thought. 'Some ex-prostitute, say. A reformed dope addict. One of the poor female devils he's helped a thousand times now—according to his tales. Good tales at that—told well. Seasoned with just the right amount of humorous self-depreciation to make them convincing . . .

'Only there's not one woman in this place who fills the bill,' the young Creole reasoned. 'It's my nerves, I suppose. After all, these last two weeks have been a strain . . .'

But, by then, he'd seen the girl. He had the feeling he'd seen her before, without having anything about her register in his conscious mind. Which, he decided at once, was not at all surprising. Busily knitting, her fingers making the great bone needles fly with real skill, the girl who sat there in a far corner of the waiting room was small, mousy, plain.

'Looks,' he thought mockingly, 'as though she just crawled out of the woodwork!'

But then, at that precise moment, he caught her at it; knew absolutely, in one-quarter or less of a heartbeat, that it was she who had been watching him all week; was just as sure upon the spur of that same instant that Bill Turner had had nothing to do with it, that whatever her motives for observing him were, they were her own.

He even had time—so swift is thought, so volatile the emotions of the young—to revise his first opinion of her. The girl who sat there with her wide, soft, penny-brown eyes flickering reflected light over his face, so that her gaze had both the feel and the texture of a caress, was—whatever else under heaven she might have been—most certainly not plain!

Then, seeing that he was—for the first time, and at long last—aware of her existence, and, to her acute shame, had seen her looking at him, perhaps—worse still!—had even recognized the quality of hopeless longing in her eyes, the unrepressed and unrepressable tenderness that a whole week of watching daily his every move had engendered in her for this—to her, at least—princely young man she already knew she could never have, she bent her head with an odd, angular, ungraceful motion, peered down at her knitting, but, as he saw at once, dropped all her stitches, making an unholy snarl of the bright wool, her fingers trembling wildly, losing all their easy skill, while a perfect sunburst of color exploded in her cheeks, almost drowning the thick dusting of freckles with which her face was covered.

He didn't even hesitate. He walked over to where she sat, stood there looking down at her. She was, he realized, not at all pretty. But she was something better than pretty. She was—alive. Wonderfully alive. Taut as a violin string. Vibrant with life.

"Drop one, purl two," he said solemnly.

She looked up at him, and he was lost. For, gone beyond her will, her warm brown eyes fixed themselves upon him, light-filled, dancing; her big, wide, full-lipped, generous mouth trembled into a smile that made him forget poor Fanny, the world, time, everything at all except this bony, exquisitely sculptured face, this nose that turned at the tip so that it seemed to defy gravity in the most enchanting way he'd ever seen, these great masses of mahogany-brown hair with reddish highlights in them that shifted as she moved.

"How—how did you know that?" she said in a low, throaty voice that was as enchanting as the rest of her, Philippe decided. "Most men have no idea—"

"Of how knitting's done? To tell the truth, I don't either," Philippe said. "But I'm an only son—and I've a flock of sisters. So I guess that after hearing Maman and the girls say them so often, those words sort of stuck. D'you mind if I sit down?"

"No—" the girl murmured, "but do you think you ought to? Mightn't—*she* mind? The—girl in one-fifteen, I mean?"

Philippe stared at her. Then he gave a little snorting laugh, and sat down in the chair next to hers.

"I can see you know all about me," he said.

"Even—to your name, Mister Sompayac," the girl said. "Wait! That's not as—as brazen as it sounds. The flowers—made me curious. That's because—I haven't been lucky, that way, I reckon. To have so—so devoted a suitor, I mean. In fact—"

"In fact, you're suffering from a chagrin d'amour at the moment, aren't you?" Philippe said.

She stared at him blankly, then her eyes cleared.

"I reckon this is the first time I ever met anyone who knew how to say those words right," she said. "Natural enough, seeing as how you're French. Creole, anyhow and—"

"Well, aren't you?" Philippe said mercilessly.

She bowed her head, looked up again.

"Yes," she whispered, "come to think of it, I reckon I am . . ."

"He's a fool!" Philippe said.

"No—he isn't. You see—he—doesn't even—know . . ."

"Why don't you tell him, then?" Philippe said.

The girl looked away from him.

"Can't," she whispered. "He—he belongs to—somebody else."

"Then he's a fool, twice," Philippe said.

"I—I don't think he's a fool at all," she said gently; then: "What beautiful roses! Where on earth do you get them this time of year?"

"Our place. Les Granges," Philippe said. "Maman has an immense hothouse—so we have flowers all year round. Would you mind telling me your name?"

"Not at all. I'm Billie Jo Prescott, Mr. Sompayac."

"Billie Jo?" he said. "Good Lord!"

She smiled.

"My father wanted—a boy," she said, "so he sort of—compromised on my names. Officially it's Wilhelmina Josephine. But I reckon I'd feel amost like shooting anybody who called me that!"

"Don't blame you. 'Billie Jo' suits you. You're not from New Orleans, though. I'm *very* sure of that!"

"What makes you so sure?" she said.

"Because I'd have seen you before now if you were," Philippe said.

"I've been here since the day you started coming—to bring flowers to your girl. And you—you didn't so much as notice I was even alive—before now, that is," Billie Jo Prescott said.

Philippe grinned at her.

"Did you want me to?" he said.

She frowned. Her frown was as delightful as her smile, he decided.

"Well, did you?" he persisted.

"That," she said primly, "is not the sort of question a gentleman asks a lady, Mr. Sompayac!"

"I'm not a gentleman," Philippe said. "Besides, we're friends; aren't we, Billie Jo?"

"I—I don't know," she whispered. "You—you're a strange kind of a boy, Phil—oh dear! I mean—Mr. Sompayac . . ."

"No, you don't. You mean Philippe. Go on: say it. I want to hear you. Please?"

She shook her head.

"I—I haven't that right," she said; then: "Do you think your girl would mind if you gave me one of those roses? Oh, not for me! It's for my Aunt Ellen. She's had a stroke—and I haven't even had time to look for flowers, so far—"

"Here," Philippe said, "take them all."

"Oh, no!" Billie Jo said. "You can't do that! Your girl—"

"Is unconscious most of the time, and delirious when she's conscious," Philippe said sadly. "Fact is, she'll probably tell the nurse to throw 'em in the wastebasket. That was what she did the last time she was awake when they brought my roses in—"

"Oh!" Billie Jo said. "Mister Sompayac—"

"Philippe. Please! There's no harm in it, Billie Jo!"

"Oh—all right—Philippe—" she murmured.

"Now I know how the voices of angels sound!" he said fervently.

"If you keep talking like that, I'll go right back to calling you mister!" Billie Jo said; then: "Tell me—Philippe—what happened to her? I—heard she had an accident of some sort—but everybody's so mysterious about it—"

Philippe looked down at the floor. A long time. A very long time. Then he said:

"She tried to kill herself."

Billie Jo's silence had texture, weight. He could feel his flesh pulping, his bones turning powder under the burden of it.

"Go on!" he all but snarled at her, "say it!"

"All right," she whispered. "Was it because of—of something you did?"

"No," he said bleakly, "it was because of something I didn't do."

Her mind, which, after all was of her times, her place,

shaped by the conventions of then-existing society, read at once into that phrase an implication it didn't really have: that he was guilty of a grave sin of omission; that he hadn't done what he was honor-bound to do. She was not yet sufficiently accustomed to his tone of voice to hear that he'd placed a small, slight emphasis upon the pronoun "I" and not upon the negative auxiliary verb "didn't." He meant, "No, it was because of something not I, but another—some others—did." She heard: "No, it was because of something I ought to have done, and failed to do . . ."

And, being a woman, she immediately leaped to the obvious conclusion—though, for that matter, most men of his times would have thought the same thing—that he, Philippe Sompayac, had refused to do right by our little Nell; for the maiden vilely seduced and basely abandoned was a stock figure of Victorian melodrama.

He was aware, finally, of the ragged note that had got into her breathing. He turned, and looked at her. She had bowed her head. When she looked up again, her eyes spilled jewels down her face, one by one, slowly.

"Oh, I say!" Philippe said.

Billie Jo smiled at him then; but she didn't stop crying. She was smiling and crying at the same time so that her face reminded Philippe of one of those April days when it goes on raining while the sun is shining and there's rainbows all over the sky.

"It's—all right—Philippe—" she said gently. "You—you're *here*, anyhow. You—didn't run away from—from your obligation. Or, anyhow, you came back. And—and you'll—make it up to her won't you? Oh, Philippe, promise me you will!"

Philippe looked away from her towards the door. When he looked back again, his eyes were very bleak. He was gazing upon the fruits of Tantalus, feeling the weight of Sisyphus' stone, attending the funeral of his every hope.

"That—goes without saying, doesn't it, Billie Jo?" he said.

# Chapter Six

But, being young, he couldn't leave it at that. He sought
her out, persuaded her, employing all of his native Gallic
charm and considerable eloquence to do it, that there was
no real harm in their remaining friends, as it were; that it
would be an honor and a pleasure—he used these exact
words; a Southern gentleman in the nineties had no fear
of a little grandiloquence, had not yet had his language reduced to the flatness and poverty his sons and grandsons
must endure—for him to beguile the tedium of her stay in
New Orleans until such time as her aunt's recovery would
be sufficiently advanced for her Uncle Oliver Prescott to
come down from his plantation—between industrial Mertontown, where the textile mills were, and the so-called
twin towns of Caneville-Sainte Marie, whose historical
designation was already a misnomer since American Caneville and Creole-Cajun Sainte Marie had long since fused
into one fair-sized, bilingual, multiracial city—and bear
the two of them, aunt and niece, away to his, Philippe's,
undying sorrow. The quotation's indirect; but the words,
the style, are his.

And, because she, too, was only human; because her
woman's heart demanded, against her will, against society's conventions, against her aching feeling that in a real
sense she was sinning against the helpless girl in room
one-fifteen—the little she could have of his presence, his
company, to store up in memory against all the bleak
years she was going to have to live without him—Billie
Jo allowed him to squire her about in the evenings after
visiting hours were over, prudently saying nothing to the
half-paralyzed hulk her Aunt Ellen had been reduced to,
of activities that, innocent as they were, would have
seemed to the sick woman the very depths of depravity.

They dined at Antoine's. Danced in the ballrooms of all
the more respectable hotels. Went to the theater, explored
the old city, with Philippe serving her as a most expert
and knowing guide. He even, in what was less unconven-
tionality than a desire to find out how her mind worked,

what her opinions on such matter were, drove her through the red light district. But in this effort to discover whether she'd make him a jealous, demanding wife, or generously allow him the freedom to go on—at least occasionally—sampling the fleshpots, that every good Creole husband considered his inalienable right, he was disappointed, for Billie Jo made no comment at all. They took long buggy rides together, talked about everything under heaven except the one subject they should have: the exact nature of Philippe's relations with Fanny. But there, a certain nicety of scruple, a native reticence on both their parts, stopped them. A pity. That one omission was going to cost them bitter pain.

"Philippe—" Billie Jo said, as they sat in his buggy by the shores of Lake Pontchartrain, staring out over the bleak, gray water, "I—I wrote Uncle Oliver last week. Asked him to—to come after Aunt Ellen—and me. Yesterday, I got a letter from him. He—he'll be here tomorrow . . ."

"But, Billie Jo!" Philippe said, "your aunt's not well enough, and—"

"My aunt will *never* be well enough, Philippe. She's going to die. If not this year, then next. Reckon passing on at home, in her own bed, would be a comfort to her—"

"Billie Jo—" Philippe said then, "d'you know what you're doing to me? I ask you—do you?"

She stared out over the waters of the lake.

"Yes, Philippe, I know all right," she said. "But you've got it wrong. Half wrong, anyhow. It's not *you* I'm doing this to. It's—us. You know that, don't you?"

"Yes," he said, "I guess I do know that. But what I don't know, Billie—is why."

"I think you do," she said then, slowly. "That is, if a body can know a thing that hasn't even had the words that fit it made up yet. The closest I can get to it is to say that short of letting myself get crowded into doing what—your Fanny—almost did, I've got to go on living—inside—with one homely speckled-faced she-critter named Billie Jo Prescott. And I can only stand that if I . . . like her a little, Philippe. The trouble is that right now, as of tonight, I don't."

He stared at her, said: "Why not, Billie Jo?"

She bent her head, whispered:

"I don't think you *want* to know that, really. Don't reckon it's good for a fellow to find out what women are really like. I wonder if it's even good for us to find it out, ourselves . . . That's one thing you've done, Philippe: showed me I'm *nothing* like I thought I was. So now I need time to get used to the real me. To see if I can learn to like myself all over again the way I truly am. I doubt it. But, anyhow, that's one thing I'm glad of: that you haven't even tried to find out for yourself what sort of— of a girl you've got sitting here next to you right now. You could have, you know. Any time you wanted to. But you've been—upright. Honorable. A perfect gentleman. I should thank you for *that,* I suppose . . ."

He studied her profile in the wash of moonlight.

"But you don't thank me for it, do you, Billie?" he said.

She stared at him, her eyes bleak with the kind of self-knowledge she could neither accept nor pardon. "No," she said quietly. "To tell the truth about it—I don't."

He sat there, very still.

'What can I say?' he thought. 'What are the words? Hell! There aren't any. The time for talking's over with. Everything that could be said, already has been. So now—'

He bent swiftly and kissed her. Even at the late, late moment, he was still unsure of what his own intentions were. But then, abruptly, all the triggers—sight, taste, touch, smell—were pulled and shot their will annihilating, mind-canceling poisons through his blood.

Suddenly, his mouth was cruel upon hers, his hands expert, betraying long practice at the removal of all the barriers to accomplished desire that the haut couturiers of the belle époque placed in a man's way, feeling her fingers gripping his wrists protestingly; but he, persisting in his efforts to lay bare at least enough of her to make that brief, unlovely buggy-seat coupling possible, felt her fingers slacken, fall away, and a burst of mocking laughter rose in him ripping obscenely heartless words through his mind:

'Good-bye, Fan! 'Cause now—'

And stopped him upon the peak of that same instant, dead, inert, detumescent, his heart constricted, clutched in a fist of iron and of ice, by—memory; but an absolutely emasculating slash of shame.

He heard, again, old Eliza saying:

"She was down there on the floor, Mister Phil. And her po' li'l hand was still around the handle of that knife. Bone it was. The handle I mean, suh. And I been to hawg killings up home near Shreveport where there was a powerful sight less blood spilt than there was all over my baby, then. But I could of stood that, I reckon. What I pure Lawd just couldn't bear was when I bent my old bones down to pick her up and I seen she was—smiling at me. With that there long knife I done sharpened myself, rubbin' it on brick dust every morning, up to the handle 'twixt her pretty li'l titties; and her a-smiling! Lawd, suh, that was when I plumb went right out of my mind!"

He sat there. What moved through his head was a kind of litany, a chant: 'Bastard bastard bastard bastard! You are, you know! The same kind of thing. To take advantage of—'

Then he heard how Billie Jo was crying.

"Billie Jo—" he said, forcing her name out through a throat constricted in the literal, physical sense by the thing in him then that had no name nor any description, but a feel, and maybe a taste. And what it felt like was a weight of darkness, and what it tasted like was a swamp slime from a back bayou, the greenest, most fetid, stinkingest abomination there is in this world.

But she didn't answer him. She couldn't.

"I'm sorry!" he got out. "You just don't know how sorry I—"

But she put her slim, freckled hand up, and laid it over his mouth.

"Don't talk," she whispered. *"Please* don't talk, Philippe! Just take me home, now. Right now, this minute. And don't say anything to me 'til we get there . . ."

He obeyed her to the letter. But when he helped her down from the buggy in front of the old St. Louis Hotel, called the Royal by its new owners, she went up on tiptoe suddenly and kissed his mouth with a slow sweetsoft trembling tenderness that came as close to crippling him as anything non-physical ever can. Then she hung back against his encircling arms and looked up at him with the gaslights turning her tears amber and her mouth quivering so that its outlines were blurred and the sobs she wouldn't let out jerking her throat in a series of quite visible pulsations that seemed to Philippe to have an independent life of their own.

"Billie Jo—" he groaned.

"That was—to say thank you, Philippe," she whispered. "For stopping. For having sense—for both of us. Only—what do I do, now? How—how does a body—live—with this kind of shame? What excuse can—a girl invent to—to go on holding her head up—when she *knows* what she is? That she probably belongs in one of those—houses—you pointed out to me down on Customhouse Street?"*

"Billie Jo!" he said.

"And me—looking down on your Fanny! Thinking that if she'd had an ounce of—decency in her, what happened to her never could have. That even—loving you, she wouldn't have let you. So how much decency did *I* show tonight? No, don't say anything! You'll only lie, try to comfort me; and you can't. Nobody could, now. Funny—"

"*What's* funny?" he said.

"You. Me. Us. The world. Only I meant funny, strange, not funny, comical. If Aunt Ellen hadn't had a stroke, I would never have come down here. If your Fanny—hadn't stuck a knife into herself over the miserable way *you* treated her, you'd never have come to the hospital, and we wouldn't have met. If Uncle Oliver had anybody up home with enough sense and gumption to run the place for him, he'd have been able to stay down here with me, and then I wouldn't have been unchaperoned for the first time in my life long enough to find out *what* I am."

"And what you are, is an angel," he said, "a saint. The sweetest, the best, the—"

"Please, Philippe!" she said; and the pain in her voice was real. "Don't say things you *know* aren't so! I'm—bad. I'm a bad girl—woman—female. Any slight claim I've got to virtue right now is due to you, existing only by—your mercy, and your grace. Or maybe because you've already got one bad memory too many, now. So this is good-bye, Philippe. No, not yet. Not quite. Tomorrow will be, though. It has to be."

"Tomorrow?" he said.

"Yes. Only because I've *got* to introduce you to Uncle

*Now Iberville.

Oliver. He'd think it was awfully strange if I didn't, after all I wrote him about you—"

"Billie Jo," Philippe said. "You can't! I won't let you!"

She turned her face away from him, stared down Royal Street.

"I don't know whether I *can* or not, Philippe," she said. "All I know is that I've got to. It'll probably kill me— being without you, I mean. I only hope it does it fast. So—so I won't suffer too much. They say dying people always tell the truth, don't they? Well, I'm dying right now. My insides are—perishing—from wanting you so much. Yes, Philippe I *do* mean in the bad way! And the—the rest of me is—being tormented to death by shame. So—"

"Billie Jo, please!" he said.

"So you'll know I'm telling the truth when I say I love you. I love you and that's the best thing that ever happened to me in my whole life. You're the finest and the handsomest and the noblest—and the best, and I'm going to go right on loving you all the rest of my life 'til the day I die. And even after that in heaven forever if the Good Lord will let me get there . . ."

"And I," Philippe said, "love you, adore you, worship—"

"No!" she said. "You mustn't say it! You haven't the right, Philippe! Not with that poor girl lying there, like that, because of you. Reckon I'll pay her a little visit tomorrow—and—and beg her pardon, now that I *know* how easy it is to end up like that. Don't worry! I won't tell her why I'm apologizing. I'll just—kiss her, and say it quiet-like inside my mind: Forgive me, Fanny—for almost cheating. For trying to steal your—beau. So now—"

"Now?" he said.

"Kiss me one more time. Then go—while I can still stand it. That's—not too wrong, is it, Philippe? To kiss you—just this once—for the last time?"

He kissed her. She clung to him and sobbed like a lost-lonesome, whipped, and motherless child until he turned her loose. Then, still sobbing, she went very slowly and quietly up the stairs and into the lobby and out of his life.

For the first time.

The next day, at the hospital, he met her uncle. Oliver Prescott was a tall man, almost entirely bald. He had a good face: lean, rugged, in-hollowed, ugly in that rough-hewn way that becomes a man much more than good looks ever do. The only disharmonious thing about his face, that weakened it, Philippe thought, was his mouth. It was full, even heavy-lipped, contrasting abruptly with the rawhide and sinewy strength of the rest of his features. It was also, Philippe realized, the most sensual mouth he had seen on a human being, man or woman, in all his life.

Then he saw something else, something that upset the easy-going dichotomy of his thinking: Oliver Prescott's mouth wasn't weak. It was, actually, as strong as the rest of his face. Even to think that called for a painful mental readjustment on Philippe's part. In his times, the expression "sensual mouth" was always preceded by the adjective "weak." To encounter a strong, sensual mouth was obscurely shocking.

He studied Oliver Prescott. Decided that his strength lay in the fact that he had come to accept himself completely. That he wasn't ashamed of the sensuality his mouth revealed. That he even, perhaps, gloried in it. Still the tall man's life could not have been a very happy one. 'His eyes now,' Philippe thought, 'are so—so resigned. As though he's lived with sadness so many years that he's come to accept it as the whole of life.' And despite the quality of immense and effortlessly controlled force his whole bearing displayed, there was great gentleness in him, Philippe saw.

"This the young fellow you wrote me about, Billie Jo?" Oliver Prescott said. "The one who's been a pestering you so bad that you want me to take you away from here?"

"Oh, Uncle Oliver, you hush!" Billie Jo said. "I wrote you no such thing, and you know it! Philippe's been a perfect gentleman. And—"

"And," Oliver Prescott said with grave humor, "sometimes *that* can be a way of pestering a filly, too!"

Billie Jo stared at her uncle.

"Reckon you're just a mite *too* smart, Uncle Oliver," she said.

"Meaning?" Oliver Prescott said.

"That—you're right," Billie Jo whispered; "I—I've got to the place where I don't *want* him to be so all-fired polite and stand-offish, Uncle! And he—he's engaged. His fiancée's here in the hospital. She's had—an accident. In fact, she's right pert' bad off, and—"

"Glad to make your acquaintance, young fellow," Oliver Prescott said. " 'Preciate your being nice to Billie. And, son, I'm sorry she took it the wrong way. That's a risk a young fellow handsome as you are always has to run with the fillies, I reckon—"

"But she didn't take it the wrong way, sir!" Philippe said. "I—I love your niece, sir. Only—"

"Only that girl is at death's door—and it's *his* fault, Uncle," Billie Jo said tartly. "So he's obligated. And even if he could break it off, I wouldn't let him. I—I'd be ashamed of—both of us for the rest of our lives . . ."

"I see," Oliver Prescott sighed. "That being so—you'll just have to get over him, Billie—"

Billie Jo smiled then, but her eyes were unclear, and mist-bright suddenly.

"You're right, Uncle Oliver," she said. "Of course I'll get over him! But you know when?"

"No," Oliver Prescott said. "When will you, Billie?"

"The day they put the pennies on my eyes to hold them shut," Billie Jo Prescott said.


"Good-looking young fellow," Oliver Prescott said, once Philippe had gone. "Good manners, too. Manly—not over-refined the way most French Creoles are. Tell me, Billie, what happened 'twixt him and this girl of his? You said she had an accident, and then you said it was his fault. Blamed if I can see how you can hold a fellow accountable for something that happened accidentally. That is, if it did. Did it, Billie Jo?"

Billie Jo looked down the corridor in the direction Philippe had gone.

"No, Uncle Oliver; it wasn't an accident," she said.

"Then?" Oliver Prescott said.

"She—tried to kill herself. And he—Philippe—admits that the reason she wanted to die was *his* fault . . ."

"Lord God!" Oliver Prescott said. "Who would have thought it? Fine, upstanding-looking young fellow like him! Got her in the family way, eh? And then—"

"Something like that," Billie Jo whispered. "I don't really know. Which reminds me: Will you excuse me for five minutes, Uncle Oliver? I'll be right back . . ."

"Why, sure, honey. Hey! That's not the way to your auntie's room—"

"I know it isn't. I'm going to—to say good-bye to—*her*. To Philippe's girl. Somehow, it appears to me I ought to. I—I sort of *owe* her that much. You wait right here, Uncle. I won't be long . . ."

Of course, since she was a girl, her presence in the corridors of the women's wing of the hospital awoke no curiosity, posed no threat to Victorian morals. Therefore, no one thought to stop her, or ask what she was doing there; and she reached the door marked 115 without any difficulties at all. She paused before it, raised her hand to knock. Then something made her stop. A sort of premonition, one might call it. But, being a level-headed young lady, she dismissed it as foolish, and knocked firmly upon that door.

She was, of course, entirely wrong not to heed and obey that sudden hunch, that inexplicable icy chill of fear. But she had no way of knowing that she was knocking on the door to disaster, begging admission to the anteroom of a curiously Dantean personal inferno, from which she would never again escape, as long as she lived.

So she waited, trembling a little, until that slow, faint whisper—that husky, scarcely audible trochee, barely stirring the still air, came through to her, not then knowing that she was going to remember it forever:

"Come in . . ."

Billie Jo pushed open the door, slipped through it into that room. Closed the door behind her. Leaned back against it. No—was slammed back against it. Smashed against it, and held there hard by the kinetic, parapsychological forces generated by that pair of eyes.

'They're not—*human!*' her stunned mind wailed. 'They don't even have any *color!* They're not blue nor gray nor—they're ice. Ice—a million years old—with fire inside it—*cold* fire that burns through without even melting the frozen lakes it's buried under. Oh, Lord, I—'

"Well?" Fanny said.

"I—I—" Billie Jo floundered. "I came to—to say—"

Her voice died. She could hear her own thoughts. They made a hurt, sick, moaning sound:

'Why—she—she's lovely! She's utterly—lovely! But she can't be! How could anybody—No! Anything—this—*evil* be lovely? But she is—she is!'

"Don't be scared of me," Fanny said in that faint ghost-whisper which was all she had left of a voice. "I won't hurt you. Can't. Come over here. That's it. Closer. So we can—chat. I can't talk—loud. Haven't the—strength. 'Sides, I want to see what you've got that made Philippe—"

"Oh!" Billie Jo said, "oh, my God!"

Fanny went on studying her. Her gaze flickered over Billie Jo's face. Billie Jo could feel that glacial reflected light searing her very flesh. It felt like ice, like flame.

"You're—cute," Fanny murmured. "Cuter'n a speckled setter pup. And you—you're a *good* girl, aren't you? Pure. Never let a fellow do anything worse to you than steal a kiss, huh? Right?"

"Right," Billie Jo whispered. "But that doesn't make me good, Fanny. Just means I'd never met the fellow who could make me *want* to be bad. Up 'til now, that is."

"But now you have. Philippe," Fanny said.

"Now I have. Philippe," Billie Jo said, and bowed her head.

" 'S all right, honey. You can have him. I'll give him to you. Tell me—how was he?"

"Oh, no!" Billie Jo gasped. "You mustn't think—"

Fanny smiled at her then.

" 'S all right, honey. I was only plaguing you. I know—nothing's happened—*yet*. That's how come you're running. Scared of—yourself, aren't you?"

Billie Jo bowed her head. The gesture was abject.

"Yes," she said.

"Don't be," Fanny said, so slowly, softly that the words, a quotation, really, "This music hath a dying fall . . ." stole unbidden into Billie Jo's mind. "With you, he'll be honorable. With *your* kind of a girl, he always is. So don't feel bad about a few buggy rides and such-like with maybe a kiss or two thrown in . . ."

Billie Jo stared at her.

"How—how'd you know?" she whispered.

"The niggers. Our Eliza's cousin's boy bellhops in the hotel you're staying at. So every time you went out with Phil, I knew it. Eliza thought she was protecting my interests—the interests I haven't got. His friends took mighty good care of that—"

"His friends?" Billie Jo said.

"Yes. Didn't you know? His buddies. And—him, too. That's how come I stuck a kitchen knife into myself. I'm not wanted, honey. *Nobody* wants me. Not Philippe. Not his jug-buddies. Not—nobody. Heck, I don't even want myself . . ."

"I'm afraid I—I don't understand you, Fanny . . ."

"Know you don't. Come closer. Lean down. I'll whisper it to you. Wouldn't want one of those busybody nurses to hear. It was like this—"

Billie Jo straightened up.

"Oh, no!" she whispered. "Oh, no, Fanny! I don't believe that! He wouldn't! He couldn't—"

Fanny smiled at her, softly, serenely.

"The next time you see him, just you ask him, honey-bunch," she said. "Hey! Wait a minute! Don't go yet! I didn't mean to upset—"

But Billie Jo had already torn open the door and fled down the corridor as though all three of the Furies were after her. She was wrong. Not even the Erinyes pursue a being already damned.

As she was. As she had been from the moment she walked through that door.

"Phil-lippe!" Odette Sompayac said. "You're not eating! Again! And you haven't—all this week! And—"

"Do not preoccupy yourself, Maman," Marie-Thérèse, his oldest sister said. "That merely indicates he's fallen in love—again. Tell me, how is she called, ta 'tite amie, Philippe? She must be quite something, her—to cost you your appetite for all of a week!"

"Tais-toi!" Philippe snarled at her. "Ta gueule, Marie!"

At which, all of his sisters, Simone, Brigitte, Françoise, Hélène, and Marie-Thérèse, herself, loosed a great peal of multi-toned laughter.

But Jean-Paul Sompayac, agent mercantile, didn't laugh.

"Ça," he said grimly, "c'est assez, mes filles! That's quite enough! And you, Philippe, will have the goodness to attend me in my study after dinner—a meal which,

from this moment on, I propose to eat—if not to enjoy—
in perfect peace. Have I at least made myself clear, mes
enfants?"

"Oui, Papa!" the girls whispered. In his own household—for all that, standing up, he scarcely could touch
his son's chin with the top of his head—Jean-Paul Sompayac was something of a tyrant. A benevolent tyrant, but
still a tyrant. The only person chez les Sompayacs who
*ever* dared cross the diminutive lion of a man was his only
son, Philippe. And even Philippe didn't try it too often.

All through the meal, which Philippe went right on
picking at, listlessly, Odette Sompayac stared worriedly
from the face of her husband to that of her son. For
Jean-Paul to call his son into his study meant that Philippe had done something absolutely horrible—again. But
she didn't dare ask what that horrible thing was. Neither
of them would tell her. Besides, it wasn't her place to. In
a Creole household, the paterfamilias was lord and master, and no mere woman would ever question that fact.

'Just when,' Madame Sompayac wailed inside her mind,
'I was beginning to believe he'd actually reformed! He's
been so good—for almost a month! And I've *never* known
Philippe to be good *that* long before!'

By that time, Jean-Paul Sompayac was finishing his
dessert, which consisted of a variety of Creole pastries:
Calas tout chaud, hot rice cakes; batons amandes, almond
sticks; pain-patate, sweet potate cake; and, of course, es-
tomacs mulâtres, which were not as cannibalistic as they
sounded, being, actually, only a kind of ginger cake. Philippe, as usual, toyed with a bunch of grapes. By his natural, frugal inclination, he never ate the Creole savories
and sweets, which was why he was hounddog lean instead
of pleasingly plump the way every other member of the
family was.

"You will serve m'sieur mon fils et moi our café noir in
my study, Pierre," Jean-Paul said to the manservant, "after which you will retire and close the door. Carefully removing, of course, your big black ear a minimum of
twenty yards away from the keyhole. You have understood me, Pierre?"

"Yes, maître!" Pierre grinned. "You wants that I bring
you your razor strop, me, maître?"

"He is a trifle old for that, now, unhappily," Jean-Paul

said, looking up at his tall son. "But do not preoccupy yourself, Pierre; I will think of something, and it will be effective, I assure you—that is if this long idiote of a son of mine cannot come up with a convincing explanation for his more recent activities. Viens donc, Philippe!"

Jean-Paul drained his cup of absolutely scalding café noir without a grimace, and put it down.

"Now," he said, "you will have the goodness to explain to me, mon fils, the nature of the activities that you have indulged in which have brought you to the attention of the police. Go on, Philippe; I am waiting!"

Philippe stared at his father.

"Papa," he said, "this time you're one up on me. I don't know what you're talking about. Truly I don't. Not at all. In fact, until this very moment, I was unaware that the police had the slightest interest in me. Do they, Papa? And if so, why?"

"Do not lie to me, Philippe!" Jean-Paul roared. His voice, a true bass, made up for his small size. At the moment, he was making the windows rattle. "I will not permit you to stand there and tell me that you are unaware that some suspicion has attached itself to your name, when three times last week, the famous detective, Sergeant William P. Turner, was seen questioning you in various establishments, and with some earnestness at that!'"

A great light broke behind Philippe's eyes.

"Oh, that!" he laughed. "Mais, Papa, Detective Turner is a friend of mine! I even had dinner chez lui a week or so ago . . ."

Jean-Paul Sompayac refrained from making his habitual comment about what peculiar people Philippe frequented. He was all too aware of his son's delight in the most unsavory companions. Besides, as he knew very well, Sergeant Turner had the reputation of being entirely upright. It was said of him that he was the only officer on the New Orleans Police Force whom nobody ever even accused of taking bribes. The thing could well be worse. Philippe might have taken up with a member of the Mafia instead. He was perfectly capable of it, his father was sure. But there was still one thing to be cleared up: Philippe's highly unusual moroseness of the past few weeks. Usually, he was a gay and laughing lad—whom Jean-Paul Sompayac, privately, and to himself, admitted he adored. So now he broached that subject.

Philippe shrugged.

"There, Papa, unhappily, Marie-Thèrése has it right," he said. "I have fallen in love—hopelessly in love."

"Why, hopelessly, mon fils?" Jean-Paul said. "Does not cette fille return your affections?"

"Oh, yes, Papa! She loves me very much—of that I am certain, moi—"

"Then there is—another difficulty, hein? Her reputation, say? What *is* she? Une demimondaine? An actress? A cabaret girl? Ou même une petite putain avec qui tu t'as couché?"

"Papa!" Philippe said.

"Well, you must admit that les filles in your life up until now haven't been exactly spotless, my son! Come on, tell me: who is this one?"

"An orphan. Et une petite Américaine. Her name is Billie Jo Prescott. She has been adopted by her uncle, who is a wealthy planter. He has a place near Mertontown; you know, that mill village about ten miles from Caneville-Sainte Marie? She is good, bien elevée, has a sufficiency of culture, is sweet—but not pretty. Which doesn't matter at all, Papa. You see, I really am in love with her . . ."

"I suppose her reputation's good," Jean-Paul said. "Mais, oui, it would be. These Calvinists are very strict with ses filles. Dommage! Look, mon fils, I'd always dreamed of your marrying a girl of our own people. A Lascals, say, or a de Pontabla, or an Arceneaux, or even a Prudhomme—"

"Papa," Philippe said, "you go too fast. Or, peut-être, not fast enough. As yet you have not even tried to find out the nature of the obstacle between Billie Jo and me. Perhaps because you don't ask the right questions . . ."

"And what, may I ask, are the right questions, my son?"

"Well, to start with, you might begin by asking me what I was doing at the home of Detective Sergeant Turner last week—besides having dinner, that is . . . No, I've got it wrong; it was week before last, Papa; and—"

Jean-Paul stared at his son.

"All right: what *were* you doing there, Philippe?" he said.

"I went there to ask him the hand of his daughter—in marriage, Papa," Philippe said.

For at least two minutes, Philippe was afraid his father was going to have a stroke. But, finally, M. Sompayac got his breath back. What came out of his mouth sounded, Philippe thought, like a steamboat whistle or a calliope.

At first all he said, or rather shrieked, was the word "merde!" endlessly repeated. Then he named the names of all sorts of unsavory and repulsive animals. But when he got around to: "Petite salope d'une putain, fille d'un vulgaire agent policier et le bon Dieu même ne sait pointe quelle sorte d'une femme!" Philippe stopped him.

"That's unjust, Papa," he said mildly. "Fanny Turner is neither dirty, nor a whore. And neither the vulgarity of her father nor the morals of her mother have anything to do with it now, mon très respecté Père. She's a good kid—une bonne petite gosse, tu sais? And I *have* to marry her. You see, I got her in trouble."

That halted M. Sompayac in midnote. He dropped weakly into his chair, mopped his forehead with a silken handkerchief, and stared at his remarkably calm and unrepentant son.

"Elle est—donc—enciente?" he whispered. "She is—with child?"

"Non, Papa," Philippe said, "at least not now. I'm afraid she lost—son—*notre*—enfant—when she stabbed herself."

Short as he was, Jean-Paul Sompayac's head almost hit the ceiling of his study as he bounced up from that chair.

"She stabbed herself!" he roared. "You mean to tell me that you, a son of mine, a Sompayac, refused to—"

"Do my duty by little Fanny?" Philippe said. The ironical side of his nature was beginning to thoroughly enjoy the simple and conventional lies he was telling now, with malice aforethought, instead of a truth—or a madness—too complicated for him to convincingly explain to himself, even, and that a person of his father's all too bourgeois mental set would *never* believe. "Mais, non; Papa! She didn't even tell me! I only found it out after she'd at-

tempted suicide. They—sa famille, les Turners, tu sais—
didn't even know whether she was going to live until week
before last. So I went there—"

"And did what you had to," Jean-Paul Sompayac
sighed. "D'accord, Philippe, I agree. You are honor-bound
to marry cette pauvre petite. But tell me, mon fils, where
is she now? At home?"

"Pas encore, Papa. Her wound was of the gravest, you
understand. She's in the hospital; New Orleans General;
the women's section. Private room 115. Why?"

"Because often, upon reflection, this kind of young girl
can be induced to see the light of reason, my son. Particularly since she's not—or no longer is—with child. Perhaps
if I were to talk to her, offer her some sort of compensa-
tion, say a voyage to New York where I have business
friends, who, at my request, would give her well-paying
employment, and—"

"Papa, no!" Philippe said. "She's only a child! No more
than fifteen and—"

"And you, my son, are even more of a lecherous swine
than I thought you were. Not to mention being liable to
legal sanctions for corrupting a minor! No matter. Decency requires sufficient imagination to see beyond one's
acts to their consequences, and at least enough intelligence
to achieve the rank of plain damned fool instead of that
of goddamned one! Unfortunately, a man needs a minimum of forty years to acquire those qualities, as I can tell
you from my own sad experience, son. But now it seems
to me plus raisonable encore to get la petite Mlle. Turner
as far away from here as possible as soon as possible. And
that, precisement, is what I am going to do!"

"No," Philippe said gloomily, "the only thing for me to
do, the only decent thing, Papa, is to marry her . . ."

"A solution to her difficulties which your very tone of
voice tells me you have scant enthusiasm for, mon fils.
And which, de plus, isn't even necessary . . ."

"But, Papa—"

"Tais toi, Philippe! I am your father, and I know you. I
will go this minute and have an interesting chat with this
little Miss Turner. And when I come back, your problems
will be over—Pouf! Comme ça!" Then M. Sompayac got
up and marched out of the study.

'Why,' Philippe thought, 'didn't I argue with him? Make him think I meant it? Only decent thing to do. I gave my pledged word to—Martha. To Mrs. Turner. And this is dirty, stinking, rotten! The kind of thing Rodney Schneider would do: Send his father to buy Fan off. Still—Billie Jo. Oh Lord, Billie Jo. Why in the name of everything unholy didn't I meet her *last* month? Oh, bon petit Dieu; oh, sainte vierge Marie—let Fanny listen to reason! I know this is filthy, cheap, ugly; but, after all, it wasn't I who made her try to kill herself, or—'

That one of the hospital's ironclad rules was that female patients could not have male visitors in their rooms unless said visitors came under the categories of husband, father, brother, pastor, rabbi, or priest, Jean-Paul Sompayac already knew. He had sat upon the committee that had drawn up the rules. But he was also aware that rules exist to be waived, especially when a member of the Board of Trustees of the hospital, which he also was, asked that they be. For, in financial, as opposed to medical, matters, New Orleans General was governed by a board of wealthy business men, Creoles and Americans alike, all of whom generously contributed to its support. Again, this was one of the points where the barriers between the two groups had broken down, to the benefit of them both. Jean-Paul Sompayac, being, as he put it, "large d'esprit," big of soul, firmly approved of the fact that American as well as Creole and Cajun indigents were admitted to the hospital's charity wards free of charge. But from there to approving of his son's marrying une petite americaine, and her the daughter of a vulgar agent policier, was a step he was very far from prepared to take.

The head nurse, who knew very well who he was, hesitated a barely perceptible fraction of a second before saying: "Right this way, Monsieur Sompayac . . ."

But, as brief as her doubt-laden pause was, as quickly as she mastered it, the astute little Creole noticed her confusion.

"It's all right, nurse," he said. "My son has—well—an interest in this young person. My *only* son; you understand? So I think I'd better see what she's like . . ."

"Of course. In fact, I think you're being—very wise, sir," the head nurse said.

* * *

Fanny looked at the short, fat, dark little man who stood there by her bed.

'So—it's true,' she told herself. 'The flowers every day—That was one thing . . . Phil's a good-hearted boy. Always has been—well—specially nice to me. Could be he—he sort of fell for me before and—and out of friendship for Rod, wouldn't . . . No, I don't believe that. But Martha said he—asked Papa for my hand. Why do fellows say "hand," when that damn sure ain't—isn't—the part of a girl they've got in mind? Asked Papa—if he could marry me, when I got well. Didn't think he was serious, really. But with his *father* coming here to see me —Lord God!'

"Good afternoon, little Miss Turner," Jean-Paul said.

"Good afternoon, sir," Fanny whispered. She was thinking: 'Phil's real nice. Good-looking, too. Better looking than Rod, even. Only he's *such* a fool! But I reckon that don't—doesn't—matter too much. Might even be to a girl's advantage, if she's got an ounce of sense in her head. Like I've got now. Like I've got to have from here on in . . .'

"How are you feeling, my child?" Jean-Paul said.

"Pretty good, sir," Fanny whispered.

'Easy, girl,' she told herself. 'He's little 'n fat; but he's all man. Where Phil got that much from, anyhow. And— smart. A damn sight smarter than Phil will ever be. One flip remark outa me and he'll . . .'

She bowed her head, squeezed her eyes tight shut, held them like that, hard, for a long moment. When she looked up again, the frost and flint were gone from her gaze. Her eyes were dewy, misty, softly glowing.

"It's—it's mighty kind of you to come to see me, Mr. Sompayac," she whispered. Her voice had breathless little ripples in it, trills. "I—I'm honored to make your acquaintance—And I hope—I hope—"

"What, child?" Jean-Paul said. His voice was very deep and—

'And sad. Mixed-up sad,' Fanny thought. 'Came here dead damn sure you wasn't going to like me, didn't you? Expecting to find a brazen hussy. Cheap li'l vulgar tart you could scare—or buy off. But now, you're not so sure, are you, li'l Mister Frog-Eatin' Aristocratic Frenchie?'

She said, whispering the words: "I hope—you—you'll forgive me for all the trouble—I caused Phil. I—I'm not good enough for him. Nobody has to tell me that—I knew it from the outset—only—"

"You're young, and—in love. Is that what you're trying to tell me, daughter?" Jean-Paul said.

"I'm young—and—and things kind of got to be—too much for me, sir," Fanny said. "Reckon you—you think I'm a bad girl—not fitten for—Philippe. For your son. And—and you're right. Reckon it *is* bad to be—stupid—and to *care* too much and—"

She bent her head and wept, really wept. She had convinced herself. At the moment, Fanny pitied Fanny with all her heart.

Jean-Paul leaned over and put an arm around her shoulder, drew her to him.

"Ne pleurez pas, ma fille!" he said. "I mean—please don't cry, my child! You—you're not what I thought you'd be. Pas de toute. Not at all—"

Fanny looked up at him with eyes that were opaque, awash, brilliantly aglitter.

"And—what am I, sir?" she whispered, brokenly. "Right now I ain't—I mean I'm not sure I know—"

Jean-Paul Sompayac studied the girl he was holding in his arms. He had never seen Fanny before, so he had no idea how she had changed. He couldn't know, for instance, that since her attempt at suicide, over the long weeks when she had been kept alive by a teaspoon of broth or two at the widely separated intervals she'd been conscious enough to swallow it without strangling, by glucose injected into her veins when she wasn't, she had lost the sum total of forty-five pounds. He saw a pitiful, pallid waif, so emaciated, so fragile, that he loosened his embrace a little lest she break. And her tiny, heart-shaped, woebegone face awoke pity in him, and something more, a strange and hurtful stab of tenderness.

'Mais,' he thought, 'elle est belle! Vraiment belle! Pâle. Douce. Belle comme une ange—ou bien comme une pauvre petite sainte martyre . . .'

"Je pense—" he began, then, remembering, switched back into English. "I think that you are—a good, sweet little girl, who has made a mistake. A great mistake. But, then, who am I to hold it against you? You must try to get well. And, after that—we'll see . . ."

"Sir," Fanny said, "you—you're being—too good to me. Too—kind. I—I'm no good. I'm a—a bad, wicked girl who—"

"Tais toi, ma fille!" Jean-Paul said, melted now, conquered, vanquished. "The past is gone. Done with. You must concentrate on getting better. If there is anything I can do for you, ma petite—my little one, you need only ask. In me, you have a friend—"

"I—thank you—for saying that," Fanny whispered. "And I—I *am* going to ask you something. I was scared—afraid to, before. Please, sir—let Phil—come to see me—I—I want to see him so bad! Don't—keep him away from me. I—I won't do—or say anything to him—I shouldn't—only—"

"You wrong me, my child," Jean-Paul said. "I have never forbidden Philippe to visit you."

"Oh!" Fanny said. Then, terribly, stormily, she started to cry. "He—he doesn't want me!" she sobbed. "Oh what did Doctor Lucien have to go and save me for? I wish I was dead, dead, dead!"

"Don't say that, ma fille," Jean-Paul Sompayac said. "That, truly, is a wickedness. And—as for Philippe, he will visit you tomorrow. That, I promise you!"

So it was that when M. Sompayac came back from his delicate errand, he walked into Philippe's room, shaking his massive head, with his face grayish, and his eyes more troubled than his son had ever seen them before in his life.

"Papa!" Philippe said.

"Pardonez-moi, mon fils," M. Sompayac whispered, "but I couldn't! I literally couldn't! Pas à cette petite angel! That little angel. Tiny, douce, blonde, pâle—so pale, smiling at me, telling me how kind it was of me to come to see her. Asking why *you* haven't been to visit her, too. Morbleu, son! Why haven't you? No Billie Jo on earth, nor mille Billie Jos, nor dix mille Billie Jos, could hold a candle to that one! Where on earth did this gross pig of a policeman get a child like that?"

"Papa—" Philippe said, "are you sure you feel all

right? Or even that we're talking about the same girl? Fanny's a plump little pigeon—gay, mischievous, fun— but an angel? Now, Papa—"

"Morbleu, Philippe! I'm not blind! Why don't you go see for yourself?" his father said.

So that next day, out of simple curiosity, Philippe did go to see Fanny. Clad in his very best clothes, and armed not only with the usual bouquet of roses, but also with a note from Martha granting him permission to call upon her daughter, since he had already discovered how strict the hospital authorities were about such things, he made his way to the desk of the head nurse of the women's section, pausing there only long enough to finish melting that stern old matron's defenses with his really considerable charm, a trait he had been born with to a certain extent, but that was now much too smoothly practiced to be wholly admirable.

"It's highly irregular!" the head nurse protested. "But I suppose this note you've brought from her mother is probably genuine, and seeing as how that not even the likes of you could get a poor child half-dead and wrapped up in bandages like an Egyptian mummy into serious mischief, I'll let you see her. But only for ten minutes, you hear? Leave those roses here. I'll have one of the girls put them in a vase, and bring them into her a little later. Mind you, I said only ten minutes, young man!"

"Yes, sister!" Philippe said. "And I thank you from the bottom of my heart!"

"Don't call me 'sister!' I'm not a Catholic," the head nurse said. "Now come along with me, young man. And keep your eyes straight ahead—in case some of those sluttish Irish biddies from the Channel have left their doors open again!"

They went down a long series of corridors until they came to Fanny's room. The head nurse pushed her white-capped head through the doorway.

"You've a visitor, my dear!" she cooed; then to Philippe: "You may go in now, Mr. Sompayac!"

Philippe went through the doorway and stopped. His breath stopped. His heart.

Fanny lay in her bed, propped up on a mountain of pillows. She weighed at the moment exactly eighty-seven pounds. Which is to say she was skeletal, her eyes blue-ringed, sunken, her cheeks in-hollowed, her lips nearly as pale as the rest of her flesh. Her almost white-blond hair had been carefully brushed and combed. But she didn't so much as glance in Philippe's direction, ignoring him as completely as though he were not there. Instead, with an odd, somehow disturbing intensity, she stared at her own reflected image in the little hand mirror she held up before her face.

Words formed in Philippe's mind: 'Good-bye, Billie Jo. Because—I can't. Not anymore. Somebody's got to accept responsibility for—evil. I guess that's my job from here on in. To comfort her, I mean. Cherish. Even—save. If any kind of salvation's possible, now. Sounds noble, doesn't it? As if I pitied her! You want the truth? Say I've looked upon this face she stole from Circe down in hell, and have taken my rightful place just behind Rodney Schneider in the ranks of utter swine! That I want her so bad I hurt. I want this scrap of milky hide stretched drum-tight over obscene bones. This perversely lovely—horror. So either I'm stark raving mad, or Fanny is a witch. For else could she lie there looking like hell's half-acre, like grim death, and convince me she is—beautiful?'

She must have heard the rasp his breath made as he let it out, because she lowered the glass and looked at him, her eyes dead level, unblinking, still. And he hung there, quivering from shock, impaled upon the ice-cold, deadly hatred in her gaze.

'But why?' his mind clawed against the frozen death he was spitted on. 'What did *I* ever do to her that she—'

Then suddenly, he knew. 'Did—nothing. Am. For my possession of a lordly dangling gut, a pair of seed sacks, to which I, like all my grunting, rooting brothers, am enslaved. For belonging to the sex that from now on she'll despise. That she'll revenge herself upon by every fiendishly dirty female trick that she—'

" 'Lo, Phil," Fanny said.

But he didn't answer her. He couldn't.

Fanny dropped her gaze again and stared stonily at her reflection in the glass. And then Philippe saw it: an absolute. Her absolute. What she'd come to now: That utter, abysmal, bottomless loathing of self that defined her. That explained what she had done. What she'd surely do again, but—flawlessly the next time. Finally. Fatally.

'If she even has to bother,' he thought, watching her from some dead-stopped hiatus, obliquely tangent to the flow of time. 'Having *this* in her is enough. Slower, perhaps; but just as—lethal.'

And shaping that thought in his mind, admitting it, accepting its iron inevitability, shattered the protective walls of ice that his—horror? terror? pity? pain?—had built around his heart, so that he could feel again. Quite suddenly, he couldn't see her anymore. She, the hospital room, the visible world, were gone, washed out by an abrupt dislocation of optical focus, the reflected light rays no longer converging, but diffused, scattered, broken into a meaningless astigmatic blur of planes and angles by the hot and bitter steamscald that surged up and blotted out his eyes.

But then, he heard her voice. It was low and vibrant, sweet, soft, almost—tender.

"Why—Philippe!" she said. "You—you're crying! And you—you mustn't! Not for me! I'm not worth it, I—"

And he was stumbling towards her like a wind-driven scarecrow, like a clockwork toy, half of whose cogs are broken, like the madman he was, or had become. When he reached her bed, he knelt down beside it, reverently, peering at her out of owlish, tear-blinded eyes, until she put out a fingertip, traced a star-track down his cheek, said:

"No, Philippe. Men don't cry. Not real man, anyhow. 'N specially not for—a whore. I'm not worth it. Not fit for nobody to cry over. So don't. You hear me, Philippe? I said—"

A knot of muscle at his temple jerked. He glared at her wild-eyed. Said:

"Don't say that. Don't ever say that again! Because nobody'll call you that, Fan. I swear before God that any man who uses that word about my wife will strangle on his own blood! I tell you—"

"Philippe," she whispered. "Papa told me that. And Martha. That you—that you've asked for me. That you want to—to marry me. Is that true, Philippe?"

"Want, hell!" he said. "I'm going to! Who's to stop me, Fan?"

She smiled at him, softly, sweetly.

"Me, Philippe," she said.

"Fan, for God's sake!" he got out.

"No, Phil. For yours. You deserve better. Much better. A—a *decent* wife. Like that cute little speckled setter pup of a girl you've been spreading yourself high, wide, and handsome all over New Orleans with. She came in here. I think she was going to ask me to give you up. But she didn't. She—couldn't. She stood there in the door looking at me, and then she started to cry. Whirled right around, and ran out of here, crying. Tell me, Phil, honey—do I look *that* awful?"

"No, Fan," Philippe said. "You look—beautiful. Like—like an angel. And I'm going to—"

"You're going to get right up from there 'n go after Miss Speckled Pup fast as you can. Girl who loves you. A good girl. Pure. Not no used, dirty, play-toy of a girl what all your friends—"

"Fan!" Philippe screamed at her, trying to stop her, knowing with a revulsion that brought a rush of nausea foaming to the back of his throat, what she was going to say.

"Have fucked. Forty-seven different ways. Made a whore out of. Less than a whore, really. Didn't even give me my cab fare home . . ."

He hung there on his knees and let—that—wash over him, hearing those words coming out of that pale, tender angel's mouth. Pronounced calmly, gently, quietly.

"Won't do that to you. You're too good, Philippe. Too fine. Martha told me 'bout that note you sent, how you tried to stop 'em. What for, Phil, honey? What difference did three more fellows make? I was already Rod's fancy gal, a cheap 'n easy little tart he was so shamed of that to get shut of her, he—"

"Fanny, for God's love!"

"Had to call his buddies in. Go shares. So—it's no good, Phil. I got that inside me—festering. And not you—not nobody—can get it out. So just you marry Miss Speckled Pup, will you, huh? She's real cute, Phil. Know what? I kind of like her. She'll make you happy, sure as hell. An' anyhow—I won't be around to get in your way—not in nobody's, for that matter—"

"Fan!" he got out; "you mustn't! You wouldn't dare—"

"Stick a kitchen knife into my left tit again? Know how

I did that, Phil, honey? I pushed it in real slow-w-w-w, little by little so I could enjoy hurting. I'd just got the last inch in or maybe not quite when I got too weak to stand up and had to lie down and 'Liza came in and found me. Only mistake I made. Should have slammed it into me, rammed it in so hard 'n fast that—"

"Holy Mother of God!" Philippe whispered.

"Don't worry about it, you sweet old long-tall froglegs-eater, you! I won't again. Don't have to. Doctor Lucien says he's gonna get me up from here. Maybe he will, this time. But I got—hellfire in me now, Phil. And it's going to burn me up. Oh, I'll last another year, maybe, or—two—or even five at the outside. But—no more than that. So forget me, hon. You go be happy. Don't even remember I ever was alive—"

The head nurse pushed open the door, looked in.

"Time's up, Mr. Sompayac!" she said.

And it was. All the time that belonged to him, that he could call his own. All up, from that hour on.

## Chapter Seven

"C'mon, Phil, lemme see 'em," Billy said. "'Cause 'til you do, I just ain't gonna believe it!"

Martha pushed open the door and came into the sitting room.

"What aren't you going to believe, Billy?" she said; then: "Oh, how nice of you to come so early, Philippe! Merry Christmas, my boy." She stopped, looked at the young Creole, and added, somewhat quizzically: "Shall I be polite—or truthful?"

"Truthful," Philippe sighed. "Though usually you manage to be both, chère madame!"

"This time, that would be difficult," Martha said, "if not impossible. You look awful, Philippe. You've lost weight, and you probably had too little to start with. There's something wrong, isn't there, my boy? Want to tell me what it is? It's been my experience that talking things out often helps. And I'm sure you know that anything, anything at all, you say to me will be kept in strictest confidence. Well, Philippe?"

Philippe bowed his head.

'It would be a relief to tell her,' he thought. 'Only, how would one go about it? Say: "Dear Mrs. Turner, I cannot marry your stepdaughter. I can't, because, just as you said I would, I've fallen in love with another girl." But I won't tell you that, Martha. I won't risk your turning one of your dazzlingly sweet, oh-so-maternal smiles upon me, patting my cheek, and gently saying: "It's quite all right, dear boy! You were *never* obligated to marry Fanny. In fact, as you may recall, I objected to the idea, rather strongly, from the very beginning . . ." And leaving me feeling myself the biggest fool who ever drew breath—as usual . . .'

He looked up again, grinned at her mischievously, said:

"I *am* troubled, ma très aimée belle-mère! You see, try as I may, I haven't been able to invent a humane, or a legal method of removing a certain gentleman from my path, or how to make my way, accompanied by his wife—and his daughter, of course!—to some Mohammedan country, where I'd be allowed to marry *both* of them. Or even figure out what all three of us—you, Fanny, and I—would subsist upon after we got there. So—"

"Ah, g'wan!" Billy said. "You don't want to marry Mama! She's too old!"

"As you may have noticed," Martha said with a smile, "the Turners, père et fils, are notorious for their really exquisite gallantry! All right, Philippe, the inquisition's over. I won't pry. I am a little disappointed, though. I thought you trusted me."

"Oh, I do!" Philippe began; but Billy cut him off.

" 'The Turners, pear at feece'?" he said. "Mama, what kind of talk is *that?*"

"It's French, Billy," Martha said, "Philippe's native language—or at least the language of his ancestors—"

"No, it ain't!" Billy protested. "Phil don't talk like that! Do you, Phil?"

"Mais, certainement, mon brave petit bonhomme," Philippe said with a smile. "Il faut que je parle toujours comme ça chez moi, si non, mon père me proportionnerait un pair de gifles magistrales!"

"Oh, no!" Billy groaned. "That ain't *human* talk, Phil! Quit it and talk like *folks!*"

"You know," Martha sighed, "I'm sure half the world's troubles stem from that particular attitude of mind!"

"And they always have," Philippe said. "Even so enlightened a people as the ancient Greeks called people whose languages they didn't understand 'barbarians,' which translated literally means 'babblers.' But tell me, ma très chére belle-mère, are we going to be graced with Fanny's fair presence tonight?"

"I—I think so," Martha said a little doubtfully. "She is—much better. Physically, that is—"

"You mean that in other ways—mentally, emotionally, say—she's not?"

"Exactly. Her—behavior troubles me, Philippe. She's—withdrawn. Silent. She always has been to a certain extent, of course; but now—"

"Mama!" Billy interrupted. "You know what Phil's got in that box? Leastwise what he *says* he's got in it: *frog* legs!"

Martha smiled.

"Have you, really, Philippe?" she said.

"Yes," Philippe said, "as a matter of fact, I have. You see, Fanny would never quite believe that we Creoles actually do eat them. So I brought along three dozen, packed in ice to keep them fresh. That's why the package is so big. Does Eliza—?"

"Know how to cook them? I doubt it. But it's simple, isn't it? Don't you just dip them in egg batter and fry them in deep fat, like chicken, say?"

"Exactly," Philippe said. "Now the problem is to persuade Fanny to even taste them . . ."

"Ah, g'wan, Phil!" Billy said. "People don't eat frog legs, 'n you know it!"

"Billy," Martha said, "am *I* a person?"

"Well—reckon so," Billy said. "You—you don't mean *you* eat 'em, d'you, Mama?"

"Every chance I get. They're delicious, son. Wait 'til you taste them and you'll see. Here, take the package out to the kitchen and give it to Eliza. Tell her that they're to be dipped in egg batter and fried just like chicken. But not too far ahead of time. They have to be served piping hot. Will you remember all that, Billy?"

"Yes, Mama. *Frog* legs, golly!"

"Wait, Billy; take this package out to Eliza, too," Philippe said, "It's her Christmas present . . ."

"May I ask what it is, Philippe?" Martha said.

"Of course. It's snuff. Imported snuff. The very finest—"

"Ugh!" Martha said.

"That, ma chère Madame Turner, is but another example of les idées fixes we were talking about a little while ago. Civilized people permit others not only their incomprehensible languages, but also their harmless little vices. Go on, Billy; take it to her!"

"I suppose that's true," Martha said. "Still—"

"Say, Phil—whatcha bring *me?*" Billy said.

"Later. When you come back from the kitchen, William the Conquerer!" Philippe said. "Or you'll only forget to instruct Eliza properly. Get along with you, now!"

"I suppose," Martha said, once Billy had scampered away, "that since you felt it incumbent upon yourself to play Santa Claus—or rather Papa Noël, as you Creoles call him, I believe—you've been quite horribly extravagant and—"

"Brought presents for the whole Turner household? Why, yes; of course. Why not? This one is for you, chère belle-mère. But, before you open it, you must pay a forfeit!"

"What sort of a forfeit, Philippe?" Martha said.

"This!" Philippe laughed; and drawing a sprig of mistletoe out of his pocket, he held it over her head.

"Now, aren't you forward!" Martha said; then very gently, she went up on tiptoe, with her head inclined at the proper angle to kiss his cheek.

But, at that precise instant, Philippe's keen ear caught an odd, faint, unexpected sound. He turned his head abruptly, with—to be truthful about it—a somewhat startled motion, for he was far from sure that a man of Bill Turner's temperament would accept with grace the gay and harmless flirtation he was always carrying on with Martha, if the detective ever caught him at it. But the result of Philippe's suddenly twisting his face and neck toward where he thought the sound had come from was to compound catastrophe, as it were, for Martha's chaste and maternal kiss, instead of merely brushing his cheek, as she had intended it to, landed full upon his mouth.

And by that iron law of fate that coincidences nearly always disarrange, if not actually derange, life, instead of the other way around, it was Fanny who stood there in the doorway, staring at them. Her eyes were the exact color of clear water reflecting a winter sky. 'Except that no water is ever that still,' Philippe thought, 'or has such bottomless abysses hidden beneath its surface, so many River Acherons feeding it—with pain.'

He had time, in that curiously prolonged interval, in that near-halting of life's normal progression, to study her. She was wrapped in a quilted pink robe, with her truly flaxen hair—being naturally of that shade of almost white blond that nobody had as yet invented the adjective "platinum" to describe—loose about her shoulders. And, though he had seen her several times since Dr. Terrebonne had allowed her parents to bring her home from the hospital, it came to Philippe that he had never really seen her before that moment if he employed the verb "to see" in its collateral sense of "perceive."

And what he perceived, with a sudden cold feeling remarkably akin to fear, was that everything he had sensed about her when he had seen her in the hospital for the first time after her suicide attempt had been true. Not only true, but, he realized now, actual understatements. The change in Fanny was so complete as to amount to metamorphosis. And the transmigration of her all-but-transubstantiated (his mind went on piling up the sonorous medieval adjectives like a crazed dark-ages metaphysician) being into this by-death's-own-subtle-alchemy-transmuted body had given her—perhaps in recompense for her famine-wasted flesh—a smoldering sensual power, little short of terrifying.

He was suddenly sure that despite Martha's and Eliza's best efforts, she hadn't gained an ounce in the almost a month she'd been in their exclusive and truly tender care, She was still—skeletal. Every bone in her face and neck threatened to thrust its cleanly sculptured outline through the taut-stretched and meager flesh that covered it. Her hands were wisps, so thin and pale that her veins made a spiderweb tracery of blue, clearly visible beneath her almost transparent skin. He could see, from across the room, the pulse in the hollow of her throat, see it halt, and flutter, then race to beat and beat and beat . . .

'She—isn't here!' he heard his own voice wailing from somewhere within the echoing cavern of pure shock all his perceptions had retreated into. 'She's teetering on the edge of—eternity. She's so—delicate—that even to breathe upon her would be a criminal offense! And, and—'

'And,' the hard-bitten, indominably realistic part of his mind added, 'what's got you reeling, cher petit ami, is the sober fact that she is—or has become—the single most beautiful female creature you've seen in all your life—'

He tried to reject that thought, for even its implications were terrifying: 'I'll never escape her now, because I—can't. Before, when she was a plump and laughing little she-thing, somewhat vulgar, a trifle gross, entirely—physical, I might have. But this haunting, delicate, exquisitely etheral—

'And goddamned perverse—' his mind put in sardonically.

'All right! And goddamned perverse—loveliness—will enslave me forever. Me and every other horny mother's son who lays eyes on her. So, I'd better make tracks, right now! Get out of here. Escape—but from—what?

'The lovely, seductive body—of this death,' his mind supplied him.

'Don't be such a sententious son of a bitch!' he shot back at his mind. But then he saw it, became aware of that last, utterly insupportable detail.

She was crying. Without a tremor or a sound—but crying.

"Oh, Fanny!" Martha moaned. "You mustn't! You really mustn't think—believe—"

"What I saw with my own two eyes?" Fanny whispered. "It—it's all right, Martha. I've known all along that it's you he's in love with, not me. Doesn't matter. Long as you don't let *Papa* catch you kissing him, that is. Well—Merry Christmas, anyhow. Guess I'll go back upstairs. Three's a crowd, isn't it? And—"

"You'll do nothing of the kind!" Martha said sharply. "Come here, Fanny. Right now. This minute!"

Slowly Fanny came into the room. Stood there. The tear streaks on her face were only a whiter white.

"Listen to me, child," Martha said. "You can't go on

torturing yourself, this way. *I* haven't rejected you. Nor your father, nor Eliza. Nor—especially not!—Philippe. What you're doing now is morbid. Of course I kissed Philippe! Though that I kissed his lips instead of his cheek was pure accident, a point you can believe or not, as you like; for I have no intention of wearying myself trying to convince you. And yes, I *do* love him very much. What mother wouldn't love such a tall and gay and handsome son? But if you put any other interpretation upon a simple gesture of affection at Christmas time, you insult me, Fanny; insult Philippe; and what's more, you insult yourself, by placing so little value upon what you have to offer a person, as a woman, even, that—"

"All right," Fanny said, in that same flat, calm, utterly weary tone of voice. "Let me make you a list, Phil, honey—of all I've got to offer you. All the things that'll make you so happy you won't be able to stand it, and'll have to burst out crying tears of joy! A—a sack of bones. With no meat—flesh—on 'em. Sick all the time. Hurting all the time. Not to mention what's inside this half-dead corpse. Used goods, Philippe. Another fellow's leavings. What he didn't even want—A cheap, dirty, little—"

"Oh, my God!" Martha wept. "Fanny, will you please, please, please—"

But Philippe had already crossed to where Fanny stood. He put a curved forefinger under her chin and lifted her face. Then he bent and—for the first time in both their lives—kissed her mouth. It was cold and trembling and tear-wet and salt, and the feel of it sent pain screaming through him. Ice-cold, destructive pain.

He drew back, looked down at her. Her eyes were so still, so fixed, that for one-half second, he wondered if they were not, maybe, blind. Then she sighed; said quietly:

"That was—very nice, Philippe. You're awf'ly good at kissing, aren't you? Now what? Do I take you upstairs so you can go to bed with me? Or what?"

"Fanny!" Martha said.

"Well, that's what kissing usually leads to, doesn't it, Martha?" Fanny said. "And, besides, what else do fellows ever want? 'Course, I'm awf'ly weak, so *that* would prob'bly kill me. But, anyhow, what's the difference? Be just another way to die. Better than a kitchen knife, least-ways, and—"

"Fanny," Philippe said grimly, "if you don't stop this, I'll slap you winding, so help me!"

She smiled at him, her mouth the palest shell-pink below whatever it was she had in her eyes, now, whatever compounded multiple of sick self-hatred and shame.

"Go ahead," she said. "You think I'd care? Or better still—shoot me. You'd do that much for a bad hurt hound-dog bitch, wouldn't you, Phil? Put her out of her misery, I mean? So—"

But, before she could say anything else, Billy burst into the sitting room.

"Mama!" he said; " 'Liza says she *knows* how to cook frog legs! Says they taste just like chicken! Do they, Phil? Hey—what's the matter with Fanny, Mama? What's she crying about?"

"Fanny's—sick, Billy," Martha whispered. "Why don't you go help Eliza cook the frog legs and—"

"No," Billy said, "I won't! 'Sides Phil ain't even showed me my Christmas present yet!"

"Here," Philippe said. "Take it, Billy-boy!"

It was a long, slim package. Billy tore into it with frantic fingers, sending the bright Christmas wrappings flying in every direction. Half a minute later, a pair of fencing foils fell out.

"Wheeee!" Billy squealed, "swords! Now I'm gonna be th' king o' the block! Any kid gets me riled, I'll stick him in the gizzard and—"

"Oh!" Martha said; then, very slowly, "Oh, my God!"

Philippe stared at her.

"Phil," Fanny said; and for the first time that night he could hear a purr of amusement moving through her voice. "Just when I was starting to think you were a mite different from the rest—"

"The rest of what, Fan?" Philippe said. "Different—how?" He was still looking at Martha.

"Different from most other fellows. Smarter. 'Cause, far as knowing what goes on inside a girl's—a woman's—head, all the menfolks I ever met, including Papa, just ain't—aren't—right bright. So if you really are planning to steal Martha from my father—"

"Fanny!" Martha said.

"You should find out something about her," Fanny went on imperturbably. "Like, say, she don't—doesn't—believe there's *any* excuse for killing people, not even self-defense. So you should have brought Billy a prayer book, maybe; or at least a wind-up train, if you didn't mean to hurt her feelings. Not swords. Nor guns. Nor knives. Nor even a bow 'n arrow, I suspect. Right, Martha?"

"Right," Martha said crisply; then: "Don't look so stricken, Philippe! How were you to know?"

"But I *did* know!" Philippe said angrily. "Which means I've been a perfect ass—again. I've heard Bill—your husband—say at least a hundred times that you believe that only peaceful means—"

"Can insure the continuity of—civilization," Martha said gently, "or even guarantee that any culture is worthy of that high name. No matter. Those button tips won't come off the foils, will they, Philippe?"

"No, madame," Philippe said gloomily.

"Good. Then I shall be spared the difficult if not impossible task of taking them away from Billy. After all, fencing's no more than a rather graceful exercise these days, isn't it?"

"You're—sweet," Philippe said, "and kind. Believe me, Martha—I do apologize—"

"Go on," Fanny said in a flat, expressionless, dead-calm tone of voice, "kiss her and make up, Phil. She'd *like* that, I'm sure!"

Abruptly Martha stood up, caught Billy by the arm.

"Come on, son," she said quietly.

"Ah, Mama—" Billy began.

"I said, come on, Billy!" Martha's voice was still quiet; but the edge in it was unmistakable, now.

"Where're you going, Martha?" Fanny said.

"Out in the kitchen, to help Eliza with the Christmas supper," Martha said. "Besides, Philippe came to see *you*, Fanny. You're a young lady, now. So, as your mother, I'm granting you the privilege of entertaining a suitor alone. At least until your father comes home—late as usual, I sadly fear. What I'm saying is, I suppose, that by now, you ought to have a sense of personal responsibility—and, if you don't, confronting—situations like this one is the best way to acquire it . . ."

"Martha—" Fanny wailed suddenly. "*Please* don't go!
I—"

" 'Til supper, Philippe," Martha said. "Be very patient
with her, my boy. There's—excellent material in her.
From her father's side, at least, the very best. I—I'm depending upon you—not to let her spoil things for everyone, by using one mistake, however grave, as an excuse to
destroy her whole life. You may find the task too much
for you. It may well be too much for any man. But, it
seems to me, you should be allowed, at the very least,
to—try—"

Even after Martha had gone, dragging Billy, bemused
by his slim and deadly-looking épées, with her, Fanny
stood there, gazing at the closed door. Then, very quietly,
she went and sat down upon the sofa, as far from Philippe as she could get.

Philippe made no attempt to sit beside her. Instead, he
stayed where he was, and studied Fanny's profile in the
warm, flickering glow of the flame from the logs burning
in the fireplace. The adjectives that came to him were
clichés, of course; but they also happened to be quite accurate descriptions of what Fanny was like now: 'Exquisite. A—a cameo. The face of a Dresden China figurine,
so damned fragile that—'

"What are you looking at me that way for?" Fanny said
sullenly. "Gives me the creeps. Like I was a bug under
your microscope, Dr. Sompayac! Or have you changed
your mind about studying medicine by now?"

"Hardly a bug, Fanny," Philippe said. "To tell the
truth, I was trying to figure out a way of describing
you—the *new* you, I mean."

"The *new* me?" Fanny said.

"Yes. Because the old you—is gone," Philippe said quietly. "I don't think she survived a self-inflicted knife
wound, say. Or perhaps she died on the operating table.
It's a pity I don't have even a tintype of her to remember
by . . ."

Fanny turned and looked at him. Her pale eyes were
very still.

"Go on," she said. "I want to see what you're getting
at, Phil—"

"Then I'll tell you," Philippe said sharply. "I don't
think that anyone, not even *you*, has the right to make

you suffer from a dead girl's sins. Especially not since those sins consisted merely of being a warm-hearted, generous little fool. Nothing worse . . ."

"Phil—" Fanny whispered.

"That's all," Philippe said firmly. "And, of course, one mistake; that of being a rather poor judge of character. But that particular mistake's common enough. It takes years for any of us to stop making it."

"More years than you've got, then," Fanny said bitterly, " 'cause you're *still* making it, right now."

"No, I'm not," Philippe said. "You know what you looked like before, Fan? You were plump and saucy and full of hell. *Very* pretty. Gay, Exciting—"

"And now—I'm not. Not any of those things," she whispered, her voice humid with fought-back tears. "I'm skinny as a rail fence. And I'm going to go right on being skinny the rest of my life, Phil. 'Cause I *can't* eat; I just can't!"

"So?" Philippe said.

"So I look like a scarecrow. Scrawny. Ugly. Half-sick—Phil! What the dickens—"

For he was kneeling before her, with his elbows resting on her knees, cradling his face in his own two hands, looking into her eyes.

"Then the good little God and his sainted Mother have blessed me, by sending me one little, skinny, scrawny, ugly scarecrow to grace my life," he said.

And something in his voice, its warmth, perhaps, its very real sincerity, got through to her, sending a wild and bitter steamscald to her eyes.

"Phil—" she wept, "you mustn't! You can't! Love me, I mean. I not only *look* awful, but I *am* awful, and—"

"Fanny," he said, "let's get that part straight, first. The way you look, anyhow. Before, that girl you—murdered—was utterly commonplace. Cute. Plump. Pretty. Like a million others. Except the hair and eyes, of course; they were, and remain, rare. But now—"

"Now?" Fanny whispered.

"You're—exquisite, Fan. You're so goddamned beautiful that looking at you—hurts. Now, instead of being just like a million others, you're one in ten million, maybe more—"

"Phil, you're crazy!" Fanny said. "I—"

But he went on in the same quiet, half-mocking, half-serious tone of voice.

"I'll grant you that you're too thin; that you look sick; and that you've got all kinds of bad, sad things you'd be better off forgetting, showing in your eyes. All three of which conditions I mean to cure, Fanny. As your doctor—and your husband, both. But, in spite of them, you—*this* you, the you who is here now, alive, present, and accounted for—are the most beautiful girl I've ever been anywhere close to, in my whole life. And the most exciting. Bones and all. Did I ever tell you you've got exciting bones, Fan? You do, y' know. I swear it!"

"No, Phil; don't swear. I—can see you mean what you say. But all that lets me know for sure is that you're *really* crazy. That you ought to be locked up!"

He jumped to his feet, put out his hand to her.

"Get up, Fan!" he said.

Slowly she got up. He caught her by the shoulder, and turned her slowly, gently, tenderly around, until she was facing the mirror over the mantelpiece. He put both his arms around her waist, and nestled his chin on her shoulder. He could feel how terribly thin she was, even through the quilted robe.

"Now," he said, "study that face. See it through my eyes. Note how perfect its lines are, how clean-cut. Look into those eyes—Lorelei's, aren't they? Iseult's? Morgan le Fay's?"

"Phil, you know how ignorant I—"

"No matter. You'll learn. Fanny, with your face reflected there, next to mine—can't you see you're—beautiful?"

She hung there, resting her slight weight against the circle of his arms.

"Phil—" she murmured, "kiss me?"

He turned her around. Very gently. Bent and kissed her mouth.

She tore her mouth away from his, and sobbed aloud, an ugly, racking, animal sound, as though the tissues of her damaged lung were tearing.

"Fan!" he said, "oh, Fan—"

"Don't—make me love you, Phil!" she wept. "Please don't! Loving leaves a girl helpless. And when it's over, it hurts too bad! So don't. Please don't. I'm begging you not to! You—you could. You're—sweet. And honorable. And

good. 'Sides, you're awful good-looking, too—better looking than Rod ever was; 'cause you look—more real, somehow. Not all pomade and moustache wax, and shaving
lotion, and silk shirts and—"

"Fanny," he said, "listen to me—"

"No, I won't!" she stormed. "I do that, and you'll persuade me! That—there's something left, I mean. A
house—with rambling roses all over it—and a nice husband in it—and—and kids. Damn it! I can see them, right
now—and they—they all look like you!"

"I couldn't have put it better, myself," he said solemnly,
"if I had tried."

"Phil—" she said, "get that idea right out of your stupid head. When I was only eight years old, Martha—
well—she said something I never did forget. She—said
I—I was *born* to be a whore. Like—my mother before
me."

"Fan!" he said.

"Didn't know that, did you? Well, she is. Maebelle
Hartman, the Queen of the Barbary Coast, they call her.
She's had *three* fellows killed over, up to now, Phil,
honey. So she's two up on me. So far, my record's—one."

"Now, Fan—" Philippe said.

" 'S a fact. Ask Papa. Ask Martha. They'll tell you
about old Mr. Jacob Fields—the poor old crazy man—
Papa—shot—for—for abusing me—when I was only eight
years old . . ."

"My God!" Philippe whispered.

"God had nothing to do with *that*," Fanny said bitterly.
"You better call on the devil, Phil. Only they won't tell
you that I went with the poor old crazy degenerate to his
house of my own free will. At eight years of age, Mister
Doctor Philippe Sompayac! So *now* you're starting to see
why you can't marry me? You—you want my randy
bitch's blood a-boiling in your *daughter's* veins, Phil?
Your son—all right. Most menfolks think a little wildness
is becoming in a boy. But s'posin' your *daughter*—turned
out to be like me? A nym-pho-maniac—layin' down for
everybody? That's what Papa brought onto himself when
he left Martha, for Mama. For a—a woman who ran off
with the first tinhorn sport who came along, and dumped
one mighty fancy package in his lap, namely, me. Her
spittin' image. Bad. Cheap. Easy—"

Philippe bent and stopped her hideous, hurtful, hateful words, by flattening them against her speaking mouth.

When he drew back a little, he could see her eyes. They were—unsettled. And unsettling. He could almost see the warfare going on behind them as she struggled to reject, what was clearly—hope.

"Phil—" she said, "when I say I'm—bad do you understand what I mean? I—I don't think you do . . ."

"That you have a normal young woman's warm blood. That you're not made of ice. That you have a certain amount of—of sensuality in your makeup. Am I right?"

"Far, as you go, yes," Fanny said. "But don't reckon a fellow like you would have much to worry about—in *that* department. You'd keep a girl—plumb worn out—and just as happy, wouldn't you?"

Philippe threw back his head and laughed aloud.

"Well—wouldn't you?" Fanny said.

"I'd surely try!" he chuckled.

"All right. But—what about all the other ways—all the twisted, poison-mean other ways—I'm—bad?"

He smiled at her, sure now, very sure.

"They—if they exist—are but symptoms of the disease of unhappiness, Fan. Cure the disease, and the symptoms disappear. And that's exactly what I propose to do."

"Phil—" she whispered, her voice hoarse, a grate, a scrape across the pain-and-pity-lacerated surfaces of his heart, "you mean you—really *would* marry me? You—you actually *would?*"

He kissed her again, gaily, playfully. Said:

"Just you try and stop me, Fan!"

"Reckon I'll have to," she said somberly. "Somebody's got to keep you from wrecking your life. So I—I'm saying 'No,' Phil. That's still—my right. Not 'cause I don't love you. Most likely I do. Or I would, if I'd let myself—"

"If you *dared* let yourself," he corrected her.

"All right. If I dared. Only I don't dare. I've been hurt—enough, Phil. No—poisoned. Reckon that would be a better way of putting it. Must be *some* way of accounting for what I did—"

"Fan, I've told you and told you—"

"No, you haven't. Not about *this,* anyhow. 'Cause we aren't even talking about the same thing. You've been trying to—to convince me that—what I did with Rod with no ring on my finger and us not having stood up before a preacher in the sight of God and man to make it right—wasn't so all-fired important. That lots of girls make the same mistake, and go on to live the rest of their lives with the fellow they made it with or even another one, and people—forget—"

"You put it very well," Philippe said gravely. "So?"

"So—far as that's concerned, I halfway agree with you. No—more than half. But even there, you don't know the whole story: About how much of the whole thing was *my* fault, right from the beginning, and how little of it was Rod's. All he did was to pay back a dirty trick I was trying to put all over him with a dirtier trick of his own—"

"Fan, please!" Philippe said.

"Don't want to hear it, do you? All right, Phil, I won't go into that part no—any—more. 'Cause when I said there must be *some* way of accounting for what I did, I wasn't talking about Rod and his buddies playin' ring-around-the-rosy with me, or even about me trying to kill myself. What I mean happened—afterwards. And if a girl can be that rotten mean lying flat on her back in a hospital bed, either she's crazy or—bad. Wicked bad. All the way through."

"Fan, I don't understand you!"

"Know you don't, Phil, honey. So now I'm going to ask you to do something. To—shoot—a filly who took a bad spill going over some jumps too high for her. Or to—save her. It's up to you to decide—"

He stared at her.

"I have decided, Fan," he said quietly.

"No, you haven't. You only think you have. So—to borrow a thing Martha always says—let's give that proposition rough proof. Tonight's—Christmas. And you're spending it—with me. So I want you to spend—New Year's—with Miss Speckled Setter Pup. Say, Phil—what's her name? I can't go on calling her *that* now, can I?"

"I think it's kind of cute, and that it suits her. But, if you must know, it's Prescott. Billie Jo Prescott. So—you're making me—a sporting proposition, eh, Fan? I'm to go up there to Mertontown and—"

"Spend New Year's with her. With Miss—what's her name again, Phil, honey?"

"Billie Jo Prescott."

"With Miss Billie Jo Prescott. That's all I ask. Will you—do that, Phil?"

He searched her face, her eyes.

"You want to make sure I'm—over her, Fanny?" he said.

"No. 'Cause you're not. And you won't ever be. I—want you to go up there—and find out something about—yourself. How—big you are. Or how little. Or how halfway in-between—"

"Fan, this is the goddamnest sporting proposition I ever—"

She shook her head. Her eyes were—'Still waters,' he decided, 'with—ice—beginning to film their surfaces over—'

"It ain't—I mean—it isn't a sporting proposition, Phil. Or leastwise it's about as sporting as a poker game with a marked deck, or a crap game where somebody's rung in a pair that's loaded . . ."

"Fanny, how on earth do you know about such things?" Philippe said.

"Papa. You ought to see his collection: Took 'em off crooked gamblers. Rings with mirrors in 'em so the dealer knows what he's giving who. Spring-loaded holders up a fellow's sleeve to shoot in a whole new marked deck when nobody's looking. Gimmick to punch tiny holes in the cards—one hole for a Jack, two for a Queen, three for a King, and four for a Ace—*while* they're being dealt. A hundred dirty, crooked tricks. Like this one. Like the one I'm laying on you right now."

"You admit then that you're—deceiving me?" Philippe said.

She looked at him, and her clear eyes darkened perceptibly.

"No, Philippe," she said, "the only person I'm deceiving—if anybody—is me."

"How?" Philippe said.

She turned away from him, stared into the fire.

"I'm telling myself—that you'll come back from up there—without her," she said quietly. "Or even maybe that you—won't go. Or that—if you do come back all by your lonesome—you'll come to see me for some other reason except to—to spit in my face. Like I deserve."

"Fan—" he said, "you mustn't—"

"Torment myself this way? Yes, I must, Phil. Only way to—to get—the evil—out. So now, tell me: Will you go to see her, Phil?"

"Do you want me to, Fanny?" he said.

"No. To tell the truth about it, no. I want you to go see that speckled-faced li'l bitch about as much as I want to stick another knife into myself, again—About what it'll probably amount to, really. Me making you judge, jury, and—and hangman, sort of."

"Fanny!" he said.

"But I think you ought to go, Phil. In fact, you've *got* to. 'Cause—if you can get past *that*—no, if we get past that, then there's a chance, hon. Not much of a chance; but still—a chance—"

He looked at her. A long time. A very long time. When he spoke at last, his voice was very deep and sad.

"Fanny—" he said.

"Yes, Phil?"

"I'll make *you* a sporting proposition. A real one, with no tricks. Deck unmarked. The dice not loaded. If I go up there—and come back without her—Wait! I admit frankly and freely there's quite a risk involved—"

Fanny stared at him.

"You—love her," she said.

"I may. I don't know. I honestly don't know. I thought I did 'til the day I saw you in the hospital—"

"And let yourself get overcome with pity," Fanny said.

"No. If it had been—if it were now—pity, I'd have no problems. What it is, I can't say, really. Or at least the words for it have fallen into disrepute these days. Call it—witchcraft. Enchantment. Sorcery. Black magic. Voodoo. I saw you lying—no, sitting up in bed, looking like something the cat dragged in—"

"Or vomited up," Fanny said bitterly.

"Or vomited up. Grim death. Hell's half-acre. A poor, miserable pitiful collection of bones trying to burst through a scrap of skin, with nothing left of *you*—the you I'd known, and even, in a way, loved; or, at least, had grown very fond of—but your eyes and hair—"

"And?" Fanny whispered.

"I suddenly realized that even like that—or maybe especially like that—you were the goddamnest most beautiful thing I'd ever laid eyes on. Eerily beautiful. Haunting. Delicate. Fragile. And yet—"

"And yet—what?" Fanny said.

"With a—a smoldering and—can I say it straight out, Fan?"

"All right," Fanny said. "Speak your piece, Phil, honey. I'm past the place where a little truth can hurt me, now."

"With a smoldering, yet goddamned perverse sensuality in you that burnt me alive, from across the room. Set me afire. All of a sudden, I wanted you so bad I hurt. And I knew absolutely, with no room for doubting, that I'll go on wanting you 'til the day I die—"

"So?" Fanny said, then.

"So, since then, I've never doubted that I love you, Fanny. I do. God yes, I do! But, to tell the truth, there have been moments when I've wondered if I ought to—if I'm being smart—"

"You're not," she said flatly. "You're being a goddamned fool, Phil."

"A condition to which I was maybe born," he said quietly. "So now, hear my proposition, Fanny! If I come back from Mertontown—free and unattached—at least unattached to anyone but you—I want you to marry me. Now. At once—not years from now. Wait! I know that physically you're in no condition to—to undertake the—well—duties of a wife. But *that* can wait. What I want is that you're bound to me by such ties as not even your morbidity of mind can break—or at least not easily. That's my proposition. Do you accept it, Fan?"

She looked at him. Looked through him. Her eyes explored intergalactic spaces, light years away from him in distance, time. Then they came back.

"Phil," she murmured, "kiss me?"

"No!" he said. "Not until you answer me, Fanny!"

She smiled.

"All right. I accept. That is—if you come back, and if—"

"If what?"

"If I'm still here—when you get here," Fanny said.

He clawed her into his arms, kissed her mouth as though he were trying to break it, tightened his clasp about her until she moaned in actual pain. Released her, stood back, raging still.

"You'll be here! You'll be here because you *must!* You hear me, Fan? You'll—"

"Be here. All right, Philippe—in one way or another, I'll—be here," Fanny said.


## Chapter Eight


Afterwards, it came to Philippe that he should have asked Fanny to explain what she meant by "one way or another;" but at that stage of their relationship, he had not yet learned that he must *never* let one of her rather sibylline utterances go unchallenged; that to do so was to have to pay—sometime later, of course—a little too high a price out of his ultimate resources, out of his diminishing store of peace and serenity; lay down too many coins minted from his pity, anger, grief, anguish, pain—and love.

But he didn't ask her that, because at that moment Martha came back from the kitchen and sat down in a straight back chair opposite them, after glancing nervously at the clock. It was clear that she'd come into the parlor because she didn't dare run the risk of having her husband come home and find the two of them unchaperoned; but it was Bill, himself, who, arriving five minutes later, pushed the question completely out of Philippe's mind.

The detective's derby and his raglan were both soaked through with rain. Martha got up at once, and went to him.

"Why, Bill!" she said; "you're wet to the skin! I knew it was drizzling a little, but—"

"Drizzling's not the word for it, honey," Bill said hoarsely; "the bottom just fell out. Haven't seen such a downpour in—"

At that moment he became aware of Philippe and Fanny. They were sitting on the sofa together. Philippe had his arm around Fanny. She was lying back against him, with her head resting in the curve of his neck and shoulder, her eyes half closed and dreaming. It was not that they hadn't had time to change so intimate a pose— in fact, Philippe was sure that Martha's rush towards the door had been designed to give them a chance to do just that—but, at the last instant, feeling him tensing, Fanny had hissed at him:

"Don't move! He's got to get used to us sometime, Phil!"

So Philippe had stayed where he was. But if there were a more uncomfortable young man in the whole state of Louisiana at that moment, Philippe couldn't imagine who he was, or envy him if he existed.

Bill Turner's green eyes were emerald glass, suddenly; a purely leonine glare. Then, abruptly, they softened.

"I say, looks like you young folks are really starting to get along," he said.

"Yes, sir," Philippe said, his voice reedy with relief. "In fact, sir—all I need is *your* consent, now, to make it official—"

Fanny sat bolt upright.

"Phil!" she said. "I didn't say I would marry you! Not straight out like that, anyhow! I only said that I'd be here when you came back—"

"Back from where?" Bill Turner said. "You're going someplace, young fellow?"

"Papa—" Fanny said, "that's—a secret. Between Phil and me, I mean. There's something I—I'm asking him to do. No, I'm making him do it. And—if it turns out all right, we'll both know that us getting married—"

"*Our* getting married," Martha corrected, involuntarily.

"Right. Thank you. Martha. From now on I'm really going to let you teach me to talk—correctly. So as not to shame Phil. But, anyhow, Papa, if what I'm asking Phil to do turns out all right, our getting married will make sense. And, anyhow, *after* he's done it, I'll tell you 'n Martha what it was. It's decent, Papa. Honorable. Only, don't ask me—or him—what it is, right now. Please, Papa! Show me you trust me a little bit, huh?"

Bill Turner's eyes changed, suddenly. They seemed to look through Fanny, focusing on something behind her, Philippe thought. At first, he couldn't figure out what that something was. Then he remembered what Fanny had told him about her mother, and he knew what Bill Turner was seeing: A double image, cause and effect viewed simultaneously, like two photographs accidentally—or deliberately; in this case surely deliberately—exposed one atop the other on the same plate. But both blurred, and fogged, and ringed about with pain.

"Don't you think," the big man said quietly, "that I've trusted you a damned sight too far now, Fanny?"

Fanny bowed her head. Looked up again. Philippe could see her face—and his own—reflected in the mirror above the mantelpiece. And what was in Fanny's eyes then wasn't to be borne. Even in reflection, it wasn't.

"Bill—" Martha whispered.

"It's—all right, Martha," Fanny said; then: "Yes, Papa—you *have* trusted me too far. And I—I shamed you. But I won't again. I don't even have to promise you—that. Just wait—'til New Year's night and—you'll see—"

"Fanny!" Philippe said.

She turned, smiled at him. If that macabre, death-in-life grimace—her lips fleshless, the skull-shape showing through—could be called a smile.

"Don't get me wrong, Phil, honey," she said quietly. "You keep your bargain, and I'll keep mine. Agreed?"

"Agreed," Philippe said; then to Bill Turner: "Mr. Turner, don't you think that we all ought to concede that the past—is dead and gone? In a week, it'll be 1896. A brand-new year, sir! And it can only be a happy one—if you don't pile too many bad memories on it."

"Spoken like a gentleman," Bill Turner said. "Your heart's in the right place, son. But it's been my experience that the only real stuff we've got to shape what our lives are going to be later on is the mud we're made out of—before the Lord breathed the breath of life into us, as the Good Book says. Mud, and muck, that's all. And we've got to pat the filthy mess into bricks—with or without straw. Way down in Egypt's land, as Eliza's good colored friends sing it. Using our bare hands. Our bare hands, son. And maybe a few other little items, like willpower, like guts, like brains, with—a level teaspoonful of—simple decency, thrown in for good measure, say. Not much to ask, is it, Phil? And whether what we build stands up, or crashes down all to hell and begone the first time some *smart* fellow who's trying to figure a way to cut himself in on the deal breathes on it hard, depends on what we *are*. Which means the past is the one thing we never get away from, son. We've got it burnt into our insides—forever."

"You're denying the possibility—of change, sir?" Philippe said.

"Right," Bill Turner said; and his voice was somber. "I'm saying that in all my life I've never seen anybody change enough for it to matter a good goddamn. Wherever people go—even into the future, son—they take themselves with them. You, me, Fanny, Martha—everybody. A pity, or a glory—depending on what you've got to take. Now, if you'll excuse me, I better go change. Reckon I've held Christmas up long enough already—"

Philippe looked at Fanny. She wasn't even crying. He wished suddenly that she would. Crying would be better. Anything would be better than the way she held her tiny figure rod-rigid and erect—'Waiting'—the image was romantic, Philippe realized; but not one jot less true for being so—'for the return of the torturers. Wondering if she'll break, this time. Cry. Grovel. Beg mercy. Or hold on. Endure . . .'

When Bill Turner came back downstairs after changing into dry clothes, his face was still troubled. With a sigh, he eased his big, rugged, square-built form down into the Morris chair and took the steaming cup of eggnog that Eliza brought him. But, before he could even take a sip of it, Billy scrambled up on his knees, with both the épées in his hands.

"Dueling swords, Papa!" he said. "Phil brought 'em for my Christmas. Now I'm gonna be th' boss o' the whole block!"

Bill looked at Martha.

"There're better things to be, son," he said. "Why don't you try for the smartest kid? The best-behaved?"

"Like Roger Dillsworth?" Billy said. "That's what everybody says about *him*. All the mamas, anyhow—"

"Well—yes," Bill Turner said. "I don't know Roger Dillsworth, but—"

"Huh!" Billy snorted. "No you don't, Papa! He's got lace on his drawers! What a sis! The fellows call him Silly Dilly—"

"Well," Martha said judiciously, "little Roger *is* a bit too delicate, too refined for a boy, Bill. But, all the same, our Billy carries things too far in the opposite direction. This morning he was telling me that his greatest ambition is to be a *robber* when he grows up . . ."

"Now, Billy-boy," Bill Turner said, "I was hoping you'd follow in *my* footsteps . . ."

"Huh!" Billy said. "Not on your life, Papa! You're a po-leeceman, and *nobody* likes po-leecemen!"

"I do, Billy," Martha said.

"Me, too," Fanny said softly.

"And I," Philippe added.

"Ah g'wan! You all have *got* to say that! You're in Papa's house—'n—'n you got to be polite! But Papa ain't *rich*, is he? Are you, Papa? C'mon, tell the truth!"

"No, son," Bill Turner said sadly, "I'm very far from rich."

"You see!" Billy said triumphantly. "Just what Eddie says! You work like a nigger, and you ain't got a pica-yune. While *his* papa—"

Bill's voice was grim, suddenly.

"And who is this Eddie's papa, Billy, may I ask?" he said.

"Mr. Sarcone. Richest man in town, and he—"

But Bill Turner's face had turned purple; he put up a hand, and clutched his own right shoulder.

"Bill!" Martha said.

"Goddamn it, Martha!" Bill Turner whispered. "You *know* Dr. Terrebonne says I mustn't get excited. But how the hell am I going to keep calm when you let my son play with the children of Mafiosa bastards like Sarcone?"

"Bill," Martha said, "I'm sorry. I'm terribly sorry, dar-ling. But you must believe me when I say I didn't know."

"No," Bill Turner said slowly, "come to think of it, how could you? My fault, in fact. Should have warned you what kind of people we've got living in this block, now. Reckon the Sarcone kid is good-looking and talks well, and all. No reason why not. Joe—his handle's really Giuseppe—Sarcone can afford to send his brats to *good* schools. Reckon he's right. Being honest doesn't pay. That guinea bastard's got his finger in every dirty deal in town. He and Tom Anderson are partners in the parlor house business; he controls every gram of cocaine that's run in from Algiers across the river; he owns half the gambling casinos and—"

"Bill," Martha said, "do me a favor, will you? Don't call Mr. Sarcone a guinea bastard, even though I suppose he *is* a bastard in the spiritual sense. Anyone who makes a commerce of drugs and prostitution would have to be. But I don't believe his being Italian—a slightly politer way of putting it, don't you think?—has much to do with it. Or with anything else, for that matter. The sort of—well—illegitimacy of soul you're referring to is rather universal, isn't it?"

"Yes," Bill Turner sighed, "it is, honey. And, anyhow, excuse me. Bad habit, I guess. Loose talk like that, I mean. Didn't intend to put *that* slant on it. Most of the Italians I've known have been damn fine folks. Martinelli, on my squad, is one of nature's noblemen. But Sarcone's *Sicilian*, Martha; and Martinelli swears that *all* the Sicilians are crooks!"

"Thereby substituting a regional prejudice for a national one," Martha said. "I know most mainland Italians don't like them. But Sicily is the poorest part of Italy, Bill. I visited it with my parents on one of our trips to Europe. So, down there, they do tend to glorify crime—as a way out of appalling misery. But if you'd ever seen how they live—"

"All right," Bill Turner said, "I stand rebuked. Only, don't let Billy play with the Sarcone boy anymore, will you, Martha?"

"You can be sure of *that*," Martha said.

"Aw, Papa!" Billy protested, "Eddie's the best friend I've got! He's always treatin' me to stuff and—"

"And I'll have you eating off the mantelpiece for a week if you *ever* take anything the Sarcone kid offers you again!" Bill Turner roared. "What's more, if you've got anything he's given you in the house, back it goes tomorrow! You hear me, Billy!"

Both Martha and Fanny stared at the big man. It was the first time he had spoken harshly to Billy, in the boy's entire—if short—life.

"Aw, Papa!" Billy whined, "that ain't fair! I *couldn't* do that . . ."

"Which means you *have* got stuff that kid's given you, haven't you, Billy?" Bill Turner said grimly.

"Nothin' much," Billy said. "Just—just a switchblade 'n a pair o' brass knucks and—"

The purple tide rose and suffused Bill Turner's face. His skin was mottled suddenly. He was trying to say something; but the words wouldn't come out. He dropped the eggnog, and his big hands came up, clawing at his high collar.

"Bill!" Martha screamed. "Oh my God! Bill!"

Philippe was beside the big man in seconds. He reached out his slim hand and literally tore the stiffly starched, high wing collar from the detective's neck. Then he bent and jerked Mr. Turner's belt loose. By then Martha and Fanny were both there.

"His shoes!" Philippe snapped. "Get them off him! Eliza! Bring me a pitcher of water! And a basin. *Cold* water, you hear me? And some cloths, towels, dishrags—anything . . ."

Eliza was back with the cold water with a speed amazing in a woman of her age.

"Oh, Mister Bill!" she moaned. "Don't, suh! Don't you up 'n die on us! You can't, suh! We *needs* you!"

Philippe bathed the detective's face with the icy water. Martha knelt beside the chair, her dark eyes appalled. Slowly Bill Turner's breathing eased; the high tide of color receded from his face. His green eyes lost that glassy look, cleared.

"Thanks, son," he muttered. "Reckon you'll make a first-class sawbones at that—"

"Philippe," Martha said, "will you help me get him up to bed?"

"Not yet!" Philippe said sharply. "I've got to see something first. Mr. Turner, do you hear me? I mean do you hear me clearly?"

"Yes, son," Bill Turner said, "I'm all right. Just got a mite too riled up and—"

"Bill, don't talk! Please don't talk!" Martha said. She was shaking.

"All right, sir," Philippe said. "Lift your right hand. That's it. Now wiggle your fingers. Good. Now do the same thing with your left. Good, again. Now your right foot—"

"I—can't—" Bill Turner muttered. "Something's holding it."

Philippe looked down and saw what that something was. Fanny. She lay on the floor with both her thin arms clasped around her father's ankles. His shoes lay to the right of her, and to the left, where she'd thrown them after taking them off. And the way she was crying was enough to make the wound of pity mortal in any man who saw her, Philippe thought.

He bent down, put his two hands unders her armpits, raised her up. She weighed nothing. She was pale wood-smoke, a barely warm misting of air.

"Now, Fan—" he said reproachfully.

"My—fault—" she whispered. "All my fault. Papa never was sick—before—before I—I turned out—bad—"

"Oh, Fanny!" Martha moaned. "You can't! You mustn't! I—"

But Fanny had caught sight of Billy's round face, from over Philippe's left shoulder. Before anyone could guess her intent, she had torn free of Philippe's clasp. She danced over to where her half-brother stood.

"And you, you little bastard!" she hissed at him, her voice rent and shaken with terrible fury, "you have to finish the job for me, d'you? I should have killed you that time I stuck you in the gut! By God, I should have killed you!"

Then she brought her right hand whistling around to explode against Billy's face. In the sudden silence, it sounded like a pistol shot. Billy hung there, too astounded to move.

"Fanny," Philippe said, "the person you *will* kill is your father, if you don't stop acting like a wild cat! Now go sit over there. Or the next person who's going to get slapped around here is *you*, Babydoll—and by *me*. You heard me, Fanny; get out of the way!"

Fanny bowed her head.

"Yes, Phil," she murmured. "Yes, darling—I'm going . . ."

The way she pronounced the word "darling" was an exact duplicate of Martha's tone, Philippe realized. Then he heard the low, throaty chuckle coming from the direction of the Morris chair.

"Son—" Bill Turner said, "you're all right! Damned if you aren't! Just what my filly needs—a stout fellow who's got something inside his trousers besides his legs. Thanks, son. And, before you ask: Yes, I can move my feet, and my toes. You snapped me out of it in time. My blood pressure's through the ceiling, Doc Terrebonne says—and any upset or too-heavy strain could bring on a stroke. But what I want to know—"

"Mama! Fanny—hit me!" Billy wailed. "Mama, she hit me—hard!" It had taken him all that time to get over his astonishment. For, in the Turner household, nobody ever struck William P. Turner, Jr. Nobody at all.

"And I," Martha said grimly, "am having an awfully rough time keeping myself from hitting you even harder, son of mine! Eliza, take him out to the kitchen—and keep him there, until I come for him, will you?"

"Yes 'm," Eliza said; then: "Mister Bill, you feel all right?"

"Just fine, Eliza," Bill Turner said. "Now take that junior candidate for membership in the Mafia out of here. I mean to eat in peace. That is, if I can eat. Can I, Doc?"

He was looking at Philippe when he said that, and grinning. It was a wan and shaky grin; but authentic for all that. 'Authentic and—gallant,' Philippe thought. 'The way Fanny's smiles nearly always are—'

"Of course," he said, "but lightly, sir. Some of the white meat of the turkey, a little cranberry sauce. Some fruit. But no potato salad, stuffing, sweets, baked yam—or fruitcake. And only a little wine, sir—"

Fanny was staring at Philippe. She had a curiously perverse smile on her face.

"Now who ever told you that you're already a doctor, Phil?" she said mockingly.

"He is, though," Martha said, "a natural one. A *born* doctor, I should say. Philippe, may I say thank you? Those words are totally inadequate for the occasion, I suspect. But, believe me, they carry an awful lot of freight: My undying gratitude, my admiration—and though I've had to acquire you as a son through indirect, troublesome, and even somewhat—dubious circumstances—my love."

Fanny made a grimace.

"That last part, he already knows," she said bitterly. "You proved it to him earlier tonight, appears to me. Before Papa came home. Or didn't you?"

"Fanny," Philippe said, his voice calm, controlled, but with a tiny rasp of anger sounding through it—very slight, but there—"don't be a jealous female, will you?"

She stared at him, and her pale eyes were very clear.

"Yes," she said. "I am, ain't—aren't I? Jealous of you, I

mean. And that's bad. 'Cause falling in love with another fellow was the last thing I meant to do as long as I lived. So—you win, Phil. I'm—helpless. Again. I love you. Only I'm asking you—to be good to me—even if I don't deserve it. No, not 'if': 'though.' 'Cause I don't. What I deserve is to be—stomped to death—and left in a ditch to rot . . ."

"Fanny, please!" Martha said.

"That's enough of that wild talk, young lady!" Bill Turner said.

"Yes, Papa," Fanny said. "Anyhow, thank you, Philippe, for saving my father. Which means you saved him and me, both. Good thing. Would have been mighty rough on Martha, arranging two funerals at the same time . . ."

"Fanny," Bill Turner said, "you mustn't think like that, daughter. If anything happens to me—"

"It'll be my fault," Fanny said. "I *made* you sick Papa; way I acted—what I did . . ."

"Well—" Bill Turner said slowly, "I reckon you do have to shoulder at least some of the blame at that. I'll admit your behavior didn't help, a thing I wouldn't even mention, if I didn't know that taking *all* responsibility off a youngster, boy or girl, just isn't smart. Because, by my lights, bearing up under responsibility is what forms character. All right. So, yes; you *helped* make me sick, daughter. You—and a mighty heap of other things. Memories. Thinking of the first-class law office I ought to have up New York way, and haven't got because I was a goddamned fool. My work. Having the kind of temperament that makes me chew my own guts out over all the dirty, stinking rottenness there is in this world that I *can't* do anything about, because some daggumed high-and-mighty muckamucks, some of our leading citizens, pillars of society and the church, have a vested interest in seeing it go on. So they protect it . . ."

He looked into the fire. Shook his big head tiredly. Went on:

"How're you going to close a whorehouse when a vestryman of St. Marks *owns* it? Or stop drug-running, when Dr. Bienvenue—one of our leading druggists, and a good Roman Catholic Creole, I'm sorry to say, son—is the *outlet* for Sarcone and that Algiers gang? How're you going

to enforce the law with a whole police force that's sold itself out, right down to the lowest harnessbull pounding
the beat—and dirt cheap at that? Every time I have to
pass through Customhouse Street early in the morning I
can see the piles of quarters the madams and the girls
leave on the doorsteps so that even the ordinary patrolman on his morning rounds will look the other way while
they're busy at making a diseased wreck out of every
young sprig in town who thinks he is a sport. And how
you're going to—"

"Bill," Martha said, "please!"

"*You're* honest, sir," Philippe said. "Everybody gives
you that."

"Yes. Me. Martinelli. Sprugs. Rogers. Maybe two or
three others. Out of the whole goddamned force, son. The
rest are eating mighty high on the hog. Taking bribes.
Shutting their eyes to what goes on every minute in the
dirtiest, filthiest, stinkhole of a burg—on the face of God's
green earth, leastways since He blasted Sodom and Go-
morrah. Aside from the footpads, slung-shot artists, bank-
robbers, pimps, drug-runners, extortionists, and the like,
you ever heard of any other city in the U.S.A. where
there's a procurement agency that specializes in finding little boys for perverts, son? Or where a lady schoolma'arm
can be convicted—and that only because I had Sprugs and
Martinelli, men who can't be bought, working with me on
the case—of supplying girls from *twelve* or *fifteen* years
old to senile degenerates, along with medical certificates
guaranteeing their virginity? Up to four hundred dollars a
filly she was getting, the bitch! And you know who sold
the poor little unbroke critters to *her?* Their own Irish
Channel mas!"

Philippe was watching Fanny's face. He knew that this
had to be stopped. Now.

"Sir," he said, "I'd appreciate it if you wouldn't undo
my best efforts. In other words, as Dr. Terrebonne told
you, you really mustn't get—"

"Excited? Right. Right as rain. But you tell me, son: In
this miserable job of mine, how in hellsfire am I supposed
to keep calm?"

"Bill," Martha said, "you *know* the answer to that. It's
very simple, dear. Your resignation, in writing, on the
Chief's desk, *tomorrow*. All right?"

Bill Turner looked at his wife. The purple tide rose in his face again.

"And live off—my woman's bounty?" he grated. "There's a word for a fellow who does that, Martha. He's a—pimp. Married to her or not, he's—"

"Mr. Turner!" Philippe said, truly alarmed by what was going on in the detective's face then, "you really must calm down! In fact, I think I'd better go look for Dr. Terrebonne right now, and—"

"No, son," Bill Turner said. "You do all right, yourself. I'll put a check-rein onto my miserable temper. You see, Phil-boy, this happens to be another—sore spot—or at least a bone of contention between the Missus and me. It so happens that her father died last year, and left her— rich . . ."

"Hardly rich, Bill," Martha said. "Say, comfortably well off . . ."

"*Rich*. That much money is a damned sight more than comfortable, Martha; and you know it. Fact is, the way the old boy left it invested for her, Martha's a lead-pipe cinch to be a millionaire—a real one, inside of five years. But my point's I'm a Southerner. And we don't live off our women; do we, son?"

"No," Philippe said slowly. "In this, Mrs. Turner, I'm afraid I'm on Mr. Turner's side . . ."

"Oh, Philippe!" Martha said reproachfully.

"You don't understand," Philippe said. "It would kill him, Marth—Mrs. Turner. It would kill him as surely as though you'd pointed a gun at his head and pulled the trigger. He'd sit there and eat his heart out, brooding over being reduced to uselessness—to a dependent's status. You should *know* that, chère madame. The quickest way to— to murder—a proud man, is to rob him of his pride. Irrational, I grant you; but there it is . . ."

Martha bowed her head. Looked up again. The tears were there now, finally; hot and bright and sudden in her eyes.

"You're—right, Philippe," she whispered. "Bill, I withdraw the suggestion—permanently. I won't make it again, ever. Forgive me, will you?"

"Forgive you? No. How's a body going to forgive the woman he goes down on his knees and thanks the Good Lord every night for merely letting him be alive and in the same world with? The question doesn't even come up . . ."

"Oh, Bill!" Martha said, and bending swiftly, kissed his cheek. She looked up again at Philippe, her eyes brimming, her lashes light-beaded.

"You see?" she said. "Remember what I told you, Philippe? That there are times—that make up for a—a lifetime of suffering? You—you've just seen happiness demonstrated, my boy—a woman's happiness, anyhow. It consists in having her man say—meaning it—a thing like that!"

"Yes," Philippe said; but he was thinking: 'With Fanny, will happiness—even momentary happiness—be possible?' He doubted it. He doubted it profoundly. So he put his hand to Bill Turner, said:

"Come, sir. You'd better take a bite to eat, then off to bed! Doctor's orders!"

"Right, Phil," Bill Turner said gruffly. "Don't reckon *I* need to say thank you, do I? You know I'm grateful, son. But speaking of *that,* young fellow; tell me: How the devil did you know just what to do?"

Philippe tore his gaze away from Fanny's white, sick, utterly pathetic face. Forced himself to smile.

"You were a textbook case, sir. And I've read the textbooks," he said.


## Chapter Nine


But his one real failure of that rare and troublesome Christmas night was not, as Philippe had anticipated they would be, the frog legs, which Fanny ate without protest—if with scant appetite—saying, "You're right, Phil, honey; they're awf'ly good . . ." but the quite unexpected detail that she flatly refused his Christmas gift. He had bought her a string of pearls—a lovely and damned expensive string of pearls. But she wouldn't take them.

"Pearls—are tears, Phil," she said. "Leastways that's what folks always say. I know it's only a silly superstition, but I don't want to take a chance. I've cried enough. Take 'em back to the store and exchange them for something else, will you, huh? A jade green comb for my hair, say . . ."

"Why jade green, Fan?" he said.

"Green—for jealousy," she said seriously. "Cause— 'cause if Martha ever kisses you like that again, I'll scratch her eyes out, so help me! Good as she's been to me, I will!"

Philippe grinned at her.

"Now I know what I'm going to ask my father to give me for a wedding present," he said.

"What, Phil?" Fanny said.

"A buggy whip. For wife-beating purposes," Philippe said.

That Wednesday evening—the night before he was to go up to Mertontown, that feared, longed-for, ambiguous, and tormenting trip, that, even with his railway ticket bought, he was far from sure he was going to make— Philippe had it forcibly demonstrated to him that his wry joke about the buggy whip made a good bit of sense. For Henri came into his study a little before seven o'clock with a note in his hands.

"Madame Eliza brought it," he said. Henri always called Eliza "Madame" because he was totally convinced that the Turners' maid-of-all-work was a *Mamaloi,* or voodoo witch-queen. Of course, Eliza did dabble in gris-gris and the simpler kinds of black magic, but for her own amusement merely; for Philippe was sure that a woman as intelligent as Eliza indisputably was didn't really believe in such ruddy nonsense herself.

'While we,' he thought with the curiously self-defeating irony he was capable of, 'light candles before plaster images with the vapid, idiotic faces of children's dolls—to exactly the same ends, and with no more rationality. Ha! Definition of religion: What *I* believe in, practice. Definition of a superstition, heresy, black magic, obscurantism, or what have you: What *you* believe in and/or practice, friend! At least when our respective brands of nonsense differ, that is . . .'

"Give me the note, vieux âne," he said.

Henri passed it over. Philippe opened it, read:

Dearest Philippe,
Please come to see me tonight. Please. It's important. I *have* to see you. Everything depends on it. Please, please, please, please!

                Fanny

He pulled his watch out of his waistcoat pocket. Looked at it. Sighed.

"You may go, Henri," he said. "There's no answer. Or rather, tell Eliza, if she's still downstairs, that I'll answer it in person."

An hour later, he sat in the Turners' sitting room, staring at Fanny. As usual, she had on the pink quilted robe, and her tiny feet were thrust into a delicate pair of bedroom slippers, decorated with a ruff of ostrich plumes. She wore her hair in a soft bun on the back of her neck, and her eyes were suspiciously bright.

He didn't like the way her eyes looked, nor the way she was smiling at him. There was something wrong about both. 'That glow in her eyes,' he thought slowly, 'is too close to—to an animal glitter for comfort. Or—to actual madness. And her smile's—perverse. Goddamned perverse—'

"Phil—" she murmured, "kiss me?"

He hung back.

'Her voice is—unnatural, too,' he told himself. 'I have never heard that throaty quality in it before. It's—rehearsed. Practiced. She's trying to sound—seductive! But why? In the name of le-petit bon Dieu—why?'

"No," he said, "I'd rather not."

Fanny stared at him

"Why not, darling?" she said.

"And don't call me dar-r-rling, damn it!" Philippe said.

Oh!" Fanny whispered; then: "Same question: Why not—Phil?"

"Don't know. No, that's not true. I do know. One: You give me the damnedest impression that you're up to something. Something premeditated, planned. And in that kind of a proposition, the man's always the goat. So let me put it bluntly: I don't like being used. Two: I'm in a mood. Can't say why, really; but I am. Three: you always called Rod Schneider 'darling' like that, rolling *r's* a little, a pronunciation unnatural in a Southerner. You probably copied it from Martha, to whom it is natural, and who sounds good doing it, which you don't, Fan. But that's not my real objection. Put it this way: When you apply the same endearment, in the exact same tone of voice to me that you used to call that randy billy goat, you can't expect me to feel deliriously happy, Fan."

"Oh!" she said again. She sat there staring at him until her eyes filled up, brimmed over, beaded her pale lashes, flashed white as the drops broke loose, fell.

'An act!' he told himself. But if it was an act, it was masterly. She got up from the sofa and came towards him, step by step, slowly. Then, when she was close enough, she sank to her knees before him. It was the first time, he realized, that he'd ever seen anyone convert that romantic metaphor "sink to one's knees" into reality. Her bones melted inside her legs, she drifted down, sighed down before him as a windblown leaf sinks, after the breeze has died. The motion was stunningly, incredibly graceful, especially in a girl who though pert and perky enough—'In her former, now dead avatar!' the thought went keening through his mind—had had scant claim to grace, had been rather clumsy, really.

"Fan—" he murmured.

But whatever he had been about to say he never finished, for she had seized his hands in hers, and turned them palms upward. Then—again with that incredible grace he had never seen before in her—she bent, and—he rejected the word "kissed" as inexact—applied her mouth, open, tear wet, adhesive, scalding suddenly, to his cupped palms, tracing miniature circles upon them with a tonguetip become a brand, searing him to the bone without losing one iota of its soft, slow, crippling tenderness.

"My God!" he whispered.

She raised her face up, smiled at him. The trembling, upturned corners of her mouth made another metaphor—'A mad female beggar juggling diamonds—' his mind supplied; but a moment later, his mind ran completely out of metaphors, of thought, of rationality, retreated into a state of prehumanity, of suspension of function, except for a kind of stunned amazement that was less than a cerebral attribute—and more.

For she came up between his knees, and cupped his

face between her tiny hands. He had a fleeting impression that they were both hot and dry. Later, thinking back over it, he realized that she must have been running several degrees of fever even then—and he cherished the thought with its accompanying diagonistic implication of delirium as a comfort against the bitter hurt she dealt him.

Once more she applied her mouth—the verb "to kiss" being again a *reductio ad absurdum* before the reality—to his, with her pale lips opened, adhesive, pressing against his so hard that she forced his teeth apart and explored the inside of his mouth with a hot, wet, serpentine tongue whose very expertness was self-defeating, because it called memory back into being with its absolute recognition of the source of her damnably practiced skill so that a sickness clawed gut-deep in him, shudderingly close to nausea. To end it, he called up rage. Putting his two hands on her shoulders, he shoved her away from him, none to gently; said:

"What the devil's got into you, Fan?"

"That—" she said, in an odd, slow, throaty voice. "The devil—what else? Kiss me, Phil, honey?"

"No!" he said, strangling on the word.

She laughed, a contralto purr, two full octaves below her normal tonal range.

"Scared, Phil?" she said.

"You're goddamned right I'm scared!" he said. "Suppose Martha or—"

"Papa. Or Eliza. Or even Billy—were to walk in here right now? Don't worry, darr—dearest. Is 'dearest' all right, dearest? I've got to call you something—sweet. Sweet as you are, you longtall old frog-legs eatin' sweetie, you! Is 'dearest' all right?"

"Yes," he groaned, "Fan—"

"Martha is over to Mary Etta Collins'—to a card party. She took Billy with her, because she's afraid that Eliza is too old to keep him from sneaking out to get into mischief with Eddie Sarcone and his gang of junior thugs. They won't be home before midnight. Eliza is calling hogs. I see you don't know that saying. It means she's snoring so loud that it sounds like the noise farmfolks make when they call the pigs in to feed 'em. And Papa won't be home much before morning, as usual . . ."

"So?" Philippe said. He hadn't known that the human voice could shake upon a monosyllable. But his did, then.

She didn't answer him, at least not verbally.

Her mouth on his made magical dissonances, a bitter combination of the screaming of his nerves and the drumroll of his blood. Her arms—no! the strangeness of that fact broke easily through the rising sexual tension in him, since all that night, something, call it the tempo, the beat, the quality of events, what you will, had, to his keen perceptions, rung false, been oddly out of tune, disconcerting, wrong—*one* arm, her left, tightened around his neck. It was not until she surged against him that he realized where her right arm was. He could feel it between them, with the fingers of her right hand tearing franticly at the knot of the silken cord that belted the quilted robe about her. He was aware the instant that the knot loosened, gave, the cord fell away.

She clawed at his wrist then, dragged his hand forward and upward so that it slid over cool, fragrant areas of tender flesh, over the all too palpable rib cage beneath, until the rounded soft resilience of her left breast was under his fingers and—

The long, long whipcord ridge of scar tissue that went on and on and on with no end to it anywhere.

He pushed her quietly, gently away from him. As his tactile sense had already told him, under that robe she was naked. She hadn't even a nightgown on.

He stood there, almost emasculated by pity, gazing at that poor skeletal nakedness, and holding hard against the feeling of desolation, of loss, of grief, that were the only emotions her starveling's body awoke in him. Then he put out his hands and gently closed the robe over pipestem legs and thighs, topped by a faint, almost invisible pale wisp of public hair, over tiny breasts, well formed and shapely enough, except that their authentic loveliness had less power to hold his gaze than did that obscenely hideous ridge of barely healed scar tissue, crisscrossed at intervals by the smaller ridges the sutures had made, and the puckering whorls where the drainage tubes had been. The great scar looped between her breasts and down her left side in a semicircle clearly showing how Lucien Terrebonne had had to open her up like a butchered she-goat in order to clean out the mess she had made of her left lung with that kitchen knife.

Then he saw how—quiescent she was. Her breath came from her nostrils sweet-sighing, slow. There hadn't been, he remembered suddenly, the slightest sign of tumescence about her nipples; nor any faint sheen of sweat upon her milky flesh. Suspicion distilled itself into cold, sick certainty within his mind. He was not without experience; he knew how really passionate women react, behave. But all the same it took him several seconds to get that, "Why, Fan?" out.

"I want you—to love me," she said in an odd, grave, little-girl's tone of voice. "You made me fall in love with you, Phil. I didn't want to; but you made me. And I—I'm my mother's own child, I reckon—I mean I suppose. Kissing and sweet talk aren't enough for me. I've got to be—to be—well—bedded, too. I remember how shocked you got when I said the real word. So I won't say it anymore. I—I *need* it, Phil. It's the way I'm made. So—get busy, damn you! Do your duty, lover! Give it to baby. Ram it up—"

It was then that he slapped her. Hard.

She hung there, staring at him. Then she threw both her arms about his neck and cried noisily, angrily, soaking his collar with her tears.

"Fan," he said sadly, "I'm sorry. But that would kill you, and you know it. It'll be years before—"

"I know that, goddamn you!" she stormed, "but I didn't want to—to have to use a kitchen knife on myself again! It hurts, Phil! It hurts something awful! I wanted *you* to do it! Finish me off I mean. *You,* Philippe, not anybody else; you understand? 'Cause when you find out how rotten, lowdown mean I've been to you, and leave me, I'll have to—so I figured this way—this way—"

"This way, what, Fan?" he said.

"*She'll* never have you, the freckled-faced li'l bitch! 'Cause my ghost would always be there between you! The ghost of the girl you killed. And, what's more, killed her in a way you'll never be able to forget. Or forgive yourself for, either, I reckon—"

"Fan—" he said.

"That way—you'll grieve. You'll spend your whole life—a-grieving and a-sorrowing. And I—I'll have that,

anyhow. Wherever I am—even if I'm screaming my guts
out down in hell, I'll know I ruined your life—and *hers,*
goddamn her! Made you both so rotten miserable that—"

He looked at her, his dark eyes almost black with pain.
Then he asked the right question: the one thing he needed
to know. Or rather, to have her confirm. For, by then, the
question had become rhetorical. He knew already. But, by
asking it, he took his first step up the bitter, stony, utterly
bleak road to maturity.

"Fan," he said, "did you want to, really? I mean—did
you actually *feel* like making love? Physically? With—
your body? Did you? Answer me! And for God's sake,
don't lie!"

She looked up at him. Her eyes were still awash. But
her mouth was—sullen.

"No," she said. "I didn't. I don't. And I never have—in
my whole life, Phil. Don't reckon I ever will. I know
some women are hot-natured, but I'm not. Martha is. So
maybe you ought to run off with *her*—"

"Fanny," he said grimly, "then—why—Rod? And why
this act? This damned fine, first-class act? Convincing as
all get-out. Why? Damn it to hell and begone, Fanny!
Why?"

"You really want to know?" she whispered. "All right.
Rod was—good-looking and rich and—and quality. So,
why not? It don't—doesn't even hurt. After the first time,
that is. Easy enough way for a girl to get herself a husband she can be proud of, Phil. It's kind of tiresome but
it ain't—isn't—*that* much of a bother. Little enough trouble for what it can get you—I thought. Only—"

"Only, what, Fan?" he said.

"Only it got me a knife in my tit—breast! I will talk
well! I will! And now, you—"

"Get to that," he said dryly. "What about me?"

"I—I love you. At least I *think* I do. And I'm going to
lose you. To her. So if I had to do that—to stop you from
going up there and seeing *her* again—if layin' down with
you on top of me—in me—and wiggling a little—
would—"

"I see," he said, almost recognizing, even then, that he
had heard the basic "why" of whoredom, the bleak, pas-
sionless chill that lies at its forlorn heart, "but what it
would do at this stage of the game is—kill you, Fanny."

She shrugged.

"What's the odds? I'm dead already. Or I will be—when you come back from up there and tell me we're quits. If you're even that nice about it. If you don't spit in my face—just like I said you would—"

"Why should I do that, Fanny?" he said.

She threw her head back. What was in her eyes now was madness's very self. Her face tightened, visibly, so that looking into it was to peer—'Into a death's head—a skull—' he thought with pity and with shock.

"Go up there and see, you damn fool!" she screamed at him, and, whirling, ran from the room.

So he did go. All the way up to Mertontown, the train ran through a blinding rain. Sitting there by the window, staring at his own reflection in the water-blurred and opaque glass, Philippe tried to tell himself that Fanny wouldn't carry out her suicidal threats—this time. The occasion was—less drastic, he believed. 'And, besides, when she sees me back again safe and sound—'

He stopped. 'Am I safe and sound?' he thought. 'Is any man ever—in this life?' It didn't help to think that, for, try as he would, he couldn't shake the nagging worry that Fanny might not even wait until his return before doing something rash—or fatal. But it was too late by then to try to remedy the situation: even if he got off at the next station and waited for a southbound train, he would gain so little time that nothing in his life or hers would be changed by it. Nothing prevented, nothing saved. So, to put down the sick unease tugging at the edges of his consciousness, he occupied himself with trying to puzzle out the whys of Fanny's behavior. But he could not; he lacked the necessary experience. Which was perhaps the greatest pity in a life torn and rent by pity, for had he known then what he afterwards came to learn, he might still, even at that late, late hour, have saved her.

It was almost dark before the ancient, creaking surrey that he had taken at the Mertontown station drew up before the porch of Oliver Prescott's farmhouse. It was, as far as Philippe could make out through the driving rain and the yellow, cracked mica windows set in the leather curtains, a rarely lovely house.

For Oliver Prescott, being a simple man, had not fallen

into the trap of building an imposing neo-Grecian monstrosity. His house was a bungalow in the French West Indian style, having one and one half storeys—the half storey being lighted with dormer windows let into a beautifully thatched roof—and surrounded by a veranda, or as the Creoles called it, a gallerie, that completely circled the house, the sweeping overhang of the roof being supported by slim, square gray cypress posts, utterly unadorned. The construction itself was the classic briqueté entre poteaux, a framework of heavy cypress posts and diagonal struts filled in with bricks and mortar, then plastered over to protect the porous Louisiana clay bricks from the eternal bayou damp.

'Nobody,' Philippe thought, 'has built a house like this in a hundred years—no, nearer two hundred—but Lord God it's lovely!'

"How much?" he said to the driver.

"Comment?" the driver said. "Que vous m'avez dit, m'sieur?"

Philippe laughed. He had been told that on the outskirts of Caneville-Sainte Marie there were Cajuns to whom English remained a foreign tongue, but he hadn't expected to find one in Mertontown.

"Combien je vous dois?" he said; then, giving way to his curiosity, demanded: "How the devil do you do business with les Américains?"

"Avec les doigts," the driver said laconically. "With the fingers. That will be—two dollars, m'sieur."

"You're a great-grandson of Jean Lafitte!" Philippe laughed, "a born pirate, aren't you? But here, take 'em anyhow! I'm in too good a mood to argue . . ."

The long, skinny Cajun carried Philippe's bags up on the porch and said:

" 'Voir, m'sieur. Merci—"

And departed.

Philippe knocked on the door. Again. And again. His elation died. The house was lighted. He could see the warm yellow lamplight glowing through every window. Strange that Billie Jo—or the servants—took so long to answer his knocking. He tried one more time, almost despairingly. Then he heard the whisper of her footsteps coming on. Hers, surely hers. No one else would walk with so light, so lissome a tread, his heart told him.

He was right. Billie Jo opened the door. She had a kerosene lamp in her hand. And seeing him, recognizing him, all the color fled her face, leaving her freckles more pronounced than ever. Even her lips went white.

"Howdy, ma'am," Philippe drawled in a heavy burlesque of the way it seemed to Creoles that all Americans talked. "Got a corner 'n a crust o' bread to give a poor lonesome feller who's come a awful long way to see a mighty pretty girl?"

Billie Jo's lips made a grim line.

"No," she said, "for the likes of you, Philippe Sompayac, no. I see you've let your hack go. Well all that means is that you'll have to walk back to town. You can leave your bags here, and come after them, later."

"Billie Jo!" Philippe said.

She peered past him at the driving rain. Sighed. Said, her voice dripping acid, triple-distilled:

"All right. I shouldn't want to be responsible for even your death, which is what you'll catch if you go out in that, though Lord knows you deserve it! Come in, *Mister* Sompayac. My uncle's not at home. I'm alone in the house, except for a couple of very old darkies. So, if you're aiming to—to take advantage of me, in your usual style—now's your chance! Only you'll know you've been in a fight, so help me!"

He stood there, searching her face. Random phrases of Fanny's flashed sudden lightnings through his mind. "For a girl to do what I did, lying flat on her back in a hospital bed, she's got to be poison-mean—or crazy." "If you don't spit in my face when you come back, like I deserve . . ." Those, and others. Combined with Billie Jo's own announced decision to visit Fanny in the hospital before going home.

"Where's your uncle?" he said.

"Out. Visiting his fancy woman—just like you'd expect, now that my poor Auntie's helpless. Men! I swear to God you all—"

"Billie Jo," he said almost gently, "what did Fanny tell you?"

"The truth!" Billie Jo snapped. "What *you* did, Mister High-and-Mighty Sompayac! She wasn't good enough for you, even though you'd got her in the family way, so you—you called all your filthy friends in and—and—Oh, Philippe, how could you?"

He looked her straight in the eyes, said:

"Good-bye, Billie Jo. I won't come back for my bags. Send them to me express collect, if that's not too much of a bother. If it is, burn them. I have a few other rags to keep out the cold—"

Then he turned and went down the stairs into the pouring rain.

She stood there, a long moment; then she came flying after him. The lamp hissed out at once in the downpour.

"Philippe!" she said. "You—you're saying that—she lied? That you—that you *didn't* do what she said? Oh, Philippe—tell me—"

He stood there, savoring the sight of the rain pouring down her small, freckled, exquisite face. He could see that much from the glow of the lighted windows. And it was precisely the extent that he had idolized her which made the anger and the pain in him so deep.

"I won't tell you a goddamned thing, Billie Jo," he said flatly, "except that maybe I was lucky to escape a woman with a mind like yours . . ." He turned; but she reached out and caught his elbow, her fingers strong and demanding, suddenly.

"Come into the house, Philippe," she said. "She—lied, didn't she? Tell me—"

"I—am a gentleman," Philippe said slowly, his voice bleak. "At least I've been accused of being one. Even by—a certain person it's unnecessary for me to name, on a certain occasion, when even *she* was willing to grant that I—behaved well. And a gentleman *never* contradicts a woman's word, *Miss* Prescott. Whether what she said is true or not, he doesn't."

"Oh, the wretch!" Billie Jo whispered, "the utterly unscrupulous, vile little wretch! To lie there like that and—"

"Lie—or tell the truth—a point you'll never know from me. So now, again, good-bye. That poor Fanny, sick, hurt, shamed, wounded unto death, humiliated past all bearing by a herd of filthy swine, was capable of—of telling you that—true or not! and believe me, you have *not* heard me deny it!—seems to me comprehensible. She was defending her little hold on hope, Miss Prescott. But that you, knowing me, having had some opportunity—to test my metal as it were, believed her without questioning strains my charity, Christian or otherwise, to the breaking point. Again, as a gentleman, it's my duty to—forgive you. And I do, freely. But I have no obligation to continue an associaton with a woman capable of believing such things of me. It would be, I sadly fear, scarcely profitable for either of us."

Then, lifting his hat, he walked away from her into the icy battering of the rain. And he didn't look back. Quite simply, he didn't dare.

When he got to the inn, he was drenched almost to the marrow of his bones; and, what was worse, he remembered suddenly that he had no dry clothes to change into, since his bags reposed still upon the gallerie of Oliver Prescott's house. He stood there before the Inn in the pouring rain, heartsick, soul sick, utterly weary, trying to puzzle out the rarely awful thing he had done. But he had to give it up. There were no answers. He admitted to himself that he didn't know why he'd treated Billie Jo so badly; or why hateful, twisted, perverse, scarred and invalid Fanny had such a hold upon his quixotic heart. The only thing he knew with any certainty was once inside that singularly dreary combination tavern-inn which was Mertontown's only accomodation for the very few travelers who had occasion to stop there overnight, despite his very real distaste for whiskey, he was going to get as drunk as an Irishman, or a lord.

So, dripping puddles with every step, he entered the common room, sat himself down as close to the pot bellied stove as he could get, and began in good earnest to drown the tormented questioning of his mind. Which probably saved him from at least two things, one of them being pneumonia.

The other thing it saved him from is more difficult to define. Philippe Sompayac was both a remarkably handsome young man, and a decidedly intelligent one to boot. He had, therefore, the natural tendency of a youth in his assured social position, well supplied with money, more often than not flattered by the attentions of the opposite sex, praised by his mentors for a scholarship unusual in his day and region, to take himself too seriously. But on that rainy night, the really formidable amount of homemade white lightning he put away caused him to quickly suspend the newborn moral sense he was already giving himself rather too much credit for, and with it, a distinct inclination towards pomposity.

In short, he became himself, a badly confused, uncertain young man with scant control over his native bent towards folly, nursing a double hurt: Fanny's appalling lie, and Billie Jo's outrageous acceptance of it as truth. And all his uncertainty, trouble, hurt, showed in his bent shoulders, in the close to tears misting of his eyes.

To a woman, that combination—his dark, Latin good looks, and his obvious sadness—was irresistible. At least they were to Marie, the inn and/or tavern keeper's daughter.

The sight of him, sitting there with the steam rising from his sodden clothes as they dried before the stove, and the bleak hurt on his face, both spurred and nerved her to immediate action, for in Mertontown, young men of Philippe's princely presence—which got more regal the drunker he became—were as rare as hens' teeth. In a word, the fair Marie, who served her father as kitchen slattern, barmaid, and come-on for the country Jakes, brought Philippe still another bourbon he hadn't even asked for. And, as she served it, she deliberately leaned towards him so far that her umbilicus would have been visible down the loose blouse she wore if her really splendid pair of mammary appendages hadn't obstructed his view. He found the obstructions pleasant and grinned at her.

"Nice—equipment you're supplied with, sweetheart," he said.

She grinned back at him; whispered:

"Lonesome, dearie?"

"Kind of," Philippe said.

"What's your room number?" Marie murmured almost without moving her lips, just as her father's bull bellow cut her off.

"Marie!" he thundered; his sense of the proprieties, which was even more commercial than a sense of the proprieties usually is, was outraged by the thought that his daughter was planning to give something away free—again.

"Twelve," Philippe said.

"You go on up to bed, sweetie—and I'll visit you later—soon as I can get the ol' coot drunk enough not to miss me," the fair and buxom Marie said.

At which art she evidently had a sufficiency of practice, for not three-quarters of an hour later, Philippe heard the knock upon his door. He got up unsteadily and opened it, whereupon Marie, all one hundred forty-odd pounds of her, cheap perfume, kitchen grease, rank armpit stench, and all, hurled herself upon him, proceeding to break his mouth against his teeth, inhale him, swab his tonsils for him, and devour him at one and the same time.

By then he was drunk enough not to be finicky. Which was just as well. Upon Marie's bountiful, and vigorously bounding, charms, he had himself a fine, busy, athletic night. In the morning, stifling the nausea that the sight—and smell—of Marie's blowsy figure awoke in him, Philippe folded a twenty-dollar bill into her sweaty palm, taking quite unnecessary care not to wake her, for not even the trump of doom could have done that by then. After that, he tiptoed from the room and down the stairs, leaving her sleeping the sweet sleep of the innocent, the charitable, the pure of heart, to whom virtue is its own reward. 'Although an occasional fiver is not to be sneered at,' Philippe thought.

In simple justice be it said that he overestimated her professionalism almost totally. Until that very night, the highest fee that Marie had received for her most excellent services had been a silver dollar. Usually she asked—and got—nothing at all, being of that rare and gallant breed of women who fornicate for fornication's own fine and pleasant sake.

So it was that some hours later, Philippe arrived in New Orleans with his halo distinctly askew, and the high-handed, firm, and lordly tone he had been determined to take with Fanny drowned under the twin tides of the damnedest hangover ever seen on land or sea, and his utter, abysmal shame.

It wasn't until the next morning that he recovered enough to go visit her, driven—quaking in his very boots all the way—by the appalling if belated recognition that Fanny *was*, after all, fully capable of carrying out her self-destructive threats, that he had been living in a false

euphoria these last two days, if not in a fool's own paradise.

When Martha, herself, instead of Eliza, opened the
door, and he saw her puffed, swollen, red-streaked eyes,
he stumbled where he stood, went so white in the face
that Martha put out her hand to steady him. He opened
his mouth, dragged air into his lungs, said the only necessary word:

"When?"

"Night before last," Martha whispered. "You'd—quarreled, hadn't you, Philippe?"

"Yes," Philippe said. "Oh, bon Dieu! Don't tell me—"

"No," Martha said. "At least—not yet. She stole my
vernol. And what with the fact that worrying over her—
and her father—has made my insomnia chronic, I had
only six tablets left. Which weren't enough—or they
wouldn't have been. Only, we missed her—after two
hours, Philippe. I thought she was in her room. But she
was lying out in the garden—face down in the rain . . ."

"Jésus!" Philippe wept.

"Don't cry, my boy. She—hemorrhaged quite horribly.
And now she's got double pneumonia. So—I'm afraid
there's no hope. I'm truly sorry, Philippe . . ."

"*You're* sorry!" Philippe moaned. "Jésus! Jésus! Jésus!
Pétit bon Dieu! Sainte Vierge! Un peu de pitié, je vous en
prie! Je vous en supplie! Ne la laissez pas mourir!"

"Philippe—" Martha said, crying too, now, "please
don't cry. It hurts too much to see *you* cry. All young
couples quarrel—that's normal. Come in, will you? Talk
to me. Tell me what it was all about. Talking does help,
you know—"

He came in. Told her. Omitting, of course, the session
with Marie. He was Gallic enough, logical enough to realize that that shoddy episode had had no real bearing upon
events. Before he had done with it, he was kneeling at
Martha's feet, with his face buried in her lap, sobbing
aloud, while, with great and maternal tenderness, she
stroked his defenseless head. For which, it is to be hoped,
a little charity will be extended him by readers of a
newer, more enlightened time. But he inhabited his own
epoch; and the late Victorian period was a sentimental,
even a lachrymose age. Now, of course, as everyone
knows, young men no longer cry.

\* \* \*

But what he afterwards came to ask himself was not a sentimental question:

"Just who was it who heard my prayer, and spared Fanny's life? God, up in heaven? His tender Son? The Holy Ghost? Mary, Virgin, Mother of us all?

"Or—the Devil?"

For a long time, observing Fanny close at hand, witnessing the appalling things she did, he put his money on the Devil. But, afterwards, he was less sure. Cruelty of that magnitude exceeded even Satan's powers. To accomplish it required—God.

Or the God behind God. The blind, faceless, eyeless, mindless Principle of the Universe. Pure Evil. Or—pure indifference, which is Evil's other face.

And colder, crueler still.

## Chapter Ten

From where she lay in her cot on the veranda of Dr. Karl Holtz's Sanitorium, Fanny could see the mountains. As always, they were blue and misty and the air that came down from their peaks was cold and sharp. She shivered a little, feeling the bite of it even through all the blankets that covered her thin body. But she didn't complain. The cold mountain air was supposed to be good for what she had now, a thing so bad and ugly that it hurt to put it into words, even inside her mind:

'TB. A couple of letters they hang onto a mighty slow and messy way of dying. Ought to throw in a few more to my way of thinking. Like say: T.B.G.Y.G. For, Too Bad, girl, you're gone. Oh, Jesus, if it would only go on and kill me and get it over with! Two years now. Two whole years in this miserable old sanitorium in this miserable little old hilltown of Ashville, North Carolina, nursing a hole in my lung that keeps right on getting bigger all the time—'cause Doctor Lucien told Papa—and Martha—that if anybody could pull me through it was Dr. Holtz. Huh! As if anybody could cure this! Who have I seen *walk* out of here in the whole time I've been here? Nobody, that's who. The ones who've stayed alive are still here, and the others they carry out with a sheet over their faces. After they've choked to death on their own blood and spit—like *I* almost did last week. Good thing poor little Susie wasn't around when that happened. Weak as she is, that would have finished her, sure as shooting!'

She lay there very still, her gaze light-locked, abstract, paler than the distant mountains.

'My own fault, anyhow. Doctor Karl says there're always TB germs in your lungs, even when you're healthy. And I haven't been healthy since I stuck that knife into myself, not to mention taking all Martha's sleeping pills 'cause I thought Phil wasn't going to come back to me. Only he did come back. Lord, is he ever a fool! I wouldn't have come back to him if it had been the other way around. If he'd pulled a trick on me half as filthy as the one I pulled on him, I'd have spit in his face, so help me! And—'

She felt Susan Beaconridge's hot, dry little hand on her arm, and turned, glaring at her very dear friend and fellow patient (out of those eyes that Sue had tried to describe to her brother Anthony in her letters several times now, but had always failed; the closest she'd got to their quality being: "They don't look quite—human, Tony; they're too pale, for one thing, and too watchful, vigilant—Oh, I can't say it right!—for another; but, anyhow, they're *so* beautiful!") and said in that harsh tone of voice she always used when speaking to people whom in spite of herself she loved:

"Sue, you mustn't! You're all uncovered again! You'll catch your death if you don't be more careful . . ."

"I've already caught my death," Susan said sadly. "I—I'm too far gone, Fanny. They brought me here too late. You, now—you've a chance. A *good* chance. Dr. Holtz says that if you'll obey the rules, rest, eat plenty of good food, get all the fresh air possible, he'll have you home again in no time at all—"

"For what?" Fanny got out in that husky whisper that served her as a voice now. "I don't want to leave *you*, Sue, honey. And I won't! You—you're the first real friend I've had in my whole life, so I'm not even starting to give you up. And you can stop all that talk about dying right now. You're *not* going to die! I won't have it! You heard me, I won't—"

Sue smiled her wan little smile.

"That's sweet of you, Fanny," she whispered. "But just how do you propose to stop me?"

Fanny sat up in her cot, tossing half of the blankets she was wrapped in aside. Her eyes ignited, made bleak fire in her face, pale as gas jets on a somber wall.

'Frost and—and flint,' Susan's mind groped for the images. 'The blue color a new knife blade gives off, when the light falls on it, and it—glitters—'

"By telling you this!" Fanny rasped, her voice hoarser than ever, which was one of the effects of the disease that was slowly killing her; but also something else, something more: a fury all the more terrible for being absolutely hopeless, grating up from her torn lung, bearing with it an undertone—of anguish, Susan realized; fiercely suppressed, but there. "If *you* die, I'll die, too! So you'll have me on your conscience, Susan Beaconridge—every time you float by on your cloud above the pearly gates and see me roasting down in hell!"

"Oh, Fanny!" Susan said. "What an awful thing to say! In the first place, even if you do die, you won't go to hell, because God is merciful and forgives sinners and—"

"And you give even the Good Lord too much credit," Fanny said. "Bet you I burst that old fiery furnace wide open when I hit! Me? Huh! Reckon I'd better tell you the story of my life all over again, just to remind you! Or, as you highfalutin' New Englanders put it, to recapitulate, sweet Sue! When I was a fat and sassy kid all of eight years old I—"

"No, you don't!" Susan snapped. "I won't have it! I absolutely will not listen to you telling all those awful lies again! Anyone can *see* you're good. All one has to do is look at you! You look like an angel out of heaven and—"

"An angel?" Fanny said. "Oh, Jesus!"

"You do. Besides, you're not going to die. You have *so* much to live for! A boy like Philippe—is he *ever* handsome!—who comes to see you every time he goes up to college and on his way back home, too, going hundreds of miles out of his way to do it—and who spends as much time with you during his vacations as Dr. Holtz will let him, not to mention all the beautiful and expensive presents he brings you every time he—"

"That's because he's a jackass," Fanny said morosely, "a sentimental jackass who only got mixed up with me in the first place because, for a reason that makes sense only to him, he felt obligated to help me straighten out the mess I've made out of my life. He's a fool. If he weren't, he would never have so much as looked at me to begin with . . ."

"Why not, Fanny?" Susan said. "You—you're so pretty! No, you're beautiful! All the interns and the younger doctors are head over heels in love with you. You get more real care and attention than any other patient in this place! Why, only yesterday, Dr. Risotti was saying—"

"Huh!" Fanny said; "That oily little dago! I can't stand him!"

"Fanny," Susan said, "please. You promised me—"

"All right. I'm sorry. I shouldn't have prejudices. That's one of the things you've taught me, Sue, darling. One of the million and one things. I used to talk like a nigger fieldhand—or should I say a colored agriculturist, Miss Beaconridge? When I first came here, I mean. Don't know exactly how you did it, but now you've got me to the place where I even *think* like a grammar book. Of course, to tell the truth about it, Martha started to teach me, already; but I just wouldn't learn. Not from *her*, anyhow. Too jealous of her, I suppose."

"Jealous?" Susan said. "Of your stepmother? What on earth for, Fanny?"

"Martha's beautiful," Fanny said slowly, "really beautiful. Her *body* is beautiful, too; not just her face. While I—if I ever do marry Phil, I'll have to keep my nightgown on, even on our wedding night—"

"Fanny—" Susan said, searching for words to express what was for her a totally outrageous thought, it being a measure of Fanny's influence upon her that now she dared express it, instead of banishing it instantly from her mind, "don't women—or at least ladies—generally keep their nightgowns on, even when they're—well—submitting—to their husbands' baser natures, say?"

"Huh!" Fanny snorted, "are you ever a sweet innocent, Sue! The only reason we Southern girls *ever* put on a nightgown—a lacy, silk transparent one, not one of those army tents you New England wear—is to get our husbands, and all the other fellows we're cheating on them with, so excited they'll *tear* it off us!"

"Now you're being horrid," Susan said primly. "You *know* I don't like hearing you say such awful things, Fanny."

"Awful truths. But, as I was saying, Sue, dearest, if I ever do marry Phil, I'm going to have to keep mine on, or else my scar will make him sick—again."

Sue let that "again" go by without noticing it. Perhaps she really didn't even hear it. The autocensorship of the Victorian female mind was often that complete.

"Why, Fanny, your scar isn't all that bad. It's just a pale line around you. One can hardly see it—"

"Now," Fanny said, stubbornly persisting in her intent.

"Now? I don't understand you, Fanny."

"It used to be bad. It stood up like a welt, and it was all purple and reddish. Made Phil sick at the stomach—"

Susan stared at her. Said, almost whispering:

"Good God!"

"Shocked you again, didn't I?" Fanny sighed. "Sorry, Sue. I—I showed it to him. The part of it I could show, without—No, that's a lie! Whether you want to believe me or not, I'm bad. I'm a bad, wicked, vicious, immoral girl you oughtn't even speak to. Phil saw that scar because I *let* him see me naked. I was trying to—to get him to go to bed with me, to say it straight out—"

"Fanny, I don't believe you!"

"God's truth. Give me that little Bible you're always reading and I'll swear on it."

"Oh, Fanny!" Susan wailed.

"He didn't though. He's decent, Sue. A true gentleman. The good Lord up in heaven only knows what he sees in me! It happend this way, Sue, honey. He had another girl and I was desperate. I was trying to stop him from going to visit her. And I would have done *anything* to stop him, even *that*. But he wasn't having any, thank you! Took just one quick look at all these bones dancing around inside my skin, and this hideous old scar, to boot, and almost tossed his cookies. Of course, I'm a little better now—I weigh ninety-three pounds. That's six whole pounds more than I've weighed at any time in the last three years—"

"Dr. Risotti says you look like a Botticelli Venus."

"Huh! I've got both my arms, or hasn't he noticed?"

"Not that one. You're thinking of the Venus de Milo. That's a statue. Botticelli was a painter. A great painter, Fanny. I've seen the picture Dr. Risotti's talking about. It's called 'The Birth of Venus.' Though some people do call it 'Venus Rising from the Foam.' It's in Florence, Italy. Of course, I'm afraid he *is* being a little fresh, 'cause the Venus in that painting hasn't any clothes on. But you *do* look like her. Very much so."

"Thanks," Fanny said. "Now lie back down and let me cover you up, or else you'll start coughing and—"

"And I'll hemorrhage again. You—you don't, anymore, do you, Fanny?" Susan said. "Not for the longest time anyhow, and—"

"*Not* for the longest time," Fanny said grimly. "Last week."

"Oh, Fanny, no!"

"Oh, Susie, yes! Who're we trying to fool, poor baby? They're going to carry us both out of here feet first, and you know it. People get well of tuberculosis about as often as chickens grow a full set of teeth. Besides, my lung *can't* heal. The lesion's too big, now. I played old Ned with it with that kitchen knife, and every setback I've had has just opened the hole I've got in it that much wider—"

"Oh, dear!" Susan said.

"Don't fret, honey. You *deserve* to live. I don't. All I've ever done all my life is to cause trouble for everybody. My father's sick, right now, because the way I acted almost gave him a stroke. And it's costing Martha a young fortune to keep me here—"

"Martha?" Susan said.

"Yes. She's rich. Her father left her an awful lot of money. Papa hasn't any. Or not much, anyhow. He's just an ordinary plainclothes detective on the police force, and he'll stay poor all his life 'cause he's too honest to take bribes. And he'll keep right on being sick because he can't stand the way the other policemen look at him and shake their heads 'cause he's got a daughter who's disgraced him. Why even my little brother Billy hates me now, 'cause all the kids put out their tongues at him and yell, 'Your sister is a whore! Your sister is a whore!' "

"Fan-ny!"

"They do. Only they're wrong. I'm not. Haven't even

that much brains. I *give* it away, Sue, darling. At least I used to. Now, there're no takers. Too afraid of finding half their damn lungs in their breakfast oatmeal every morning. Perks up the appetite no end, Susie, dear. Shredded pulmonary tissue à la carte, garnished with tubercular nodes, and some really tempting blood and spit. Oh *do* forgive me, Miss Beaconridge! I meant to say saliva, and—"

"Fanny—please!" Susan got out. Her voice choked in her throat. Drowned.

"Oh, I *am* sorry!" Fanny said. "Don't cry, Susie! *Please* don't cry! You know I just can't stand it! Here, let me kiss you. Is that better?"

"Y-y-yes—" Susan whimpered. "Fanny—do you ever—kiss—Philippe?"

"And give him—*this?* Not on your sweet life, Sue-baby. I may be lower than a worm's belly-button, but *that* low I'm not. I get awf'ly tempted to at times, not only because I'm in love with that sweet little old longtail gumbo guzzler; but because if I messed him up this way, that freckled-faced, scrawny li'l setter bitch could never have him!"

"Fanny, there's no understanding you! Two minutes ago, you were saying that your lung—couldn't heal and that you—"

"I'm going to die. I know that. So what you mean, sweet Sue, is why should I care what Phil does after I'm gone? But I do care. I want to ruin his life for him. Make him so damn miserable he'll cut his throat. From ear to ear."

"But, Fanny! You love him! You just said—"

"That I love him? I do. But I'm not like you, sugar plum; I'm crazy. Poison-mean lowdown rotten crazy. Besides, there're two sides to everything, Susie, dear. Just like a silver dollar's got heads and tails, the other side of love is—hate. I love Phil. I love him with all my heart, and a few other parts of me that it wouldn't be ladylike to mention, setting aside the fact that I'd shock the living hell out of one poor sick little upstate New York girl, if I were to. But he's so goddamned good and sweet and gentle that he gets me wild. What I mean is that I hate his gentlemanly, well-bred, aristocratic guts, Sue, about as much as I love his crooked grin, and good looks, and broad shoulders and—oh, hell, skip it! That part's all imagination anyhow, damn it! Besides, he's a man; and I despise men! All of them!"

"Including your own father?" Susan said.

Fanny stared at Sue. Her pale eyes darkened perceptibly.

"Him—more than anybody," she whispered.

"Oh, Fanny!" Susan said.

"He made me what I am!" Fanny said, her voice dark, rent and shaken with a mortal fury, it seemed to Sue. "Even when I was knee-high to a grasshopper, he used to—to sort of push me off. I suppose it was because I look just like my mother. And *she* did him dirt with another fellow. But girl babies just naturally adore their papas, Sue. Way we're made. So I grew up missing that—being loved, I mean. A girl-child's birthright, Martha says. So, after fifteen years of being looked at like something that had just crawled out from under a rock—a wet and clammy rock, Sue-baby—I sort of blew up. Accounts for Rod, I suppose. Sold myself down the river to get even with Papa—"

"And now—you're even, Fanny?" Susan said tartly. "Why, yes; I suppose you are. You've made your father sick—and you're at death's door. Even if you—recover, you can never be more than a semi-invalid, at best. You've already cheated Philippe—and yourself—of the beautiful children you'll never be able to have. Oh, yes; you're even all right. Now, tell me: How does it feel?"

Fanny stared at her friend. She didn't say anything. She just sat there, looking at Susan. The expression on her face was strange. Her lips moved, finally, shaping words; but she spoke so quietly that Susan had to lean forward to hear.

"You win, Sue-baby," she whispered. "That round's yours. Looks like the only person I'm even with is *me*, doesn't it? 'Cause I sure Lord threw the book at myself, as the lawyers say. Drew—a hanging judge. Got the—death sentence. And you know what? It's going to be soon. Next week, maybe. Or tomorrow. Or maybe even—today. I've got that feeling I get when it's going to be bad. And, since what you said is God's own ugly truth, what am I hanging around for, anyhow?"

"Oh, Fanny!" Susan all but wept. "Don't talk like that! Philippe's coming—he'll be here day after tomorrow,

remember? You—you're going to live! We're both going
to live! We're going back up to Troy Female Seminary
and study hard and graduate and you'll meet my brother
Tony and maybe—maybe . . ."

Susan's voice, faltered, died. She tried to go on talking
in order to distract Fanny, at least, but her throat was too
constricted by pure terror to let sound pass.

Fanny didn't answer her. She sat there, and what she
was doing was remembering: calling up in precise and
pitiless detail all the things she habitually fought down by
sheer, ferocious will because she had known from the outset, with a conviction proof against all argument, that to
dwell upon them, to sort out and catalogue her private list
of horrors, was to invite madness or death, or both. But
now she sat there with all her defenses down considering
them; acknowledging the brutal fact that at only seventeen years of age, she had already reached rock bottom;
that she had absolutely nowhere to go, that all roads were
closed to her—except the final one.

The effect of that recognition was curious to watch.
And to Susan, who loved her, utterly appalling. All the
blue left her irises—that pale, misty shade of a winter sky
far out on the rim of the world, at best only an approximation of a color—deserted her, fled. Her eyes went
opaque, lightless, dull, trying to wall Susan's face out, to
bar time, the world, memory, thought; but they could not.
Helplessly, hopelessly, she sat there; her fixed, mindless
stare, breaking up now, becoming unsettled, dissolving
into the shifting, brilliantly luminous facets of a grief, an
anguish, that she had borne thus far at an absolutely intolerable cost, and which had to be ended now, because
bearing them even one second longer had become a simple impossibility.

She sat there without motion, soundless and remote,
head up, erect, unbreathing, her cheeks awash and glistening. Then, abruptly, a shaking got into her thin body. She
shivered violently, as an animal shivers. As a small dog
does who is soaking wet and cold and starving and lost.
Finally, utterly lost.

"Oh, Fanny!" Susan wailed. "I'm so awfully sorry! I
shouldn't have said that to you! That was rotten of me!
You know I do love you! I didn't mean—"

But she might as well have not been there. Fanny went

on crying. It was impossible to tell at what point the sobs that racked her, no less terrible for being completely silent, changed, or were allowed to change—a point about which Fanny, herself, would or could never be certain— into the kind of coughing fit she had trained herself to avoid at all costs, for her two hands flew up and covered her mouth, so that it was not until some moments later that Sue became aware that the gesture was not designed to stifle the sounds of weeping, but rather to hold back that thick, hot foaming rush that was pumping out between her fingers now, dyeing her arms red to the elbows, streaking the front of her gown at first, then, as her hands came away from her mouth in her final, despairing effort to gulp air, flooding the gown, plastering it to her tiny, fragile body.

Susan's screams split the very sky. She was still screaming like a wild thing when the three interns got there. They bore Fanny away in their arms, having seen at once that there was no time to spare, not even the little it would have cost them to go after a stretcher.

And it was Fanny's good fortune, or her bad, that Dr. Guillermo Risotti, Dr. Holtz's junior partner in the management of the sanitorium, was on duty in surgery that day. Seeing who the patient was, he did what he had to, took at once and without hesitation the very nearly mortal risk involved. That is, he simply pointed at the huskiest of the three interns, growled: "You! Roll up your sleeve!" and performed a transfusion then and there.

Which, of course, would be—some five years from that day—routine procedure, after certain simple precautions had been taken; but, in 1898, the world had two years still to wait before Karl Landsteiner of the Rockefeller Institute would publish his masterly paper on the four imcompatible blood groupings in the human race. Nor was the rejection mechanism by which the body protects itself against invasion by foreign cells understood. All doctors knew was that at least three times out of five, transfusions killed the patient, and in a rather horrible manner at that. Therefore, in 1898, what Dr. Risotti did for Fanny amounted to very nearly criminal malpractice. To the orthodox, to offer in his defense the fact that she would have been dead within the hour without that transfusion was but to beg the question.

* * *

And Dr. Karl Holtz was orthodox. Even his selection of Risotti as his assistant and junior partner was, to a certain extent, proof of that. For, in all the years after emigrating from his native Austria to the United States, Karl Holtz had never even considered taking on a native North American doctor for this demanding position, muttering "Dummköpfe und Esels!" under his breath every time anyone suggested it. He had found Dr. Risotti in Cambridge, Massachusetts, barely making ends meet by combining an almost nonexistent practice with tutoring Harvard Medical undergrads. In fact, the Dean of the medical school—where Karl Holtz was, at the moment, giving a series of lectures on his eminently sound, for the times, methods of treating tuberculosis—had recommended the young Italian immigrant doctor as being absolutely brilliant. An interview with Guillermo Risotti had all but overcome Karl Holtz's stubborn Teutonic prejudices against all Latins—even Louis Pasteur—as scientific incompetents and mental featherweights; and he stifled his lingering doubts with the consoling thought that Risotti had been solidly trained in first class *European* medical schools. But now, learning of the terrible risk his assistant and partner had taken, all his prejudices came back with a rush.

"You know what happens half the time, Guillermo!" he roared. "They die! Of hemolysis, pure damned oxygen starvation! And when we perform the autopsy, what do we find? Not a red corpuscle left! Every single erythrocyte dissolved! Every artery, every vein choked with bluish black gook—hematin, the refuse of dead hemoglobin! You Latins! Is there no way to make responsible, scientific doctors of you?"

Dr. Risotti's face darkened. Milanese born, a graduate of Torino, Padua, and Rome, he considered himself a better doctor than Vienna-trained Karl Holtz every day in the week and twice on Sundays.

"Is it," he said icily, "responsible to stand by with folded hands, mein Arzt, and let a patient die? Besides, if you would kindly stop bellowing like a Teutonic bull, Karl, I might be able to point out to you that the girl's alive, and seemingly recovering . . ."

"Seemingly! We need at least another twenty-four hours

to be sure. Hemolysis takes from twelve to forty-eight hours to set in and—"

One of the interns pushed open the door without knocking, and said in one long breathless rush:

"'Scuse me, sirs! But that young fellow's here. The Frenchie who comes to see Fanny. And he wants to know if he can—"

"See her? The answer to that one is hell no, Tom! Now get out of here! You heard me, Tom; I said—"

"But, sir—that girl—she—she died. Hemorrhaged during the night—and wouldn't call anybody. Stuck her poor little face into the pillow and—"

Karl Holtz turned on Guillermo Risotti like a lion.

"You see!" he roared. "I told you transfusions were too damned risky! What have you got to say for yourself now, doctor?"

Risotti bowed his head, looked up again. His dark eyes were unashamedly wet.

"Only that Fanny was much too beautiful to die," he whispered. "Santa Maria, what a waste!"

Tom, the intern, stared at them both. Then he burst out:

"Not her, sir! Li'l Fan's doing fine. The other one. That poor li'l vingary Yankee—Sue Whatchamaycallit—"

"Susan Beaconridge," Karl Holtz said slowly, "worth ten of Fanny Turner by any rational standards. And that's a considered, scientific judgment. I could sustain it, but to do so, I'd have to go into little Miss Turner's personal history, which wouldn't be ethical—"

"Nobody's asking you to, Karl," Doctor Risotti said. "Poor little Sue. I liked her, but—"

"But she was plain, so she didn't have you and the interns trooping into her room all night long to see how she was doing, so—she died. One might almost say of neglect, eh, Guillermo?"

"She had only to ring her bell!" Dr. Risotti said.

"Dr. Risotti, sir—" Tom said, "I—can explain that, if only you'll let me. At least I think I can—"

Dr. Risotti looked at Dr. Holtz.

"All right," Karl Holtz said. "Speak your piece, Tom!"

"She 'n Fanny—had words. Ruthie—I mean Miss Simpson, the afternoon nurse in that section—told me that the little Yankee cried all evening long. Seems she said something so rough to Fan that poor Fan started sobbing and brought on a fit of coughing. And hemorrhaged—as you all know. So I reckon she—Sue—blamed herself for what happened to Fan."

"All right," Karl Holtz said tiredly. "You've had your say, Tom. But if I hear this theory of yours anywhere outside that door, your internship at Holtz Sanitorium is over. Do make myself clear?"

"Yes, sir! I won't breathe a word to a living soul, sir!"

"See that you don't. Now get out of here, will you? Dr. Risotti and I have things to discuss—in private!"

"Yes, sir!" Tom said again and fled.

Dr. Risotti looked at his senior partner.

"He implied—suicide, Karl," he said.

"And he's probably right—in a way," Dr. Holtz said grimly. "That evil little witch! Is there no end to the harm she's capable of?"

"You're referring to Fanny, Karl?" Dr. Risotti said.

"I am. And if you knew her better, you'd—"

"Still say she's Venus, rising from the foam. You can't see it because she isn't hefty enough to suit your Teutonic taste for beef. She's Botticelli, not Rubens. Fragile, delicate, haunting. Her beauty is—eerie, somehow. Not of this world—"

"There, you're right. That lung's not healing, Guillermo. Another hemorrhage like this last one will finish her. And even if she manages to avoid that, I'll give her six to nine months at the outside. No more. And before you say so, I agree it's a pity. She's a lovely child. And all the things wrong with her, all her destructive personality traits, to quote the alienists, as those windy exponents of the pseudo-science, psychology, now call themselves—by God, Vienna's fairly infested with those charlatans these days!—are results, not causes. But, fond as you are of her, you'd better get used to the idea that she's slowly dying. She is, you know."

Guillermo Risotti bowed his head, looked up again, said:

"I sadly—agree. But do me one favor, Karl . . ."

"Which is?"

"*You* tell young Sompayac. Don't wish that dirty job off on me," Dr. Risotti said.

# Chapter Eleven

Philippe stood there. He looked first at Guillermo Risotti, then at Karl Holtz.

"You mean to tell me," he said, "that there's *nothing* you can do? That medical science knows so little that Fanny has to die? All right, all right! Not only my Fanny. Thousands of people every year, everywhere, from this damnable white plague! You're saying that in all the world, there's not one doctor, one scientist, who knows any way of stopping people from dying in this monstrously ugly fashion?"

Karl Holtz stared at the young Creole.

"You are, I believe, a medical student, are you not, Monsieur Sompayac?" he said.

"Yes," Philippe said. "Harvard. I still have another year to go before I graduate, though."

"Do you? Ach, even so! You are not a first-year student. And yet not only do you use such totally unscientific expressions as 'white plague,' but you have the need to ask me a rather stupid question. What precisely do they teach you up there, young man?"

Philippe stiffened. Then slowly, ruefully, he smiled. "I apologize, Doctor," he said. "Yes, I suppose I do know the answer to that question. Almost rhetorical, isn't it? If we catch the patient early enough, with rest, fresh air, a rich and varied diet, we can, in many cases, arrest the progress of the disease. If not, the patient dies. But, in Fanny's case it seems to me that—"

"We undertook her care in time? Ordinarily, I should say so, yes. But her case was not ordinary, as you should know, young man. A lesion the size of the one she had in her left lung the day she was brought into my sanitorium normally takes months, even years to develop. Only—"

"She produced it herself, in five seconds flat; with a kitchen knife," Philippe said grimly, "then interrupted its healing with a second suicide attempt. Is that what you mean, Doctor?"

"Exactly. Only I should use 'terminated' instead of 'interrupted' as far as healing is concerned, Mr. Sompayac. And you may count that second attempt as successful. She will die of it. I give her less than a year at best."

Philippe looked down at the floor. His big, bony hands knotted into fists. A year or two earlier, he probably would have shaken them at deaf heaven out of his rage, his grief. But his scientific training had led him to suspect that heaven was not only deaf, but untenanted. Morally, this second hypothesis was more nearly acceptable to him; a man can resign himself finally to helplessness and hopelessness. But to that absolutely fiendish cruelty which, considered against the long horror of mankind's history, the concept of a supreme being implies, neither resignation nor acceptance is possible. Fanny's brief, pitiful history alone was enough to make him reject it with all his whole being.

Even so, Karl Holtz saw the gesture and bristled.

"We cannot cure late tuberculosis, Mr. Sompayac!" he said harshly. "No one can, so far as I know, in any country on earth. Do you think we like it, that we *enjoy* seeing people—all kinds of people, not merely one pretty little girl you happen to be in love with—die? We curse our own ignorance hourly, I assure you! The best of us work ourselves into an early grave trying to cure what no man can cure—"

"Karl," Guillermo Risotti said suddenly, "I just thought of something!" Remember what I told you when I came back from my vacation in Italy last year?"

"Hummph! About some charlatan who claims—"

"One minute, Karl! Carlo Forlanini* is *not* a charlatan! He is one of Italy's greatest medical men. When I talked to him, he was understandably reluctant to reveal his methods; stated that he needed many more cases to be sure. All I could get out of him was that he somehow im-

---

*One of the great figures in medical history, Dr. Forlanini performed the first artificial pneumothorax operation circa 1892 or '93, and published his report on the value of collapsing the damaged lung by introducing air under compression into the chest cavity, thus immobilizing the lung so that even large lesions could heal, in 1894. In 1906 he published a study of twelve years of largely successful practice of this technique. But it was not until John B. Murphy of Chicago started using this method successfully that it caught on in the U.S.

moblizes the damaged lung long enough for it to heal, and . . ."

"Nonsense!" Karl Holtz roared, "Utter nonsense, Guillermo! Immobilize the lungs! Next you'll be telling me that he stops a cardiac case's heart for a couple of months to give it a rest! Why . . ."

"We'll do that, one day," Dr. Risotti said quietly. "Rerouting the blood through some sort of electrical centrifuge, say, while the tired old heart takes a vacation for a week or two. But if you had been using your ears, Karl, you would have been aware that I said *lung,* not lungs. Most people have *two,* is it not so? And if they're both damaged, not even Dr. Forlanini can do very much with the case. But my colleagues in Torino report that given *one* fairly sound lung, he saves the patient nearly every time. The whole medical profession of Italy is intrigued. Only, he's not telling. Not yet. Wants to be sure . . ."

"Commendable!" Karl Holtz snorted; "An Italian who can keep his mouth shut!" He stopped short and glared at Philippe. Then he turned back to Dr. Risotti. "Now see what you've done, Guillermo!" he said. "Look at him— fairly trembling! How many times have I told you that there's nothing crueler than to raise false hopes!"

"You're wrong, sir," Philippe said quietly. "One thing is—no hope at all. This Dr. Forlanini, sir—where does he operate? In Rome?"

"No," Dr. Risotti sighed. "In Pavia. He has a clinic there. A good clinic, Mr. Sompayac. He's modernized it completely. But in a way, Dr. Holtz is right. It will do no good at all to write him. The circumstances being what they are, he wouldn't even bother to answer you, I'm afraid . . ."

"I have no intention of writing him," Philippe said, "I'm going to Italy to see him and—"

"Bring him back across the Atlantic to save one lovely little Botticelli Venus—at the cost of deserting for months all his own gravely ill patients, Mr. Sompayac?" Dr. Risotti said. "There is such a thing as medical ethics, you know—"

Philippe stood there. Looked at them. Said: "Dr. Holtz—could Fanny—"

"Stand an ocean voyage? Now, today—no. But if she recovers a bit from yesterday's hemorrhage, possibly. The ocean voyage might even be good for her. Only—"

"Only what, sir?" Philippe said.

"The practical difficulties would be immense, young man. Most people have an unreasoning fear of tuberculosis, fostered, may I say, by the kind of medical sensationalism which pins such dramatic labels on it as 'The White Plague!' You'd need an attendant private nurse along, who'd have to sleep in Miss Turner's stateroom. To find a nurse willing to risk fifteen days' constant exposure to the disease would be a task I shouldn't like to undertake. What's more, you'd have to advise the ship's medical officer, and obtain his consent and through him the steamship line's, to bring your fiancée aboard. Considering that commerically, the line would risk hundreds of cancellations should the news get out—as it would, I assure you! I don't—you don't need to be especially clairvoyant to guess what the ship's doctor's answer would be—"

Philippe went on looking at Karl Holtz.

"Go on, Doctor," he said.

"All this, assuming you have obtained her parents' consent to both voyage and the operation, Mr. Sompayac; she is not of age, and though you seem to forget it, not yet married to you. Then you're also making the quite unwarranted assumption that the Italian wizard—what's his name, Guillermo?"

"Forlanini, Carlo Forlanini," Dr. Risotti said.

"That Doctor Forlanini will be willing to accept Miss Turner as a patient once you reach Italy. He may not, you know. His clinic may not have a bed available. His examination of your fiancée may lead him to conclude that the risk involved is too great—"

He stopped short, looked at Philippe, said a little angrily:

"Nothing I have said has made the slightest impression upon you, has it, young man?"

"No," Philippe said. "The difficulties you've enumerated exist—I accept that. But solutions to them, or ways around them also exist, Doctor. Because there's one thing you may both be certain of, gentlemen: I refuse to let Fanny die!"

"You'll pit your will against—God's, then?" Karl Holtz said grimly.

"And the Devil's!" Philippe said. Then: "Please, sir, may I see her now?"

Karl Holtz bowed his immense and shaggy head.

"Why not?" he said, almost to himself. "What she needs is a miracle—and who knows? Maybe you will provide it. The young and the mad have worked wonders before now. Jawohl! Yes, you may see her. Try to instill in her a desire to live, young man. That is one of her problems. Perhaps the chief of her problems. No doctor in history has ever succeeded in saving a patient who wants to die, as your little Miss Turner does, I'm afraid. And I shouldn't attempt to convince her that life itself is good— a most debatable notion, young sir!—but that she is worthy of what it has to offer. All her destructiveness, whether inwardly or outwardly directed, stems from that: her profound, deep-seated feeling of unworthiness . . . Bah! I talk like an alienist! And all alienists should be arrested for fraud."

Philippe smiled at the old Austrian, then.

"And so should you, sir," he said. "For the one you commit every day . . ."

Karl Holtz stopped short, glared at Philippe.

"I don't follow your meaning, young sir!" he said.

"The fraud of pretending not to have a heart," Philippe said. "Now I'd better go see Fanny. By your leave, sir?"

"Ach Gott, yes! *Get out of here!*" Karl Holtz said.

Looking at Fanny, where she lay on her bed, Philippe almost lost his uncertain hold on hope. He was torn simultaneously by both rage and despair. He didn't know which of two insane impulses he wanted to give way to more. To bury his face in his two hands and weep, or pick up a chair and hurl it through the open window. But he restrained both impulses. Giving vent to them wouldn't help anything. He knew that very well. And what was worse, they might even harm Fanny, tip the balance she lay trembling in, the scant inch it needed to drop her out of life.

Very quietly, he sat down beside her bed. The room was cold. All the windows were open. Fanny lay there, bundled in blankets, her eyes closed, her fair hair spread out over the pillows, her face, her lips, distinguishable from the bed sheets chiefly by being even whiter than the sheets themselves.

Philippe sat there a long time, staring at her. He suspected that she wasn't really asleep, but was pretending to be in order not to be bothered. The pulse at the base of her slim throat—the adjective slim was his; scrawny, fleshless, skeletal would have been far more accurate—was too irregular to denote sleep. There was a hint of conscious agitation in it; of annoyance, even. But there was nothing he could do. Fanny kept her eyes closed, refused to move or speak. So pauvre, brave Philippe waited, manfully outdoing Job.

'In the name of the good little God,' he groaned inside his mind, 'how does one convince a girl of anything when she won't open her eyes or say one single word?"

Then the way occurred to him. It wasn't very original, but it was effective, decidedly so. He bent over and kissed her icy mouth.

Fanny's eyes flew open; huge and startled. Her two hands came up, pushing. But he paid them no attention and they had no strength at all. He went on kissing those parchment-dry lips, faintly bitter-tasting—the after-effects of some medicine or another, he supposed—that were as cold as the lips of a statue or a corpse, until very slowly they warmed, moistened, slackened, parted, moving under his in a perfect agony of tenderness, of longing, trying to invent a tactile language, a braille code of the flesh in order to communicate to him all the wild, sweet, wondrous things she didn't even know the words for, at least not the kind of words that wouldn't cheapen or demean them.

But then, abruptly, the feel, the candid ardor of her lips changed, metamorphosed into bitter grief, anguish, loss; he tasted the renewed welling up of the psychosomatic (forgive the anachronism; he will learn the as yet uncoined word before too many years have passed him by) wounds that more than her diseased and damaged lung were killing her, in the hot flooding wetness, the sudden salt between his mouth and hers. He drew back at once, looked at her, whispered:

"Fan—"

"No! No!" she stormed at him. "You mustn't kiss me, Philippe! You'll catch—this! And—and you'll die! Haven't I got enough dead people on my conscience now? That—

old man. Sue—I murdered her, Phil! I killed her just like I'd used a knife! And Papa—dying inch by inch because of me. I couldn't stand it if you caught this, Phil. And I'd know! Even down there in hell where I'm going, I'd know!"

He smiled at her, said:

"I'll be there before you, Fan, heading the reception committee. Because you're going to live to be ninety-seven years old and you're going to have sixty-nine grandchildren, a hundred and four great-grandchildren, and . . ."

She stopped crying, almost; whispered:

"Quit plaguing me, Phil; will you, huh?"

"I'm not. I swear it by the good little God. But there's one item we have to consider first: To have all those grandchildren, we have to make a few children to start with, you and I. What do you want first, Fan, a boy or a girl?"

She looked up at him and her mouth trembled into a smile.

"Oh, you!" she said. "Phil, you know darn well I'll never be able to . . ."

"I don't know it darn well, Madame Sompayac, ma chère petite épouse! Things have changed. There's a doctor in Italy who has been curing people far worse off than you for years now. I'm going to take you to him. And afterwards we'll just have ourselves one mighty fine honeymoon in Italy. We'll drift down the canals of Venice in a gondola, throw pennies in the Trevi Fountain in Rome, eat huge, huge slabs of bologna at the foot of the Spanish stairs, washed down with gallons of Chianti, twine yards and yards of spaghetti around our forks . . ."

She giggled, suddenly.

"Phil, honey," she husked, "will we ever quit eating long enough to—to make love?"

"Oh, we'll go to Capri for that," he said airily. "After I've fattened you up enough to stand it. Even so, we'll probably end up like Grand-père et Grand'mère in that daguerrotype Papa has—"

"And how'd they end up?" Fanny said.

"It was like this," Philippe said solemnly. "Grand-père was the soul of politeness. La grande, politesse française, tu sais? Always bowing and scraping and popping up like a Jack-in-the-box when a lady entered the room. But in that photo he's sitting down, while pauvre Grand'mère's standing up. . . ."

"So?" Fanny said.

"So I asked him why. 'Grand-père,' says I, 'Pourquoi tu t'es assis, lorsque Grand'mère est debout?' "

"Oh, Phil!" Fanny protested, "you *know* I don't understand a word of French!"

" 'Grandpop,' says I, 'why're you sitting down while Grandma's standing up?' "

"And?" Fanny whispered.

" 'Mon petitfils,' says he, 'Grandson, that picture was taken the day we came back from notre voyage de noce—our honeymoon. And, bon Dieu!—I was too tired to stand up—while your grandmother—la pauvre!—she was too sore to sit down!' "

Fanny threw back her head and loosed a peal of clear, silvery laughter. But, in midnote, it broke into something curiously like a sob. Abruptly, she turned away from him. To his vast astonishment, he saw her shoulders shake.

"Fan!" he said.

She whirled to face him, her pale eyes streaming.

"Phil—" she whispered, "would you—would you—have told *her*—a dirty joke like that?"

"Would I—have told whom—? Oh, hell! You mean Billie Jo, don't you?"

"Yep. Never can remember her name, the speckled little bitch! Mainly because I don't *want* to remember it, I reckon. But it just rolls off your tongue, doesn't it? Anyhow, tell the truth: Would you have told her—a filthy joke like that? You'd have had more respect, wouldn't you? Remembered that she—that she's—pure. That she's never been—anybody's fun-filly, play-toy girl—nobody's dirty little whore!"

"Fan, I'm going to hit you, if you don't stop this!"

"Go ahead!" she sobbed. "That's all I'm fit for, isn't it? Kind of cheap little tart a fellow feels free to slap around, not never a girl who—"

"Fan," he said suddenly, flashing his crooked grin, "the last night I went out with Billie Jo, I tried to remove her pantalettes!"

Fanny stopped sobbing, peered at him.

"And she slapped you winding!" she husked.

"Want to bet?" Philippe said.

Fanny sat up in bed, her pale eyes afire.

"So!" she whispered. "You—you say you love me—and here you are—bragging about—about doing your dirt with other girls!"

"Jealous, Fan, bébé?"

"Phil, you know darn well, I'm—Oh, Christ! How can I be? What right have I to plague you about *anything* you do?"

"You have every right, Fan," he said quietly, "because I've given it to you. I love you and nobody else. It's a matter of fact, I didn't. Couldn't get 'em off. They were buttoned up the back—and there were all those hooks and eyes. Besides I'm sure her Aunt Ellen sews her into 'em to make sure nobody samples the goods ahead of time—and—"

"Phil," Fanny whispered, her voice a grate, a scrape, barely audible, "the truth—what *did* happen?"

"Nothing," Philippe said. "If you want me to, I'll swear it on poor Grand'mère's grave."

"No, you're telling the truth—so far. Only I'm not going to let you off that easy. Next question, Monsieur Philippe Sompayac! *Why* didn't anything happen? And don't tell me *she* stopped you. She wouldn't have. That day she came into my room she had the—hungriest look a lone and lonesome female ever hung onto her face! So don't you sit there and tell me that she—"

"Stopped me? No. *You* did."

"Me? Huh! How the dickens could I have? Why, I was lying flat on my back in the hospital and—"

"Nevertheless, you did. I remember you—lying there like that, and I couldn't. I simply couldn't either betray my pledged word, or even *be* the kind of bastard who'd shamed you so. No, worse. Because I already promised the good little God that I'd spend the rest of my life taking care of you; so proving that I was as randy a billy goat as Rod Schneider at the expense of another poor innocent became unthinkable. Yes, yes, for her sake, too. But mainly because I'd already said that 'for better or for worse, in sickness and in health, 'til death us do part' in my heart to you, Fan. And those aren't words to be taken lightly."

She sat there. Then suddenly, wildly, she put out her arms to him. He drew her to him, feeling her trembling under the coarse gown, the utter, fragile, weightlessness of her; but at the last second, she buried her face in the hollow of his throat, croaking.

"Don't kiss me, Phil. I want you to so bad my mouth hurts; but don't! TB's awfully catching and—"

"TB is *not* awfully catching," he said firmly. "If it were, every mother's child on earth would have it because we all have the germs in our throats and lungs. Only we have to get sick of something else or—"

"Stick a knife into our guts," she said harshly.

"Or stick a knife in our guts, or take too many sleeping pills, or do something else equally stupid and destructive to weaken ourselves enough to catch it. So now, kiss me. But first, let us remind you of something else, Fanny—"

"What else, Phil?"

"You belong to *me*. So you have no more rights over yourself. You can't cheat me anymore. You've *got* to get well—for my sake. Because—because I need you, Fan. Because I can't live without you—and I won't. Life would have no meaning—"

"Oh, Phil!" she said, and started crying again.

He put a finger under her chin and lifted her ghost-white, tear-streaked face. Kissed her mouth a long time, but very gently.

"Fan," he said, "I'm going home tonight. I have to browbeat the money out of my stingy old pirate of a papa to take you to Italy. That's no problem. I'll do it somehow, even though he has had some bad business reverses, lately. The real problem is you. In one month's time you have to be strong enough to travel. Which means you must eat, rest, and—and stop brooding over your imaginary sins! You owe me that, Fan. You owe me—sons. I'm the *last* Sompayac. Are you going to end a *family?*"

She stared at him.

"Phil—" she whispered. "You think that Italian Doc can get me well enough to—to have *babies?*"

"I'm sure of it. D'you want to, Fan?"

"Oh, Phil!" she breathed. "Do I? Dozens of 'em! A house full of brats, all yelling at the same time, and fighting and playing and smashing things! Can you think of anything more—beautiful?"

'Yes,' Philippe thought. 'Your face, now. At this instant in time. Perhaps only one of the pre-Raphaelites could paint the Madonna-like, unearthly purity of it . . .'

The odd part about it was he was absolutely right. Her maternal instincts, her desire for motherhood, were very nearly the strongest emotions that Fanny had. Her face, at that moment, was truly angelical.

"Phil," she said in a breathless rush, "if your Papa won't give you the money, ask Martha to! She will— Please, Phil! Don't stand on pride! We can pay her back later, after you're a famous doctor with rich and important patients and—"

"One nice fat little blonde wife and ten kids?"

She smiled at him but her eyes were sad.

"Ten—I can't promise you, Phil. But one—yes. Even if I have to die to do it! One little black-haired, black-eyed, crooked-mouthed little devil who—"

"Will adore sa petite maman, even as his father does," Philippe said and kissed her.

Such a simple, normal thing they asked of life. But still, too much. As simple, normal things so often are. That is, if either simplicity or normalcy even exist as such.

Which, considering what life is, the complications of the human psyche, and how things in general work—or rather don't—would be devilishly hard to prove.


## Chapter Twelve


Jean-Paul Sompayac lifted his head and studied his son's face. But he didn't roar. When he spoke, his voice was quiet. Too quiet, Philippe thought.

"So, now I am to supply you with the small sum of five thousand dollars—or more if I can spare it—so that you may take la petite et si angelique Mademoiselle Turner, ta soi-disant fiancée, to Italy, where this worker of miracles can cure her? I *have* understood you correctly, have I not, my son?"

"Yes, Papa," Philippe said.

"Suppose I refuse?" Jean-Paul said.

"I'll get the money elsewhere. I should regret to have to, but I will."

Jean-Paul bowed his head; looked up again.

"You say cette pauvre petite will die without the operation?"

"Yes, Papa. It is her only hope," Philippe said.

"I see," Jean-Paul sighed. "Very well, Philippe—I'll advance you the money. Wait! Control yourself, mon fils! I suspect you'd better listen to *all* I have to say before you start hopping up and down like un singe and grinning like an imbecile. Because I'm going to have to put certain conditions upon this affaire, I'm afraid . . ."

"What kind of conditions, Papa?" Philippe said.

Jean-Paul frowned.

"I'd better start with the principal one, I suppose," he said. "If I invest in this wild gamble to save Mademoiselle Turner's life, it's only because simple humanity demands that much of me. But, in return, I must ask your solemn promise that you will renounce all thought of marrying this young woman . . ."

"Papa!" Philippe said.

"Calm yourself, my son! A little reflection should convince you that I'm being exceedingly just with you—far more than you deserve. I don't even believe I need state my reasons; you know them as well as I do. You've lied to me about a number of things and failed to explain others, such as why in the name of all the saints you felt it necessary to assume the responsibility for that vacherie to end all vacheries* those American unspeakables you called your friends perpertrated upon this poor child. Wait, Philippe! I'll listen to your explanation of that particular folly later. Now, I haven't time. I say only that it had better be a good one; for, at the moment, I don't know whether my relief at finding out that you weren't after all, goatish enough to participate in une affaire so ugly and so—say—messy as that one outweighs my worry over the possibility that your reaction to it may well indicate that all is not right with your head, my son! Because of all the possible explanations for your behavior in that matter—rushing off to demand of her father the hand of a girl whom you, personally, had *not* dishonored—the

---

*Literally "cowishness." Why the French attribute to the gentle bovine the sort of behavior we call swinish, the writer doesn't know.

only two that make any sense at all are a nervous break-down or an attack of insanity!"

"Papa, I—" Philippe began.

"Tais-toi, imbecile! You thought I shouldn't bother, or should be unable to learn, such disquieting and piquant details about this young woman you offer me as a daughter-in-law as the fact that at age fifteen the little demoiselle was already la petite maîtresse of young Schneider. That beyond that, she had ceased to be vierge at age *eight;* something of a record, n'est-ce pas? Ah, si—bien entendu, a violation. By an aged degenerate whom Monsieur Turner killed. And well done. I applaud him—"

"Papa—" Philippe groaned.

"You depended upon my being stopped by a matter of common knowledge, called into question by absolutely no one at all, that Monsieur Turner is an upright and an honorable man. Mais—sa femme? Not his present wife, whom I have made it my business to meet. She is a lady. Une grande dame. That time, your friend Turner was wise. But the other one? His *first* wife, whom he was obliged to divorce. The *mother* of la petite Fanny?"

"Papa, you aren't going to visit the sins of the mother upon the head of the daughter, are you? Ça, c'est pas de toute juste!"

"No," Jean-Paul said quietly. "No. The sins, of course not. But certain—inherited tendencies, disons-nous? As little Mademoiselle Turner has already demonstrated. A daughter doesn't *have* to follow in her mother's footsteps, mon fils. Even among our soeurs religieuses, our good Catholic nuns, one can find some whose mothers were abandoned females. I happen to know that as a fact. But they instinctively rejected the sort of life their mothers had led, turned to piety, good works, grace. Mais—ta 'tite fiancée, mon fils? Did she not set out from infancy to demonstrate that she was—toute justemente—her mother's daughter?"

"Papa, you don't understand! There were reasons, pressures upon the poor child, things that—"

"I know. As there are upon us all. Upon ta mère, my son, and upon your sisters. Only they did not succumb to those reasons, pressures. Which is a certain rude measure of worth, isn't it? All men—and all women, though we like to deny the latter ugly fact—have carnal desires. The decent resist them, Philippe, until they can be sanctified before the good God in his temple to the increase of Christians. It's as simple as that . . ."

"Papa, you're being hard!"

"I know. Unfortunately, it is necessary. Let us leave the moral side of the question, Philippe. You could argue, more sensibly, that many a man has married une demi-mondaine, even a prostitute, and, after having borne her away to a city where she was not known, lived with her in honor and in peace. In some cases, the women so uplifted, saved, have made excellent wives. You could have advanced that argument, my son, and I should have been forced to grant you your point . . ."

"So?" Philippe said.

"But, even granting it, I shouldn't be inclined to give you leave to follow so altruistic a procedure. My objection to it, in your case, is twofold: you are my only son, and you are the last *male* Sompayac. With you, our family will die, if you do not father sons. The more, the better, say I!"

"You object to your grandsons having Fanny for a mother, then?" Philippe said.

"Not especially. Our first female ancestor in the New World—deny it as we will—was probably one of the Correction Girls, one of the several hundred prostitutes deported from La Salpetrière prison in Paris to Louisiana to serve as wives for the early settlers—a rude lot themselves, I assure you! What I object to is your marrying an invalid, a woman who probably can *never* give you children, Philippe. I have seen la petite Mademoiselle Turner, remember. She seems to me a delightful child, well worth saving, whatever her mistakes, her sins. But for her féerique, angelique beauty, she is not worth ending la famille Sompayac for! Not she, nor any other girl, my son."

"Mais, Papa—if she is completely cured, she *can* have children. Healthy children. Several of Dr. Forlanini's ex-patients have subsequently given birth without incident and . . ."

"A speculation. Besides which there is—Les Granges. There is this house—nearly two centuries old now. A whole weight of honorable tradition that it is your duty to sustain, my son. The mere fact that now, as conditions stand, with her name already become a theme for scandal throughout our city, you would have to abandon New Orleans, leave all the fine and worthy things that I and your ancestors have built, to marry a girl of dubious virtue, and even more dubious health, is sufficient to make me oppose this match, Philippe. But enough of this! I shall write you the check. You need not say anything to Mademoiselle Turner now. Wait until she is somewhat recovered, before—"

Slowly, sadly, Philippe shook his head.

"No, Papa. Do not write it. I prefer to get the money elsewhere, with no strings attached," he said.

"Well, son?" Bill Turner said. "Martha tells me you've been waiting for me to come home more than three hours. A long wait. I'm doggoned sorry, but in this miserable work I'm in, my time is never my own. A drink, then? A little whiskey and—That's right, you don't drink, do you?"

"No," Philippe said, "and even if I did, I wouldn't tonight. Mr. Turner, I want you to do me a favor—a great favor. And the first part of that favor consists in sitting down and listening to what I've got to say without getting excited. Frankly, you don't look too well to me. And the last thing in the world I want to do is upset you . . ."

Bill Turner stared at the young Creole.

"Fanny is—worse," he said. Without a rising inflection. Making a statement of it, not a question.

"Yes, sir," Philippe said. "In fact, sir, madame, she's slowly dying."

"Oh, my God!" Martha said, and buried her face in her hands.

"Wait!" Philippe said. "Dr. Holtz says there's no immediate danger. He gives her eight, nine months—perhaps a year."

"Hell!" Bill Turner said, "that's nothing. No time at all. Oh Jesus! My poor little baby. And I—I never was good to her, really. Blamed her for—for looking like her ma—as if she could help *that*. God, son, I . . ."

"Mr. Turner, please!" Philippe said. "I didn't come here to bring you bad news. Nor to raise false hopes. But there is a chance. A fairly good chance, from what I've been able to find out. There's a doctor in Italy named Carlo Forlanini, who has been saving eighty percent of cases like Fanny's ever since 1894——"

Martha looked up. Her dark eyes still bright with tears; but she blinked them away now, sat there, listening, attention in every taut line of her.

"I don't know how he does it. I only know——on the basis of information given me by Dr. Risotti, the assistant head of the sanitorium, you know——that he *does* save people who up 'til now would be considered hopeless cases. All that Dr. Risotti could find out was that his method involves surgery. So we would have to take Fanny to Italy, since no one knows the actual operational procedure except Dr. Forlanini, himself. And he's understandably reluctant to reveal it . . ."

"Why understandably, son?" Bill Turner said. "Hell, even if he lets other sawbones in on it, he'll still get rich! And he can't operate personally on all the patients who need it. That's a physical impossibility, it seems to me . . ."

"That's not the reason, sir," Philippe said. "According to Dr. Risotti, Carlo Forlanini is a true scientist. And he wants to be sure that his procedure works in the majority of cases. He has to operate and operate again——a hundred times, two hundred——follow the subsequent history of his patients to see what happens to them before he dares——no that's the wrong word!——before he has the right to tell other doctors: Do it *this* way! Or else he becomes morally responsible for the deaths of patients caused by a faulty procedure he has advocated."

"I see," Martha sighed. "So, Philippe, as I understand it, you're suggesting that we ship Fanny to Italy while there's still time?"

"Not exactly," Philippe said, "there's considerably more to it than that——including the reason I waited until Mr. Turner came home before presenting my idea. The truth is, it wouldn't have been honorable to propose this to you behind his back . . ."

"Hell, son," Bill Turner said, "if there's any one human being on God's green earth I trust, it's you! Next to Martha, that is . . ."

"Thank you, sir," Philippe said, "I'm truly honored. The trouble is it's going to cost a lot, anywhere between five and ten thousand dollars. And I haven't the money. Papa wouldn't give or lend it to me. I asked him for it this morning, and he refused."

Martha stared at the handsome young Creole.

"Might I ask why, Philippe?" she said.

"You may. I was going to tell you anyhow. Papa didn't refuse outright. He—he'll give me the money, if I'll give Fanny up. If I—don't marry her, I mean . . ."

Bill Turner's green eyes flared. Then the light in them dulled.

"I see—" he said bitterly. "Yes—it's all over town. That my daughter was young Schneider's riding filly—playtime girl. And Schneider and his friends have seen to *their* versions being noised abroad that Fanny stabbed herself out of jealousy because of that young swine's attention to another girl; nothing more, nothing worse than that—"

"Bill—" Martha said,

"So I don't blame your father!" Bill Turner said. "If the boot were on the other leg, I shouldn't allow my Billy, say, to marry a filly with a reputation like the one my daughter's got! Your old man is well within his rights, Phil. Nobody can deny him that!"

"Don't—judge him too harshly, sir," Philippe said. "If it were merely a matter of Fanny's reputation, I'm sure he'd consent. But I'm his only son, and the last Sompayac. His real and chief objection is that I have no *right* to marry an invalid. That I have a duty to continue his line. Selfish, perhaps even irrational, I grant you; but—understandable from an emotional point of view, isn't it sir?"

"Yes," Bill Turner said sadly, "entirely understandable, Phil. Hell boy, he's right!"

"No, he is not," Philippe said quietly. "If the good God, who is all-powerful, grants me freedom of will, no human father can order his son's choice to this extent! I—I refused his check, sir—madame. I placed Fanny's life in danger, gambling on the hope—"

"That *I'd* advance you the money?" Martha said. "Hardly a gamble, Philippe. Wait, I'll write out a draft now—this minute. How much do you need? Don't worry, Bill will let me do this, and even if he wouldn't, this is one time I'd defy him!"

"Don't you always?" Bill Turner groaned. "All right, son—name it. Hell, it's already yours!"

"I'd say—five to ten thousand. I don't really know. But please! Don't write a check yet, Mrs. Turner—"

Martha smiled.

"Bill knows you call me Martha when he isn't around," she said. "He doesn't mind, Philippe. Says it's rather a compliment to an old woman, my age. Didn't you, Bill?"

"Didn't say woman," Bill Turner growled, "I said bag. Old bag your age flirting with boys! Anyhow call her Martha, son. Makes her feel young and kittenish and there's no harm in it . . ."

"All right—Martha; don't write it yet. Mr. Turner, are you willing to—or even in condition to—do without your wife for six months—a year? Because you'll *have* to come, Martha. It's quite impossible to hire a trained nurse to make the voyage. None of them will accept the risk involved. And there *is* a risk. Not much, but still a risk. You see—you'll have to sleep in Fanny's stateroom, exposed to contagion for fifteen days at least and—"

"So?" Martha said.

"By God, sir!" Philippe said, "do you know what an angel out of heaven you've got?"

Bill Turner smiled.

"I know, all right. And there's just one of her. After the good Lord made her, he broke the mold. But tell me: How much danger is there—"

"For a healthy person, very little," Martha said. "And I'm as healthy as a horse! The trouble is—you, Bill. How on earth will you manage—?"

"Got three months' vacation with pay coming to me. And this time I'm going to take 'em. And *rest*, darn it! I promise you, myself, and almighty God that, Martha. I'll take Billy to the country and do nothing more strenuous than fishing all summer long. By then we should know how Fanny's getting along, shouldn't we, son? Hell, I may well join you in Italy. Always did have a hankering to see Rome—"

"You do that, sir," Philippe said. "But now, Mr. Turner, will you do me—Fanny, all of us, one great favor? It's—a bitter pill to swallow; but I—I need your help . . ."

"Name it, son!" Bill Turner said.

"Come with me tomorrow to call upon my father— Wait! There're a few things that he, and only he, can do, and we've *got* to win him over—"

"What things, son?" Bill Turner said.

"No steamship line would take a known tubercular aboard—not without an awful lot of pressure from someone who has the power to apply that pressure. As my father does. His business connections in New York are first-rate, sir. I've worked out all the details: first of all secrecy. We'll have to hire a whole parlor car, put in our own bedding, utensils, plates, silver, tablecloths, napkins, and so forth aboard it—and whatever special foods Fanny will need, even to get her to New York from Ashville. There we'll have to sign her into an isolation ward in one of the hospitals until sailing day. The night *before* sailing, we must arrange to bring her aboard and into her cabin without anybody's seeing us, except such officers and crew as can't be avoided. And we will have to invent a first-class cock-and-bull story for *their* benefit—I'd say we describe Fanny as a cardiac case, whom we're taking to a foreign specialist for a delicate operation. Everyone knows heart attacks aren't contagious. Will you join me at home at—four o'clock tomorrow afternoon, say, sir? Papa will have finished both his lunch and his nap by then, which means his mood will be at its best. Anyhow, I don't think he'll refuse. He was willing from the first to try to save Fan; but I just couldn't accept the string he tied to the package, sir—"

"All right," Bill Turner said, "four tomorrow it is, son!"

"Thank you," Philippe said; then to Martha: "One more string. And this one *I'm* going to tie. This has to be a *loan,* which I'll pay you back. Fanny's not your daughter, and she will by my wife. The responsibility's clear, I think. You can go easy on the interest rates, if you like; but a loan it has to be!"

Martha smiled at him.

"Dear boy," she said, "dear prickly Southern boy! All right. It's a loan. Which, when you pay me back, I'll put into stocks and bonds with your first child's name on them. Boy or girl, but the *first.* Agreed? You'd better agree, Philippe! What means have you to stop me?"

"None," Philippe said ruefully. "All right. Fair enough! Now, let's get to work, shall we?"

The session with Monsieur Sompayac was short, and not at all bad. He only bristled once.

"I am not an ogre, sir!" he said. "Of course I'll pull every wire there is to pull. I should never forgive myself if your daughter died through a failure of simple Christian charity on my part. My only objection to this marriage was that, under the existing circumstances—"

"I understand that," Bill Turner said stiffly. "In fact, I agree with you. I, too, would forbid a son of mine to marry a girl with the kind of reputation my daughter unfortunately has acquired. Which is neither here nor there, now. It's not my daughter's reputation, but her life that's at stake. You've agreed to help. I thank you for that, from the bottom of my heart. The question of Philippe's and Fanny's eventually marrying can very well wait until we see whether my poor child's going to be around to marry anybody; and if her health will permit her to, even if she is . . . Which closes the subject, for the moment, anyhow, doesn't it?"

Jean-Paul Sompayac looked at the detective.

"Spoken like the gentleman you are, Mr. Turner," he said, slowly. "Come, let us bury the hatchet, shall we? May I offer you a brandy? A good brandy, Silver Ribbon, which means a hundred and twenty-five years of aging; not that urine de cheval they sell with three stars on it! And I'll drink a toast—to Philippe and to Fanny, that the bon Dieu grant them every happiness!"

"Papa!" Philippe said.

"Yes; I withdraw my objections. I'm a sentimental old fool, I suppose. You'll have your check tomorrow, with no strings attached. There, there! Don't act like a Creole; you'll shock our guest!"

For Philippe had bent his tall form almost in half in order to take his father in his arms and kiss his cheek.

To Bill Turner's eyes, the spectacle was ludicrous, but it was also moving. He was sadly aware he'd never have such love, or such respect from his own son. So, clearing his throat, he said:

"About your check, Monsieur Sompayac, I'd like to suggest that you limit it to whatever your son's steamship fare and other expenses will be. Fanny's and my wife's—who'll accompany her, of course—are quite another matter . . ."

"But, Mr. Turner—" Philippe began.

"Wait, son. You call yourself investing in a future wife. But until you're able to accomplish that, Fanny's not your responsibility, she's mine. And the whole thing's a gamble, anyhow. This Doctor Forlanini may refuse to operate, or he may operate and fail. So I think we should both cut our losses: You accompany Martha and Fanny to Italy, since I can't, paying your own expenses. But the rest is up to me. Agreed?"

"It's fair enough, Philippe," Jean-Paul said. "Besides, to insist upon doing everything yourself is to quite unnecessarily wound Mr. Turner's pride. It's agreed then. Now, sir—about that brandy?"

"Happy to try it—but make it a light one, will you, sir?" Bill Turner said; then touching his chest: "This old ticker's a little the worse for wear—"

Afterwards, remembering it, Philippe decided that the long voyage to Italy was one of the good times in his life. To his vast relief, and Martha's, they were blessed with uniformly good weather, for which they were duly grateful. Because in Fanny's case any prolonged siege of seasickness would have been dangerous indeed; vomiting all too often induces hemorrhages in a lung with a lesion in it, Karl Holtz had warned them. But if the sea did not actually achieve the glassy state of the popular metaphor, it was gentle enough; so much so that by midvoyage, Fanny could spend hours bundled up in blankets in a deck chair in a sunny corner of the upper deck, from which, of course, Hendricks, the ship's doctor, had carefully separated all other chairs, except two for Philippe and Martha, by a prudent five yards' distance, at least.

And that, of course—coupled with the huge freshly painted signs: "Reserved for Monsieur Sompayac, Mrs. Turner, and Miss Turner," attached to the backs of their chairs—only aroused the curiosity of the other passengers to a fever pitch. But there was something in Philippe's bearing, and perhaps even more so in Martha's, that gave the curious pause. And since the three of them always took their meals together in Fanny's stateroom—an arrangement suggested by Dr. Hendricks, who was absolutely petrified by his fear that they might start an epidemic aboard—not even mealtimes served as an icebreaker for all the middle-aged matrons simply dying to penetrate the mystery of the actual, as opposed to the stated, relationship between the dark Latin couple and the tiny,

frail blonde girl who obviously could have no blood kinship with either of them, and who was just as obviously
gravely, if not fatally, ill.

Of course the members of the one society that is truly
international, if not universal, the Sisterhood of Long-
Nosed Post-Menopausal Females, soon observed that Martha and Philippe occasionally left Fanny quite alone in
her chair, while they took a turn about the deck. And
armed with the misinformation from a steward that Fanny
had, he thought, heart trouble, the moment the first opportunity presented itself, the most redoubtable among
them, a hugely upholstered dowager who gloried in her
powers as self-appointed guardian of public morals, not to
mention the possession of an extraordinary olfactory sense
for sniffing out the faintest whiff of the gamier sorts of
sin, pounced. Flopping down in Philippe's vacated chair,
she cooed:

"All by your lonesome, dearie? Tell me, how's that little
heart, today?"

Fanny turned those pale eyes upon her for one full
minute without blinking. But Mrs. H. Morton Whitney
had the hide of a rhinoceros, or of the she-walrus she
rather resembled.

Oblivious to the astonishing fact that she had at long
last met her match, and ignoring, to her rapidly increasing
peril, Fanny's look of incredulity and contempt, Mrs.
Whitney ploughed on, full steam ahead:

"Would you like me to get you something?" she
bleated. "A cool drink, maybe? I should think your—
family shouldn't leave you alone like this! With a bad
heart, it's always—"

This time that ice-blue gaze stopped even her.

"There is nothing wrong with my heart," Fanny said.

"Oh!" Mrs. Whitney said. "Then I've been misinformed. But you *are* ill, aren't you, dear? Tell me, just
what *is* it you've got?"

Fanny looked Mrs. Whitney up and down, very slowly.
Then her gaze came to rest, all frost and flint, dead-level,
still. Her rather husky voice came out evenly, quietly,
flatly, as though she was discussing the weather or the
time of day.

"Well, if you must know, I've got syphilis, ma'am," she
said.

* * *

"Fanny, in God's name!" Philippe said. "Why did you tell that fool woman that? Hendricks almost had a fainting fit! Finally told that old she-walrus that your heart condition made you morbid, so that she shouldn't pay attention to what you said. But name of a name—syphilis! Why on earth did you pick *that* one?"

"The other one's too long. Gonor—Gonor—Gonor—what, Phil?"

"Gonorrhea? Oh no you don't! Fanny, if you say that to one of those busybodies I'll wash your mouth out with soap, so help me!"

"Then I'll vomit. And I'll have a hemorrhage and die. What you want anyhow—leastways after we get to Italy. Then you and Martha can just stay—set up housekeeping together and—"

"Fanny!"

"You think I haven't got eyes? Round the damn deck, arm in arm, while I sit here and—and brood. Tell me, Phil, honey—is she *good* in bed? I kind of think she is. Papa always looked satisfied and happy as old hell, at least until he got sick and—"

Philippe stared at her. Then very slowly he smiled.

"Believe it or not, I don't know," he said. "Are—you?"

Fanny bowed her head.

"No," she whispered: "I'm terrible. Rod always said so, anyhow. Cold as ice. Tell you what, you come to my cabin tonight—after midnight—and—and—and find out. Of course *that* will kill me too; but maybe I'll die happy. Philippe! What are you grinning at?"

"You," he said, and kissed her.

"Oh, Phil," she wailed. "I feel so—so miserable! I'm—I'm scared! Before I wasn't, but now I *am*. You know why, dearest? 'Cause now I *want* to live. I want to live and marry you and have your babies and make you happy! And I'm not going to. Because people never do get what they want. At least I don't. And—"

He kissed her again.

"Phil!" she husked. "You keep this up and you're going to catch TB! I've told you and told you not—"

"To kiss you?" he said, and did so, again.

She lay there against him, very quietly. Then, suddenly, mischievously, she giggled.

"Phil, honey—can I tell them leprosy?" she said.

He threw back his head and roared.

They went ashore at Genoa because, since only one hundred twenty-two kilometers separate the two cities, it is the nearest seaport to their destination. And they had three pleasant days in that magnificent city, while Philippe arranged for their transport up to Pavia. He was able to reserve a first-class railway compartment for the three of them with the greatest of ease, but he pretended to be having great difficulties over the matter, in order to wander around Genoa without bringing Fanny's wrath down upon his head.

At which, be it said, he failed. Being, as were nearly all upper-class Creoles of his times, a lover of the fine arts, it seemed to him unthinkable—the more so because Fanny, on Dr. Hendrick's orders, *had* to rest three or four days anyhow before being subjected to the jolts and fatigues of a train trip through the mountains—not to take advantage of this opportunity to see whatever Tintorettos, Titians, Michelangelos, and Raphaels the excellent museums of Genoa might afford.

But, to his astonishment, he discovered that it is in the powerful genius of the lowland painters that the galleries of Genoa excel. So bemused was he by the fact that in this Italian city, one can see more of Van Dyck's masterpieces than anywhere else in the world with the possible exception of that great painter's native Holland, that he forgot to keep his mouth shut, and raved about the wonders he had seen in the Palazzo Bianco, the Palazzo Rosso, and the Gallery of the Spinola palace. Worse still, he came back to the hotel with his hands full of postcards and small reproductions of the immortal Flemish School: prints and lithographs of the works of Van Dyck, Rubens, van der Goes, Joos van Cleve, et al . . .

Fanny took one look at them, then snatched them from him, and threw them on the floor.

"*Fat* naked women!" she screamed. "No wonder you—you *hate* me! I'm as skinny as a rail fence—and I always will be! So go away and—and let me die in peace! I *knew* that was why you wouldn't that time and . . ."

She saw Martha staring at her, and subsided.

"Don't pay me any mind, Martha," she husked. "I'm

crazy. You know that. 'Sides it's an insult to you, too! You're not built like the side of a barn, either!" She bent and picked up one of the prints, stood there looking at it as though it were something loathsome.

"Ugh!" she said. "Just look at her! Rolls and rolls of lard! And with *these*—she ought to be able to feed all the bambinos in Italy at the same time!"

Philippe grinned at her.

"She's not Italian, Fan-baby," he said. "She's Dutch. Rubens painted that one!"

"That's right," Fanny said, "she's blonde, instead of dark like an Italian girl would be, isn't she? Even down *there*. Huh! Got that in, didn't he? You men! I swear to God that all of you never even think about anything else!"

"Fanny," Martha said, "I suppose it's a waste of breath to tell you—again—that you really shouldn't say such indelicate, unladylike things. I've told you that at least a thousand times, now. But I simply will not stand here and let you doubt the love of a man who has done all that Philippe has for you, then add injury to insult by screaming at him like a fishwife into the bargain! That, child, is just a little too much!"

Fanny turned, looked up at Philippe. She stood there a long, long moment, halted, arrested, dead stopped, somehow, making an almost intolerable hiatus in the endless motion of time, before she started to cry in that awful, soundless way she had.

"I'm—just no good, Phil-honey," she said brokenly. "I'm rotten all the way through. Poison-mean. And if you had an ounce of sense in your head you'd . . ."

She stopped short, for he was holding both his hands out to her; but, strangely, he had them closed into fists. Nodding first toward one fist then toward the other, he said,

"Choose, Fanny!"

"You—you've got something for me?" she said in an odd, grave, little-girl's voice, "a—s-surprise? Oh, Phil, I don't dare! I'll guess the wrong one! You know I never have any luck!"

"Try!" he said gaily. "If you guess right, it'll mean that your luck's changed!"

She stood there. Then she took a trembling, tottering step towards him. When she was close enough, she dropped to her knees, and laid her cheek against his hand.

"I—I love you," she murmured. "You—you don't have to bring me things, Phil. Even if this hand is empty, I love you. I want you to know that. 'Cause—'cause if I've guessed wrong—"

Her voice changed then, darkened, coarsened, shook with what was clearly horror—but she went on with it, shaping her thought into words with a conviction so complete that listening to her, both Philippe and Martha forgot to breathe.

"It means—I'm going to die," she said slowly, "just when I've got you to live for. Just when my life could maybe be happy, sort of, anyhow. And I hate that! I *want* to live! I want to live and love you and have babies and—"

Very slowly Philippe opened his right hand. In it a magnificent handcarved cameo gleamed. It was a very nearly perfect reproduction of a Luca della Robbia piece, done by a craftsman of matchless skill.

Fanny stared at it. Her pale eyes gleamed, took fire.

"Oh, Phil!" she breathed. "Oh Phil—nothing could be as beautiful as this! Nothing in the world!"

"*You* are, right now," Phillipe said, trying to keep the shake out of his voice.

And that was one of the good times. Perhaps even the best. For, two days later, they went up to Pavia—to meet their collective destiny, their fate; which, as sententious as it sounds, was, for all three of them, neither more nor less than true. Of course, they didn't know that then. Ignorance is sometimes kind.

Is knowledge—ever?


## Chapter Thirteen


Martha stood at the intersection of the Via XI Febbraio and the Viale Matteotti. She, as any good Victorian was expected to, had her Baedeker in hand. She had just come out of the Church of San Pietro in Ciel d'Oro (dutifully translated for her by the Baedeker as St. Peter in the

Golden Sky) where she had seen the tomb of no less than Saint Augustine, himself.

But she didn't remember anything about the church or the tomb or all the beautiful things in the shop windows of the Strada Nuova, the principal shopping street of Pavia, through which she had passed on her way from the pensione on the Via Mazzini where Philippe had found them rooms.

Which was a pity, a very great pity. But the reason she didn't remember the considerable number of monuments and historical sites she had already seen was the same reason that she had the morning free to go sightseeing in the first place:

Fanny wasn't at the pensione anymore. She was in the clinic, in the operating room, where now, at this very moment, perhaps . . .

But it was that, especially, that Martha didn't dare think about, or rather imagine, for to call the attendant images too precisely to mind was to invite a kind of suffering she wasn't sure she had the strength any longer to endure, so she deliberately tried to substitute for them a mental picture of their first interview with Dr. Forlanini, remembering how he—a very handsome man, she'd decided, with his short, iron-gray beard and huge, bushy moustache, contrasting oddly with his close-cropped hair, or what was left of it, because the good doctor was rapidly becoming bald by that late date—had stared at her and Philippe in pained astonishment before turning to the translator that Thomas Cook and Sons, Limited, had provided them:

"From America, you say? The United States? Ah, sí! But it was not wise of you to come so far—crossing the whole ocean, Dio Mio!—without consulting me by mail beforehand. In the first place, I have no beds available, though that difficulty can perhaps be overcome; but in the second, the operation is delicate, difficult, even dangerous and—"

"Please, sir!" Philippe burst out, "I didn't write for that precise reason! For fear that you might refuse! Surely you haven't forgotten how it feels to love one person with all one's being! You're not an old man, Doctor!" He whirled upon the translator, all but crying:

"Quickly, my friend! Tell him I just couldn't let her die!"

Dutifully, the translator had put all that into classic Tuscan. Dr. Carlo Forlanini looked at Philippe. A glow of something like pity showed in his eyes. Before he even spoke, Martha had been sure that the young Creole had already won.

"Very well," the doctor said with a slow smile, "such truly Latin impetuosity in an American deserves a reward, is it not so? You may bring the signorina tomorrow. I will examine her—with the magic rays of the good Dr. Röntgen*—whose apparatus since last month I have had installed. But I cannot, until then, promise you to accept her case. If my examination shows that the operation is feasible, I will operate. But I will not kill your cara signorina because your desperation tells you something should be done. Is that understood, young man?"

"Of course!" Philippe said. "Bless you, Doctor!"

"Amen to that," Martha said.

The next day, after the examination, Dr. Forlanini looked from one of them to the other, then said slowly, thoughtfully:

"Very well, I will operate—though the case of the signorina is a very bad one. I warn you, she may die. But the lesion interests me; I have never seen one quite like it before. It looks more like a wound than a tubercular cavity—hm-m-m, strange—"

Philippe started to open his mouth, but Martha gripped his arm, fiercely. He waited, trembling a little.

"But, in a way, that is an advantage. Its edges are so—clean, even neat, that they should knit very well, despite the size of the lesion. So now I will venture to make an odd, even drastic prediction: either this little lady so beautiful and so young will die on the operating table or shortly thereafter, or she will recover, say, ninety, ninety-five percent of her health . . ."

*Wilhelm Konrad Röntgen of Roentgen discovered X-rays on November 8, 1895, and announced his discovery to the world on January 6, 1896. It was greeted with great enthusiasm by the medical profession. By late 1898 (the time of Fanny's operation), a good many hospitals and clinics were already using the remarkable discovery.

Dr. Forlanini smiled then at Philippe, a little mockingly; said to the translator:

"Tell the young signor that I will also answer the question he has not dared ask me. Yes, the young lady, if she survives the operation itself, will be able to present him with all the great, golden, bouncing bambini that his heart may desire. For, despite her thinness, she is very strong. If she were not, she would have been dead at least a year ago—"

He paused, frowned a little; nodded to them both.

"In any event, waiting will not help. She will not grow stronger with that hole in her lung, but only weaker. Therefore, with the permission of la signora, her mother, and yours, of course, young sir, I will operate—tomorrow—"

And that, in a way, was why Martha found herself wandering, Baedeker in hand, through the streets of the lovely old city. To sit in the austere waiting room of Carlo Forlanini's clinic had been more than unbearable, it had been unthinkable. The only alternative open to her had been just as bad; in fact, it had taken just one hour of pacing up and down her room in the pensione with her nerves crawling like live snakes beneath her skin, to drive her out into the streets of Pavia—alone.

Philippe, of course, was at the clinic. What was more, clad in a white surgical gown, he was actually watching the operation itself.

"How could he!" Martha thought, more in astonishment than in anger. She knew Philippe far too well to attribute this behavior of his to hardness of heart. It was only that when a man's love for a woman was rivaled by his love for an art, a profession, or even a hobby, it was always the woman who came off second-best.

But still, she had been shocked to hear Philippe beg "the immense privilege" of being permitted to witness the operation. 'What sort of privilege is it,' Martha wondered, 'to witness one's beloved being cut open like a butchered lamb?' Philippe had been quite persistent about the matter, told Dr. Forlanini that he was a medical student, showed his credentials to prove it, said:

"I should count it as an honor if you would let me attend. Perhaps in the future—always with your written

permission, Doctor!—I, too, may be able to save lives in
my own country in this wonderful way—"

Dr. Forlanini frowned, studied Philippe's papers, and,
nodding to the translator, said:

"A year at the least before you graduate, is it not so,
young man? And another two of internship? Va bene!
You may watch. But even so, I want your solemn word as
a gentleman that you will not attempt to duplicate this operation until you have five full years of surgical practice
behind you—"

"You have it," Philippe said, when the translator told
him that.

"And you will not faint, young gentleman? I know! I
know! By now you have dissected cadavers, watched
bloody abdominal surgery, et al! But our patient is the
little Fanny whom you love. Una donna molto cara
per Lei, no?"

"Caríssima. But in spite of that, I will not faint," Philippe said.

'It's the way men are made,' Martha conceded again,
now. 'Always they manage to keep one curiously icy inch
of emotional distance from us. Even when they love us,
truly. As Bill loves me, and Philippe loves Fanny. "A
man's love is a thing apart, but 'tis a woman's whole existence . . ." Who said that? Lord Byron, wasn't it?
Strange, I don't remember . . .'

She looked up the Street of February the Eleventh
towards the huge frowning battlements of the building
that stood in a little park almost directly in front of the
church she had just visited. She looked at her Baedeker.
The building was, according to the guidebook, the Castello Visconteo, now converted into a museum. It had a
famous archeological collection, with many statues dating
from Roman times. The Baedeker rated at as being well
worth a visit . . .

With a sigh, Martha started toward the entrance. She
was very tired; but she wasn't even aware of that. She realized that she probably wasn't going to be able to recall a
single detail from the museum any more than she remembered St. Augustine's tomb, or the frescoes, statues, and
windows of San Pietro in Ciel d'Oro. But it was something
to do. And even this somnolent tourism was better than
sitting in her room in the pensione, waiting hour after

hour until Philippe finally came back to tell her . . .

"Oh, God!" she whispered and started walking again, towards the Castello's door.

An hour later, Martha started back down the Strada Nuova. She wondered wearily if she'd even recognize the Via Mazzini when she got to it. Then she remembered it was exactly three streets before one reached the most imposing landmark in Pavia, the Duomo San Michele, that ancient church which boasted the third biggest dome in Italy, so that, even if she accidentally passed the street where she lodged, she had only to retrace her steps when she got to the church. That is, if she didn't decide to walk on through "the picturesque ancient quarter" until she reached "the Ponte Coperto (Coperto Bridge) with its splendid view of the Rio Ticino (Ticino River)."

But before she had time to even think about such decisions, she saw Philippe's tall figure racing toward her through the crowds. She stopped where she was, unable to take another step. Her mind stopped—her heart.

'Why do I love her so?' she thought bitterly. 'She's wild and savage and bad-tempered and impossible and not even mine. And yet—and yet—'

By then Philippe was close enough for her to see his face. He was smiling at her. No, he was grinning so broadly that another inch would decapitate him, Martha thought. She put out a hand and steadied herself against the wall of a store. Then she bent her head and wept, freely, stormily, joyously, letting it all out: all her worry, grief, terror, pain.

"A marvel, Martha!" Philippe was exulting. "A marvel and a miracle! He makes a little incision—about here. Claps on the hemostats, put a pair of forceps on each edge of the wound to hold it open; then zap—into the pleura! Pokes in this tube—sterilized, of course—and gives a signal to his assistant, who fires up the little compressor—electric, I think it is—and z-z-z-zhish! The pleura's full of air! And since our lungs are nothing more than spongelike affairs kept more or less inflated because the air we inhale is under greater pressure than the little there probably is in the thorax and the pleura anyhow—at least until we exhale, Martha—when Dr. Forlanini pumps all that air under terrific pressure into the pleura, it natu-

rally collapses the lung, thus *forcing* the sides of the lesion
to come together. What's more, with several pounds per
square inch extra pressure from that compressed air on it,
that lung *can't* move! Even when Fanny inhales, it can't.
She'll have to get along on the other one for the duration.
That's the beauty of it, don't you see? He sews up the patient with all that air trapped in the pleura and—"

"Philippe," Martha said, "do I gather from all this absolutely incomprehensible medical jargon that the operation was successful? That Fanny's going to live?"

Philippe's expressive young face darkened.

"Dr. Forlanini thinks so, yes, Martha," he said slowly.
"but it'll take twenty-four to forty-eight hours to make
sure . . ."

Afterwards, neither Philippe nor Martha could ever
bear to remember that particular forty-eight hours. It was
not only that it came close to breaking both of them, that
silent waiting, that murderous ordeal of maintaining de-
corum, composure, despite the very nearly crippling degree to which they both were suffering; but afterwards
each of them had to face, individually and alone, the same
utterly merciless conclusion:

"And I endured that—for *this!*"

Philippe, who was of a decidedly philosophical bent,
spent a goodly part of his remaining years (pitifully few,
all too brief, for in his private Upanishad it was written
that he was not to see his thirty-second year) trying to de-
cipher the why of what—through Fanny—had happened
to him. And the only conclusion he could reach was that
in Pavia, the Devil had once more won the toss.

For it all fell out so neatly. Step by step it all went
slowly, inexorably wrong, while seeming to go right. First,
there were the delays.

For, even after the second set of X-ray plates showed
that the lesion in the collapsed lung was healing very well
and cleanly, so that Dr. Forlanini was going to be able to
draw off the compressed air within another week or two,
and allow Fanny to use both her lungs again, Martha
found, to her astonishment, that the assumption she'd
been making all the time, that is, that she'd be able to
take her stepdaughter back to New Orleans as soon as she
was up and about, was neither feasible or even possible

from the medical point of view.

For, when she mentioned it to Dr. Forlanini, he began to talk very fast in a tone and voice that indicated real distress.

"What's he saying?" Martha demanded.

"That it is impossible," the translator said. "You cannot take your daughter home for another six to eight months, signora. The postoperative care is crucial. Dr. Forlanini says he cannot run the risk of having you, her family— with the very best intentions, naturally!—kill a patient he has almost saved. Her lung is healing, true. But she has tuberculosis still. Now, he must cure that. Of course, with the lesion healed, his chances of success are much, much greater. But it will take time. You understand this, my lady?"

"Yes," Martha said; then, looking at Philippe: "Oh dear."

"Well," Philippe said sadly, "there goes graduating with my class. Six or eight months, bon Dieu! I could never catch up! Oh, well—"

"Oh no, you don't," Martha said. "It's back to school for you, young man! We'll wait, Philippe. Next June, you come for us. Bring Bill, if he can come. And we'll have a really splendid vacation! You and Fanny, Bill and I. Because by then—"

"Oh, Martha, I couldn't!" Philippe began.

"You want a demonstration of what a mother-in-law I can be?" Martha said. "By August fifteenth, at the very latest, you'd better be on a boat!"

And he was. His Gallic logic told him that losing six months to a year from his studies would scarcely arrange his future. To marry Fanny, he had to be able to support her; and his already injured pride made the thought of having to seek his father's aid in maintaining a wife that his sire really didn't approve of painful indeed.

But before he went, he had the joy of seeing Fanny walking about the clinic's gardens, with the palest of spring roses beginning to bloom in her cheeks again. What's more, she no longer objected to begin kissed; but even begged kisses of him at every conceivable opportunity. And best of all, she laughed frequently and gaily, became mischievous as all get-out, and something of a tease.

" 'Til June," she told him solemnly the day he left, but

with her hoarfrost eyes alight: "The *first*, Phil! Because by the *second*, I'm going to catch me one of those pretty, girlish-looking Italian boys who're always calling me 'la donna piú bella di mondo' and turn him every way but loose! And that's a promise, so help me!"

"I'll bring Grand-père's dueling pistols with me," Philippe said.

"You'd better!" she mocked; then, as always, with mercurial suddenness, her mood changed. She clung to him, shuddering. "Oh, Phil," she whispered, "if you don't come after me as soon as you can I'm going to cry so hard I'll burst loose on the inside and *bleed* to death! I don't think I can stand it anyhow—'til next June! Oh, Jesus, that's forever! Phil, honey, do you *have* to go? Couldn't you study medicine over *here?* Dr. Forlanini could teach you and—"

"In *Italian?*" Philippe said. "Lord, Fan—give me a chance, will you? I've got to make enough money to buy soup and potatoes twice a week, or how the Devil will we ever cover these bones of yours?"

"Phil," she said seriously, "I'm going to stay thin, likely. My stomach is all shriveled up. I *can't* eat. I've told you and told you! So if you want a *fat* wife, like in those pictures, you'd better find somebody else, 'cause sure as the dickens, I—"

"What would you do if I did?" he teased.

She looked him straight in the face and said it then, slowly, carefully, but with such complete conviction, that he couldn't find the breath to answer her.

"You know what I'd do. What I did do when you went to see *her*. Only better. Making *sure*. So if you really want me around instead of six feet under, you'd—"

He caught her by the shoulders and shook her until her teeth rattled. Then he kissed her.

"Arrivederci, Fan," he whispered. And his cheeks were wet. She clung to him and shivered and sobbed and shook like a demented creature, until Martha came up to them and drew her away.

Then Philippe went down the walk toward where the fiacre waited to take him to the Stazione Principe to begin his journey. His long, lonely journey. Longer, lonelier, and far more obscure and serpentine than he then realized or knew.

Which, since life has its inevitability built in, was just as well.

## Chapter Fourteen

Fanny looked out of her window. It faced directly north, in the direction of the famous Carthusian monastery, La Certosa di Pavia, and, beyond that, the great city of Milan. But she couldn't see anything beyond the garden walls, because a fine misting of rain whispered down through the trees and shut out the world like a drawn curtain. She hoped the rains would stop soon, because any day now Philippe would arrive to take her back home again. Philippe, and Martha.

Her head came up, proudly.

'I have been brave,' she thought. 'I have been very brave. I stayed here all by myself—and I did what Doctor Carlo told me—and now I'm well. I even learned some of this crazy lingo. "Good morning. No, I don't want anything. Has the mail come yet? No, I don't want anything. Good night." What else do I need to say?'

She glanced down at the two letters in her lap. She didn't need to read them because she knew them by heart. Phrases from Philippe's rippled through her mind:

"Although, as you may recall, my dearest, I started medical school in January 1896, by dint of much hard work, and going without sleep, I shall graduate in June—next month, think of that!—with my class, and if you will pardon my lack of modesty, with honors, too. Ours will have the distinction of being the very last class to graduate in the nineteenth century—though by the time I finish my internship and hang out my shingle with M.D. on it, the twentieth century will be two years old . . ."

'And all that,' Fanny thought with wry amusement, 'to tell me that he'll graduate this year, instead of next! I'm glad, though. Means we can get married that much sooner. I—I love Phil. He's not right bright, some ways; but wasn't for him—where would I be? What chance would I have—to hold my head up? To be somebody. A doctor's wife *is* somebody, isn't she? Of course we can't live in New Orleans; but in New York, say, I'll be—a lady. Nobody'll ever know—about my past. And I'll go on studying and learning and watching my grammar and my manners and—And he'll *never* be ashamed of me, never!'

She remembered, suddenly, the letter she had written Philippe, the one his was the answer to. It had been very short. And, as always, she refrained from mentioning that Martha was no longer with her, that she was all alone in Dr. Forlanini's clinic, in Pavia, Italy, half a world away. 'Wouldn't do to upset him right now,' she had thought. 'He's got to keep his mind on his books. 'Cause if he fails his exams, we'll lose a whole year!'

"Dearest Phil," she had written. "I'm well. Not one of those damn little bugs in my lungs or blood, or anywhere, Doctor Carlo says. So now I've only got fifty-three more nights to cry myself to sleep, hugging my pillow, and praying to the Lord to turn it into you. I get so scared, sometimes, that you'll find out how awful I really am, and leave me. I mean go back to Miss Speckled Setter Pup. That is, if you haven't already. Oh Phil, if you don't come soon, I'll die! I love you. Ditto ten million times, Fanny."

She smiled, thinking: 'I wouldn't die, though. Not for him, nor for any damn man. I was a fool. Things got to be too much for me. But no matter what happens from here on in, I won't bow my head, nor shed a tear, let alone do something as stupid as punching holes in myself and swallowing pills! I'm—pretty. I'm very pretty. Even Doctor Carlo calls me "la bella signorina Fanny"—and his eyes kind of light up when he looks at me. For a girl who's smart, good looks can mean an awful lot. Used right, they can buy her damn near anything . . .'

'Phil. Yes, of course; Phil. But there's many a slip 'twixt the kiss and the lip, as the saying goes. I'm going up. I'm going to be—rich, and—respectable. A Lady. With Phil, if I have any luck. Pushing him so that he climbs mighty high. That kind of brains he's got. It's *people* he doesn't understand. But—if that fails—if something happens—'

She paused, crossed her fingers superstitiously behind her back like a child.

"Which heaven forbid!" she murmured, fervently. But, all the same, she went on with her thought: 'If that fails—I'll find me somebody else. Richer than Phil. Better-looking. And I'll—'

She stopped, shook her head.

"Bad luck, thinking like that, Fanny-girl!" she told herself, sternly. "Think about something else. Think about— Papa. Poor man, he sure does have rotten luck, doesn't he? Especially with his children!"

She remembered the day the cable had come; even the date was graven in her memory: January 3, 1899. All of six months ago, now. Martha had looked up from it, and her brown eyes had been—appalled.

"It's—it's your father, child," she whispered. "He—he's had a stroke. This cable's from Dr. Terrebonne. It says Bill's out of danger; but—"

"You want to go home. To him. To Papa," Fanny said. "Please do, Martha. I—I'll be all right. I'm practically well now, anyhow, and—Papa *needs* you. He always has, and he always will, I guess. While he's managed to do without me mighty nicely!"

"Fanny, please!" Martha said.

"Sorry," Fanny whispered. Then suddenly, she bent and kissed Martha's cheek.

"Go to Papa," she said quietly. "Go save him. 'Cause if anybody can do that it's you. Besides, if you stay here because of me, and—and something—happens to Papa—I'll never forgive you as long as I live, so help me God!"

So Martha had gone. And two months later, Fanny had had the first letter from her, which was about as fast as a body could expect, since boat mail between New Orleans and Italy took a minimum of thirty days.

'That little bastard!' Fanny thought furiously. 'Why can't *he* behave himself? Papa fairly dotes on him and yet he's always in trouble. I hope they whip his skinny little ass for him twice a day and three times on Sundays in that school!'

She referred, of course, to her somewhat less than beloved half brother. For Martha had written:

"To put it bluntly, daughter, the Turners are again in very bad odor in New Orleans—and this time because of my well-bred, gentlemanly little son! Your father's stroke, Fanny, was caused by his shock, outrage, and despair at the fact that when Eddie Sarcone and his gang were arrested while breaking into a sporting-goods store, prominent among the culprits was your so very angelic brother. To make matters even worse, our Billy confessed that their object was to steal *guns* which they planned to use, to quote my darling boy's marvelously chaste language, to 'stick up' a local bank . . .

"Of course, due to your father's excellent and hard-earned reputation for honesty, Billy was released to our custody. And, already, with the judge's permission, he has been shipped off to a military academy in South Carolina whose iron discipline is famous, and whose headmaster is well known for having made irreproachably honest men of a good many delinquent boys—

"But enough of sad news! Your father, child, is much better. He will, to tell the truth about it, never fully regain the use of his left leg. But he can get around the house now with the aid of a stout walking stick. And the chief of police has reserved a desk job for him down at Head-quarters for whenever Bill feels up to going back to work, which is a great relief to me, because if your father had to depend upon my bounty, I'm sure he'd die of heartbreak, just as Philippe once said he would . . ."

'I'll have to be careful of Papa,' Fanny thought. 'Mustn't *ever* do anything to upset him again . . .' Her pale eyes lighted suddenly, with that kind of wry amusement that comes from bitter and perfect self-knowledge. 'Leastwise I mustn't let him find out anything I've done that would get him wild. 'Cause if Martha hadn't been able to come back after me with Phil—and she sure Lord thought she wouldn't be, sick as Papa was for so long—I wouldn't have bet a plugged lead picayune on what might not have happened on that steamer trip back home with Phil right there within reaching distance and Martha two thousand miles away!'

Her smile faded. She reached down and picked up Martha's latest letter, read again, for what must have been the twentieth time:

"The reason I haven't written you in so long, child, is that I simply didn't know what I could tell you. I even feared for a while that I was going to have to ask Philippe to go over there *alone* to bring you back, with all the risk of a hideous scandal that procedure would have entailed. I feared it not because I don't trust Philippe or you," ('If you do, you're a damn fool, Martha, dear,' Fanny thought. 'Anybody who trusts a fellow and a girl off by themselves for fifteen whole days in a place where they can get at each other needs her head examined!') "but because, as you well know, neither you nor Philippe need be guilty of the slightest impropriety for wagging tongues to blacken your names forever—by which I mean, sadly, more than they already have. In my desperation, I even thought of suggesting to Philippe that he ask his mother, or one or two of his sisters, to accompany him; but then I remember, from one or two remarks he'd inadvertently let slip, how strained his relations with his family already are, because of you.

"But, fortunately, all that is past. Your father, three weeks ago, took a decided turn for the better; largely, I firmly believe, because he *willed* himself to, in order to free me to fetch you home. Best of all, I have been able to hire an excellent trained nurse to take care of him; and even have averted the outbreak of open warfare between her and Eliza!

"Therefore, child, since Philippe graduates June fifth, you may expect us any day from June twenty-second on. It will be a happiness to see you, especially since in his last letter, which Detective Sergeant Martinelli was kind enough to translate for us, Dr. Forlanini says you are entirely well. For which, God be praised and thanked!

"Look your prettiest for Philippe. Your father sends love. And so do I, Martha."

"June twenty-second," Fanny muttered. "And here it is the twenty-fourth, and they haven't—"

But, at that very moment, as if in answer to her words, Sor Giulia pushed open the door and squeaked:

"Il fiacre! Tua mama! Il signorino giovanni! Oh, signorina Fanny, che felicità!"

Fanny didn't know where she found the words, but in one long, breathless, horribly garbled phrase, she made Sor Giulia understand that Philippe was to be detained until she was dressed, until she made herself pretty. Whereupon the little nursing sister kissed her ecstatically, called her "La donna piú bella di mondo!" and fled down the stairs.

In Dr. Forlanini's office, after having received the disappointing news that he would just have to wait a little

longer before the bella e dolce Signorina Fanny would be
ready to receive him, Philippe fidgeted, stared blankly,
rapped his own knuckles, and the like, presenting so perfect a portrait of a blithering idiot—or its exact synonym,
a young man in love—that the good doctor was moved to
say to Martha, through, of course, that necessary evil, the
interpreter:

"Shall we excuse the young gentleman? You and I, signora, can very well attend to the tiresome and prosaic
details of medicines and business without him. And Sor
Giulia tells me that la signorina your daughter has passed
a most unhappy week, awaiting his arrival. He can wait in
the garden until she is ready to come down. Shall we give
the young lovers our *beneplacit* for a while, madame?"

"Of course!" Martha laughed.

"By now, la signorina is already in the garden," the interpreter said. "Sor Giulia told me she would be ready in
five minutes. And, as ten have already passed, I think—"

The only reason that Philippe didn't anticipate the
Wright brothers' invention of successful heavier-than-air
flight by a full four years was that he, at the moment, actually was lighter than air. Atune to all the celestial music
of the spheres, he soared, floated, windborne and adrift
upon the bosom of a soft and rosy cloud. The pity of it
was how soon that mood would pass, how easily he—as
every man of woman born!—would fall victim to time's
merciless erosion of his very capacity for wonder, so that
never again would he be able to capture the exact quality
of that moment in either memory or imagination, no matter how hard he tried. Perfect happiness is so rare, so
fleeting, that we soon teach ourselves to doubt its very existence, retouching our mental picture of the past in more
somber colors, forgetting, or not daring to remember—lest
the contrast prove too painful—that once we were young,
and once, very truly, there was joy.

But in the garden he halted, became not only heavier
than air, but rooted in the earth. Yet he was extraordinar-
ily alive, alert, aware, his perceptions so sensitized that it
was as if he'd been plunged into a galvanic bath. His skin
tingled; every nerve in his long body became a thorough-
fare over which uncounted legions of invisible ants
marched with sextuply uncounted, vibrating feet. His dark
eyes dilated, catching the Renoir quality of that light,

palely luminous, sun-filtering, misty, for it had been raining that morning so that every leaf, petal, blade, in that garden was asparkle with myriad brilliant droplets now that the clouds had fled, making a perfect setting for a living portrait that was less Renoir than Reynolds, less exuberant rosy flesh than the sort of pale and exquisite perfection in which Sir Joshua excelled.

Fanny was dressed in white. Her hair was pinned up with the coiffure that later generations would call the Gibson Girl hairdo, after Charles Dana Gibson, the artist who fixed forever the distinctive traits of an age in some ways more remote from ours in its habits of thought than was Augustan Rome. She had a fan in her hands—but why go on? Description is subjective and therefore meaningless; any detailed listing of her dress will not make you see what Philippe saw, still less feel what he felt. Say merely that effect of those details, combined, blended, heightened by his will to love, his longing, his carefully sublimated lust, were overwhelming.

She was smiling at him, and her lips, though still pale, were discernibly pink at last. Her cheeks were the color of one variety of dogwood, her face the color of the other; and, her eyes—No. It cannot be said or written. There are no words for that special almost-but-not-quite color that were Fanny's eyes, especially when they were busy— though her pale lips went on smiling all the time—at performing the alchemy of fracturing light, pouring it down her cheeks in liquefied jewels that danced upon the wildly trembling corners of her mouth, to flesh-white fire as they broke free to fall and fall and fall.

'Oh no!' Philippe's stunned and reeling mind protested, arming its defenses against the crippling onslaught of wonder, 'no one could be this beautiful! They lied to me. My Fanny—died. And this—this is a ghost. A changeling angel sprite who—'

But she had put out her arms to him. From across the garden, he could see them tremble. He did not, odd as it may seem, odd as it later seemed even to him, go flying to her. Rather he tottered, stumbled, jerked like a spastic, his control over the very movements of his fine, lean, athletic body gone from him under the impact of this small, slight miracle of femininity returned to him from the very edge of, if not beyond, the grave.

Even when he was close enough, he did not take Fanny in his arms. Instead, he flopped down upon his knees, making a curiously sodden thump, and ruining his trousers almost beyond repair; it had been raining, remember, and what was underfoot, once he'd left the graveled path, was thick, unromantic mud. Then he took her two tiny, wildly trembling hands, and kissed them with the aching reverence of a true believer before the image of his adored and blessed saint.

Which was more than Fanny had bargained for, or was inclined to bear. She jerked her hands from his, clawed her fingers around his ears—sizable enough, but neither as long or as hairy as his behavior demanded that they be—yanked at them until she'd brought him to his feet, went up on tiptoe, and kissed his mouth.

And that kiss, too, was a perfect demonstration that every really vital moment in our lives must of necessity be granted the honest respect of silence, because language by its very nature distorts and falsifies emotion, overstates it into ludicrousness, or understates it into a sort of curiously Anglo-Saxon attitudinizing.

Say merely that on a bright, rainwashed morning in an Italian garden, Fanny reinvented for herself the kiss as a means of communication. She told Philippe, with soft warm pressures and tear-salt tremblings, that she loved him; she got over to him an all but maiming tenderness that very precisely defined the common frontier of joy and pain; achingly, she braille-spelled longing, need, and faint, still scarcely breathing, hope. But no slightest hint of animal passion—to quote that most marvelous of all Victorian clichés—reared its ugly head.

In short, absolutely nothing marred the crystalline perfection of that moment. They lived, for some ten minutes anyhow, a little idyll: a good, lovely, satisfying, and regrettably vanished Victorian word.

"Phil—" she said, "lift me up! Catch me by the elbows and lift! Go on—please!"

He did so, his eyes alight and puzzled. She was, to his strong arms, weightless as so much air.

"You see!" she said triumphantly. "Ninety-seven whole pounds! And I'll make a hundred yet! Just you wait!" Then she saw the gleam of amusement in his eyes.

"Phil—" she whispered, "I'm—I'm still awfully skinny,

aren't I? Not like those girls in those pictures you bought in Genoa. So—so I'll *never* please you! You said you wanted a nice *fat* blonde wife who could give you ten kids, while I—"

"While you're a nymph of the airy regions," he said solemnly, "and the single loveliest human female into whom the good little God ever blew the breath of life. Fan, Bébé, looking at you hurts. You're so damned beautiful that half the time I only remember to breathe after I've turned a noticeable shade of blue. And I *don't* want you fat. You were before, remember? Fat and pimply and miserable. Then you got to be plump and cute. Pert and perky as all get out. Gave everybody ideas. Even me. So—"

Her pale eyes flickered reflected light over his face.

"And now I *don't* give you ideas?" she said.

He stared at her.

"Yes," he said finally, "you do. But they're different, somehow. Blasphemous as it sounds, I'd say they're kind of—holy. Before, I used to speculate about what a night—or a weekend—I could have for myself if I could sneak you off somewhere—"

"And now?" she said, holding him with that still, dead-level ice-blue stare.

"Now I don't even think about *me*," he said slowly. "I don't exist. Or if I do, it's only as half of *us*. And I don't want a night, or a weekend, or a year. I'll settle for a lifetime, though even that's too short. I ask only of le bon petit Dieu that, when I quit this vale of wrath and tears, He allow me to wake up in heaven and find you at my side."

"Oh, Phil!" she breathed, and started to cry.

"Fan!" he said.

"You shouldn't!" she sobbed. "You mustn't, Phil! Say such beautiful things to me, I mean! It's bad luck! I'm not worth it! I'm a bad girl, remember! You're only getting second-hand goods—No! *Fourth*-hand, really! 'Cause—"

He bent and flattened her ugly, hateful words against her speaking mouth.

She nestled against him like a tiny, captive bird.

"Phil—" she said, "you won't mind if I don't get fat, will you? I don't think I can, anyhow, so . . ."

"Lord!" he laughed. "Speaking of monomania! Ma chère Fanny, why would any man in his right mind change perfection? And that's what you are now, my love. I solemnly forbid you to gain another ounce!"

She giggled a little, said:

"Phil, honey—when are we going to get married? Soon? Oh, I do hope so, 'cause . . ."

He frowned.

"Not for a long time, I'm afraid," he said sadly. "More than two years at the very least. The New York State Medical Board requires that all medical grads put in that much time before we can even take the examinations for the license to practice. Two years of internship, I mean, before I can hang out my shingle with M.D. on it. And that is even if Papa's august French friends *don't* keep their promise—an appointment to the Pasteur Institute in Paris. If they do, that'll set me back still another year . . ."

He stopped, looked at her, said:

"Oh, Lord!"

"I'll die!" she got out. "I'll plain curl up and die! Three more years! Oh, Jesus, Phil; I couldn't stand waiting *that* long! I simply couldn't! Let's run off! Elope—I'll get a job—as a waitress or something. I—I'll scrub floors! And I've got enough frocks to last me ten years anyhow, and I hardly eat anything at all, so . . ."

"Fanny!" he said, outraged now, wounded in his pride.

"Phil—" she said. "Don't some fellows get married *before* they pass the Medical Board? *Some*, anyhow?"

"Jeunesse dorée," he said, "millionaires' sons with doting papas. And my father is neither a millionaire, nor doting; in fact, he—"

She didn't even hesitate. With pure destructive instinct, she plunged a finger into that open wound.

"Doesn't approve of me. And has some nice sweet little Creole girl with a letter from the mother superior of the convent school stating that she's a certified, grade-A virgin, so pure that not even the Holy Ghost could make a little Jesus with her, all picked out and—"

"Fanny!" he roared.

"Well, hasn't he?"

"No," he said, "and he rather likes you. His only reservation is that he's afraid your health will prevent you from presenting him with grandsons."

Again she made one of her breathtaking changes of

mood. She stared at him with eyes alight and dancing, filled with all the mischief in this world.

"Phil!" she breathed, "Martha and Doctor Carlo're sure to talk all morning what with that little fibberty-gibbet of an interpreter to slow them down. So—let's sneak up to my room and make your papa a grandson! Then you walk in with me, with my tummy poking out a mile and a half, and say: 'Papa, you've got to help us out! You wouldn't want your first grandson to be a li'l bastard, would you? Besides, it's time I made an honest woman of poor Fan, don't you think?' And—"

He stared at her. Decided, after a long moment, that she was joking. It was the only thing he dared allow himself to think.

"Come off of it, Fan!" he laughed. And looking up, he saw Martha and Dr. Forlanini coming towards them down the garden path. That sight filled him with vast relief. He wondered, suddenly, with something very close to fear, what that homeward voyage was going to cost him out of his ebbing reserves of good intentions, will.

But he had time at least to put that one more question to her, before they were close enough to hear.

"What would you have done if I'd seriously taken you up on that?" he said.

Fanny looked up at him, unsmiling, her pale eyes cool and still.

"Gone upstairs with you. Made us a baby. Or tried to, anyhow," she said.


## Chapter Fifteen


Philippe was playing shuffleboard with a group of the younger male passengers when he saw Fanny coming towards him. She was dressed all in brown and green, colors which became her wonderfully. She had on a brown felt hat with a beaver-fur band, but sporting a huge green lace bow just above the front brim; and a sleeveless beaver jacket and muff protected her from the fresh sea breezes. Her dress had sleeves, though; tight-fitting brocaded brown and beige velvet sleeves—for the huge leg-o'-mutton sleeve of the past two decades had finally gone out of style in 1897. Under the jacket, she wore a vestee of draped green satin, and a cream-colored lace bow about her neck. Her incredibly tiny waist was tightly belted with brown satin, and her long, light-brown cloth skirt with inverted pleats swept the deck. All in all she was a sight to gladden any man's heart.

Philippe put down his long push-stick, picked up his jacket, and slipped into it.

"Your fiancée, eh, Sompayac?" one of the other players said. "By Jove, she's absolutely stunning! When are you going to present me, old fellow?"

"Never," Philippe said, and moved off to join Fanny.

"'Lo, Phil," she said in that slightly husky voice her now-vanquished illness had left her with permanently, it seemed. "Kiss me?"

"No!" he said.

She looked at him. Said: "Oh!"

He offered her his arm. She took it. They moved off down the deck.

"Phil—" she said, "you—you're mad at me, aren't you?"

"No. Not mad—if by mad you mean angry. Mad in the sense of being crazy over you, yes."

"That's—sweet. Now, kiss me!"

"I said no, didn't I?"

"Why not, Phil?"

"And turn off that plaintive little-girl's voice, will you? You *know* why not."

"'Cause people can see us? What difference does *that* make? We're engaged, aren't we?"

"*Not* because people can see us. I couldn't care less . . ."

"Then why not, Phil, darl—dearest?"

"Because I'm *human,* Miss Frances Turner! I keep on kissing you and one of these days I'm going to let out a fearful howl, catch you by the hair, and drag you down to my cabin, that's why!"

"Oh, goodie!" Fanny laughed, and clapped her hands in pure delight. "Now you've *got* to kiss me, Phil! But don't drag me straight down to your cabin; three times around the deck first, so everybody can see, first, huh? Shock all those nosy old busybodies right out of their long drawers!"

"Fanny, you're incorrigible!" Philippe said.

"No, I'm not," Fanny said. "I just love you, that's all. I *love* kissing you. It makes me feel good. Would you rather that you gave me the horrors?"

Philippe looked at her.

"For the duration of this voyage, yes," he said.

She laid her hand on his wrist.

"Phil—I—I make you suffer—don't I?"

"Yes, Fanny, you do."

"I'm sorry."

"Forget it. Now I'll kiss you. Just once."

"On one condition, mon amour!"

"What condition, Fanny?"

"That you make that one kiss last ten minutes. Agreed?"

"Hell, no! You want me to burst?"

"No. I want you to let out that fearful howl, catch me by the hair, and—"

"Fanny—no. Seriously."

"Phil—what's wrong with me?"

"Wrong with you? Nothing, now, I hope."

"There is. I'm—not a girl. Not really."

"If you're a boy, that makes me a pervert."

"Oh, fiddlesticks! That's not what I mean. I—I'm—a cripple, sort of. I—I love you. I love being kissed. But it—it doesn't—doesn't—"

"Have the slightest effect upon you. In other words, by your own admission, you're as cold as ice. Which, contemporary standards to the contrary, is abnormal. And that, Fan, frightens me. I darned well don't want a submissive, dutiful bride. I want une petite amoureuse who'll climb all over me!"

"But, Phil, *good* girls don't—can't—"

"Merde!" he howled.

"Phil—" she whispered.

"Yes, Fan?"

"I—I wasn't *always* like this. Cold, I mean. *They* did it. Rod and—"

"Fan, if you mention that bounder's name to me one more time, I'll feed you to the sharks!"

"Don't feed me to the sharks; catch me by the hair and—"

"Why should I? When ice touches me, I turn blue!"

"Phil—have you ever thought that—that with *you* I might not be? Cold, I mean? You're—sweet, kind, gentle. You'd never—"

"Fan, if you start making comparisons, I'm going to slap you winding!"

She whispered the word "sorry," looked away from him over the rail. Her eyes seemed to darken a little. To catch something of the sea's own color. She was silent for a long moment. Then, softly, slowly, sadly, she said: "We —we get there tomorrow, don't we? This is our *last* day at sea, isn't it?"

"Yes," he said.

"And tonight's our last night, isn't it?"

"Yes, why? Fan! *Now* what the Devil?"

"I was so hoping she'd go to *sleep,*" Fanny sobbed, "real sound sleep, Phil! I've lain there and watched her out the corner of my eyes. But just let me move and her eyes fairly pop open! She—she doesn't trust me, that's all!"

"Should she?" Philippe said, gently.

"No—no! With you, no. Not one minute. 'Cause I— I'd do anything to be alone with you. You—you could— cure me, Phil. Melt all this ice I've got walled around my heart. If anybody on earth can, it would be—you. And I—I want to *try.* Don't you see, love? We're going to have babies, you and I—lots and lots of babies. And babies are—a kind of art, aren't they? Like those pictures and statures you're so crazy about. You said the things Michelangelo did were so beautiful 'cause he made them with—love. How can I make a beautiful little Phil Number Two if I'm—stiff as a board and scared to death and —hurt—and sick to my guts and trying not to throw up?"

He bent then, and kissed her mouth.

"I don't think you need worry about that," he said.

That night there was a farewell ball in the steamer's main lounge. But Fanny wouldn't go. She wanted to walk the promenade deck with Philippe in the moonlight. But after less than ten minutes of that, she kissed him convulsively and fled weeping to the cabin she shared with Martha.

"So endeth my romantic voyage," Philippe thought morosely, and descended to the ship's bar where he solaced himself with a Hines, Ruban Argenté; for his father had formed his taste in fine wines and cognac very well indeed.

But, once reaching his stateroom, he found it impossible to sleep. Moonlight poured through the porthole, silvering all the room. He sat there in his nightshirt, thinking:

'Is she beginning to thaw? Or are her maternal instincts getting the better of her? I'd swear that her desire for motherhood is the only pure, unmixed emotion she has. She'd put up with a man for that. Accept our incomprehensible and faintly repulsive attention because she so longs for a child. And this is the girl whom all New Orleans has—has branded a whore. Rod—now. Handsome enough beggar, to tell the truth about it. And poor Fan thought she was reaching far above her station; was willing to accept—concubinage as a means to winning him over to honorable matrimony. She was a fool. A sin of which all humanity is guilty. Oh hell, I—'

And it was then, at that precise instant, that he heard the knock on his stateroom door. He sat there frozen, not even breathing. The knocking came again, a light, faint, brushing sound, completely different from the businesslike rapping that the stewards made. He knew then, with appalling certainty, he knew.

'I'll—have to let her in,' he groaned. 'If someone passes down that corridor and sees her there—Oh bon petit Jésus! What on earth am I to—'

He opened the door.

Fanny slipped through it like a wraith, closed it behind her, leaned back against it. Her face was ghost-white. She was shaking.

"Phil," she said in that odd, grave, little-girl's tone of voice she always used when what she was saying was important to her. "If you ask me to get out of here, I'll go. I won't cry or scream or make a fuss. Only—"

"Only what, Fan?" His voice was strangling him. It took him four tries to get those three words out.

"Only—please don't. This—this is our last chance, Phil. In three years, anything could happen. I—I could get sick again. Die, maybe. You could change your mind—go back to her. To Billie Speckled-Tail, I mean. Phil—do you know what I'm asking you for? No, begging you for, really?"

"No," he croaked, "put like that, I don't. What are you, Fan?"

"For—a memory. One good memory, Phil. To keep— all the rest of my life. Only one I'll ever have, likely . . ."

"Fan—" he groaned, "I—"

"Wait! Don't say anything yet. Let me finish. I've told you a million times that I'm—bad. And I am, too. Some ways, I'm awful. I'm poison-mean. Hateful. Full of dirty tricks. But *that* way I'm not, Phil. Not at all. Because— bad women—enjoy it, don't they? I—I don't. I *hate* it. It's horrid. Messy. Disgusting!"

He smiled at her, a slow, warm relief stealing through his veins.

"Then, my darling Fanny," he mocked, "what in the sacred name of the good little God are you doing here?"

"Begging—my husband—for a little love," she whispered. "Hoping that—he—he's different from the—rest. That he's not—a wild animal—trying to pound a girl to pieces—rip her in half up the middle—yelling awful dirty filthy words at her all the time—all the miserable little no-time-at-all it lasts—then flopping over—asleep before his head hits the pillow—stinking of sweat and snoring like a hog—"

He stared at her, his dark eyes soft with pity.

"You've had it—rough, haven't you, Fan?" he said.

"Yes, I have," she whispered. "And still—in spite of all that, I—I want you so bad I hurt! So please, Phil! Do I have to get down on my knees? Or don't you have any pity?"

He stared at her. Said one word slowly, softly, but with a rising inflection.

"Martha?"

"Asleep. She's quit locking her vernol up—now she knows I want to live now. Tonight she had a headache— so I rang for the steward to bring her some hot milk. I slipped four vernols in it before I brought it to her. And gave her another one of the aspirin she asked me for."

"*Five* vernols! Sacre nom!"

"It takes twenty to kill a person, Phil. I know. Six of them only put me to sleep that time you went to see *her*—even though I already had a hole in my lung you could shove your fist into. Martha'll have a worse headache tomorrow, but she'll be all right. So—there's no danger. You—you aren't going to send me away, are you?"

He looked at her. Sighed. Shrugged his shoulders:

"No, Fan," he said. "I'm not going to send you away—"

Physical love is a schizoid thing—which is the basic reason that all attempts to write about it inevitably fail. Who can read of Lawrence's lovers, now, whipping each other's naked bodies with flowers in a pouring rain without being seized with incredulous—and yet acutely painful—laughter? Who, in the future, will be able to even comprehend Roth's wild, antic, but basically sad savaging of emotion? Donleavy, perhaps—for he retains a bittersweet whiff of tenderness; but Updike, say; and the rest? Or shall we return to Hemingway's moving Spanish mountain? Dear God!

Was then, de Maupassant right when he accused God of perversity for having combined the organs of procreation with those of excretion, and made the continuity of the species possible only through the most preposterous of activities, carried out in an utterly ridiculous posture? Yes. Why yes; of course. But also wrong. Because, being a writer, one of those pitiful emotional cripples who distil their own frustrations into words, he was incapable of understanding—love.

An old-fashioned word, what? Truly mid-Victorian. High time we brought it back. The trouble is that those who believe in it, understand it, *can't* talk or write about it. Before one's holy of holies cast off your shoes. This ground is sacred ground. In the presence of the Mysteries, be silent, and be still. And, above all, don't watch! Voyeurism is a vice. A sick, sad, cowardly vice. If in the orisons of this or that particular nymph, our sins be all remembered, let us have at least displayed the intestinal or the testicular fortitude of participation!

But, you say, you're curious. And your curiosity is legitimate. Fanny's and Philippe's individual and/or collective futures may well depend upon that midnight session in that steamer cabin's bed, you insist. Whether it goes well or badly may be the hinge upon which fate in all her ponderous idiocy turns. You'd determine the future then, upon a nervous case of ejaculato praecox? Or upon the psychosis of an unthawable frigidity? You're within your rights. The Romans used chicken guts. To each, his own.

You still insist? Very well. We'll draw that red plush Victorian Curtain of Charity aside. Indulge you your masturbatory fantasies. There they are. They're quite naked, thank you. They're better looking than most. Fanny's great scar has faded considerably. To one who had never seen it before, it would wake curiosity, not revulsion. They are duly limb-entwined, impenetrant, engulfed—or perhaps engorged would be the better word—

They're bedewed with sweat, making a fine sheen on her snowy flesh, and on his lean, bronzed form. And de Maupassant is right; the position's preposterous. There's something infinitely sad and comical about a pair of small white feet waving in the air on either side of a lean brown rump, muscular as all get-out and hairy enough to justify Darwin, isn't there? And the motions—pelvic writhe, partial withdrawal, total repenetration, buttock tension, thrust, and heave (yet, in this case, somehow, always gently) *are,* let us admit it, more than a trifle absurd.

But you've seen all this before, even—a consummation devoutly to be wished!—indulged in it yourself upon occasion. So what is so remarkable about this performance?

What you don't see. What description must leave out. The reasons that they fail. The powerful presence of nontactile, invisible, nonolfactory factors. (Curiously enough, they always leave that rich assortment of aromas out, too, don't they? Forgetting, or perhaps ashamed of, that characteristic of our animal natures. Stupid of them! What intoxicant can be more heady than our beloved's natural smell?) The leitmotifs, often contrapuntal, this solemn, horizontal dance is danced to, really.

"Such as?" you ask.

Such as intention, will, state of mind. The regard the lovers have for one another when fully clothed. Admiration. Respect, love, hate. The whole compendium of human emotions which culminates in this—or make it impossible. For, after all, tactile sensation has its limits, and all the variations of position in the Kama Sutra, even eliminating from the outset the excessively contortionist, and the actually painful, become eventually both tiresome and a bore. Which, of course, reduces the purveyors of panting prose to the frustrated to falsifying—not lying, conceivably, perhaps; but selling out *their* fantasies—so that what you buy is a substitution of their sick dreams for yours. Nothing more. The reality is another thing.

For some fortunate few, a glory. For the rest—well, you can always swap door keys, can't you? Exchange your disappointments. Spread the misery around. While, of course, indulging in such of today's fashionable practices as require neither virility, potency, femininity, nor tenderness, but only a strong stomach and a high threshold against the onslaught of nausea.

So here we have Philippe and Fanny—to borrow today's language—balling, screwing, fucking, making love. The last, gentle reader, believe it! Only the last is true. They are making love. And *that* is what is remarkable.

For love-making is a demanding occupation. All tender giving, sharing, asking nothing. Offering: "See what I have—and all for you!" Philippe, for instance, didn't have a thought in the back of his head about his own pleasure, that vastly overrated carnal joy. Rather, the opposite was the case. The degree of restraint, of self-control he was exercising was monumental, and very close to self-inflicted torture. A modern would have called it masochistic. But let us dispense with the labels, shall we? They serve as blocks to communication; being meaningless, really, they distort meaning; that is, when they don't destroy it—

Philippe, actually, was trying to make Fanny happy. Fanny, not himself. He was very slowly and tenderly and carefully trying to enable her to find joy. To take pride in her own body, and glory in its uses.

And Fanny was attempting to prove to herself that what men and women do together in the dark need not be ugly, hateful, messy, or disgusting. That the flesh has its own language, silent, tactile, worshipful, and tender. That those who love, learn that language, finally, learn to achieve fusion. That "ye two shall be one flesh, no longer twain!"

Too much to ask for a single night, perhaps. Sexual love, like skilled dancing, is learned behavior. Still, our pair had the saving grace of totally unselfish intent. What they also had was recognition. He:

'This is not any hired, bought, persuaded female body I am belaboring in the dark to ease the ancestral beast-thing howling in my blood—this is *Fanny!* My Fanny! It is my Lady. Oh, it is my love!'

And she:

'He's—so good. So—gentle. He doesn't hurt me! He doesn't even want to—and—and—*this* feels so good! Slow. Slow. Easy—slow. Oh Jesus! All the time I've wasted up 'til now—and Oh! It's happening! Just a second then—it was—there, again! It is! What I thought couldn't maybe. There's nothing wrong with me! I'm—human. I'm a real live, honest to God, girl! There now—almost—only a little more, a little, little—more. There! If he'll only—only—'

Speaking. Saying:

"Phil—"

"Yes, Fanny?"

"Love me?"

"Yes."

"Love me?"

"Yes."

"Love me!"

"Now?"

"Now! Oh, Phil! Oh, Jesus! Oh sweet—Oh my love—"

Lying there in his arms. Crying. Good tears. Healing tears. The tears of joy.

So now let's draw that red plush brocaded Victorian Curtain of Charity the hell back again, shall we? Leave Philippe and Fanny alone. They've earned their momentary peace.

You're disappointed? One rather hopes so. Go buy your fantasies somewhere else.

Or, better still, go learn to—love.

## Chapter Sixteen

All the time it had taken to dock, retrieve their luggage, and go through the customs, Martha had been trying to think of that word. At first she had believed that it was her lingering and totally inexplicable drowsiness—it had taken four cups of scalding black coffee to even wake her up enough to attend to the business of disembarking—that wouldn't let it come to mind. But, even after that, during the three days they had lingered in New York, indulging Fanny's quite understandable desire to see the big city, since she hadn't been able to on their outward-bound voyage to Italy, Martha had searched her mind for the exact term to describe Fanny's face. The change in it. The way it was now. Still the word wouldn't come, even though she had persisted. On the long train trip south, she had "cudgeled her brains," as a popular phrase of the day put it, to find an adjective exact enough to define that look glowing softly in her stepdaughter's eyes, hovering almost luminously about the corners of her mouth.

But it wasn't until now, at long, long last, as the train came snorting and panting into Terminal Station on Canal Street itself, that it came to her. And with such impact that she said it aloud.

"Radiant! That's it!" she said. "Why, you're positively radiant, child!"

Fanny smiled at her.

"You mean my nose is shining? Or that I'm pretty? Which, Martha?" she said.

"Neither," Martha said. "I mean something altogether different and much more important, I suspect—"

Philippe, who had been gazing absent-mindedly out of the train window, turned to her.

"What did you say, Martha?" he said.

"That Fanny is—radiant. Look at her! Have you ever seen anyone look happier, Philippe?"

But Philippe didn't even glance at Fanny. Instead, he went on looking at Martha—a trifle too long. A tide of darker color rose in his face. Abruptly he dropped his gaze.

"No, never—" he said, shortly, miserably aware even as he spoke that his hesitation, his very tone of voice, had been as close to an open acknowledgment of guilt as it was possible to make, with the sole granted exception of an open confession before witnesses; especially when the aching fact that Martha's intuition, her perceptiveness, bordered upon the miraculous was taken into consideration.

He was right. Martha sat there facing him like one

transfixed; her breath itself halted upon the felt vibrations of what she'd heard in his voice, that almost imperceptible undercurrent of—

'Remorse?' her stricken mind demanded. 'Shame?'

She sat there, rigid with shock—because she knew. Suddenly, completely, appallingly, she knew. Gone beyond her will, her memory mercilessly supplied the corroborating details: The box of vernol, entirely and unexplainably missing. The maddening drowsiness it had taken her all day to fight off. Fanny's pale eyes, blue-ringed, a little sunken, her lips, usually almost colorless, which on that morning had been as close to a natural human pink as she had ever seen them; perhaps even beyond it, approaching a shade of rose, actually.

There there was something else; something that tugged at the edge of her consciousness, now. Why had she so much as noticed Fanny's mouth, anyhow? What had called her attention to it? Now, effortlessly, pitilessly that detail came to her, too. Fanny's lips had been distinctly swollen!

Martha bowed her head, fighting for self-mastery. 'What should I say?' she thought. 'What's to be done now? Oh Dear God, what if she's—'

But with abrupt mercy, at that precise instant, a vagrant memory struck, called into being, surely, by an unconscious association of ideas: On her own belated honeymoon, she and Bill had gone to Niagara Falls. And in the morning, leaving him still sleeping, she got up, crossed the bedroom and looked at her own face, reflected in the mirror above the vanity, fully expecting to see it—changed. And it had been. That was the first time she'd ever seen the kind of soft pure radiance that glowed in Fanny's eyes, now.

'Then,' she thought fiercely, rebellion in every fiber of her, 'if he can make her look like this—he's perfect for her. Vows or not. Printed words on a paper or not. And goddamn the Queen!'

"Philippe—" she said quietly, "if you ever have—a problem—I mean one that you *can't* discuss with your father; if you should suddenly find that you need a fairish amount of money, say—for reasons that you're almost certain he wouldn't approve of—will you come to me?

Pride, under some circumstances, is a luxury none of us can afford—"

He stared at her. 'Does she,' he thought, 'mean what I *think* she means? Yes. Almost surely yes. My God, but she's extraordinary! Not one word of reproach—just expressing her willingness to—to see us through. And I can't even tell her—not to worry—that I took a gentleman's precautions. So—'

But in 1899, the words, the way to tell the truth about what had happened, did not exist. He could have told Bill Turner, or his own father; but Martha, never; he said:

"If such a situation should arise, I'll come to you, Martha. You have my word."

"Good!" Martha said.

He went on looking at her; then he said:

"D'you know, Martha—you don't belong to your world—not at all. No, wait! I don't mean the obvious fact that you were born to be a duchess, at the very least, and ended up married to a gumshoe—"

"Philippe!" Fanny said, "don't you dare talk about my father like that!"

"He taught me the word, Fan," Philippe said. "And the fact that I don't admire his profession has nothing to do with the fact that I do admire the man. I admire him tremendously. He's wholly admirable—and his friendship honors me, not the other way around . . ."

"That's better," Fanny said. "That's a whole lot better, Phil!"

"All right. As I was saying, Martha, you don't belong to our world in time, either. You were born a hundred years too soon. Like all really worthwhile people, you're more in tune with the future than with your own day. Bill calls you a bluestocking; but you aren't, really. You're something better: you're a person—a truly magnificent person—something we rarely, if ever, allow a woman to be. You're broadminded, tolerant, understanding . . ."

"Philippe," Martha said crisply, "I shouldn't push those aspects of my personality too far, if I were you."

"I don't mean to," Philippe said. "On the other hand, I might—mildly—point out to you that my concepts, my standards, remain what they were, Martha. And though I should never claim perfect rectitude, I think I can claim two other things that are perhaps even more important: a rather unshakable sense of personal responsibility and—old-fashioned as it sounds!—a gentleman's word . . ."

"I thank you for that, Philippe," Martha said.

Fanny stared from one of them to the other.

"Oh Lord!" she said, "you're talking English—I know you are; but all the same, I didn't understand a word either of you said!"

"Which is just as well," Martha said; then, to Philippe: "I don't believe Fanny's a part of her world, either. One could hardly call her a proper Victorian, could one?"

"No—but she'd like to be," Philippe said slowly. "And given a chance, she'll get to be. You're a rebel, Martha; but Fanny's—an exile. You, consciously or unconsciously, reject our milieu—or at least the falsity, crudity, and hypocrisy in it. While Fanny *wants* to belong; and due to what was mostly just plain darned bad luck, has never been allowed to. I only hope that when I bring her back into this plush and gilt and gimcracky world of ours, she won't find it stifling. I often do. Well, here we are, I do believe?"

Martha glanced out of the pullman car's window. Philippe saw her face go white. Then she was up and running down the aisle. He got up, took Fanny by the arm.

"Come on!" he said.

When they got to the platform between the cars the train was still moving. But they could see Bill Turner standing there on the siding with Martha. She had jumped from the car without waiting for the porter to lower the stairs, or for the train to come to a full stop, which, considering the length of the skirts a lady wore in the 1890s, and the number of petticoats she had under them, had been exceedingly foolish, involving as it did the risk of a broken leg, if not a broken neck.

But, now, hearing Fanny's soft, helpless "Oh, Phil! Oh, Phil—he looks *awful*," Philippe understood why. Martha still had her arms about her husband and was crying. Bill Turner patted her cheek clumsily with his one free hand—the other gripped the stout walking stick he needed to get about now—and growled:

"Now, Martha! Now, now, Martha! Don't—you mustn't—"

"But you shouldn't have come to meet us, Bill!" Martha

stormed. "You simply shouldn't have!"

He looks, Philippe thought with aching pity, like death's own twin brother!

He helped Fanny down from the car. She made a wild dash towards her father. But a yard away from him she stopped, and burst into a galestorm of sobbing.

"Oh Papa!" she wailed, "you look so *awful!*"

Bill Turner took his arm from around Martha's waist, drew Fanny to him, kissed her wet cheeks. And this unexpected gesture of tenderness from him came close to breaking her. She clung to him and sobbed and sobbed until both Philippe and Martha had to draw her away.

"Now baby, now baby—" Bill mumbled. "You'll ruin your pretty eyes a-crying that way! C'mon now, let me look at you, missy!" He put his hand under her chin and lifted her face, stared at it a long moment, then got out in a husky whisper the two slow words: "Lord God!"

"Papa!" Fanny said then, fiercely. "If you—if you say I look just like—Mama—I'll throw myself under the next train that comes by!"

"Then, baby," Bill Turner said, "you're going to live to be a hundred. Because you don't look *anything* like her anymore. When you were plump, you did. Maebelle ran to beef. But now you're something else again. A *real* beauty, I'd say. Delicate, fine. Don't you agree, Phil? And excuse me, son—for not saying Welcome Home afore now—"

Moved by a sudden impulse, Philippe put his arm about Bill Turner's shoulders and hugged him as he would have his own father. But he didn't kiss his cheek, as he also would have done to his father without a second thought. That would have been too much. Americans found such demonstrations of affection between men embarrassing.

But Bill Turner's face flushed with real pleasure at the gesture.

"Glad to have you back, son," he said; then: "Join us for supper tonight? Something's come up—and we've got to have sort of family conference. I'd like to count you in on it, Phil. It sort of concerns you, seeing as how you're almost family now—"

Philippe felt as much as heard the note of unease fairly crawling through the big man's voice. He stared at the detective. You could still legitimately call Bill Turner big;

but that bigness was all bones, now. His suit hung loosely off his great frame. And Fanny was right: he looked awful. He was one of those square-built men to whom a certain stoutness is essential; and his present thinness was painful to look upon.

"Sir," Philippe said. "I'm afraid I can't, tonight. You see—"

"Oh, Phil!" Fanny wailed.

"Now, just you behave yourself, Miss Frances Turner!" Martha said grimly. "Philippe, since you seem to need reminding, has a father, a mother, and a goodly number of sisters, all of whom he hasn't seen in almost a year because of you. So, under the circumstances—"

"I don't care!" Fanny cried. "They don't count! He doesn't belong to them anymore, Martha! He's mine, you hear me, mine!"

"Lord!" Bill Turner said. "Women! And in spite of all we know about 'em, we go right on marrying them. All right, son. Another night, then; but come to see me as soon as you can. It's important, mighty important . . ."

"Bill," Martha said, "he *knows* about Billy's trouble. I told him."

"Not that, honey," Bill Turner said sadly. "Something else, something a darned sight worse than that. And I don't believe Phil's folks know about it yet; just heard it myself, day before yesterday; but the only fair thing is to give him all the facts so he'll be prepared when they do find out. Because they will—everybody will—that's just the trouble!"

"Couldn't you tell me *now*, sir?" Philippe said.

Bill Turner frowned.

"No, son," he said. "Hardly the place for it, seems to me. We've got to have quiet and privacy both to discuss this. By the way, isn't anyone coming to meet you? Your Pa at least? 'Pears to me that—"

"Bill," Martha sighed, "at times you're positively— dense!"

Fanny whirled then, came over to Philippe with what was half a skip and scamper, half a dancing step. Like all her movements now, it was very graceful.

"But *I'm* not," she whispered. "You didn't tell them, did you, Phil? You didn't notify them that you were coming for fear that they *would* come to meet you and find you here with me. So—now—go home! Run home to your mama and your sisters—little Creole boy! You don't have to come to see me *ever* again—since you're that *ashamed* of me, forget me, will you?"

"Fanny!" Martha said, "if you don't stop behaving like a wildcat I don't know what's going to become of you!"

"I do," Fanny said. "I'm going to hell on roller skates! When Phil lets his family break us up, the way they're trying to—I'm not going to stick a knife in myself or take too many pills. I'm just going to go—bad. The way they already say I am. Follow in Mama's footsteps likely, and—"

Bill Turner's big hand came down on his daughter's shoulder. He whirled her around, as effortlessly as though she were a china doll.

"That," he said, "is one thing that's never going to happen, Fanny. Because I'm not going to let it. Before I'll allow you take that road, I'll strangle you with my bare hands. You hear me, daughter?"

"Yes, Papa," Fanny whispered, then: "Papa—you mean you—you *care* about me, that much?"

"Yes, baby," Bill Turner said. "You're *my* daughter, and I care about you that much."

"Oh, Papa!" Fanny said, and threw herself upon her father so hard she almost knocked him down.

The pullman porter touched Philippe on the arm.

"Your bags, sir," he said, "and the ladies' . . ."

Philippe tipped him, said: "Call me a baggage porter to take 'em all out to the gate will you?" Then turning to the Turners: "I'll try to get away for coffee, anyhow, tonight—" he said.

"No," Martha said, "don't. Please don't, Philippe. One lesson, my boy—no woman wants a man to make a slave of her, that's true enough. But just the same, she instinctively despises a man whom she can rule. Make Fanny respect you. You'll have hell on earth with her if you don't. And keep the love of your family if it's humanly possible to do so. No one can blame them for their point of view. If this little idiot would use her head, she'd realize that it's up to *her* to convince them—by becoming the sort of wife you're entitled to, and deserve—"

Fanny stared at Martha.

"You—you mean I'm not—still, Martha?" she quavered.

"You're not," Martha said firmly. "You're ignorant and gauche and your manners are atrocious. And the reputation that makes Philippe's family reluctant to accept you didn't create itself, child. You have to shoulder a certain amount of blame for it—to quote your father here—even if only through sentimentality and folly rather than any innate viciousness on your part. From where I stand, Philippe's patience with you has been astonishing. I assure you nine men out of every ten would have left you long ago—instead of spending time and money he can ill afford to save you, cherish you, lift you up—"

"Martha—" Fanny whispered, "you—you *hate* me don't you? You think I'm *awful!*"

"Sometimes I come pretty close to it," Martha said grimly. "But the truth is, I don't. I'm afraid I love you, child. Or else I'd keep my mouth shut and let you put on those roller skates you mentioned. I've always had a weakness for cripples, I suppose; birds with broken wings and the like—"

"Cripples!" Fanny gasped; then: "Yes—I see what you mean. I am, aren't I? Crippled—my mind, anyhow—and my heart—"

She turned then, went up to Philippe.

"That's why I mostly can't help being so awful, Phil, honey," she whispered. "When you're always—hurting—you get so you want to hurt back. So you hit out at whoever's close to you, whether they're the ones who made you hurt in the first place or not. So now—I beg your pardon, humbly, and from the bottom of my heart. I don't want you to leave me—ever. If you do, I'm sure I couldn't live—"

"Fanny," Philippe croaked, "I—"

Fanny turned her face toward her father.

"Papa," she said with immense dignity, "d'you mind if Philippe kisses me good-bye? He wants to, and I want him to. And we're engaged. Please, Papa?"

"Of course," Bill Turner said. "A kiss never hurt anything. 'Specially not in a railway station. Lord, I'm tired! Appears to me we've been here for hours—"

"We have," Martha said. "That's enough, you lovebirds! Tell Philippe good-bye, Fanny, and come on—"

But Fanny stayed where she was—in Philippe's arms.

"Phil," she said, "why's that old nigger woman staring at us like that? She knows you?"

Philippe turned. But the black woman, dressed in a stiffly starched nursemaid's uniform and leading two small white children by the hands, was not one of the Sompayac's servants, as he had feared when Fanny had called his attention to her. Nor was she employed in the home of any one of his family's close friends, or else he would have recognized her. But she *was* staring. There was a look of outraged shock on her massive and immensely dignified face.

And that, in itself, was enough. That she knew him was evident. And the consequences of this unknown Negro nursemaid's reaction to his having kissed Fanny in public were as inevitable as death and taxes. By tonight, at the worst, by tomorrow afternoon at the best, his mother would have received a full—and suitably embroidered— account of his scandalously public misbehavior.

His heart sank to his boot tops. For there was one neuralgic detail that he hadn't, and couldn't, tell Fanny: His father, mostly to maintain a semblance of peace chez les Sompayacs, had allowed his mother to believe that he had *sent* Philippe abroad as his, and the company's, business representative, in the hope that once his only son and heir had seen how the import-export business was run, how great was its scope, its importance, he might well be persuaded to drop cette drôle d'idée of studying medicine. But now the fat was in the fire indeed.

'They,' Philippe thought, 'serve as the chorus in all our tragedies, don't they? The bearers of tidings, usually ill. Their vengeance, I suppose for all we've robbed them of: freedom, dignity, pride—'

"Well?" Fanny demanded.

"Don't know her," he said shortly. "Probably shocked at seeing me kiss you like that."

"Hm-m-m!" Fanny said. "Shock her some more, Phil—huh, please?"

"No you don't, young lady! You've made enough of a spectacle of yourself already, it seems to me," Martha said. "Now, come on!"

# Chapter Seventeen

Fanny looked at her father. Her eyes didn't move. They might as well have been made of gray-blue glass for all the expression they had in them. 'Except no glass could ever be that pale,' Martha thought, 'nor any artisan—or artist, for that matter—duplicate that color—if it *is* a color, really. Sometimes I doubt it.'

"Don't look at me like that!" Bill Turner said, fretfully. "Fan, makes a fellow's flesh crawl, to tell the truth about it! Swear to God if I believe you've heard a word I said. Lord, child, I'm doing the best I can! I—"

"You're—getting rid of me," Fanny said, her voice flat, toneless, chill. "I've been home maybe four, five hours, and already you want me out of your sight . . ." Her voice rose, edged: "Papa, listen to me! I didn't pick my mother! *You* did! I can't help it if I remind you of her. This is my home—and I want to stay in it! You—you're my father—and I—I love you. Though Lord knows why, the way you treat me! I can start school in September. Oh, Papa—let me have *one* summer at home with you and Martha and—and Phil. Yes—I admit that, too! A girl's got a right to a little courting, hasn't she? Oh, *now* I see! That's it, isn't it? You—you don't trust me, do you? You're *sure* I'm going to turn out just like Mama. So you keep pushing me off and pushing me off and pushing me off—until you don't give me any choice! One of these days I'm going to say to myself: 'All right, Fanny, your papa thinks you're no good! So why fight against him? Get yourself a thin silk dress and go stand in line in Frankie Belmont's Parlor!' "

"Fanny!" Martha said.

Bill Turner bent his head. The gesture tore Martha's heart. And Fanny's. It was the first time that either of them had ever seen him acknowledge defeat.

"Papa!" Fanny sobbed. "I—"

"The day after you do that," Bill Turner said quietly, "you can change into a black one, baby. To wear to your old man's funeral. You would have that much respect, wouldn't you?"

Fanny came flying to where he sat, threw both her thin arms around his neck, buried her face against his collar, shivering, sobbing, babbling:

"I didn't mean it, Papa! You *know* I didn't mean it! Only I—"

Bill Turner looked up at his wife.

"Tell her the truth, Bill," Martha said. "Can't you see it's the only way?"

Bill put his arms around his daughter's waist, drew her down until she was sitting on his knees. "Listen to me, baby," he said. Then he told her.

Fanny listened, her face growing whiter and whiter, her eyes twin polar stars, reflecting the color of a fjord, until he had finished.

"That's it," he said sadly. "That's why you've got to leave New Orleans, Fanny. You see that, don't you? I even wrote to that school you mentioned in your letters: the one you and that girl friend of yours were thinking about going to. The little girl who—who died . . ."

"Sue Beaconridge," Fanny whispered.

"Yes. And, like I said, I wrote that school. But it wasn't until yesterday that I heard from them; mainly because the name's been changed. It's called the Emma Willard School now—not the Troy Female Seminary. And it's been called that for some years, so I don't see—"

"How poor Sue got it wrong?" Fanny said. "She didn't. She told me the new name, but she said all the old families in Troy went on calling it the Female Seminary out of force of habit. I guess I just didn't remember the new name, that's all . . ."

"Anyhow," Bill Turner went on, "they've got summer courses, and since you've got an awful lot of back schooling to make up, I thought—"

"All right, Papa," Fanny whispered; "I'll—go. You're right. I have to go, don't I? To give me 'n Phil even a ghost of a chance, I have to. Oh, Jesus! What did she have to come back *here* for? To ruin everything for everybody! And to pull a low-down, dirty, filthy stunt like that! So that *everybody*'ll know what kind of business my mother and your wife—your ex-wife, anyhow; that's where you've got it all over me, Papa! You could divorce her; but I'll never get her rotten blood out of my veins!—

is in. Of course Phil's folks will break us up, now. Who wouldn't? Don't blame 'em! Oh, why'd she have to come back? Tell me that, Papa, why?"

Bill Turner looked at his daughter. His eyes were very bleak.

"You hit it the first shot, honey," he said. "She came back—at least she chose New Orleans to come back to—deliberately. And for the reasons you said, child. To ruin everything for everybody. Her way of getting even, sure as hell's afire. I—bested her. Took *you* away from her. Got married again to a good woman. Stayed honest. Been—happy. Too much for Maebelle to take, I reckon. So—"

He shook his head, fell silent. None of them said anything. 'What is there,' Martha thought, 'really to be said?' The silence lasted a long time. A very long time—until, finally, Fanny broke it.

"Papa—" she said, "can I go out for a little while?"

"Lord God, child; it's almost nine o'clock at night!"

"I know that. But—I've got to talk to Phil, Papa. Warn him. It's not fair not to. So I thought—"

"Now, Fanny," Martha said, "you simply can't go knocking on a young man's door this time of night and asking to speak to him. That, child, would give his family an even worse impression of you than they have right now . . ."

"I know that, Martha. And that's *not* what I mean to do. I'm going to take a cab down to Dr. Bienvenu's drugstore. He's put a telephone in, Eliza was telling me. And I know from Phil that Mr. Sompayac has one, too. So I'll just call and ask to speak to Phil. *That's* not so bad, is it?"

"Well—no," Martha said doubtfully. She was thinking: 'How does morality cope with scientific innovation? Does physical absence change—or modify—intent?' She said:

"But surely you don't mean to shout all this over a telephone in a drugstore full of people! Dear God, Fanny! That would be the very worst thing you could do!"

"No 'm," Fanny said. "I'll tell Phil—to—to meet me—in front of the St. Louis. Papa, please! I'll make him bring me home before eleven o'clock! But this *can't* wait, don't you see? I've got to get him prepared before somebody springs it on him cold. Like Rodney Schneider, for instance. Wouldn't that make a rotter like him happier'n old

Ned—to be able to tell Phil *who* Maebelle Hartman *is;* and *what* she does for a living!"

"It probably would," Bill Turner said soberly, "all the more so because he and his gang have already become steady clients of Maebelle's establishment. All right, go call Phil; but—Martha, don't you think you ought to go with her? For appearance's sake, anyhow?"

"No," Martha said, "with me along, they couldn't talk freely. And Fanny's right; Philippe must be told as soon as possible. Putting it off is too dangerous. You can trust Fanny, Bill. She's been through an awful lot—and it's matured her, more than you think. Very well, young lady. But eleven o'clock means eleven o'clock, you hear me?"

"All right," Bill Turner said. "But if you get here one minute late, daughter, nineteen years old or not, I'll have your hide!"


Philippe broke off the glowing description he had been giving of Italy's glories, architectural and otherwise, and stared at the door of the dining room. He was sure he'd heard a faint noise outside in the hall. He hesitated a long moment, then went on again. Thinking: 'Nerves! Damn it all, I'd feel better if that nigger nurse maid had already got the bad news to Maman, instead of having to wait like this for all hell to pop loose!' He said: "And then, from Perugia, I went down to Assissi to see the relics of St. Francis and Ste. Claire; but—"

He stopped short, because the door definitely *was* opening. Everyone stared at it. Then Henri, Philippe's manservant, stuck his head through the opened door, quickly got out the French equivalent of, "Oh, excuse me!" and closed it again, but not before giving a most significant toss of his head in the direction of the stairs.

"That's odd!" Marie-Thérèse said; "I've never seen Henri act like that before. Come bursting into a room without knocking I mean. Philippe! I'll bet you brought him some Italian wine as a present!"

"No, I didn't," Philippe said, "but I did manage to get a few bottles of Chianti Ruffino and Vino Blanco de Orvieto in unbroken—"

"And undrunk?" Brigitte teased.

"And undrunk," Philippe said easily, "for you, Papa. Still, Marie-Thérèse has a point. From the way that fat scoundrel acted just now, I'd better take a look to see whether they're still tightly corked. Excuse me a minute, all. I'll be right back. With the bottles, Papa. I strongly suspect you'd better lock 'em up!"

But, the minute he started up the stairs toward his room, he saw Henri at the head of them. At once, with a fine sense of theater, the little Creole mulatto winked one eye at his master, and placed his index finger across his lips.

Philippe looked nervously over his shoulder. The door of the sitting room was still closed. Taking advantage of that fact, he dashed up the stairs, two at a time.

"What passes with you, vieux âne?" he demanded, sotto voce, once he was close enough.

"Her!" Henri gasped. "Cette Fille! Mam'zelle Turner! Dans votre chambre, maître! I slipped her up the back stairs, me. I told her 'n told her 'twas not right for a young lady to visit a young gentleman here; but she wouldn't listen! Said she had to see you! Said she was desperate and—"

"Douce enfant Jésus!" Philippe said.

"Ce n'était pas de toute ma faute à moi, maître!" Henri groaned: "She was—hysterique—you know, her? Crying and wringing her hands. I was scairt she'd start in to scream. 'N—'n—you knows damn well down here, maître, white girl all by herself wit a black boy starts in a-screaming, that nigger's *daid*, him—afore nobody starts in to ask her why . . . Please, maître, I—"

"It's all right, vieux âne," Philippe said. "Wait! Don't go! I'm going to need you in a couple of minutes. Stay here by the door."

Philippe pushed open the door a scant inch. Stopped dead. Instead of standing by the window, or sitting in his chair, Fanny lay stretched out in his bed. Of course she was fully clothed; but if his mother or his sisters came up those stairs right now, that would have made very little difference.

He opened the door, slipped into the room, hissed:

"You get up from there, Fanny!"

"Why?" she mocked, smiling at him, although by the light of the gasjet that Henri had thoughtfully lit before summoning him, he could see that her eyes were swollen almost shut from crying. "What better place could I be,

mon amour? Place I mean to spend all the rest of my life
in. Tell you what, Phil, hon—you better hire us a good
cook, else you'll starve to death. 'Cause I sure don't mean
to get out of bed for our first six months of married
life—or let you get up either! So—"

"Fanny, in God's name, will you get up from there?"

"No. Your Papa comes up here and finds me in your
bed, he'll *make* you marry me, honorable as he is. You're
going to tell me he wouldn't?"

"No," Philippe said flatly. "But my mother would cut
her own throat on the church steps the day the ceremony
took place. And that, ma chère Fanny, carries considerable weight with Papa—"

Fanny stared at him. Her pale eyes darkened a trifle.

"And—with you," she whispered.

"And with me," Philippe said. "Now, will you get up
from there?"

Fanny looked at him; turned her Medusa's, Gorgon-
Head's, Basilisk's gaze upon him, pierced him through
with twin spears of light, unwavering and undimmed by
the liquid crystal that brimmed over from her eyes. She
came upright very slowly in the bed, swung her legs from
the side, stood up.

"All right," she said. "I'm going. Good-bye, Phil. But
don't come to my funeral. You're not invited."

"Fanny!" he said.

"I thought you loved me. Should have known better.
From experience, even. Anytime a girl's fool enough to let
a fellow get up in between her legs, he—"

Philippe caught her by the shoulders and shook her
hard enough to almost snap her neck.

"You little fool!" he grated. "Just when I had everything all arranged—or almost—you have to come here
and ruin it all! Now come on! We're going to have a talk,
you and I, Miss Frances Turner! That is if I don't take a
buggy whip to you the way I ought to!"

"Phil—" Fanny whispered, making of his name a
moaning sound.

"Come on!" he said. "No, wait! I've got to arrange
things first. Stay right where you are; but don't even
breathe, damn you! I'll be back in a sec—"

He went outside. Fanny pressed her ear up against the
door, heard him say:

"Tell Papa I was called away. An emergency. Yes, yes! Tell him it had to do with Mademoiselle Turner—he'll believe that—but you don't know the details. Non par le pétit bon Dieu! Not now—give me five minutes to get her out of here!"

They tiptoed down the back stairs together. The door of the kitchen was open. Philomèle, the cook, was bustling about before the range. Philippe gripped Fanny's arm so hard she almost cried out from the pain; but seeing his intent, she subsided. The minute Philomèle turned her immense back to the door, Philippe yanked Fanny past in it one wild rush. Thirty seconds later they were running down the back alley. When they got to the sidewalk, they stopped.

"Phil—" Fanny moaned.

"Shut up!" he hissed. "I've got to find us a cab!"

Getting a hanson proved easy enough at that still early hour of the night; but, once they were inside it, Philippe pushed up the little trap door in the top, and said to the driver, who sat above and behind the cab itself on a high seat, with the reins by which he guided the horse trailing across the roof.

"Martin's Livery Stable—on Poydras Street. And quickly, my good man!"

Fanny stared at him, her eyes luminous in the darkness.

"Why're you taking me to a livery stable, Phil?" she said.

"Because tonight, bébé, considering all the things we've got to talk about, three's a crowd, even if one of 'em's only a cabdriver," Philippe said.

Half an hour later, this time in a rented buggy, drawn by a rented horse, they set out again.

"Phil—" Fanny said, "don't be mad at me—please, huh? I *had* to come. I even went down to Dr. Bienvenu's drugstore and called you on the telephone, first. I looked up your Papa's number in the book and gave it to the operator—after Dr. Bienvenu had cranked his arm half off to get *her* to answer. But it rang and rang—I could hear it, Phil!—and nobody answered it!"

"Of course not, Fan. The telephone is in Papa's *office*, not at home. And at that time of night there's nobody there. Papa refuses to put a 'phone in the house. Swears Maman and the girls would call him up all day long so he'd never be able to get any work done—"

He stopped, looked at her, sighed a little.

"All right," he said. "I'm not angry anymore. At least not *very*. But before you start in to tell me why you just had to see me at almost ten o'clock at night—that is, if you even had a sensible reason, which, knowing you, I doubt—let me say this: Fan, you've just got to give me time to win Maman over. Of course, Papa's on our side; but when Maman really gets started she's too much for even him, and she's heard—"

"That I'm no good. A cheap, dirty, little—"

"Fanny, goddamn it; don't you start *that* again!"

Fanny turned away. Turned back to face him.

"Phil—" she whispered, "kiss me?"

He obliged.

"Hm-m-m—" Fanny murmured, "don't quit, Phil. Kiss me some more. Some slow sweet long time more—"

"No, damn it!" Philippe said.

"Why not, mon amour?" She pronounced the words "mon amour" with a perfect accent, having learned them from Philippe himself.

"Because—hell, Fan? You *know* why not!"

"Don't care. No, that's not right. Not quite, anyhow. I—I *want* to. Don't you?"

"Yes. But we can't. Not now. Not tonight."

"Same question: Why not, Philippe, mon amour?"

"Because—oh, Christ! Because I fully intended to stay home tonight—en famille, Fanny. And I didn't—"

"Bring your overshoes along, so now you're afraid of getting your feet wet?" Fanny said, bitterly.

"I'm afraid of giving you a baby out of season," Philippe said bluntly, "so quit this, will you?"

She stared away from him out into the night.

"That's the difference between us," she said softly, "no baby of yours would ever be out of season far as I'm concerned. He'd be—mighty welcome—anytime he showed up. Anytime at all. But then that's because I *love* you, while you don't—"

"Merde!" Philippe howled, and dragged her into his arms. But she kissed him so softly, sweetly, gently that the mounting passion in him died. When he turned her loose, she lay against him, pillowing her head upon his shoulder.

"Phil," she said, "take me someplace—and—and find us

a justice of the peace. Right now. Tonight. Wait! I'm not asking you to—to give up being an intern. Like you said, you've got to make a living for both of us. I just want to be married to you before you go. I'll wait. And I'll be good. I won't even look at another fellow sideways 'til you come back, so help me! And—"

"Fanny," he said sternly, "you know what you're asking? That *your* father, your poor sick father, go on supporting *my* wife."

"Oh Jesus!" Fanny said. "What do you have to be so doggoned honorable for, Phil? That's *not* what I'm asking—not at all. 'Sides, I'll get a job—support myself. Would that make you feel better?"

"Considering the kind of job—if any—you could get with your education, or rather the lack of it; no, Fan," Philippe said.

"Phil—I wish you'd get that ramrod the heck out of your backbone—just a little," Fanny said. "You can't be honorable all the time. You can't be. Or this plain damn stupid, either. It'll cost you too much—"

"It'll cost me more not to be," Philippe said.

"As much as not giving in a little is going to cost you?" Fanny whispered.

"And what, may I ask, is that going to cost me?" Philippe said.

Fanny looked at him; across his mind formed, all unbidden, the images, the valley of the shadow, with eyes—again the words grew in him, hugely symbolic—pale as death is pale, big with ten thousand years of pain.

"Me," she said. "It's going to cost you—me, Phil. But I reckon that doesn't matter very much to you, does it?"

He took her small, heart-shaped face between his two hands, bent and kissed her mouth.

"*You* be the judge of that, Fanny," he said.

"All right—" she sighed. "I reckon you *do* love me—a little bit, anyhow. So now I've got to tell you—how come—why, we can't wait, I mean. My mother, my real mother—came back to New Orleans last month. Just like she left, on the arms of a tinhorn sport—name of Hartman, this one. Seventy-odd years old. Rich. And a jackass. But then a fellow who'd take up with Mama would have to be, wouldn't he?"

"Fan—" Philippe began.

"Let me finish. She's taken his name. Calls herself Maebelle Hartman, now. And he's set her up in business—the only business she knows: bustle hustling—peddling tail. Only she's too old to hustle her own these days. Must be plumb worn out by now—"

"Fanny!" Philippe said.

"You figure it, Phil. At twenty-five fellows a night, three hundred and sixty-five nights a year, multiplied by—let me see—thirteen years she's been at it now, at least that folks *know* about—Of course you have to subtract four or five nights twelve times a year for her monthlies, if she even did subtract 'em—"

"Petit enfant Jésus!" Philippe said.

"Adds up to quite a crowd. You work it out, lover. I never was any good at arithmetic. Anyhow, she's back. And in business. Number Two-Twenty-Two North Basin Street, if you're interested in changing your luck—or something. Got herself a whole stable of riding fillies for dead-game sports. Like Rod Schneider and pals. They've quit patronizing Frankie Belmont's place altogether. Mama's girls are better-looking, I'm told. Fresher. Less beat up. Got more changes of gait. The talk is that there's *nothing* a fellow can think up they won't do—"

"Dear God!" Philippe whispered.

"So there you have it, lover. The reason you've got to marry me right now—or never. Because when your folks find *this* out, as they will, not even *you* can be fool enough to believe that they won't invent some way to break us up. Have you declared insane, maybe, and make it stick. 'Cause marrying the daughter of a woman who is a whore way out in San Francisco, California, is one thing; but getting hitched to a girl whose mama is the madam of a parlor house right here in New Orleans is damn sure another—"

"It'll make no difference," Philippe said, lamely. "I—"

"That is, if you can even *stand* being married to me, knowing. 'Cause I can tell you right now before you open your mouth what you're going to say. That we can live up North. New York, maybe, where nobody knows me. Only *you'll* know me. You'll remember that before you married me I'd been to bed with Rod Schneider every damn time he crooked his little finger in my direction. That he and his three buddies played ring-around-the-rosy, or musical chairs, or spin the bottle—grown-up style—with me the same night. That I came down to your cabin on the steamship and begged you on my knees to do it to me—"

"Fanny, for Christ's sake!" Philippe said.

"And then one day I'll start noticing that when you're holding li'l Phil, or little Susie—name I picked for our girl, after poor Sue Beaconridge, hon; hope you don't mind—in your arms, you're sort of examining them real close to see if they look like you really. And you'll drive off to attend to your house calls, and maybe kill a patient with the wrong pills because you can't keep your mind on your work for wondering who's warming your bed for you every time you leave home. And the worst part about it would be that I'd just have to bow my head and cry my eyes out and take it. 'Cause I *couldn't* leave my babies. I *couldn't*, Phil! Not like I could leave everything right now, if you decide you don't want me. Reckon I'm a damn fool to love you that much. But I do. I can't help it. So it's up to you, Phil. You make up your mind. I won't hold it against you if you think you'd better give me up. Only sensible thing you could do, really—"

"And you," he said, harshly, "I suppose you'll make your usual threats if I *were* to call it quits, Fan?"

She looked at him, and her eyes were very bleak.

"Kill myself, you mean?" she said. "No, Phil. 'Cause that way I wouldn't be around to enjoy seeing you suffer. I've got a better way now. Reckon I'd just put on a silk dress and join the lineup in Mama's parlor. You could come to visit me. For you it'll always be free, honey. I'll fix it up with Mama so that—"

"Fanny, I'm going to slap you in a minute!"

She smiled at him slowly, tenderly.

"Phil, honey—would it *really* hurt you if I did that?" she said.

His voice came out with a grate in it, a shake, a tearing.

"Hurt's the wrong word. It would—kill me, Fan," he said.

"Oh, Phil!" she said, and kissed him. She nestled there in his arms, quietly, her eyes flickering pale summer lightnings against the night.

"Funny thing," she said; "that's exactly what Papa said

when I told him I'd probably end up in some parlor
house's lineup."

"You told your *father* that?"

"Yes, I was—upset. No—that's not true. I was poison-
mean mad and yelling like a drunken nigger market
woman. 'Cause you see it was Papa who told me about
Mama's coming back here. Swears she only did it to get
even with him. He's probably right, at that. Only he wants
to send me away. Tomorrow. The next day. To a girl's
school. Even picked the one I'd told him in my letters I'd
like to go to: the Emma Willard School in Troy, New
York. That's the school poor little Sue and I were planning to go to, together."

"But, Fanny!" Philippe said, his voice reedy with relief,
"that's just perfect! I'll be interning in New York City, so
we can see each other at Christmas and Easter and—"

"See each other, how? As man and wife—or as a dead-
game sport, sneaking his fun filly up the back stairs?"

"Fanny, for God's sake! Oh, all right! We would see
each other as a properly engaged couple, you wearing my
ring on your finger for all the world to see. And as for the
back stairs, that would depend entirely upon you, ma
chère Fanny! All you'd have to do would be say, meaning
it, 'No, Phil.' And that would be that."

She looked away from him, said, very quietly:

"No, it wouldn't, as you know damn well. I might say
it; but I'd never *mean* it. I'm my mother's daughter, Phil.
Hot as a two-dollar nickel-plated pistol. For you, anyhow.
Good girls can say 'no,' 'cause they don't even *like* being
loved. With you, I love it. I want it all the time. Want
you all the time. Can't sleep for thinking how nice—No!
that's the wrong word!—how damn fine, lovely, great,
wonderful it would be to have you there loving me to
sleep, taking all the time in the world about it—slow—s-
s-slo-ow-w—all night maybe—and—".

"Fan, for God's sake let's change this subject, shall
we?" His voice had thickened. He sounded as though he
were strangling.

She smiled at him, said:

"You see? Phil, honey—turn this damn nag down that
little road. Over there. To your right, dearest! Lots of
trees, don't you see? Nice and dark—"

"Fanny, no! I told you I didn't bring—"

*ged up against him, found his mouth—
'...God!' he groaned inside his mind. 'Dear God help
me! I

He turned the horse into the little road.


## Chapter Eighteen


Fanny sat there at her desk. But she wasn't listening to
the lesson. American Literature One, The New England
Poets, Miss Maud Barlett, Instructor. She was looking out
of the window toward where the elms and birches shaded
the campus of the Emma Willard School for Young
Ladies in Troy, New York, without seeing the lovely trees
any more than she heard Miss Barlett's lecture. What she
was doing was smoldering with an irritation little short of
actual anger. And the subject of that irritation was, as
usual, Philippe Sompayac.

'He shouldn't have been so—relieved,' she thought bitterly. 'Relieved—nothing! Plain damn happy—that what
he was so scared of happening—didn't. So he was right—
so it would maybe have ruined everything for us to have
to get married in a hurry. I was relieved too—in a way—
but he shouldn't have been so *glad!* Couldn't half read his
darn letter, his words were dancing so all over the page—
from joy . . .'

Her pale eyes were glacial suddenly.

'Makes me wonder—if he was just glad he didn't have
to marry me right then—or if he's not maybe hoping
he—he'll *never* have to. No—that, no. 'Cause when he
says that he didn't even know what love—what making
love, anyhow, could be like 'til he met me, he's telling the
truth. Lord, what a night! Thought I was going to die.
That my heart was plain going to stop—Jesus! Feeling
*that* good *hurts.* You just know you aren't going to be
able to stand it. And—and you don't! You—die. Just for
a sec—you die dead—and—and go to heaven and roll
around on all those soft pink clouds—'til your mind
comes back and you hear yourself—begging and praying
and crying—

Her head came up. Her gaze became more distant still.

'Martha *knew*. Only she didn't say anything to Papa.
Thank the Lord he was asleep when I got in! Must have
been way after midnight—and—she looked at me, looked
at my mouth—Lord God, but my lips were swollen from
the way he'd mashed 'em up—and at my eyes, and she
knew. That I—that I'd been doing *that*. Being bad. Huh!
If that's bad, don't show me anything good, Lord Jesus!
But she didn't say a word—Likely because she's a real
honest-to-god female woman herself, so she—understands—'

The glow in her pale eyes dimmed. The hint of blue in
them slid downscale into gray—into fog and frost, wintry
bleak.

'I was happy,' she thought sadly. 'For almost a month I
was—happy. Then—damn!—right on schedule, like clockwork—No little Phil. No little Sue. No—nothing. Oh,
Lord. S'posing I *never* can! Supposing I've messed myself
up too much with that kitchen knife or the vernols—or
just being sick too long—or the operation or—'

She was aware then of the little stirring in the class.
Miss Barlett's voice had changed somehow, become purr-
ing, warm. As a sort of echo, belatedly captured, what
she was saying came over to Fanny.

"Norma! How nice! You're early, my dear. Fall term
doesn't begin—"

"Until next week," the really lovely, truly musical contralto voice answered her. "I know that, Miss Barlett—
only I got bored at home—nothing to do—so I persuaded
father to let me come—"

Fanny turned in her seat and looked at the newcomer.
The girl was very tall, and willow slender. She had brown
eyes and chestnut hair and she moved with a grace that
Fanny hadn't the words to describe. "Sylphlike" would
have come close to it, but the abysmal poverty of Fanny's
vocabulary forever robbed her of the power of making
such literary flourishes. What she thought was: 'She
moves so—so nice! I mean nicely. Delicate-like. Graceful.
And she's pretty, too. Odd—but pretty for real—'

"May I stay and listen in on this class, Miss Barlett?"
the girl called Norma said. "Since I've decided to become
a teacher, myself, it's—most instructive to watch how a
past master of the art does it—"

Maud Barlett hesitated. A tide of red rose in her

cheeks. She was visibly embarrassed.

"Well—yes, I suppose so, Norma," she said at last.

'That was funny,' Fanny thought. 'Acted like she didn't *want* her to stay. Don't see any harm in this long-tall girl's visiting—listening to the class. None at all . . .'

But what she did not, could not, know was that the causes of Maud Barlett's embarrassment lay not in the visit, itself, however inopportune, but rather in the identity and the personality of the visitor; and still less could she know that her—Fanny's own—presence in the class both deepened and intensified it. For already—innocently, involuntarily, and without even a ghost of a notion what the trouble was all about—Fanny had become involved in the curious relationship between Norma Tilson and Miss Barlett. Worse still, by simply being there, she had changed the carefully preserved parallelism of their lives—side by side, but *never* touching—into a triangle, a geometric figure having three aching points of contact, at least painful, if not actually destructive, to each of the three lifelines thereby connected. For since the moment she had first laid eyes upon the frail, pale, classically beautiful Southern girl, Maud Barlett had been just a little insane on the subject of Fanny Turner. "She looks just like a Rossetti painting!" she had said so many times to Mrs. Redfern, the headmistress of the school, that that outwardly glacial statue of New England granite with the frost lines showing through had been moved to say:

"Constrain your enthusiasms, will you, Maud? They might be misinterpreted. And there were other schools of painting beside the pre-Raphaelites, y'know. As far as your *very* strange little Confederate is concerned, I'd suggest you take a look at Reynolds—"

Whereupon Miss Barlett had—at least at what reproductions her personal volume of Hendrick's *History of English Painting* contained—and had come fluttering back to announce that Mrs. Redfern was entirely right.

"Of course I am," Mrs. Redfern said dryly. "The girl's a real beauty—a classical beauty. But I'm not sure she belongs here. Could become a problem, y'know—"

"A problem—how?" Miss Barlett had gasped.

"For one thing—her age. She's nineteen, older than nearly all of our seniors. And her ignorance is absolutely abysmal. I have yet to discover a single item of elementary schooling about which she has the faintest notion. Of course she has had to stay out of school several years because of illness—"

"Illness?" Miss Barlett whispered. "The poor dear! No wonder she's so pale!"

"She was in the same sanitorium with our dear departed Susan Beaconridge, and apparently they were fast friends. That's one of the reasons I took her—one of the two reasons—"

"And the other?" Miss Barlett said.

"Her stepmother is Martha Brantley. Martha was a freshman at Vassar when I was a senior. New York City family; but—solid. Brantley, Brantley, Brantley, and Cook, Corporation Lawyers. I did hear that Martha married—badly—one of her father's law clerks, who turned out to be a—womanizer. Apparently the child's *his*, but not hers. I don't know the details. Anyway, Martha wrote me from Italy, more or less appealing to me to admit her stepdaughter. The husband, one Turner—imposing name, nice aristocratic ring to it: William Pelham Turner—had written me several times before, but I'd been noncommittal until I heard from Martha. But now, Maud, I wonder—"

"I think you're being prejudiced!" Maud Barlett said hotly. "You just don't like Southerners—"

"A justifiable prejudice if there ever were one! But it isn't that. The girl's—strange. Her eyes—well—"

"Her eyes are *beautiful!*" Maud breathed.

"Maud, dear, your enthusiasm for feminine beauty seems a trifle excessive in a female—even, at times, to me," Mrs. Redfern said dryly. "And again, I must beg you to curb your public expression of it. There are people who might not understand your exquisite sensibilities. I was on the verge of writing the Reverend Doctor Tilson, suggesting that his daughter Norma might be happier somewhere else—for all that she's our very best scholar . . ."

"Oh, no, Jane!" Miss Barlett breathed. "You wouldn't!"

"I most certainly would—and I definitely will, the next time she's caught exchanging long, soulful kisses with an innocent schoolmate—and a freshman, at that—"

"Not so very innocent," Maud said tartly, "if she *let* Norma kiss her like that."

"Jealous, Maud?" Jane Redfern said.

"Oh, no! Jane, you don't believe—" Maud Barlett gasped. "You cannot possibly think—"

"I neither believe, nor think," Mrs. Redfern said calmly. "I know you much too well, my dear Maud; including the fact that your personal moral standards are very high indeed. All I'm trying to point out is that a schoolteacher must emulate Caesar's wife: live entirely above even base and baseless suspicions. So, therefore, Maud, when dear Norma returns for her senior year this fall, I hope you will refrain from walking across the campus together with your arms about each other's waists; and, as of today, I shall expect you to cease and desist from boring all and sundry with your paeans to Frances Turner's beauty. No school, nor any schoolmistress, can afford—and I do mean financially, my dear!—the splurge of withdrawals, not to mention the sudden decision of a great many wealthy alumnae *not* to send their daughters to their alma mater, that such unsavory gossip can cause. Have I made myself clear?"

Maud Barlett drew herself up very stiffly.

"Entirely," she said; "So much so that my resignation in writing will be on your desk tomorrow morning!"

"I'll tear it up if it is," Jane Redfern said, with a snort of quiet laughter. "Good English teachers are too hard to come by for me to let the best I've ever had go because every time she lifts her head out of her books, she leaves her brains behind. The subject's closed, Maud; I, for one, have no intention of raising it again—unless you force me to. But I hardly think you will; after all, you're not altogether a fool."

At which Maud Barlett had stormed out of the office of her employer—and lifelong friend—with the tears of helpless rage stinging her eyes.

But she had been more careful, nerving herself to be almost stern with Fanny now, telling herself that her indulgence of the girl's failings and lack of application had no deeper motivation than pity—for in the early fall of 1899, the word "latent" was still absent from the vocabulary of psychologists, and no one dreamed that a silly schoolgirl "crush" could mar and distort a woman's entire subsequent existence. As it had Maud Barlett's, a condition all the sadder for the fact that Maud had never set sail for the fair Isle of Lesbos, and never would; all her Sapphic

Odes remained unheard, unsung, even unwritten, somewhere below the level of her conscious mind.

But if she was unaware of her motivations, and even
upon occasion, and to a certain extent, lied to herself
about them, Maud Barlett was keenly alive to her reac-
tions, and almost childishly indulgent of them. Noting,
now, how Norma Tilson was staring at Fanny—'Literally,'
Maud thought, 'devouring the poor child with her
eyes!'—she gave way to an impulse that really wouldn't
have stood close scrutiny, not even her own, and said, her
voice breathless and a little thick:

"Fanny, my dear, will you recite 'The Village Blacksmith' for us? Surely you know it by now."

White-faced and stricken, Fanny got to her feet, darting
imploring glances for help about the class. But her classmates stared back at her, some of them already beginning
to smile in cruel anticipation of her failure.

"Under the village chestnut tree—" she began; but
there she stopped. The rest of it just wouldn't come.
'Damn stupid old poem!' she thought, 'I hate poetry anyhow—and, besides, how's a body supposed to remember
verses when she's got as much to worry about as I have?'

"Go on, Fanny," Miss Barlett said, hopefully, already
lost and bemused in her contemplation of all that pure
and classical loveliness.

Fanny tried again—and once more got no farther than
the chestnut's leafy shade. Maud Barlett saw Norma's
rather full lips curl into a small, slight, utterly contemptu-
ous smile.

"For goodness sakes, Fanny!" she said now with real
exasperation. "Can't you *ever* remember anything?"

Fanny bent her head. Her eyes felt like they had sand
in them. 'I won't cry!' she told herself, 'I won't!'

She lifted her face, turned Maud Barlett to stone with
that ice-gray, off-blue, mindless, soulless, unwavering
stare.

"No 'm," she said. "Reckon I can't. Just plain *born* stupid, I guess."

"Try!" Maud said, her voice stark-naked, the longing in
it displaying—and she all unknowing!—even its private
parts. Norma Tilson stopped smiling, stared from teacher
to pupil, her brown eyes questioning. Fanny tried, but she
couldn't; she truly couldn't.

And, in that repeated failure, Polly Stevens, who sat just behind her, saw her opportunity. Now Polly was not attending the summer courses because of poor scholarship; next to Norma Tilson herself, Polly Stevens was the brightest girl in the whole school. She was there, with three whole months to make up, because her incorrigible mischief-making had finally forced Mrs. Redfern to suspend her for half a semester. To her now, so splendid, so golden an opportunity as Fanny's dumb-beast flounderings presented was simply not to be missed. She bent over her notebook, scribbling busily. And, by the time Fanny had reached, for the third time, her dead end, "Under the village chestnut tree—" Polly was ready. Deftly she flipped the torn-out page from her notebook around Fanny's trembling form, so that it slid soundlessly upon the desk. Fanny bent her head again. Her pale gaze fell upon the huge block printed words. She looked up, triumphantly, and her voice rang out loud and clear:

"Under the spreading chestnut tree
The village blacksmith squirms.
For he's been eating chestnuts
And they are full of worms!"

The silence was absolute. It had thickness and texture. Then it broke apart. Exploded. The classroom rocked with a gale of silvery, girlish laughter. But Norma Tilson didn't laugh, or even so much as smile. She stared at the younger girls, her brown eyes icy with contempt.

"Fan-ny!" Miss Barlett gasped. "How dare you! I'll not tolerate—"

Then she saw Fanny's face. She had, of course, no way of knowing that Fanny was hearing simultaneously two waves of merciless youthful laughter widely separated in time. At her first dance, her schoolmates had laughed at her like this, because she had been grossly fat and pimply. And now, again, these new schoolmates, whom she had thought to hold off, if not dominate, by her really exquisite slender beauty, acquired at the cost of a literal, physical descent into hell itself, were laughing at her; but this time because she was an ignoramus and a fool.

She stood there a Galatea returned to her original condition, because no Pygmalion ever was, and the gods never kept their pledged and promised word. Except that no statue of marble or of ivory could have been so still, so unbreathing, or spilled pure anguish distilled into shifting facets of fractured light from those pale dead-soul's eyes—Dead, dead, dead, and damned! Maud Barlett's pity-wracked mind wailed.

Slowly, slowly, Fanny slid down the glissandos of her classmates' laughter—beginning to falter now—into her seat. Then she bent forward, burying her face against her crossed arms on her desk, and wept with a fury all the more cataclysmic for the fact that from between her ferociously clenched and grinding teeth, no slightest sound escaped.

The laughter stopped. Halted in midnote. Died. The girls stared at her, as she bent there shuddering and shaking under the paroxysms of a rage so pure, so foreign to their youthful, and hence limited, experience, that they had no way of recognizing it for what it was, still less of suspecting how murderously, suicidally she turned it in upon herself, blade down and breastward driving, conditioned as she was by then past the point of instinctuality to a belief indistinguishable from conviction in her own worthlessness, to a remorseless, implacable self-loathing, even more destructive than the kitchen knife or the sleeping pills had been; because, at worst, all those merely physical instruments of self-injury could have cost her was her life.

And by then she knew, had been taught, beyond all questioning or doubt that there are things much more to be dreaded than the simple, and often merciful, act of dying; for she, herself, had endured them, lived past them, though each time at a marked increase in the really fearful price she had had to pay, must go on paying still for the doubtful boon of existence: the death by silent inanition of her every hope, the steady weakening of her resistance, her nerve, her will, the slow erosion of *what* and *who* she was, becoming progressive, cancerous, and hence ultimately fatal to that peculiar and individual entity suffering in the world; though her body, that apparatus of flesh with all its tiresome, unlovely, even faintly disgusting functions, lived on, surviving the assaults that had first wounded, then maimed, and would finally leave cataleptic and comatose, if not dead, its indwelling Gnostic host.

But she could not have explained these things to Miss Barlett, or to her classmates, because quite simply, she hadn't so much as the words to—if the words for what she had already suffered, endured, even exist as such. At describing hell even great Dante failed.

Yet among all those present, there was one to whom explanations of any sort were totally unnecessary. For by then Norma Tilson was already out of her seat and up the aisle, her hand extended to touch Fanny's wildly trembling form.

"Norma!"—Miss Barlett's voice was a whipcrack—"I must ask you *not* to interfere! I propose to handle this matter in my own fashion. Please take your seat, I beg of you!"

Norma stared at Miss Barlett in utter shock. For the first time since they had known each other, Maud Barlett had spoken harshly to her. Then, again with that sylphlike—and curiously sibylline—grace, she turned and went back to her seat at the back of the room.

"Polly Stevens!" Maud Barlett said, her voice trembling a little with fury, "stand up! This is *your* doing, isn't it?"

"Yes, Miss Barlett," Polly wailed, "but—it was only a—a joke! I thought she'd know—realize—"

"Remain standing, Polly," Maud Barlett said, "stay right there where you are, while I tell you *why* Fanny didn't know it was a joke. Some of you older students remember Susan Beaconridge, don't you?"

"Yes, Miss Barlett—" the girls whispered.

"Well, she and Fanny were in the same sanitorium together—fighting for their lives, while you were learning all the things that Fanny doesn't know. Susan lost that fight. And I'm sure that up in heaven where she is, she isn't very proud of her schoolmates today. Fanny chose to attend our school out of loyalty to her—absent friend. I suppose, having known Sue, she thought she'd be among kindly, decent, civilized young ladies—instead of having for classmates a pack of female laughing hyenas—"

She saw, with an obscure and perverse sense of triumph, that more than half the girls in the room were crying, now. Even—a fact that increased her satisfaction all the more—Norma Tilson's eyes were wet.

"That's all I have to say," she said icily. "Class is dismissed. I shan't report this incident to Mrs. Redfern, nor take any further action—except one: You, Polly Stevens, must apologize to Miss Frances Turner, here and now! All right! Let me hear you!"

"Fanny—" Polly got out. "Please! Don't cry anymore! I'm sorry! You don't know how sorry I—"

Fanny raised her head, turned in her seat, faced Polly. Said, in a husky whisper of a voice:

"Why? It—isn't *your* fault—I'm an ignorant fool . . ."

Then she stood up, gathered her books together, and walked out of there. And the silence attendant upon her going was louder than any cry.

But she had not crossed half the campus before Norma Tilson caught up with her.

"Hello, Fanny—" Norma said, making a double trochee of the words. "I'm Norma. Norma Tilson—and we're going to be friends, you and I—"

Fanny stared at her. Norma shivered. 'Those eyes of hers,' she thought, 'would unnerve a stone statue—or even a dead person!'

"Are we?" Fanny whispered. "Why, Norma?"

"Because—you're beautiful. And I simply adore beautiful people, and beautiful things. Besides, it seems to me you need my help. I'll be blessed if I'll stand idly by and allow a stupid little creature like Polly Stevens to torment you, make you cry . . ."

Fanny went on staring at Norma; but now a little of the glacial hardness of her gaze softened, thawed ever so slightly.

"Doesn't matter," she muttered. "Besides it wasn't *her* I was mad—angry at, anyhow. It was me—I *hate* being so stupid; and everytime I *think* I'm getting a little smarter, something like *that* happens just to remind me I'm a fool."

Norma took her gently by the arm.

"I'm quite sure you're not, Fanny," she said crisply. "In fact, you impress me as being *very* wise. What you're doing is to confuse ignorance, which is simply not knowing—largely, in your case, because, having been sick and confined to a sanitorium for years, your opportunities for acquiring even a nominal degree of culture were distinctly limited—with stupidity, which is the inability to learn . . ."

'My God!' Fanny thought with awe, 'she talks just like a book . . .' She said, morosely: "If I'm not stupid, Norma, I sure Lord don't know who is!"

"Oh there're a good many stupid people in the world, a remarkably sizable portion of whom attend the Emma Willard School for Young Ladies," Norma said, "but what I propose to demonstrate to you, Fanny, darling, is that you're not numbered among them—"

Fanny studied her.

"Demonstrate it how?" she whispered.

"By tutoring you. You'll forgive my lack of false modesty if I tell you I'm the best scholar in the history of this school. In fact, I'm only quoting Mrs. Redfern when I say that. She looked up the records and found out that no girl who has ever been here, not even she, herself, ever made higher grades than mine. By that token, I'm eminently qualified to help you. And by another—that your—your great beauty—and your, well, call it personal charm—appeal to me, I'd be glad to, if you'll let me. Will you, Fanny?"

"I—I'd be ever so grateful if you would, Norma," Fanny said.

"Then, come on," Norma said. "No better time to begin than right now!"

They walked across the campus together, entered the dormitory, climbed the stairs to Norma's room. Norma opened the door, stood aside for Fanny to enter first; and, as she did so, a ray of afternoon sunlight fell on the photograph she had on the night table by her bed. It was of a tall, blond, exceedingly handsome young man, breeding showing in every line of him, an expression of cool hauteur, of self-recognized distinction lending an air of not-quite-sulky boredom to his aristocratic face.

"Who's *that?*" Fanny breathed: "Lord, Norma, is he *ever* good-looking!"

"Tony," Norma said dryly. "His parents and mine have the weird idea we should marry each other. Tony goes along, from sheer inertia likely, the cold fish! If you think he's good-looking, I'll make you a present of him, Fanny—duly gift-wrapped in Christmas tinsel. I'd be deuced happy to be rid of him—he bores me *stiff*. Oh, I say!

Come to think of it, you should *know* him. He's your—
your late friend Sue Beaconridge's brother—"

Fanny stared at that picture. And, for the very first
time a truly disloyal impulse towards Philippe stirred in
her mind; 'Watch out, Creole boy!' she thought suddenly,
'there're a heap more fish in the sea, y'know. Bigger fish.
Richer. Better looking . . .' But she stifled it at once, telling herself: 'You ought to be ashamed of yourself, Fanny—thinking a thing like that!'

Aloud, she said:

"I've heard an awful lot about him from Sue, but I've
never met him. He never did come to see her at the sanitorium while I was there—"

"He wouldn't," Norma said. "Tony loves Tony, period.
And with an all-consuming passion. Forget him. Sit down,
darling. Let me see—where shall we start?"

"Please, Norma, do you—do you think you could teach
me to talk—like *you* do? Saying the words right—all
crispy-like and fine? Like you could see 'em printed on the
air. And the—grammar. Never a mistake—not one. Like
a book talking—so—so refined—so elegant—"

"Which are two words, Fanny, dearest," Norma said,
"that elegant people, refined people *never* use. If you *are*,
they're unnecessary, don't you see? There, don't look so
stricken! Of course I can, you poor baby! Tell you
what—let's just talk—I'll listen to you—*without* correct-
ing you today. In order to get an idea about what you
*usually* do wrong. All right?"

"All right," Fanny said. "What'll we talk about,
Norma?"

"Anything your little heart desires, baby girl," Norma
said.

Fanny thought about that. Then she pointed towards
Anthony Beaconridge's photograph.

"Him," she said, "let's talk about him—"

Norma frowned.

"Fanny—don't tell me you're—a bit boy-crazy?" she
said dryly. "For if you *are* you'll disappoint me—deeply."

"No," Fanny said, angrily, "I *hate* boys, the bastards!
But—"

"That—" Norma purred, "is distinctly better. Only a
trifle inconclusive. You finished your sentence on a rising

note, and with the conjunction 'but'—indicating, shall we say, some reservation about the basic illegitimacy of the male sex—"

"No," Fanny said, the words of Philippe's last letter smoking through her mind, "I haven't got any reservations, Norma. What I started to say was what faster way can a girl go up in life besides riding on some damn man?"

"Usually," Norma said bitterly, "it's the other way around—at least as far as the riding's concerned, Fanny. But, either way, it's a distinctly whorish thought isn't it? Oh no, I don't disapprove! We should use them, the idiots—while preserving all our own personal liberty. All right—the subject's Tony—dear Tony. Why his ears aren't as long and hairy as they should be, I'm sure I don't know—What do you want to know about him?"

"Where does he go to school?" Fanny said. "Harvard?"

"Heavens, no! He hasn't the brains to get into one of the Ivy League Schools. He's a townie. That is, he goes to Rensselaer Polytechnic, right here in Troy. And the only reason they don't kick him out is that the Beaconridges are prominent contributors to the institute's endowment fund. Beyond being a perfect idiot, intellectually, his accomplishments consist of playing polo, very well indeed, tennis, average, sailing, first-rate, seduction of any halfway willing maiden, zero. He's awful at it. Even creatures who don't even remember when, where, or with whom it was they misplaced their alleged virtue laugh at him.

"In short, Tony is an ass—an insufferable, dim-witted, pompous ass whom I fell heir to because my mother's both a Troy girl and an alumna of this school, so she can't even imagine there are wider horizons. To her, beyond Troy lies only heaven—which is something in the nature of an understatement rather than an exaggeration of her point of view. Hence—Tony. Truth to tell, I'm rather fond of him—my maternal instincts I suppose. Anyone as backward as Tony stirs pity in me . . ."

"You sure make him sound like a prize catch," Fanny sighed.

"Oh he *is!* As you probably know, the Beaconridges are filthy rich. Say! Why don't you set your cap for him, Fanny? Then you could stay here in Troy—and you and I could see each other as often as we liked."

Fanny looked at her.

"You're from here, too?" she said.

"I should say *not!* I'm from New York City—we've a townhouse in the east seventies. You'll see it, though, when you spend Christmas with me this year."

'New York,' Fanny thought, 'where Phil is. And this rich, dumb pretty boy is *here.* Heck, I even know his address. Poor Sue gave it to me. So—play it smart, Fanny Turner! From now 'til Christmas this one—*dear* Tony. Then at Christmas, Phil—And betwixt and between, this long-tall off-horse kind of a girl to teach me all I need to know—'

"What are you smiling about so sweetly, Fanny?" Norma said.

"Nothing—no, that's not so. I was thinking how lucky I am—meeting you and all," Fanny said.

"Now that's my darling girl!" Norma said, and, bending, kissed Fanny on the mouth. Lightly, tentatively, playfully. For the first time.

It wasn't to be the last.


## Chapter Nineteen


"C'mon, li'l Southern gal! Pucker up you-all's sweet li'l ol' lips 'n give a Nawth'n genmun a kiss, will you-all?"

"Tony," Fanny said crisply, "who on earth *ever* told you that we Southerners talk that way? We don't, you know. Not even the nig—the colored people—speak so badly. For instance, we only say 'you all' to distinguish between you, singular, and you, plural—a useful distinction, you must admit—"

"And you talk just like Norma, damn her," Tony Beaconridge said gloomily, "even to her la-di-da pronunciation. Pedantic as old hell. Induces a squeamish feeling in my solar plexus—or somewhere a little south of it, anyhow. But, as I was saying before I was so rudely interrupted, how's about a little kiss, Fanny, darling?"

"No," Fanny said primly.

"Why not?" Tony Beaconridge said.

"First and foremost, I shouldn't like to be expelled

from school. If you were even the slightest bit observant, my dear Tony, you would have seen by now that both Miss Barlett and Mrs. Redfern are looking at us—though 'glaring' is a lot closer to what they're *really* doing at the moment. Secondly, you smell like a horse—a most unappetizing aroma, I assure you. And last but not least, I don't think it's at all wise to get seriously involved with a man who honestly thinks that knocking little white balls around a field with a wooden mallet from horseback is the be-all and end-all of existence."

"Blasphemy!" Tony cried. "To defame the noble game of polo like that!"

"If you did it walking, it would only be croquet," Fanny observed.

"Oh, Jesus!" Tony said.

"Don't be profane, Mr. Anthony Stuyvesant Beaconridge," Fanny said in her best, letter-perfect imitation of Norma's tone, vocabulary, and even her crisp, New England accent: "By now, surely you should be aware that I don't approve of that sort of thing . . ."

She was enjoying herself hugely. 'I've got it! I've got it!' she exulted in her mind. And, in sober fact, she had. What she had suddenly reached and passed, after the long torture of being hammered at, day and night, by Norma, was one of those abrupt and mysterious breakthroughs in the learning process, that no psychologist has ever been able to adequately explain for all that they are, actually, almost a commonplace. After having lingered for weeks on the plateau of having to form her sentences slowly, word by word, consciously remembering the relationship between noun, adjective, pronoun, verb, adverb, dependent clause, prepositional phrase, and the like, one morning she simply woke up with the pent-up flood of language broken through the dam of her repressions, hesitations, doubts, fears.

She hadn't even known it, until meeting Norma, she said, without even thinking about it:

"Strange—I feel different this morning. Or the world does, rather. Can't say why, really." She'd pronounced rather "rawther" and can't "cawn't" without being conscious of it at all.

Norma stared at her, and whispered:

"Go on, Fanny! Don't stop! *Please* go on!"

"Go on, where? It's utter nonsense I'm sure; but all the same I—"

She stopped, her pale eyes alight.

"Norma!" she gasped, "I—"

"You're talking!" Norma wept. "You're really talking, Fanny! Like a human being at last! Oh my darling, I'm so happy for you!"

Then wildly, passionately, Norma swept Fanny into her arms and kissed her mouth.

Thinking about that, Fanny's pale eyes darkened, went smoky gray, opaque. 'We're—lovers, Norma and I,' she told herself bleakly, 'and that's *awful*. How did it happen? I—I've always *adored* boys. No. Isn't it rather that I've always loved anyone—or anything—that can give—my body—pleasure?'

She sat there, bundled up in furs, looking out on the snow-streaked, muddy, polo field. She and Tony weren't alone—most of the students of the Emma Willard School and the Rensselaer Polytechnic Institute were there to watch Tony's privately organized polo team—limited to those students wealthy enough to own and maintain their own strings of ponies—defeat the team from Yale. Actually, to call their opponents the team from Yale wasn't quite true either, for no college or university supported, or even listed, polo as an officially recognized sport. Most of the opposing team *were* from Yale, however; but as was also the case of Tony's own, it included players who weren't students at all, but simply wealthy—and exceedingly idle—young sportsmen.

"Fanny—" Tony said, pleadingly.

"Leave me alone, Tony; can't you see I'm thinking?" Fanny said. And she was, the thoughts running bleak and bitter through her mind?

'How did I get into—*that? Oh, Jesus—that!* Like I did every other stupid mess I've got into in my whole life—by being a damn fool. Couldn't I have *noticed* the way she was? Always hugging me, kissing me on the mouth—and a little longer each time—with her own mouth opened—and—and hot—and wet. Then—touching me. Her hand on my knee while she was explaining the difference between a transitive and an intransitive verb and how to tell a gerundive from a prepositional phrase. Or accidently brushing her hand across my bust—so that her fingers rubbed me where I'm sensitive—where any girl is, I suppose. Made me feel—all tingly. And I never could swear she was doing it—on purpose. I was too worried about—*me.* That *I* was getting—excited. *That* way. And—and with another *girl.* Until—finally I—I had to—to go back to that—bad habit I'd thought I'd got rid of, overcome—again. Almost every night, so I could get some sleep . . .'

She went on looking past Tony, *through* Tony, thinking with sad anger:

'Oh, she was smart! Little by little, getting me so mixed up until I *cared* about her in other ways, too. Like—like being upset and—and hurt by the way she treated me when Polly or Agnes or Irene or any of the other girls were around. So—cool. A little sneering. "Now really, Fanny; must you be *quite* so stupid, my dear?" She never said mean things like that when we were alone. And me putting my heart on my sleeve and going up to her room and—Oh, Jesus!'

That memory was particularly bitter. She'd gone up the stairs, pushed open the door to Norma's room and burst out:

"Norma, just you tell me one thing: Why do you treat me the way you do in front of the other girls?"

Norma put down the book she was reading, carefully marking the page with a decorative leather bookmark, looked up at Fanny gravely and said:

"And how *do* I treat you, my darling?"

"As though—as though you *hated* me! What's the matter, Norma? Are you ashamed of me? I know I'm only a poor little stupid Southern girl who—"

"Is utterly lovely," Norma breathed, and getting up from her chair, took Fanny in her arms and kissed her slowly, lingeringly on the mouth. "All right, Fanny, darling—time we had it out. I—was only protecting you. A good many of the girls around here suspect me of—of being a Lesbian, to call it by its correct name. So, since I didn't want you to suffer because of my unfortunate reputation, I—"

"Norma," Fanny said, a little plaintively, ashamed at having again to reveal her ignorance, "what's a Lesbian?"

"A woman—who loves other women," Norma said, quietly. "Loves them in preference to, and to the exclusion of, men. That's what the word means. It's derived from the name of the Greek island of Lesbos, where the immortal poetess, Sappho, lived. She wrote the most beautiful love poems in human history, all of them addressed to—girls."

"But I love you," Fanny began, "and I don't see how that would make me—" She stopped, her pale eyes very wide. "Norma—" she breathed, "when you say 'loves' d'you mean 'makes love to?' With—with their—bodies, I mean?"

"Yes, Fanny," Norma said.

Fanny hung there, staring at her.

"And—*are* you? *That?*" she said.

Norma bowed her head. Looked up again. Her brown eyes were full of tears.

"A Lesbian? Yes, Fanny; I'm afraid I am," she said.

Fanny went on staring at her.

"But how?" she said. "A woman *can't,* Norma! She hasn't got anything to—to—"

Norma studied Fanny's face, her eyes. Decided—correctly—that there was no revulsion, but only curiosity, there. In her own dark eyes, hope took fire.

"A lot you know about it, poor baby!" she said. "Shall I—shall I show you—darling? Wait—you don't have to *do* anything, yourself. I'll manage for both of us quite nicely, thank you! Would you like to—to try?"

Fanny didn't answer her in so many words. She stood there rapt, her lips a little parted. Swiftly Norma bent and kissed them, slipping a hot and busy tonguetip between them into the bargain. Kept it up until she had the response she sought. Drew back, smiled at Fanny, very tenderly, murmured:

"Go—lock the door, will you, sweetheart?"

Fanny did so; turned back to Norma, trembling a little.

"And now?" she got out, half-strangling on the words.

"Take off your clothes. All of them, darling," Norma Tilson said.

Fanny sat there, staring out over the Polo Field. Tony had left her, gone to play the last chukker. The match was tied; but he had some hopes of winning, still.

'I—like it!' Fanny thought bitterly. 'So that makes me one, too, doesn't it? A—Lesbian. A woman-lover. Norma makes me feel better than any damn man I ever knew.

Even—Philippe. Says—being a woman, herself—she understands *what* a girl wants, needs: slowness—gentleness, sweetness—And she does, too! 'Course what she does—what *we* do—isn't any more than what I used to do all by myself, most of the time. Except she does know just *where* to—to touch—and how easy—soft-like—and just how long. But the—the other—? Lord Jesus! *Now* I know what old man Jacob Fields was trying to do! That way she—she drives me crazy—right out of my stupid mind. But I won't—what's the word?—reciprocate. Because if anything's unnatural *that* is! Perverted. Ugly. And she keeps on trying to get me to—to do *that* to her. Only I won't! I won't! I won't!'

She sat there, the misery in her eyes very cold and still.

'Then why don't I stop her from doing it—to me? 'Cause, if I don't, one day I'll have to—to satisfy her that way. And I'll be gone. I'll be a *real* one—like she is. If I'm not already. Kissing and touching are half-way normal, anyhow. But—making the scissors? What does she call it? Some damn Latin word. Tree—something, tribadism—that's it. And even that's pretty close to being queer, for a fact. But the *other*—soap and water and cologne be damned, that's—filthy! Down there we—'

She saw Tony come striding back towards her, leading his pony. From the look of triumph in his eyes, she realized that his team had won. It was the only way she could have known, because she hadn't watched the game.

'Why *can't* I like him?" she thought. 'He's awfully good-looking—and not half as dumb as *she* tries to make him seem. Only—she's always trying to *give* him to me—because with him for my husband, I wouldn't have to go back down South—and she'd move back here to Troy—where her mother's family came from anyhow—and she and I could go on doing filthy Lesbian tricks with each other for the rest of our lives. And that spoils Tony for me. He's—good as gold. Fun. Sweet, really. Rich. And more than half in love with me already. But I *can't* like him because I always see him through *her* eyes, somehow. If she even had enough respect for him to be jealous, I—'

She studied Tony's tall, lean, athletic form.

'I should *let* him!' she thought viciously. 'Maybe that would cure me—make me a girl again!'

But then, suddenly, her eyes cleared. 'No,' she whispered, 'that would be cheating on—Philippe. Norma doesn't count. She's only a girl. But with Tony, I'd *really* be cheating and—'

A burst of joy exploded behind her eyes. It transformed them into twin artic stars, matchlessly bright.

'Christmas!' she exulted. 'Only two weeks away! I'll send that letter to Papa! Asking him to let me spend the holidays with Norma, like she's been begging me to. And another one to Phil, telling him *not* to go home to New Orleans for the holidays, 'cause I'll be coming to New York with—a friend. And I *will* too. Go to New York with Norma, I mean. But the minute I get there, I'll go find poor Phil and—and turn him every which a way but loose! Every night all night long 'til this—this slime is burnt out of me. 'Til I'm a real, honest-to-God all-female girl again! And if this he-man Mary ever tries to lay a finger on me again after I come back, I—I'll kill her, so help me!'

She was aware, at last, that Tony was standing there gazing down at her. His blue eyes were very dark and troubled, suddenly. When he spoke, his voice was uncertain. A shake had got into it.

"This really ties it!" he muttered. "And all these years I was so completely sure I never would—"

"That you'd never *what,* Tony, dear?" Fanny said.

"Fall in love," Tony said ruefully. "Only I'm afraid I have. And with *you,* Fanny, darling. Just then you—your eyes—I see *now* what poor, dear, Susie meant. Her letters, y'know. Always trying to describe their color to me. Confound it! They're just too beautiful. And so are you. I mean it. It suddenly occurred to me that I can't possibly live without you. Will you please make an honest man of me, my dear? At Christmas time, say. We could get my Uncle Cabot to officiate. He's rector of Christ Church, y'know and—"

"Oh, don't be silly, Tony!" Fanny laughed. "I neither whinny nor neigh, and I detest oats! I'm a girl, dear boy, not a horse. And you only love horses. You said so, yourself!"

"Up 'til now," Tony said. "I—I'm serious, Fanny. I love you. Will you become Mrs. Anthony Stuyvesant Beaconridge the Third? Or perhaps it's the Fourth. Never can remember—there've been so deuced many of us—"

Fanny sat there. She thought: 'Lord! What do I do now? A chance like this! The chance of a lifetime, and I—'

She said:

"Tony—I—I don't know what to say. I—I'm terribly honored and flattered, but—"

"Please, Fanny! Don't say no! Think about it. Take from now 'til the Christmas holidays to think about it! Take the holidays themselves. Take 'til next spring. But don't send me to a drunkard's grave! I—I'll go straight to perdition, I swear it! Ever see *Ten Nights in a Barroom*? That'll be *me,* if you don't stop freezing me to death with those eyes of yours, turning them into millpond ice every time you look at me, and open up those still-unkissed—by one poor devil named Tony Beaconridge anyhow—lips and say at least, 'Maybe, Tony, dear—' That much, Fanny? Dearest, darling Fanny—at least that much?"

"All right," Fanny said gently. "Maybe, Tony. I—I like you a lot. In fact, I'm terribly fond of you. But, as of now, I don't love you. If you were a little more serious, perhaps I could learn to. But I really shouldn't like for my children's futures to depend upon—an idler, a wastrel, a ne'er-do-well—all of which you *are,* Tony, dear! Having your father leave you all that money *is* important to me. It's my stepmother, not my father, who's rich. And she'll probably leave hers to my half-brother, not to me. You see? I'm being honest. Much too honest for my own good, likely. Quite frankly, I shouldn't like being poor. And with you, my darling Tony, very probably, I should be just that. For, judging from what I've seen of you, you'll run through your father's money so darned fast that—"

"That's enough! You're looking at a reformed character, Fanny! Tomorrow evening after classes at the institute will see me in the old man's office busily poring over the blinking books, damn them! And this coming spring I'll actually graduate from Rensselaer instead of flunking out as usual. That's a promise. Oh, why the devil did this have to hit me on a polo field? Where I can't even kiss you! Oh, good heavens! I—"

Fanny smiled at him softly, sweetly.

"There'll be time enough for that—later, Tony, darling," she said.

* * *

She sat in her room, staring at her books.

'I was plain, downright rotten, this time,' she thought. 'Philippe—has done everything for me. Saved my life. Gave me a chance to go up. To be somebody. Only— being married to him means we'll be dirt-poor, for a while. 'Til he starts making money at practicing medicine. If he ever does. Because that old Creole witch of mother of his will *make* his father cut him off without an Indian-head copper if he marries *me*. But I love him. I *do* love him, truly. Yet Tony's *so* good-looking. And so god-damned *rich!* Oh, Lord, I—'

Norma pushed open the door and came into the room. Fanny stared at her.

"Norma!" she said; "are you crazy? I thought that we agreed *never* to go to each other's rooms in the daytime—only very late at night when everybody else is asleep? And never to be seen together on campus un-less—unless—"

"There are others present. And even so, to be distinctly cool to one another. Of course, darling! And it's worked out beautifully, hasn't it?"

"Yes. But now you—"

"Came to see you. To—congratulate you, my dear. Tony. *That* arranges matters oh, so neatly, doesn't it? Ties everything up in pink silk ribbons for a fact! Polly Stevens was sitting right behind you when he proposed. So now it's all over the campus—"

"Oh, Jesus!" Fanny said.

"Marry him, sweetkins! The gilded oaf! Don't you see how *perfect* he'll make life for the two of us? The perfect foil, smoke screen, camouflage, or what-have-you. Already he's done us a world of good."

"How?" Fanny said.

"By giving you an absolutely perfect certification of normal heterosexuality. And in public, too! We needn't be quite so circumspect from here on in; with Tony as your fiancé, nobody will dare accuse us—don't you see?"

"Norma," Fanny said, "we've got to—to *stop*. I—I don't want to be—unnatural. I want to be myself—a girl. A real honest-to-God *feminine* girl who—"

"Oh, that you are, darling," Norma purred. "If you weren't, *I* wouldn't love you!" Then she bent and kissed Fanny's mouth. Fanny's two hands came up, pushing. But, without even changing her position, Norma slid her right hand up the left leg of the knee-length, lace-trimmed pantalettes that Fanny wore.

"Stop it!" Fanny whispered. "Stop that, Norma! I said—Oh! Oh Lord! Oh Jesus. Oh, please, Norma! I—Oh—"

"*Now* I'll stop it. 'Til tonight, darling. About two thirty, as usual. And leave these ruddy things off, will you? They only get in the way . . ."


"You sent for me, sir?" the short, thickset little man said.

Anthony Beaconridge II looked him up and down, slowly, from the beet-red face, bisected by a classical handlebar moustache, and half-strangling above the high, stiffly starched wing collar, past the loudly striped pink and blue shirt, to the waistcoat whose checks fought an anguished, screaming war with the stripes of the shirt, to the huge, silver-plated watch chain that crossed the ample abdomen, to the brown derby posed in the man's left hand, to—

He stopped. It wasn't worth the bother. 'Vulgarity, thy name is Hawkes,' he thought, and turned to his secretary. "That will be all for today, Miss Milhaus," he said. "Take the rest of the afternoon off. This—gentleman and I have quite a session coming up, I'm afraid . . ."

Miss Milhaus stared at Hawkes with frank and open disapproval. Then she turned back to her employer.

"Very well, sir," she said. "And—and thanks for the afternoon—"

Don't mention it, my dear," Anthony Beaconridge said. He sat there calmly until her heels had clattered out of earshot before opening his mouth.

"Good afternoon—" he said, bringing the phrase almost to a full stop before adding, very slowly, "Hawkes." The pause was deliberate, for among the many things that Mr. Beaconridge knew about Hawkes was that his name actually was Jones, the little man having adopted the pseudonym for professional reasons—'In the forlorn hope,' Anthony Beaconridge suspected, 'that people will one day call him "Hawk-eye Hawkes"—or something along that line . . .'

"Good afternoon, sir," Hawkes said. "What is it this time? More labor trouble? Don't see why, what with the salaries *you* pay, Mr. Beaconridge. Downright generous, if you ask me . . ."

"No," Anthony Beaconridge sighed. "The problem is—personal, this time."

He paused, stared at Hawkes inquiringly. Hawkes drew himself up stiffly, came in, right on cue:

"You know you can rely upon my discretion, sir!"

"Yes," Anthony Beaconridge said grudgingly, "I suppose I can, at that. Very well. To make a long story short: It's my son, Tony—the Third. And the last, likely. No use saving the name for *his* son. Anthony Stuyvesant Beaconridge the Fourth would look silly on a manual laborer, wouldn't it?"

"Now, sir—" Hawkes protested.

"That's what *my* grandson will be, six months after Tony gets his hands on my money," Anthony Beaconridge said gloomily. "One of the reasons I sent for you. The subject's Tony. My son. 'The Well-Known Polo-Player and Sportsman' to quote the illustrated papers. Two days ago, he suddenly discovered an all-consuming passion for, of all things, work. In fact, he's in the outer offices now, getting in the way, cluttering up the place, and, in general, making a perfect ass of himself. An even bigger ass, in fact, than he was born to be . . ."

Hawkes studied his employer.

"I wouldn't call that bad, sir," he said. "Always did say the boy had the right stuff in him, and—"

"If he has," Anthony Beaconridge said, dryly, "it has never been discernible before now, not even under microscopic examination. Oh, come off of it, Hawkes! You know damed well that even your sterling talents would be hard put to run to earth a more perfect specimen of utter uselessness than my Tony. He's the exact illustration of the old adage: Shirtsleeves to shirtsleeves in three generations. It's no sense trying to hide from *you,* anyhow, that the Beaconridges, while older than the hills, and as aristocratic as all gèt-out, were as poor as churchmice until my father's time. He made himself a carload of money by tying in with that Montague woman's invention. Since most people just *won't* wash their filthy hides, detachable

collars and cuffs make sense.* *I* have at least maintained
the family fortune. But Tony will reduce the Beaconridges
to beggary again within six months after my departure to
whatever award awaits me, above or below—"

"Oh above, sir!" Hawkes said piously, "surely above!"

"Not bloody likely!" Anthony Beaconridge snorted.
"I've more than my share of sins upon my soul, Hawkes;
and I've enjoyed every damned one of them, I can tell
you that! But to get back to Tony. I have, naturally, taken
the usual precautions: ironclad trust funds and the like.
Enough, I should say, to make his future foolproof. But
not goddamned foolproof, as he's demonstrating right this
minute! All this new-found initiative of his, Hawkes—if it
were his own idea, I'd be overjoyed. I'd even take the
trouble of trying to teach him the rudiments of good business practice. But it *isn't*. It was suggested to him by a
certain young person—a very clever young person—of the
opposite sex, naturally—who is seeking to forestall whatever possible objections I might have to her, personally.
Which means the goddamned fool has fallen into the
hands of an artful, designing woman!"

Hawkes nodded sagely.

"The ladies," he observed, "have been the ruination of
many a good man, sir—"

"And the *making* of many another. Like my Nellie, say.
Perhaps if she had lived, she could have done something
with this braying young ass I've sired! But that's neither
here nor there, now. What *is* here, rather too much so,
Hawkes, is this young female person. A student at the
Emma Willard School and—"

"But, sir!" Hawkes protested. "What better credentials
could you ask? If Mrs. Redfern accepted her, you can be
sure that—"

"Her background and her morals are above reproach.
Ordinarily, I'd agree with you, Hawkes. But this time I'm
not so sure. It seems to me Jane Redfern slipped up this
once. I've talked to her, of course. And the little, the very,

---

*In 1825, Mrs. Hannah Lord Montague, a Troy housewife,
noting that her husband's collars and cuffs became impossibly
dirty long before the rest of the shirt, invented the detachable
collar and cuff to save herself from having to do too much
laundering. Her invention became the basis of a thriving in-
dustry in that city that lasted through World War I.

very little she knows about this Miss Frances Turner is—
well—disquieting. One: the girl's an ex-tubercular. She
was in that North Carolina sanitorium with my poor departed baby—and apparently has briskly *used* the friendship she *claims* she had with Susan, while there, as a lever
to pry her way into our world—which, with all its faults,
doubtless seems a trifle superior to whatever milieu she
came from—or else why would she try it? Jane Redfern
knows nothing about her family. She does know her
stepmother, one Martha Brantley, distinguished New York
City family. But one doesn't inherit tendencies from a
*stepmother*, Hawkes! About the father—a William Pelham Turner—nothing, not even his present occupation.
Used to be a law clerk in the Brantley offices, and was,
I'm told, *kicked out* for unsavory behavior: women,
mostly. The mother—less than nothing—no one has been
able to discover what her very *name* was. Which is, of
course, where you come in, my good man—"

"You can count on me, sir," Hawkes said. "One question—if I may, Mr. Beaconridge: The girl—have you seen
her, talked to her? If so, how does she strike you?"

"Circe. Lorelei. Morgan le Fay. Guinivere and Iseult all
rolled into one." He stopped, aware of the blank expression on Hawkes' face. "What I mean is that she's absolutely stunning. Breathtaking. But—cool. Self-possessed. A
heart-breakingly beautiful face—with a she-devil's mind
behind it. Don't ask me how I know that. Call it intuition—tailored by sad experience. She'll wreck my boy,
Hawkes. Squeeze him dry and toss the husk aside. And
fool though he is, I'd like to prevent that—"

"You can count on me, sir," Hawkes said again.

"I know that, goddamn it! The place to start is New
Orleans—that's where this little person hails from. The
time, *now*. You have time and to spare to catch the
twelve-oh-one down to the city; and make connections
with the Southern & Central's eight-fifteen that goes
straight into New Orleans without a break. I've got your
tickets here. Pullman accommodation, so you'll arrive
with your wits about you. And here're two thousand dollars cash for your expenses—small bills so you won't attract too much attention as a spender. Reservation at the
St. Louis, confirmed by wire. Anything else you need?"

"This—" Hawkes consulted his really remarkable memory, and came up at once with the name, "Mr. Turner's address? A good description of *him*, at least, sir? Or even of Mrs. Turner—the former Miss Brantley, I believe?"

"Sorry—can't oblige. But to a detective of *your* talents, Hawkes, those obstacles are small. Be off with you, now! Time's a-wasting. And report to me personally; put *nothing* in writing. No letters, no telegrams, understand? Female secretaries aren't to be trusted in such matters. Well, Hawkes?"

"I—I'll do my level best, sir," the man called Hawkes said.

And in the quiet confidence of his tone, a hypothetical listener, thinking about the outcome, already inevitable from that moment, might have sensed or felt a whole series of not exactly rhetorical questions that said outcome raised: Does the quality of remorseless implacability lend tragedy to a chain of events having intrinsically neither dignity nor meaning? Is absurdity necessarily comic? Should the foot poised above the wildly scampering cockroach be considered a motive for laughter?

Not to the cockroach in any event.

So, with all due rites and respectful ceremony, let us trot out the rotund, obscurantist, golden-sounding words: Inescapable destiny. A woman's fate.

Fanny's? Yes. Why yes, of course. But not hers alone. No man is an island, John Donne wrote, using the word "man" with unconscious, and primitive, male chauvinism to include "woman," too, one must suppose. And those peculiarly Donnean funeral bells, when at last they'd begin to toll, would lift their muted clangor above a hecatomb sacrificed to the obscene gods of venegance by one small, white, slender hand.

For every man or woman who made the monumental error of underestimating Fanny Turner paid dearly for that miscalculation—in many cases, the ultimate price. Medea would have understood her very well, one thinks.

Which is a way of defining her, isn't it? Or trying to. So be it. Let it rest. Let it be.

"Send not to inquire for whom—"

# Chapter Twenty

"And just where d'ye be a-going, Tim?" Molly Hawkes said to her husband.

Hawkes looked at his wife—all two-hundred-odd pounds of her—and under the imposing handlebar moustache his small mouth curled into a grimace clearly intended to indicate acute distaste.

"Told yer oncet already, Mol," he said—for Tim Hawkes's mode of speech varied in direct proportion to the social position of the person whom he was addressing, grammatical correctness and nicety of pronunciation being reserved for the Anthony Beaconridges of this world—"New Orleans—job for th' boss. Confidential. Can't tell yer no more about it . . ."

"I know *that,* Tim," Molly said, "but seein' as how yer train don't leave 'til after midnight, what I wanna know is where ye be a-going right *now*."

Timothy Hawkes, né Jones, took a long black cigar out of the Japanned lacquer box on the sideboard, sniffed it lengthwise with a connoisseur's appreciation, cut off the tip of it with the solid gold cigar-cutter that was a token of his employer's appreciation of the really excellent services he had rendered Beaconridge and Co. in the matter of the labor troubles of two years before, lit it very slowly, wreathing his rather roundish head with clouds of fragrant smoke before even condescending to answer his wife's question.

"Out," he said, and taking his derby off the hat rack, he fitted it with some care to the properly rakish angle above his left eyebrow.

"Yer goin' to see *her,*" Molly said querulously.

Tim Hawkes looked at his spouse—from head to toe, and from side to side—the lateral, horizontal gaze, due consideration being given to Molly's build, taking him almost as long as the vertical one.

"Could be I am," he said calmly, "takin' into account what a foine example of love 'n beauty I got me at home . . ."

"Men!" Molly shrieked. "His boss sends him off for th' blessed saints thimselves don't know how long—and instid o' spendin' his last evenin' at home with his ever-lovin', off he goes to visit a filthy hoor! 'Cause if Myrtie Tolliver ain't a hoor, I ain't iver seen one!"

"Go sneak a glint at yer blessed mither's picture, then, Mol—to refresh yer memory," Tim said and walked out the door.

He made his way—by an exceedingly roundabout route, for it certainly wouldn't do for his relationship with Myrtle Tolliver to be brought to his employer's attention—until he came to the neat, ivy-covered cottage where Miss Tolliver lived. Tim Hawkes paid the rent for the cottage, giving Myrtle a sealed envelope every month with enough of "th' long green" in it to take care of that matter and also to buy whatever little geegaw might strike her vagrant fancy. But though the little detective prided himself upon having risen high enough in the social and financial scale to afford a kept woman, aping his betters even in that small and piquant detail, the fact of the matter was that Myrtle was largely self-supporting, holding a job in the telegraph office, interestingly enough procured for her by Timothy Hawkes himself, which, instead of being in any way altruistic on his part, was merely another evidence of the inherent shrewdness that had made him the past master of his unlovely profession he indisputably was.

He knocked with careful firmness on Myrtle's door.

She opened it a crack, peeked out, said listlessly: "Oh—it's you. All right—c'mon in . . ."

Tim Hawkes strode into her parlor, leaned forward to "buss her a good 'un," but Myrtle turned so that his kiss landed on her high cheekbone.

"Overjoyed to see me, ain't you, Luv?" Tim said sarcastically.

"Tim," Myrtle said, "it ain't that. You know I—I care for you a awful lot. But you're a married man. And this—is wrong, Tim. It just ain't—right."

"Righter than what you was doing in New York City, Myrtie," Tim said, and had the satisfaction of seeing her dark eyes fill up with tears.

"I was—hungry, Tim," she whispered. *"Too* hungry—too damn long. You know that. Never figured that when you showed up and saved me from that life—it was to put me into another just as bad—"

"*Not* just as bad, Myrtie," Tim Hawkes said. "You'n me wuz meant for each other—and just because there ain't no way I can get shut of that fat sow I'm harnessed to don't mean—"

"Tim," Myrtle said, "why don't you—let *me* go? Stop holding what you know about me over my head? Let me live decent—I could, Tim! I had a good reputation 'til I got fed up with that miserable clerking job in th' five 'n dime, and ran off down to th' city. Maybe I could even meet me a nice single feller who—"

"Quit dreaming, baby!" Tim said, quietly, "you're mine and don't you niver fergit it. Feller what slips a hoop o' gold on yer pinky is gonna find out before morning that his one 'n only has peddled her dainty li'l bustle from Times Square to the Bronx and all pernts in between. So don't try to pull a fast one, Myrtie. Fact is, I didn't come over t'night to plague you with my lovin' attentions—"

"Thank God for that much, anyhow," Myrtle said.

"Though wasn't for the fact that gettin' you into the mood would take me so damn long I'd probably miss my train, I just might change my mind," Tim said.

"Please don't, Tim," Myrtle whispered. "I—I just don't feel like it tonight."

"When do you, ever?" Tim said bitterly; then: "No matter. The truth is, Myrtie, I'm here on business—got a little job for you to do."

"Oh, Jesus!" Myrtle said, "not *again!*"

"Now, Myrtie," Tim said, "listen to me—"

"No!" Myrtle stormed. "I won't listen, Tim! I—I really loved you—up until then. 'Til two years ago. 'Til you made me copy down every telegram them poor fellers sent—and them just trying to get their natural rights, and the rights of them poor female critters that old pirate Beaconridge fair *starves* to death. Working stiffs just like my poor old daddy. And I helped you get the goods on 'em. Pinned that 'Labor Agitators' tag all over 'em. Fixed it so they'll *never* get a job again not only here in Troy but not nowhere in the New England states. Blacklisted 'em for fair! I used to hide my face every time I ran into one of them poor fellers—in rags they was, and their faces sunk in from being *hungry,* Tim! And *I* did that, or leastways helped you do it—black-hearted scoundrel that you be!"

"No, I ain't," Hawkes said mildly. "What I am is practical, Myrtie. My old man was a working stiff, just like yours was. Only he taught me sense. 'Timmie, me bye,' he used to say, 'niver kick aginst th' pricks.' Or 'Whin ye have yer head in th' lion's mouth don'cha go an' tickle th' beastie's tongue.' So I played it smart. Since any fool could see that th' likes of me didn't have a Chinaman's chance of licking people like th' Beaconridges, I ups and joins 'em. Myrtie! Right now 'tis a lead-pipe cinch that I'm old Tony's right-hand man. Proof of that is this job he just give me. So now just you sit there like the good girl you damned sure ain't and listen to what I have to say, will ya?"

Myrtle Tolliver looked at the dapper little detective.

"All right," she said, her voice burdened, freighted with the weariness of one all too accustomed to defeat: "anything you say, Tim—"

"But," Myrtle protested, "say this girl *does* come in to send a wire—how am I going to know her?"

"She's got to sign it, hasn't she? And put her right name and address on the bottom. Miss Frances Turner, the Emma Willard School. You see—?"

"But Tim, Christmas time so many of those schoolgirls come in that I might not—I mean she just might get past me—"

"No, *she* won't. Had her pointed out to me this afternoon. Blonde as a Swede. Hair damn near white. Strikes you, Myrtle. And then there're her eyes. Damnedest eyes you ever did see, baby. Ain't got no proper color at all. I suppose you could call 'em blue, but if they are, it's the color ice turns sometimes. And again you could call 'em gray. Truth is, they ain't neither one. Spooky as all get out. Like she wasn't altogether human, really—"

"Tim," Myrtle whispered, "s'pose she—she really is in love with young Tony. S'pose—she—she's a *good* girl who'd make him a fine wife and—"

Tim reached out an immaculately manicured hand and patted Myrtle's thin cheek—

"In that case, neither she nor you have anything to

worry about, Myrtie, 'cause anything we find out will help
her along instead of hurtin' her. You see that don't you?
Good thing about this private detective business, baby.
We're after the *truth*. Many's the time I've been able to
say to a jealous feller: 'No, sir, you're wrong. Wife's good
as gold. Only place she goes is to the hairdresser's 'n to
church—' "

"I—I hope you'll be able to tell Mr. Beaconridge something like that this time," Myrtle said.

"Me, too. But I doubt it," Hawkes said.

"Why, Tim? Why do you doubt it?"

"Don't know. Instinct, maybe. But this li'l missy's been
around. Got the boldest, brassiest stare a feller ever did
see. And the day she figures out that the only way to get
her pinkies on the Beaconridge millions is to play the
maiden wronged, she'll unbutton young Tony's fly 'n take
it out of his pants all by herself . . ."

"Why, Tim—what an awful thing to say!"

"Awful truth. Now give me a kiss, baby. I got to go
pack me duds," Timothy Hawkes said.


Fanny sat there with her eyes alight, reading her father's letter. When she had finished it, slowly and carefully she tore it into tiny pieces, and, going down the hall
to the bathroom, flushed the pieces down the toilet. Then
she came back to her room, and waited. Just as she had
expected, half an hour later, Norma appeared.

"Well," the tall girl said a little harshly; "have you
heard from your father yet?"

"Yes," Fanny said, "this morning—"

"And—?" Norma said.

Fanny sighed theatrically.

"It's bad news, Norma," she said. "He says I can't—
that I haven't been home in so long and—and besides my
brother Billy's coming home for Christmas—and—"

"I see," Norma said. "Well—better luck next time, my
darling. Perhaps we can start working on the idea of your
spending the Easter holidays with me—or even the summer vacation—"

'I'll see you dead and in hell, first!' Fanny thought; but
she said smoothly: "Easter—almost surely. But I wouldn't
count on the summer vacation. Papa doesn't trust me *that*
much. Fears I'll get into mischief if I'm out of his sight

too long, though I'm sure *your* particular variety of it would *never* occur to him . . ."

"That's the beauty of it, darling!" Norma laughed. "One of its many beauties. As a matter of fact, I never could see why people object to Sapphic love so violently. There's not the faintest chance of your returning home with your dear little middle bulging with forbidden fruit, which is what comes of letting *men* perform their appalling brutishness upon you—"

"I wouldn't know," Fanny said. "Tell you what though, Norma, dear—if Phil comes home for Christmas, maybe I'll be able to give you a first-hand report—"

"Fanny, you wouldn't!" Norma said; then, bending closer: "Oh yes—you would, wouldn't you? In fact, I rather suspect you *have* . . ."

"Well as long as it remains only a suspicion, I'm quite content, thank you!" Fanny said. "Now if you'll excuse me, dear. I must go out—"

"Go out—where?" Norma said.

"Telegraph office. I have to wire my father. Want to come along?"

"No—no, thank you!" Norma said. "I *hate* going downtown. But then, you *know* that, don't you? Quite safe to ask me, wasn't it?"

"Oh don't be a ninny, Norma!" Fanny laughed and kissed her cheek, whispering against her ear, "See you tonight, my dearest . . ."

"Yes," Norma said bleakly. "Yes, please do. We—we have so little time . . ."

Fanny left the two girls she had had to find to accompany her—for it was an ironclad rule of Mrs. Redfern's that no girl, not even a senior, was allowed to go downtown alone—outside on the sidewalk, and went into the telegraph office. The minute she came through the revolving door, Myrtle Tolliver recognized her. 'Please,' Myrtle prayed inside her mind, 'don't send a wire! And if you do—make it something ordinary. Like—meet the ten fifteen or—'

But Fanny had taken a blank and was scribbling busily. She finished it within minutes, and, approaching the window, thrust it through.

Mechanically, Myrtle began to count the words—for it

was her job to tabulate and receive payment for the charges before passing the telegram along to the telegrapher. Then she looked up and her brown eyes were appalled. The telegram was addressed to one Philippe Sompayac at an address in the east fifties, New York City. It read, very simply: "Get rid of your roommate, I'm on my way. Love, Fanny."

"You—you're sure you want to send *this,* Miss?" Myrtle whispered.

"Yes," Fanny said crisply. "What concern is it of yours, may I ask? You're most certainly not my mother."

"No—I'm not," Myrtle said. "But—as one girl to another—I—I made this kind of mistake myself once. And—and I've suffered for it, ever since—"

Fanny stared at her, congealing the blood inside poor Myrtle's veins.

"It so happens that I am not you—thank God!" she said with icy, perfect control. "I know how to manage whatever I choose to do very well indeed, if that's any comfort to you. Besides, it's none of your business, anyhow. How much will the wire be, please?"

"Three dollars and a half," Myrtle Tolliver whispered. She thought: 'Oh damn you to hell and back again, you stupid little bitch! I was depending on you—sort of—to—to help me get free of him. Of that little rotter. But you've torn it now, dearie. For both of us. So don't expect any mercy from me!'

"Bill," Martha said; "Somehow I can't help feeling that it wasn't exactly wise to let Fanny go to spend the Christmas holidays in New York with this Tilson girl—a person neither of us knows—"

"Reckon you're right, honey," Bill Turner said; "but what choice did I have—except the choice between bad and worse, if you get what I mean? Never a night passes that there isn't some uproar or another in that parlor house of Maebelle's. Night before last, Mrs. Kunemann—the draper's wife, Sam Kunemann's, you know—took six shots at one of Maebelle's sluts and missed her every time—from damn near pointblank range at that. I happened to be passing by—and you know what I did? I hung back and waited until the harness bull on that beat showed up. Then I sent him in to make the arrest. For the first time in my life, Martha, I was derelict in my duty. But I didn't have the simple guts to go into Maebelle's place and give her the satisfaction of laughing in my face—"

"You—happen to pass by that place quite often, don't you, Bill?" Martha said softly.

"Now, Martha! You know damn well—"

"That it's simple curiosity—or horrible fascination—one of the two. Yes, Bill; I do know that. But the next time, *do* go in. I want you to."

"Martha!"

"I *want* you to see her. For I have, darling. Oh, well, I'd might as well confess my sins! I've done something, Bill, that I *knew* you wouldn't approve of. Last week, while you were in the hospital for your checkup—and the rest Dr. Terrebonne knows you won't take at home—I got your friend Sergeant Martinelli to take me down there and point her out to me. So, if you have any lingering doubts, any—wonder, say, about what dear Maebelle's like now, you have not only my permission to go to see her but my fervent desire that you'll do just that! She—she's disgusting, Bill. Enormously fat. Obscenely so. Her breasts are the size of watermelons. She has a glittering gold tooth in the front of her mouth. Front and center, to replace the one her pimp knocked out of her head, I'm told. She smokes long black Cuban cigars just like a man. Her clothes—how can I describe them?—grotesque comes pretty close to it, I'm afraid. She doesn't dress like a whore—far from it! None of the girls that Martinelli pointed out to me have anything like her appalling lack of taste. In fact, most of them were rather discreet, really . . ."

"You mean that Martinelli—"

"Actually took me on a tour of Storyville? Yes, Bill. But only because I asked him to. Don't scold him, please! The poor dear fellow, he was *so* worried! Kept saying: 'But Mrs. Turner, this is no place for a lady—' "

"It *isn't*," Bill Turner said grimly.

"Nor for a man, Bill. Not a real man. A true one. But I'm happy I went. I needed to see her, dear. To—to set my heart at ease. And my mind, as well. I came back convinced—that virtue *is* its own reward after all. That decency *is* worth all the efforts, all the resistance to temptation we poor, flighty females must make to maintain it. Their faces were—horrible, Bill. Even the pretty ones. There was so much hatred in their eyes—for the world, for men—for themselves. And the strangest thing happened: Just as we were getting into a cab to come away a man passed by—a very old, filthy, dirty man—with his hands full of—whips, Bill. Switches. Cat-o'-nine-tails. Buggy whips. Bull whips. Thin, flexible steel rods—"

"Joe the Whipper,"* Bill said. "I know. Awful, isn't it?"

"Flagellation. A perversion, I'm told. But, in this case—is it? Isn't it that—they've sunk so low that pain—simple, comprehensible, physical pain—is a relief? That loathing themselves, despising what they do—they seek the surcease of punishment? Offer up to—almighty God their blood and stripes and welts—in penance, say? In contrition for—for *joyless* sin? Oh, Bill! That's truly dreadful, isn't it?"

"Yep. And that's why we've got until next summer to figure out another scheme to keep Fanny the hell away from here. Maybe you'll have to take her abroad again and—"

"Bill, I simply don't believe there are any such thing as inherited tendencies in this particular sense. Look at you—you're so honorable it hurts! And throughout all their history my people have been virtual paragons of honesty; yet our Billy came close to turning out a thief. You must get out of your head that Fanny will inevitably follow in Maebelle's footsteps. Life just isn't that simple, nor that orderly, dear—"

"Maybe not, but I'm sure Lord glad Fanny's in New York. Wonder what the devil she's doing right now?"

It is, perhaps, some slight proof of Heaven's occasional mercy that he did not, could not, know.


"Please, Fanny!" Philippe said. "I couldn't eat another mouthful! You want me to burst? Who on earth ever

*Joe the Whipper unfortunately actually existed; and even more unfortunately performed for a fee the functions herein ascribed to him. The reader interested in such matters is referred to Asbury, Herbert: *The French Quarter* (Garden City Publishing Co. Inc., Garden City, New York 1938), pp. 388-389.

taught you to cook like this?"

"Liza," Fanny said, "when I was quite small—or rather, young. Because I most certainly wasn't small in those days, was I?"

"And—you've learned to talk—beautifully," Philippe said—sadly, Fanny thought—"As well as Martha does, if not better . . ."

"I know," Fanny said. "Kind of a dirty trick, isn't it? Mean. Unkind . . ."

"Unkind?" Philippe said.

"Yes. Plays old Ned with all the excuses you've thought up for yourself by now. For *not* marrying me, I mean," Fanny said bitterly. "I'm a first-class cook. A better than fair housekeeper. I dress well; I've stopped being—loud and vulgar, say. And I've acquired enough book-learning—or shall I call it 'general cultur,' Monsieur Sompayac?—to keep people from finding out just how ignorant I really am. By now, you're pretty sure that I won't disgrace you in public, that you'll never feel ashamed of me again. So—now tell me: what is it, Philippe? Does the fact that—that I *enjoy* going to bed with you shock you? If it does, I'm sorry. You know all about my life—my past. Every dirty, stinking bit of it. So what sense would it make for me to pretend to be the sweet innocent at this late date?"

Philippe stared at her, and the thing he had felt—or sensed—the morning after their first night together was in him again, and it was very bad.

'Look at her,' he thought. 'Douce enfant Jésus, look at her! Standing there staring at me out of those eyes—that are the smoke from a soul burning in hell, maybe. Lord God, what a thing to think! So don't think it. Think that—that she's beautiful. That she's utterly—lovely—'

He stopped and his gaze darkened. Perception rode in upon him. He was seeing Fanny now, really seeing her, and the sad, bad, cold, sick feeling was getting worse all the time.

'But she—*isn't!* She is *not* lovely. She is beautiful: completely, terribly beautiful; but not lovely. Maybe that's it; perhaps that's why for all of this week, I've felt like Faust bargaining with the Devil for my immortal soul! Scared spitless! Oh, God, I—'

"Philippe—" Fanny said.

"Wait," he said. "Don't move! Let me look at you. Let me study the way you are right now so that I can figure out, try to understand—"

"What?" Fanny said.

"Don't know. You, probably. Me. Fate. Destiny. Existence. God. The Devil. Goddamn it, Fanny, keep still!"

"You're—crazy, mon amour," Fanny murmured.

"Right. A lunatic. Insane. Now will you keep still?"

"All right," Fanny said.

'Beautiful,' he thought, 'but not in—in a sensual way. This beauty—is cold. Yet *she* is not. Far from it! That's—another of—of her endless contradictions. How can a beauty like this—eerie, unearthly, angelic, and a few hundred other adjectives du même style—house a Maenad's soul?'

He went on staring at her. She frowned at him, said: "I asked you a question, Philippe!"

He said: "Later. Please. This is important, believe me."

She pouted, said: "Oh, all right. But I'm going to sit down. I'm tired. I *should* be, shouldn't I?"

"Yes—" he whispered, thinking: 'Nothing applies—nothing out of my past experience has anything to do with her. Before, when I realized I was getting too deeply involved, as it were—all I had to do—is what I've been doing all week. That's always been the sure cure. Because sex is romance's deadliest enemy. To see a girl, dressed all in white, standing in an Italian garden, say—in a pale blaze of sun—surrounded by lilacs—looking exactly as though Sir Joshua Reynolds had painted her, cool, remote, lovely—is one thing. But to wake up in the morning and find her stark, mother-naked at your side is another. Or it always has been—up until *this* week—'

"Now, Philippe—" Fanny said.

"Don't interrupt me! I'm thinking. I'm thinking profound, weighty, yet lovely thoughts. All of them about you, my love!"

"All right," Fanny said, and held him with her eyes.

'How does one rid one's self of that Reynold's portrait? Why, bed with it, of course! Because once you've wrecked their careful grooming, played hob with that air of—of immaculate, spotless purity they cultivate so assiduously, as a defense against our carnality, likely, and thereby against their own!—have seen their hair loose and tangled, made

them pant and sweat and—and yes, goddamn it, stink!—
used them, forced them to acknowledge their animality,
the spell is broken, the magic gone—'

He stared at Fanny's profile. She had turned away from
him and was looking out the window at the stream of
horse-drawn vehicles passing in the street.

'Then,' he continued his wry, ironic chain of thought,
'in that one utterly dismal moment—when the heat's out
of you, and your eyes see what's *there* instead of what
your heart—correction!—what some damned brainless little glands have told them to—your goddess slides back
into—woman once again. Damned imperfect, rather vulgar, lumpy, pimply, sagging, with enough hair on her
legs—and between them—to prove there's ape in her ancestry, too. Female. A she-thing, bitch-thing, lying there
with the sweat pouring out of her, gape-legged, used, with
your male muck oozing down the insides of her thighs,
sprawled out like a damp rag doll on the wet, stained,
twisted sheets of some cheaply rented bed. And your glorious love affair has become just another casual fuck.
That's it, mon vieux, that's all!

'But with—her—with Fanny—it doesn't work out that
way. Not at all.' "Why doesn't it?"

"Why doesn't what?" Fanny said; and he realized that
he'd spoken aloud.

"The question's rhetorical, ma bien aimée! I'm—getting
at something. Something important. So leave me be, will
you?"

"All right," Fanny said. "I—like it when you're crazy
this way. It's—nice. Makes me think you—you care for
*me* a little. I mean—the *real* me—not just the—ninety-
seven pounds of hot she-meat that lies there and—and
wiggles to give you pleasure."

"All time, of course, being terribly bored, and not enjoying herself at all," Philippe said solemnly.

"Philippe—" she whispered, "I—I'm awful—aren't I?
Depraved, or something. A—nymphomaniac—Oh, Jesus,
I get so scared sometimes! Of—*me*. Of what an awful
bitch I—"

"Stop it, Fan!" he said, then: "Be patient with me—a
minute longer. Two. I've got to work this out. It's important—"

"All right—mon amour," Fanny said.

'It doesn't work. I don't know why. But in her uniquely perverse case, my appetite "doth damned well grow with increase of that it feeds upon!" Who said that? Shakespeare, I think. Yes, Shakespeare. Hamlet, some place. So now I look at her—and get this awful feeling of being—enslaved. Enslaved—hell! Worse! Addicted like any dope fiend to this Circean witchcraft that turns me swine! To that—that unspeakable soft slow mucoid almost prehensible cling and twist and scald that—drains me, empties me of manhood, leaves me witless, witless, trembling, blind—melts my brains into spermatazoa and milks me of my life, my life!

'So—enslaved. Addicted. Besotted. Damned. Or—in love. Jésus! All I know is that I'll go on wanting her forever; I'll scream her name from the hottest pit after she's tossed me into hell. But—escape her? Never! Don't even want to, really. By my side—my wife. To love, honor and cherish—God!'

"Aren't you—ever going to answer me?" Fanny said.

"I was trying to figure out—how to," Philippe said, slowly. "In a way, you're right. Innocence is irretrievable —so to pretend it, is stupid. But it isn't that which bothers me. Or not entirely. Of course, you do shock me at times. I really didn't know a girl *could* get that much fun out of it."

Fanny slipped out her chair, came around the little table, and stood there before him, looking into his eyes.

"I'm going to tell you something I really shouldn't," she said a little harshly, "mainly because it's much too flattering, I suppose. I—I didn't before. Before that— first time—with *you* on the steamer—I *never* had, felt *anything,* I mean. With Rod—I hated it. It was awful. But it so happens I love you. I love you all over—inside and out. I wake up in the morning and see you lying there beside me—and I—I feel like singing. I don't know whether you're a good lover or not—that you're better than *he* was goes without saying—but you don't even have to be. All you need to be is you—and that does it, love! So right now you're looking at the happiest girl in the whole wide world—and the saddest—and the scaredest—I mean the most frightened—"

"Why, Fanny?" Philippe said.

"Because—something's come between us. Something—

new. Not Miss Speckled Setter Pup. Not even—your
mother. But something. And you're hiding that something
from me. What is it, Philippe? Another girl? If it is—you
can tell me. I'm all done with my suicidal mania, thank
you! Of course I'll cry my eyes out—but I'll get over it.
Get over—*you* even. And that, come to think of it, is the
saddest thing of all."

" 'Men have died, and worms have eaten them,' " Philippe quoted somberly, " 'but not for love . . .' "

"A pity," Fanny said. "What better reason for dying
could a person have?"

"Now, Fanny!" Philippe said.

"I won't harm myself, Philippe. Tell me—is there—another girl?"

"No," Philippe said at once, and with obvious sincerity.
"You're the only girl in my life, Fanny. And God willing
you're the only one there'll ever be—"

She bent then and kissed his mouth, slowly, lingeringly,
taking all the time in the world about it. Drew back,
looked at him.

"Then what *is* it, my love?" she said.

Philippe's eyes were bleak with actual anguish.

'I wish I could tell her,' he thought. 'But I can't! I can't.
That Papa's friends came through. A little behind schedule—but they came through. Inside of a month I'll be in
Paris—studying at the Pasteur Institute—doing my internship at La Salpêtrière—so instead of passing the Board
next year—it'll be two more at the very least—maybe
three. She—she'll be so disappointed—so hurt. If—only I
could marry her and take her with me! But that's—impossible. I haven't a picayune beyond what Papa sends me—
and Lord knows asking him to support the wife Maman's
dead set against my marrying anyhow would be a damned
sight too much! Oh, petit bon Dieu, I—'

"What is it, Philippe?" Fanny said.

"Don't know—nerves, I suppose. I—I keep thinking
how rough our first years together are going to be. Maybe
I'll be able to get a country practice. The farm folks pay
the Doc in produce, you know—chickens, eggs, pork, and
such like—So that way we wouldn't starve—not quite
anyhow—"

"Philippe," Fanny said, "has—your mother—turned
your father against us?"

"No—not entirely, at any rate. But she just *won't* get reconciled to the idea, especially since—"

"*My* mother came home to open the biggest parlor house in Storyville," Fanny said.

"Yes," Philippe said. "Lord, Fanny—That *is* awfully rough to take!"

"Philippe—" Fanny whispered, "you—you want me to get out of your life? I will, you know. I—I love you that much. Enough even—to give you up—it that's what you want."

"That's not what I want, as you know damned well!" Philippe howled, almost strangling on the words, the tears he was fighting back scalding his throat like live steam. "I want you by my side—forever. I want you to be the mother of my sons. I want—our daughter—to be your image. To look and act exactly like you, Fan. Even if—she's—a trifle naughty, I'll forgive her, knowing where she got it from. Oh, petit enfant, Jésus, I—"

"Phil—" Fanny breathed, "you—you *meant* that, didn't you? You really, truly meant it. So right now I'm happy that it feels like I'm going to die. And I will, too if—if you don't—"

"If I don't what?" Philippe said.

"Take me to bed—right now. Make us our little Susie—or our little Phil. That's what I want. Right now. In spite of everything. You hear me, Phil?"

"Fanny, you're crazy, you know!"

"As a loon. Over you, mon amour," Fanny said.

And then it was over, their illicit idyll, their stolen, premature honeymoon. Fanny Turner took a train back up to Troy, New York. Philippe Sompayac embarked upon a steamer bound for France, vowing to himself, 'I'll write her the minute I get there—the very minute—she'll forgive me—when I explain that I just didn't have the heart . . .'

But, as he should have expected, that proved impossible. Matriculation, getting himself oriented, making the not exactly easy transition from his heavily patois-laden Louisiana French to the classic, racy speech of Paris, all delayed him. When he did write her, it was far too late. Which made no difference really. Since their last night together, it had already been.

# Chapter Twenty-One

"You miserable, disgusting little liar!" Norma said.

Fanny looked at her. Smiled. Said:

"All right. Since I disgust you, why don't you get out of here? For good. I mean, I'd appreciate it, really. Do me that favor, Norma; please."

"Oh, I will," Norma said; "I mean to. But not without first giving you a piece of my mind, Fanny, darling! Thought you were smart, didn't you? Since you knew I *hate* going downtown, dealing with ordinary people—the dull, plebian clods!—you thought I shouldn't bother to inquire into your activities, didn't you, Fanny, dear? Your clandestine and oh, so delicate activities! But I did. Something told me to. Something in your behavior just didn't ring true. So I checked at the railway station, at the ticket office, my dearly beloved! Described you to those grubby clerks—and who could forget *that* hair; *those* eyes? You, my darling Fanny, spent the Christmas Holidays in New York City. Alone? Perish the thought! Then—with *whom?* That question presented slight, even negligible difficulties, I assure you! From the station itself, I rang up the Beaconridge residence, asked to speak to dear Tony. 'Why, yes,' says he, 'as a matter of fact I *did* spend Christmas in New York. Why, Norma?"

"And?" Fanny said.

"I said: 'You know damned well why, Tony!' and hung up on him. So now the oaf probably thinks I'm jealous of *his* activities! Dear God! 'Lay not that flattering unction to thy soul!' In any event, I'm waiting, Fanny Turner. For an explanation. For some sort of explanation that makes sense. You *refused* my invitation, swearing you had to go home to New Orleans. But instead, you—"

Norma's voice slid down the tonal scale into silence. Her brown eyes opened very wide. Then she went on, whispering, her voice hoarse with what was clearly horror, her words a shudder with the actual, honest nausea that she felt:

"You went to New York. In order to—to—my God!"

"Go on, Norma," Fanny said. "Say it."

"I can't! It's—too—too—utterly disgusting. You—sweet, clean, delicate you—spread out like a sacrificial lamb—while he—snorts—and plunges—and rips into you with all that—appalling male brutishness—dear God, Fanny! Why? I'm trying to understand, believe me!"

Fanny's long, dusty golden lashes came down, almost veiling her eyes.

'So Tony was in New York, Christmas,' she thought. 'Good. That might help. Depends on how—gallant—I can fool him into being. If I have to. And I just might have to. Anyhow I'm awfully glad I never told this he-man Mary where Phil was—or anything much about him—mainly because it didn't seem right to even mention his name to an oddball, wrong-go, off-horse, weird critter like this. Oh, Jesus; why doesn't he answer my letter? Of course it's all my fault. That last time I—I didn't even give him a chance to—to use one of those hateful dead feeling things that men—Oh Lord! So now—'

"I'm waiting, Fanny!" Norma said.

"I fail to see why I owe you an explanation, Norma," Fanny said, "not to mention that there just isn't any I could give you that you'd understand. Because to do that you'd have to be what *I* am—a woman. A real, honest-to-God female woman. And that, Lord knows, you're not! I *like* men, honey. In fact, I adore them the way that nature intended a girl to. I put up with your messing around, mucking about with me—because I needed the things you could teach me—how to talk well, to dress discreetly, how not to be gauche, commit faux pas. And I thank you for those things, truly . . ."

"You're—incredible!" Norma said. "Simply incredible!"

"No, I'm not. You're the incredible one, honey. Proof of that is that you don't even know which end of you is for what, and that neither one of 'em is for another woman. Because not one of your filthy, abnormal, Lesbian tricks is any substitute for what a man—a *real* man—has got hanging between his legs, although it doesn't always *hang*, thank goodness!"

Norma clapped her hands over her ears.

"I simply will not listen to such—filth!" she said.

"No," Fanny said, *"listen*—I suppose not. But if what you *do* isn't filthy, seems to me that Webster, or somebody, needs to invent another word. Kissing—well, let's call it kissing anyhow, for argument's sake—is just fine— but, as broad-minded as I try to be, it seems to me that kissing ought to stop—somewhere above the waist, Norma dear. And I'm not talking about morals. I'll admit mine are nothing to brag about, though I contend that if you're going to be immoral, *men* are the creatures to do it with. What I'm talking about—is hygiene, cleanliness, fastidiousness, maybe. But then, you wouldn't understand that, either, would you?"

Norma stared at her a long, slow time.

"So—" she said bleakly, "it's—all over between us, Fanny?"

"All over," Fanny said. "No hard feelings, Norma?"

Norma looked down, stared at the floor. Looked up, again.

"Yes," she said icily, "there very definitely *are* hard feelings, Fanny. You—you've cost me too much—time, devotion, worry, trouble—love. If I can—I'll ruin you, make you suffer a thousandfold for the way I'm suffering now. So, you'd better be very careful what you do, and how you do it in the future. Because, if you don't—"

Without even knocking, Polly Stevens pushed the door open, squealed, "mail call!" and clattered off down the hall.

Fanny jumped up, her pale eyes ablaze. Norma stared at her.

"So—" she whispered. "It wasn't—Tony!"

Fanny stopped in the doorway, turned very slowly, smiled.

"How would I know?" she mocked. "With all your attention to—well, grammatical niceties, Norma, dear, don't tell me that you didn't notice that throughout our conversation I consistently said 'men' plural. So don't absolve dear Tony of—sin. He could be the guilty party. But then so could any number of—dear friends and gentle acquaintances of mine—all of whom wear trousers. Of that you may rest assured. And to prove that *I*, at least, haven't any hard feelings towards you, dear—come along with me to get your mail—"

"No," Norma said, her voice gone toneless, dull. "who'd write me, Fanny? Strange—I've just realized that I'm going to—die—all alone . . ."

"Doesn't everybody?" Fanny said, and went through the doorway.

Since it was Miss Barlett's unvarying custom to distribute the mail in alphabetical order, it took her some little time to get to Turner. Long before she had, Fanny could feel that vile, green-tasting sickness rising in her again—as it had every morning for a week now. 'And my period's two weeks late,' she thought sadly. 'No, nearer three. Oh Lord, don't let me throw up! Not now, not here in front of everybody. Miss Barlett's pretty innocent—but Polly Stevens is as smart as a whip. Jesus! How many times have I heard her and Irene Lodge talking about girls they knew who got "caught"! As I'm caught now. I—I thought that if this happened I—I'd be so happy. And I am, too—in a way. Or I would if he—if Phil would only answer my letter. He's had plenty of time. All—of eight days since I wrote him telling him what I thought: that I'm—pregnant. I'm going to have a baby. *His* baby. Little Phil—or little Sue. Oh Lord make it look just like him—either way. Boy or girl—'cause—'

"Miss Polly Stevens!" Maud Barlett said.

'That means—I'm next,' Fanny thought. 'Let her say it, Jesus! Please God, let her call my name!'

"Miss Frances Turner!" Maud Barlett cooed. *"Two* letters for you, my dear! Why, aren't you the lucky girl!"

Fanny got up slowly, putting one slim hand to the base of her throat and thinking fiercely: 'Stay down, damn it! Toss my cookies, and they'll *know,* they'll know!'

She took the letters from Miss Barlett. The first one was from Martha. Impatiently she flipped under the other. Then a shaking got into her. She quivered like an aspen in a high wind. Her pale eyes widened, widened, until they threatened to eclipse her face. Her lips went white.

For that second letter was her own. The one she had written Philippe nearly ten days before. On the envelope, someone—his landlady probably—had scrawled: "No longer at this address. Forwarding address unknown."

She stood there, holding that letter, and shook. From somewhere, ten million light years away, it sounded like, Polly Stevens's voice came over to her:

"Why—Fanny! You—you look so awful! Are you ill?"

"No," she grated. "I'm just fine, Polly." Then, more to

be doing something, anything, than for any other reason, she tore open the envelope of Martha's letter. But her hands were shaking so that she dropped it, scattering its many pages all over the floor. Polly Stevens, Irene Lodge, Dorothy Meadows, and another girl helped her gather them up. She was aware that they were all staring at her—even Miss Barlett—and with real concern.

"I—I guess I don't feel very well at that," she murmured in the direction of Polly's ear. "Wrong time of the month and—"

Then with that cruel inevitability that bad news seems to carry with it, the words of the uppermost page came clear: The fifth page, which ordinarily it would have taken her a fairish amount of time to get to, since she was anything but a rapid reader:

". . . met by accident, Monsieur Sompayac, down on Canal Street this morning. Of course, he's always been most polite to me; but today he was even affable. Told me that he'd heard from your Philippe—from Paris, which was a thing I didn't know, though I suppose that you did, dear. Some friends of the family who apparently hold high positions in the French government got Philippe appointed—as a student of course—to the Pasteur Institute, and he's to continue his internship at La Salpêtrière Hospital and the Hôtel-Dieu. The only regrettable thing about it, M. Sompayac says, is that Philippe must remain abroad all of three years—I know you must be unhappy over that detail, but—"

'Three years.' Fanny didn't think those words, she heard them. They rang in her ears like—church bells—all the great bronze cathedral bells in the world lifting their deafening clangor at the same time, tolling the funeral of her every hope. 'Three years. Three years. THREE YEARS!'

She started towards the door, crumpling Martha's letter into a damp ball in her fist. But she didn't get there. Even at that late date, one year before the Victorian era would be officially over, there were still women who knew how to slip gracefully to earth in a beautifully staged swoon. But Fanny wasn't one of them. She simply went down head first, striking her face against the floor so hard that her teeth tore the inside of her upper lip, and a small flood of red poured out of her mouth. From somewhere, very far away, she could hear the girls screaming.

She went on hearing them, faintly, for perhaps a second longer. Then she neither heard, nor saw, nor even sensed anything. For being, as she was, nobody's proper Victorian, her swoon was real.

"Please, Mrs. Redfern," Fanny said, "don't send for the doctor! It—it's nothing really. Just a weakness. It—just comes, sometimes. Dr. Forlanini at the clinic in Italy said it would be years—before I get over it. If I ever do. I—I didn't tell you about it before for fear you wouldn't admit me to the school! And I—I *wanted* to come here *so* badly. You see, I promised Sue—"

She bent her head and cried, daintily, prettily, softly.

Jane Redfern stared at her.

'The girl's got her points,' she thought. 'Good material, there. We'll make something of her yet.'

"I have to, child," she said gently, "for your own sake, dear. Don't worry—we won't send you away unless Doctor Lewis thinks it's absolutely imperative. Now, try to rest. Norma and Polly will sit with you—Won't you, girls?"

"Of course, Mrs. Redfern!" Polly said; but Norma merely nodded, grimly.

'Oh Jesus!' Fanny thought. 'The doctor! He'll just look at me—and he'll *know*! Why'd I have to go and faint like a damn fool? My—condition—I reck—I guess. Well— I've torn it, now. That lying, heartless, no-good— Oh Jesus! Paris! Even if I wrote him right now and he wrote me right back and then got his father to send him the money to come home to—to marry me, my tummy would be poking out a mile and a half before he got here, and everybody would know. That is, if—'

She stopped and her pale eyes went arctic, glacial, the anguish in them frozen, deep.

'If he'd even—bother to come. 'Cause he *knew*. About his appointment to that French medical school, I mean. Already, at Christmas time, he knew. He had to. And still, knowing he—he took advantage of me. I *know* he didn't—didn't use—protection that last time; but there were a couple of times before when I don't think he did either! Why not? What were the odds? Knock the stupid little bitch up, then skip, brother! To gay Paree! Wine, women, and song. While I—while I—'

She bent her head and wept, stormily, terribly.

"Fanny, please!" Polly Stevens said.

"Let her cry," Norma Tilson said, harshly. "Sometimes it helps—makes a person feel better, Polly . . ."

"Oh, dear!" Polly said, "but the *way* she's crying—is just too awful, Norma! I think—"

"I said let her!" Norma said.

Dr. Lewis had come, and gone—prescribing, before his departure, a tonic, and all sorts of broths and strengthening foods.

"The poor child's plain undernourished, Jane!" he said to Mrs. Redfern. "She needs to gain a minimum of twelve pounds, though twenty would be better. Those Europeans! The surgery seems to have been neat enough, but the postoperative cure must have been dismal, to leave her in such a weakened condition! Let her catch a cold and she'll be right back where she started from. I'll look in again from time to time. Pretty little thing, isn't she? Delicate—fine—"

"Yes," Jane Redfern said.

And Fanny lay there, weak with relief, because the bearded, fierce-looking old doctor hadn't even glanced at the lower part of her body.

'I suppose I don't *look* like a bad girl,' she thought. 'That's why . . .'

She looked at Polly, who sat by her bed.

Polly was showing an unusual devotion, while Norma no longer even looked in to see how Fanny was.

'Norma hates me now,' Fanny thought, 'but looks like Pol is really on my side for a change. Part of it's because she's ashamed of that dirty trick she pulled off on me with that poem. But, anyhow, it's just as well. Right now I need all the help I can get. Got to do something fast. Phil is—out. Oh, Jesus, how that hurts! But even if he were to—to try to do the right thing by me, he'd still be too late to save me from being disgraced. That is even if I could depend on him, which after the way he's acted I sure Lord can't! Besides I—I'll still have *his* son. Or his daughter.

And nobody can take that from me, even if I do have to call it—her, him—by another name. Like—Beaconridge, say. I'll always know. Oh I can't do this to poor Tony! It's too rotten! Only I've got to. I've got to. Tony is—a dear. Good-looking. Sweet. and *rich*. And—and he loves me. Wants to marry me. So—'

"Polly—" she said.

An hour later, Polly Stevens, accompanied by Irene Lodge, was already on her way. For though trusted upper-form girls were allowed to go downtown upon request, they had to go in pairs. Not that Jane Redfern believed that any of her young ladies would get into serious mischief; the rule was laid down to still the townspeople's too-ready tongues. Even on the day that she'd sent that fatal wire, Fanny hadn't been alone. But she'd chosen Gertrude Walker and Lillian Fisby to accompany her that day, having observed that they were the dullest, most stupid girls in the whole school. Today, however, fortunately or unfortunately, Fanny's schemes worked like well-oiled clockwork. Since the labor troubles of two years before, Mr. Beaconridge had placed a uniformed guard before the door of the shirtworks, a stout young man of considerable physical strength; the only flaw in the arrangement being his youth, though perhaps his plebian status had something to do with it. In any event, it was laughably easy for two decidedly pretty, aristocratic young ladies to get the guard to leave his post to go fetch young Tony from the offices upstairs, due consideration being given to the fact that said young ladies weren't above flirting with the guard to accomplish their ends.

The minute Tony came down, Polly slapped the carefully sealed envelope into his hands and said: "From Fanny!" Then the two of them were off, leaving a trail of girlish giggles bubbling behind them on the frosty February air.

Tony stood there, staring at that note. Joy, tenderness, desire, even love stole over his almost too-handsome face. He tore open the note, read:

Dearest Tony—I must see you. Tonight. Drive down Ferry Street—a little after midnight. I'll be waiting

on the corner of Second.* I know this sounds awful—but it isn't. I—I've just got to talk to you
*alone*—that's all.

Love,
Fanny.

They sat in Tony's smart little rig far out on Brunswick
Road, by the shores of Ida Lake.

"It's cold!" Fanny complained. "Haven't you got any
place where you could take me—where we could be
alone, so I can talk to you without other people listening,
and at the same time we wouldn't freeze to death?"

"Well," Tony said slowly, "I do know a place—but it's
got kind of a—a bad reputation, Fanny. Jacob Reisling's
Tavern, out on this same road—but further out. About
three miles beyond the city line. Only—"

"Only what?" Fanny said.

"People—men and women go there to—to be together.
People who shouldn't, I mean. Married women—who're
—well deceiving their husbands. And vice versa. Young
couples who—don't want to wait to make it legal. You
see?"

"Yes," Fanny said, "is this—Mr. Reisling—discreet?"

"Fanny!" Tony said.

"Don't get me wrong, *Mr.* Beaconridge!" Fanny said. "I
only want to talk. About—something—very important to
me—and maybe even to you, as well, but you'll have to
be the judge of that. I've already taken an awful risk, slipping out at night like this—and it seems to me that if we
could go to that place—and have a rum punch or a hot
toddy or some eggnog—while we talked—we'd probably
be in less danger of being seen by people who'd tell Mrs.
Redfern—*or* your father—than in a more respectable
place. Am I right?"

"You are," Tony laughed. "Old Jake is a friend of
mine. He'll put us in a back booth with curtains where
nobody'll see us! So—"

---

*The Emma Willard School, now at Pawling and Elm Grove
avenues, formerly occupied the present site of the Russel Sage
College for Women, at the northwest corner of Second and
Ferry streets.

"So come on!" Fanny said.

"Fanny!" Tony said worriedly. "You shouldn't! That's the fifth toddy you've had, and—"

"Don't care," Fanny said, in an elaborately thickened tone of voice. "I'm—so blue, Tony! Oh Lord, but I need consoling—"

"What's the matter, doll?" Tony said, tenderly.

"Well—Oh, all right! Gonna tell you th'—th' truth. That time—you—you asked me to marry you—on th' polo field, remember—?"

"Yes, dearest," Tony said.

"I turned you down. Not because I didn't like you; I did. I do. Maybe I even love you—I don't know. I'm so-o-o-o mixed up."

" 'Sall right, darling," Tony said.

"Tony—I—I had me—another boy. Fiancé, I mean. We were planning to get married. Don't look so hurt! But at—at Christmas time, we had a terrible fight. And—we broke up. So now I—I miss him something awful. At least I *think* I do—"

"But you only *think* so, Fanny?" Tony said.

"Yes. Every time I think of him—of Phil—the next minute I think of you. I—guess I could have written him a dozen times by now—and made up—but every time I started to, *you'd* get in the way. I—I'd remember how you looked that day on the polo field, and—"

"Fanny, dearest, darling—forget him! I'm here—and I love you. I swear—"

"Don't swear. It's—naughty. Tell you what—Tony—O—how's about a little—kiss, huh?"

"Fanny!" Tony said.

"Wait! Gonna tell you why. Got to be honest, with you. Want to see if—if I *like* kissing you. If I do that means that I—don't *really* love him, doesn't it? At least I think so. Don't you?"

"God, yes!" Tony Beaconridge said.

"Oh, Tony!" Fanny wept. "We—we shouldn't have! Oh, what a fool I've been! Just because I had too many toddies! And was blue—and—and—now you'll *never* respect me again!"

"Respect!" Tony said. "Wrong word! Worship, honor,

cherish, adore! We'll elope—right now—tonight. I was a beast, Fanny! Thought I had—my animal nature under better control than that—Will you forgive me, my dearest?"

"No!" Fanny stormed. "You—you hurt me—something awful, Tony. I—I've never done *that*—been *bad*, really *bad*—before. Of course, I have kissed Phil—but—"

"Don't mention the bounder's name to me!" Tony said.

"Don't call—Phil—a bounder, Tony," Fanny whispered, brokenly. "He—always—respected me. And you *didn't*. So now—"

"I'll make it up to you, dearest! We'll go rouse out the justice of peace this minute and—"

Fanny stared at him. 'This is it!' her mind exulted. Then abruptly that exultation died. 'Don't be a fool, Fanny-girl!' she told herself. 'Do it this way and his old man will cut him off without a red copper. Play it smart, baby! If you have to marry a boy *this* stupid, at least make it pay!'

"No, Tony—" she said.

"Why not?" Tony said.

"Your father. You'd better get his consent. I shouldn't want him to—to think badly of me. Besides, I—I've always wanted a formal wedding. Me—all in white—I guess I can *still* wear white in this case, can't I? Since it was you, who—"

"Was a rotter! A beast! An utter, lustful swine! Oh, Fanny, I—"

"You—were—sweet," Fanny murmured, tenderly. "I think I—I'm going to like having you for a husband—now that I know—what it's like. Making love, I mean. I thought—it was going to be—awful—and it—it wasn't. Of course, it *did* hurt—at first—but—"

"I'll speak to Father first thing in the morning!" Tony said.

"No, don't!" Fanny said. She thought: 'Don't let him spoil things, the damn fool! I can take a chance for a while. It'll be—at least the middle of April before it begins to show. But I—we—have got to do this again—several times more. So when I tell you I'm—caught—you'll believe me. Maybe I'll be able to teach you to be good at it—a little. 'Cause Lord knows you aren't! Quicker than a jackrabbit—almost as bad as Rod was. But

I think I can teach you. You—you're finer; got good blood, good breeding—so—so controlling yourself, being gentle shouldn't come too hard to you.'

"Why not?" Tony said.

"Better to—to go at this gradually, love. Let him—see us together. Get used to me. Get to—to like me—a little, first. You understand?"

"Of course!" Tony said. "You're right, darling."

But she wasn't. The trouble was, of course, that she had never even heard of a man called Hawkes. And, although Tony had, he was totally ignorant of what Hawkes's actual function was.

"There is a tide in the time of men's lives, which, taken at the flood—" And all the grand and sonorous rest of it. Fanny's very shrewdness, you may observe, had defeated her. For had she gone with Tony to a justice of the peace that very night, who knows? Both she and Tony were of age, and his father hated public scandal. Ergo . . .

In any event, that particular enterprise of great pitch and moment had already had its current turned awry and lost the name of action.

It and her life. Her life.

## Chapter Twenty-Two

Norma Tilson was walking down First Street with Maud Barlett—for to such a pass had her loneliness brought her that she'd been forced to resume her neutral, and neuter-gendered, friendship with the English teacher—when the strange young woman came up to them.

"Please, miss!" the young woman said. "Could I speak to you—in private—a minute? Believe me, it's important!"

Norma stared at the thin, dark, much-too-intense young woman.

"Am I supposed to know you?" she said. "I'll admit there *is* something familiar about your face; but for the life of me I can't place you . . ."

"You *do* know me," the young woman said, "but you ain't—I mean aren't—acquainted with me. We come from too different walks of life. I work in the telegraph office. I've taken telegrams from you half-a-dozen times, Miss. That's how come my face is familiar to you. My name is Myrtle, Myrtle Tolliver, at your service, miss . . ."

"Well—Myrtle," Norma said, "what can I do for you?"

"Ask this lady—she's a teacher, ain't she?—to excuse you —a sec. What I got to tell you—ain't for her ears . . ."

"If it's not fitting for me to hear," Maud Barlett said firmly, "I simply can't permit a student of mine to listen to it. Come along, Norma!"

"No 'm," Myrtle Tolliver said, "you're getting me wrong, ma'am. Didn't say it wasn't fitting. Maybe it *is*, for all I know. What I mean is—that this matter is—awful delicate, ma'am. And seeing as how you're a teacher, you'd maybe be honor-bound to—*do* something about it. Something that sure as the dickens would do more harm than good if I know anything about people. While this young lady could likely clear the whole thing up by saying a word or two in the right quarter—"

"You mean," Maud whispered, "that one of our girls is—in trouble?"

"Yes 'm. *Bad* trouble. So bad you'd have to expel her, ma'am. A pity. But if this young lady would speak to her, get her to—to mend her ways, quit what she's doing, *you'd* be spared an awful lot of pain and trouble, the school would be saved from an awful messy scandal, and the girl in question could finish with her class 'n nobody'd be the wiser. You see?"

Maud Barlett stared at her, guessed, with sure intuition, who the culprit was. And, upon the spur of that same moment, retreated from the knowledge. She achingly, abjectly admitted that, to the actual, irrevocable certainty that her doll of Dresden china, her delicate portrait of a high-born lass stepped coolly, freshly, fragrantly out of a canvas by Sir Joshua, a half-smile on those shell-pink lips, a cerulean mist hovering about those eyes, was indulging—the pain was blade-keen, remorselessly thrusting—in the grosser forms of carnal sin, she much preferred even the faintest, most tenuous doubt.

"I see," she whispered. "All right, Norma, go listen to her—you have my consent."

Norma stared at her, and involuntarily a smile of pure contempt tugged one lip-corner upward. For a fraction of a second, half a heart beat, less, it flickered there, then was gone.

"As you like, Miss Barlett," she said, and moved off, down the street, with Myrtle Tolliver.

"It's *her*—" Myrtle said quickly, "your little blondie friend—the one who looks too blamed pretty 'n sweet to be for real—"

"Do you," Norma said icily, "know her *name*, by any chance?"

"Yes, miss—it's Turner. Miss Frances Turner . . ."

"I see," Norma said. "Go on—please—"

"Tell her"—Myrtle all but wept—"that th' old man *knows*. That he's had 'em followed. That every time they go to that place—"

"I think you'd better speak clearly, Myrtle. I assume that my dear friend Miss Turner is half of that 'they.' But the rest of it eludes me. Who is the old man? And to what place do you refer, exactly?"

"Why—you—don't know? Thought everybody knew who the old man is. Why, Mr. Beaconridge, of course. Damn near owns this burg, don't he, and—"

"I'd thank you to watch your language Myrtle," Norma said, "especially if you want me to go on listening to you—"

"Yes 'm," Myrtle said, contritely, "sorry, miss—that slipped. I won't use strong language agin. Mr. Beaconridge knows that—that her 'n young Tony is doing what they hadn't ought to—leastwise without having stood up before a preacher or a justice of the peace, first. He's had 'em followed. Every time they go out to old Jake Reisling's place on Brunswick road—"

"Seems to me I *have* heard whispers about that place," Norma said. "Sort of a tavern, isn't it?"

"You could call it that," Myrtle said. "What it really is—if you'll pardon th' blunt language, Miss—is a house of assignation. Every Troy girl who's fell from virtue in th' last twenty-five years, lost it there—"

"Including *you*, I dare say," Norma said.

"That," Myrtle said flatly, "is none of your goddamned business, miss—and I *don't* apologize for the rough talk. I'm trying to help, and you're making it hard for me. So now you tell me, you want to hear this, or don't you?"

"Sorry," Norma said. "I *do* apologize. I can. Mainly because noblesse does oblige, I suppose. All right Myrtle, please go on."

"All rightie. Mr. Beaconridge—has put a fellow onto 'em. A feller I know—private detective. Even sent him down to N' Orleans to check on your little friend—"

"And," Norma said, "what did he find out about her down there?"

"Won't tell me. Close-mouthed sort of a fellow. But he admits it's plenty. Says that if Mrs. Redfern knew one per-cent of what *he* knows about your little friend she'd *throw* her out of the school head first!"

"I see. But there's one thing in this wild tale of yours, young woman, that doesn't hold water: how on earth could Tony Beaconridge take Fanny Turner *anywhere* unchaperoned, the rules of our august institution being what they are?"

"He does, though. Two 'n three nights a week. She simply waits 'til everybody's asleep 'n sneaks out. Shinnies down the drainpipe next to her window. Climbs th' gate. She's quick as a cat 'n just as surefooted. Tony waits for her a little ways down Ferry. I've *seen* 'em do it. My friend let me come along with him that far, oncet. Then he sent me home. Says Jake Reisling's Tavern is no place for th' likes of me—"

"I'm sure he's right," Norma murmured. "And I do thank you, Myrtle—from the bottom of my heart. I'll speak to Miss Turner—very firmly, I assure you. I only hope she'll listen to me."

"Oh I know she will—I used to see th' two of you to-gether—and you were very close. She fairly dotes on you, miss—I—I kind of like her. Got spirit, that little girl. Only she's making a *bad* mistake this time. She hasn't got a Chinaman's chance of marrying Tony. She'd be better off sticking with that French fellow in New York—"

"What—French fellow—in New York?" Norma whis-pered.

"Name of Sompayac—or something like that. I kind of figger she spent Christmas with him, judging from that telegram she sent. That little girl sure gets around. But she'd better quit it—latch onto a *good* man, before her re-putation gets to be *too* bad—"

"I'm sure—you're right," Norma said. "But just one thing more—Myrtle. Just *why* are you doing this?"

"Don't know. To—to make up for something—I did wrong myself. Oh no! Not *this* kind of thing. But a sort of a dirty trick I was forced into— But that's another story, miss. 'Pears to me you'd better get back to the teacher-lady. She's getting impatient . . ."

"Right," Norma said, "and I do thank you, Myrtle. You've done *me* a very great favor, truly—"

"Well?" Maud Barlett said when Norma came up to her.

"She's—right," Norma said gently. "It *really* isn't for your ears, Miss Barlett. It would—place too great a strain on your affections—and your sense of honor. Put them in opposition, as it were. Let me handle it—or try to. If I fail, then I'll come to you. Agreed?"

Maud Barlett stared at the tall girl and her eyes were troubled. And more than a little frightened, too.

"Very well, Norma, agreed," she said.

"I still insist," Jane Redfern said fretfully, "that this is undignified, unworthy of—either of us, my dear! Don't know how I could possibly have allowed you to talk me into *this*. To skulk in the shadows like—"

"Sssssh!" Norma said. "Here she comes!"

Fanny came running down the gravel path until she reached the iron gate. It was, of course, both locked and bolted. But Fanny lifted a dainty foot, clad in a stylish buttoned patent-leather shoe, as high as the bolt, showing in the process not only her petticoats, but a pair of the ruffled, lace-trimmed, knee-length pantalettes of the type affected by actresses and other women of dubious virtue, and swung herself up on the gate. A little leap and her gloved hands deftly caught the top bar; with surprising strength, she drew herself waist-high, hip-high upon it, swung her legs fetchingly, if with complete immodesty, across it, and waited. A second later, Tony Beaconridge sprinted out of the shadows and held up his arms. Fanny leaped down into them, and lifted her mouth to be kissed.

But Tony failed to oblige. As he turned his face away from her, the light from the gas lamp by the gate fell fully on it, and both Norma and Miss Redfern could see the flash and glitter of his tears.

"Tony!" Fanny gasped; then softly, pityingly: "What's wrong, love? Why—you're crying! You actually are!"

"I—I told—Father," Tony groaned. "And now I—I wish to Christ I hadn't!"

"He—he doesn't—approve—of your—doing your honest duty by me?" Fanny said quietly. "Is the Beaconridge name—too good—to give to the child you've got me with, Tony? Is *that* what you're trying to say?"

"No!" Tony all but screamed at her, "but he says—and he's right!—that it's too good to give to the girl whose *mother* runs the biggest sporting house in New Orleans! To the girl—who—who tried to kill herself when the fellow she was the mistress of—at only fifteen years of age—my darling Fanny!—left her for another, more decent girl! And he says that I *can't* give my name to a baby I haven't the slightest proof is actually mine—since you spent the whole Christmas holiday in New York in the apartment of a French Creole from New Orleans named Philippe Sompayac! And it's no damned good trying to lie to me; I've seen the actual telegram you sent him: 'Get rid of your roommate, I'm on my way. Love, Fanny.' Oh, Christ and Saint Judas, I—"

"That miserable, meddlesome, long-nosed little bitch!" Fanny whispered.

"And you—pretending you were drunk that first time! Fighting me off—but not too hard! And afterwards—after you'd *really* got me hooked—all those nights, saying as though you were ashamed almost to death, but couldn't help yourself: 'I guess it's all right, Tony—since we're as good as man and wife already, anyhow—Besides, Oh Lord—I *need* your lovin' so!' "

Fanny stood there. She didn't cry. She looked at Tony. And behind her eyes, quite visibly, something started dying. Tony stood there watching it die—a long time, a very long time; and the spectacle—that minature Roman Circus going on inside those semantically irrelevant entities we are pleased to call her mind, her heart, her soul—was almost unbearable. For in Fanny, hope was, had always been, a dumb-beast thing; so what young Anthony Beaconridge watched was a chained and idiotic mute being nibbled to death by the rats of time, voicelessly deprived, by a process whose cruelty was nothing less than obscene of (and this, perhaps, was the subtlest of all the tortures her epoch inflicted upon all those who, like Fanny, were born incapable of conforming to its mores) the existence that it, poor dumb-beast hope, had *never* had any right to.

"All right, Tony," she said, finally. "Help me back up over the gate, will you?"

"Aren't you—" he got out, "going to say—anything? Defend yourself—even a little? Please, Fanny! Say it—it isn't so! Tell me that—Hawkes got you confused with somebody else! That Myrtle Tolliver made up that telegram of yours she gave him and he turned over to father. Don't—don't *kill* me like this! Tell me they're wrong, even if you have to lie!"

Slowly Fanny shook her head. As small, as slight as she was, in that moment, the motion became as ponderous as time—freighted with the only thing she had left: a certain irreductible reserve of—dignity, say:

"No, Tony—they're not wrong—and I won't lie," she said softly, "not anymore, leastwise. I'm sorry it turned out this way. I'd have made you a good wife. We would have been—happy. If—people—and God—and His twin brother—His Siamese twin brother, the Devil—had let us alone. My first baby—wouldn't have been yours—that's true enough. But *all* the rest would have been. And—you'd have loved—even this first one, Tony—'cause it's going to be—beautiful. I made sure of that. I picked out for its father the best and smartest and kindest and handsomest man in the whole wide world—"

"Philippe—" Tony said, bitterly.

"Philippe. But you're not far behind him. 'Course you're kind of stupid, but you make up for that by being—so nice, Tony. So—good, really. And you know what? It was getting so that when I said to you 'I love you'—I wasn't lying anymore. Not even a little bit. Too bad, isn't it? Oh, well—Tell me: Would it be a kind of insult—for a no-good little bitch like me to—to ask you to—kiss her good-bye?"

"Fanny!" Tony wept, "I don't care! Even if—if you've been the biggest whore on earth, I love you! I don't give a damn who the father of your little bastard is! Come on! We'll get old Justice Weatherby and his wife up and—"

"Oh don't be an utter ass, Tony," Fanny said wearily. "Help me back up over the gate, will you?"

Jane Redfern came out of the shadows, then. Her face

of New England granite was—shattered now, the frost
lines showing white.

"That won't be necessary, young woman," she said. "I'll
unlock it. Good night, young Mr. Beaconridge. I'd suggest
that you go home—and meditate upon your sins—not the
least of which is that—of folly . . ."

"Please, Mrs. Redfern," Fanny whispered, "don't send
my father a wire. Write a letter—and not to him. Address
it to my stepmother. I'm asking you that. No, I'm begging
you. Please."

Mrs. Redfern stared at Fanny, finding, to her own astonishment—and disgust—that she had to blink her tired
old eyes furiously in order to clear them enough to bring
the girl's white face into sharp focus.

'She moves me,' she thought. 'She has me close to tears.
This utterly vicious little minx who—'

She said, dryly:

"If your father's good opinion means that much to you,
Fanny, it seems to me you should have avoided the—the
well—sort of activities that have brought you to the state
you're in . . ."

"Yes 'm—" Fanny said. "His good opinion does mean
that much to me. Only I found out a long time ago I
could never have it, no matter how I tried. Other fathers—pet and spoil their only daughters, sort of—and
kind of make it easy for them to be good. Most girls can
say, 'Oh I *couldn't* do that! What would Papa think!' But
I *knew* what my father would think about *me*—nothing.
Getting the best marks in the class, or the worst, would
pull the same kind of little grunt out of him. Being an angel—or a devil, he—"

She stopped; and her pale eyes misted over suddenly.

"No, that's not true. Not quite, anyhow. He *does* care
about my being *bad*. He cares—terribly. That's why you
*can't*, wire him, Mrs. Redfern, you *can't*. Listen to me,
please! I—"

"One moment, Fanny!" Mrs. Redfern said. "You said
something—or started to—that interests me profoundly.
Because, if you meant to imply that your father's lack
of—of affection was one of the *causes* of your getting into
trouble, you confirm a thing I've noticed myself. Nearly
all the girls I've had to expel from this school came from

disharmonious—or even broken—homes. But I don't understand the attitude you attribute to him. You are—as
you know only too well—an exceedingly attractive young
woman. Very pretty. No, more than pretty; one might
truthfully call you beautiful. Most fathers would dote on
such a daughter as you. How then can you explain his attitude?"

Fanny bent her head, looked up again.

"I—I look just like my mother," she whispered, "and
she—wrecked his life."

"I see," Mrs. Redfern said. "So you're afraid that if I
wire—or write him, he'll be—especially harsh—even brutal—towards you?"

"No 'm. 'Cause he won't. He won't lay a finger on me.
What he'll likely do is drop down dead."

"Now, Fanny!" Mrs. Redfern said.

"It's the truth, I tell you! When I got into trouble the
first time—I was only a kid, fifteen years old, and so
blamed starved for a little affection that I let the worst,
cheapest, rottenest tinhorn sport anybody ever did see
make a fool out of me—my father got so sick we thought
he was going to die. And, after that, when my brother
Billy got mixed up with a gang of underage crooks, Papa
had a stroke! Dr. Terrebonne says that the next bad shock
he gets will kill him! So I'm begging you not to—"

"And yet," Mrs. Redfern said slowly, grimly, "knowing
*that,* you still—did this—repeated the offense that almost
cost your father—his life!"

Fanny stood there. She didn't say anything. Her mouth
came open a little. Her lower lip quivered like an idiot
child's. Slowly she slid down into the chair opposite Mrs.
Redfern's desk, without so much as a by-your-leave,
lunged forward until her head struck against the mahogany desktop with an audible thud, and started to cry. Never before in her fifty-odd years of existence had the headmistress seen—for, as always, Fanny's paroxysms were all
but silent—anyone cry like that. Thirty seconds later, she
was sure she never wanted to again.

"Child—" she said, imploringly.

Fanny looked up, her eyes pale, no-colored blind scalds
of pure anguish in the streaked and glittering plains and
angles of her face.

"I should be—killed!" she said. "Dead. A bad way—

that takes—a long time—and—and hurts something awful. So bad I'd have to scream my filthy guts loose and choke to death on 'em trying to throw them up. I should be beaten to bloody rags and thrown into an open drainage ditch full of green slime and garbage and turds of human shit, for the maggots to eat—and the buzzards —and—"

"Fanny!" Mrs. Redfern said.

"I'm—awful," Fanny whispered. "There's nothing—or nobody—lower—than me. And now—I *can't* do anything about it. I can't even stick a knife into myself again—or take too many sleeping pills or—or anything. 'Cause that way—I'd kill—my baby. And I can't do that, Mrs. Redfern! I can't!"

'I,' Jane Redfern thought with aching pity, 'have played God—again. Sat in judgment over—a human being. Over this poor, sick, tortured, more than half-demented child. Judged her—without mercy. Without taking into consideration that "why" always outweighs "what" in the scale of God.'

She said: "Now you go too far, child. I suspect that you—drifted into sin—through thoughtlessness, weakness of will, stupidity, rather than through any innate viciousness on your part. Very well, I'll write your stepmother. I knew her; did you know that? We were—schoolmates at Vassar, long ago. She was an excellent student—and a very fine person."

"Not was—is," Fanny said slowly. "She's been the best mother to me—any girl ever could have. And—and the best sister too. She's tried every way under God's own heaven, Mrs. Redfern—to—to reform me—to save me. Only what was needful—she couldn't do. Nobody could. I guess. Not even the greatest doctor in the world—"

"And that is?" Jane Redfern said.

"Open my veins. Drain every drop of my mother's filthy whorish blood out of me. Put—somebody else's blood into me. A good woman's. Somebody—decent."

"Fanny," Jane Redfern said, leaning forward, across the desk, "you mustn't—despise yourself this way. You simply mustn't. You're young. And you've a lot to live for, now. Your child—however conceived—will need her mother—"

"*His* mother. 'Cause if it's—a girl I—I'll drown it, so

help me! Better that, than letting it grow up to be a whore like me!"

"Fanny!" Mrs. Redfern said.

"I'm sorry. Besides that was a lie, anyhow. I couldn't kill my little Susie—Oh, Jesus!"

"Now what?" Mrs. Redfern said.

"I promised—Sue—Sue Beaconridge I—I'd name my first girl-baby after her. But can I? Can I hang the name of a girl who's probably looking down from the pearly gates and crying her poor sweet eyes out over the things she sees me do, onto a little bastard? Oh, I'm sorry! I mean—onto an illegitimate child?"

"Of course you can," Jane Redfern said gently. "You see, Fanny, there's no such thing as an illegitimate child. There are only illegitimate parents. Now go lie down. Rest. You're excused from all classes. And I'm afraid I must ask you to remain in your room—for your own sake, mainly, until we hear from your stepmother. I think you've already found out that our young ladies can be most unkind. I hope they haven't heard anything of your—trouble. But I'm afraid that if they haven't, they soon will. As long as we have day students, and our better homes employ local people as servants, no secret is safe. I'll have your meals sent up to you and—"

"Don't bother," Fanny said. "I couldn't eat now, Mrs. Redfern; I purely couldn't!"

"You'll have to, I'm afraid. I'll have Dr. Lewis look in on you tomorrow. I ask only that you stay in your room—voluntarily. That you give me your word to that effect. You may, of course, leave it to—to go to the bathroom—or to come here—or to go to Church—that is, if I can find another girl of your persuasion—you're Methodist, aren't you?—to go with you, now. Or I can ask the Reverend Mr. Rounley, rector of Trinity Methodist Church, to visit you if you like—"

Fanny shuddered.

"No, don't," she said, "please don't, ma'am. Don't suppose anybody could pray me out of—the bad place, now; and listening to it would only make me feel worse. Mrs. Redfern—can I have—visitors? I mean can any of the other girls—Polly—or Norma—or Irene, say—come to see me while I'm under house arrest?"

"House arrest!" Mrs. Redfern gasped. "What a phrase! You're not, Fanny; by any means! Your confinement—is to a large extent voluntary, which I ask you to submit to, for the good of the school. But, as for visitors, I'm afraid that's impossible. When the story—and the nature—of your difficulties get out—as they will, you know—some of the parents might object rather violently to their daughters' having visited you. You must realize people aren't very tolerant, child, especially in questions of well—personal morals. If there's anything else you want though, any books, something special to eat, or—"

"No 'm," Fanny said. "May I go now, Mrs. Redfern?"

Mrs. Redfern looked at her, sighed: "Yes, I suppose you'd might as well," she said.

Fanny lay on her bed and stared up at the ceiling of her room, her eyes the color of an August sky when the sun has washed most of the blue out. They flickered their gaze against the dingy white plaster, desperately braille-coding her thoughts, making a rapid pointillism of the somber images moving through her mind.

'I'm done now, finished. So forget me, damn it! Think—about—my baby. What to do—about it. Papa'll make me put it out for adoption, sure as hell. Martha'll—want to keep it, maybe; but—she'll be afraid to stand up to Papa—for fear he'll get too excited and—'

She stopped, her pale eyes brilliant in her white face.

'If he doesn't before that. When he sees me. When it—hits him that I've disgraced him again. That his daughter is—in the family way, knocked up, bigged, pregnant, going to be an unmarried mother, carrying some tinhorn sport's bastard brat in her stupid belly 'cause she didn't even have sense enough to keep her drawers on, and her legs together. So he *mustn't* see me! Not ever again! Not him nor Martha nor Billy nor Phil nor anybody I knew before. Go down to New York. Get myself a job—

'That I'll get fired off of the minute my belly starts to swell. Go down to New York to starve and freeze and die in a gutter somewhere taking my baby—with me. So what *can* I do? What do I *know* that'll keep me alive long enought to—'

She sat up in bed, jackknifed up, her eyes appalled at first, then sick, swimming, resigned.

'That. What else? What Martha said I was born to be.
What Lord knows I'm good at to judge from Rod and his
buddies and—and Phil—and Tony. That. I'm finished,
anyhow; but maybe I could put my baby out to board
with a good, decent poor family, and go to see it week-
ends and—and maybe it would have a chance—even if
it's a girl—

'I'll go there. To—to Mama's. She'll take me in, all
right—if only to laugh her head off at Papa behind his
back. She'll be even then—so even that she won't even
need to tell him. Just knowing it herself will be enough—'

She lay back down. Closed her eyes. The tears stole out
from under her eyelids, ran down her face, one by one,
slowly. Her lips moved, shaping words that turned out to
be a prayer:

"Do whatever you want to with me, Lord: but give my
poor baby a chance, a chance!"

And it was then that she heard the faint knocking on
her door. She opened her eyes, said:

"Come in!"

Polly Stevens jerked open the door, slipped into the
room, closed the door behind her, leaned against it, got
out finally:

"Oh, Fanny! Oh Fanny!"

"Oh Fanny, what?" Fanny said.

"The girls! They—they're saying the most horrible
things about you! That you—you got caught—with Tony
Beaconridge out—at old Jake Reisling's place! And that
the two of you were—in bed—and with no clothes on
and—"

"Fucking like crazy?" Fanny said, solemnly.

"Fanny!" Polly gasped. She knew the word. Her family
was rich enough to afford grooms, stable keepers, coach-
men, and the like, so inescapably she had heard it. Victorian prudery rarely extended to the lower orders.

"Well, we damned sure weren't waltzing," Fanny said,
"or playing croquet, either one."

"So—" Polly breathed, "it's—true!"

"Yes. And no. That—I—I've done what I shouldn't—
what no girl should 'til after she's married, is true, Polly.
But that Tony and I were caught doing it—or even out at
the Reisling place—isn't. We were caught right outside the
Ferry Street gate of this school, with all our clothes on,

talking to each other. Of course, I *had* slipped out, and it *was* after midnight, but that's all."

"And you—you're going to be expelled for that?" Polly said. "Why I call it a dirty shame!"

Fanny stared at Polly, thought about what to say. Then said it, carefully.

"No, not for that—Polly, have you ever been in love?"

"God, yes!" Polly breathed, without having to think about it.

"And—you didn't—you *never* have—done—what you shouldn't?"

"No-o-o—" Polly said, a little uncertainly, because human nature being human nature even in the late Victorian epoch, Polly had at least to consider how much territory that "what you shouldn't" embraced.

"All right," Fanny said, "but answer me one thing, Polly—telling the truth, because not only can you be certain-sure that the truth will stay right here between you, me, and the bedpost, but you can be twice as sure that nobody would take my word for it *now*, even if I were to repeat what you said—*Why* not, Polly? And if you don't trust me—or yourself—enough not to lie, skip it, will you?"

Polly hung there, and her soft, deep-blue eyes opened very wide.

" 'Cause—" she whispered, " 'cause Joe and I have never been alone together anyplace where we *could*, I suppose. Lord knows I—I've wanted him so darned bad that I hurt! So that I couldn't sleep all night long and—"

"And had to get up 'n take a cold shower," Fanny said calmly, "I suppose you're going to say. I've told that same goddamned lie, myself, many's the time. The truth—is not so—*nice*, is it, Polly?"

Polly quivered there, rigid with shock. But it was the shock of—recognition, of acknowledgment, Fanny saw, and knew that she had won.

"Sh-sh, honey," she said gently, almost tenderly, "don't admit anything, not even to me. This is *my* old-time country-revival confessin' session—and only because you—and all the world—are going to find out anyhow, so lying makes no sense. Say—I was more—well, brazen than you were—and stupider—so I let myself get shown that my busy little pinky was no substitute for a man. So—I got caught. Yes, Polly, exactly what you're thinking: I'm going to have a baby—"

"Oh—you poor thing!" Polly breathed.

"Poor fool," Fanny said bleakly. "No better nor any worse than a million girls before me, and a couple of million that'll come after me, I suppose. And if you've let all the nice-Nellies who sold the whole female half of the population a bill of goods get to you—just remember this: They're calling the Good Lord Himself a damn fool—"

"Fanny!" Polly said.

" 'Cause if He wasn't smart enough to make women *like* it, considering all the pain and worry and trouble it causes them, then the Devil sure as hell *did*, which means Old Nick is one up on Him, right?"

"Right," Polly whispered; then, firmly: "Per-fect-ly right! For if that isn't the truth, I've never heard it!"

"Good," Fanny said. "The only trouble—is that Mr. Beaconridge's dug up something, or had somebody *invent* it, that has made Tony—doubt me. I—I don't even know what that something is, but no matter; I may have nothing else left, but I've got my pride, Polly. Only I need help— need it awfully bad. Will you—will you take one more note to Tony for me? The last? Being real careful, of course, so that nobody'll know it was you who—"

"I don't care!" Polly said hotly. "They aren't being fair! I'll do it, Fanny. Is there anything else you want?"

Fanny looked at her, then said slowly, calmly, softly, so that it wasn't until afterwards Polly recalled something in that too-quiet voice had made her shiver:

"Yes. Can you ask one of the townies—one of the day students—where a girl named Myrtle Tolliver lives?"

"I—suppose so. Never heard of her, though. Who is she, Fanny?"

"A girl—no, a woman—I owe something. I'd like to— to give it to her, before I leave here," Fanny said.

The very next afternoon, Polly put Tony Beaconridge's answer into Fanny's hand. When Fanny opened it a shower of twenty-dollar bills fell out, and lay crisp and green and new on the coverlet of Fanny's bed.

"My—God!" Polly said.

"Yes," Fanny said, "I asked him for money, Polly. To—get away with. So I won't be here when—my father comes. So I can start—all over far away, where nobody knows me. Give—my baby a chance to grow up—decent. Was *that* wrong, too, honey?"

"No," Polly said, "not at all, Fanny. Oh—by the way, Miss Tolliver works in the telegraph office!"

"I knew that," Fanny said. "What I want to know is where she *lives*—"

Polly searched in the pocket of her apron and came out with the note.

"She lives—at Six-Twenty-Four Oakwood Avenue," she said.

"Yes," Jane Redfern said, pure outrage shaking her voice, "we do have a girl named Frances Turner here. But I cannot imagine anything she could have done that would cause police officers—*uniformed* police officers—to enter *my* school to look for her! I definitely think you owe me an explanation, sir!"

"Well, ma'am," Chief Schuykill said uneasily, "it's this way—this—gentleman"—he jerked his finger over his shoulder at the small and dapper man who accompanied him and the other patrolman—"has sworn out a warrant for her arrest and—"

"And who may *you* be?" Jane Redfern said.

"The name's Hawkes, ma'am," the dapper little man said, "Timothy Hawkes, at your service. I work for Mr. Beaconridge—in a confidential capacity, you might call it. And Myrtle—the victim—is a personal friend of mine. Oh, I realize you're concerned about the good name of your school, ma'am—and I don't blame you for it. But that's just *why* you'd better turn this little she-devil you took in by mistake over to us—voluntarily. Wouldn't like to have to go get a court order or a search warrant and—"

"Mister—Hawkes, "Jane Redfern said, "would you mind telling me *what* this is all about?"

"Yes 'm," Tim Hawkes said. "It's like this, ma'am. Poor Myrtie's all alone in the world. And me—and my missus, ma'am—are the only real friends she's got. So when Fred—the telegrapher, ma'am—rang me up and told me Myrtie hadn't showed up for work this morning—I dropped by to see if she was sick or something—"

He stopped. Waited.

"Go on," Jane Redfern said.

"She wasn't sick. What she is—is blind, ma'am. Though Dr. Lewis thinks a little sight can be saved in her left eye. But—nobody can save her looks, ma'am. And she was fair-to-middling pretty, that she was! Sulfuric acid is an awful thing—"

"Sulfuric acid!" Jane Redfern said.

"Yes 'm. Figures, doesn't it? You've got a first-class laboratory here, I've heard—for your chemistry students. And since Mr. Beaconridge put me on the case from the first—he wasn't starting to let his only son marry the likes of this Turner female, ma'am; and can't say I blame him!—I knew all about it, including the telegram this little dilly of yours sent to that French feller she spent the Christmas holidays with in New York. Now, what I figure is that the Turner girl must of found out that poor Myrtle *showed* me that telegram and—"

"Threw sulfuric acid in her face? Impossible, Mr. Hawkes! Impossible and outrageous! Why—"

"Please calm down, ma'am. Neither you nor th' school is to be blamed 'cause this Turner creature wasn't what you thought she was. You—you got hoodwinked this time, I'm sorry to say. Supposing you do just two things: Send somebody to ask the chemistry prof if a whole bottle of this acid—*this* bottle, ma'am; it was lying on the floor next to poor Myrtle—isn't missing from the lab shelves. And somebody else to bring this little missy down to your office so that we can ask her a question or two. Take us five minutes or less to find out whether it *was* her. And, if it wasn't, we'll go away real quiet, apologizing humbly for bothering you, ma'am. Isn't that—fair enough?"

Jane Redfern stared at him bleakly, the first cold, slimy worm of doubt beginning to gnaw at her intrepid heart.

"Yes, Mr. Hawkes—it is fair enough, I suppose," she said.

"Why, yes," old Professor Briggs said, "that's one of our flasks, all right. Missed it this morning. Who took it, Norma? *You?* Why the devil should you do a thing like that? Vitriol's dangerous, young woman! And—"

But Norma was gone, reeling away from the door of the lab, a prey to the most abject and miserable of terrors the flesh is heir to—the fear for her very life. She went down the stairs three at a time, crossed the campus at a dead run, flew up the stairs of the dormitory towards her room.

"I've got to get away!" she moaned inside her mind. 'If she did that to poor Myrtle, who was actually trying to help her, what mightn't she do to *me*, who—'

She put out her hand to jerk open the door to her room. And it was then that she saw the little white triangle under the edge of her door.

She stared at it, not daring even to pick it up.

But she did finally, opened it, read:

"Don't worry. I despise you too much to even hate you. Because to hate, you've got to care about a person a little. And I don't, can't care about—a thing. Besides, you've already had enough of my acid, haven't you—from the place I'm most acid, where any woman is—considering one of the things it's used for. So good-bye; get yourself another lollipop, honey. Or a mouthwash. Your breath stinks—and so does your soul, if you've got a soul—which I doubt. But as I said before, don't worry, you're in no danger from me. To kill a thing like you would be to do it a favor. I hope you live a hundred years. Can you think of anything worse? Fanny."

Norma sat there, a long time. She didn't cry. She just sat there. Finally she said aloud, whispering the words:

"No, my dearest. I can't think of anything worse. Largely because you're right—there isn't anything worse, is there?"

Then very slowly, she got up and went down the stairs.

So it was that when Maud Barlett came back from Fanny's room, and Norma Tilson returned—considerably later—from the chemistry lab, their reports were in a way, much the same.

Yes, a bottle of sulfuric acid *was* missing from the stores.

And so was Fanny Turner—from the school.

# Chapter Twenty-Three

"Miz Mae—" Louella said, "young lady out front axin' to see you, ma'am . . ."

Maebelle Hartman looked at her maid, and, as always, approvingly. Louella was, to quote the late Major Julius Hartman, Maebelle's soi-disant husband, "a fetching piece of coal-black ass, if there ever were one! Tempts even me to change my luck, by God!" And the Major had been a connoisseur of such matters up to the moment—not two weeks before—that he had gone to his reward, by way of a heavy meal, followed by a heavier drinking bout, followed by the attempt, at seventy-five years of age and two hundred sixty-two pounds, to sample one of the more luscious of Mae's commercial wares.

"Got a handbag on her, Lou?" Mae Hartman said.

Louella loosed a high-pitched, peculiarly African snorting giggle.

"Yes 'm," she said, "but a mighty little 'un, Miz Mae. Li'l ol' teensy-weensy bag 'bout *this* big." She made the gesture of outlining its dimensional limitations with her slim, black, long-fingered hands.

"Big enough for a lady's pistol, anyhow, Lou," Mae Hartman said.

"Well, yes 'm. But she don't look mad. Not like that Miz Kunemann—Lord, was she ever a rotten shot!"

"Thank God!" Mae Hartman said. "Go on, Lou—what does she look like?"

"Sad," Louella said.

"Is she—alone? Or got her fancy man with her?"

"This 'un ain't got herself no pimp, yet," Louella said.

"She holding her breath, Lou?" Mae Hartman said.

Again Louella loosed her high-pitched giggle

"So's her belly won't poke clear over into the next parish, ma'am?" she laughed. "No 'm. She ain't showing yet . . ."

"But she *is* knocked up, eh Lou?"

"Not so's a body could tell it, Miz Mae. But she *is* got that peaky look around her eyes. 'Sides, who ever heard

tell of any *other* reason for a good-lookin' young gal to
show up all by her lonesome in a place like *this?*"

Maebelle Hartman reached out a pudgy hand—ablaze
with gemstones on every fat finger including her thumb—
and absentmindedly took a cigar out of a miniature black
coffin, complete to the silver cross and the letters R.I.P.
engraved in the plaque on its lid. She contemplated the
cigar a moment, then, fishing in her bag, came out with a
heavily ornamented switchblade knife. That knife was one
of the most cherished of her souvenirs. She herself had
dug it out of the pockets of Joselito Sotomayor on the occasion of Theodore "Terrible Ted" McGaw's having fired
the sum total of twelve forty-five caliber bullets into the
Mexican's slight frame in defense of that remarkably nonexistent quality, her honor—eleven of them after Joselito
was already down and dead as a doornail, which, of
course, required the Texan's having to stop and reload his
shootin' iron after the first six shots. And Ted had been
all for reloading the Colt for another go at Joselito still,
but eighteen bullet holes in a ninety-eight pound corpse
had seemed a trifle dismeasurate even to Mae, so she had
pointed out mildly to McGaw that he'd already messed up
the poor little greaser more than somewhat, and enough
of a thing was enough.

Standing there, contemplating what twelve forty-five
caliber slugs fired from pointblank range had done to the
seventeen-year-old Mexican, Mae was dismally sure that
this time Ted had gone a mite too far, and that remedial
measures were necessary. It was then that the idea of
searching for Joselito's knife had come to her. For sure as
old Nell, Mexican midwives tucked a switchblade into a
little greaser's diapers the minute he was born. Having
found it, she opened it very carefully and placed it in
Joselito's hand, thus sparing Ted even the relatively slight
difficulty that killing a Mexican in California in defense
of a white woman, whore though she might be, would
have caused him.

After the inquest was over, she'd asked the presiding
judge for the knife. He had given it to her willingly
enough, saying: "Souvenir, my hindquarters! Tell you
what, Mae; you use this greaser toadsticker on McGaw
and I'll hand down a verdict of justifiable homicide on the
spot, without even calling court into session!" She'd trea-

sured it ever since, more as a reminder of her own clever-
ness than anything else, for it troubled her not at all that
Joselito's sole offense had consisted of sticking his face
almost into kissing distance of her own and murmuring
plaintively, "¡Toda mi fortuna por una noche contigo!"—
unless due consideration be given to the fact that Joselito's fortune (one peso and one real) wouldn't have
bought ten minutes of her time, not to mention a whole
night, even at the prices she was forced to be content with
in those days.

Carefully she cut off the tip of the expensive Cuban
cigar with poor Joselito's knife, and sat there thinking a
long time before lighting up. Then she peered at Louella
through the cloud of fragrant smoke, and barked:

"C'mon, Louella! Quit holding out on me! What d'you
think of her?"

It was a question she often asked, for it was Mae Hartman's considered opinion that Louella Thomas was the
smartest woman, black or white, she had known in all her
life. And, be it said in passing, that her opinion was
shared—at least secretly—by a good many people who
knew Louella—Les Nouvelle Orleanais paying the slim
black girl the ultimate compliment of labelling her "Crazy
Lou." Now a "crazy nigger gal," by the curiously pragmatic unwritten laws that actually govern Southern behavior—the written ones being almost totally unworkable on
certain levels—was any black woman so damned smart
that she'd gained the privilege of telling white people exactly what she really thought of them, depending upon the
matchlessly skillful use of a self-depreciative gesture, a
certain ambiguity of phrase, or a pleasant laugh to save
herself from the disaster whose edges she was constantly
skirting. It was a privilege that no young Negro man ever
enjoyed, being permitted only to exceptionally intelligent
black serving women and a very few crotchety, half-blind,
tottering elders, fondly labeled, "crazy ol' Uncle Ben," or
the like.

But there was another aspect to Maebelle Hartman's
relations with her maid that was much more difficult to
define. It consisted basically of an intense, almost compulsive desire to "bring Louella down a peg or two," as Mae
herself put it. And it was a tribute to Mae's own intelligence that she never attempted to do this by the methods
any other Southern white woman would have almost in-

stinctively employed: shouting at her, calling her names,
trying to humiliate her verbally, or even slapping or kick-
ing her. She didn't because she knew they wouldn't work.

The one thing that would have delighted Mae's almost
placidly evil soul would be to learn that Louella had finally succumbed and gone to bed with any one of the numerous clients who offered her money—more in some
cases than they paid for the services of one of Mae's
girls—to do just that. But, when questioned about the
matter, Louella's answers, while always skirting that
knife-edged line beyond which her listeners would almost
surely have had their suspicions—that the offense implicit
in her tart remarks was both conscious and intentional—
confirmed to their outrage and to Louella's immediate departure for a better world, had at least the saving grace of
never being based on conventional morality, quite possibly
because Louella knew damned well that was the one thing
neither Maebelle nor her clients would believe.

"Lord Gawd, Miz Mae," she'd whoop, "what I wanta
go and let one of them there gentlemens push his po' li'l
puny half-a-inch-long white folks' think up 'twixt my legs
for? You ever seen how a real big black buck nigger's
hung? Heavy ain't the word for it, ma'am! They's *tons* of
hot 'n lovin' *black* man down there, I kin tell you! Not to
mention yards 'n yards!"

Or: "Hit's like this, Miz Mae. Got myself a *man*. Lettin' alone th' fact that he'd sho' as hell stick a butcher
knife into my belly-button and walk all th' way around
me holdin' onto the handle effen I was to look sidewise at
any critter other than him what wears pants, he keep me
so damn wore out the one night you lets me off and I gits to
see him that I just ain't got no ambition to try nobody else!"

So now, Mae sat there, holding all two hundred-odd
pounds of sweaty, sticky, perfumed and powdered flesh
absolutely still, which was something of a feat, because often the remoter portions of her jounced and jiggled without Mae's being aware of it, and waited for Louella's answer, the feud between them temporarily suspended, as it
always was when business in its primary aspect of dollars
and cents was the subject under consideration.

"This 'un, ma'am," Louella said slowly, "would make
you a fortune. For one thing, she's five o' ten times pret-

tier than any gal you's got in the house. But that ain't the main thing, Miz Mae—hit's the *way* she's pretty that counts . . ."

"I'm listening, Lou," Maebelle Hartman said.

"Remember that place you told me 'bout you was in once down in Cuba when th' madam used to dress the gals up like *nuns?* Make 'em tell th' customers that they was only doing it temporary to raise money for an orphan's school or such like? Get them Cuban fellers so excited they'd fair tear them religious robes 'n rosary beads in crucifixes right off 'em, you said."

"Yes," Mae said, "but what's that got to do with our visitor, Lou?"

"Her face. Hit's—so—innocent, ma'am! So—*pure.* I know! I know! She's sho' to be knocked up. She's likely done laid down 'n spread her legs for every man in whatever town she comes from what could still git it up. 'Cause she's got a look that's bold as brass, I kin tell you. She's plumb a nach'l born ho'. But it don't show—leastwise 'til she look at you straight in the face. Learn her *not* to do that—look at menfolks straight-like, I mean—learn her to hang that angelbaby sugarpie face of her'n down like she was 'shamed o' herself 'n timid 'n shy—'n to flutter them long straw-colored eyelashes to her'n at the gentlemens real demure like and—Lord Jesus!—she'll have fellers like young Mr. Schneider—and even fellers not so young like that dago gangster gentleman, Mr. Sarcone—crawling right up the wallpaper by they fingernails!"

Maebelle considered that.

"Send her in, Lou," she said. "No, wait! First you get that handbag away from her, just in case!"

"All rightie, Miz Mae," Louella Thomas said.

Fanny sat there in the Rose Parlor and waited. It was some measure of what her stay at the Emma Willard School and her association with Norma Tilson had—perhaps unfortunately—done for her that she was painfully aware that the furnishings of her mother's establishment, touted in the Blue Book as being "fully the equal of those in any palace belonging to European royalty," were actually in such thunderous, crashing, overwhelming vulgarity

and bad taste that words to describe them eluded her. She
had just hit upon the expression "whorehouse gothic" as
being apt enough, when "that uppity black wench of a
maid"—her own immediate definition of Louella's disturbing quality—came back into the room.

"Miz Mae'll see you now," Louella said. "Oh, by the
way, you'd better leave your bag on the table, over
there . . ."

Fanny was aware by then that Louella was carefully
avoiding the word "miss" when speaking to her.

"I will *not*," she said icily. "Just you tell me one thing,
nigger girl: why should I do a thing like that?"

"No reason," Louella said blithely. "You purely ain't
got to, honey. But then neither is Miz Mae got to see you.
And believe you me she *won't* long as you's got that there
bag in your hands."

Fanny stood there, lashed from two sides at once by
rage—and despair. But she controlled herself, said:

"Why? Does she think I might have a knife in it—or a
gun?"

Louella stared at her, then loosed that peculiar snort of
laughter.

"You's smart, ain't you, honey?" she chuckled.

"Don't call me 'honey!' " Fanny flared. "Call me 'miss'
as you should!"

"All right, *miss*," Louella said. "I'll call you anything
you want me to—up to and including a chile o' Gawd.
I'm plumb downright obliging, that way. But whether I
should o' shouldn't is another matter. Depends on what
*you* mean by 'miss,' honey. Just for curiosity's sake what
*do* you?"

"Why—" Fanny got out, her cheeks aflame, "a—an unmarried girl—of course."

"Right," Louella said, "that's part of it—'n the other
part's a young, unmarried girl what ain't never had her
cherry busted. If you can say that, I *should* call you miss.
If you *can't*, I shouldn't. But since I'm a nice, sweet, obliging soul who's perfectly willin' to call you any damn
thing what makes you feel good, it don't make no nevermind neither way, do it—*miss?*"

'I should kill her!' Fanny thought. 'Why, the uppity black
bitch, she—'

"Tell you what, honey—I mean miss. You lemme see

what you's got in that bag—or more to the point, what
you *ain't* got in it, and you can take it with you. 'Cause
you hit th' nail right on the head. There's a mighty heap
o' rich, respectable white ladies who just might try to do
Miz Mae in, though Lawd knows *she* don't make them
ever-lovin' husbands come here. One of 'em even tried it
some time back, only she couldn't shoot shit off a
outhouse floor. That'd be the best way, I reckon."

Fanny held her breath, counted up to twenty, waited
until the rage that tore her subsided. Then she said:

"All right, have a look, if you like."

Louella took the bag, opened it a crack; then snapped it
shut at once with only half a glance at its contents.

"Now, honey—I mean miss," she said, "first you take
ever livin' bit of that long green foldin' stuff out o' heah,
and keep it in your sweet li'l lily white hands. 'Cause I
done lived this long and stayed th' hell outa th' ice house,
by being smarter than any white woman born, even *you*,
miss. Ain't even starting to give you a chance to say:
'There was a hundred 'n fifty dollars in it and now there's
only a hundred 'n thirty.' C'mon now, take it out!"

"All right," Fanny said mockingly. "Since you think
you can't resist temptation—"

"Honey, I couldn't resist temptation, wouldn't have me
no damn maid's uniform on. Or you think I couldn't get
myself a good price for mine, from white gentlemens bent
on changing they luck, effen I wanted to?"

Fanny smiled at her then, really smiled. There is a
point beyond which pure brass-bound nerve is irresistible.

"You know—I kind of like you," she said. "What's
your name?"

"Louella," Louella said: "What's your'n, honey?"

"Fanny—" Fanny said, "Fanny Tur—Smith."

"Th' hell you say!" Louella hooted. "Ain't nobody
pretty as you ever been named Smith, honey. Forget it—
hit's no skin off my nose—and *nobody* ever uses they
right name in a place like this, anyhow. C'mon now—take
all that money out and lemme see . . ."

Fanny did so.

"Well—you's clean," Louella said, "long as you ain't
got no toadsticker in your garter . . ."

"Want to see?" Fanny said.

"Naw. You ain't the type. C'mon now."

"Tell me, Louella," Fanny said as they went down the hall, "why *do* you work as a maid? You really are pretty for a nig—a colored girl. You could make yourself a lot of money, I'm sure . . ."

"Honey," Louella said, "I got me one bad habit: I likes *menfolks*. And *menfolks* is the one thing you don't *never* find in a ho' house."

Fanny stopped short, stared at her, whispered:

"Why not, Louella?"

"Honey, may the good Lawd Almighty save me from a feller what has to *buy* hisself a piece of pussy. Proof positive he ain't worth goose shit on ice in th' hay. News gits around. Us wimmenfolks just will talk too damn much, y' know. One gal tells another one, and fore you know it, feller what's all wool 'n a yard wide, if you gits what I means, has to step over the gals all spread out with they drawers already off that's done laid theyselves down on the banquette front of his house. But the po' critters what makes ho'-house madams rich comes to places like this 'cause they ain't even man enough to thaw they old ladies out more'n once every six months, or the other kind thats scairt they's gonna give way to they nach'l impulses an' kiss that pretty li'l altarboy one Sunday mornin'. But a *real* man, never! Well, here we be . . ."

Fanny stepped into the room and stopped dead. Stared at that painted mountain of human flesh, at that full-moon-shaped face, at those two red lips, folded caressingly around the butt of a long black cigar. Nausea rose in her in wild blinding waves; she fought against it desperately, thinking:

'No. I'll never tell her I'm her daughter. I'll never admit that even to God in prayer. Just have to take a chance on whatever I've got to offer—my looks—such as they are, and—'

But Maebelle Hartman had taken the cigar out of her mouth and was smiling at her. Fanny saw the great gold tooth in the center of her mouth that had earned her the name of "Brasstooth Mae" in certain quarters, the theory being that Mae was much too tightfisted to invest in gold for such a purpose, and thought: 'This is *my* mother. This—*thing.*'

"Howdy, li'l missy," Mae said in her best fake-Western accent. "What can I do for you?"

"Give me a job," Fanny said coldly.

"Now, do tell!" Mae marveled. "And just what kind of a job do you be a looking for, li'l missy?"

"Oh, don't be tiresome, Mrs. Hartman!" Fanny said. "I didn't come here to play games. I know, and you know, the only kind of job that you have to offer. So the only thing we need to discuss—are the conditions and the—the remuneration—say . . ."

"Now listen to her!" Mae said. "Go on babydoll, keep talking! You're just what this ol' place needs, damned if you ain't!"

"I'm—just what your place—needs?" Fanny whispered.

"Yes. The grand duchess. Educated, ain't you, baby? That's all to th' good. We'll bill you as—the Princess Olga Salosowski—from Poland. You wouldn't submit to the King o' Poland's or the Tzar o' Russia's lecherous embraces and therefore you had to flee. Now, having fallen on evil times, you—"

"I'm peddling my dainty tail just like any other whore?" Fanny said. "The whole thing's ridiculous, Mrs. Hartman. In the first place I'm a—Louisiana girl. Some of your clients might well know me. And—"

"Oh shit!" Mae said. "But never you mind, honey—I'll think of something. Now you tell me—where was th' *last* place you worked?"

Fanny's pale eyes opened wide.

"If—by worked, you mean *this*," she said quietly, "I have *never* worked before . . ."

"Wal, now," Mae said, "reckon *giving* it away does come under th' heading of *fun*, don't it baby? All right. Police looking for you any place?"

Fanny stiffened. 'They could be now,' she thought bitterly, 'but I'll never tell *you* that, you miserable old bag!'

"No," she said crisply. "No, of course not! Why do you ask me such things?"

" 'Cause I got to, if I want to stay out of the cooler, honeybunch. So now I'm gonna ask you one more question. And you either answer me the strict, gawd-blessed truth, or you get up and walk right out that door. In this case, as any fool can plainly see, lying don't make no sense. So all right, here goes: C'mon, baby, tell ol' Mae: How many months are you gone?"

Fanny stared down at the floor. Looked up again. Her face was very white.

"One—" she whispered. "A little more—Oh, Mrs. Hartman—please!"

"Honeybunch," Mae Hartman said tiredly, "nine out of every ten of your kind of innocent-looking young girls who walk through that door looking for a place here is in the family way. And mostly they're plain poison as far as th' business is concerned. But in your case—I plain don't know. You've got something, baby. Looks, for one thing. You're a real beauty, for a fact—like I was in me younger days . . . Another thing you've got is brass. Never a tear. No act—put to me straight. So—maybe you'll do. Now about your li'l bundle. We'll get you rid of it first thing. I know a real good snatcher who—"

But Fanny was on her feet, and what was in her eyes stopped even Maebelle Hartman.

"Good-bye, Mrs. Hartman," she said, very quietly.

"Now look, honeybunch—" Mae began.

"I came here," Fanny said, "because all I've got is a finishing-school education. You know what that means, ma'am? That I'm trained to be decorative—and useless—a wife for some *rich* man. So since—that's out—since no decent fellow would marry me now, I was willing to do *this*. But for only one reason, Mrs. Hartman—to give my baby a chance. I wouldn't do it for *me*, ma'am. Only to keep my baby from starving. I—I thought that maybe that in exchange for *all* my earnings for a year—two—you name it, ma'am!—you'd keep me while I was useless—let me have my child, allow me to put it out to board with a *decent*, poor family where I could visit it my days off, try to bring it up to be a good girl—or boy—and never let it find that its mother was—a whore—"

"Pipe dream!" Mae snorted.

"Maybe. But since you don't seem willing to give me that chance—good-bye, Mrs. Hartman. No hard feelings. And thanks, anyhow, for listening to me—"

"Wait, child!" Mae said. "Where're you going when you leave here?"

"Frankie Belmont's. Of course her place isn't as—as grand as yours, but I think maybe she would oblige as far as my baby's concerned . . ."

Maebelle thought about that. Decided that this pale little snow princess of a blonde was probably right. Frankie was one of the few madams in the trade who had a reputation for being a sentimentalist. It was rumored that two or three of her girls kept farmed-out bastards on their earnings. But even before that, Mae had decided another thing: She damned sure wasn't going to let a beauty of this caliber, a living fortune poised on its two dainty round heels, walk out the door if she could help it.

"And—failing her?" she said.

"The Arlington. The Annex. Even—Mahogany Hall—if I have to."

"Jesus!" Mae screamed. "You know *what* Mahogany Hall is?"

"Yes," Fanny said evenly. "A colored cathouse. But since most of the girls are quadroons or octoroons—all I've got to say is that my mother was nearly white, and my father was a German or a Swede. There're girls there as blonde as I am."

"And d'you also know," Mae said, "that Tuesday nights—they entertain rich *niggers?*"

"Yes," Fanny said. "But with the luck I've had lately, might not be a bad idea to change it, don't you think?"

She got up and put out a slim, gloved hand to her mother.

"Sit down, you damn li'l fool!" Mae bellowed. "You ain't going nowhere!"

"Aren't I?" Fanny said. "Who's to stop me? You try to keep me here against my will, and I'll see that this place is padlocked. I've got friends in high places, in case you don't know."

"Name one!" Mae snorted.

Fanny held her with her eyes.

"Detective Sergeant William P. Turner, for one," she said quietly.

"Jesus!" Mae shrieked. "My *ex!* And wouldn't he just love to shut me business up, th' sanctimonious bastard! But you know that, don'cha, missy? Tell me: He th' one who knocked you up?"

Fanny hung there rigid with shock. But her recovery, as always, was quick.

"Mr. Turner, as you should know, is an honorable man," she said.

"Ain't no such animal, once a he-male critter gets a

whiff o' fresh, *young* tail," Mae said. "I got *preachers*
'mongst my clients, girl! But no matter. I don't aim to
keep you nor any filly whatsoever here 'ginst her will. I'm
not a fool, honeybunch. Sit down, will you, 'n let's talk
business. You're dead set on keepin' th' kid?"

"Yes," Fanny said.

"All right," Mae sighed, "agreed. It's a fool stunt, but I
was a mother oncet, myself. My kid'd be about your
age—only I'm afraid she wouldn't have your looks.
She's—sickly, TB, th' poor baby—"

"You—you haven't seen her lately?" Fanny ventured.

"No. She's up north someplace 'n school. Bill—my
ex—your friend 'n protector—sent her up there to get her
away from my bad reputation. Don't blame him. Best
thing he could have done. Where were we? Oh yes, terms.
One year of your take to compensate me for th' trouble of
your lyin' in, medical expenses, putting out th' kid to wet
nurse 'n board—and th' loss of yer time oncet yer belly
gets too big—though some types likes 'em that way . . ."

"Never!" Fanny said firmly.

"Oh, all right. When can you come?"

"Now. I can—just stay. That is if you'll send somebody
with my baggage checks to the station to bring my things
here . . ."

Mae stared at her. Threw back her head and loosed a
thundercrack of almost baritone laughter.

"You're all right, baby!" she boomed. "Damned if you
aren't! Dead-game li'l filly, aren't you?"

"I—suppose so," Fanny said. "I—take after my mother
in that. I'm told."

"Then yer ma must be quite a girl!" Mae laughed.

"Oh, she is!" Fanny said, bitterly.

Maebelle Hartman reached up and put her pudgy hand
on the bell cord. But she held it there without pulling the
cord.

"Jesus!" she said, "I forgot th' main thing! What's your
name, missy?"

Fanny looked at her.

"Does it matter?" she said.

"Yep," Mae said. "To th' public, you can be the Princess Liechtenstein; but *I* gotta know your handle. Your
real one. Safer that way. Protects me—and gives me a

chance to protect you. C'mon, missy—what'd your mama call you?"

"Fanny. Fanny—Turner," Fanny said.

"Je-ho-sha-phat!" Mae bellowed. "That's the moniker I hung on *my* brat. And—and you said you knew him!— that he was a friend of your'n—Baby, you don't mean to tell me that you—"

"That I'm *your* daughter? No, Mrs. Hartman; most definitely not. That my name also happens to be Turner is a—simple coincidence, that's all. So far as I know there's no kinship between Detective Turner and me, whatsoever. Besides—wouldn't you *know* your own daughter if you saw her?"

"No," Mae said gloomily, "been too damn long. All the same, I ain't sure I like this. Blonde filly the right age, same name—"

"But definitely not tubercular," Fanny said calmly. "Even if you want to accept two awfully unlikely propositions, Mrs. Hartman: One, that your own daughter would deliberately choose to try to enlist in a sporting house run by her own mother; and two, that she'd give you her right name if she did. It's strange that your poor sick daughter and I have the same name; but wouldn't her name be Gloria Smith, say, if she were standing here in my shoes?"

Mae thought about that. The effort was painful. Fanny watched the struggle with carefully concealed enjoyment. 'Now,' she thought, 'I don't have to worry my head remembering some damn-fool name that doesn't belong to me. And the *best* lies, anyhow, are the ones that stick closest to the truth. Besides, brass-monkey nerve is exactly what I've got to have from here on in, so I might as well start exercising it right now.'

"You got a point there," Mae said, "but—"

"Mrs. Hartman—you were married to Mr. Turner once, I believe."

"Yep. Why?"

"Then you know him. How much chance would *his* daughter have of walking in *your* door? And in New Orleans itself? I ask you!"

"Ha!" Mae said. "Bill would take every inch of skin off her poor little ass right down to the bloody bones! Damn but that li'l silver-blonde top-piece o' your'n *works*, don't it! All right, missy—but I swear to God you had me scared there for a minute!"

She gave the bell cord a hard pull. In a few minutes, Louella appeared.

"Bring us some champagne, Lou," Mae said, "to celebrate th' li'l princess here's joining us." She turned to Fanny. "You ain't adverse to a li'l snort, are you, honey?" she said.

"Of course not," Fanny said. "In fact I rather like it."

Louella looked at her pityingly. Because, from past experience, she already knew what Maebelle was going to do. But it wasn't her place to tell this little blondie that. Louella always knew her place and kept to it when the matter involved was that of a white girl's going to hell by the fastest route. For that was exactly where most of them belonged, she figured. Still, she couldn't keep from feeling sorry for this one, a little.

"All rightie, Miz Mae, comin' up!" she said.

Half an hour later, Maebelle rang for her again. When she came into the room, the first thing Louella saw was the blonde girl, stretched out on the floor. She looked as though she were dead. Louella didn't turn a hair. She'd seen this sort of thing before, several times.

"Yes 'm?" she said.

"Fool girl took with cramps," Mae said, "and now she's up 'n fainted on me, Lou. Looks like a miscarriage, don't it?"

"Yes, 'm, Miz Mae, it sure do," Louella said solemnly. It looked like nothing of the kind and both of them knew it. What it looked like to Louella was that something had been slipped into Fanny's glass of champagne. Knock-out drops, for instance—a preparation that every madam in the trade found useful for subduing bumptious guests and—and well, emergencies like this one.

"See if you can get Dr. Baines on th' telephone," Mae said. "And I hope to God he ain't drunk—"

"Never seed him when he wasn't," Louella said. "But seeing as how he's th' best baby-snatcher in th' business, drunk or sober, don't 'pear to me hit makes no nevermind—"

"Oh, get out of here, and call him!" Maebelle Hartman said.

"You's th' boss, Miz Mae!" Louella said, and loosed her bitter, mocking laughter.

The first thing that Fanny became conscious of was that she hurt. The lower part of her abdomen felt like it had hot coals in it. She put down her hand and explored herself there—and her fingers touched a neat, well-made, elastic suspender belt to which a soft, thick sanitary napkin made of endless layers of gauze and cotton was attached. She lay there, frozen. Then she pushed her fingers under that napkin. They came out red and thick and sticky with her blood.

She turned then and saw Louella sitting in a chair beside her bed.

"What—happened?" she said, dully.

"Took yo'self one sip too many, honey," Louella said. "Got dizzy 'n—'n faint like—so you axed Miz Mae where was your room 'cause you felt like you needed to lay down. So Miz Mae rung for me to show you were it was. But by the time I got there you'd done fell down flat on your pretty face, chile. And when me 'n Miz Mae picked you up, we noticed you was bleedin' like a hawg at fall killin' time. So we sent for the doc—and—well—I'm might sorry, honey, but you done lost your baby, to say it straight out . . ."

Fanny stared at her. She didn't say anything. She didn't even cry. She simply turned away from Louella and faced the wall. Her lips moved soundlessly, forming words. In a way, all things being considered, they made a kind of sense:

'All right. You're—one up on me—God. Or old Devil. Or both of you. Or the one of you that's both of you at the same time. 'Cause you could—do *this*—couldn't you? You let 'em nail your own son to a cross—and die like that. Hurting like that. Crying out to you that you'd let him down. So—what the hell was—my baby—to you? Or me to you? Or anybody to you, for that matter? Bugs—to step on—that's all.

'Y' know what? I've spent my whole miserable, fucked-up life trying to be good—and not quite making it. So—all right. So now I quit. I'm never going to try—anymore. 'Cause what good is being good? What goddamn good at all?'

"Chile—" Louella said, pityingly.

Fanny didn't answer her. She went on thinking:

'Look out hell, here I come! But not by myself. Leading a parade. Every sorry bastard who gets in my way. Every whining bitch who ever crosses me. Right down to this snotty black one sitting here—

'Gonna make the whole—damned—world—sorry—I was ever born. Make 'em curse the miserable old slut who birthed me—for not drinking a quart of turpentine, or sticking a knitting needle up herself—and throwing this one more long-gone tiny little slimy bloody mess out with th' slops! Make 'em moan 'n shake 'n cry every damned time they even hear the name Fanny Turner. And that's a promise. You hear me—God?'

A tall order, you say? One that inevitably she must fail at? You're right. Why yes, of course you are! But then in human terms, neither success nor failure is an absolute; you'll grant that, won't you? Besides, when you're dealing with this sort of relativity, viewpoint is all-important. To an ant, even a child's foot is the end of the world.

For it is a simple fact, and verifiable as such, that the viewpoints of nearly every human being, male or female, black or white, young or old, who ran afoul of Fanny Turner after this time in her life, this nadir of her existence, this perigee of her orbit about the doom that had become her lodestar, however tangential, oblique, marginal, casual, meaningless their encounters with her were, coincided, were in absolute agreement. Asked, they all swore by their sacred honors, by whatever they held dear, believed in, by their fear of hell, their hope of heaven, that she, Fanny Turner, kept that promise.

To the letter.

## Chapter Twenty-Four

Before Louella had got anywhere even close to the Blue Parlor, she could hear Estelle screaming. She stopped where she was, waited until she heard Estelle screech:

"And let me tell you one more thing, Fanny Turner—" before moving on, towards the door.

'Her agin,' she sighed. 'Lawd, but that there chile's done took out the first 'n only original patent on gitting folks riled. Ain't a gal in th' house what wouldn't cut her throat from ear to ear for her, 'n that's a nach'l fact. Even Miz Mae at times. Like this mawning, fer instance—'

Then, as usual without knocking, Louella pushed open the door.

Fanny was sitting by the window, buffing her nails. Occasionally, she opened her mouth and blew on them gently. But, for all the attention she paid to Estelle, or the steady stream of curiously unimaginative invective with which her "fellow Cyprian"*—to employ one of the Blue Book's more fanciful metaphors for the profession—was blue-smoking the very air, Estelle might as well have been a piece of furniture.

And, because she had worked as a maid in both the Arlington and the Annex before entering Mae Hartman's service, Louella waited, with the patience, or the resignation, instilled in her by four or five years of witnessing scenes like this one almost daily, until Estelle momentarily ran out of breath. Then she said, very quickly, before the tall, skinny prostitute could gulp enough air to go on screaming:

"Miz Mae done sent for you, Miz Fanny—"

"Very well," Fanny said. "Tell her I shall come along—presently—"

"Oh Jesus!" Estelle shrieked. "Listen to her! The gawddamned grand duchess! Presently, my ass! If I ever catch you mincing down the hall agin when Beau Dan comes to take me out, I'll wring your whorish li'l neck with my bare hands!"

Fanny went on buffing her nails.

"Miss Fanny," Louella said, "Miz Mae's awful mad. Wouldn't keep her waitin', I was you."

Fanny looked up at Louella.

'She ain't—human—' Louella thought, for the hundredth time. 'Look at a body like that 'n *freeze* 'em to death, for fair. But you ain't a-gonna stare me down, you

---

*Aphrodite is supposed to have arisen from the foam near the Island of Cyprus. In the Greek Legends, she is sometimes called Kypris.

brass-assed li'l chippy! Just you hold your breath 'til *I* blink!'

"Awful bad temper Miz Mae's got, honey," she said.

"You go tell Mrs. Hartman," Fanny said, "that I'm busy—"

"Busy doin' *what?*" Louella said.

"Dusting off and polishing up the only first-class goods for sale in her meat market," Fanny said imperturbably, "as she knows damned well. Considering the clientele *I've* brought her, she can afford to be patient. And if she isn't, she might as well be, because until I decide to go to see her, she can sit there and wait. With all she's got to sit on, she should be comfortable enough—"

'God's truth,' Louella thought wryly. 'Miz Mae's got th' biggest, fattest ass in seven states and forty parishes—'n every sport in town—'n three-quarters of the respectable gentlemens, too—is outside th' door pantin' to see this little ice-water bitch-kitty afore we even opens up. Still I can't take Miz Mae no sich answer. She blow up sho'—'

"Miss Fanny—" she began.

"You heard me the first time, Lou," Fanny said. "Any rough talk from Old Puss-Gut, and I'll walk out that door—and leave her to depend upon her fugitives from Crib Row, present company *not* excepted. That is, if there *is* someone present. Seems to me I heard a noise. Rather like barking. Or howling. Or maybe I merely *smelled* something rotten: A whiff of L'Eau de Franklin Street,* shall we say?"

"Franklin Street!" Estelle gasped. "Why you miserable li'l straw-haired bitch, I'll—"

Then she started towards Fanny.

Fanny raised her eyes to Estelle's face. The effect was curious to watch. It was as if Estelle had run up against an invisible wall. She stopped. Hung there, trembling.

'Don't know how she do it,' Louella thought. 'Turn them no-color eyes o' her'n onto a body 'n stop 'em cold. Don't hafta talk, answer back, cuss at 'em. She look and—'

---

*At this time, most of the Cribs, indescribably filthy one-room shanties containing no other furniture than a bed, were on Franklin and St. Louis streets. The asking price of their immates was twenty-five cents.

"Estelle," Fanny said quietly, "you were about to do something—rash. Don't. Not now. Not ever. Or you just might find yourself peddling your syphilitic tail in hell. And discovering that down there, there're no takers. Which *would* be hell for you, wouldn't it, my dear?"

She stood up, stretched luxuriously, yawned.

"God, how these stupid bitches bore me!" she said. "Oh well, I'd might as well pay a call on Old Puss-Gut. She can be amusing—especially when she's mad. Coming, Lou?"

Louella glanced at Estelle. The tall girl was actually crying.

'From being mad at herself,' Lou thought, 'for lettin' this here ice-cold, mean-all-the-way-through li'l critter make her take low agin—'

"Yes 'm," she said. "I'm coming—"

Once they were out in the hall, she looked at Fanny, curiously.

"Miss Fanny," she said, "you ain't a-fixin' to take up with Beau Dan, is you?"

Fanny stared back at her.

"And—if I were?" she said.

"Don't," Louella said.

"I'm not afraid of Estelle, Lou," Fanny said.

"You, honey," Louella sighed, "ain't afeared o' the old Devil, far as I can see. Don't even reckon you's rightly scairt o' the good Lawd. That ain't what I mean."

"Then what *do* you mean, Lou?" Fanny said.

"That pimps is poison, honey. 'N *him* more than the rest of 'em."

"Why?" Fanny said.

"Why is pimps poison? Or why is Beau Dan worse poison? Which, honey?"

"Both. Start with the general. We can get to the particular, later."

"Well, for one thing, they ain't menfolks. Not for real, leastwise."

"Now, Lou!" Fanny laughed. "You're beginning to sound like a broken-down gramophone—You said *that* about the clients, remember?"

"Was I wrong?" Louella said.

Fanny frowned.

"No," she said, "as a matter of fact, you weren't. But

you don't mean to tell me that a big, good-looking hunk of man like Beau Dan—"

"Ain't worth a damn in th' hay? Naw. 'Cording to Estelle, he pretty good. Not that she'd know for real. What I means, honey, is that to be a ho's fancy man a feller's got to be lower 'n a rattlesnake's belly-button. He plumb got to hate his own mama, let alone all the rest of wimmenfolks. Tell me something, honey, you ever been in love?"

"Yes," Fanny whispered.

" 'N how you feel ever time your feller cut his eyes sidewise at another gal? Tell me *that*, Miss Fanny, will you huh?"

"Like—slapping him winding," Fanny said, "and scratching *her* eyes right out of her head—"

"Not t' mention snatchin' her bald-headed on top o' that," Louella chuckled. "Me, too—many's th' time I done felt like that, honey—lettin' alone the times I actually done wiped up half o' Burgundy Street with black she-ass. 'N menfolks is even worse—when it come to bein' jealous, I mean. So now you takes a feller—a big, tall, handsome red-haired feller with sideburns and a moustache like th' woods on fire that folks call Beau Dan O'Conner. Best lookin' *white* man I ever did see—that is, effen you don't look at his litte bitty poison-mean blue eyes. A feller what not only knows his women is layin' down 'n spreadin' wide for two dozen other fellers every night, but what takes th' money she gits for doin' it. Jealous? My ass, he is! He too busy out lookin' for mo' po' sorry would-be menfolks to jazz* his old lady for a sawbuck—"

"So?" Fanny said.

"So maybe I was born stupid, but a man what won't chop my kinky black head with a ax so hard he split me in two right down to my belly-button I even *looks* at another feller out the corner o' one eye, that man I don't want, don't need, ain't got no use for, 'n kin do without—permanent. You hear me talkin' to you, honey?"

"Yes," Fanny said, "and you're right. The fellow I was in love with said that I ever did anything like this, he'd die. And he meant it—then. While my father—"

*This is the original meaning of the word. By extension it became gradually applied to the musicians who played in the Parlor Houses, still later to their music.

She stopped then. Totally. Her slim, exquisite body. Her eyes. Her heart. Her breath.

"Miss Fanny!" Louella said.

"Where is he now?" Fanny was thinking, the thought moving through her like a blade, 'where is poor Papa? Nobody's seen him—in months. Maybe he's still up there—looking for me. That is—that is—if he—if he—'

She felt Louella's hand on her arm.

"You ain't a gonna faint, is you, honey?" Louella said.

Fanny shook her head, stinging the hot, salt, blinding spray from her eyes.

"No, Lou; I'm not going to faint," she said. "And—and don't worry. Taking up with a thing like Beau Dan is the *last* thing I'll ever do. Well, shall we bed the lioness in her den?"

"Fanny," Mae Hartman bellowed, "you gone crazy, girl? Tell me that, you little bitch! You tryin' to *ruin* me? Get us all *killed*? This place set on fire in the middle of the night? Or—"

"I suppose," Fanny said, "that you're referring to Mr. Sarcone—and the fact that I refused to go upstairs with him. Did he bother to tell you—why?"

"Lord God!" Mae shrieked. "She sits there on her narrow little ass so proper-like and asks damn-fool questions! If you don't know by now that in this business there *ain't* no reason for turning a customer down you—"

"One moment, Mrs. Hartman," Fanny said in her best, most irritating imitation of Norma's crisp New England accent. "*I* have reasons for refusing. And I will refuse whenever it suits me to. I am *not* an employee of yours. In a way, we're partners. Sharecroppers, one might call it. Splitting the profits from the sale of some awf'ly shoddy goods. So *you* don't tell me what I may or may not do. Rather late in the day now for that, I should think—"

Mae Hartman stared at Fanny. The reddish-purple tide of anger drained abruptly from the Madam's fat face, leaving it grayish-white. Like dirty bread dough, Fanny thought.

"No; he wasn't lying," she whispered. "He purely wasn't—"

"*Who* wasn't lyin' Miz Mae?" Louella said.

"Later," Mae said grimly. "I was telling this stupid little slut that—"

"No, you weren't," Fanny said. "I was telling you, Mrs. Hartman. I agreed to work here—if you can call bustle-hustling, tail-peddling, work. Oh, but you can; can't you? It *is* work. The nastiest, stinkiest, filthiest work there is. And the hardest. Well, I've kept my bargain. But more than that I will not do. Because I *didn't*, one, agree to take part in the exhibitions on that little stage in the Green Parlor, or, two, to indulge your clients in their whims and fancies, beyond doing it in the Crystal Room—though God knows what fun a man gets out of seeing himself snorting and bucking and sweating on a whore, multiplied a thousand times by all those mirrors. In short, my services don't include being beaten bloody, or pretending the poor little puny things nature cursed them with are either lollipops or peppermint sticks—to mention only the most usual of their perversions. And, last of all, I won't even attempt to delude them into thinking I *like* doing it. They pay to use a worn-out hired cunt. If they want an act, let 'em go to the theater."

Mae sat there.

"Jesus H. Christ!" she said.

"Miz Mae—we got t' *do* something, us," Louella said. " 'Tain't only Mr. Sarcone—that po' young feller Mr. Schneider—th' po'lice done throwed him in th' ice-house agin last night. Drunk 'n disorderly. Don't know 'zactly what Miss Fanny done to him, but—"

Fanny laughed suddenly. The sound of her laughter was very clear. It sparkled with amusement like the bubbles in champagne.

"If you must know, Lou," she said, "I fell asleep. While he was busy, I mean. Why not? There's nothing Rod Schneider can do that could keep a girl awake, really. But it seems that he was laboring under the misapprehension that he meant something to me—that he was responsible for my downfall, which is true, in a way, and that he was the grand passion of my life, which isn't, and never was. So the fact that his—lovemaking—wasn't even enough to keep me awake upset him, rather badly, it appears. The poor bastard! And the next time—"

"You give him his money back," Louella said.

"Jesus!" Mae screamed.

"Yes. Why yes, as a matter of fact, I did. Didn't seem fair to take money under pretenses false to that degree,

Lou. I've never tried to fool our clients into believing that I like what I'm doing; but at least most of them manage to enjoy themselves to a certain extent, anyhow. It would seem that I'm warmer and softer and wetter than their own five flying fingers, but beyond that the difference is slight. But he—he had a miserable time—trying to—to, well—arouse me, get me excited. I told him not to waste his time—that I was frozen all the way through. Then he asked me if he were responsible for my frigidity—I really think the poor bastard would have been *proud* of that!—of the miserable way he and his three friends treated me—"

"Jesus—" Mae whispered to herself, "it checks! It's *so,* all right. Every damn word that Joe—"

"What checks? What's so?" Fanny said.

"Nothing. Get on with your tale, missy!" Mae said.

"All right. He wanted to know if the time he got me drunk and turned me over to his three friends had had that effect on me. I told him no—that with—my lover—another ex-friend of his, I'd been able to get there *every* time, and sometimes four and five times to his once . . ."

"An' you tol' him," Lou put in tartly, "that you'd had a schoolchum *girl*friend oncet—one of them butchgals, bull-daggers, dykes, what could do it better than *him* . . ."

"Another highly unpleasant truth I might have spared him, eh?" Fanny said, her voice cool, pleasant, amused. "No matter. If any son of a bitch ever had it coming to him, it's Rod Schneider. But, anyhow, to date I have *never* refused him, you'll admit that won't you, you goddamned burr-headed, liver-lipped black spy?"

"Ain't spyin'. Don't give that much of damn, honey. I'm a maid—and that's honest work. So what a ho' do or don't do is no skin off my flat nose. Hit's just th' po' fellow tol' me—he was cryin' like a motherless chile, fer a fact—an 'bout th' time after that, too—when you let him agin—let him try, anyhows, but by then you'd done got him so upset he couldn't even git it up no more—"

"But that was all of two weeks ago!" Fanny said.

"Knows that. Only you got him so worried he had to try somewheres else. Same thing. He *can't* now. He really can't. He been down th' line—every parlor house in Storyville, 'n most o' th' cribs, too. Po' feller! He th' joke of the whole red-light district—all th' ho's laffin at him.

Nigger gals on Franklin—gals from Smoky Row—done hung mo' down nicknames on him! Like Limber Rod Schneider—or Danglin' Daddy Rodney—or reciting real slow-like: 'His rod 'n his staff don't comfort him.' Po' feller. He almost out of his mind—"

Fanny threw back her head and laughed aloud.

"That's enough!" Mae Hartman snapped. "So now you're even with young Schneider. With th' feller who ditched you, staged a circus with you for all his friends. Caused you to try to kill yourself. Twice. A kitchen knife *and* sleeping pills wasn't it? Now tell me—just what have you got against me—*daughter?*"

Fanny stopped laughing. Her voice cut off in midnote. Her silvery blonde head came level, was still. Totally still.

"Who told you *that?*" she said.

"Joe Sarcone. Wouldn't believe it at first. Couldn't. Then I started in to remember—how you said that Bill was your protector. How shocked you looked when I asked you if you was layin' down and putting out for *him*. But you admitting to the name Turner throwed me off. That called for more brass than I thought you had. And the way you lied—with them goddamn dirty ice-water colored eyes of yours dead still—when I asked you if you were kin to—Bill. To your Pa—"

"Mrs. Hartman—"

"Mama. Call me Mama. I got some rights to you, now, me girl!"

Fanny stood there. Then she leaned forward and put her two hands palms down on Mae's desk.

"I'll see you in hell, first, you miserable old whore," she said.

Mae stared at her.

"All right, missy," she said at last, "but if you think you can get next to me by riling Joe Sarcone up, you got another think coming. Setting aside the fact that as you oughta *know,* I never left you—You was *taken* from me by the sore-headed old sanctimonious bastard of a Pa o' yours—Joe Sarcone is on *my* side. He *told* me about you turning him down—asked me to say a word to you—as mother to daughter. That's how it all came out—How his kid used to play with your half-brother—and—hell—the whole story of your damn-fool life. Too much to expect a daughter of mine to have brains enough to keep her skirt-tail down and her drawers up, I suppose. Anyhow, back to Joe Sarcone. Next time he ask you to go upstairs, you *go*. You hear me, child?"

"I hear you. But I'll be damned if I will. In the first place you haven't heard the whole story: That even setting aside the fact that I can't abide dagos anyhow, and the other fact that Joe Sarcone looks like a bullfrog, I *didn't* refuse him the first time. That was the second. The first time he set out to demonstrate what a purebred Sicilian stallion he was, though bull would be more like it. And he hurt me. He was goddamned rough. Not queer-rough like the types who want to beat on a girl with the buckle-end of their belts and who can't even come 'til they hear a poor bitch screaming—no. He's normal enough. Only he's got to prove to himself that he's twenty-five years old instead of the fifty-five or sixty his baptismal certificate's probably got on it—and since he is strong and better preserved than any old bastard that age has got any right to be, he damned near pounded me to pieces. So I wouldn't take him on the next time. So now, he's got a new one. He is, he says, in love with me. He wants, he declares, to set me up in a little house, for his exclusive use—like those quadroon placées in the old days, eh Lou? And my answer to that—"

"Was to tell him to go fuck himself up the ass with any available blunt and dirty instrument," Mae said grimly.

"My, my!" Louella said. "That was telling him, wasn't it? You *really* tol' him that, Miss Fanny?"

"I did. And I'd tell this miserable puss-gutted old slut—who was trying to get him to raise the ante from five to ten thousand dollars before she'd *sell* me to him like a nigger before the war—the same thing, except that she'd probably enjoy it, that is, if she can even *find* her asshole among all that lard. But Joe Sarcone is finished, far as I'm concerned, and I don't care if he's the head of the Black Hand and the Mafia combined!"

"So—" Mae said slowly, "you *knew!*"

"Of course. Only, Mama Mia, the day they took that mess of blood and—and slime that would have been the goddamnest most beautiful baby *ever* born into this world, 'cause I—*we* made him with so much *love,* a thing an old Puss-Gut like you would *never* understand, and carried it out with the slops, was the day that anybody could make me do anything got ripped right out of the calendar. I know Joe Sarcone could have me murdered, only what in the name of Christ, and Him crucified, makes you think I'd *care?* Why, I'd thank him! I promised Papa I wouldn't try to kill myself again; and even at that I lied a little, maybe, because what the hell is *this* but a slower way of doing it? Looking into the mirror and having a filthy whore look back at me doesn't help my appetite, Mama, or my health, either one—"

"Fanny—" Mae began.

"I've stopped being human, Mama. I'm just a hole for a man to push his thing up into and wiggle and buck and pump and swear 'til he comes, spewing all his slimy muck into me, getting 'rid of at least some of the items that are griping his stinking guts—the way friend wifie *always* treats him, for instance, or how the boss took half a yard of hide with the hair left on it off his behind in the office the other day, or the fact that he *knows* he isn't—to quote Louella, here—worth gooseshit on ice in *any* department where manhood's called for—though about that, how would I know? God knows this is the last place you'd ever find a man . . ."

"Fanny," Maebelle said slowly, "last fellow who got Joe mad, they took him down to that meat-packing plant Luigi Boasso owns down on Gallatin Street—a blind, naturally, 'cause Luigi is one of Joe's boys—and hung him up on a meat hook—alive. Then they took turns at him for three whole days before the Lord had mercy on him and let him croak. Stout feller he was. Knew him well in the old days—"

Fanny looked at her mother.

"So?" she said.

"I grant you getting knocked off ain't so much. Long as it's *fast*. But screeching and begging and praying for 'em to finish you *is*. Joe's boys are—experts, baby. They know just when to stop—for a while that is—so you won't even so much as faint and spoil their fun."

Fanny looked at her mother, and her blue-gray eyes were cold and still.

"You're forgetting a few things, Mama," she said. "I weigh ninety-three pounds soaking wet. I've undergone major surgery *twice*. I wouldn't last a quarter of an hour, no matter *how* expert they are. And, as I said before, I'd thank them . . ."

"Lawd Jesus!" Louella said.

"Lou," Mae said, "what *are* we going to do with her?"

"Leave her be," Lou said. "Ax her to be kind o' nice to young Mister Schneider th' next time. Pleasure him sweet-like—make him *think* he's pretty good. Apart from that, Miz Mae, why don't we turn this here quirk of her'n—being *cold* I mean—to the house's advantage: Offer a—prize. Ten dollars in free trade to any feller than kin git a rise out o' her? That way we—"

Mae stared at her maid.

"Lou—" she said, "did I ever tell you you're a fuckin' black genius?"

Louella loosed her high-pitched giggle.

"No 'm, you purely never did," she said.

"But," Mae said, "what about Joe Sarcone?"

"Mr. Sarcone's—a gentleman," Lou said. "You 'splain things to him. Like th' baby's delicate—no rough stuff. Missionary style, tha's all. 'N—gentle. 'Bout settin' up housekeepin', our baby don't like the idea of being a partner to him cheatin' on his old lady for *real*. Buyin' a piece ain't so important—just a slip, kind of. But cheatin' *permanent* is a sin—a *mortal* sin if I 'members my catechism right. He a *good* Catholic. He'll 'gree to that. Only our baby'll have to oblige him oncet in a while. You will, won't you, Miss Fanny? 'Specially if he promise not to play so damn rough?"

"All right," Fanny said wearily, "what difference does it make? What difference does anything make now?"


## Chapter Twenty-Five


During that same week, three things happened. "The moving finger writes, and having writ"—this short and simple line, stops dead, appalled. How to begin? With whom or what or where?

The theme, actually, is evil. (We aren't going to be afraid of the *big* questions, are we?) And the varied motivations—good, pure, worthy, noble, idiotic, insane, bad, impure, unworthy—that drive men to it; for impulses of all these categories did, in simple fact, impel all three actors in the—drama? melodrama? tragicomedy? slapstick (with the reservation, of course, that the custard pie to the victim's face had as its chief ingredient oil of vitriol, and the clown would never get up from his pratfall) farce?—towards Fanny Turner, as moths swoop and flutter towards a candle's flame . . .

And having once begun (for the above paragraph is a beginning of a sort, isn't it?) in what order shall we catalogue the events of that week? Chronologically? By their relative importance? By their results?

By none of these. By no order at all in a world from which order and meaning both have fled. Scramble the numbers, say number one on this list is number three, and number two is the sine of the complement completing (or extending to?) the perpendicular of the angle of contact of their brief tangents with the arc of her life, and hence the cosine of their fatal earthward plunge. Say all three add up to (or subtract downwards toward) tragedy—a most sententious word. But this is an old-fashioned, a Victorian novel. It has a beginning, a middle, an end. Its absurdity consists in not recognizing life's absurdity, in stubbornly attempting to give meaning to meaninglessness. Or form to amorphousness. Who knows?

So—tragedy. If the word chokes you, spit it out.

That week (where the hell *were* we, anyhow, by God?) as we have already said, three things happened:

Timothy Hawkes got off a train in New Orleans; William Pelham Turner wrote his wife, Martha, a letter; and Rodney Schneider got drunk—again.

Three things. And two more which cannot be added to the other three to make five, because they were of a different nature. Three apples and two oranges do add up to five pieces of fruit; and even if you add three apples (the forbidden kind, naturally, from the tree of self-knowledge, sure to get you permanently expelled from Gan Eden!) to a (sudden, smashing) stone and a blade (designed, perhaps, to sever your living from your life), you've still got five *objects* though that's loosening categories past absurdum. But what if you try to add three apples (of vengeful purpose, of bitter resignation, of abject despair) to a very sour lemon (Beau Dan O'Conner's vagrant, unpolarized desires) and the whole impossible combination to (the rage that burned in Fanny's slender form devouring her little by little, slowly) a flame?

All right! All right! The play's the thing! (The hell it is! *Why* is always worth ten of *what;* but who has the time—or the talent—to convince you of that?) One day that week, Fanny had—or took—a day off, by which it is meant that she slept 'til noon, got up, bathed, dressed, and went out, with no intention of returning until the following morning. She did this at least once every week, and sometimes twice, having convinced her mother that if she didn't, she'd go crazy.

"What did Beau Dan do?" you ask. Simple. He followed her. Let's imitate him shall we? Let's do the same. Keeping a discreet distance, of course, behind them both. The outing will be instructive, you may rest assured. That is, if you're wise enough, tolerant enough, to accept the fact that people are normally inconsistent to the point of being contradictory. It will, it is only fair to admit, prove utterly confusing to those who believe in such elementary categories—if not semantic irrelevancies—as good and bad.

On the day we are concerned with here, Fanny was dressed all in white. Squarely atop her head she wore a broad-brimmed picture hat, covered with egret and ostrich plumes. Her high-buttoned shoes were of snowy suede, and the buttons themselves—on her dress as well as her shoes—were of mother-of-pearl. But the remarkable thing about her costume, as well as her cosmetics—a lip salve paler than a baby's blush, the faintest hint of rose touched with matchless skill to her all-but-colorless cheeks—was their discretion. No one who did not know her would have dreamed she was from Storyville; nor, for that matter, would, such a hypothetical observer, a least if he were a native Orleanais, have assumed that she was from the Garden District, or even from the more aristocratic streets of the French Quarter, for the obvious reasons that the tastefulness of her dress, and the quiet distinction of her bearing, could not have been matched by the proudest names of either section. It is only a slight exaggeration to state that the stage had perhaps lost what might have been one of its finest talents in Fanny Turner.

Walking along some four yards behind her, but, with
the skill of an experienced footpad—a profession he had
followed most of his early life—on the banquette, or sidewalk, of the opposite side of the street, Beau Dan O'Conner found himself being torn two ways at once. Which is
to say his habitual mode of being, behavior, thought,
fought total warfare with that aspect of his personality his
contemporaries would not have scrupled to call his better
nature. He was outraged to find that one facet of himself
he hated most stirring stubbornly back into life: the more
so because he'd believed it dead and buried long ago.

'Going soft!' he raged, employing even in his thoughts
the sort of Irish comic's brogue straight out of a third- or
fourth-class minstrel show he'd adopted as a part of the
public image he was forever trying to project in order to
hide from the world all the dismal things he knew about
himself, not to mention the appalling ones he suspected,
'softer than me old grandmither's curds 'n whey!
Blessed saints take a gander one and all! An angel. A
tiny whiff o' sweetness a-floatin' down th' banquette over
there—And damn me for Paddy's pig from th' Emerald
Isle if her sweet li'l tootsies so much as touch th'
ground—

'Stop it, Danny-boy,' he told himself sternly. 'Get a grip
on the nerves; use the old bean for a change, will you?
That's yer fortune tripping along there so ladylike and
fine. Not just the usual rake-off of ninety-five percent of
her take; but one or two *real* jobs and ye're in clover! She
could do it—talks like a duchess 'n looks like a queen!
Get her dainty little hooks into a bloke who's *niver*
walked the shady side before, and by me sainted mither,
I'll be driving a four-in-hand, and living at the Saint
Looie! Only—'

He stopped still, shivered like a wet dog.

'Only—she gets t' me. Makes me—wonder how'd it be
to live decent—go straight. With her as the little woman.
Houseful o' brats. To wash 'n comb 'n shepherd off to
Mass. 'Cause she—could do it. Save me. Cure me of—'

He lurched forward again, almost running, the taste of
nausea thick and vile at the back of his throat. He was
gripped by a feeling that he would have been hard put to
describe: the sensation of vertigo that hits a man after he
has stepped back from the roof-edge of an immensely tall

building; the recognition that the peril he'd escaped had been mortal. As it had been. Fanny's cool and silvery beauty had brought him to the verge of admitting to himself consciously a thing about his own basic nature, his way of being, that he could not yet, at that stage of his existence, accept, any more than he could accept the idea of his own death.

'I'm all mixed up,' he moaned, 'worse than a snake-bit hounddog ripping open his own belly to drag out his poisoned guts. Them filthy dago bastids! Stinking Sicilian scum, they—'

Then he saw Fanny had lifted her frilly white parasol, and was signalling a cab.

He looked around wildly. Fortunately for him there were several hacks and hansoms clip-clopping through that street. He waved one down, jumped in, snarled the phrase that the dime novels and penny dreadfuls of the nineties had already made a cliché of:

"Follow that cab! Look alive, man; don't lose it!"

To his relief, keeping in sight the hansom Fanny had taken turned out to be an easy matter. She obviously was in no hurry, for, after having given the driver the address she wanted to go to, she did not again lift the little trapdoor in the cab's roof to ask him to whip up his ambling nag.

She got out of the cab in the busiest shopping district on Canal Street; entered successively a store specializing in children's clothing, a toy shop, and a confectionery. In each case two or three unctuous and servile attendants came out with her, their arms piled high with packages. With a cool and regal gesture, she indicated to each in his turn that he was to wait for her on the sidewalk until she had finished her shopping.

'Holy Mither of God!' Beau Dan breathed. 'She's spent a pretty penny, that she has! Got to take this little girl in hand before—'

Then it hit him.

'A kid! She's got a bastid brat stashed away somewheres sure as old Paddy was a lover of the pork! And that means—'

But he wasn't yet prepared to go into what it meant. Besides, he hadn't the time, for, at that very moment, Fanny swept imperiously out of the confectionery with

the fat little Creole who was its owner behind her, as
laden with burdens as the others were.

Beau Dan stifled his first impulse, which had been to
approach her, lift his boater, offer to get her a cab, help
her with her packages. It was, he decided, much too soon.
He had one unvarying rule when dealing with men and
women alike: 'Get something on 'em, Danny-boy! Then
make 'em dance to any tune you feel like fiddlin'!'

The only problem with this procedure was that once a
woman had embarked upon making a public career out of
being "notoriously given to lewedness" to quote the city
fathers' rather comical phrase, getting something on her
became an exercise in futility, for what extortionary
threats could be effective against a woman who had absolutely nothing left to lose? Even menacing her life made
no sense when she knew as well as you did you were
damned unlikely to carry out a murder that would cost
you her earnings in the future, and a long jail sentence if
not the gallows to top the matter off.

That was one of the two reasons Beau Dan had turned
from straightforward blackmail to the subtler variety of it
that pimping was, the other reason being that Joe Sarcone's Mafiosi had effectively closed all the other avenues
open to his peculiar talents in his white, trembling, ice-
cold, sweat-wet face.

So he had learned to use his striking handsomeness, his
devilish Irish charm, to great effect, combining them,
when necessary, with the only menace that meant anything to a whore, to "Mess up yer pretty phiz more than
somewhat," since the loss of a harlot's beauty, such as it
was, meant the loss of her livelihood, a hideously scarred
face being a sure ticket downward to Crib Row, if not to
actual starvation.

But if there were anything that living by his wits taught
a man, it was to be a better than average judge of character. The first time that Fanny Turner had fixed (and
transfixed) him with her gaze, with that ice-cold, unwavering, deadly stare, not even challenging really, lacking
the faintest trace of any emotion whatsoever, unless it
were contempt, he'd realized that none of his usual tactics
would work with her. To get her to open her arms, her
thighs, and her pocketbook to him was going to take some
doing, he saw. And, because it was, it became the ruling

passion of a life singularly devoid of passion in any real sense. "Got to have her!" Beau Dan had told himself, morning, noon, and night ever since: "By all the saints, I've got to!"

So now, riding behind her in still another cab, he meditated upon what use he might make of his near-certainty that she had a child, once he'd found out just where she'd put the little bastard out to board. The possibilities were numerous: If the brat were an infant still—as judging from Fanny's own age it almost had to be—he'd pull a snatch, kidnap the little beggar; for although he was absolutely incapable of harming a child, Fanny didn't know that. If, however, the child were somewhat older—as it could be; he'd known Irish Channel drabs to drop their first at age thirteen—he'd threaten to carefully explain to it just how its Mama made her living. 'That'd get to her!' he exulted, ' 'cause sure as St. Pat chased the slimy twisters out, she—'

Then he saw that Fanny's cab had stopped, and he sat back against the seat of his own, confounded. They were at the corners of Gravier and South Liberty streets, and that low red brick building was the Creole Orphanage run by the Ursuline Sisters.

"They'd niver!" he gasped, "take a whore's bas—"

Then he stopped. 'Oh, yes they would,' he realized sadly. 'They wouldn't hold how he was got 'ginst the kid. What's surprising is Mother Catherine's lettin' her visit it. Rough edge to her tongue she's got, has Mother Kate—'n no patience at all with human failings—'

He waited until Fanny had got down and entered the orphanage, accompanied by the cabdriver, who bore in his arms all the packages she couldn't carry herself, before getting down and dismissing his own cabby.

'Damn me for a sinner,' he thought, 'she's fair crossed me, that she has. A brat put out to board with a family is no trick at all to get me paws on, but how in the names o' Saint Patrick and Saint Jude I'm a going to pick out *her* bairn amidst all the little squealers the good sisters have got stacked up in layers in there?'

He decided then to wait outside until Fanny came out again, and trust to luck. Some of the younger nuns weren't immune to the old blarney, especially when employed by a trickster of his skill. Then he saw something:

the brick walls surrounding the orphanage, while high, had decorative openings in them at intervals—to let a little light and air in, he supposed. Tall as he was, a bit of a stretch would be enough to—

The thought was the father to the deed. Poised there on tiptoe, Beau Dan was able to see Fanny. She was seated on a stone bench in the garden of the orphanage, surrounded by a swarm of children. She was busily engaged in handing out toys and candy—not, as he'd expected, to one particular child, but to them all. Near her, three sisters were taking the clothes out of the boxes and holding them—in order, it was obvious, to get a rough measure of what would fit whom—against small, ecstatically wiggling forms.

Beau Dan could hear the children.

"La Dame Blanche!" they were squealing: "Comme elle est bonne! Comme elle est belle!"

Having lived in New Orleans since his father had brought the family over from the slums of Dublin where he, Beau Dan, had been only nine years old, O'Conner had no trouble understanding them.

'La Dame Blanche, the White Lady' he translated inside his mind. 'Why damn me wicked soul to perdition 'n back agin, it fits her!'

He moved from his vantage point to another inlet in the brick wall much closer to where Fanny was. By the time he'd got there, the Mother Superior of the Ursuline Sisters had come out of the orphanage, and put out her hand to Fanny.

What happened next not only caused Beau Dan to shiver, but also, with the reflex of long habit, to make the sign of the cross above his sinful heart. For Fanny immediately dropped to her knees, took Mother Catherine's big, red, work-hardened Irish hand in two slim white ones, and kissed it with reverence, with awe, with—devotion.

"Damn me!" Beau Dan groaned, "that ties it! Whore or not, th' filly's got goodness in her! I can't. Sweet Mother Mary 'n Your Darling Boy; but I—"

"Get up from there, child," Mother Catherine said. " 'Tis not fitting for you to treat me so. Have you thought over what I told you?"

"About—taking instruction?" Fanny said sadly. "Yes, Mother Catherine—only—I—I can't—"

"Then I'll button me lip," Mother Catherine said jovially. "Far be it from me to try to convert any Christian from the branch of the faith she was born to. The Church holds that our Father God will accept a true devotion however mistaken. And, after all, you *do* believe in our Lord and the Holy Virgin, don't you, child?"

"Yes," Fanny whispered, "at least I *think* I do. Sometimes, anyhow. It's not that, really. I never was a *good* Methodist, to tell the truth about it. And—now, when I go to church—and that's at least once every week—I go to *your* church, Mother Catherine—"

Mother Catherine looked at the three younger nuns and all four of them fairly beamed.

"Then ye're on the true road to Salvation, my child," she said. "And that being so, I'll tolerate no further shilly-shallying, you hear me? I'll ring up Father Du Bois this instant! He'll set up a schedule for you—"

Then she saw—and Beau Dan, his ankles beginning to ache from being poised on tiptoes so long, also saw—the rarely awful way that Fanny was crying.

"I—can't— " Fanny got out finally, in a voice that was hushed, choked, fragmented even by a true grief, by a curiously naked pain, "I—I'm—bad, Mother Catherine. Immoral. What you'd call a fallen woman, I suppose. Not fit to touch these poor innocent babies' hands. You're being too good to me when you even let me come here and—"

"Child," Mother Catherine said, "I knew you were a sinner. But that you're bad, I don't admit. Good people sin—and bad people sin. The difference is that the bad feel no remorse. I guessed what your trouble was the first day you showed up without a ring on your finger, and fairly smothered yourself in bairns! But I kepy my mouth shut, waiting to see if I could pick out which o' the wee ones is yours—"

Fanny stared at her. Then, slowly, she shook her head.

"None of them is, Mother Catherine," she said. "I—I lost mine. It—it didn't even come to term. I—I fell down and—"

"And, seeing that you were no longer in the family way," Mother Catherine said grimly, "the man in the case ran off like a rat and—"

"No," Fanny said, "he didn't even know. I—never told him—"

"Married, wasn't he?" Mother Catherine said.

"No. He—he'd gone abroad to—to finish his studies. Medicine. There—there was no way I could have let him know—"

"I see," Mother Catherine said. "Forget him, child. Do as I tell you. Go to Father Du Bois. Take instruction. Embrace the one true faith. Then find yourself a fine young Catholic fellow. Get married. Have children of your own."

Wearily Fanny shook her head.

"Who'd have me now?" she said.

"You'd be surprised," Mother Catherine said. "And—even failing that—*we'd* have you. You could always come to us as a novice—a girl who loves children the way you do would be immensely valuable here—"

"Me?" Fanny said. "You'd take me—as—a *sister?* Me—a wicked, bad, low—"

"So were some of God's greatest saints, until they repented, child—" Mother Catherine said.

"This," Beau Dan groaned, "I gotta put a stop to—right now, if not sooner! To hide all *that* under a Sister's robes! To give all that sweetness to a passle of orphan bastids who—"

Fanny was still crying; but there was a new look in her eyes now—a glow like starlight, Beau Dan thought. Then it died.

"No," she said with almost infinite weariness, "it's too late for me, now."

Her voice, speaking, made Beau Dan shiver. 'An' me worryin' about her takin' th' veil' he thought. 'More likely she'll go off the end of a pier some dark night. Oh, Jesus, I—'

Then he stopped thinking altgether, bemused by, and lost in, the contemplation of that face.

When she left the orphanage, walking, Beau Dan followed her. His plans were in ruins. Fanny had told the bitter truth when she'd said she had no child; he was absolutely, and sadly, sure of that. "Just have to trust to luck," he muttered, and fell back a pace or two for fear that she might become aware of him.

He soon realized Fanny's stroll was aimless. In fact, it

had as little destination as her life had now. But Beau Dan followed her doggedly, still trusting in his luck. And, as is so often the case with the Devil's own, it was very good indeed.

Fanny started towards the Quarter, walking down Gravier itself in the direction of the river. Soon, Beau Dan knew, she would have to turn left on any one of the half-dozen or so streets that would take her across Canal into the Vieux Carré itself. But she did not turn on either Rampart or Burgundy or Dauphine, keeping on until he was beginning to worry if her destination were not the river itself, if she weren't in such a mood of despondency, of despair as to cause her to go off a wharf's end in broad daylight, when he saw she was going to pass directly in front of Tom Anderson's Stag, which worried him even more, or at least more immediately, because it was one of the most notorious saloons in the city.

Still, beyond a few hoots and catcalls from the drunks on the banquette outside it, she had no real trouble. At least not at once. She was already well beyond the saloon when a young man reeled out of its swinging doors and rushed unsteadily after her. Beau Dan recognized him at once, noting that though he was hatless, and his clothes in some disarray, the quality of the latter was rich and fine.

'That bastid Schneider,' he thought. 'Estelle told me he was still after her. 'N drunk as a Belfast Bogside Padre, as usual—'

Another thing that was, or had become, usual was that Rodney Schneider was alone. These days, his friends, Joe Downey, Tim Waters, and Hank Phelps, found his black ill-humor too hard to bear—and saw no reason to bear it, now that Rod had become the laughingstock of the district. A dead-game sport has followers; a poor, weak fool, none. Which means there's a rough sort of justice in the universe, after all. Or does it? Depends on your point of view.

Beau Dan quickened his pace, closing the gap between them. Then he broke into a pounding run. For Rodney Schneider had Fanny by the arm and was pulling at her ferociously.

"Right now!" he was screaming, his voice high, hysterical, woman-shrill: "We're going to the justice of the peace, Fan! I'm going to make it up to you—the way I treated you, I mean! Make you my wife in the sight of God and man!"

Fanny stared at him. Then she opened her mouth—not much, barely parting her lips, really—and loosed an almost soundless purr of laughter. And that sound, faint as it was, had a quality in it that made the flesh along Beau Dan's spine prickle with sudden cold.

"And just what could *you* do with a wife, Rodney, darling?" Fanny said.

"Love her! Treat her like a queen! Give her kids!" Rodney was sobbing. "Nothing's wrong with me! You—you just—got me upset and nervous and—"

But by then Beau Dan was there. He lifted his straw boater with elaborate grace.

"This masher—annoyin' you, Miss Fanny?" he said.

Fanny stared at him. A light appeared in her eyes—a speculative sort of gleam, glacially calculating. Was even this opportunity to put the final seal upon her vengeance worth the obvious and continuing dangers of getting herself involved with Beau Dan? Then she decided that it was, or rather that the dangers were nonexistent. Using and then discarding such a thing as the pimp was, she was suddenly sure, no problem at all.

"Why, yes, Mr. O'Conner," she said quietly, "as a matter of fact, he is. Make him stop it, will you?"

"Be off with you, me fine lad," Beau Dan said gruffly. "Sure 'n twould be a sin 'n a shame to mess up such a pretty, girlish face . . ."

"Why, you pimping bastard!" Rodney screamed, "I'll—"

Beau Dan put his right hand into his pocket, spreading all his fingers wide. They slid easily into the loops of a pair of brass knuckles. He kept it there until Rodney threw his first wild, totally ineffectual punch. Then Beau Dan set him up with a jolting, almost professional left, and crossed with that armored right. Fanny had moved a discreet yard away by then, but even so . when those gleaming hoops of brass crashed into Rodney's face, she had to leap backward farther still to avoid being splattered by his blood.

Rodney hung there, dazed. Then he opened his mouth and spat out three of his front teeth.

And Fanny Turner looked at him and slowly let her

lips curve upward in a smile that would have shocked speechless anyone who knew her, even—or maybe especially—her fellow inmates of number Two-Twenty-Two North Basin Street, because it was, in contradiction to everything her acquaintances believed of her, sensuality's very self.

"Go on, Beau Dan," she said calmly, her voice soft, pleasant, warm: "Give it to him. Take him apart, will you?"

Beau Dan looked at her. He was remembering how she'd looked, kissing Mother Catherine's hand, the gentle Madonna-like glow in her pale eyes as she had held the orphaned children in her arms. But he shrugged off this enigma, as he did all of the wonders and the mysteries of life.

'Wimmen!' he thought, 'there's no understanding 'em nohow!'

Then he moved in upon Rodney Schneider. With four blows deliberately held in check so as not to knock his victim down, depending, actually, upon the massive weight of the brass knuckles rather than on sheer force, he closed both Rodney's eyes, broke his nose, and fractured his jawbone in two places. After that, with young Schneider out on his feet, lightly, playfully, Beau Dan cut his face to ribbons.

Fanny stood there, watching that, observing with detachment how those flashy good looks that had been one of the causes of her life's fatal divergence from society's norms were being not so much ruined as obliterated, erased, and that soft, luxurious—in the word's antique sense—smile, never left her face.

Beau Dan stood back, not even breathing hard. Then, lifting his polished brogan, he kicked Rodney Schneider carefully between his opened, loosened thighs. The screech Rodney let out was the scrape of glass on stone, shrill, high, all gone, terrible.

Slowly he buckled before Beau Dan. But, at the last instant, the big man's hand shot out and caught him by the throat. O'Conner jerked that bloody, utterly ruined face to within inches of his own; snarled:

"Let this be a lesson to you, me boy!"

And kissed Rod's broken mouth.

He jerked his head sidewise to see whether Fanny had

seen that. But, if she had, she gave no sign.

She was smiling at Beau Dan, her pale, almost colorless eyes alight with something that he had neither the intelligence nor the sensitivity to comprehend, and that would have horrified him if he could have defined it.

"I suppose I'll have to—reward you for your heroism, shan't I?" she said, her voice a little harsh, having a throaty quality to it he had never heard before.

"You're damned right you will, Fanny, me girl!" Beau Dan said happily. "Come along—I'll hail us a cab. Take you out to dinner—and after that, I've got the classiest diggin's you ever saw on Dauphine Street—"

But Fanny shook her head.

"I prefer to fight my battles on neutral ground," she said. "What do you say to May Evans's, Beau Dan?"

Beau Dan frowned. May Evans ran a house of assignation at 1320 Conti Street. It was one of the best and most discreet in the city. Then his face cleared. Aside from the fact that it was going to cost him money, the results would be the same. From that day on, Fanny Turner would be his woman.

They moved off, leaving Rodney Schneider lying on the banquette, sobbing and choking on his own blood and vomit. The barflies, the hangers-on, were beginning to edge towards him now, their abysmal cowardice beginning to recede at the sight of Beau Dan marching away from there with Fanny on his arm. Five minutes later, Mike Higgins, Tom Anderson's barkeep at the Stag, called an ambulance. Rod was in bed with his jaw wired shut for three months. When he got up again, he looked like a broken-down pugilist—except that no ex-pug was ever that thin, or had an expression quite like that one in his eyes.

Two weeks after his release from the hospital, he disappeared from New Orleans forever. What became of him, what his subsequent fate was, no one has ever bothered to ascertain. Rumors floated back: That he was drinking, or had drunk, himself to death. That he was in jail for life, for the murder of a prostitute who'd spurned him, repelled by his broken face. That he was in a Northern lunatic asylum, chained to the wall and howling. That he was dead by drunken mischance, by suicide, by starvation.

Does it matter, really? Rodney Schneider was gone. As late or soon all men go. That his defeat was public and obvious made it differ only in degree from the quiet and secret capitulations the flesh is ever heir to, but not in kind. For birth itself is where death starts; and implicit in every man's beginning is his end. So, Ave atque vale, Rodney Schneider! Requiescat in pace. De mortuis nil nisi bonum, we agree. Which compels us to silence, doesn't it? For beyond the fact that Omnia mors aequat, what good could we say of you?

Before dawn that next morning, Beau Dan woke up to find Fanny fully dressed, her hair already combed, carefully fitting the egret-and-ostrich-plumed hat to her head.

"Where th' hell d'you think you're going?" he roared at her, in his best woman-dominating tone of voice.

But she only smiled at him, her eyes untroubled and unafraid.

"Back to Mae's," she said, "And thanks for a wonderful evening, Beau Dan. As Estelle claims, you really *are* pretty good . . ."

Beau Dan grinned at her.

"I'm the *best,* baby!" he said. "All the fillies can tell you that—"

Fanny shook her head.

"The best, no," she said quietly. "You aren't even anywhere close to him. But—pretty good, I'll grant you. Mainly because—the matter doesn't even interest you, does it? You—react enough to perform; but that's all. But you're—bored. Which is insulting to a woman, really. And, since you're bored, you can keep it up, go through the motions, anyhow, for as long as it takes to satisfy most women, I suppose—"

"I satisfied *you!*" Beau Dan said.

Fanny smiled.

"*Did* you?" she said.

"Well—you damn sure acted like it," Beau Dan said, a little uncertainly.

"Maybe I'm a good actress," Fanny said.

"Jesus Christ!" Beau Dan said. "You mean to tell me that you—didn't? Not even a little bit? In the names of all the saints, Fanny, I—"

Fanny crossed over to the bed. Sat down. Bent and kissed him slowly, lingeringly on the mouth. Straightened up, smiling.

"Let's say I appreciated your efforts," she said, "such as they were, Danny-boy. And to prove it, put your hand under that pillow, will you?"

Beau Dan pushed his big hand, with the red hairs on the back of it gleaming like fox-fur in the glow of the incandescent lamp, under the pillow. It came out with a twenty-dollar bill in it.

He stared at her, and his little blue eyes were sick, suddenly.

"You—you're *paying* me?" he said. "Goddamnit, Fanny! I niver in all my life—"

"Took money from a woman? Is *that* what you're going to say? Now really, Beau Dan!"

"No," he said slowly, "I wasn't going to say that. All right, the fillies give me things—tokens of their esteem—but mainly it's because I do them favors: protection from toughs; get up bail money for 'em when they get pinched; find 'em a sawbones not only willing to snatch the li'l bundle some too-healthy sport's left 'em with, but good enough not to kill them in the bargain. I but *can* say, on me sainted mither's grave, that this is the *first* time in all me days that a filly ever paid *me*—for this!"

"And you're ashamed of that? Why should you be? You amused me. I actually did enjoy myself—in a way. Men pay me for that sort of amusement, so what's the odds? Besides, Mister Big Beautiful Beau Dan O'Conner—I wanted to make it clear where we stand. I'm not Estelle, nor any other of your tarts. You don't own me. I don't need you, don't want you, have no use for you—except for such occasional amusements, for which I'll gladly pay—if for no other reason than to keep the record straight—"

"Goddamn it woman, you're calling me a he-whore!" Beau Dan roared.

"A compliment, really. Means you've got something *worth* buying. A lot higher in the scale of things than a pimp, don't you think? But then everything is. Because there's nothing lower, is there? Not even a whore. Which is why we keep you around. Makes us feel better . . ."

"Jesus!" Beau Dan all but screamed.

" 'Bye, now, Beau Dan," Fanny said, and bending once more, kissed his mouth.

He stared at her. Then he put out his hand with the twenty-dollar bill in it.

"No," he said, "for you, Fan, baby, it's always free. That's one thing. And another is you're going to need me. For one little girl all by her lonesome, this old life is just too goddamned rough. So take back your twenty, honey, and buy some more gumdrops for them sniveling orphans of Mother Kate's—or some red woollen longies to keep their poor li'l bare asses warm come winter. 'Cause—strange as it may seem to you—this way, Beau Dan O'Conner just ain't for sale."

Fanny looked at him, and laughed, suddenly making that sound again: a low, curiously throaty gurgle of amusement he had to strain his ears to catch.

"Aren't you?" she said. "Too bad. Like every female born, I dearly love a bargain. But keep the twenty anyhow—as a souvenir. Frame it and hang it over your bed to show to your riding fillies. Tell them a woman gave you that—as stud fee. Something to brag about, don't you think?"

"Don't brag," Beau Dan said slowly, "don't have to. Me wimmen do it for me."

"Among whom," Fanny said, "you'd better not ever try to include me. I'm not anybody's woman, except my own. As I said before, I don't need you. I don't need any man. I'm a free soul. Beyond God's reach by now—and even the Devil's, maybe. Funny—"

"What's funny?" Beau Dan said.

"The—reason I'm free. I suppose it's the only way any human being ever gets to be, really—"

"And how's that, baby?"

She stared at him, and her eyes went opaque suddenly.

"All right," she said, "I'll explain it to you, so you'll know what you're up against. It's because I don't give a damn. Nothing matters to me. Absolutely nothing. Not even my life. If you were to pull a gun on me right now, I'd simply move in closer to make sure you wouldn't miss. Most people knuckle under to force—or to threats, don't they? But how can you threaten a woman who's got not a blessed thing to lose, Beau Dan? Who'd count being put out of her misery—a favor?"

He peered at her shrewdly.

"Supposing I was to threaten to mess up that lovely little phiz of yours more than somewhat, Fan?" he said.

She stared back at him and her eyes were somber. She was remembering Myrtle Tolliver.

"Now that *is* an effective threat," she said slowly. "You do know women, don't you? Most of us put our looks above our lives. Only—don't try it, Dan. You start roughing me up, and you'd have to kill me. And that, apart from calling for the kind of balls that really work, which means the kind *you* haven't got, would be bad for business, wouldn't it? Even an occasional twenty is better than nothing, it seems to me. Besides, there're people who just might take offense. A certain gentleman on the Police Aids* who has half a cemetery full of crooks to his credit by now, for one. And another—who might invite you down to that meat packing plant on Gallatin Street for an interesting chat. So don't be unnecessarily tiresome— please?"

She stopped then, staring at Beau Dan's face. It had changed. His sturdy, masculine good looks departed on the spur of that same instant for parts unknown. Everything in his countenance pinched, tightened. For the first time, she realized how small his mouth was for so big a man, remembered, almost hearing it inside her mind, Louella's remark about his "little bitty p'izen-mean blue eyes."

'Why,' she thought wonderingly, 'he looks just like a child. A *girl*-child—who's been beaten—and tormented— and abused—*that* way. Because there must have been a time when—rape—was possible even upon him. When he was an altar boy in the cathedral, say. But what did I say that made him—remember?'

Then it hit her.

"Want to tell me about it, Beau Dan?" she said. "About your *last* visit to Luigi Boasso's packing plant?"

"Get out of here!" Beau Dan screamed at her. "You filthy little bitch! I'll kill you if you don't!"

It was, Fanny realized, the voice of a woman, a reedy, nerve-edged soprano that vibrated from his mouth.

---

*In New Orleans, Detectives were classified as Police Aids, for reasons known only—and that dubiously—to bureaucracy and to God.

"You mean you'd like to," she said, sadly, "if you had what it takes to do it—only, you *don't,* do you?"

Then, her eyes soft with pity, she put out her hand and ruffled his bright red hair. She had a certain weakness for children, especially damaged children, even when they came garbed in the big, muscular carcass of a man.

Then she turned and walked out of there. Before leaving, she paid May for the use of the room, too, thus becoming doubly guilty of hubris, a word she didn't even know. But to the gods—or the principle of mindless malice that controls all of human fate—ignorance is no excuse for breaking the law.

So she would pay for it, and dearly, before that week was out.


## Chapter Twenty-Six


The first thing that Martha did, after reading the letter from her husband was to rush over to Sergeant Giovanni Martinelli's house with it. Her own experience had long since confirmed Bill's statement that Detectives Martinelli, Sprugs, and Rogers were the only completely honest men—besides himself, of course—on the New Orleans Police Force. Yet, although Martinelli and his wife Lucia were the sole members of Bill's Diogenesian Circle—as Martha called it—who were not of her own completely Anglo-Saxon background, it was precisely they whom she found most congenial, their Latin warmth and gaiety striking a responsive chord in her own psyche—"Likely because," as she only half-jokingly told them, "some not so remote female ancestor of mine probably let the local Italian greengrocer thaw her out when her old vinegar-bones of a husband wasn't around; there must be some way of accounting for dark hair and eyes like mine popping up every other generation or so in a family of blonds, mustn't there?"

When Gino Martinelli opened the door, she didn't even say "Hello" to him, but thrust the letter out with an abrupt and awkward gesture completely at odds with her usual unstudied grace.

Martinelli took the letter, stood there holding it while his dark eyes searched her own.

"Read it," Martha said.

Martinelli moved over closer to the gas lamp. Martha could see his lips moving as he spelled out Bill's none-too-legible script.

"I give up," he read slowly. "I've spent all my money, and too much of yours, Martha; but I can't find Fanny. I'm beginning to believe she's not even here. Of course I did trace her this far. That's why I stayed. Most fugitives think that the Big City is the perfect place to drop out of sight in, and mostly they're right. But I had what I thought were some special advantages. In the first place, I'm a trained detective; and I don't think I'm doing anything else but stating the simple truth when I say I'm a good one; in the second, there are certain courtesies that the police departments of every good-sized city extend one another; and, in that regard, New York's finest have been very fine indeed. And the third thing is that Fanny's a pretty spectacular-looking young woman. It's been my experience in running down female crooks that to dye hair like my poor lost baby's is only to call attention to it more, and, besides, there's no way she could dye those eyes.

"But, in spite of all that, I can't find her. With the help of the plainclothes squad here, I've talked to the madams of every sporting house in New York—and Lord knows there're a lot of 'em—shown them her photograph, naturally—but none of 'em have seen her. So, maybe you're right about that—maybe she wouldn't take that road . . . I checked all the hospitals with her—well, delicate condition in mind. No soap. The women's prisons. The morgue. I've looked at every young white female suicide they've brought in since I've been here; and although more than one of them had been in the East River or the Hudson a sight too long to be really recognizable, I'm sure none of the ones I've seen was her.

"Funny thing: while I was looking for her, Timothy Hawkes—you know, I told you about *him*—was tailing *me*. Reckon he thought I'd lead him to her. Seems that the Tolliver woman was his light of love; and he's fairly boiling to get even. And, yes, all my investigations show that Fanny actually did do the awful thing he accuses her of, and that I wrote you about. And that, to me, means my poor child is not quite right in the head—if she ever was, which looking back over her life now, I'm inclined to doubt.

"But, to get back to Hawkes. He's pretty good. A real pro. No one who hadn't summered and wintered with this lousy profession the way I have would have even noticed him. But he seems to have given up, finally; this last month I haven't seen him at all.

"So, honey, next week I'm coming home. I'd come now, except that I've got two more slight leads to run down. I honestly don't expect anything to come of them; but I don't dare not look into them, just in case.

"Glad Billy's doing so well in school. Sending him there was the right move—if only to get him away from the Sarcone boy. Because although folks generally don't believe it, the Mafia *do* sometimes take non-Italians in to do some of the dirtier, riskier jobs for them, cases where their operator can be sacrificed—arrested or killed—and the fact that he has a good Irish, or German, or even English name will throw the authorities off the track.

"Fact is, I've got reasons to suspect that a certain small-time Irish crook, well known in New Orleans's sporting circles, and, who, beyond having one or two prostitutes he lives off of, has no visible means of support, is in their pay. Name of Dan O'Conner. When Joe Sarcone and Company wiped 'Yellow Dog' O'Mallory's gang off the face of the earth, they didn't kill Dan for some reason or another, although he was the youngest member of it, and present at the shoot-out. Some say it was because he wasn't but fifteen years old at the time, and pretty as a girl, so that even those Sicilian bastards didn't have the heart. But there was more to it than that—

"Lord, I ramble, don't I? Reckon it's to keep my mind off my own troubles. You know what? If I don't find Fanny this next week—and under conditions that would give you and me a chance of saving her, I hope I *never* find her. Better that way for all concerned. Don't think I could stand any more real bad news. Anyhow, as I said before, next week I'll be coming home—to you. Don't think I'll ever go away again. I miss you too damn bad.

"All my love,
                    "Bill"

Detective Sergeant Giovanni Martinelli handed the letter back to Martha, and his dark eyes went darker still.

"Oh, Jesus!" he said.

His wife Lucia looked from him to Martha. She had almost conquered her Latin woman's suspicion that any woman whosoever was after her tall and handsome husband, at least in Martha's case. Besides, she genuinely liked Bill Turner's wife. She had had so many convincing proofs that Martha was entirely free of anti-Italian prejudice—peculiarly virulent in New Orleans since the murder of Police Chief David Hennessy and the subsequent lynching of no less than eleven of her compatriots some ten years before*—that she had come to accept her as fully as she had long ago accepted Bill Turner.

"What is it, Gino?" she said.

Sergeant Martinelli looked at Martha.

"Tell her," Martha said.

"She's—*here*," Gino said. "The girl, Lucy. Bill's daughter. Martha's—stepdaughter. In a *cathouse*. And you know what'll happen when Bill—"

*Hennessy was killed by Mafia gunmen on Oct. 19, 1890. A bribed and intimidated jury acquitted the eleven Mafiosi charged with the murder on March 13, 1891, whereupon a vigilante committee, in a notice signed by 61 prominent New Orleans citizens, called a mass meeting at Henry Clay's statue (then at the junction of Royal and St. Charles Streets on Canal; it was moved in January 1901 to its present location in Lafayette Square). From there the mob marched—after having procured arms at a local sporting-goods store, probably on Canal Street itself—on the Parish Prison in Beauregard Square, entered it, and shot nine of the accused men to death, dragging the other two out and publicly hanging them.

The case had international repercussions. Italy broke off diplomatic relations with the U.S.A., and there was even talk of war. Finally the American Government paid the ridiculous indemnity of twenty thousand dollars to the Italian Government —not quite two thousand dollars a head—and the matter was quietly dropped.

Many authorities hold that the Mafia was never again a power in New Orleans' underworld. The writer does not agree. There is abundant evidence to indicate that they merely adopted what were later to be called Cosa Nostra tactics—operated with greater cunning and subtlety, concealing their activities with the skill that has made them the powerful organization they are today.

Lucia looked at Martha.

"Then he mustn't find out," she said.

Martha bent her head. When she straightened up again, her brown eyes were sad. No, more than sad: resigned.

"In *this* town, Lucy?" she said.

"We gotta try, anyhow, Martha," Lucy said. "The men on the force respect Bill. Even the worst crooks, the ones who're a disgrace to the uniform, do. If Gino—and Sprugs and Rogers—would—well sort of pass the word around that *nobody* is to shoot off his lip in front of Bill, maybe—"

"And maybe not," Martha said.

"Well—" Gino said, "Bill is on a desk job now. And that bum leg of his keeps him from getting around too much, so—"

"He'll find out," Martha said. "You know him, Gino. You *know* he will—"

"Yes," Gino said, "but—later. After you've had time to—to sort of break it to him gently and—"

Martha looked at him. Through the wall behind him. Through all the intervening space from where they were to past the point where the last spiral nebulae dim away into the final dark. Then her gaze came back again.

"Gino," she said, "tell me—how. How *does* one say it really? 'Look, Bill, I hate like hell to tell you this, but your daughter—your only daughter—is a whore'?"

"Jesus!" Gino said.

"You know any other way of putting it?" Martha said. "*Is* there any way of keeping this miserable little bitch from killing *her* father and *my* husband—which is precisely what she's set out to do?"

"Now, Martha," Lucy said, "why would she even *want* to do a thing like that?"

"She does," Martha said wearily. "Believe me, Lucy, she does. In a way, she has always wanted to, without even knowing it herself, maybe. Bill was—a bit too strict with her. Too stern. He never would—or could, for that matter—show her how much he loves her. Said that every time he looked at her, he saw—her mother's face looking back at him. Everything she did—every gesture—reminded him of that woman. So—"

"So she's gone there," Gino said. "To her mother. To Maebelle Hartman—"

"As she threatened to do at least a dozen times when she'd quarreled with Bill," Martha whispered. "And the last time when she screamed at him, 'All right, Papa— since you're so sure I'm no good, why fight it? I'll just get myself a thin silk dress and stand in the line in Mama's—' No. That's not right. She didn't say Mae's. She said 'in Frankie Belmont's parlor.' But the effect is the same, isn't it?"

"Santa María!" Lucy said.

"And he told her—" Martha went on in the same flat, almost toneless voice, "he said—"

"What?" Martinelli said.

" 'If you do—you'll have to change into a black one that same day. You would have that much respect, wouldn't you, daughter—?' And he meant it, Gino. Billy's—trouble—almost killed him. But, even so—*she* started it. Trying to commit suicide over that worthless Schneider boy—"

She stopped then. She and Detective Sergeant Martinelli stared at one another. A long time. A long, slow, dead-stopped awful time.

"You've heard what's happened to him, Martha?" Gino said. "To young Schneider?"

"Yes," Martha said. "The telephone is an invention of the Devil, isn't it? I'm sure that every nosy-Parker busy-body in town has had one installed—I've had that proved to me this week."

"They called you up—to tell you *that?*" Lucy said.

"No. They had their maids and cooks call Eliza. I had to put her to bed—and give her a vernol to stop her from crying and carrying on so. Scattergun tactics, Bill would call it: two birds with one shot. One poor, old, defenseless colored woman who loves Fanny. And one white one, less poor, less old, with a defense or two left, maybe. I can say, 'She's not mine; she hasn't a drop of *my* blood in her veins,' can't I?"

"Only you won't," Gino said.

"I won't. She's Bill's, and therefore mine. And by all the worry and suffering she's caused me, all the pain. So two shot-down birds, Gino! And it hurts. God, *how* it hurts! Tell me—tell me, how's young Schneider?"

"Bad. His face is a mess. Jaw's wired shut. Doc Schloss says there's maybe brain damage; but until the patient can talk, he can't make sure. Poor bastard! That roughneck used brass knucks on him . . ."

"Over her. Over—Fanny," Martha said.

"Yes. And I swear to God that Bill's plumb downright clairvoyant, sometimes. Got second sight. Take this letter. Right out of a clear blue sky he—"

"I don't remember his writing anything about Rod Schneider—" Martha said.

"Schneider, no. But what made him mention Beau Dan to you in his letter, Martha? You ever heard of that filthy pimp before?"

"No," Martha said. "Beau Dan? Oh, I see: this Dan O'Conner he says is in Joe Sarcone's pay?"

"Yes. And he's right. That little mick—he wasn't more than fifteen, then; that was four or five years before the Hennessy case, Martha—swore to Sean O'Mallory he had a verbal message from Joe—an invitation to a peace conference, to divvy up their turfs, the fruit docks, the gambling joints, racetrack betting, and the sporting houses, on a friendly basis—and *personally* led O'Mallory into that blind alley where Joe's hoods were waiting for 'em—with Mafia guns, double-barreled shotguns sawed off to less than a foot long and loaded with buckshot. You could have put a baseball in the hole in O'Mallory's belly those hand-cannons left. Lord knows I've no reason to love the Irish, but even a bastard like Yellow Dog and his cheap John plug-uglies deserved better than that—"

"I—I'm afraid I'm a trifle dense tonight," Martha said. "But I really don't follow you, Gino. I fail to see the connection between this—O'Conner, isn't it? Yes. This O'Conner's playing Judas Iscariot and—"

She stopped. Said:

"Oh!" Then, "Oh, my God!"

"Yes," Martinelli said. "It was him who did the job on Schneider. Like you said—over Fanny. Seems he's added her to his string. That's how come Bill's mentioning him in his letter hit me so hard. I hate to admit it, but I'm superstitious. I know that educated people like you would call it a coincidence; but Madre di Dio! This kind of coincidence I don't like . . ."

Martha put out a groping hand, found a chair, pulled it towards her, sat down.

"There's nothing worse than—a whining woman," she

said, "one of those females who tells her friends her troubles over and over and over again. So I won't. I'll spare
you a recapitulation of all the things I've put up with, suffered, endured, for Fanny's sake. Besides, you know them
all, anyhow. But looking back over my married life there's
one question that keeps nagging at me: What on earth did
I do it *for?* In God's own holy name, Lucy—for *what?*"

"I don't know for what," Lucy said. "All I do know is
that you'd better stop brooding over it, Mona mía, before
you make yourself sick. How's about a shot of Mama's
Guinea Red? Make you feel better, sure . . ."

"All right, but not just a shot, Lucy. Tonight I need a
gallon," Martha said.

Fanny looked at the clients in her mother's Rose Parlor.
Early as it was there were nevertheless a goodly number
of them. But most of them ducked their heads, turned
their faces, or otherwise avoided her gaze. She knew why.
These were the ones who had already gone upstairs with
her, some of them as many as ten times before giving up,
and snarling: "Damn li'l bitch is frozen all the way
through!"

'Fools,' she thought. 'Poor cruddy bastard fools. You
get what you give. And when you've got nothing you give
nothing and that's just what you get. Complaining about
your wives. Jesus. A man doesn't have wife trouble. Not
ever. Even if he's married to a marble statue right out of
the cemetery a man can melt that statue. Make it pant.
Moan. Beg. But men don't come here. Men don't have to.
Men have women—for free. I mean—for love. Like Phil
had me. A man can make the sky fall in on you every
time. But you cruddy poor weak bastard scum— Half an
hour to even get it up. Then three seconds flat before it
falls. Fumbling around like a beggar with the blind stag-
gers. Coming all over the bed sheets before you can even
get it in. Then blaming me. Frozen Fanny, the icebox girl.
Jesus. Because I won't play games. Pretend I'm in love
with every crud who's got a sawbuck in his pocket. Go
into the big act: "Oh Sugar! You're driving me wild! It's
so go-o-o-od I can't stand it! I'm going to screeeam in a
minute!" Shit. Gooseshit. Frozen Fanny, the icebox girl.
Right. Goddamned right. Whom it takes a man to melt.
Like—Phil—'

She frowned suddenly.

'I get there sometimes with Beau Dan,' she thought. 'Why? Because he's slow—and powerful—and lazy—and doesn't give a damn. But—it's different. Not like Phil— *Nobody* could be like Phil. Sweet baby Jesus, I miss him so!

'Still, Beau Dan's better than nothing. The hell he is! I get a bigger thrill playing with myself.' She smiled bitterly, thinking: 'You cruds. Every girl in the house does that *every* damn night to get some relief. Twenty-five cruddy bastards a night and not one of 'em capable of satisfying a girl. Oh no. You all want wrong-way business. French arithmetic: Soixante-neuf. That doesn't call for *anything* does it? You don't even really have to be able to get it up. And because I *won't*, you say I'm cold. Jesus. I wish I had me a man. Right now. I wish just once a man would walk in that door. Take me upstairs and wreck the goddamn bed. Make me scream the roof down. I want that. I need it. Gentlemen, I've got news for you: a hotblooded girl is better off in a convent than in a whorehouse. 'Cause at least there they feed her saltpeter and she doesn't get tormented all night long by bastards who have neither their brains, heart, guts, dick, nor balls in working order—"

Then she saw the little man.

What attracted her attention to him was the fact that he was new. And a stranger. More than a stranger—an outlander, in the German sense, for no native Orleanais of the class who could afford Mae's fees would have been found dead in the clothes this little fellow wore. A high wing collar of pristine celluloid that was choking him to death, almost. A shrieking green ascot tucked into a burgundy waistcoat, across the bosom of a pajama-silk shirt whose three-inch-wide stripes of rose and—'And bayou-slime green,' Fanny decided—alternated with a crash like a summer thunder. 'And—Lord God!—a checkered Prince Albert! But with those stripes what else could little Sergeant Shits put on, I ask you? And bulldog brogans, shined 'til you could see your underdrawers in them if you stand too close to him—Lou swears that's why the Mother Superior makes the convent-school girls scuff their Oxfords with sand and dirt. Might wake up some boy's carnal nature—Oh, brother!

'And pipe that moustache! Shades of John L. Sullivan!

As Mama always says, "Now I've seen everything with the hide left on it!" And—Oh Christ, oh Lord, oh Jesus, here he comes! Straight as an arrow to—*me'*

She said:

"Go away. You're too little. Be a mortal sin to teach you mannish tricks. Tell your Papa to take you somewhere else to get broke in . . ."

He stood there, grinning at her. She shivered suddenly. And violently. There was something in the little man's grin that—His voice came over to her, silken smooth, with a marked trace of an Irish brogue in it.

"Miss Fanny Turner, I presume? Late of the Emma Willard School, Troy, New York, right?"

"Who—" Fanny's voice faltered, "just who the devil are *you?*"

"The handle's Hawkes, Fanny me girl," the little man said. "Timothy Hawkes—And I've come a long way jist to see yer bonnie blue—gray—Hell, what color do yer eyes be? No matter. Le's go upstairs. Have a little chat, jist the two of us. More cosy that way, right?"

Fanny stared at him. She was afraid. She who'd thought she was past all fear. She didn't like the feeling.

"You—you've got to ask Mam—I mean Mrs. Hartman—first. Stand all the other girls a drink. House rule."

"All right," Hawkes said. "After all the trouble and expense ye've alriddy cost me, me foine lass, a bit more don't make much difference. Where's ye darlin' mither anyhow?"

"Over there—" Fanny said, and pointed.

Hawkes sauntered over to where Mae sat, behind her desk in the lobby, keeping a watchful eye on all her girls. They were all beautifully dressed, in expensive evening gowns. They kept their eyes downcast, conversed with would-be clients in demure and dulcet tones. Some of the other houses permitted their girls to sit around in their underwear, or even, sometimes, entirely nude; but Mae was too shrewd an observer of human nature to fall into such crass and stupid errors. Goods too openly on view, merchandise that could be handled before purchase, automatically lost value in the prospective customer's eyes. And since what she was selling was the pretense of love, it paid to accompany it with a counterfeit of romance as well. She ritualized her commercial arrangements so that

her clients found themselves forced into an abbreviated
charade of formal courtship which, for all its patent falsity, was somehow forlornly charming. The result of this
was that Mae lost—at least temporarily, because most of
them were back on the turf in a year or two—more girls
by marriage to clients than any other madam in Storyville. This troubled her not at all, because she knew from
observation as well as from her own personal experience
as Bill Turner's first wife that the only legend falser than
that of 'The Whore with the Heart of Gold' was that
other only a trifle less beloved of our Victorian forebears,
'The Fallen Woman Redeemed by Love.' Whores, as any
fool could plainly see, made the world's worst wives.
Having to stick to one poor bloody sod bored the piss
out of 'em. In her long and dedicated life of commercial sin, Mae witnessed forty-five marriages of young prostitutes. Of that forty-five, thirty-nine ended in divorce,
desertion, or separation, three by suicide, two by murder,
and exactly *one*—apparently—succeeded.

Of course Mae was incapable of realizing that a woman
who had as much wrong with her as it took to become a
whore in the first place could never fit in normal society.
She put the matter on a simpler basis.

"Prairie gopher shit!" she used to bellow through her
cigar smoke. "Man what marries himself a poor, worn-out
cunt is a fool!"

But now, Fanny saw, she was playing her favorite
role—that of the grande dame, housemother to a school
of charming, and charmingly available, young ladies—to
the hilt. The cigars stayed in their coffin; her booming
laughter—"Sounding jist like," Terrible Ted McGaw always swore, "the bawl a yearling lets out when yer
gelding knife drops his poor li'l balls onto th' lone
prairie"—was held down to a ladylike note. And the
strange little Hawkes seemed much to her liking—'Probably,' Fanny thought bitterly, 'because he's loud and vulgar
enough to suit even *her*—'

Then she saw Mae was beckoning her with the bejew-
eled lorgnette whose lenses were plain window glass—Mae
had the eyesight of a bald eagle or turkey buzzard, the
late Julius Hartman always swore—and she got up and
sauntered listlessly over to join them.

"This gentleman, Fanny dear—" Mae said archly,

"would like a little chat with you in private—upstairs. I've given my consent—that is, if *you*'re willing. Are you, dearie?"

'Oh Jesus,' Fanny thought. 'Oh Christ. Oh hell.'

She said: "All right, Mrs. Hartman. Give me ten minutes—then send him up."

It was all of three hours later that Louella noticed that she hadn't come down again, and that struck the shrewd black girl as odd, knowing Fanny as she did by then.

'Strictly a short-timer, Miss Fan,' she thought. 'Turns 'em out in ten minutes. Less. Five sometimes. But three whole hours—Lord God.'

She went up the stairs herself, knocked discreetly on Number Thirty-Three, the bedroom in which Fanny usually entertained her clients. There was no answer. Boldly Lou pushed open the door. Stepped inside the room. Stopped. Let out a little choked-off scream.

Fanny lifted her head. She had been vomiting onto the rug. Her eyes were absolutely terrible.

"Get me—Beau Dan—Lou—" she said.

"I'm agonna git you a doctor, me," Louella said. "He done damn near kilt you. Jesus! Who'd of think that little feller was one of them men folks what loves to *whup!*"

Fanny twisted her neck awkwardly, looked at her own naked back. It was a mess, crisscrossed with several ugly striped, blue-ridging, oozing red. But she comtemplated that spectacle a long time, and with care. As if it meant something to her; suggested something. "Killed me, no," she said. "I'm tougher than I look, Lou. Besides he only hit me—ten times. With the buckle end of his belt, though. Said—it was only—a—a sample—"

"You didn't yell," Lou said accusingly. "You didn't sing out for help. You—let him. I done tol' you 'n tol' you, Miss Fanny, them fellers what likes to whup on a gal is dangerous. Maniacs. Oughta be locked up. I plain just don't understand how come you—"

"Let him? Had to," Fanny said, in a croaking whisper; then: "Goddamn it, Lou! Go get me Beau Dan!"

"Th' doc first," Lou began; but Fanny screamed at her:

"Hell, no! I got to show Dan—my back like this."

Lou looked at her pityingly.

"He won't do nothing," she said. "Maybe he'll even *like* seeing it, him."

"I—know that," Fanny got out, "but I won't have the doctor—not yet. Because all I want Dan for is to take a message—to Joe Sarcone. Tell him to come here—tonight to see *this*."

"You means," Lou whispered, "you wants that little whuppin' feller—*daid?*"

Fanny looked at Lou.

"He—did more than beat me, Lou," she said. "He made me—do *that*. What I swore I'd never do. Why th' hell do you think I was throwing up?"

"Jesus!" Louella said.

"Besides—he'll be back. To take me away with him—so he can beat on me *every* night. Make me—"

"Polish his knob for him," Louella supplied.

"That's a nice polite way of putting it," Fanny said. "And the bad part about it is—I'll have to go. He—he's got something on me, Lou. Something I did. He could send me to jail—for life. And that's the one thing I couldn't stand. I told him to go ahead and kill me—but he knew better. Said, 'You'd like that, wouldn't you, me lass? Outa yer misery. Hell no. Ye're gonna live 'n suffer like Myrtie—' Oh, shit!"

"I ain't heard no names," Louella said, "and effen I is, I done forgot 'em already. Damn fine forgettery I'se got, me."

"All right. Get me Dan, Lou. The doc—later. I can stand this. I've stood worse. You hear me. Got get him, damn you!"

"All right, Miss Fanny, I'm going, me," Louella said.

"Fan, baby," Beau Dan all but wept, "I'll kill him, myself! Show me th' cruel bastid what did this and—"

"No," Fanny said; "You couldn't kill a flea, Beau Dan. Beating a fellow up is all you're capable of—and even then it depends on who the fellow is, doesn't it? What have you and I got to hide from one another? I'm an ice-cold filthy whore and you're a pimp and a bully and a coward. So maybe we were made for each other after all. Water seeks its own level, doesn't it? Even drainage-ditch water like us. Oh, shit! I hurt worse than old hell and you make me lie here and argue with you! Do as I say,

Danny-boy! Go get me Joe Sarcone."

"Fanny," Beau Dan got out, "you just don't know what ye be a-askin', girl!"

"Yes, I do," Fanny said. "He'd come. You know damn well that for me—"

"Yes. Him and every other mother's son in this rotten burg. That ain't the catch, doll. Joe will be here with bells on the minute he gets your message. 'Tis there the trouble lies, lass—"

"Don't call me lass!" Fanny screamed at him. "That's what *he* kept calling me all night. While he was beating on me, I mean. Kept saying: ' 'N how did that one feel, me foine lass? Just a downy tickle, wasn't it?' And then, 'Wham!' another one. With the buckle end of his belt, naturally—"

"All right—" Beau Dan said. "All right, Fanny, me doll—I won't call you that. What I was trying to say to you was that getting to see Joe Sarcone is damned nigh impossible. Those Sicilian thugs of his take it as a matter of course that anything in pants is out to do Joe in—and the fact that they're ninety-nine-and-a-half percent right makes trying to see him a might risky business—"

"Try—" Fanny whispered.

Beau Dan stood there. He wasn't thinking, really. What he was doing was remembering. He knew Joe Sarcone's Mafiosi wouldn't kill him. He'd been safe from the Sicilians' tender mercies since the night he'd played the Judas-goat and led poor Yellow Dog and his boys like lambs to the slaughter into that blind alley where Joe's gunmen waited. His stomach turned over, even now, remembering that. The price at which he'd bought his immunity from the Mafia. The bodies of twelve murdered men of his own race, his own kind.

So now the Sicilians wouldn't even beat him up. All they'd do would be to—remind him. And he couldn't be reminded of that. Because, like Fanny, he too had learned that there were, after all, fates worse than death. And being forced to admit, acknowledge, *what* he was, was one of them.

He couldn't. He simply couldn't.

That was the reason he had never told the story to a living soul of *why* he'd fingered Sean "Yellow Dog" O'Mallory and his plug-uglies for Sarcone's outfit. He had excuse enough. Any member of New Orleans's under-world would have accepted it as a more than valid expla-nation if he had said:

"They grabbed me. Pulled a snatch. Kept me down in Luigi Boasso's packing plant for three whole days—"

Just to mention the meat-packing plant on Gallatin Street would have justified him forever in the eyes of ev-ery small-time crook in town. Because any of the drunks and derelicts who frequented the two-block-long alley that was all Gallatin Street was, had heard, on more than one occasion, the screams coming through even the two-foot-thick brick walls at two o'clock in the morning. Not that they ever mentioned it. To do so would have meant that they too, would have paid the slaughterhouse floor a visit, and though it was true that, infrequently, a visitor to the building walked out of it again on his own two feet, no one of them was ever the same again.

Not even Beau Dan O'Conner.

And that was the thing he never could explain. He had no single scar to show. The Sicilians hadn't hung him up on a meat hook, pushed through a loose fold of his own flesh, and burnt his feet with cigar butts, or pulled out his fingernails one by one. No. Instead, by sure, if diabolical, instinct, seeing the face of an angelic choirboy he'd still possessed at age fifteen, his willowy, much-too-graceful form, they'd simply stripped him of his clothes, and used him sexually, taking turns at him as though he were a girl.

So if he went there now he'd escape unhurt. His body would, anyhow. And what real harm could come from their jeering at him, saying: "'Allo, Danny-boy! You sucka me da cock, no? Or you want that I give it to you uppa da ass? Only you ain't so pretty any more!"

No harm. Except one. His own destruction, living. His own involuntary abdication from the rank, rights, and privileges of manhood to descend into the half-world of creatures with men's bodies and women's instincts, feeling, souls. Because the reason he couldn't face Joe Sarcone's "famiglia" was simple: They knew a thing about him he had concealed from all the world, even most of the time from himself: The worst of the torture they had inflicted upon him was—

He had liked it.

"Please, Dan—" Fanny said now. "You do this—and

I—I'll do anything you say—even—"

"Be *my* girl?" Dan said.

"Even—that," Fanny said bleakly.

"Then done it is!" Beau Dan said, and went out of there, running toward the stairs.

But at Joe Sarcone's headquarters, he was agreeably surprised. None of the Sicilians ribbed him, reminded him they had possessed his body. They'd said simply, " 'Allo Dan—you wanta see da boss? Wait a minute. I see if he gotta da time ta talk to you."

"Tell him—" Dan got out, "it's important. Tell him Fanny sent me. She's been hurt—a feller tried to—to kill her—"

Afterwards he would remember the courtesy they had shown him, and curse himself for a fool. Because when Joe Sarcone's boys started being nice to an outsider, a nonmember of the famiglia, it meant that Joe had found a use for him, was planning to make of him a tool. And what happened to Joe Sarcone's tools was notorious. Once used, they were broken and thrown away.

Less than a minute later he was in Joe's office. Joe sat there, a squat, powerful bullfrog of a man, gazing at Dan through a fog of cigar smoke. He didn't so much as offer the pimp a chair. He said, softly, slowly:

"This some kind of a trick, Dan?"

"Jesus, Chief!" Dan said, "do I look like I'm tired of livin'? Would I have come in *person?* I ask you."

"You went to Yellow Dog in person, after my boys got through with you," Sarcone said.

"All right," Dan said, "tell your boys to keep me here 'til you phone 'em it's all right to let me go. With a gun in the back of my neck if that makes you feel better, Chief. But you go to Mae's. Jesus—take twenty of your hoods with you—and circle the block three times to make sure Sean and Company ain't risen from the grave—'cause who the hell else could touch you, now? Then when you've seen what that bastid did to Fan, you—"

"And what did this bastard do to Fan?" Joe Sarcone said.

"Beat her," Dan said. "Buckle end of his belt. I wanted to get her a doctor but she wouldn't let me. Said she wanted *you* to see her back first . . ."

Joe Sarcone looked at Dan. Got up. Nodded to one of the Sicilians. The man ran his hands all over Dan's body. Stepped back, said.

"He's clean, Boss. Not even a shiv, let alone a heater."

"No—brass knucks?" Joe Sarcone said with a grin.

"Oh Lord, Chief—" Dan began.

"He had it coming, that young pup," Joe said. "Come on, Danny-boy. I'm taking you with me. Frankie, you 'n Pete come with us. Not that I expect any trouble: Danny, for once, is telling the truth."

Joe Sarcone stood there looking down at Fanny's back. It wasn't a pretty sight. Not at all. Joe didn't say anything. Slowly he sat down on the edge of the bed. "Frankie," he said, "run down to Doc Bienvenu's and ask him to send me up some of that special salve he made up for me the last time I got hurt. He'll know. Give him a twenty for it and tell him to keep th' change—Get going, now—"

He waited very quietly the ten minutes or so it took Frankie Francesco to get back with the salve. Then he began to rub it into Fanny's hideously striped back, his big, square muscular fingers as gentle as a woman's.

"Thanks—Joe," Fanny whispered; "but—I didn't ask you to come over here—for this—"

" 'S all right, bambina," Joe said. "I know why you sent for me. It will be taken care of. Tell me his name."

"Hawkes," Fanny got out. "Timothy Hawkes. He—he's a detective. Not a police detective. A private one."

"Description?" Joe Sarcone said.

"Little fellow. Shorter—than—than Frankie. A big bushy moustache like John L. Sullivan's. Loud clothes—very bad taste."

"He proved that tonight," Joe said. "Address?"

"Don't know. Some good hotel, though. He seems to have plenty of money."

Joe looked up at Pete and nodded. Pietro Dominici got up at once.

"Try the Royal, first," Joe said. He went on rubbing the salve into Fanny's back.

"Any *reason* for this, bambina?" he said. "Or he just a maniac, this fellow?"

"There's—a reason," Fanny said. "Do you mind if I don't—talk about it, Joe?"

"Not at all," Joe said. "Smart not to talk. There—it's all gone. Feel better now, baby? Or shall I send for more salve?"

"It feels—just wonderful," Fanny said. "Joe—I've got to tell you something. Any time you want to—visit me, go upstairs, even stay the night, you're welcome. But beyond that—no. So if you don't feel like doing me this favor gratis, I—"

He put out his big hand and patted her wan cheek.

"No strings, bambina. I'm an old ugly dago who looks just like a bullfrog, just like you said. I won't bother you again, ever. Besides, taking care of this little matter will be a real pleasure."

He got up, quietly.

"C'mon, boys," he said; then: "Not you, Dan. You stay with her. You don't want to get mixed up in this. I'll tell Mae you're up here. And Lou. Better still, I'd advise you to stroll around downstairs a while, let a few of the girls know you're stayin 'all night—"

Beau Dan looked at Joe Sarcone. Licked bone-dry lips, said:

"Why, Chief?"

"No reason. Just might not be a bad idea for you to be able to *prove* where you were tonight. Fool stunt that, smashing up the Schneider boy. Gave you a reputation. Linked your name to Fan's in the public mind—"

"Chief, I—"

"I approve. Long as you're good to her, Dan. If you're not, if ever you start slapping her around, Luigi'll send you a special invitation. And maybe the boys won't be so nice, next time—"

"You—" Dan croaked, "don't have to worry about that, Chief. I—I love Fan—I—"

Joe Sarcone looked at him, said:

"Yeah. I suppose you do." Then: "Come on, boys."

Miss Milhaus picked up the cone-shaped earpiece of the telephone from its cradle hook and put it gingerly to her ear. Then her eyes widened and widened until behind her thick-lensed glasses their pale watery blue image was enormous. She said:

"Yes, sir, Chief Schuykill, I'll ask him . . . Yes, sir; he's here. Just a minute, sir—"

She looked at her employer.

"Mr. Beaconridge—it's Chief Schuykill—the chief of *police,* sir, and—"

"Oh, Jesus!" Anthony Beaconridge groaned. "What's Tony done now?"

"It—it's not Tony, sir," she said. "Oh, Lord! You'd better talk to him yourself, sir!"

Mr. Beaconridge took the telephone, barked into it: "Yes, Chief?"

Then his fine, aquiline, aristocratic face melted into the ludicrous loosening, softening, slackening of shock, of astonishment.

"In a *trunk,* you say? Addressed to *me?* . . . In God's name, man! . . . What's that? . . . Yes. Why yes, of course, I'll be right down—"

Half an hour later he stood in the morgue with the chief of police and the city coroner. The trunk stood there on a table in the icy room.

"Brace yourself, sir," the chief of police said. "He ain't pretty—"

Then he lifted the trunk lid.

Anthony Beaconridge reeled away from that table. Bent in half. Vomited. Said:

"Oh God. Oh Christ. Oh Jesus."

"Is it?" Chief Schuykill said.

"Yes," Mr. Beaconridge whispered. "Yes—it's Hawkes, all right. Of course I can't be absolutely sure, but—"

"Edwards called me," the chief said heavily, "from the freight depot. Said he had a trunk there—addressed to you—and that it was stinking up the whole place. So I went there, and—"

"Sir," the coroner said, "have you any idea who might have—"

"Done this? No. Of course a man in Hawkes's profession inevitably makes enemies; but God Almighty! Who ever did this was—a fiend!"

"But somebody—who knew your address, sir—and that Hawkes worked for you? Why even *I* didn't know that."

"His wallet," Anthony Beaconridge said. "He always carried an open letter of credit from me. I trusted him—and he never abused my trust. He only used that letter when on a job for me. So this time I'm sure no bank wherever he was will bill mine. He told me he was going away on a private matter. Rotten luck, isn't it? Even that lead is closed."

"I've put a tracer on the trunk, sir," Chief Schuykill said; "for what that's worth, which ain't much. The line it came in on runs clear down to Natchez, Mississippi. And naturally the fellow who did *this* didn't put his return address on the label. Hell, sir, it could have been shipped from damn near any place between Natchez and here. Frankly, the chances of us finding out who the murderer was are pretty slim—"

"Work of a lunatic," the coroner said, "which makes matters even worse. Fingers—chopped off. Toes, too. A meat cleaver, I'd say. Nose, ears, even—I beg your pardon, sir—his privates—So I'd say—"

"That—we'd better notify his widow," Anthony Beaconridge said. "That's all anybody can do now . . ."

He was right. It was.


## Chapter Twenty-Seven


"Uncle Oliver," Billie Jo Prescott said, "promise me something—"

"What, child?" Oliver Prescott said.

"While I'm gone—stay away from *her*. From that woman. You owe Aunt Ellen that much respect. After all, she's not even cold in her grave, and . . ."

Oliver Prescott stared at his niece. Tried to see—to discern—from her expression whether she had asked him that because she'd finally heard something. Whether she knew *why* he was all but forcing her to take that European grand tour with the Thorntons. 'So she won't be here when it happens,' he thought sadly, 'when that scandal's all the way out and spreading over the parish like a brushfire whipped up by a high wind in August— 'Course Ruth ain't even showing yet, but—'

He leaned closer. Decided, with immense relief, that there was no hidden motive behind Billie Jo's words. She, he was sure, still didn't know. Her request had been a coincidence, a lucky hit—nothing more.

He went on studying the girl. What he saw didn't please him. Billie Jo was very thin now. She'd always been slender; but now she was thin. 'No—scrawny,' his mind supplied. 'All bones. And nerves you can see crawling underneath her skin. What can I say to her? For her own sake—*not* building up a defense in this terrible business about Ruth? That every man who isn't a fool makes his own rules, constructs his own morality? And every woman, too. Only she's young—and, admit it, Oliver—a fool. She—should have gone to bed with young Sompayac. I'd have beaten her to death if I'd found it out, but there was no reason for me to have found it out—except pregnancy, maybe. And even that could have been arranged, adjusted, taken care of—particularly since that young Creole was obviously a gentleman . . . If only she'd even *look* at another boy. If only she wouldn't persist in this truly idiotic romantic folly—'

He said, mildly:

"I thought you *liked* Ruth, child."

Billie Joe sighed.

"I did. I do," she said. "She's—lovely, Uncle Oliver. And sweet. I can't say she's good—because all my life I've been taught—by *you*, Uncle, as well as by poor Auntie—that—adultery, to say it straight out and ugly—is a sin. I suppose you can say that it's only half the sin it was before, since Aunt Ellen's passed on. I mean it isn't *double* adultery any longer, is it? You *can't* cheat on a dead woman, can you? But there's still *her* husband. There's still Lennie Colfax—"

Oliver Prescott snorted.

"Oh, I'll admit he's nothing much! But what difference does that make? Don't vows mean anything? When a woman promises to 'love, honor, and obey,' she also promises to do so 'for better or for *worse*'—not to even mention 'in sickness and in health'—'til death us do part.' *Death* Uncle Oliver, not the divorce courts! Which isn't very likely is it? He'll *never* give Ruth a divorce. What he'll do is *hire* somebody to kill you. Or arrange an accident—since he's too big a coward to face you like a man—"

"Baby," Oliver Prescott said, "you've been reading too many novels."

"Maybe. But that would be just Lennie's style. Ugh!

He's—slimy. Crawly. Repulsive. And—"

"You're—justifying Ruth's behavior, Billie," Oliver Prescott said, "and—mine."

He saw her eyes flare; heard the sharp intake of her breath.

"Oh, Uncle!" she wailed. "You've—admitted it! And—and you shouldn't have! Not to me! Not ever to me. I—I've been accusing you for years and—"

"You're a big girl now, Billie Joe," Oliver Prescott said. "Time you learned the fact of life."

"But I know—No. *That* isn't what you're talking about; is it?"

"The birds and the bees? Where babies come from? No, child. Sit down, will you? Listen to your poor old sinner of an uncle?"

She sank into the big rocking chair. In it she looked absurdly small and fragile. A great wave of tenderness engulfed him, seeing her like that.

"Billie," he said, "I'm going to have to use some pretty abstract terms. But you're smart. You'll follow me. No—there's another way. Going to ask you a few Socratic questions: One: Is it wrong to kill a human being?"

"Yes!" Billie Jo said. "Of course, Uncle Oliver!"

"*I* killed a man once, Billie," Oliver Prescott said.

She stared at him, whispered, her voice beneath the threshold of audibility: "Oh, Uncle Oliver!"

"An old colored man. A crazy old man who should have been sent to a lunatic asylum years before. What happened was this: a little girl got lost. A *white* child, honey. And our friend Lennie Colfax *claimed* he saw Uncle Ben leading her away into the woods. Nobody else saw that. But, then, Uncle Ben wasn't properly respectful towards white people—especially not towards white folks like Lennie—"

"Which means he *wasn't* crazy," Billie Jo said.

"Honey, when you get to the place where you realize it's the *world* that's crazy, and imposes its standards and conceptions of sanity on the rest of us, you'll be all the way grown up," Oliver Prescott said.

She stared at him again, said:

"Go on, Uncle Oliver."

"All right. They found the child dead. Not a mark on

her—her clothes untorn. Exposure, likely. But two hundred sane, respectable, good white citizens went and got
poor old Uncle Ben, and chained him to a green log
soaked in kerosene—the *log,* honey—not Uncle Ben—and
set it afire—"

"Oh, Uncle Oliver!" Billie Joe said.

"I'd followed 'em. With my deer rifle. Winchester .30-
30. I was young in those days, and I had the damn fool
idea that maybe I could face down that whole mob of
good, respectable, entirely sane white citizens and make
'em turn one poor disrespectful crazy-like-a-fox old nigger
loose. Only I got there too late. He was already burning.
No. Roasting is more like it. And screaming. That was
twenty-seven years ago and I still wake up nights with
those screams inside my guts, baby, not in my ears. So I
shot him. Four hundred yards, no deflection. Best shot I
ever made in my whole life. Hit him right between the
eyes. He didn't even kick. I was proud of that shot. I still
am."

Billie Jo's penny-brown eyes widened, widened. Her
mouth came open a little. The freckles on her face stood
out starkly against the sudden white.

"Baby," Oliver Prescott said, "I'm asking you all over
again: Is it wrong to kill a human being?"

She went on looking at him. Said, harshly:

"I see. You're saying that circumstances change things.
Even good—and evil."

"I'm saying that every man and every woman—especially folks with blood in their veins—has to find out
what's good for him or her and what's evil—the only reservations being having a decent respect for the basic
rights of other folks—"

"But Uncle," she said, "that's a moral anarchy!"

"Lord!" he laughed. "My baby's eddikated, fer a fact!"

"Stop teasing me!" she pouted; then: "Isn't it?"

"Maybe yes, maybe no. Morality is a set of rules set up
by society to protect itself. If we go around making li'l
bastards all over the place, it costs society money to keep
'em in orphanages. If I've got to send my children to
school, feed, clothe, house them—not in the order
named—plain common sense, or—another fancy name for
human jealousy and selfishness—dictates that I make

damn sure that my woman didn't get at least some of 'em
with the fellow down the road—not to mention the sneaking suspicion I've got clawing at my guts that she just
might like *his* lovemakin' better—"

"Uncle Oliver, you're *awful!*" Billie Jo said.

"Ain't I, though?" he chuckled. "I sometimes think this
old world would be better off if marriage were declared a
mortal sin, outlawed, and everybody had to pay a headtax
for the state support of children he or she'd got with
whomever happened to strike his or her vagrant fancy at
the time. Folks would sure as hell be a lot happier!"

Billie smiled then, slowly.

"You—could be right, Uncle," she said. "But what
about that respect for the basic rights of others? Doesn't
that include the right to keep your own wife? Even if
you're—a thing—like Lennie Colfax, say?"

"Not if she wants to go. Because then you're reducing
marriage to involuntary servitude. And seems to me ol'
Abe Lincoln took care of that quite some time ago . . ."

She sat there staring at him. But now there was a new
thing in her eyes.

"So," she said, "you won't promise me to stay away
from Ruth Colfax while I'm in Europe on this trip you insisted that I take with Mr. and Mrs. Thornton and those
idiotic Thornton girls?"

"Billie," he said gently, "no offense meant, honey; but
I'm forty-eight years old—and I kind of reckon I can
manage my own affairs. In other words, baby, it ain't
rightly any of your business."

"Then," she said, "since I've reached and passed my
twenty-first birthday, Uncle Oliver—*last* year, remember?
—neither will I promise you to—to be good—while I'm
in Europe!"

He looked at her, and his eyes were sad.

"Never asked you to, Billie," he said.

Her brown eyes gave a startled leap in her freckled
face.

"Oh!" she said; then: "Oh, my God!"

"I do ask you one thing, though," he said solemnly.

"And that is?"

"Not to tell me anything I could do without knowing
when you come back. Better like that. Maintaining—one's

privacy is a mighty fine thing, Billie—"

They heard then the squawking of the bulb horn on the Thornton's victoria, as it wound up the road behind their dappled gray pair.

"Uncle—" she whispered.

"They tell you how long 'til sailing time once you get to New Orleans?" he said.

"Yes. Three or four days. Time for me to buy the rest of the things I need."

"Want me to take a breather and come see you off?"

She shook her head.

"No. Please don't, Uncle Oliver. I—I couldn't stand it. Seeing you there on the dock alone, I mean. I'd run down the gangplank at the last minute and—"

"Don't be a fool, child," he said.

She laughed then, a little shakily.

"I don't mean to be, Uncle Oliver. Not ever again," she said.


"Gawddamn it!" Estelle was screaming, "wasn't enough for you to make him cheat, was it? Hell, all pimps cheat! But you hafta keep him all for yourself, d'you? I don't give a shit if he jazzes you oncet in a while; but this business of not lettin' him see anybody else—not lettin' him take me out—"

Fanny didn't even turn her head from where she stood by the window, looking out into the driving rain.

'Make her shut up, God,' she half-prayed, half-swore, 'or else I'll kill her. Cut the poor bitch's throat to stop the noise. I've got a headache. I *need* some quiet. And it's the wrong time of the month. Jesus! Couldn't you have figured out a less messy way of doing things? So all right— so that's the way our female plumbing works—but the rest of it—why do I feel so goddamned *mean?* Every month this time I have to get a grip on myself or else I'll do something that I'd go to jail—or swing—for. Jesus— look at that rain! Bastardy rain. Bastardy world. Full of people more full of shit than a Christmas turkey. Like Beau Dan—the creature that this creature wants—I wonder—if he—isn't? Like that, I mean. At least a little? Took me to that house on Lafayette Street—corner of Baronne. Said I'd get a kick out of watching them. Miss

Big Nellie. Lady Richard. Lady Beulah Toto. Lady Fresh.
Chicago Belle.* Niggers and white men—all dressed up
like women. Dancing with each other. Kissing each other
on the mouth. Feeling each other up. Made me a little
sick at first—then it *bored* the piss out of me. But *he*
wasn't bored. Far from it! Maybe that's why he *never* really gets excited in bed. Not like a *man* gets excited. Like
Phil did. Only Phil had learned to control that excitement—but I could feel it. Throbbing. Threatening to burst
any second—until I caught it from him like a fever. A
goddamned big fine wonderful broiling hot fever. Down
there. Ha! In the swamp under the bushes—at first.
Then—Sweet love, my love—all over. Only I didn't have
to control it, 'cause he could always catch up with *me.* So
I could just turn loose go wild go crazy explode burst die
go to heaven singing hallelujah and come back alive again
—slow, slow—melted all gone loose peaceful happy . . .

'But Dan—all right. He's better than nothing. Nothing
being the clients of this august establishment. But it's not
the same. It—is—not—the same.'

"You bitch!" Estelle screamed. "One of these days I'm
going to—"

"Have a shit hemorrhage, faint, and fall in it," Fanny
said. "For God's sake, Estelle, can't you be quiet? I've got
a headache. And when I have a headache, I get to be un-
predictable. I just might *do* something to you—"

"Like what?" Estelle sneered. "You little half-assed yel-
low-haired li'l—"

But Fanny didn't hear her. She was peering out into the
driving rain. She saw that haunched, stocky, forlorn figure,
lurching through it, supporting himself upon a heavy
cane, swinging his bad leg in a convulsive, almost desperate effort to force movement from that part of him that
was already dead.

'Again!' Fanny thought bitterly. 'Why does he always
pass this way? It's *not* the way home. Is he hoping to see
Mama? Or—me—?

'No. That, no. Mama says he doesn't know I'm even
here. That the harness bull on this beat dropped around
to ask her to do all she could to keep him from finding

---

*The address and the names are both a matter of historical
record.

out. Said it might be too much for him—

'Shit! It wasn't too much for you, was it, Papa—dear,
darlin' Papa—to treat me like something the cat puked up
on the parlor rug? To *never* say a kind word to me? Oh,
no! It was always Billy this—and son that—although that
little rat-bastard was a born sneak and liar and thief
and—'

Then she felt Estelle's hand upon her shoulder.

She whirled. Faced Estelle. Stopped the tall girl's breath
with that look of hers. But worse now. Ice-cold premeditated murder distilled into rays of light.

"You *touched* me," she whispered. "You actually
*touched* me. I told you *never* to do that. I warned you
never to put your filthy, cunt-smelling, syphilitic hands on
me. So now I'm going to kill you. I'm awf'ly sorry, but no
goddamned miserable bitch-kitty of a whore can touch me
and go on livin'—"

Estelle backed away from her.

"Now, Fanny—" she got out, "I—"

Fanny flipped her skirttail up to her waist and reached.
She had a knife in her garter. A switchblade. Beau Dan
had bought it for her at her request after Hawkes had
beaten her bloody. Now, when she went upstairs with a
client, she slipped it deftly under her pillow. That way
there was no real danger of any unknown sadist's repeating Hawkes's offense, or even of some well-known
client's—too far gone in his cups usually—trying to force
her to perform fellatio on him, as occasionally, even yet,
despite, or maybe because of, her known refusal to indulge in oral sex, one of them occasionally did.

Her small, slim hand came out with the knife. She
touched the catch. The blade flipped up into position,
caught the light, glittered. It was then that Estelle started
to scream.

Outside on the banquette, Bill Turner heard her. He
stood there, shivering like a wet dog.

'That's—not fake,' he thought. 'Somebody's being hurt
in there. Hurt bad.'

He listened. The scream came again. Louder, now.
Shriller.

'Got to go in there,' he told himself. 'My duty. Can't
let—Mae cower me. Must prevent—a murder. Because
that's sure as hell somebody getting killed—'

He lurched forward to the stairs. Up them onto the stoop. Put out his hand and twisted the door knob. The door wasn't locked. He had known it wouldn't be. Storyville parlor houses never locked their doors. He limped forward toward where it seemed to him those screams were coming from. Entered the Rose Parlor. Saw one girl—the tall, skinny, dark-haired one—backing away from the other, the one whose back was turned towards the door, towards him. It was the tall whore who had screamed, was screaming still; but, he saw to his relief, she hadn't a scratch on her, at least so far. He saw the other one—tiny, dainty, silvery blonde; his trained investigator's mind registered the necessary, identifying details—closing in slowly, steadily, murder glinting bluely from her fist; and he, thinking, 'She's new; I don't know this one. A bad-acter, though, little as she is,' took a step forward and saw who the blonde whore was.

He opened his mouth. The name wouldn't come out of it. He choked on that name. He could hear it in his ears, amid the sudden roaring; but he couldn't say it. It turned bile in his throat; turned blood. It was strangling him and he couldn't force it out. But he must have, finally. He must have got it through his clenched and grinding teeth, through his locked, knotted, jerking jaws, through the froth of blood and foam on his already turned purple lips.

"Fanny—" Bill Turner must have said.

Or something sounding enough like it to make her turn, stop, hand there for that brief fracturing of the stuff of time—some milliseconds, we'd call it in our superior and scientific age—it took him to die. And even after that for some micro/milli/nanoseconds more, she didn't move. Very likely, she couldn't. Then her fingers opened. The knife clattered against the floor. She took a step forward towards that not yet inert, still feebly moving, jerking, twitching bulk on the floor. Said, tentatively:

"Papa—"

Then again:

"Papa—"

A whisper, faint, all gone, no sound, nothing:

"Papa—"

Her knees buckled under her. She slid down, sighed down, bonelessly crumpling until she was lying across him. Her hands came up, clawing at his head. It was a stone of flesh. It had the terrible inertia of inanimate things, death's own immovable weight. But she lifted it with desperate strength, saw his eyes wide open, sightlessly glaring at her, the accusation in them eternal now, and bent and kissed his half-opened mouth with wild, mad, senseless, utterly sensual passion, thrusting her tongue between his dead lips as if he were her lover.

As, to her, he was. As all unknowing to her conscious mind he had always been. The first male being to reject her, scorn her, awake in her that fury of which hell hath not the like.

The first to die for love of her, if we except old Jacob Fields; if we strike a senile craving for infant's flesh from the lists of things that men call love. For Hawkes didn't count. His motivations put him on a different list: those who let their hatred for Fanny Turner blind them, make them fatally underestimate her. And Rodney Schneider, at that moment, was still alive.

So let's leave Fanny for a little while, then, shall we? Leave her rocking back and forth, cradling her dead father's head in her arms, trying to break through the numbing, all but paralyzing shock that gripped her, enough to even cry.

Only one other death will grieve her more than this.

And—

Mourning does become Electra; doesn't it?


Billie Jo Prescott walked by the telephone on the reception desk in the Royal Hotel's lobby—it had occurred to no one at this time to put one in every room, any more than anyone ever dreamed that two or three bathrooms really weren't enough for all the rooms on a given floor—and stared at it longingly.

She'd been doing that for three days now. Tomorrow she was going to sail for Europe with the Thorntons and she still hadn't got up the nerve to do what she wanted to do, what in a very real sense she had to do.

'Suppose,' she thought with something akin to terror, 'he hangs up on me? He could. Maybe he even should. Brazen hussy calling a man's office to ask him for his son's address in Paris. So she can look him up when she gets there. He—he'll think she's—planning to—to do what

fast people are usually supposed to do in Paris. Have an
affair with his son. With Philippe—'

She stopped dead and the blood rushed to her cheeks so
hot and red that it drowned all her freckles.

'And—*aren't* you?' she asked herself pitilessly. She
stopped there and thought about that. One of the advantages—or disadvantages—of having been brought up by a
man with a mind as iconoclastic as her Uncle Oliver's was
that she was very often—though not always—capable of
seeing things from an independent, even unconventional
point of view.

'No.' she told herself now, 'quite honestly, no. I'm planning no such thing. I reckon that what I meant when I
told Uncle Oliver I wouldn't *promise* to be good is that
it—could happen. And it—could. Things could—get to be
too much for me. And—for him too. But I'll take my Bible oath right now, swear on poor Aunt Ellen's tombstone, that I'm going to be mighty, mighty careful.
Avoid—temptation. Try not—even indirectly—to lead
Philippe on—'

She hung there, her mind and her heart both wailing.

'How can I even *not* lead him on when I don't even
know where he *lives*—in a city as big as Paris?'

And then, almost as if in answer to her doleful cry, she
heard the newsboys shouting:

"Extra! Extra!! Famous Detective Drops Dead! William
P. Turner Dies of Shock! Finds His Daughter in a House
of Ill Fame!"

She stood there frowning. Then her brown eyes opened
very wide. 'Turner! That's her—name! Fanny Turner!
And Philippe told me that—her father was a detective!'

She whirled towards the bench near the front door
where the bellhops sat, waiting to be called to take a newcomer's bags or perform some service for a guest.

"Captain," she said, trying to keep the shake out of her
voice, "will you have a boy get me one of those extras,
please?"

"Yes, ma'am!" the bell captain said; then loudly:
"Front! Go git th' little lady a extra! Git a move on,
now!"

She didn't even go back upstairs. She sat there in the
lobby reading that story in the *New Orleans Picayune*.
When she had finished it, her face had changed. There

was a new thing in it, now: determination, maybe; resolve; a decision so firmly made that it lent her an aspect of serenity.

She approached the bell captain again:

"Captain," she said, "will you get me a cab, please?"

"She says—" Yves Martin, Monsieur Sompayac's secretary—female secretaries being all but nonexistent in Creole business offices so far, largely because Creole wives knew their husbands far too well, "that she's a friend of Philippe's—and that she *must* see you, Patron. Swears it's important—"

"Is she—well—upset—or—?" Jean-Paul Sompayac said.

"Neither. Neither hysterical nor—with child. In fact, she is entirely calm, Patron. And so far as Mister Your Son's amatory proclivities are concerned, considering how long he has been abroad, she ought to be as big as a house, or even have her little package of joy in her arms. And neither painful fact is the case. To me, Patron, she seems a young woman well reared, perhaps even—untouched, if you understand me—"

"In New Orleans?" Jean-Paul snorted. "Don't be an ass, Yves! A young person who has the audacity to come to my office and—"

He stopped, peered at his secretary, said:

"Très calme, hein?"

"Même tranquille," Yves said.

"Very well, Yves," Jean-Paul Sompayac said, "show her in."

His first reaction, when Billie Jo came quietly into his office, was: 'My son has taste. This one is *very* fine. Not pretty—but interesting. Which often enough is the better choice.' He said:

"Good afternoon, young lady. Have the goodness to take a chair."

"Thank you, Monsieur Sompayac," Billie Jo said, and sat down.

Jean-Paul peered at her a long moment. He liked what he saw: 'Good bones, excellent—bearing, posture. Signs of good breeding; Yves may be right. Même—vierge peut-être. Au moins, elle n'est surment pas une fille perdue—' He said:

"May I ask to what—circumstances—I owe the honor of this visit?"

"That's—difficult to explain, sir," she said quietly. "'First permit me to introduce myself. My name is Prescott. Billie Jo Prescott—"

She waited, apparently expecting the name to mean something to him. It didn't. The sole occasion he had heard it had been too long ago—and much water had passed under the bridge since then. She said, a little uncertainly:

"I—I guess—Philippe must—never have told you—about me—"

He frowned, thinking back. He had an excellent memory; but this name eluded it.

"He may have, Miss—Prescott, isn't it? But I am an old man, and very occupied—very busy. If you would be so kind as to mention the circumstances, tell me something of your relationship with my son, perhaps, then—"

"I met him," Billie Jo said, "in the hospital. I went there to visit my Aunt Ellen—who'd had a stroke. And his—his girl—his fiancée Miss—Turner—was there. It seems that she—that she—but surely you know that, sir!"

"Yes. Unfortunately, yes. Ma foi! Now I remember! He told me he was in love with a little American girl—from Cainville-Sainte Marie or Mertontown—"

"From neither place, sir. From a plantation near both of them. He—he told you that, sir? That he was—in love with me, I mean?"

"Yes. To the extent that he asked me to get the Turner girl to release him, and—"

"But she—wouldn't," Billie said.

"To tell the truth, Miss Prescott, I never asked her to. I saw her lying in bed, so small so frail—her wound was—very grave, you understand—and I let myself be overcome by pity. I have often regretted it. I'm not sure that the little Miss Turner is really suited to be—my son's wife—"

"She's not," Billie Jo said flatly, "but I don't think you need worry about that anymore, sir."

"And—you'll forgive an old man's curiosity, Miss Prescott—what are *your* feelings towards my son?"

Billie Jo bent her head. Then she faced him, almost proudly.

"I love him, sir," she said. "If—he'll have me, I'll

marry him, now that he's free. I—hope—you won't object. Philippe made it very clear—that aristocratic Creole fathers don't approve of little American nobodies—"

"And if I *did* object?" Jean-Paul said gravely; but there was an amused crinkle about the corner of his eyes.

"I'd still marry him. I'd feel sorry—that you didn't—don't approve. I'd rather have—your friendship. And—his mother's. But I wouldn't give him up. I—can't sir. I love him—too much."

"Good!" Jean-Paul laughed. "But I don't object—daughter. Philippe told me you were a very well-reared, and—a—well—decent—girl. These are not the dark ages. Naturally his mother and I would have preferred his marrying a girl of our people, but—"

She smiled then, for the first time; but her eyes were misty.

"I—I thank you, sir," she murmured. "I—I'll make it up to you. I've already started learning French. Of course I haven't got very far, but—"

"I say!" Jean-Paul Sompayac said, "why don't you—and your chaperone, of course—come to dine with me and Madame Sompayac tonight? I'd like her to meet you very much and—"

Billie Jo shook her head.

"I—I haven't that right, sir," she said. "At least not yet. If I were Philippe's fiancée, I'd accept with pleasure. But I'm not. So far, he's still engaged to—Miss Turner. That he *can't* marry her, that such a marriage is impossible—no; it's *unthinkable*, now, sir—he doesn't know yet. That's the reason I came. I'm going abroad, with some friends of my uncle's. Mr. and Mrs. Albert Thornton, and their daughters Charity and Hope—on a grand tour—sort of—"

"And one of the places you're going to visit is Paris, hein?" Monsieur Sompayac said.

"Yes. I—I found out he was there only last month—Madame Pluchêt told me. It seems your wife and daughters have their clothes made in her shop, too. I saw two of your girls there—they were chattering away in French with Madame Pluchêt, so I didn't understand what they said; but one of them—Brigitte, I think her name is—looked *so* much like Philippe that I couldn't resist temptation and asked Madame Pluchêt what her name was. And when she said Sompayac—I—well, you *know* how women are, sir—"

"Don't I, though!" Jean-Paul groaned. "I've a house full of them!"

"I sort of led her on—got her to talk about your family. Though *rave* would be more like it. As far as she's concerned, there's no better in New Orleans. She swears you're related to—to the Bourbons. To the royal house of France—"

"She may be right," Jean-Paul said with wry amusement. "Nearly every very old Creole family in New Orleans seems—or *claims*—to be. And all for the same reason: that some certain ancestress of theirs in the reign of Louis XIV, the Sun King, was *very* naughty, indeed! Frankly, I doubt all such claims. They are so numerous as to be—well—beyond even kingly powers, shall we say?"

"I see," Billie Jo said. "But all kinds of things happened back then, didn't they? Anyhow, sir—what I came for was to ask you for—Philippe's address. I—I know that sounds awfully forward. It *is*, isn't it? Only—sir—it's my life— I'm fighting for. If I can't have Philippe—be his wife—I'll be nobody's. I haven't *looked* at another boy since I met him. They—they don't *exist*."

"That daughter, is an exceedingly foolish point of view. No man is worth that much, and especially not my Philippe! But I have no objection at all to your having his address. It's Numero Onze Rue de Saints Pères, Number Eleven Street of the Sainted Fathers. That's in the Latin Quarter, you know. But you'd better learn it in French or you'll *never* get there—"

"I thank you, sir. Would you—write it down in French for me?"

"But of course!" Jean-Paul said, and did so.

He passed the sheet of paper over to her. She took it, said: "Thank you, Monsieur Sompayac. You've been very kind." And stood up.

"One moment, Miss Prescott!" he said. "Don't you think you ought explain to me *why* you think it is—or has become—impossible for my son to marry the little Miss Turner?"

She stared at him.

"Haven't you seen—the *Picayune*, Sir? The extra that came out not a whole hour ago?" she said.

"No," Jean-Paul said, "I seldom read the English-language papers. There is—well—a certain vulgarity about them that I find distasteful. And the *Picayune* has a notorious weakness for issuing extras with very slight justification. I did hear the newsboys shouting; but since they always shout, I—Very well, tell me, ma fille, what was in the *Picayune* that has anything to do with Mademoiselle Turner? With Philippe's marrying her, I mean?"

"This—" Billie Jo said; and handed him the extra.

He took it, read the headlines; then the story beneath them. When he looked up, his eyes were troubled, even—sad, Billie Jo thought.

"I see," he said slowly. "A pity, a very great pity. He was a fine man, Monsieur Turner. We were never friends, but I respected him. He was worthy of any man's respect—and his admiration too, for that matter." He paused; looked at her, at this small, thin, freckled-faced girl with her big wide mouth and turned-up nose and penny-brown eyes who could be now salvation of a sort for his son, for Philippe. He said:

"You're right, of course; this marriage has become impossible. But then I suppose, it always was. Do you mean to—to tell Philippe this, show him this paper?"

"Yes," Billie Jo Prescott said.

"Take my advice, daughter; don't. Let me write him, first—send him a copy. *Before* you reach Paris. Human nature is strange, my child. Men always harbor a certain resentment against the bearer of ill tidings. He will be—crushed by this, I assure you. Then, when he is at his spirits' lowest point—at the nadir, even, of his despair, *you* will appear to—"

"Catch him on the rebound?" Billie Jo said bitterly.

"Mais non! To lift his spirits high again. To convince him that there is goodness, sweetness, decency in this world. If that circumstance helps your cause, my child, to me it seems no more than fair—"

"I—I thank you, sir," Billie Jo said. "Well—good-bye, sir—"

"Not good-bye, daughter. It's au revoir—isn't it? At least I hope so," Jean-Paul Sompayac said.

Fanny went running through that street. She had thought it was Burgundy Street at first; but now she was sure it was Hellfire Avenue, Brimstone Boulevard, Inferno Road. Drunks swayed toward her, too far gone to be dangerous, really. Inside the opened doors of the cribs, the crib girls sat, stark naked, peering out at the passers-by— with dull, blank, mindless eyes. Some of them openly sniffed cocaine, lifting the white powder to their nostrils with a teaspoon. Others were smoking opium or hashish. Still others had the insides of their arms covered with scars where they'd injected heroin into their veins, usually with the point of a safety-pin—hypodermics cost too much. And the rest were drunk.

Fanny didn't think about that. All the parlor house girls knew what being a crib girl meant. The last stop before the river, or the morgue. There were all colors of them from jet black to snow white, because the City Fathers didn't enforce segregation in Burgundy Street except to forbid black and white whores to live in the same house, a rule that couldn't be enforced anyhow, since the Orleanais legally maintained the ridiculous contention that anybody with one drop of Negro blood in her veins was black, which often meant that a pure Scandanavian type was held to be a Negress while a swarthy, coppery-complexioned Italian or Spanish girl ten shades darker than she was officially white. So the police had given up trying to decide who was mulatto, quadroon, octoroon, or white and let Burgundy Street the hell alone.

It would have been more to the point for them to have decided who had syphilis and/or gonorrhea, since on Burgundy Street there was neither the weekly inspection and prompt treatment that the parlor houses insisted upon for pure business reasons, and the answer would have been easy: close to one hundred percent of the crib girls were—often visibly and hideously—diseased. A goodly number of them were insane, or on the road to becoming so. And since, at twenty-five cents to half a dollar a tumble, they were hard put to even buy the narcotics that dulled the pain of their abysmal existence, not to mention the food they largely went without, soap was a luxury they couldn't afford. The stench that boiled out from those opened doors would have made a billy goat heave.

'Or a buzzard,' Fanny thought. 'This is where you'll end up,' she told herself: 'This is just about your style, you miserable murdering little bitch! You should have gone with Hawkes. Let him beat you bloody every night the way he swore he was going to. He'd have killed you finally, but what's the odds? Only you let Joe scare him off, drive him away—so now you've got to find this other one, find that dirty old man who—who'll do the job. Or else you *will* end up here. You will!'

But she wouldn't end up on Burgundy Street. She knew that very well. Parlor house girls very seldom did. The reason they didn't was simple: during its long existence Storyville averaged from seven to ten successful suicides a month. Nobody ever even tried to count the unsuccessful attempts. In point of fact most of the attempts were only temporarily so, for when a girl became so despondent that she wanted to kill herself, she'd try it again and again until finally the vernols worked, or the small twenty-two caliber ladies' pistols most of them used didn't hang fire, or the old-fashioned straight razor she'd stolen from her pimp bit deep enough into her throat. Because the infant (and dubiously scientific) science of psychoanalysis hadn't got around to considering the poor, tormented creatures called—with totally unconscious irony—filles de joie. Nobody realized that for a woman to become a whore she had to be quite desperately sick in the first place—though not quite as emotionally disturbed as her pimp, and only a trifle more so, perhaps, than her clients.

As sick as Fanny Turner was that night. As sick as the pale blonde girl, her long hair streaming out behind her as she ran through Burgundy Street in search of—

Well, call it surcease, penance, expiation, say. Because suicide—death by her own slim hand—had become too simple, was no longer commensurate with what was in her now. Too simple. Not enough to pay for—the murder of her father.

She had to stop suddenly, her way blocked by a little knot of people. Crib girls mostly, wrapped in ragged, indescribably filthy bathrobes, a few drunks, some male whores who had drifted down from the "meat rack," the corner of Burgundy and St. Louis where they hung out, thrusting their pelvises forward to show their wares through their skin-tight pants, hoping to attract some rich degenerate—as homosexuals were universally called in that illiberal epoch, their condition not yet having been reduced from a psychosis, to a neurosis, and finally to a mere "variant life-style" as in our oh-so-enlightened day—

She started edging around the group. Then she saw what had engaged their attention: A woman lay on a piece of carpeting on the sidewalk, with her skirt rolled up around her waist. A man was on top of her, in her. They performed busily while the crib girls and the drunks and the rough-trade punks egged them on.

"Got it, fifteen-cents gal! Do it to him good! Or else he ax you a dime change!"

She had heard about that but she hadn't believed it: That there was in New Orleans a category of whores lower than the crib girls: the roofless, homeless sidewalk girls who sold themselves for fifteen cents, a dime, a nickel, a poorboy sandwich—and on the banquette itself, in full sight of all the world.

But there were. In those good old days, there were.

She moved on. On the edge of the crowd she saw a crib girl staring at her. This one didn't appear to be drugged, or even too drunk to understand. Fanny stepped up to her, holding hard against the nausea the crib girl's bitch-stink awoke in her, leaned forward, and whispered that name.

"Up there," the crib girl said. "Four houses farther on—other side o' th' street. He won't, though. You's too white."

"Thank you," Fanny said.


William Pelham Turner's funeral was a splendid affair. The whole New Orleans Police Department turned out for it. The Mayor, the City Council, the Aldermen, the Board of Trade. Almost every crook in town, and few came to rejoice—they, his worst adversaries, had respect-ed him. The Mafia sent a tremendous wreath of blood-red roses. It was labeled "The Italian-American Protec-tive Association." Joe Sarcone came in person to pay his honestly felt respects. Long ago he'd learned that Bill Turner could be neither bribed nor intimidated, which left him with the sole alternative of ordering him mur-dered: but by that time, Sarcone, a complex, subtle, and intelligent man, had conceived so deep an admiration for Bill's sheer guts that he'd had the word passed around that anyone who harmed a hair of his red head would have to answer to him, the boss. Which was why, maybe,

Bill lived so long. A pity. To have been gunned down, like Chief Hennessy, by the Mafia would have been a better death. It would, at least, have had a certain style.

There were countless people he had befriended, people of every race, creed, and color. More than one of them could say things like:

"Didn't even turn me in. Took off his belt and whupped my black ass proper. Then took me home 'n stood by while Pa did hit all over agin. I niver stole another red copper after that, I tell you—"

Or:

"Caught me sneaking into Tilly Hendrick's place with Jim. Says to me: 'Aren't you Molly Hughes—Brad Hughes's daughter?' And when I mumbled 'Yes,' he says: 'C'mon, daughter, I'm taking you home.' And when Jim cursed at him, he took off his coat and his gun, laid 'em on the banquette and beat Jim to a pulp with his fists. Then he took me home—and spent a whole hour pleading with Pa *not* to throw me out, to give me another chance. Even to go easy on me with that razor strop of his. Ha! I was eating off the mantelpiece for a month! But I—stayed decent—married a good man and—look. *His* daughter didn't. I wonder why? Likely being a detective he never was at home enough to watch her proper—"

The Reverend Mr. Watkins, the Methodist minister, preached a moving sermon, leaving not a dry eye in the church. At Metairie Cemetery, some of the police had to hold back the crowd of the curious.

But, standing there, listening to the scrape of the brick-layers' trowels as they sealed the coffin in the plain over-shaped tomb,* with Billy sniffling on one side of her and Eliza wailing aloud on the other, Martha saw, with immense relief, that Fanny wasn't present. 'Better like that,' she thought, with a sadness too deep to leave room for anger. 'Half of these people came in the hope that she'd appear—break down, faint, make some sort of terrible scene. They don't know her. And now I wonder if *I* do— if I ever did—

'What *will* she do now? They said—they had to tear

---

*In New Orleans, until quite recent times, burial in the earth was forbidden by law, largely for quite mistaken and unscientific health reasons.

poor Bill's body from her arms by main force. That she was—crazy. Literally insane with grief. Some of them even told—Maebelle—told her mother—to lock her up. "Or else you'll find her—floating, four or five days from now—" That—was what they said.'

Martha stood, her face hidden by her widow's veil, lost in a very private world.

'And—they will, too. Only—'

She shivered suddenly; went on with her thought:

'Is it wrong, God, to let the hopelessly disfigured, maimed, crippled—the souls damaged beyond repair—die? Isn't it even a kindness, maybe—a mercy? "Thou shalt not kill!" Not even—oneself, dear Lord? Not even when—cancer is devouring one's bowels and the pain—is far too great? Not even a down and thrashing horse with his shinbone punching through his flesh? Not even a dog a brewery wagon's run over, smashing his spine above his hips and leaving him to drag himself toward the banquette, howling? Not—even—a girl—poor, lost damned—who without really meaning to, has—murdered—her father? Not even—a child—a forlorn child who has been reduced to—to the unspeakable obscenity of—selling—her delicate body—nightly—to the goats and monkeys of this world?

'I ask you, Lord. Because if—there're no exceptions, I stand here at my husband's grave—a sinner. I—wouldn't try to save her. I'd grant her—the mercy—of letting her die. For no one, not even you, almighty God, could make me condemn her to—this life, this life!'

Then it was over, the long ordeal of the funeral, the visits from all those come of offer her their condolences, what help they had to give, the telephone calls. Martha sat there in the silent house alone. Billy was asleep. Eliza was also. The furniture was shrouded with clothes, waiting for the movers who'd come tomorrow to take it to a warehouse until she could decide what to do with it. The train tickets—hers and Billy's only, for Eliza would remain in New Orleans with relatives, enjoying a generous pension for life from Martha—were bought. She was going to take her son, her only souvenir of years of trouble, sorrow, and great happiness, back to New York, leaving those years (of trouble, of sorrow, of happiness) behind her forever, fleeing her private ghosts—of memory, of pain.

But there was one thing she had to do first: To say good-bye to Bill. To say it alone, not as a part of the Roman circus his funeral had been. So, before going to bed, she telephoned the cab company and asked them to have a cab at her door at eight o'clock in the morning. She'd have time: she and Billy were taking the night train to New York, with a drawing room, complete with berths already engaged. With the help of vernols she'd sleep at least one-third of the long journey north.

It was still misty that next morning when she got to the cemetery. Under the trees it was very quiet. Birds twittered and sang above her head. She felt—a kind of peace invade her. Bill was dead—and at rest. Nothing would trouble him again. What even Fanny did from now on, he wouldn't even know. It came to her then that this idea was a rejection of the basic tenets of the Episcopal faith she had been brought up in. But that didn't trouble her too much. She realized it had been a long time since she'd really believed the teachings of her church, or of any church, for that matter. She prayed, she believed in God; but she had reservations about the nature of the Deity. She wondered if the pronoun He was really applicable; and if He (It/The Force Behind the Universe/The Ice Cold Mindless Indifference Controlling the World) was even aware of one tiny, burned-out cinder-speck of a planet, far out on the edge of the universe; and still less of the featherless naked bipeds which swarmed over it in their hideously insane fashion, attributing to themselves the lordly name of homo sapiens, and declaring themselves worthy of the attentions of a god.

She wondered if immortality would even be endurable, even granting the existence of that semantically irrelevant entity men called the soul. If death, being, as she knew it to be, annihilation, a sleep, and a forgetting, were not, after all, a kindness—since life always, late or soon, got to be more than people can bear.

She was thinking all that when she reached his tomb. But then she stopped thinking altogether, for she saw Fanny lying before it, face down on the ground.

She took a step towards her, towards that tiny, crumpled, inert form. Another. Bent to touch her, to see if—

Stopped. Hung there till the trees, the tomb itself, the harsh cacaphonic shrilling of hideously mocking birds, stopped still again, ceased to revolve with maddening, torturous slowness about her defenseless head.

She lifted her veil threw it back. Stood there. 'Oh God,' her mind wailed, her heart, even her pity-wracked and tortured flesh, 'Oh God Oh God Oh God Oh God.'

Fanny was dressed in white. In a long white lace-trimmed stylish whore's parlor dress. Only it wasn't white anymore. From shoulder to knees it was red. And in ribbons. It and the tender flesh beneath it.

'Who?' she asked herself: 'Who—did—*this?* Beat her—to death? Brought her here—'

Then, raising her eyes, she saw the handprints and kneeprints in the soft earth where she, Fanny, unable to walk, stagger, totter, anymore had dragged herself to the tomb. Trailing her dress through the mud, leaving a smear of half-dried—

'Oh God!' Martha thought again; 'God God God!'

And bent to her, saw that, pitifully, tragically, she lived still, but having no time to think about that, about what it meant, her whole mind filled to bursting, to the point of explosion, with the realization, the recognition, the acknowledgment:

'She—did it herself. Hired it done. Paid that filthy old madman to do it. Because—a knife wouldn't do. Pills. Poison. The river. Not even a gun. Dying wasn't enough. It had to hurt. It had to be—a horror. It had to equal—what she'd done—to Bill. Oh God, Oh Jesus, I—'

She whirled, already running, towards the gate. Her cab waited for her there. She leaped into it, said:

"The nearest hospital. One that has ambulance service. And fast. Fast as you can. Please."

She was in time. "Prompt medical attention," the *Picayune* put it, "saved the distraught girl." Afterwards, looking back, Martha realized that she had failed to carry through her carefully thought-out intent; that she had been guilty of an abysmal cruelty, only slightly mitigated by the fact that its motivations had been instinctive, well-meaning, kindly.

She had condemned Fanny Turner. To life. And to memory.

A whore's life. A patricide's memory.

Than which conditions there might, conceivably, be something worse. But, offhand, she couldn't think of what it was.

## Chapter Twenty-Eight

It was still raining. Oliver Prescott peered through the windows of his bedroom out into a dismal landscape: The rain, like a gray curtain shutting out the light; the puddles in the road, black-silver, reflecting a somber sky; and, in the road, in the fields, under the trees, everywhere the mud, dark, amorphous, all-encompassing, Louisiana bayou mud, absolutely the muddiest mud in the whole bleak, fouled-up world.

He stared at that mud, remembering how it had sounded, splashing against *her* coffin lid; the obscene sucking sound it had made as they lowered the simple, oblong black box into it, while he and all the other mourners had stood there like bifurcating—and surely poisonous, his mind added bitterly—mushrooms under the umbrellas, while the rain came whipping down.

'What,' he thought, for at least the ten-thousandth time in the year and three months that had gone by since that rarely awful day, 'am I going to do now? What—on earth—am I going to do—*now?*'

He turned away from the window, and stared at his face in the mirror. Swore at his own reflected image with quiet violence:

'You horny old bastard! Wasn't for you, she'd be still alive! Fifty years old, and you *still* can't leave women alone. Couldn't leave—Ruth alone. And all the time you thought you were playing it smart. No—young fillies for you. Pick out a woman near your own age. Ruth was—forty-one when she died. Only eight years difference between us. Fine woman. Good-looking. More than good-looking—after I taught her what it was to *be* a woman, a real honest-to-God *she*-woman, after all those years of being married to that neuter-gendered nothing—she started in to being plumb downright—beautiful. She—glowed. What I put into her made her glow. Carnal knowledge—

hell, yes! But used like Pygmalion used his carving tools—to create a woman. To free my Galatea from that—rock of pure damn misery that held her—dead, already dead in life, Jesus!'

He went on, staring at his image.

'Thought we'd die together. Never figured—on this. On being alone in my old age. On being this goddamned lonely. Was a hell of a lot more likely that Lennie would get one of us—or both. 'Cause he was trying. Like a rabid fox, never showing his hand. Gave her that skittish gelding that any damn noise, even a dead leaf blowing down an empty road, would spook. Changed the landmarks at Deadman's Jump. Gave that feeble-minded nigger a new shotgun and told him to shoot a mess of birds for supper next to the path we took . . .'

He remembered all that. All Leonard Colfax's attempts at murder. So carefully planned, all of them. A new riding horse as a present on his wife's birthday, a hammerheaded beast that would have killed any horse-woman in the parish—except Ruth, whose very voice seemed to soothe the beast's uncertain temper. Then going out at night and digging up the crooked pine tree—which, miraculously having, some years before, survived being seared by a lightning bolt into a shape any Japanese arboriculturist would have envied, had served Ruth as her landmark for the easy jump over Merry Creek, no more than a couple of yards wide at that point, that she had to take on her way home from her rendezvous with her bald, middle-aged, but absolutely tireless lover—and moving it, replanting it in another spot only a few yards downstream so that it pointed to Deadman's Jump, the name itself indicating what it was: a place where the creek suddenly dropped down over a little waterfall to leave a bank twenty-five full yards high on the near side, murderously screened by a thick growth of underbush so that you couldn't even see it until you were over it and falling; and on the far side marshlands, bayou swamp, stretching out to hell and begone, out to death and forever.

Afterwards, Ruth could never explain what had made her stop, pull that hammerhead, hardmouthed gelding up.

"Seems to me I heard something, the sound of the falls, maybe. Or maybe it was him—hidden in the bushes—waiting to see me die. To see the adulteress punished for her sins—since he knew that nobody in this world cared enough about him to pick up a pebble to toss in my direction, let alone take part in a biblical stoning party. So I pulled up and was left alive to—"

"To go and sin no more?" Oliver had asked her gravely.

"Sin?" she'd answered him, her voice slow and clear, with deliberation in it, reason; but something else, too, surety, conviction. "Staying with *him* is the sin, Oliver—not this. Being alive—for the first time in thirty-five years is no sin. Being the woman the good Lord intended me to be. And—if I hadn't heard—whatever it was I heard—if I'd taken that jump and broken my neck as he fully intended for me to do, I'd have died happy, Oliver—died a real woman, a complete one—fulfilled—and—and grateful, sort of, to maybe even the Lord, and certainly to you—for having made me one, granted me my birthright, you could call it—any woman's for that matter; though mighty few of us ever 'get to know what—and how—it is—"

"And what and how is it?" he said, only half-teasing her, wanting to know.

She'd smiled at him, then, whispered:

"A dissatisfied body—*can't* house a contented soul, Oliver. You've taught me that. And the reverse of the same coin, which is more important. You only find contented souls in bodies that feel like mine does now: warm, glowing. At peace with itself—and with the world. And discontented souls—shrivel up, dry up, start to die, even before the body does. I know. There's nothing worse than a dead soul . . . Mine was—'til you sort of resurrected it, brought it back to life . . ."

Lennie had waited a full six months before trying again. Before giving a feeble-minded Negro fieldhand on his place a brand-new shotgun and telling him to go shoot birds in the middle of the night next to that road. And again luck, chance, fate, had intervened. Oliver had ridden back with her farther than usual. Out of a feeling of—unease, of disquietude, a premonition, really. Because she had never allowed him to ride home with her, for fear that what every living soul in the parish already suspected be confirmed beyond hope of denial by some chance eyewitness: that she, Ruth Colfax, was Oliver Prescott's mistress; and that she had been ever since last year, 1895, the

whole thing having started three months to a day after he
had brought his paralyzed wife home from New Orleans.

And the feebled-minded black had fired off both bar-
rels of his new sixteen-gauge at a flock of birds existing
surely only inside his addled head. But Oliver was with
her. Oliver Prescott, who even at forty-six, his age at the
time, could still outride any man in the parish. He'd
caught up with that spooked, wildly plunging gelding of
hers in less than twenty yards, swept her from her little
English sidesaddle with one arm, pulled his own mount
up, and watched the gelding plunge on until he reached
the creek. Without Ruth to guide him he didn't jump in
time; landed awkwardly; came down, and broke his leg.
So Oliver had shot him. And brought Ruth to within a
quarter of a mile of her own door. Closer than that, she
wouldn't consent to—largely because in those days poor
Ellen was still alive.

'And because of—Billie Jo,' he thought. For, finally,
Ruth had got over feeling guilty as far as Ellen was concerned. She had early discovered that Oliver Prescott
didn't lie, not even to defend himself. And in one certain
way, in the way that in the late 1890s *nobody* talked
about, his marriage to Ellen Tyler had been pure hell.
"An Eskimo's hell," he had put it. For Ellen Tyler was
the type of the Victorian "good" woman; which meant she
was frozen to the marrow of her very bones.

"While I," he told Ruth sadly, "am purely one horny
poor old sinner! Always have been—always will be.
And—for the last six—no, nearer to eight—years, she's
asked me kindly to—to leave her alone. Suggested that I
go down to New Orleans once in a while—to let off
steam—"

"And have you?" Ruth had said.

He'd grinned at her, crookedly.

"Left Ellen alone—or gone down the row on Customhouse Street?" he said.

"Both," she said, and sat there, waiting.

"Left Ellen alone, yes," he said. "Gone whorehoppin',
no. Ain't made that way, Ruth. Never was a fancier of
used and raddled she-meat—"

She stared at him, said:

"How you must have suffered!"

"And you—didn't, before?" he said.

What she said was evidence of one of the basic differences between men and women.

"No," she said, "now—knowing it anyhow. When you—despise a man—*this*—is sickening, Oliver. And since I was being a good and faithful wife I didn't know that it—quit being sickening mighty fast when you love the man in question. That it gets to be a joy. No—a glory."

"Then you still won't—even ask him for a divorce?" he had said. "After Ellen's gone, I mean. Doc Volker gives her only a year or two—at best . . ."

She shook her head.

"No," she whispered. "I—couldn't face your niece, Oliver. She's—so straight, your Billie Jo. So—appallingly—decent! I started to say innocent; but it's not innocence, really. Of course she *is* innocent; but—"

"But not ignorant. Besides which, she's got blood in her veins. Took after *my* side of the family."

"And she *knows*. I met her downtown the other day. She looked at me—and made me cringe, Oliver. I felt—dirty. She turned those big brown eyes of hers on me and studied me with great care—looking at me with the same expression on her face that most women get when they look into the snakepit at the zoo—and—"

"Hell, Ruth, baby—she *likes* you. And you're wrong; she doesn't know one damn thing! I've kept her in the dark about us, and—"

"Don't be too sure about that, Oliver," Ruth had said.

'Good thing Billie ain't the prying type,' he thought, ' 'cause if anybody—anybody at all—had mentioned Ruth's condition—to her, she'd have *known* why I was packing her off to Europe. Only luck I had: that she was willing to go. Hell, she wanted to! And now I know why. But it worked out all right for both of us. She wasn't here when it happened, which suited *me* just fine. And she got her heart's desire. Which maybe suited *her*. Lord, I miss her! Still, abroad, two whole damn years, with that husband of hers. Costing me—and *his* pa—a pretty penny to keep them there. No matter. She seems to be happy enough. At least I hope she is. Be no justice in the world if she isn't, after waiting and suffering so long. Wonder when they'll be coming back? Last time Billie wrote me—nigh onto four months ago—she said they'd be packing the minute he passed the French medical board. Didn't even seem worried that he even might not pass, seeing as how he's got so far ahead in his studies that the Frenchies are letting him take it *this* year, 1902, instead of next, like he was supposed to—'

He turned away from that window, opened the bureau drawer and got the newspaper clipping out. It was yellowing a little. After all, it was two years old. He smiled sadly, looking at it. There were several things about it that amused him. The first of these things was that it had appeared *only* in *L'Abeille*,* the French-language newspaper, and not in the *Picayune*. That showed with brutal clarity what the Sompayacs actually thought about the people they persisted in calling "les Americans," just as though they themselves had not been Americans for three full generations now. It proved that they cared so little about Protestant and Anglo-Saxon opinion that they hadn't even bothered to announce the wedding to those— barbarians and semi-savages—who knew no French. The rest of his amusement came from the contents of the clipping itself. It was much too explanatory, verging upon being a virtual apology to the aristocratic Creole families for Philippe's having married "une petite Americaine" instead of one of *their* daughters as he should have, and gave reasons that they would well understand, in these difficult times, for his having done so.

The clipping read:

PHILIPPE SOMPAYAC S'EST MARIE A PARIS.
ETUDIANT DE MEDICINE EN FRANCE, FILS DE M JEAN-PAUL
SOMPAYAC, PROMINENT HOMME DES AFFAIRES NOUVELLE
ORLEANAIS,
PHILIPPE SOMPAYAC EPOUSE JEUNE AMERICAINE A PARIS.

M et Mme Jean-Paul Sompayac annoncent le mariage de son fils, Philippe, à Mlle Wilhelmina Josephine Prescott, Louisiane, elle aussi, provenate de la Paroisse de St. Josèphe. Le mariage, solennisé par l'Eveque de la Ville Lumière, Monseigneur François

---

*It wasn't until 1925 that the editors of *L'Abeille* were forced to admit that there weren't enough people who could read French left in New Orleans to support a French newspaper and suspended publication.

Plaque, a eu lieu à l'église de St. Germain des Pres,
le cinquième du mois passé.

Quoique la nouvelle épousée est orpheline, néanmoins
sa situation dans la vie est aisée. Adoptée par son
oncle, M Oliver Prescott, riche planteur de la banlieue
de Caneville—Ste. Marie, à un âge très court, depuis
la mort tragique de ses parents, son charme de petite
enfant a bientôt été cause de qu'il l'a fait sa seule
héritière. M Prescott, lui, est veuf, et sans enfants.

De la famille du jeune mari, c'est tout à fait inutile
écrire, parce que tout Nouvelle Orleans sait d'abord
qu'elle est une des plus vieilles et distinguées de la
Louisiane et même de la France . . .

He smiled again. 'They really laid it on the line, didn't
they? Wedding solemnized by no less than the Bishop—
and even if my poor baby is both American and an orphan she's an heiress—'cause *I'm* a rich planter who's a
widower and hasn't any brats, so—'
He stopped, stared at that phrase.
"M Prescott, lui, est veuf et sans enfants."
Said: "Oh God."
He could hear Hans Volker's voice speaking even now.
"I came to you, Oliver, because it's yours. It has to be.
You're not going to stand there with your bare face hanging out and try to convince me that Lennie Colfax is capable of fathering a child. Apart from the fact that I have
technical and medical reasons for knowing he's as sterile
as a mule, all you've got to do is to look at him. Now
wait! Don't get up on your high horse, damn you! I'm neither your father confessor nor a self-appointed censor of
public morals. You don't have to admit anything—not
even to me, though I thought we were better friends than
this. All you've got to do is talk to Ruth. Make her see
that she's got to let me abort that foetus. Or else she'll die.
She's too damned small, her pelvis is too narrow, and goddamn it all to bitter hell and back again, Oliver, she's
forty years old!"
"Forty-one," Oliver had said.
"You're conceding me my point. And don't even start
in to tell me the names of all the women in this parish

who've had brats clear up 'til age forty-nine. Their last child—their eighth or ninth or tenth—or in the case of the Cajuns and the Negroes their twentieth, sometimes—not their *first*, Oliver. I'd stake my medical reputation on the opinion that no woman over forty years of age can give birth for the first time in her life and survive the ordeal—even when she's big and husky instead of being a tiny, delicate creature like Ruth. Only—"

"Only what?" Oliver had prompted.

"Only she's in love with her unborn child's father—though she stubbornly won't pronounce his name—Love being, by any rational man's definition, a state of temporary insanity most people get entirely over by the time they're thirty. So she is calmly, even cheerfully, prepared to die to bring a duplicate of such peerless worth, such sterling quality into this miserable fornicated world. And on one issue she stops me cold—"

"Which is?" Oliver Prescott said.

"I cannot swear the child would die. Quite the contrary. If I performed a caesarian in time—deliberately murdering that poor, dear, loving, idiotic woman in the process—the little bastard has almost an eighty percent chance of survival. The real point is that unless I abort her now, Ruth has none. Jesus, Oliver! If I drop the case she'll get one of the local Catholic quacks whose rules say that the woman *must* be killed to save the child. But I—can't stand this! I don't have a dark-ages mentality—"

"I see," Oliver whispered. "I'll talk to her, Doctor Hans—"

And he had—repeatedly. Stormed at her. Swore at her. Wept. While she sat there, her arms folded around her swollen belly, and smiling her slow and secret smile.

In the end, not even the child had lived. It had been a tiny, beautifully formed boy. They'd buried it in the same coffin with her. She'd lived long enough to request that.

'What,' Oliver Prescott thought again, 'am I going to do now? What—on earth—am I going to do—now? Besides leaving women to hell alone, I mean—'

He smiled at himself with sad self-knowledge, knowing that he wouldn't do that, because he couldn't. He was, of course, nobody's satyr; but then neither was he a monk. 'I'll wait another year,' he thought, 'then go down to New

Orleans. Find myself a nice woman—a widow, likely. Get married again. Better to marry than to burn. And up in heaven—if there's any such place—Ruth'll realize it's not because I didn't love her, but because I *did*. Because she showed me what happiness was. If I hadn't met her before Ellen died—if I'd judged by that ice-cold misery I had with my wife, I'd have gone down the row in Storyville to cool off rather than *ever* thinking like this. But Ruth showed me a man and a woman together, united, loving can be the finest thing in the world. And I want that. I need it—and there's no reason not to now that my baby's taken care of . . .'

Being a clear-thinking man, he felt great sorrow, but little guilt, over his part in Ruth's death. They'd both honestly believed that the possibility of a pregnancy resulting from their liaison at their ages, and with the previous evidences of two long-time childless marriages on both sides, was remote indeed. They had been wrong. "Because," Ruth said, when she was sure of her state, "a love this big, fine, wonderful had to—create life, Oliver—leave its image in the world . . ."

And her death had been no way his fault. She had died of her own free will, or rather on the accepted terrible gamble that she could survive bearing his child, of the maniacal force with which the maternal instinct can grip a true woman, a real one. He would have had the abortion performed without even her knowledge, or her consent, if that had been possible, and if he could have found a doctor willing to do it.

For at that extreme, even so enlightened and liberal a physician as Hans Volker drew the line.

He was thinking all that, coming to what should have been an eminently sensible decision over the question of how to bring order and peace to his declining years, when he saw the mailman drive his buggy up the road, pause before the metal mailbox on the gatepost, and put a letter in it.

The letter was, as Oliver had hoped, from Billie Jo. Then, to his joy, he saw it had been posted not in France but in New Orleans itself. He shoved it into his inside coat pocket to keep it dry, and rushed back into the house to read it.

"We'll be home next week," Billie Jo had written, "and to *stay*, Uncle Oliver. For two most excellent reasons: I convinced Philippe, or rather allowed him to convince himself, that we'd be years getting started down here, since New Orleans is, if anything, over-supplied with practicing physicians—while Caneville—Sainte Marie needs doctors desperately, as Doctor Hans is always preaching—because of the yellow fever from Nelson Vance's man-made swamps, as he calls the marshes where the muskrats breed. The other reason is that I have already had a sight too much of my mother-in-law! The very day we arrived she turned and said to one of the three hundred and fifty sisters Philippe apparently has (I exaggerate, of course! It just *seems* that there are that many of them) and remarked that I was "Assez moche—même laide—" Whereupon in my best Parisian accent—I've had lessons every day while we were in Paris, and Philippe swears I'm a natural linguist—I said:

" 'Ne pensez-vous pas, chère Madame, que c'est Philippe, luimême, et pas sa mère, qui devrait juger cette question? Vous lui trouvez avec une aire mécontente?'

"And left her speechless! Never occurred to her I could understand her horrible Creole patois, much less answer her. On the other hand Papa Sompayac is a love!

"Anyhow, I'm *dying* to see you! I've so much to tell you. I'll probably rattle on for weeks—Meanwhile amuse yourself with another clipping. From *L'Abeille*, naturally; parce que, *personne*, mon cher Oncle, mais *personne* would be found dead with the *Picayune* in his hands—

"All my love—and Philippe's
"Billie Jo"

The clipping was on a par with the wedding announcement. It said that the brilliant young physician Mister The Doctor Philippe Sompayac had returned from his studies at the Pasteur Institute from which he had been graduated with the very highest of honors, and fresh from the practice of medicine among the poor of the Hotel God, and the unfortunates ("Read *whores*," Billie Jo had written in the margin) of the Saltpeter Works ("Meaning," Billie Jo annotated at the bottom of the clipping, "not that they make gunpowder in the prison but they feed the women prisoners saltpeter to—well—oh, heck, I am *married* after all!—to inhibit their carnal desires!"), to employ his profession for the benefit of his native state . . .

It went on to explain who Philippe's parents, grandparents, and great-grandparents were, apparently having forgot that in the piece about the wedding, it—the selfsame *L'Abeille,* or at least some editor thereof—had declared such information unnecessary. Then in closing—as an after-thought!—one line:

"The young Doctor Sompayac is accompanied by his wife, Madame Sompayac, born Prescott."

Oliver Prescott threw back his head and laughed aloud.

Perhaps he shouldn't have laughed, since his laughter conceivably threw him headlong into the category of those Whom the Gods Would Destroy, and First Made Mad.

And surely he wouldn't have laughed if he had known all the trouble that news story was going to cause.

For, three days before that, Louella had come into the Blue Parlor with a copy of *L'Abeille* in her hands. Louella knew about Philippe. By then, she knew Fanny's entire history. She was, in actual fact, the only person in all New Orleans whom Fanny confided in. Her being black had, of course, a great deal to do with it—made it easier for Fanny to talk to her, tell her things she simply couldn't bring herself to reveal to a person of her own race. And Louella's unfailing tact, her wit and patience, her real and growing fondness for Fanny, made the matter all the easier.

"Look-a heah, honeychile," she whispered to Fanny, so that none of the girls in the Parlor could hear. "Hit's 'bout *him,* 'bout you *ex.* The feller you swears to Gawd is the only one you ever did *love.* Only I çain't tell you what hit says—this here damn newspaper is printed in Gumbo filé for a fact."

Fanny took the paper. Stared at it as though her pale eyes by concentrating their reflected light like twin magnifying glasses would burn holes through the page. But she couldn't figure it out. At the Emma Willard School, she had begun studying French; but no one had been able to get a single word of it through her head.

She looked up then, swept the faces of all the other

whores in the parlor with her gaze. Came to the one she sought; said, crisply:

"Josette—will you come over here, please?"

Josette came to her at once. All the girls at Mae's were desperately afraid of Fanny by then. They heard of Rodney Schneider's supposed—and supposedly horrible—death. They had witnessed her father's, given eager ear to the wild rumors still being floating about in New Orleans's underworld as to what actually had happened to the man called Hawkes at the hands of Joe Sarcone's executioners. And there was in Fanny, now, an icy, maniac force, all the more frightening by being kept under perfect control. She seldom spoke to anyone; she performed her duties to the clients with a frigid, insulting indifference that had driven more than one poor devil half out of his mind. And to date, no one had won Mae's standing offer of ten dollars in free trade—or even in cash—to any man who could arouse her. She was known, and gloried in the title, as "Frozen Fanny, the Coldest Strumpet in Storyville."

Saddest of all, by then her title was almost the literal truth.

And yet, possibly because of that, her beauty remained intact and untouched. Generally speaking prostitution is a vertically mobile profession. Only its direction of movement is inevitably downward. A few pretty girls—a very few, because one of the things that *makes* a woman pretty is intelligence—become, by some misfortune, whores; but their beauty begins to fade the first year of active practice, and is gone—entirely gone—by the third. Which was why shrewd madams, like Mae, constantly changed their stock. Even so, it speaks volumes about the neuroses, psychoses, or what-have-you of the clients, that they could continue to pay good money for the dull, dumb, sick ugliness of even the best of whores.

But Fanny was—or appeared—immune to this iron law. Her fragile, ethereal beauty seemed proof against the grinding destruction of that life, being diminished not even by her really notable collection of scars: from two major operations, from the stripes the late Timothy Hawkes had given her, from the absolutely murderous whipping she had paid Joe the Whipper to administer after her father's death, screaming at the half-insane old man, crazed beyond control by the sight of her bloody purpling flesh: "Don't stop, damn you! Keep it up! Beat me some more! More! To death, you hear me! Beat me to death!"

What saved her finally was that she lapsed into unconsciousness and Joe came to himself in time. There is some evidence that Joe was not of pure Caucasian ancestry; perhaps the fear of being the victim of a lynch mob stole through his demented brain. Anyhow, he stopped in time. And Fanny employed the last of her strength to reach her father's tomb. And Martha—

But you know all this, don't you?

Josette came to her at once. Fanny looked at her said:

"Come into Mama's sitting room with me a minute, will you, Josette?"

Josette stared at her.

"I—I never said word about you, me!" she quavered: "Crois-moi, Fanny—I mean believe me, I never—"

"Oh shit, Josie," Fanny said, "I'm not after you for anything. I just need you to read something in the French newspaper for me. You can, can't you?"

"Bien sûr!" Josette said; her voice reedy with relief, "down there on the bayou where we'uns lived I never even heard folks talk English, me, Fan, 'til I was ten years old! Where's it? This paper—"

"Not here," Fanny said. "I don't want the other girls to hear. Come into Mama's sitting room like I said. She's upstairs asleep, this time of the afternoon, you know."

Josette went with her, read that article. The same one that Billie Jo had sent to her uncle.

Fanny sat there gazing upon the Gorgon's head, counting the twisting serpents of Medusa's hair. Or was it her own reflection glaring from her perfidious lover's shield that had turned her to stone? Who knows?

Josette, frightened, let slip the first muted note of a beginning scream.

Fanny stirred, gazed at her, said:

"Don't have to tell you what'll happen to you if you say one word about this to those sluts out there, do I?"

"No-o-o, Fanny!" Josette breathed, "I keep my mouf shut, me! You knows that."

"All right. Now do me a favor, will you? You know that old French photographer the girls call Papa? The one who's always trying to get 'em to pose bare-assed?"

"Yes, I know him all right. He named Bellocq, him."

"You know where he lives? Where his studio is, I mean?"

"No—but when I gits off tomorrow, I ask Louis. He know, Louis. Louis know damn near everthing, him . . ."

"You do that, then come and tell me," Fanny said.

Three days after that, Fanny knocked on the door of E. J. Bellocq's studio. The odd, dwarfish, exceedingly ugly little photographer answered it himself. He could afford neither a receptionist nor even a laboratory assistant. He never was able to afford one. He spent most of his life photographing boats, machinery, and dressed and undressed whores, none of which kept him from being one of the greatest photographers of all times*—which in its turn didn't keep him from dying poor, alone, and completely unknown.

"What can I do for, mees?" he said in a high-pitched, heavily accented voice.

"Take a picture of me—naked," Fanny said.

Bellocq looked at her then. Waggled his strangely shaped head from side to side, smiled.

"That be wan dam' fine picture, mees!" he said.

## Chapter Twenty-Nine

Four theses to be nailed to a church door:

Character is Fate.

There are only two sins which life itself recognizes as such and punishes implacably: Weakness and Stupidity.

There *is* Justice in Life (the reservation being made at once that said Justice has absolutely nothing to do with morality, sexual or otherwise, ethics, fair play, or any man's concepts of good or evil. Adolf Hitler died not of being a megalomaniacal monster [an ethical concept] but of being a military idiot [an actual one]. And his death

---

*As visitors to the New York Museum of Modern Art's exhibition of his collection of Storyville Portraits in 1971 should be aware.

was much easier than that of millions of presumably good
and decent people whose crimes consisted of being weak,
defenseless, and credulous—in other words a combination
of thesis one and thesis two):

But no mercy.

Philippe Sompayac sat on the gallerie of Oliver Prescott's house, talking to his uncle-in-law. Billie Jo was there
with them, but she didn't join in the conversation. She
simply sat there, smiling to herself with quiet amusement.
Catching Philippe's eye, she tossed her head with a slight,
almost imperceptible motion in the direction of the house,
and closed one eye in a maddeningly provocative wink.

'Oh damn it!' Philippe thought, 'damn it all to hell!'

"Yes, Son," Oliver Prescott was saying, "the big problems hereabout are ignorance and poverty. Don't know
why, but there's something about textile mills—Mertontown's only source of income—that plain reduces people
down to morons. The number of mill-women's children
that are *born* feebleminded would amaze you. My guess is
that working conditions undermine the women's health—
and their husbands'—and the children being born of stock
we'd cull the hell out of any decent barnyard come into
this world more and more backward every generation.
Plumb—natural. What with the wages people like that old
pirate Winthrop Bevers pay, they can't even *eat* decently,
let alone afford proper medical treatment; while here—"

Philippe was looking at Billie Jo and thinking:

'The house is too small. *You know* it's too small, Billie.
Slightest noise can be heard all over it. Makes me nervous. Freezes me up. I should oil those bed springs, damn
it! But what about those operatic arias you've occasionally
given out with—and at the worst possible moments—my
dear?'

"While here?" he prompted, aware at last of Oliver's
pause.

"Yellow fever. Of which the prime cause is our
swamps—Doctor Hans swears that they weren't always
this bad. He's sure but can't prove it that Nelson Vance
dammed up this end of Merry Creek at the point that
Bayou Flêche should drain off into it, so as to extend the
muskrats' breeding grounds. If there ever were a case of
extorting one's bread from the sweat of other men's faces,
that's it. Those poor Cajun trappers—but you'll see them

soon enough. No group is worse off than they are—"

"Not even the Negroes?" Philippe said.

"Not—much," Oliver Prescott said. "And they'll soon be getting some relief, far as medicine is concerned. Doctor Hans is putting a bright colored boy through medical school—smart as a whip, that Mose. Swears it's to get the niggers off his back; but he's lying, a little. Hates like the dickens for folks to find out how good-hearted he really is . . ."

'We'll have to find a house of our own,' Philippe thought, 'for here, our—nocturnal intimacies—are getting shot all to hell. Even at two o'clock in the morning, who can be sure the old boy is really sound asleep? Puts a constraint on me—on us. Rather spoils things, in fact—'

He looked sideways at his wife, gave a slight, negative shake to his head. Whereupon Billie Jo pouted, theatrically. She was teasing him, and he knew it. The matter really wasn't *that* pressing. After all, there was still two o'clock in the morning. The real trouble was going to be getting away after they'd found—or built—a house of their own. Oliver Prescott obviously believed that his was big enough for the three of them, and was just as obviously delighted to have them there.

'He's lonely, poor old fellow,' Philippe thought. 'That business about Mrs. Colfax must have been rough—'

Billie Jo had told him the whole story. So far, she had no secrets from her husband, and clearly expected him to share his every thought with her, as well. Philippe had his reservations about that; but he was at least smart enough to keep them to himself.

'I'm—happy,' he realized now, 'very happy. And he—Oliver—is largely responsible for it. He brought her up to be—a human being. To—accept life. Of course she couldn't entirely escape—our times. She was much too rough on the old boy when she told me about his affair with Mrs. Colfax. Said he was too old to be indulging in such behavior. But I wonder. Is a man ever too old to go off his rocker over a woman? Oliver damned sure isn't. He's more alive—more vital than most men half his age. I'm sure that *I'm* not going to abruptly turn *monk* after forty-five, or even after sixty, if I can help it!

'But still she—and Martha Turner—are the two women least contaminated with Victorian prudery that I've met in all my life. Far less than—my poor, poor Fanny—dear God! How did that happen? How *did* she fall into that? She *accepted* all the rules; only she couldn't—or wasn't allowed to—keep them. That damned old bitch of a mother of hers was around her neck from the beginning like the Ancient Mariner's albatross. And whoredom's peculiarly Victorian, isn't it? The reverse of the coin. The *bad* woman to contrast with the good. Even to "protect" the good, lest she suffer from our unbridled male passions. Passions she isn't supposed to have, or share. Merde! Whoever dreamed up the idea that embracing a rigid, unmoving, revolted statue of ice was either desirable or even natural?

'Anyhow, Victorianism is dead, or it should be. Since the author of it went to her own reward last year,* maybe people will break out of her whalebone corsets and rediscover that physical love is one of God's greatest gifts to mankind. So, thanks, old boy—for making it possible for me to have a warm and loving wife—without the slightest taint of that—well—viciousness, perversity—that poor Fanny damn well had. With Billie—it's *great*. Fine. Wonderful. Especially now that she's got over the idea that she ought to be ashamed of enjoying herself in bed. Best foundation a marriage can have. Makes it solid, unshakable—'

"When is Doctor Hans coming for you?" Oliver said.

"Doctor Hans?" Philippe said; then he remembered: "Tell me, Uncle Oliver, why does everybody call him that? I mean Doctor Hans instead of Dr. Volker?"

"Affection," Oliver said. "Gratitude. Sometimes both. Hans Volker is one of the finest human beings the good Lord ever blew the breath of life into. Oh he'll bark your head off; try his damnest to convince you he's the roughest, meanest, horniest-hided old bastard on the face of the earth, when the fact is he's just the opposite. I found that out when Ruth—Oh, hell! Sometimes I talk too damn much. Sign of old age. Tell me son, when is he coming to ride you round the district and point out all our natural impediments to good health?"

"About six," Philippe said. "Why, Uncle Oliver?"

"No reason," Oliver Prescott said, with a wide grin on

*Queen Victoria died January 22, 1901.

his pleasantly ugly face. "Reckon I'll mosey on down to the south acres—some drainage ditches down there need fixin'. I'll try to get back by six myself. Want a word with Doctor Hans. Meanwhile, why don't you young folks go take a nap? Settles the stomach after such a heavy meal—"

Then, looking at his niece, he gave a slight toss to his head in the direction of the house; and winked his eye exactly as she had done, making it abysmally clear that he had seen her playful gesture.

Billie Jo blushed scarlet as a peony.

"Why, Uncle Oliver!" she gasped. "You mustn't think—"

"Don't think," Oliver Prescott chuckled, "know. One advantage of stayin' young at heart, honeychile: ain't forgot how being really young feels . . ."

Philippe threw back his head and laughed aloud.

"Don't go, Uncle Oliver!" he quipped, "or else I'll sure as hell have to fight her off. And I'm too young to lose my boyish laughter . . ."

"You're—awful, both of you!" Billie Jo fumed. "Wicked! Mean! Why—"

"Ain't we, though?" Oliver said complacently. "See you later, Phil—Go easy on him, honey; he's down to skin and bones now!"

Then with that loose-jointed, slouching grace of his, he went down the steps, and around the house toward the stables.

"Come on!" Philippe said.

"No, I won't!" Billie Jo said. "We're going to sit right here on the porch—"

"Until he's out of sight," Philippe said.

"All afternoon! To—to punish you for—saying that awful thing—about fighting me off and—"

"And also to punish one very naughty little girl, for making suggestive gestures and winking her eye," Philippe said solemnly.

Billie Jo bent her head. He could see her shoulders shake.

"Now, Billie—" he said reproachfully. He got up, went over to where she sat. Then he saw she wasn't crying. She was laughing.

"Oh, Phil, darlin'!" she gasped, "wasn't I awful! And

he—he saw me! Of course, I was only joking; but—"

"Were you, Billie?" he said, and kissed her.

"Mm-m-m—" she said; "well, half-joking anyhow—and—Philippe! You stop that!"

"Why?" Philippe said.

"We're on the front porch, for one thing. And he hasn't even had time to saddle Bess yet, and—"

"And what?" Philippe said.

"We're going to stay right here on the front porch—and wave him good-bye. Stay sitting very calmly like an old, old married couple until he's out of sight, at least, and—"

"And after that?" Philippe said.

"Oh you *are* wicked, Philippe!" she said.

"And aren't you *glad!*" Philippe said.

She looked at him, and her brown eyes were merry.

"Yes," she said: "I am glad, lover. Now go sit over there—out of kissin' distance. Out of—touching distance—at least 'til Uncle Oliver is out of sight. We owe him *that* much respect, anyhow . . ."

The only trouble with that was before Oliver Prescott was completely, out of sight—his mounted figure, though dwarfed by the distance, being still clearly visible on the high ground between the house and the south fields—the mailman came.

"Come'n git it, folks!" he sang out. "Package! Too big to git in th' mail box. 'Sides, it's marked fragile . . ."

Before Philippe could move, Billie Jo dashed down the stairs. He ran down them behind her. Of course, he could have overtaken her at the first stride; but he didn't, deliberately slowing his pace in order to enjoy the sheer pleasure of watching her run. She was a doe-thing—a gazelle, all slender grace. Most women—because of their pelvic structure, he knew—looked like hell, running; but Billie Jo didn't. She ran beautifully— 'Just as she does—everything,' Philippe thought.

But by the time he reached the gate she had the flat, rectangular package in her hands. She looked down at the handwriting, saw that it was feminine, exquisitely formed, an almost copperplate Spencerian script that was expert indeed.

He could see the color drain out of her face, leaving the freckles bolder than ever. But she waited until the mailman had said, "Evenin', folks," and had driven off, before saying:

"It's—addressed to you, Philippe. And *only* to you. Not to Mr. and Mrs. Sompayac. And a *woman* wrote this. Well, Philippe—"

"Now, Billie Jo—" he said, and grinned at her: "You aren't going to hold my past against me are you?"

But he could feel the corners of his mouth jerking a little, so he knew how shaky that grin was. Then, as he reached out to take the package, the shaking got into his hands as well. Because he already knew who had sent him that package; very dismally and certainly, he knew.

The handwriting had changed, of course; but then, it had begun to change even before he'd left for Paris. The letters she had written him twice or three times a week while only the few miles between Troy and New York City separated them had shown even from one to the next a truly amazing progress in penmanship.

'She was—not stupid,' he thought, 'not ever stupid. In some ways she was *very* intelligent, even—brilliant. Only her mind was always dominated by her inclinations. What she liked—what interested her—she learned effortlessly. Like this—like to form these beautiful loops and curlicues, these exquisite letters. Dress. Correct English. Etiquette. Fastidious grooming. All—trivialities. All superficial things. Designed to impress other people, make them believe she was—the lady she longed to be—

'But anything more? Who knows? In all else her taste was execrable. She was incapable of understanding the simplest poem; any music more complicated than a dance tune left her cold—and she couldn't even grasp what it was that made me haunt the museums of Italy. Did she *ever* read a book? Yes—novels. Trashy novels—in which the heroine sins, repents, and is redeemed by the love of the insufferable kind of prig novelists call a "good man." And I—

'I'm standing there like a long, gangling ass, afraid to open this package because Fanny sent it. What's worse, sent it *here*. Which means she knows, has been told—'

"Open it," Billie Jo said.

"Billie—" he croaked.

"Open it!" Billie Jo said.

So because there was nothing else to do, he did. Stood

there, holding that photograph, Bellocq's absolute master-piece, that supremely beautiful portrait of a supremely beautiful woman, staring at it, rapt, nerve-ravished, lost.

Fanny lay, facing the camera, on a wickerwork chaise longue, her hair was loose. It lay over one shoulder, its true platinum shade darkened a little by the failure of the slow emulsions that were all turn-of-the-century photographers had to work with to catch the true intensity of its reflections. But her eyes were not darkened. Being, as they were, very nearly colorless anyhow, the silver salts had reproduced them perfectly. They seemed to follow him with their gaze. He knew they were going to haunt him forever.

Her head rested upon a pillow that had a floral pattern printed on it, dark, stylized, curiously abstract. Her lips were unsmiling, a trifle sullen, actually. And he stood there holding that picture, and shaking a little harder, a little more visibly every second, because he could taste them. His memory turned acutely tactile and reproduced the tart flavor of them, hot, wet, clinging, negating or abolishing his mind, annihilating his will, hollowing out his middle suddenly, then filling it up again with—what?—vitriol, maybe. And ground glass.

She was naked. But the word was wrong. Even the substitution of the French word *nude* that English-speaking people use to distinguish between the way a statue is naked and a living woman is, didn't work now. He remembered suddenly his former mistress Lillian, and how distressed he had been the first time that he'd seen that she had two or three coarse black hairs fringing the dark, muddy-colored nipples of her breasts. Nakedness—was, well, a yellowish bead of sweat stealing down from an imperfectly depilated armpit. A spray of pimples marring a beautifully rounded buttock. Blackheads in the creases of a pretty nostril; a tiny pustule on an almost perfect chin. Even skin roughened by a draft, or calves displaying a hint of ancestral pelt, however downy.

Fanny was unclothed; but she lay in a glow from the studio's skylight, in an aura that today's photographers, with their miraculous films, their strobes, fill-ins, spots, floods, umbrella reflectors, shutters fast enough to catch the image of a rifle bullet in flight, lenses made of rare-earth glasses, apertures up to $f$ 1.1, cannot duplicate. Perhaps because we are all science—and this was love. Devotion. Worship.

Bellocq had photographed what Fanny's beauty had made him feel. Had reproduced that feeling so that it came through to the viewer undiminished, undisguised, and undefiled. The ugly, misshapen, dwarfish photographer had been privileged to look upon beauty bare, and had responded not with desire, but with awe. And that awe worked its humble worshipful magic on the viewer. Only the supreme painters of the female nude excelled— and even this is not so great a measure as one might assume—the work of art that Papa Bellocq had achieved that day.

Fanny's pose, Philippe saw, was not entirely graceful. One arm was half hidden by the curve of her hip, the other rested beneath the trunk of her body, and was bent awkwardly, making what could be seen of her hand look deformed. Her breasts were a little larger in proportion to the rest of her than he remembered them; but still rather small, still firm as an adolescent girl's, and the palms of his hands, his fingertips, his mouth, ached suddenly, damnably with their weight, softness, warmth, texture, taste.

Her legs and thighs were long and slim; and—as if to lend humanity to so much perfection—her feet were noticeably dirty. He was aware finally, belatedly that something was wrong with that photograph, something missing from it. Then almost at once he saw what it was: the glass-plate negative had been retouched with a master's skill. Bellocq had carefully removed every trace of the scars from her two operations. He had not, however, as most photographers do, etched or brushed out the feathery spiraling of blonde pubic hair; nor had Fanny— as most models do—lent a curious coy obscenity to the photograph by putting her hand in her lap or tossing a shawl over her genitalia. She simply lay there unsmiling, naked and beautiful, taking her own nakedness and her beauty as matters of course, perfectly normal things, put into the world to lend that world a little joy, assuage some also perfectly normal hungers, grant the male half of humanity a little temporary peace.

She had signed it, "All my love, always, Fanny." Then under that, an afterthought, a sort of postscript: "When you get tired of her, come back to me. I'll wait for you, forever."

He felt then, the light, trembling touch on his arm, and the world, reality, now, shuddered back into focus. Turning he looked into the face of his wife. Of the wife he had already lost.

"Shall I—" she said, her voice flat, twanging, dull, "pack my things? Or are you going to pack yours?"

"Billie!" he said.

"Choose, Philippe. 'Cause one of us has got to leave. We—can't stay together, not after this."

"Billie, for God's sake!" he said. "Just because Fanny sent me her picture in the altogether, you—"

"No, Phil. Not for that. For—what your eyes did looking at it. Your hands. Your mouth."

"And," he croaked, "what did they do?"

"Went—to bed with her. Right here—before my eyes. I won't live a lie, Philippe. When I repeated 'forsaking all others,' I meant it. I won't put up with a ménage à trois—even if one of the three is only a memory—"

"Billie!" he all but wept.

"Not when the memory is that strong. Not when it made you forget I was even alive and standing here next to you. So—let's say good-bye, Philippe—right now, before we do each other any more harm. It—it was-nice-knowing you. I'm going to remember you all my life—"

She saw his big hands grip that photograph convulsively, start to twist, and said:

"No, Phil—it—it's too beautiful. She's too beautiful—go to her. Yes, I said: Go to her. Save her—from that life. After all—*you* put her into it."

"I put her into it!" Philippe howled.

"Yes," Billie Jo said, and handed him the sheet of notepaper. "This fell out of the package. Naturally, you didn't see it. You were too busy committing—mental adultery. But since the Bible says 'As a man thinketh in his heart, so is he,' the sin's just as great, to my way of thinking. And I read it. I apologize for that. It wasn't addressed to me. But as your wife—I thought I had some rights in the matter. I was wrong. I see I haven't any rights to you, have I?"

"Billie—" he whispered.

"And I—apologize—for another thing," she went on slowly, crying now, at long last crying, but keeping an almost brutal control over herself in spite of that. "I beg your pardon most humbly, Philippe—for coming after you—to Paris—like a brazen hussy. I thought—that she—that she was out of your life. But she isn't, is she? And she'll never be . . . Go on, read it! Won't take you long. Took me—only a couple of minutes, although you gave me time to read the whole Bible from Genesis to Revelations twice over—while you were—looking at her like that. You heard me, Philippe, read it!"

He took the note, read:

Dear Phil:

So now you're married. And to her. To Billie Speckled-Tail. Tell me, has she got freckles on her bottom, too? No, don't tell me; I couldn't care less. I hope you'll be very happy with her. Oh hell, that's a lie. I hope you'll be so damn miserable that you'll feel like cutting your own throat—and hers, the scrawny, spotted little bitch!

Got you on the rebound didn't she? Told you about me. What I'm doing. The truth. I'm a whore. I sell myself to dozens of men every night. It's fun. I have a great time. I love it. Some of 'em make me scream the roof off!

That's another lie. It's awful. I wish I were dead and in hell, instead of alive and in hell. I killed my father. But you know that. It was in all the papers. Bet she sent you a bundle of them so you'd know.

But what you don't know because the papers didn't write it clearly was that afterwards I paid a crazy old man to whip me to death. Only he lost his nerve and didn't quite finish me off. You should see my back. It looks like a zebra's. All scars.

It—and my heart. Only the ones in my heart don't heal. They bleed all the time. In the night I can hear 'em go drip, drip, drip—hear my insides crying.

For you. And for our baby. I lost him, Phil. That was why I went to Mama's. I had to have some way to support him, since you'd gone off to Paris without telling me you were going and when I wrote you to your New York address to tell you I was pregnant my letter came back marked "not at this address." And after I got to Mama's and begged her to keep me 'til I had my—*our*—baby, promising her that I'd do that—be a whore—to pay her back, I fell down and lost it.

So—I stayed. Nothing else to do. I couldn't go back home. Couldn't face Papa and Martha and not even Eliza. You know me—so you know when I'm telling the truth. And this is the truth. If you want me to, I'll swear it on poor Papa's grave—and on the grave that my—our—poor little bastard hasn't even got, because, you see, he wasn't even fully formed.

Now you know. Don't let it bother you, Phil. Forget it—just like you forgot me—and go be happy—if you can.

Fanny

He looked up then to face his wife. But by then he couldn't even see her. He heard her voice saying pityingly:

"Don't, Philippe! Oh, please don't! Please!"

Afterwards he wondered what instinct it was that made him say the right things; though maybe it was more than instinct—it was—defeat, surrender—truth in him up to the hilt like a blade and his life welling up around it—but anyhow he put his hand out to her and said quietly:

"Don't leave me, Billie. Don't you see I *need* you more than ever now?"

"Need me—for what?" she said; but it was an honest question without bitterness or sarcasm either one.

"To—oh hell, Billie! To heal me—to cure this one poor pill-pushing quack of a sickness that isn't even in the medical books. But that could kill him, even so. Because—a man—could die of—hating himself this much. Of despising himself—for—a liar, and a cheat, and a lecherous swine—"

"Philippe—" she said.

"Because she isn't lying in that letter. I ran off like that. I didn't know she was with child, but that's no excuse. I ran off because I didn't have the heart, or the simple guts, to tell her that I'd got my appointment to Paris—when she was so—happy. I was too stupid, and too weak, to spoil that happiness—when that was the only honest thing to do. And, au fond, I know now that I *never* wanted to marry Fanny Turner; while from the very day I met you I always wanted to marry you—"

"Now, Philippe!" she said.

"God's own truth. You know I sent my father to—"

"Ask her to give you up? Yes. He told me that. All right. But tell me something else. Say the only two things that'll make me stay with you. That is, if you can. Without lying, I mean. Tell me you never loved her. Tell me you don't love her now."

Philippe looked at her. Studied that taut, fine, intelligent little face; decided that to lie now, under these particular—and damned peculiar circumstances—was not only demeaning, but idiotic as well.

"Your price tag's too high, Billie," he said slowly. "When you make a man bend that low even for the privilege—and it *is* a privilege, I grant you—of staying with you, you break him in half across the middle. So you lose both ways. I tell you the truth, and you lose a man—flawed, imperfect, as who isn't under heaven, baby?—but still a man. I lie to you and you keep a cripple. A moral cripple, the ugliest kind there is . . . So here goes: the truth, ugly as all get-out—but having its own peculiar value. And since you've set yourself up as judge, jury, and executioner: hear it: I loved Fanny. I still do. I'll probably go on loving her 'til the day I die. I hope not. But it doesn't depend upon me. It depends upon—you."

Billie Jo stood there. Except for her freckles all her face was white. Even her lips.

"Then, I reckon," she whispered, "that the only thing I can say is—'Good-bye, Philippe—' "

"Goddamn it, Billie, you listen to me!" he said. "Are you a woman, or aren't you?"

"If *you* don't know that by now, I'm sure I—Oh! That's not what you mean is it?"

"Yes, and no. What I mean mostly is are you a grown-up woman with brains in her head, or a romantic little moron who's prepared to wreck her own marriage and her husband's life before she'll face up to reality? There isn't any Santa Claus, Billie. Fairies don't exist. I doubt that even God does, now. I think he died of disgust at watching the antics of people like *me*, long ago—"

"Philippe—" she said.

"Item one—and get this through your head, Billie!—There has never been a monogamous *man* in the whole of human history, and there never will be. Any man who says to any woman I love you and nobody else on earth *may* be telling the truth at the time he's saying it, though I doubt even that. But if he says he never loved any other woman he's a liar; and if he says he's never going to, he's a barefaced, goddamned one. And I suspect that if women ever faced up to the truth about themselves they'd have to say the same thing—though I do give the fair sex slightly higher marks in the fidelity department—"

"Don't," she said ominously, "especially not when the provocation's gross."

"I haven't offered you any provocation—yet," he said quietly. "I've been a good and loving husband and an absolutely faithful one. You know that, Billie. What you don't seem to know, or at least refuse to get through your head, is that a man may be torn in half between two women both of whom he loves—a word broad enough to cover a multitude of sins, baby—one of whom he neither likes, respects, or needs—but loves, yes. Hell, yes! Just as a drunk loves liquor, and a dope addict loves the opium that's curdling his brains into a useless mass of gray dough inside his head—"

"That's not love," Billie Jo said, "that's—"

"If you say lust, I'll hit you, so help me!" Philippe howled. "Hear this, woman! I lust after *you*, goddamn it. You're a hell of a lot better in bed than she ever was. I love your pointy little tits, and your rounded little tail, and what's between your legs, too. Is that vulgar enough to suit you?"

"Oh, Philippe!" she moaned.

"And if you were a *real* woman, you'd glory in it. I wouldn't need to go on to say what you also already know: that I love your pert and perky little mind, your great goodness, your tenderness, your warmth—hell, *you!* I want you to be the mother of my kids. I need you. I respect you. Without you my life would have neither meaning, nor hope. So now that's enough. I don't mean to either grovel or beg. All right, Billie—now it's up to you. Shall I pack? You want to throw away a husband that you went to considerable trouble to get because of a *picture?* A bare-assed picture, I grant you; but still a picture—"

"Not because of a picture," she got out, "but—"

"Because of a sin I did after you'd already tossed me the hell out of your life? What goddamned business of yours was it, Billie? What business of yours is it now?"

She bowed her head. Looked up again. Smiled at him. Her tears ran into the upturned corner of her mouth. She could taste them. They tasted as salt and bitter as old hell.

"None, Philippe," she said. Then: "Oh Lord, but are you ever a fool!"

"Stale news, Billie," he said. "What am I being a fool about now?"

"Not knowing I would have been running down the road after you screaming for you to come back before you were even out of sight. Not realizing that if you *ever* leave me for any reason whatsoever, I'd do just what *she* did—only better. Philippe—do me a favor. Give me that picture, will you?"

Without the slightest hesitation he handed it to her. Stood there, smiling at her, said:

"What are you going to do with it? Burn it?"

"No," she said. "I'm not that big a coward. Going to hide it though. From you—and from Uncle Oliver! If he ever sees *this*—horny as he is—he'll purely climb up the wall. But the day our oldest boy gets into mischief—this kind of mischief—"

"I hope to God it *is* this kind!" Philippe said.

"Me, too," Billie Jo said, "the other kind's too awful, isn't it? Anyhow, the first time he does and you're dressing him down because of it, I'm going to dig this out and show it to him right in front of you, saying, 'Look, son— what a fine example your Papa set you!' "

He bent his tall form and kissed her. A long time. A very long time. And after that it was all right. Perfectly all right. Because when he turned her loose, she said:

"Philippe—how long is it 'til six o'clock?"

He fished in his waistcoat pocket for his watch. Got it half way out before he saw her face, and remembered—or was reminded—of what the afternoon's program had been, and maybe now was, all over again. He threw back his head and roared.

"Who the hell cares?" he said. "Time's a-wasting, Billie—come on!"

She hid Fanny's picture. Hid Bellocq's absolute masterpiece. Hid it so well that not only was Philippe never to see it again in his life, which didn't really matter one way or another; but also that her Uncle Oliver, who did find it, finally, or rather had it delivered to him by fate's own—in this case appropriately black hand, only got to see it *after* she and Philippe had moved away from his farm, so that there was nobody to explain things to him, which sure as hell did matter, as we shall presently see.

So now, Gentle Reader, go back to the beginning of this chapter and reread the four theses fluttering from their nails in the church door. Especially the last one.

Because there isn't, you know.

None at all.


## Chapter Thirty


One day in mid-August 1903, about a year after her very nearly successful attempt to wreck Philippe's and Billie Jo's marriage, Fanny, beautifully dressed as usual, set out for Beauregard Square, to visit her lover, Beau Dan O'Connor—in jail.

Looking out of the window of her cab, she could see that New Orleans was—reluctantly and regretfully, of course—entering the twentieth century. All the downtown streets had electric lights now instead of gas. Not one horse-drawn street car was left; electric trolleys banged and rattled over the iron rails. Even in the short distance she had ridden (for she always walked until she was well beyond the confines of Storyville, hating as she did for even a hackie to know what she was) she had seen no less than four automobiles*: one steamer, two gasoline buggies, and one stately electric, though she lacked com-

---

*In 1900 there were 8000 automobiles in the U.S.A. By 1905 there were 78,000. The writer couldn't find the figures for 1903, but a shrewd guess would be nearly 50,000.

pletely the technical knowledge to classify them as such. She wondered idly how it would be to ride in one; but dismissed the notion as silly, for she held, as unshakeably as did ninety nine and ninety seven hundredths percent of her contemporaries, that the noisy, smelly, unreliable things would never replace the horse.

At the prison she got down, and went through the visitors' entrance to the checkroom, where she was required to leave her handbag (a lady's handbag was quite big enough to conceal a gun or a knife to be passed on to a prisoner bent upon escaping) the pie or cake she always bought him at a local bakery (like most essentially childish men, Beau Dan had a sweet tooth) for the same reason, to be passed on to the prisoner only after it had been carefully probed for a weapon, or a file, or a hacksaw blade baked into it; and, here of late, even her hat, since some weeks before a prisoner had almost got away after thrusting a lady's hatpin into a guard's right eye.

'They needn't worry about Dan', she thought bitterly; 'he hasn't got what it takes to break out of a wet paper bag, let alone a jail. And yet, I miss him—really miss him. Definition of reaching rock bottom: when you start to miss a thing like Dan . . .'

'And yet they made me wait three months before they'd even let me see him—'cause they've got him on that dangerous prisoners list. Charged with armed robbery—what a laugh. I *never* believed that. The minute Lou told me. I saw through that particular little farce—'

"Fecal matter, Lou," she had said, "bovine or equine, you take your choice. But excreta pure and undiluted . . ."

"Honey," Louella said, "talk simple-like, will you, huh? When you pulls that highfalutin' Grand Duchess Olga speechifyin' on me, you just plain *loses* one po' li'l thickheaded colored gal—"

"Oh hell, skip it," Fanny said. "You know Dan, Lou. So don't you stand there with your liverlips flapping in the breeze and start in to tell me Dan tried a stickup. He plain hasn't got the nerve to point a gun at a four-way cripple, no arms, no legs, let alone a man—"

"Done beat up a powerful lot o' fellers, from all I heard tell," Louella said.

"Drunks. Poor little scared rats half his size. Get on

with it, Lou; but don't try to make me believe that Dan pulled a heist—"

"Did, though. Feller named Angie. Eyetalian gangster feller. Mighty mean, him. Only thing I can't figger is how come that Angie even called in th' bulls. Up to now every feller what ever talked rough to him is pushin' up daisies—and that includes some o' Mr. Sarcone's boys. All the same, 'cording to what *I* heard, Angie took Dan's heater off him real gentlemanlike and called the police. Don't sound right, do hit?"

"Hell, Lou, it doesn't even smell right," Fanny had said. "Breaking and entering, I'd believe—maybe. Shoplifting, purse-snatching—picking pockets, no; he's too damn clumsy. But what I can't figure is why he needed to steal at all; can you?"

"Me neither—not with all the foldin' green stuff *you* lays all over him, honey, not to mention—"

"Estelle. Josette. Adele. Rose—and maybe a few others I don't even know about. That's what you were going to say, wasn't it?"

"Honey," Louella said, "I ain't never opened my big, wide, flapper-lipped mouf. Not even to breathe. That's how come I got this color—not breathing. Turned blue, then mortified on me, fer a fact—"

"Don't worry about it, Lou," Fanny said. "I won't carve them up. I couldn't care less. A faithful pimp—and a faithful whore, for that matter—are contradictions. But this *is* the goddamnedest thing! Reckon I'd better skip down to the cooler and talk to that boy—"

But talking to Dan that day turned out to be an impossibility. An attempted holdup automatically placed a man on the dangerous felons list, a class of prisoners whose privileges were distinctly limited. In fact, she had had to wait three months, until Dan's positively angelic behavior during the probationary period convinced the warden that it was safe to let him have visitors. More than convinced the warden, in fact; made him wonder how the hell a type like Dan had ever got up the nerve to pull the stunt he was accused of, and had confessed to, against a character like Angelo Marchesi. "A frame-up, sure as hell," he told the assistant warden. "He's fronting for somebody—and Angie knows it. Or else Dan would have been the guest of honor at the big Irish funeral, for a fact!"

But when, after her long wait, Fanny was finally allowed to visit Beau Dan, it took her all of five minutes to get the truth out of him; and, as usual, the truth was somewhat less than pretty.

"Joe—" he whispered through the wire netting separating them. "The Chief. He *called* me. I owed him a couple of favors. More than a couple, to tell the truth about it, not even counting the one he did *you,* takin' care of that detective feller—Hawkes, the name was, wasn't it? Anyhow this Angie—Angelo Marchesi is his handle, baby—was moving into the Chief's take on the fruit docks. Protection money, you know, honey. Been warned a dozen times—but that's one tough little guinea bastid, that Angelo. So the Chief decided that Angie had to—well, get lost. Go swimming with a couple o' bags of scrap iron for life preservers, for instance—or come out as the *lean* in Luigi Boasso's ground steak, maybe—"

"And Joe called *you,*" Fanny said, "to do *that?* To *kill* a man?"

"Sh-sh-sh!" Dan hissed. "I'm in for a stickup, Fan, baby. A simple heist—not no attempted murder . . ."

"Get on with it," Fanny said. "Why'd Joe pick you for a job like that?"

" 'Cause I ain't no dago," Beau Dan said.

Fanny sat there, looking at him through the wire screen.

"That Angie's fast with a heater," Dan sighed. "Any guinea what started in to take him was going to wind up awful dead. So Joe figgered that it had to be somebody what Angie wouldn't suspect—a red-haired Irish feller like me, for instance—"

"Whom—" Fanny said evenly, "he could deny any connection with—and who could, and probably would, be sacrificed to get the heat off him and his pals. Dan, I swear to God, sometimes I think I'll have to send you through college to educate you up to being even a moron."

"You think I didn't see what Joe was up to, baby?" Dan whispered. "That was exactly why I bungled the job. Fiddled around so long that Angie got suspicious: Then I pulls me heater 'n blasted twice—for the effect, honey. Missed him cold both times—on purpose, naturally— threw me iron down on the floor and put up me hands—"

Fanny smiled then, a very slow and secret smile.

"The wonder is that he didn't kill you, even so," she said.

"Talked him out of it. Told him I had to come gunning for him or visit Luigi's packin' house—agin. Pointed out to him that if I'd really wanted to let a little daylight through him, he'd be a piece of guinea mackerel by then, 'stead of standing there pointing his cannon at me. 'Lord, Jesus, Angie,' says I, 'I missed you twice from three feet! Don't nobody shoot *that* bad.' "

"You might," Fanny said, "if you don't shoot any better than you lie, Danny Boy, you could have missed him from three inches—"

"Aw hell, honey—" Dan began.

"Oh come off it, Dan," Fanny said, "you know damned well that if you'd even started to pull a gun out of your pocket around a nervous type like Angie, you'd be the *late* Beau Dan O'Conner right now—"

"Aw, Fanny—" Dan said.

"Shut up. I'm going to tell *you* what happened: You sidled up to Angelo and said out of the side of your mouth: 'Look, Angie, th' heat's on fer fair. Chief sent me to blast you. But, seeing as how I don't hold with killing nohow, and what with I ain't got nothing agin' you personal, I thought—' "

Beau Dan stared at her with pure undisguised admiration, but absolutely no shame.

"Honey, did I ever tell you you're a witch?" he said.

"Yes, only you spelled it a little differently," Fanny said. "Now go ahead, tell me about the deal you fixed up with Angie—"

"Didn't fix up no deal," Dan said. "Told him the truth. That I had to come gunning for him or the Chief would see that it was *me* who headed the missing persons' list, tomorrow. And I sort of hinted that after all, I could of put at least one slug into his carcass if I'd really had a mind to, since it hadn't even occurred to him that a nice redheaded Irish feller like me had been sent to do him in—"

"So?" Fanny said.

"So he shakes his head and says: 'All right, Danny, I believe you. But one good turn deserves another don't it? Give me yer cannon, will ya?' "

"And you gave him your gun?" Fanny said. "You actually trusted Angelo Marchesi *that* far?"

"Had to take th' chance, honey. So I passes over me iron. And he takes it, aims at the chair he'd been sittin' in, and blasts a hole in the back of it. Then wham! Another one right through a big picture over his desk. 'My mama-in-law gimme that 'un,' he says, 'always did hate th' damn thing. This way it looks good, eh, Danny-boy? For Joe's sake. You tried 'n missed. But anyhow I'm gonna do you a *real* favor. I'm gonna call th' bulls, and charge you with an attempted stickup. That way, by the time you gits outa da icebox. Joe *might* let you live long enough to catch a slowboat fer some place like Shanghai, China. In jail, you're one nice *live* Irish fella; you walk outa that door and you're *dead*, Danny. Catfish bait—that is if Joe don't call in Luigi to mess you up a little, first—"

"Dear God!" Fanny said.

"And he's right, Fan," Dan had said somberly. "When I get outa here, you 'n me have got to find us some other turf—a long way from N' Orleans, fer a fact. I've told the warden I don't want to see no *men* visitors—'cause Joe just might figger that I crossed him as far as Angie is concerned and have a couple of the boys come here to send me home to me eternal rest—"

Fanny smiled at him mockingly.

"What makes you think I'll still be around when you get out, Dan? After all, that judge threw the book at you. And seven years is a long, long time."

"Won't be seven years, honey. What with Angie pullin' wires to get me out, and time off for good behavior, five'll get you ten I'll be out of this cooler in two. That's one thing. Another is, the kind of a itch what makes a girlie take on another feller soon as her One 'n Only is out o' sight, you just plain ain't got. *I* take mighty good care of you in that department, but even with all *your* opportunities, so far you ain't found *nobody* else what *can*. Am I right?"

"Yes," Fanny sighed, "you are, Dan. Mainly because the kind of a fellow who could get a rise out of me wouldn't be found dead in a whorehouse. And my chances of meeting gentlemen socially are nil. But don't give yourself too much credit, Danny-boy. All you do is—outlast me, sort of. So with you I manage to get

there—again, sort of. But it is not—what I remember—
from the one time in my life I had me a *man*—"

"Fan, honey—" Dan said. His voice had a quaver in it.

"Forget it," Fanny said. "That's not a problem. Not a
big problem anyhow. What *is* a problem, Dan—is that by
crossing up Joe Sarcone, you may have cut me off from
some help it looks like I'm going to need—goddamned
bad—"

Beau Dan stared at her.

"How come, honey?" he said.

"I'm being followed again. Dan, do you know just *how*
Joe got rid of Timothy Hawkes? He—Hawkes I mean—
really had reasons to hate me. Good reasons. But he
didn't impress me as the sort who'd send another fellow to
do his dirty work for him. He'd do it himself. So when he
didn't come back after so long a time I figured I was
safe—"

"You are," Dan said, "from him, anyhow. Forever."

Fanny looked at Dan. Her mouth was ash-dry suddenly. She put out her tongue-tip and licked her lips. The
gesture was nervous, compulsive.

"Dan—" she whispered, "you don't mean that he—that
Joe—"

"Yes, honey," Dan said, "yes. Just what you're think
ing. But don't let's neither one of us say it out loud. Better
like that. Safer."

"Oh my God!" Fanny breathed.

"I thought you *knew*," Dan said.

Fanny shook her head.

"No, I didn't," she said: "Stupid of me, I must admit. I
should have, knowing Joe. But I didn't—I honestly didn't.
So—now this new one. What d'you think, Dan? A friend
of Hawkes? Somebody that Mr. Beac—his boss has hired
to find out what became of that little curd?"

"Honey, how would I know? What's this new fellow
like? And one other thing: He ever been to Mae's?"

"He's tall," Fanny said. "Bald-headed. Ugly. Thin.
Dresses well. Carries himself—like a gentleman. Quite
old—more than fifty, I'd say. And he hasn't been to
Mae's—yet. And the damnedest part about it is—he
doesn't look like a detective at all. Or act like one, either—"

"The good ones never do," Dan said.

"I know. But this fellow looks like the type who would *never* get mixed up in anything—as *slimy* as detective work. He's got such a—a *good* face, Dan."

"Thought you said he was ugly—"

"He is. But if I were a man I'd rather be ugly the way he's ugly than handsome the way Rod Schneider was before you ruined his looks for him, if you get what I mean."

"Yes," Beau Dan said sorrowfully. "I was a pretty young'un, myself. It's—rough. Older wimmen—and—hell, degenerates—always after you. Better to be ugly, man-sized. Fan, baby—tell you what: Take a chance. Let him pick you up. Maybe he don't *know* what you do fer a livin'. After all, you're so goddamn careful—"

Fanny stared at Beau Dan.

"You know," she said, "you could be right, Dan. The first time I noticed him I was on my way to—Mother Catherine's—to take some things to the kids . . ."

"Thought you was scared to go there anymore. That business of about yer old man, I mean—"

"I was. But I needn't have been. Mother Kate reads nothing but the catechism, the prayer books, and such-like—and the rest of the nuns are Creoles—which means apart from religious books they only read *L'Abeille*. And my father's—death—wasn't printed in *L'Abeille*, nor—"

"What you did afterwards," Beau Dan said. "Lord God, Fan baby, I niver in all me days heard tell of anybody who—"

"Let's not talk about it, Dan," she whispered. "But about this man, you're right. He's always started tailing me once I was well beyond the district. And I've always managed to shake him before going back—"

"Which mean he either ain't a detective at all, or a rank amateur," Beau Dan said. "Tell me another thing Fanny, me girl—does he look—rich?"

"I'd say—yes. Why yes, decidedly so. Why, Dan?"

"No, reason, yet. Do as I tell you, honey. Drop yer hankie o' something. Delicate like. And then—"

"Time's up!" The guard in charge of the visiting room said.

So when she came out of the prison, Fanny didn't take a cab. Instead she walked, tripping along on her high-buttoned shoes, the very picture of womanly grace.

Within five minutes she was aware that the tall man was following her again. She slowed her steps until he had almost caught up with her. Then abruptly, she whirled, faced him.

"You've been following me for days," she said evenly. "Would you mind telling me why? *Before* I call a policeman, I mean?"

"Lord God, miss," the tall man chuckled, "if following a pretty girl was a crime they'd have to build a mighty heap of new jails. Didn't mean to give offense. And if I have, I apologize. Don't be mad at a poor lonely old fellow, will you?"

In spite of herself, Fanny smiled a little.

"You—shouldn't be lonely," she said. "You're not the handsomest man I ever saw, but you aren't all that bad looking. Surely all the girls you've known mustn't have turned you down. There must have been at least one willing to say 'yes.' "

"Meaning have I got a missus?" the tall man said. "The answer to that is no, miss. I *had* one, yes. But the good Lord called her to her reward some time back."

"And you've remained faithful to her memory ever since?" Fanny said, mockingly.

"To tell th' honest truth, no. But the only other female I really cottoned to was married to another fellow. So—"

"So now you've taken to following girls in the streets?"

"No—not girls. One girl. You."

"Then we're back to my original question," Fanny said tartly *"Why?"*

"That there's a long story, miss—'Pears to me it could be better told sitting down, over a bite of something to eat. What would you say to Antoine's, for instance? It's plumb nigh supper time right now . . ."

Fanny considered that. She had never so much as seen the inside of Antoine's although she'd lived in New Orleans most of her life. During her childhood, her father simply hadn't made money enough to take his family to restaurants of that caliber; and, as a woman, her profession made her being invited to respectable places out of the question. No man was going to run the risk of taking a known prostitute into a restaurant where his wife's best friend, or, worse still, his mother-in-law, might be sitting at the very next table.

So out of simple curiosity, if no more, to Fanny a chance to dine in New Orleans's finest restaurant was not to be sneered at. That was one thing. Another was that there was something—well—intriguing, if not actually charming about this tall, thin, bald, ugly, middle-aged man.

"Very well," she said primly, "I accept—upon your promise to comport yourself as a gentleman should. But, first of all, I should like to know your name—"

"Th' handle's Prescott, miss. Oliver Prescott," the tall man said. "What's yours?"

Fanny hesitated. The name was familiar somehow. Then it came to her. Prescott was *her* name. The girl Philippe had married. That little freckled-faced bitch who— And this man *was* old enough to have a daughter Billie Jo's age, so—

"Tell me, Mr. Prescott, do you have any children?" she said.

"Nary a chick nor a child. Never was lucky, I reckon. Me'n the missus adopted a baby girl though. Niece of mine, in fact. My poor brother's baby. Him and his missus passed on during an epidemic. Yellow fever. Up our way we suffer an awful lot from that. Swamp country, y'know—"

"And—where is she now?" Fanny said.

"My niece? Married and moved away. Same parish though, so I see her and her hubby right frequently. But all the same I get mighty lonely rattling around in th' house all by myself. That's howcome I came down to N' Orleans in the first place . . ."

"To visit—our celebrated fleshpots?" Fanny said bitterly. "Storyville, for instance?"

He stared at her. Frowned.

"Lord no, miss," he said quietly. "I was kind of hoping I'd meet me a nice woman—not too young, late thirties or early forties, who'd—well—be willin' to comfort my declining years—"

"And yet," Fanny said, "You followed *me*. Do I look forty to you?"

"God Almighty, no! I'd give you nineteen or twenty, no more."

"You're wrong," Fanny said. "I'm twenty-three. But it seems to me, Mr. Prescott, that you really haven't explained what your intentions towards me are, or why you followed me in the first place."

He looked at her, and his eyes were sad.

"I haven't got any intentions towards you, miss," he said quietly. "A dinner, a little chat to fill up a little space in all this loneliness, that's all. And I followed you because I just couldn't help it. Curiosity at first—and then it was a sentimental old fool's hoping against hope that his first guess about you was wrong . . . Only it wasn't. I see that now."

"And what was your first guess about me?" Fanny said. To her own surprise a catch had got into her voice; the question came out in little spurts of breath. It sounded timid, shy, half-afraid—even a trifle flirtatious, which wasn't the way she'd meant it at all.

"Let's—skip that one, miss," Oliver Prescott said gravely. "Too nice an evening to spoil, don't you think? Now do me a favor, will you? Give me a name I can call you by. You've been avoiding telling me yours for the last ten minutes. If you've got a reason you don't want me to know it, I'll respect your wishes in the matter, like a gentleman ought to. But I can't go on calling you 'miss' all evening can I?"

"No, I suppose not," Fanny said. "And there's—no reason why you can't know my name. It's Frances. Frances Turner. But call me Fanny. All my friends do."

She stood there a moment, searching his eyes, waiting for them to change, to flare in recognition, in dismay at that name. Only they did not. They didn't, because it was the first time Oliver Prescott had heard it spoken in all his life. Billie Jo, on the day of his first encounter with Philippe in the hospital, had referred to Fanny as "Philippe's girl," not by name. And, upon their return to the plantation, the whole matter had been dropped by mutual, if silent, consent. Billie had been obviously suffering; just as obviously the subject of Philippe and his nearly tragic relations with "his girl," nameless still to Oliver Prescott, was extremely painful to her. And Oliver was a kindly, sensitive, and, best of all, a tactful man, who hadn't wanted to distress his niece. So, in those days, the question of who "Philippe's girl" was simply hadn't come up.

And afterwards, when Billie had come back from France, married to Philippe and glowing with visible happiness, Oliver had been quite content to let the old scandal—if it were even that—molder in its grave. He certainly had no intention of disturbing the newlyweds' charmingly harmonious existence by digging up a matter best forgot . . .

On the other hand, he *had* read the stories in the *Picayune* about Detective Sergeant William Turner's death, and his daughter's bizarre and insanely cruel suicide attempt thereafter. But he read the *Picayune* daily, and it, like most of the papers of the epoch, served up such lurid bits to its readers in every edition. During the same week that Fanny had hired Joe the Whipper to beat her to death, one distraught maid had hurled herself from a third-story balcony to impale herself fatally upon an iron picket fence in the gardon below, and another had soaked her clothes and her bed with kerosene, laid down, and lit a match. So, having no associations for him—as it would have had, if he'd known it as Philippe's girl's—the name Fanny Turner had slid easily and quietly out of his memory. He remembered the story, of course, but only as 'Some detective fellow who dropped dead in a sporting house on finding his daughter was an inmate there. And afterwards the poor li'l bitch tried to beat herself to death—'

Fanny let her breath out, slowly. She thought:

'He doesn't know about me 'n Phil. She probably never even mentioned me to this old bald-headed turkey buzzard. Thank God! So now all I've got to do is play my cards right and—and I'll be out of Storyville, for good. Married to—this one. To this old fart who'll sleep like a top all night long every night—while I—pry Phil loose from her. Drag him away to—to New York, say. Or even Paris. Live the way I was meant to. Oh, Lord, let me do this one thing right . . .'

She smiled at Oliver Prescott, slowly.

"All right, Mr. Prescott, let's go have supper at Antoine's," she said.

Life punishes implacably only two sins: Weakness and Stupidity. What's more, it takes a peculiar delight in coming down like a collapsing brick wall upon those most foolish of all fools: The ones stupid enough to believe themselves clever.

Two more quotations, more or less apt:

"He was very suspicious and hence an easy dupe,"—Somerset Maugham.

"You can fool all of the people some of the time, and some of the people all of the time; but you can't fool all of the people all of the time."—A certain rail-splitter from Kentucky and/or Illinois.

To spell it out, generally speaking, trickery on the order that our little Fanny is planning now doesn't work, not because it is bad or immoral (it works even less when it is perfectly good, absolutely moral; you ever try keeping a surprise party a secret from its beneficiary, say?), but because the degree of talent, will, intelligence, necessary to make it work would preclude its even being attempted, since a person so endowed would realize from the outset how hopeless it is to try to control all the known factors involved, much less the unknown ones which will always pop up in absolute conformity to Murphy's Law:

"Anything that can go wrong will; and at the worst possible moment."

Such as, for instance, the moment that Fanny, her pale eyes misty, glowing (good champagne always had that effect upon her) leaned forward across that table in Antoine's and murmured:

"Come on, Oliver—be nice. Tell me—Why did you follow me? The *truth*, I mean."

He looked at her, and that rough-hewn, remarkable face of his that resembled, in some ways, that of the rail-splitter quoted above, and in others the black basaltic head of Julius Caesar in the British Museum was sadder than ever.

"Don't insist, Fanny," he said. "I'd rather not."

"But I do insist!" she pouted. "You're an awful old meanie, Oliver! I—I thought you liked me."

"I do like you, Fanny," he said gently. "Too much. Far, far too much."

"Then tell me!" she said.

"All right. On your own head be it, child. I followed you because two weeks ago, a nigger woman on my place brought me a picture of you. Her son found it, wrapped very carefully in oilskin, and hanging from a cord let down almost to the waterline of a well in the east section of my place. A well we don't use anymore 'cause the water in it has gone bad. Worth a man's life to drink it. As whoever it was who hid it there had to know—"

Fanny sat there, seeing the Gorgon's head—again.

"She'd taken half a yard of black hide off that fool kid's hide. Because the picture—your picture—had had a certain effect upon the little nigger. Caused him to indulge in a practice that's reputed to drive men crazy. Though if it does"—Oliver loosed a dry little chuckle—"there's no such thing as a sane man—"

'Nor a sane woman either,' Fanny thought. But she didn't say that. She didn't say anything. She waited, help-lessly.

"So I came down to New Orleans—to meet a nice widow woman some friends of mine had sworn was just the girl for me; it's hell to find out just what your friends think of you, child, at least judging from the perfect frights they throw at your head—and happened to see you pass by Tom Anderson's Stag on Gravier—where I was drowning my sorrows."

'Oh Jesus!' Fanny wailed insider her mind. 'That tears it!"

"And," she said, somberly, "you asked them who I was and they—"

"No. As a matter of fact, I didn't. I simply got up, threw some money onto the bar to pay for my drinks, and followed you. I reckon I was hoping you weren't the girl in that picture . . ."

Fanny held him with those eyes of hers, whispered:

"Why, Oliver?"

"Because you have the face—of an angel, child. I hon-estly think you're the single most beautiful woman I've seen in all my life. And your beauty is—so classical. So serene. So—pure . . ."

Fanny bowed her head. Stared at the table. A long time. A very long time. Then she looked up, faced him. In the flickering light of the candles on their table, her tears made a double parade of fireflies down her cheeks.

"Oh, I am sorry!" Oliver said. "I didn't mean—"

"You didn't mean anything," Fanny said. "Reckon it was that word 'pure' that got to me. Because I was once.

So long ago I can't even remember how it was, Oliver. And for your information: Yes, I'm a whore. A high-class one, maybe, but still—a whore."

Oliver Prescott stared at her; said, quietly:

"And you—*hate* it; don't you child?"

Fanny sat there looking at him, and letting the great tears slide unchecked over the—to him at least—absolutely exquisite contours of her face. Told him unthinkingly and without calculation the most nearly perfect lie possible: the lie whose stunning force derives from the fact that every single word of it is true, achieving falsity only by reason of their being taken out of context.

"I've tried to—to kill myself three times, now, Oliver. The first two times cost me three whole years in a hospital—and two operations. You couldn't see the scars—in that picture of me, 'cause he, Papa Bellocq, touched 'em out of the negative. And the last one put me back in New Orleans General for three months. But the next one—will put me in my grave; you can be goddamned sure of that."

Oliver put out his big, brown, work-hardened hands and caught hers between them. He could feel them wildly trembling, like small white captive birds.

"There'll be no next time, Fanny," he said. "You must promise me that."

"No!" she stormed at him, "I won't promise! Tonight when I go home, I—I'm going to use a gun! And it'll be all your fault, Oliver! Yours, damn you, yours!"

He kept her hands imprisoned between his own; said, gently:

"Why mine, child?"

" 'Cause," Fanny sobbed, "I *knew* you were following me, right from the first! And—and I let you—'cause I thought—I thought—"

"What, Fanny?" Oliver said.

"That you—could be—my way—out. Out of Storyville —which is just another way of saying out of hell. You— you've got such a *good* face, Oliver. So—so kind. I thought I could keep you from finding out—what I was. Trick you into falling in love with me—even marrying me—and taking me out of this life. And you wouldn't have been sorry either! God knows I'd worship on my knees any man who'd—save me, lift me up, take me—"

"But what if the man in question doesn't want to be

worshiped, Fanny? What if he insists—sentimental old fool that he is—upon being—loved?"

Fanny looked at him, said:

"You think—that that—wouldn't come, Oliver? All by itself, I mean? If you're half as good, as kind, as you seem to be—learning to love you would be a mighty easy chore, I think. And—if you're half the man you look to be, it would be an awful pleasant one as well—"

Oliver Prescott sat there.

"Lord, Fanny: what am I supposed to say to *that?*" he said.

"Nothing," she whispered. "Just—just tell me one thing, Oliver: Do you *know* how that picture of me got to be on your place? Whom it was intended for, I mean?"

"Not for that horny little nigger, that's for sure!" he chuckled: "Tell me, Fanny, whom *was* it intended for?"

"You—don't *know?*" Fanny said. "You really don't, Oliver?"

"Of course not," he snorted. "How could I, child?"

She examined his face, his eyes; saw he was telling the truth; said slowly, softly:

"Oliver—let me keep that secret, will you? It may be the last one I'll ever keep—surely from *you* and maybe from anybody. I'll say this much though—it wasn't intended to be on *your* place. I—I don't even know how it got there."

"All right, child," he said; then: "Blues gone? You're over all those wild impulses, aren't you?"

She shook her head.

"No, Oliver. I—I'm going to kill myself. Maybe not tonight. But—sometime soon. When I'm—alone—and there's no one there to take my two hands between his big rough ones and—and comfort me, sort of. One night—no, one morning—when I look in the mirror and see my face tired, gray colored, kind of, my eyes sunken in with blue circles all around 'em, my mouth all mashed up and bruised, blue splotches on my shoulders, my arms, my thighs—my—my tits—hurting where some real gentlemanly type has bit 'em—smelling their randy billy-goat stink all over me, and trying to wash to scrub to get clean—and knowing and knowing—"

Her voice died on her. Drowned.

"Child," he said, "please!"

"Knowing I can never get clean 'cause the—the stink—the filth is on my very soul. Looking at my face in the mirror and wanting to heave, and saying over and over again: 'You whore, you nasty stinking dirty whore. Buzzard's pyke. Polecat's vomit. You chamber pot for them to spew their filth into. You cunt. You—' "

"Stop it!" he said then sharply. "You stop it, Fanny!"

She bowed her head. Looked up at him. Said with a kind of achingly pitiful idiot's cunning:

"Oliver—do me a favor, will you? Come home with me—spend the night. On no! Not—to—to the place I—I work at—but to a little place I've got of my own. You— you don't have to—to make love to me—though to tell the truth, I wish you would. That's up to you. And, any-how, the occasion's free of charge, my friend! But *be* there, anyhow. Don't leave me alone tonight, Oliver. I'm asking you that. No, I'm begging you. Please."

He looked at her, made, being who and what he was, the only decision possible for him to make, that choice wry, out-of-joint, maniacally, absurdly, fatally wrong:

"All right, Fanny, let's go," he said.

And, taking her arm, took, at the same time, his first step down that well-known road, paved with the notori-ously slippery building materials that the wise old saw (or dreary old cliché if you will) attribute to it, towards that justly celebrated tropical resort reserved exclusively for fools. Even kindly, bald-headed, middle-aged fools.

A pity, isn't it? But then, what isn't in this, to quote Voltaire's *Candide,* very best of all possible (miserable, fucked-up) worlds?

## Chapter Thirty-One

Beau Dan stared at her through the thick wire netting that separated the prisoners from their visitors. Then a wide grin split his face.

"Say that agin, baby!" he said.

"It's—it's true, I tell you, Dan," Fanny whispered.

"He—that old man—wants to marry me. To take me out of this life. And—I'm going to be honest with you, lover; I'm—tempted. He owns one of the biggest plantations in the state. And—"

But she couldn't say the rest of it. 'And he's—so *nice*. So goddamned gentle. Kind. Got a sense of humor, too. And—Lord God! Who would have thought it? Who ever would have thought that he—that he—'

Her mind groped for the words, for the images. It was not that she lacked either words or images to describe the coupling of two naked opposite—or rather complementary—gendered bodies upon a narrow bed. Rather it was that the words and the images she ordinarily would have used had suddenly become plain damned wrong. Because they didn't describe what had happened between her and Oliver Prescott. Not at all. They simply didn't apply. To use them was to be talking about something else. What went on every night, say, in Storyville; not what she had done with Oliver. That was another thing altogether. That existed in another kind of world, only obliquely tangential to the one she habitually lived in.

The closest she could get to the reality of that night was to think: 'Like—Philippe. Only—better. Much, much better. Like maybe Phil will get to be when he's that old and has had that much practice. But—Oh Jesus! that was wrong. I—I *cheated* on Phil. I really did. Three years in a whorehouse—and thirty thousand men—since that Christmas—and I—I gave myself. All of me. Let go. Joined in. Got there—how many times? Don't know. Too many to count, one right after another after another after another like a string of firecrackers. Oh, Lord, I—'

"Do it, baby!" Beau Dan laughed. "Don't you go 'n miss a chance like this! Set us up on easy street for the rest of our natural lives!"

Fanny stared at him, uncomprehending.

"Set *us* up on—" she began.

"Easy street. Yep. Listen to Danny the Wizard, will you, now? Sure and a chance of a lifetime like this don't come every day, me girl! Marry the old sod. And in two years' time, when I get out o' the cooler, I puts in me appearance, big as life 'n twice as handsome—waving a wedding certificate, with a prior date on it, me doll, under the old fool's nose. Respectable gentleman farmer like him will cough up more than somewhat of the coin o' the realm to stave off a public scandal, or I miss my guess! You see that don'cha, love o' my life?"

'No,' Fanny thought, 'you're wrong. A man like Oliver would ram your fake license down your filthy throat, and kick your worthless ass so hard he'd break your back teeth out. Still—I'm afraid. I'm scared of him—of Oliver—I'm afraid to get—hooked on him—like Jane is hooked on cocaine. Lord Jesus! A man who can turn your whole body into—a guitar, and—and play that kind of *music* on it—Lord God!'

She said:

"Where would you get your prior-dated wedding license, Dan?"

"Simple," he said. "We fix it up with the prison chaplain. For—next week, say. Get hitched, for real. How does that strike you, Fanny, me girl?"

"No," Fanny said. "It doesn't strike me, Dan. I like you a lot. I'm even fond of you the way a mother is of a backward child. But I don't want you to have any hold on me. Not legally, anyhow. Nor him, either. Nor—anybody. But still to get out of Storyville—out of this life—I'd—"

"Wait!" Beau Dan said. "You know Madge Dennison—over at Frankie Belmont's place?"

"Yes," Fanny said. "Why?"

"She's me missus. In the *church*, Fan. Didn't work out—so we separated. But we're both of the mother church, me girl. So—we can't divorce. Which means that when you and me call in the prison padre and jump over the broomstick together, that pretty certificate, ribbons, seals, and all won't be worth the paper it's printed on. But 'twill be enough 'n to spare to pry you loose from Old Money-Bags—bringing said bags along, to be sure!"

'And,' Fanny thought grimly, 'enough for me to put your good for nothing carcass back into the cooler on a bigamy charge the minute you start believing that you own me—as you just might—if I let you push me into this—'

She said:

"I'll have to think about it, Dan—"

"All right," he said. "Think about it, 'til next visiting

day. But, by all the saints, Fanny, don't you go 'n ruin a chance like this!"

Going back to the flat she had taken over from Dan since he'd been jailed, Fanny tried to reason things out. But she couldn't, really. Precise reasoning calls for an un-flawed mind, an undamaged nervous system, and—well, a certain emotional security, say—none of which poor Fanny had by then. Which meant that what she called reasoning went like this:

'I hate him. He's old and ugly and he fucks too good. He'd make—a slave of me. I wouldn't be able to get away from him to leave him, not even for Phil. Oh, Jesus! I—I love the old bastard. I do. I almost do. I must, or else how could I have—I used to sit there and sneer at all those miserable cruds who come to Mama's and pay good money for a girl to help them fool themselves into believ-ing that they're men. Every night I'd tell myself if only a *man* would walk in the door just once. Take me upstairs and wreck the bed with me. Make me scream the roof off, and—'

She stopped still, her pale eyes flaring with sudden won-der.

'He doesn't. Make me scream, I mean. Or pound me and the bed to pieces. Still he's—powerful. Like the ocean. Rolling on and on—but gentle and—and he *knows* too goddamned much! About—how women work. About how *I* do, anyhow. Hours 'n hours of—touching—lazy-like, as if he wasn't really interested, wasn't even trying. And kissin''—Jesus, who *ever* taught him all that? And then—and then he makes me *wait*. He knows when I'm almost there—and slackens off—and starts up again—and slackens off 'til I'm almost out of my mind—until I have to ask him, beg him—and even then he won't—until he's sure that when it happens—when I come—it's damned near going to kill me—'cause feeling that good is the scariest, hurtingest, most godawful great fine wonderful beautiful—thing—in the world—'

She started walking again, towards the flat. Faster. Fast-er. Until she was running, praying, sobbing:

'Let him be there. Oh please God let him be there. I know this is wrong I shouldn't I can't I won't but sweet baby Jesus let him be—there—'

He was. Sitting there in Dan's mangy, scuffed leather chair, and smoking a cigar. A glass of bourbon sat on the little table by his side. He smiled at her, said:

"Well, Fanny, have you decided?"

She leaned back against the door, fighting for breath. Slowly she shook her head, whispered:

"Can't—can't do this to you, Oliver—You—you're too good. Can't—ruin your life—You—deserve—a good, decent woman—who'll—"

He put the cigar down.

"That," he said gently, "is precisely what I mean to make of you—"

Her pale eyes went mist-silver, opaque, then they blazed.

"You fool!" she said, her voice hoarse, a shudder. "I'm a *whore*, remember? A born whore, Oliver. I've been one all my life. Nobody can make me decent. I'd cheat on you the morning after our wedding night. With the postman, the iceman, your hired hands—"

"My hired hands," he chuckled, "are niggers—"

"Ha!" she said, "think I wouldn't change my luck with some big black buck if I got a chance to?"

"No," he said, his voice still cool, amused; "I *know* you wouldn't, Fanny. You've neither the—imagination, nor the guts to do a thing like that. Besides, I flatter myself by thinking that I'd never leave you with either the breath or the inclination—"

"You—old bastard!" she screamed at him. "You old ugly bald-headed bastard! You ought to be in the old folks' home instead of running around trying to fuck every young gal you see! I hate you! I hate everything about you! I wouldn't marry you if you were the last man on earth! I'd *rather* be a whore than your wife, don't you understand that? I'd rather be a Burgundy Street crib girl charging twenty-five cents a tumble! I'd rather be a fifteen-cent sidewalk slut before—"

He stood up very slowly. Crossed to where she stood. Bent and kissed her open, still-screaming mouth. Went on kissing it until her slim white hands came up, and moved through the thick, iron-gray hair he had at the temples, on the back of his neck, everywhere, in fact, except on the glistening bald crown of his head. She came away from the door, fitted her body into his, curving into him, moving.

He drew back, smiled at her.

"Come on!" she husked, "do it to me, Oliver. Let me show you my professional style. Prove to you what a no-good randy bitch you want to marry. All the tricks. Forty-seven positions. Polish your knob for you if you like that. Sixty-nine. Get you so damn disgusted that—"

"I'll leave you? It's—a sight easier than that, child. All you have to do is to ask me to, meaning it. Tell me, Fanny; do you want me to go?"

"Yes!" she shrilled. "Get out of here! I hate you! I hate—"

He turned her loose. Picked up his hat. Smiled at her, a little sorrowfully.

"Good-bye, Fanny," he said.

She backed away from him until her hands, groping behind her found the doorknob. But she didn't twist it. She leaned back against the door, staring at him.

"Oh, Oliver!" she wailed, and started to cry.

He came up to her, caught her by the shoulders, very gently. Stared into her small, pitiful, tormented face.

"Why do you torture yourself this way, child?" he said.

"Because—because—I'm—no good," she sobbed. "I'm not even fit to live, Oliver. And—I—I'm *used* to being miserable. It's—what I deserve. No. It's less than I deserve. I deserved to be killed—by inches—to be beaten to death and—"

"You tried that once, didn't you?" he said gravely. "Judging from the scars on your back."

"Yes," she said, "only the fellow I paid to do it lost his nerve and—"

"Don't talk about it," he said. "That's over for you now, Fanny. All the sorrow, all the pain. You're starting from scratch, child. And with my help—and maybe God's—you'll make it—"

"Will I?" she said morosely. "I doubt it, Oliver. That's what makes what you're doing—so awful. Mean. Cruel."

"Cruel?" he said.

"Yes. You—show me—happiness. Like a Canal Street shopkeeper filling up his window with cakes and pies and candy and rolls and Christmas turkeys in front of a starv-

ing beggar kid who's standing there shivering in the rain
with his nose pressed up against the glass—"

"No," he said. "I'm opening that window, Fanny. Handing you those pies, cakes, turkeys. All you want. Everything your little heart desires . . ."

"You think I can eat 'em?" she whispered. "You think
my stomach isn't too shriveled up by now? You believe I
could *stand* being happy, Oliver? You think I wouldn't go
crazy—crazier than I am now, I mean—remembering all
the dirty, rotten low-down, filthy things I've done—and
sitting there by your side, a respectable married woman?
Knowing I ought to have been hanged by the neck 'til I
was dead dead dead a hell of a while ago?"

"You've done nothing," Oliver said firmly. "After all,
you were forced into this life and—"

"Oliver, Oliver!" she said, pityingly, *"nobody* was *ever*
forced into this life. Whores are *born.* Say—a decent
girl—was starving—or her baby was—and she tried *this,*
as a way out. She'd be dead of pure disgust in a week. Or
screaming her guts up in a lunatic asylum. And, most of
the time it's not even a lack of money. Most girls—
drift—into this, just 'cause that's the way they're made.
After they've lain down for every man in town free of
charge, for the hell of it, they wake up one morning and
realize they're done for in that town, so they have to
move on or make the only thing they know how to do—
sort of—pay. And the sad part about it is they aren't even
hot-natured, really. A hot-natured girl is—more careful.
She—sort of—well, respects her body—'cause it's always
reminding her it's there. That she's got dynamite between
her legs, all set to blow her life all to hell—"

"Fanny—" Oliver said.

"But the ones like me—who started layin' down 'n
spreading wide—'cause it seemed such an *easy* way to be
popular, Oliver; the ones it means nothing to because they
don't even warm up enough to feel anything, who can
equal a whole night's fuckin' with a pair of silk stock-
ings—"

"I wish you wouldn't use that word," he sighed.

"You want me to pretty it up? All right. I'll say sexual
intercourse. Better, huh? The ones who know they're
cheap goods from the outset, who learn to despise them-

selves from the time they're little girls, Oliver; they're the
ones who end up like me, an ice-cold no-good hussy
who—"

"You, Fanny," he said, "are anything but cold—"

"With *you*, I'm not. I reckon that's because I—I love
you, Oliver. Even when I'm screaming at you, and calling
you every dirty name in the books. In all my life I've only
met one another fellow—I wasn't cold with—and I was in
love with him, too. Only—only—he got sick of my rotten
temper, bad disposition, and immoral ways, and married
somebody else. He was smart. *You're* being a fool if you
keep this up—"

"I'll take the chance," he said. "Fact is, I've got to. You
leave me no alternative, Fanny. For instance, what would
you have done if I'd walked out of that door just now?"

"This!" she hissed at him. Her hands moving, blurred
sight. She flipped her skirt up to her waist and reached.
Her fingers closed on the switchblade, drew it from her
garter, touched the button, flipping the blade into place,
arched it upward in one smooth-linked blindingly fast
chain of motions; so that as swiftly as he lunged towards
her he was almost too late; the point of the knife had already entered the flesh of her throat, and his efforts to
tear the knife from her, successful as they were, widened
the penetration into a nasty gash that bled and bled and
bled.

When he had bandaged her throat with his big, square,
work-hardened hands, he sat there in the scuffed and
mangy chair, holding her in his arms like a child, like the
pitiful, lost, forlorn child that to him she was, and stroked
her bright hair.

"Fanny," he sighed, "what on earth am I going to do
with you?"

"Love me," she murmured. "Take care of me the way
you're doing now. Be good to me. Gentle. Make me
feel—wanted. Needed, even. And—and beat hell out of
me when I'm bad!"

"I reckon I'll have to, once in a while," he said. But
there was a hint of quiet, playful amusement in his voice.

"You will," she said seriously, "or else I'll make you
miserable, Oliver. I have, every single person who's ever
tried to be good to me, so far. I'm perverse. Oliver. Crazy.
Mixed-up. Twisted—"

"Stop it, Fanny!" he said; them: "All right, when do we make this—legal?"

She looked away from him, and that look of idiot's cunning, insane craft, was back in her eyes.

"Week—after next—if you still want to by then, Oliver," she said.


## Chapter Thirty-Two


On the train up from New Orleans, Oliver Prescott had time to spare for thinking about the thing he'd done, the step now irrevocably taken. He had read somewhere that the very purpose of the great English public school (why the hell did the English persist in labelling "public" schools that were about as private as any institution ever is in this world?) was to train a boy to have his second thoughts first.

'Doesn't apply in this case,' he thought. 'About Fanny I was never deluded, so all my first thoughts were second ones in that sense. The minute I saw that picture, my immediate reaction was: Lord God, what a pretty little whore! Obvious. No decent woman would have lain there like that mother-naked and stared into the lens of a camera a man was pointing at her. Wonder if that photographer was—one of her lovers? And if that picture was taken before—or after—as it were?

'Careful, Oliver!' he told himself sternly. 'Get off that track. That way lies—misery. You've married a public woman. Tormenting yourself about her past is more than futile; it's idiotic. It's the future you've got to take care of—if you can. With dignity. With grace. Or more accurately with what dignity and what grace you can manage to apply to all the perfectly hellish situations that can, and damned likely will, arise—"

He turned to his bride, his breath catching in his throat, as always, at the sight of that cameo of a profile outlined against the train window's sooty glass.

"Fanny," he said casually, "did you ever know a couple of fellows named Forsythe Bevers and Stanton Bruder?"

She turned to him, very slowly; and her pale, almost

colorless eyes were filled with light so that the line "Two of the fairest stars in all the heaven, having some business, do entreat her eyes—" crashed into his mind.

"No, Oliver, I never did," she said. "Why?"

"No reason," he said, a little gruffly.

She went on staring at him; then very slowly her dusty straw-colored lashes beaded brilliantly with hurt, dripped brine-salt, white-fired anguish down her face.

"Fanny!" he said.

"It's—no good, Oliver," she whispered. "Don't you see it's no good? We've been married all of two days and already you—you're starting in to—to torment me—and yourself—about my past . . ."

"Wasn't your past I was thinking about, child," he said gravely, "but your future—our future. Those two names I mentioned are this parish's version of dead-game sports. They both make frequent trips down to New Orleans, even live there part of the year. So I thought—"

"That they may have been clients of mine," she said bitterly. "And if they were, any chance of—our being able to—to live in peace up here—in this beautiful, beautiful country—is already shot to hell. That's what you meant, wasn't it, Oliver?"

"Yes," he said, "that's what I meant."

"I—don't know, Oliver," she said. "I honestly don't know. I'd have to see their faces. Gentlemen don't present their visiting cards, or a letter of introduction to—a whore."

"It's all right, child," he said gently.

"No, it's not all right, and you know it," Fanny said. "I can only tell if—they've been customers at Mam—at Mrs. Hartman's—when I see them. And by then, it would be too late, Oliver—far too late—"

He smiled at her, cheerfully.

"This is a mighty big country, child," he said.

"Oh, Oliver!" she wailed: "You mean you—you'd give up your plantation, move away from here—because of *me?*"

"I'd buy another one," he said. "Growing oranges out California way always did strike me as a mighty fine way to live—"

She pushed her slim hand through the crook of his elbow, leaned her fair head against his shoulder. He could smell her. She smelled of fine, expensive bath soap, of rice powder, of the faintest, most delicate perfume anyone could possibly imagine.

'Lord God!' he thought, 'how did she *ever* get into that life? She's the direct antithesis of what a body'd expect to find—hell, what one *does* find—in a sporting house. She is tiny, fragile. Exquisite. And most of the time, except when one of those black moods hits her, she talks like a New England schoolmarm. Didn't need to buy her new clothes. Her taste is just about perfect. Didn't own one loud, gaudy—all right Oliver, say it—whorish lookin' dress—'

"Oliver," she murmured, "I—I love you. You believe that, don't you?"

"Yes, child," he said. "The real question is, Do *you* believe it?"

She lifed her face from his shoulder, looked at him.

"I know it," she said gravely. "Back then when you started following me—no, it wasn't then. It was after you told me your name, I was—planning to use you. To—to get away. Even to—to get to see—the fellow I sent that picture to. I thought that if I could see him again, I could persuade him to leave his wife. Run off with me—"

"Which meant," Oliver said, the pain in his voice almost unnoticable but very deep, "that you were planning to leave *me,* as soon as you possibly could."

"Yes," Fanny said. "I *was* planning that, Oliver. But now I'm not. I stopped planning it—on our wedding night."

He looked at her.

"Mind telling me why, Fanny?" he said.

" 'Cause—'cause—Oh, Oliver! You were so—so good to me! So gentle. So tender. You—treated me just as if I'd been—a *good* girl. One who'd *never* had a man before. All evening you treated me that way. Until I—I started to *feel* like one. All—timid—and fluttery and—and shy—and afraid, too! Just like a *decent* girl would be on her wedding night. And—afterwards—it was—so beautiful, Oliver! You—you made love to me—as though you—you were *worshiping* me! My body, anyhow—"

"And your soul," Oliver said gravely, "your lovely, little, curiously undamaged soul. In spite of everything, Fanny."

She looked at him, and shook her head.

"There, you're wrong, Oliver," she said. "It *is* damaged. Maybe even beyond repair. Oliver! When we get there—to Mertontown, don't let's get off! Let's keep right on going. To—to some place else. Where nobody knows me. Where maybe we'd have a chance . . ."

He took her small, exquisite face between his two hands, held it imprisoned, gently, tenderly, firmly.

"You're saying that there *is* someone up here who knows you, child?"

"Yes," she whispered, brokenly. "Him. That fellow. The one I sent my picture to. Oliver—I want you to—to listen to me. I'm going to tell you about him—about how it was I got into—into the bad life. 'Cause it was his fault—a little. A very little. Most of it—nearly all of it—was mine—"

Then she told him. Simply. Truthfully. All of it. Except that she never once said Philippe's name, or mentioned any particular detail—such as, for instance, that her lover had gone abroad to study medicine—that would have enabled her new husband to guess it.

'She's telling the truth,' Oliver thought. 'Why is the ring of it so—unmistakable?'

"Only I—I fell down," Fanny finished quietly. "Had a miscarriage. And—and stayed on at Mrs. Hartman's place, anyhow. I should have cut my throat, first!"

"There's a lot of truth in that old saw that while there's life, there's hope, Fanny," he said. "About this fellow now, want to tell me *who* he is?"

She shook her head. The gesture was freighted with misery.

"No," she whispered. "Not yet, anyhow, Oliver. Not ever, if I don't have to. He—he's a gentleman. I'm certain—sure he won't open his mouth . . ."

" 'Pears to me he can hardly afford to," Oliver said grimly.

"He can afford to," Fanny said. "If you don't see that, I've wasted my time telling you all this, Oliver! None of it was his fault. None at all. I reckon he was scared to tell me he was—going away—that he *had* to, really—'cause he knew what an awful disposition I have—and didn't want me to start screaming and cursing and maybe throwing things and—"

"I see," Oliver said. "Listen to me, Fanny. Everybody makes mistakes in this world. The trick is not to compound them. And from the little you've told me of your life, it seems to me that that's precisely where you've always fallen down. And that's where I mean to take over: to see whatever mistakes you make from here on in—and you will make some, child, being human—will stay just that, mistakes, nothing worse. I won't let you compound 'em into tragedies . . ."

"I told you that was all you had to do: Love me—and take care of me," Fanny said.

And then they were there, at Mertontown, anyhow; and Fanny saw to her relief, that nobody had come to meet them at the station. She'd been half afraid that Oliver had notified Billie Jo, sent a wire to his niece, which, after all, would have been a perfectly natural thing for him to have done. Then it came to her that her husband had had time and to spare to *write* Billie Jo; and that, if he had, he almost surely had mentioned her, Fanny's, name. If so, the fact that Billie Jo and Philippe hadn't come to meet them at the station, instead of being a reason for feeling relieved, was its exact opposite: a sign, a portent of impending disaster.

She turned, looked at Oliver, said:

"Didn't you—didn't you—let your niece—know we were coming, Oliver?"

"Yes," he said calmly. "Only I asked them not to meet us, Fanny. Too blamed much trouble. They live pretty far out. On the other side of Caneville-Sainte Marie, in fact, so didn't seem right to make 'em drive twelve or fourteen miles, seeing as how they're always hacks for hire in front of the station . . ."

"And—and did you—tell her—what my name was? My maiden name, I mean?" Fanny whispered.

"Come to think of it, don't think I did," Oliver said. "Matter of fact, I'm pretty sure I didn't. Just wrote I'd married the prettiest little girl in the whole wide world— and the sweetest—though that last part ain't always true, is it?"

"It—it'll get to be, Oliver," Fanny said. "Just—have patience with me, will you?"

Then when they were in the hack, rolling through the

green fields under the silvery streamers of Spanish moss hanging from the live oaks, pass the bulbous trunks of gray cypress standing in the fetid swamp water, she said another thing, whispering it so that the driver wouldn't hear:

"Oliver—you—you want children, don't you?"

"Well, child, I could be past the age to manage it—but yes, as a matter of fact, I do. Do you, Fanny?"

She clung to his lean, muscular arm with both her slim, white ones.

"If I could, I'd make him stop this surrey right now— and go over behind those bushes with you, lover! Oh Oliver, Oliver give me a baby, will you? Tonight even? Will you please?"

He laughed then, but his eyes were misty suddenly. Never before had he heard such naked longing in a human voice.

'All she needs,' he thought. 'All she ever needed, right from the first. Manage that, you horny old bald-headed turkey buzzard, and this will *work,* damned if it won't!'

" 'Pears to me that that's up to the Good Lord in a way, Fanny," he said, "but you can rest assured I'll give the matter one whale of a try!"

They were swinging around the last curve before his house, and he was thinking, 'Nobody ever told me that pity—compassion—was a mortal sin. But maybe it is. On life's terms, anyhow. This lovely, forlorn child—unmans me with pity, weakens me with compassion, plays ivy to my oak—and could destroy me. Because more than one damned fine swimmer has been dragged down by the frantic struggles of the drowning bather he dived in to save. Will I—a noble thought engendered by an erect male organ and a pair of aching balls!—be able to save Fanny as I mean to, want to? Or won't she involve me in her private doom? The hell that somebody seems to have built into her psyche since babyhood? What I did—marrying her—was by every moral concept I've ever heard of— good. But was it? Won't my so-called kindness turn out to be suicidal in one sense, and ultimately destructive to the object of its attentions in another? Besides, whoever proved that being good has any real connection with what goes on in life?'

He gave a little snort of almost silent laughter.

'Put it another way, Oliver! Who is to be more pitied: the blind love and/or lust besotted fool? Or the intelligent, ironic, self confessed and knowing fool—who takes the high road to hell by deliberate choice, and with his eyes wide open? So go to it old goat-boy, pan-piper, grizzled satyr! There's a new melodrama on the boards, with you as the male protagonist: *The Fallen Woman Redeemed by Love*. And the argument is this: If you can make this slender middle (thy belly is like unto a stack of wheat!) swell before a year is out, you've got a chance. A slim chance, but still—a chance. If not—'

Then he stopped thinking altogether, and sat there, peering at the rows of buggies, surreys, victorias, buckboards, even wagons, drawn up before his house. There were more than two dozen of them, and he could have named the names of every one of their owners by his quick and certain recognition of the horses and in some rare cases, mules, hitched to them. He sat there, sweating, a fact that the warmth of that early September day had nothing to do with at all. Then he felt Fanny's hand on his arm.

"Oliver—" she whispered, her voice taut and vibrant with pure, naked terror. "That's—your house, isn't it? And all those people—?"

"Are my friends," he said, keeping his voice steady with immense effort, "come to welcome us home, Fanny—"

"Oh, Oliver!" she wailed, "I'm so scared! Oliver, please! Tell him to turn around before they see us! I—I can't face 'em! I can't, Oliver! I'll be sick! I'll—throw up! I'll—"

"You'll walk through that gate on my arm, with your head high, Fanny. A lady. A great lady—and my wife," he said gravely.

She turned to him and her eyes were luminous suddenly.

"You—meant that, didn't you?" she said in an odd, grave, little-girl's tone of voice.

"I meant it," he said.

"Oliver—kiss me?" she whispered. "Oh please, Oliver, please!"

He bent to her, touched her lips. But she clung her mouth to his in a long, long, shuddering blind scald of al-

most feral passion, that went on and on and on until it
died down, slackened, softened. Her mouth came away
from his. He could feel her warm, soft, childishly sweet
breath stirring against his face. Her eyes were still closed.
Then they came open and vindicated one of the hoariest
of literary clichés: they had stars in them. 'The morning
and the evening star singing together, chanting hosannas
unto God,' he thought.

"*Now* I can do it!" she said, "Now I can, Oliver!
'Cause I am now, aren't I? A lady, I mean. And your
wife. Come on, my dearest darlin' husband! Let's go!"

She came up the path to the house on his arm. But before they were halfway there, people came storming out
of it and surrounded them.

Fanny heard the names that Oliver said, presenting
them: Douglas Henderson, his fiancée Grace Harvey from
New Orleans, a couple so young that she realized at once
they had to be Billie Jo's and Philippe's friends, not Oliver's; Father Gaulois, the Catholic priest. Father Rayn,
the Episcopal minister; Dr. Hans Volker; Nurse Jenny
Greenway, a pretty, bespectacled young woman with a
face almost as freckled as Billie Jo's; old Winthrop Bevers
of the Bevers Knitting Mills, and Mildred, his wife; Jan
and Hilda Muller, local storekeepers and amateur musicians; Marvin Roberts, the photographer; Editor Tyler
Blakewell of the Caneville *Clarion*—and more, many
more, but she couldn't keep even the first names in mind,
because she was too busy searching among the people who
had them penned in, surrounded—all of them laughing
and talking at once, saying things like, "Oliver, you old
cradle robber, you! Lord God, look at her! Saint Peter
went to sleep and left the pearly gates open, so help me!
I've seen some pretty wimmen in my time but this li'l girl
beats 'em all!" and young Doug Henderson roaring,
"Somebody catch a hold onto Oliver! And one of you
ladies sit on Grace! 'Cause I'm agonna kiss me the bride
or bust a gallus tryin'!"—for Billie Jo's face, for
Philippe's.

But she didn't see them, then, because all the men
present, including not only two late arrivals who came up
the path behind them—and whose names, Oliver told her,
were Nelson Vance and Leonard Colfax, neither names or

faces registering in her consciousness at the time, surely
one of heaven's occasional mercies—but also both men of
the cloth as well, a fact that shocked her a little, availed
themselves of the privilege of kissing her, while all the
women wished her happiness and most of them also
hugged and kissed her and treated her with such friendli-
ness that she started to cry—thereby winning over even
the few envious and suspicious females to whom her great
beauty had seemed at least a threat if not a mortal offense, causing them to surge forward, clucking like hens:

"The poor baby! You've upset her, carrying on so! A
pretty timid child like this and all you horny old rapscal-
lions kissin' and mussin' her up! Come on, child—we'll
take you inside—need to lie down, don't you?"

"Y-y-yes," Fanny stuttered, "I—do—I reckon. I'm—
awful tired—and you—you've all been so—so *good* to
me, I couldn't help cryin'. I'm sorry—I—"

"Don't be, childt," Hilda Muller laughed. "Just come
with us. Get you away from the mens, billy goats and
monkeys, they be—all. Even mein Jan! Ha! First time he's
got a chance to kiss a pretty girl in twenty years!"

Then with women on both sides and behind her, she
started, or rather was half-carried, up the stairs onto the
gallerie, only to stop dead.

Because Billie Jo stood there, staring at her, with pure
and undisguised horror in her dark eyes, while behind her,
Philippe stood, or rather swayed, looking for all the
world as though he were going to reverse the traditional
rôles of the sexes at any moment now, and collapse before
them all in a dead faint.

Then Fanny, having no time for thinking, in that situation where thinking would have been useless or dangerous
or worse, anyhow, did by pure instinct, perhaps, what she
had to, and hence the absolutely right thing to do: She
took a quick step forward, grabbed Billie Jo's hand,
leaned forward and kissed her face, and hissed into her
ear, desperately:

"Please. Please, Billie Jo, please. Give me a chance.
You've got to. You must. 'Cause if you don't, I'll be dead
this time tomorrow afternoon. I swear that on poor Papa's
grave. It's—my life I'm begging you for, you hear me!
Please, Billie Jo. Please."

Billie Jo shrank away from Fanny's touch, her kiss, opened her mouth to say—

What? Who knows! Who in this world of sin and sorrow will ever know? For by then she had seen how Fanny was crying, witnessed that silent, bitter, cataclysmic, utterly bottomless grief, suffering, pain, that face of Niobe witnessing the tortured dying of her eldest child, that poor, pitiful, fragile creature men called Hope, and it—whatever she, Billie Jo Sompayac, had intended to say—vanished out of time and mind leaving only pity in her like a blade—the suicidal blade it was to all those who felt that particular emotion, peculiarly mistaken and misplaced when applied to such damned souls as Fanny Turner was by then, to that very nearly perfect replica of one of the Erinnyes clothed in slender flesh, to that implacable carrier of the germs of disaster, destruction, even death. But Billie Jo did not, could not, know that then, so she said quietly:

"Welcome home, Fanny," hearing behind her the rasp of Philippe's breath as he let it out on the halted, dead-stopped, utterly silent air.

But it, all of it, the scene, the interaction, the charged, blue-smoked, whining, spark-shot tension between the two of them, had gone far too long for even the dullest woman alive not to have noticed it. Seeing their faces, their eyes avid, their mouths slackened and salivating with the lust after scandal which is the most truly sexual, most nearly orgastic emotion that the majority of women ever know, Billie Jo rose to the occasion, to nobility even, said, with a rueful, controlled, beautifully staged laugh:

"All right, ladies—I'll 'fess up! Fanny and I are—old friends. At least I *hope* we can be friends now. She was—engaged to this long tall stupe who's trying to kick a hole in the gallerie with his heels, crawl into it, and pull the planking over him. And I—well, to tell the honest truth—I *stole* him from her. Ancient history, now. Besides, reckon I did her a favor: I left her free to marry a far better man!"

"That," Fanny whispered, an edge of bitterness vibrant in her voice, "is the ugly truth, if I ever heard it!" Then she put out her hand to him, murmured: " 'Lo, Philippe—" making of his name an incantation, a little prayer.

He took her hand, swayed then gray-faced, speechless, silent, stunned, and the tension was back again. But Billie Jo again saved the day, going beyond nobility, this time, achieving a sort of magnificence. She said:

"Oh for heaven's sake, Philippe, kiss her! I don't mind—"

So he did. It was the briefest, clumsiest, poorest excuse for a kiss that any woman present had even seen; and, as such, it broke the tension, for all of them began to laugh and tease him:

"Oh, boy, Doctor Phil—you're gonna have to give up all your patients out this way! A body wouldn't dare call on you, knowing that your missus will be waitin' up with the rolling pin when you get back!"

"Lordy! He drives in this direction—and Oliver'll shoot him! Oliver misses and Billie Jo'll crown him! Poor ol' fellow! You're really twixt 'n between the Devil and the deep blue sea, now, son!"

But Billie Jo had taken Fanny's arm.

"Come on, dear," she said, "I'll show you where everything is. Reckon you want to—to freshen up, even lie down a spell—before dinner, don't you?"

"Yes," Fanny whispered: "And—thank you, Billie Jo."

"Don't mention it, Fanny," Billie Jo said. "Now, come on."

But when they reached the bedroom, Billie Jo closed the door firmly, in the rest of the women's faces.

"Now, girls," she said, "the rest of this conversation's private, if you don't mind. I'd like to—to make my peace with Fanny—sincerely. And I can't, with an audience. I—I treated her rather badly, it appears to me now. So— if you please?"

Fanny stood there waiting, until they had gone away. Then she said:

"All right, Billie Jo, speak your piece."

"I—don't know what to say," Billie Jo whispered. "Philippe—told me that—that letter you wrote him—"

"The time I sent him that picture of me—naked," Fanny supplied.

"The time you sent him that picture of you—naked," Billie Jo said quietly, "was—true. That he—did that. Deserted you. Only he says he didn't—know—about—the child—"

"He didn't," Fanny said.

"All right," Billie Jo said. "That's—water under the bridge, now; isn't it? But—my Uncle Oliver is another matter, it seems to me. Did you *know* who he was when you married him? That he was *my* uncle, I mean?"

"Yes," Fanny said, "he told me."

"Oh," Billie Jo said. "Oh my God!"

"Wait, Billie Jo," Fanny said. "I didn't marry Oliver for any of the reasons you're thinking now. I asked him on the train coming up here to—to take me some place else. I didn't come to this parish to—to ruin your life, nor to steal Phil back from you. I married Oliver to get out of that life. I love my husband. I respect him. I mean to be a good wife—if you'll let me. If you—and the world—and maybe even the Good Lord—will give me a chance. Like I said—it's my life I'm pleading for, Billie. You break me and Oliver up—and you maybe even could—and this time tomorrow, I'll be dead and in my grave. I swear that on poor Papa's tombstone. And on the one me and Phil's poor little bastard hasn't even got."

Billie Jo stared at her.

"So," she whispered, "I'm supposed to have pity on you. And I do. Believe me, I do, Fanny! But I wonder if I have enough—to—to aid and abet you in fooling my poor old senile uncle—to let him go on living in a fool's paradise, believing he's married a decent girl. I wonder if there's that much pity in the whole world . . ."

Fanny bent her head. Looked up again.

"That there's a bell cord, isn't it?" she said. "And if you pull it, a colored woman will come up here, won't she?"

"Yes, Fanny," Billie Jo said. "Why?"

"Pull it. Send her to—to call Oliver. Tell him I—you—we—have got to talk to him. Then, when he comes up here, you tell him that. That he's married a whore. Go on, Billie! Pull it."

Billie Jo stood there. Something Philippe's father had said to her long ago—on the day she had met him in fact, stole into her mind: "All men resent the bearers of ill tidings, child . . ." She knew her uncle. She realized that he'd never be able to forgive her for wrecking his fool's paradise, destroying his illusionary world. At his age, a man had seen his dreams die one by one—of malnutrition, of inanition, of ugly, brutal reality's savage blows.

She couldn't do it. Fanny had her. This lovely, pale, silvery little witch had won.

"No," she said, "I won't. I can't. Fanny! What on earth!"

Because by then, Fanny had crossed to the bell cord and given it an almost savage tug.

"I won't!" Billie Jo said. "He'll be too—hurt, Fanny! And don't you go and tell him either! Because if you do—"

But then she heard Cindy's footsteps coming on. The black girl pushed open the door, said:

"Yes 'm, Miz Billie?"

But Billie Jo didn't say anything; she couldn't.

"What's your name, girl?" Fanny said.

"Cindy, ma'am," Cindy said.

"Cindy. Well, Cindy, go ask my husband—Mister Prescott—to step up here a minute. Tell him it's important. Tell him to please hurry. You understand?"

"Yes 'm," Cindy said, in a frightened tone of voice. Then she was gone, scurrying off down the hall.

"Fanny!" Billie Jo all but moaned.

"I asked you," Fanny said, "to—give me a chance. To save my life, Billie. And you wouldn't. You weren't really willing to. You didn't have—the charity, as the Good Book says. Or the understanding either. So now you're gonna learn—and you're gonna pay for your learning, too—the way I paid for mine—with a mighty heap of sleepless nights, getting up in the morning with my eyes swollen shut tight from cryin'—"

"Fanny, please!" Billie Jo said.

"What I said to you. Please, Billie Jo. Please. And you—"

Oliver Prescott pushed open the door, stood there looking at the two of them.

"Oliver," Fanny said to him, "you know how I got all those scars on my back—all those whip marks, don't you?"

"Yes, child," Oliver said, his voice deep, and sad, "*you* told me."

"Well then—she—knows, too. She—read it in the paper. How poor Papa dropped dead. And—*why*—"

"I didn't read anything about any whip marks!" Billie Jo said angrily. "Your father never touched you, Fanny!

Oh what an awful liar you are! He just—"

"Dropped dead," Oliver Prescott said quietly, "at finding out that his daughter was an inmate of a parlor
house. That's right, Billie. That's the truth. But all the
same, Fanny's whole back is covered with scars—of
whiplashes that cut to the bone. She was in the hospital
another three months because of that. Because of the
rarely awful way she chose—to die—"

"Oh, Uncle Oliver!" Billie Jo said.

"So now you know. I suppose you thought that she was
deceiving me about her past. You're wrong, child. To
date, my wife has yet to tell me one single lie. I married
her *knowing*, Billie. All her mistakes, errors, sins—follies.
Because she wouldn't lie to me, refused to even try to de-
ceive me. Tried time and time again to send me away—"

"That's a lie, Oliver," Fanny said. "Oh I *said* that all
right; but I never meant it. I'd be dead and buried now if
you'd left me, and you know it!" She whirled then, faced
Billie Jo, her eyes blotted out, opaque, and crystalline.

"You know how I got him, Billie?" she whispered. "I
begged him on my knees to marry me, and take me out of
that life! I swore, meaning it, that I'd kill myself if he
didn't save me from being a whore. 'Cause there's nothing
worse! Nothing in this world. Nothing in hell itself, Billie.
What you do with—Philippe—is a glory—or leastwise it
ought to be—'cause it's him, Philippe, you're doing it
with. The man you love. But imagine havin' to do *that*
twenty times a night with any stinking, hairy, old goat
who hasn't had a bath in the last ten years, just 'cause he's
got ten dollars! Men—you hate on sight. Creepy, crawly,
slimy men. Crazy men who—want to—to do dirty, unnatural things to you—perverts who want to make you—"

"Fanny!" Oliver said.

"All right, love, I'll stop it," Fanny said. "So I begged
him to save me. And you know him. You know he's the
best and kindest and the sweetest man in the whole wide
world. He let himself be overcome by pity. And raised me
up—out of the gutter. Out of that slime and filth. Made
me his wife. And I was grateful, at first—"

"But now you're not?" Billie Jo said.

"Now, I'm not. Now—" Fanny said, and whirled,
graceful as a ballet dancer, flying weightlessly to where
Oliver stood, and coming to earth as a white bird, a swan,

swoops in, a poem of pure motion, until she was lying collapsed and boneless on the floor, her two arms about his ankles, her mouth pressed, open and shuddering convulsively, against his dusty shoes, the whole wild, insane, melodramatic action robbed somehow—by her obvious sincerity, by her desperate hope—of both absurdity and embarrassment, leaving only—truth.

"Oh, Fanny!" Billie Jo said.

"Get up from there, child," Oliver Prescott said sadly.

"No. Not 'til she sees how I love you. Not 'til she knows that I live scared to death of losing you. That you smile at me and my heart starts in to singing like all the birds in all the treetops in the world. You frown—even a little frown—and I can't even breathe. My heart stops beating. I start to die. Tell her that, Oliver! Make her see that she couldn't *give* me Philippe now! 'Cause I wouldn't be able to wait all the years it'll take him to get to be what you are right now—that is, if he *ever* does—"

"Fanny—" Oliver said.

"She *knows* you. She's your niece. You raised her. So she ought to be able to see that a man can be old and skinny and bald-headed and ugly—and—and beautiful— just plain beautiful—on the inside at the same time! Oh, Oliver, I—"

He bent, raised her up, held her in his arms, smiled at his niece, his eyes a little misty, too.

"You see how it is, Billie?" he said gently. "Can't you find it in your heart to forgive an old fool?"

"Forgive?" Billie Jo said, slowly. "It's—me who stands in need of—forgiveness, Uncle—and of prayer, too, like that hymn the colored people sing. Reckon I didn't even understand what Christian charity meant, before now. And Uncle—I congratulate you—on your—your marriage—and for being both a Christian—and a man. Fanny—"

"Yes, Billie Jo?" Fanny said.

"I—wish you every happiness. Will you—let me kiss you, please?"

"Of course," Fanny said. "I always did like you, Billie Jo. You know that, don't you?"

So now, let's draw the Victorian Curtain of Charity over this scene. It's getting to be embarrassing. It no longer rings true. Yet it was true. Many touching, sentimental things are.

At some certain moments, intervals, periods, of our lives that is. But to demand permanency of them is to ask too much.

The terrible foe, the implacable enemy—is time.


## Chapter Thirty-Three


One rainy October morning, approximately one month after Oliver Prescott's return from New Orleans with his bride, Dr. Hans Volker drove his buggy up the winding gravel road that led to the Sompayac's little bungalow—actually it was a clapboard shotgun cabin, not much better than those of the more affluent Negroes and poor whites—and stopped before their gate. Wearily, he climbed down from the buggy, went up on the little stoop, and knocked on the door. His call upon his young Creole colleague was neither social nor professional. The truth was that he had heard that between Philippe and Billie Jo, things were going very badly, indeed. And, since he was fond of them both, he had come to do what he could.

Therefore, when Billie Jo opened the front door, and he saw that she had been crying, he wasn't surprised. Philippe was only a step behind her. He had his bag in his hands, his hat on his head, and his raincoat draped about his shoulders. To judge from the expression of suppressed anger on the young Creole's much too thin, far too tired face, they had been quarreling again. Bitterly. As usual.

Hans Volker pointed to his colleague's bag.

"Is this call absolutely necessary, Phil?" he drawled.

"No, it isn't!" Billie Jo burst out. "It's just an excuse—to get out of the house. To get away from me!"

"Put it down, son," Hans Volker said mildly. "Fix a tired old sawbones a snort of bourbon and branch water. Yes, I'm going to poke my nose into your business. You can tell me to go to hell—after I get through doing it. But damned if I'm going to stand idly by and let two fine young folks ruin their lives mainly because they're suffering from a disease they'll be over with in a few more years, namely, youth. 'Cause that's all that makes 'em keep tearing the hide off each other over things that ninety-nine out of a hundred ain't even so—"

Philippe smiled then, sadly.

"I'll never tell *you* to go to hell, Doctor Hans," he said. "Appears to me you're the wisest man I've known in all my life. And I'll be glad to listen to anything you have to say. Though whether this scrawny little freckle-faced broomstick rider I was fool enough to marry will or not, I can't say. She can be reasonable, sometimes. But mostly it's when she's asleep . . ."

"Well, I never!" Billie Jo gasped. "Doctor Hans, can you give me a lift? Over to Mertontown. I want to talk to Attorney Wilton, about how to get a divorce!"

"Billie," Hans Volker grinned, "remember that time you played hooky from school when you were nine years old? Got lost in the Bayou Flêche swamplands?"

"Yes," Billie Jo said, and the corners of her mouth began to twitch, despite herself.

"And what happened?" Dr. Volker said.

"*You* found me," Billie Jo said, "and spanked my hindquarters so hard that I had to eat supper off the mantelpiece. Uncle Oliver was away from home. Only thing that saved me from getting *two* whippings the same night, I reckon—"

"You ain't much bigger than you were then," Hans Volker pointed out dryly, "and if you don't stop talking this particular brand of dadblamed rot, I'm going to fetch Phil the hairbrush!"

"Men!" Billie Jo said. "Always stick together, don't you?"

"Not necessarily," Dr. Volker said. "I just might be on *your* side, when I find out what the trouble is, Billie. But I'm certain-sure that whatever it is, breaking up a going concern is no way to arrange matters. Go get me that snort, son—then tell an old party what this is all about. You been playing around with Abbie Fontaine or Meg Clouter, say?"

"No," Philippe grinned, "but thanks for the tip, old-timer! With all the love and affection I get around here these days, I just might look up the two ladies in question—"

"Phil-lippe!" Billie Jo said.

Hans Volker took off his overcoat and handed it to Billie. Sat down on the sofa. Said:

"Come sit here beside me, child—Tell an old party what's bothering you?"

"It's—her!" Billie Jo said. "Fanny! Hasn't been married two whole months—and already she's cheating on my poor old fool of an uncle! And he—Philippe—won't let me tell him! Mainly because he's in love with her, himself."

Philippe came in with the bottle, the pitcher, and the two glasses on the tray. Just in time, Hans Volker saw, to overhear Billie's last remarks.

"Now, Billie," he said.

"It's the truth! You admitted it yourself that time she sent you that picture! A photograph of herself, *stark naked,* Doctor Hans! With a note on the bottom of it, telling him to get rid of me! And—"

"Sometimes I get awfully tempted to do just that. Using an ax!" Phillippe said.

"Stop it, both of you!" Hans Volker said. "Look, Billie, Oliver's no fool. He—"

"About *her,* he is!" Billie Jo said; "and this long-tall pillpusher is even worse! I grant you she's pretty. No, she's beautiful. But that way she's got of looking so sweet and pure while all the time—"

"Billie, you shut up!" Philippe said.

"I won't shut up! While all the time my uncle found her in a whorehouse! In Storyville at that! The same whorehouse that my dear darlin' sweet ever-lovin' husband put her into! So there!"

Hans Volker stared from one of them to the other. Said, very softly, "Lord God!" Then, "Make that a double snort, son. Reckon my nerves could use some extra calming after *that* one."

Philippe poured. His hands shook so he spilled the whiskey. Billie Jo was crying—again.

"Son," Hans Volker said, after savoring his drink, "is any of those wild remarks your missus just gave out with—even slightly—true?"

Philippe looked at him. Sighed.

"All of them are, I'm afraid," he said.

"Jehoshaphat!" Hans Volker said; then: "Want to tell

me about it, son? I'm nobody's father confessor, and God
knows I was no saint in my younger days. But, maybe,
knowing, I could help head off trouble, somehow. Oliver's
just about the best friend I ever had in this world. And
he's the *last* man I'd ever have believed would pull a fool
stunt like this!"

"He did, though," Billie Jo sniffed. "She knew just how
to get to him. Worked on his pity. Swore she'd kill herself
if he didn't take her out of that life!"

"And she would have," Philippe said quietly. "She's—
not entirely sane, Doctor Hans. If any *woman* ever is! But
Fanny, less than most of them. She's alive today only because Lucien Terrebonne—you know him, don't you?—is
the damned best surgeon God ever blew the breath of life
into—"

"Second best. I've got a protegé who's even better.
Name of Childers. You'll meet him soon. He's coming
back up here to practice. I'll grant you Terrebonne's an
ace with a scalpel, though. Go on, Phil. Tell me what happened—"

Philippe told him. All of it. Or rather what he believed
was all of it. For the young Creole physician had never
even heard of Norma Tilson, Anthony Beaconridge III,
Myrtle Tolliver, and Timothy Hawkes, or even of Joe Sarcone's subsequent relations with Fanny. Which was just as
well. Philippe Sompayac was not the world's strongest
character. It could, conceivably, have been more than he
could have borne to have known or learned that much
about the woman whom, despite himself, he loved.

Hans Volker shook his head.

"I've argued and argued with Duncan Childers," he
said, "that those Vienna witch-doctors—alienists they call
themselves, nowdays; fancier than psychologists, I suppose—are wrong. But damned if this poor child's—"

"Poor child!" Billie Jo snorted.

"A little charity, Billie, Christian or otherwise," Hans
Volker said mildly. "Damned if this poor child's case
doesn't fall right in with their thinking, as I understand it,
or at least, as Childers explained to me. Poor little
Fanny's had it rough, hasn't she? Profound emotional
shocks in childhood—the feeling of being an outcast, because of her mother, likely—one really filthy deal at the

hands of those young swine—your apparent and unintentional desertion of her—the loss of her child—enough, I should think to—"

"To make a vengeful little monster of her!" Billie Jo said.

"Whose ends, you, Billie Jo, are aiding and abetting," Hans Volker said dryly, "at least as far as that business of revenge is concerned—"

"Aiding and abetting—" Billie Jo gasped.

"Yes. I take it one of her prime aims is to break the two of you up. And you're helping her do it. Your husband, child, hasn't been anywhere near her. If he had, twenty-five patients of mine would have rung me up in half an hour to give me the dirty details. You know this parish, Billie. Do you think anybody could get away with anything in it—as far as this man-and-woman business is concerned, anyhow?"

"Uncle Oliver did," Billie Jo said.

"No, he didn't. Everybody knew about him and Ruth. But most folks hate Lennie so damn bad that—Jesus!"

"So—" Billie Jo whispered, "you *have* heard that, haven't you, Doctor Hans?"

"And rejected it out of hand as ridiculous. I'll admit my first reason for rejecting it was that I thought little Fanny was a decent young woman, as angelic as she looks. But even setting that aside, what does anybody *really* know?"

"Enough," Billie Jo said. "She rides by the Colfax place—alone, in that little buggy Uncle Oliver gave her . . ."

"But she does ride *by* it," Philippe said. "Nobody has ever seen her go *in*."

"You see, Doctor Hans? Defending her tooth and nail as usual! That's the kind of loving, faithful husband *I've* got!"

"Billie, for God's sake!" Philippe said.

"All right," Billie Jo said, "I'll try to be fair. She rides up to the edge of Lennie Colfax's place—and slows that gray horse of hers down so slow he's almost crawling. Then, as my sweet, disinterested, fair-minded *faithful* husband claims, she goes right on by. But as soon as she's out of sight, that slimy, crawly, fat little toadstool of a man comes out—and follows her!"

"Source of your information?" Dr. Volker said.

"His people. Lennie's colored people—at first. But after they'd spread the news around—"

"As they always do when it's going to cause whitefolks some pain," Hans Volker observed dryly. "Can't say I blame 'em. Good enough vengeance for the way we treat 'em, I reckon. Go on, Billie—"

"People started watching. White people. And it's true. That's just what happens!"

"But," Hans Volker said; "after *that?*"

"After that," Philippe snorted, *"nothing!* Nobody, even the longest-nosed old scandalmonger in the perish has *ever* been able to find one single person who's seen 'em together. Not one. Plenty of folks have seen her shopping, gadding about, having tea and cakes in the tearoom. But nobody, I repeat, nobody has seen them together—"

"Philippe—" Billie Jo said, "that doesn't mean a thing, and you know it. Before we were married, there were a couple of times we—well, wanted to—to be together, all by ourselves—and nobody saw *us*, either. Anybody with a little brains in his head can arrange it—"

"So that old witch Charity Mance keeps on making a fortune performing abortions," Hans Volker said wryly, "and so that the parish bastardy lists keep right on increasing year after year—"

"Why Doctor Hans!" Billie Jo said. "You don't think that I—that we—"

"I don't think anything," the old German-American doctor said. "I merely grant you your point, Billie Jo. Any couple bent on a little private spooning, or fornication, or adultery can always find ways of throwing the nosy-Parkers off their tracks. I'll admit you've demolished my first objection: that little Fanny was too good for that kind of hanky-panky. But, damn it all, my second one still stands: What on earth could she, or *any* woman for that matter, see in Leonard Colfax?"

"As a man—nothing," Billie Jo said quietly, "but—as an—an instrument of torture—to *break* my poor uncle, where could she find a better, Doctor Hans?"

"But why would she want to harm Oliver? He saved her, lifted her up, treated and treats her as if she were—"

"That," Billie Jo said, "precisely that. Tell Doctor Hans *your* theory, Philippe."

"She—hates herself," Philippe said slowly. "No, worse.

She loathes, despises, herself. Utterly, Doctor Hans. If Oliver would beat the hell out of her every night, slap her around, treat her like dirt—like the dirt she believes she is, she'd crawl on her knees to kiss his feet. But let him, or anybody, treat her halfway well—as I have reason to know—her contempt for that person becomes absolute. The only reason on earth she still displays any interest in me is that I—accidentally if you will, but actually—treated her badly. And if this little idiot I married would forget the whole thing, we—"

"*We*, nothing!" Billie Jo said. "Even forgetting Fanny, Doctor Hans, setting her dirty tricks completely aside, I contend it's no fun being married to a man who *admits* he's in love with her. That, it seems to me, is a little too much!"

Hans Volker turned to Philippe.

"And *are* you in love with the little dilly, son?" he said.

"Yes," Philippe said, "but—"

"But he also loves me," Billie Jo said acidly, "so I'm supposed to forgive him because he manfully refrains from committing adultery—out of respect for me, and Uncle Oliver. I'm supposed to put up with the crumbs of his affection, to see him growing thinner every day, wandering around like a ghost, mooning over her! I won't settle for half my husband's love, Doctor Hans! I want it all! And, if I can't have it, I'll—"

"Smash your dollhouse. Throw all your toys out into the rain. Behave as childishly as possible. Lord God, Billie; sometimes I think love ought to be banned by law! Or our conception of it, anyhow. Stupidest damned idea there ever was. And relatively new, at that. Throughout most of history, people got along without it, very well indeed—"

"Now, Doctor Hans!" Billie Jo said.

"As a basis for matrimony, anyhow, Billie. Very few people in ancient and medieval times got married for love. Marriage was considered too serious a matter to base upon a temporary adolescent aberration that all normal people are entirely over by the time they're thirty. Romantic love—bah! Romantic nonsense!"

Billie Jo smiled at him; said, quietly, a little cutting edge of triumph in her voice:

"You, Doctor Hans, married young. People still talk about your touching devotion to your wife. She died—

when was it?—nearly twenty-five years ago. And you not only haven't married again, you've never even *looked* at another woman, folks say. And now you play down romantic love! Whom are you trying to fool, Old Party?"

Hans Volker threw back his head and laughed aloud.

"Not you, at any rate, baby!" he chuckled. "Unnecessary. You manage that chore for yourself, quite nicely. Let me set the record straight. I *was* in love with Margaret. Devoted to her, likewise. But when she died, I was the most *relieved* man in the state of Louisiana. Wouldn't admit it at first, even to myself. Took me a whole year to realize how goddamned *peaceful* not having her underfoot was. And whether I've ever looked at another woman or not—under conditions where my personal freedom and my privacy both could be preserved—is my own business, Billie. Maybe I have, maybe I haven't, I ain't a-sayin' and that's that. It's a fact that I haven't married again, but the reason's hardly romantic: I simply decided that if a woman as good, as true, as loving, as devoted as Meg was, could be as big a pain in the fundament as she likewise was, I wanted no further part of the fair sex—at least not on a permanent basis, anyhow!"

Philippe's roar of laughter made the windows rattle.

"Why Doctor Hans!" Billie Jo said.

"Listen to this old party, child. Seems to me we miseducate our young people—especially our daughters, on that score, damned badly. Songs. Poems. Stories. Plays. Novels. All about true love. Honey, there *isn't* any such animal—at least not in the sense of persistence or permanency. Absolutely no kind of love endures. The best two people bound together more or less legally for a lifetime can expect is to learn to like each other, a much more acceptable and certainly more lasting condition than the fevers and chills of romantic love. The second best is a wary, intelligent recognition and acceptance of—or maybe a resignation to—each other's manias, faults, and follies. The third best—if all else fails, of course—is divorce. And the last is murder—which Phil has probably found out by now can be a mighty appealing thought at times!"

"Doctor Hans, you're awful! As bad as Uncle Oliver is, sometimes," Billie Jo said.

"Worse. I'll cheerfully admit, Billie, honey, that my Meg frequently entertained the idea that I'd make a mighty delectable corpse. Fact is, every time she started humming the 'Merry Widow Waltz,' I used to get out of the house!"

"But," Billie protested, "how can you—how can anybody be *happy*, if he thinks like that?"

"Wrong question, Billie. The right ones are: Does happiness exist? And even if it does, is it possible to attain it?"

"Doctor Hans, the philosopher!" Philippe said. "All right, give us the properly Socratic answers to those Socratic questions, Old-Timer!"

"Not with an empty glass in my hands I won't!" Hans Volker snorted. "Damned if the whiskey don't flow like glue around this house!"

Philippe filled his glass and his own.

"Give me—a little bit, honey," Billie Jo said. "It tastes awful, but maybe it'll relax my nerves—"

Philippe poured her a stiff one, added water, grinned at her.

"All you want, Billie!" he said: "Maybe it'll stop you from being so goddamned mean!"

"Happiness," Dr. Volker said sententiously, "*does* exist."

"Surprise!" Billie Jo said.

"It does," Dr. Volker went on. "Sometimes it even lasts a reasonable length of time. Up to about twenty seconds, say. Time enough for any rational adult to realize all the fallacies it's based on. And that it's largely irrelevant, anyhow. Most people tend to confuse contentment with it, just as they confuse resignation with contentment. What I'm getting at, child, is that most of the things that you're working yourself up into a stew over don't matter, 'cause they just ain't so. I've known hundreds of married couples and every one of 'em believed that everybody else was lovin', faithful, happy, and what-have-you—except them. I have *never* known a happy married couple like in the story books, Billie. Aside from the fact that their complementary genitalia do fit rather well most of the time—a little of which I recommend for bad nerves and as an alternative to throwing things, child—men and women are just too goddamned different—mentally, morally, emotionally, for anything more comfortable than an armed truce to be possible between them . . ."

"Doctor Hans," Billie whispered, "I—"

"So don't drive him into her arms, daughter. Arms, hell! Don't drive him up between her legs, which is where he'll end up, if *you* don't keep him worn out 'n happy the way a good wife should. And appreciate his honesty—he admits the little dilly gets him worked up. Hell, she gets *me* worked up, and everything else in pants—"

"Including Lennie Colfax!" Billie Jo said tartly.

"I doubt that. He's just trying to pay Oliver back—for Ruth," Hans Volker said, "and I'll bet my bottom dollar he'll get nowhere. Not because li'l Fan's too good, but because her *taste* is—to judge from the fellows she's picked so far. Phil—and Oliver. Mighty fine, Billie. Mighty fine. Now I'd better be getting along. Some of these old bags who've phoned me *might* be sick for real. I doubt it, but I better look in on 'em anyhow. And appears to me I'd better have a little chat with Oliver one of these fine days—"

"Oh, Doctor Hans!" Billie Jo wailed. "You won't tell him that I—that we—"

"I won't tell him a damn thing, baby! Just offer him a shoulder to cry on, if he wants to," Hans Volker said.

A shoulder that in sober truth Oliver Prescott was going to need. For when Fanny gave Billie Jo that impressively theatrical (straight out of *Way Down East, St. Elmo,* and *The Orphans of The Storm*) demonstration of how much she loved Oliver, she was telling the strict, literal truth. A month later, by the rainy October day we have come to now, asked by her observant, and therefore worried, husband if she still did, she dutifully answered: "Of course, dearest!" but by then she was lying.

On the morning of the day that Hans Volker visited the Sompayacs, Fanny was writing a letter—and to black Louella, of all people:

"Dear Lou—" her flying fingers shaped the whorls, loops, tracings of her singularly beautiful script. "Here's a money order for twenty-five dollars, just like I promised. You can cash it at the nearest post office. Then for God's sake grab yourself a train and come up here like you said you would the last time you wrote. Being my personal maid won't be much work: I've got that dumb bitch Cindy for all the hard chores; what I really need you for, honey, is to talk to. To have somebody around who speaks my language—a *born* whore's language, to say it straight out and ugly, although I take your word for it when you say you never were.

"You won't be lonesome. There's some mighty fine-looking colored gentlemen up here. And when they get a look at you with that figure, and the way you dress, not to mention the fact that these dumb nigger wenches up here don't even know how to straighten their hair the way you do, you'll have 'em climbing up the walls.

"Lou, honey, I'm so damn *bored* I could scream. My hubby's a natural lamb. But who the fuck wants a *lamb?* I'd settle for a wild, unbroke stallion, if you get what I mean. No, don't get me wrong! He's all right in *that* department. Better than all right—mighty fine, girl, mighty fine! But—oh hell—he's so—gentle. Treats me with such respect. He has yet to slap or pinch my ass playful-like, even in private. Jesus! Who can *stand* this much respectability?

"We go to church every Sunday, even though my hubby isn't very much of a believer, and me—even less. After all the good turns the good Lord has done me so far, reckon Him and me are quits. But Mr. Prescott holds—and he's right, Lou—that we'd better put up a mighty big front so that nobody will get ideas. So we go and I doze all through the sermon. We're Episcopalians —like all the High-and-Mighty Muck-a-Mucks up here. We look down on all the other kinds. Father Rayn— that's right, *Rayn*, not Ryan—just dotes on me. Wants me to sing in the choir—Lord God! I should do it— give out one Sunday with one of the songs the girls used to sing in the Green Parlor. That would really rock 'em back, wouldn't it? Like: 'Bertha is a highborn lass. How delicately she goes back on her—'

"Oh, skip it! Never thought I'd miss Mama's, but I do, I was miserable there, but I was never bored. Looks like I can stand being miserable, but being *this* bored, I just can't take.

"The worst of it is that there's no way I can see *him.* You know who. She watches him like a hawk, the speckled-faced little bitch! And, Oliver—my husband—watches *me.* Says he trusts mè, but he doesn't, really. Besides, I'm not even sure I want him anymore. In New Orleans and New York he was so—so elegant. Now his clothes are baggy and awful and he's thinner than ever and his face is tired and he looks just like what he is, a horse-'n-buggy back-Parish country doctor! And he looks unhappy too. She hasn't even given him a kid. Bet she freezes his balls off, that's why.

"Though maybe not. I treat my hubby just royally in that department, mainly because I want a baby so damn bad that some times I'm tempted to go out and steal one—or put a couple of other fellows on the job—and still no luck. Maybe he's too old. Or maybe I messed my insides up too much that time I fell down and lost mine. Or maybe my poor little thing's worn out from overuse!

"Anyhow I reckon I'll be glad when Dan gets out of the ice-house and comes after me. Dan's not worth gooseshit on ice, but then I'm nobody's prize, either. Reckon we suit each other. A whore and her pimp. Drainage-ditch water seeking its own level. Running together.

"There's a fellow up here who's after me. A widower fellow. A little younger than Oliver. Fat, soft, slimy. Makes a body want to puke just to look at him. But still, in spite of that he fascinates me. Like a snake—a cold, slimy snake—fascinates a bird. He'd be lousy in the hay. Never met a fat man yet who wasn't. Still, there' something about Mr. Colfax—or maybe it's just 'cause my hubby can't bear the sight of him. Mighty bad blood 'twixt the two of them, Cindy tells me, but she's scared to tell me why—swears Mr. Prescott would have the hide off of her in strips—Funny, my husband's so damn good and sweet and kind and lovin' and perfect that I'm getting so I can't *stand* him. I'd like to know why he and Mr. Colfax *hate* each other. Useful information you're gonna pry out of Cindy when you come . . .

"Go see Dan for me. Give him a kiss. He won't mind. You can bet your sweet life you won't be the first colored girl he ever kissed. Hell, Dan will try anything, including Chinese and Malay—whatever that is.

"Come up here quick as you can. I'll be waiting.
> "Love,
> "Fanny"

When she had finished the letter, Fanny didn't call Cindy, and tell her to send a boy, riding a mule for slightly greater speed, into town to post it. Instead, dressed in her warmest clothes—for although that late October day of 1903 wasn't cold, it was raining as usual, and to a person as thin as she was, its dampness posed a very real threat—she went out to the stables and ordered Isaac, Oliver's groom, to hitch up her gray gelding Danny Boy to her buggy.

She often drove into Mertontown alone, nowdays. This, and other signs and portents of her growing restlessness, troubled Oliver more than he would admit, even to himself. But he was far too intelligent to forbid her to do so, especially since, up to the moment at least, the world's second-oldest sisterhood, the Devotees of Character Assassination Through Vicious Gossip, had been able to find so little remiss in Fanny's behavior that the worst abjective they had been able to apply to her was "Flighty."

She got in the buggy and drove off, saying to Isaac:

"Tell Mr. Prescott I'll be home about suppertime—got some shopping to do—"

This, too, was the truth, in part. Today, October twenty-seventh, was Oliver's birthday, a fact that he himself had forgotten. But in the first euphoria of her marriage, and of her escape from Storyville, Fanny had wormed out of him both his birth date and Billie Jo's, as well as the date of Philippe and Billie Jo's wedding anniversary. Philippe's birthday she already knew. All these data she had copied down in a little notebook, with a view of demonstrating to Oliver what a thoughtful little woman he had married. On her last trip to Mertontown, she had already bought Oliver an expensive gold watch— so expensive, in fact, that this drive into the parish's closest approximation of a city was the third it had taken to accomplish the matter. On the first, she had had to be content with merely ordering it, since in a place like Mertontown nobody, with the sole exception of Winthrop Bevers and his son Forsythe, had money enough to buy that kind of watch. But Fanny wouldn't take a substitute. She wanted that make of watch and no other, because it was the make that the richest and flashiest of Mae Hartman's clients carried.* Therefore the local jeweller had

---

*Carried*, not *wore*. In 1903 a man who would have dared wear a wristwatch—if indeed such a thing existed—would have been admitting effeminacy.

had to order her one—with its accompanying heavy gold chain—from New Orleans. The second trip had been devoted to examining and admiring the watch, and ordering it engraved with the lines: "To My Beloved Husband, Oliver, on his birthday, October Twenty-Seventh, 1903."

Today's trip was to complete the whole thing: to bring her gift home in its tooled Morocco leather box. In part.

Because none of Fanny's trips into Mertontown had been wholly devoted to the purchase of Oliver's birthday present. A large part of the interest—"thrill" would have been at that stage too strong a word—she got out of the five- or six-mile drive consisted in slowing Danny Boy to a creeping walk and taking the longest possible time to cross that part of the Colfax farm that bordered on the road.

She was aware that Lennie Colfax was there always watching her, behind closed shutters, peering out at her like some dead-white, repulsive toad. Why this fact, and the man himself, fascinated her, she could not have said, not even to herself.

'He's so goddamned ugly,' she thought. 'Crawly. Soft. Like the kind of grubworms you find in a rotten tree stump. And yet—and yet—'

She was thinking that when she got to the edge of the farm. Then she caught her breath, held it. For Leonard Colfax was standing there by the gate, looking down the road in the direction from which she came. Obviously he was waiting for her. When he saw her, he grinned.

Fanny let her breath out slowly. Drove on towards the gate.

When she was close enough, Lennie took the straw out from between his teeth. He had very thick lips—'Like a nigger's!' Fanny thought—that were a curiously leprous pale pink in keeping with the rest of his very nearly albino complexion. Due to a congenital defect, a deviated nasal septum, he breathed through his mouth, so that his thick, wet lips were never closed, and a phosphorescent slime of saliva was always visible in their corners. His hair was white-blond. The same color, in fact, as Fanny's own, except that it was maybe a trifle lighter, less silvery, more nearly a dead moss-white. His nose was too short, so that his nostrils flared above his gaping upper lip, and his watery blue eyes were even smaller—'And meaner' Fanny thought—than Beau Dan's own.

He was short and fat. His face displayed a brace of chins, ill-shaven, and a pair of mournful hounddog jowls. His belly hung over his belt. And yet his arms and legs were pipestems, and the seat of his pants sagged over buttocks so flat as to be practically nonexistent.

'Jesus!' Fanny thought, 'What a creature!'

"Howdy, Miz Prescott," Leonard said. "Long trip into Mertontown—"

"It is, Mr. Colfax," Fanny said, in her best imitation of Norma Tilson's crisp New England accent: "but, unfortunately, it happens to be necessary—"

"Break it a little," Lennie said. "C'mon on up on the porch. Set a spell. Chat. Widower feller like me gits awful lonesome, sometimes—"

Fanny smiled at him.

"Today, I can't, Mr. Colfax," she said. "My errand's— urgent. Some other time, perhaps—"

"Gonna stay long?" Lennie said.

"Why—no, I suppose not," Fanny said. "I—I only have to pick up a—a gift I bought for Oliver. Today's his birthday and—"

"I know. Gitting along, ain't he?" Lennie said.

"Oliver's not *old!*" Fanny protested.

"For *you*, he is," Lennie said. "Why don'cha stop a spell on your way back then? Got some mighty fine elderberry wine. Made it myself. The ladies hereabout all say it's the best. Don't drink it myself. I like good likker— but for the ladies it's all right. Sweet. Mild. Not too heavy . . ."

Fanny stared at him. Said, astonished at the falter, the hesitation, in her voice:

"Well, I—I don't know, Mr. Colfax—it might—cause talk. After all I am a respectable married woman and—"

Leonard Colfax grinned at her, sure now, very sure.

"Gate'll be open. You see anybody on the road you drive on by. You don't see nobody, you turn that sassy gray in here and drive round in back o' the house. Your rig can't be seen back there—Fanny. I'll be waiting for you, you hear?"

Fanny opened her mouth to say, "I'll see you in hell, first!" but what came out a little breathlessly was:

"Well—maybe—I—I won't promise you, though—"

But she would. She knew she would. What she didn't know was why.

When she came back, with Oliver's birthday present in her purse, the gate was open, and no one was in sight. She turned Danny Boy's head into it, drove around back of the house. Lennie Colfax was waiting for her in the kitchen. He had on a bathrobe. Under the bathrobe he was naked. Like that, he was, if anything more repulsive than ever.

"Why, Mr. Colfax!" Fanny gasped.

"Hell, honey," Lennie said. "I don't believe in wastin' time. Have a snort to calm your little nerves. Then git out o' your things. Got a powerful hankering to see what you look like in th' altogether—"

"Well, I never!" Fanny whispered.

"C'mon now, Fan," Lennie crooned.

Ten minutes later, they were both stark naked and abed.

It was truly awful.

"Reckon you better help me, honey," Leonard said. "Ain't as young as I used to be."

Fanny put down one slim hand and caught hold of him. He went on kissing her breasts, sucking noisily, wetly, greedily at her nipples. She stroked him gently, squeezed him, tugged at him, jerking angrily, fiercely, until at long, long last, he began to swell into her hand.

The minute he entered her, he came.

But she wouldn't let him off so easily. She wrapped her legs around his waist, in a viselike hold, and writhed, and bucked, and twisted and ground upon him until his detumescence was overcome. Then she stabbed her nails into the greasy softness of the flesh of his back; hissed at him:

"Roll over, damn you!"

He did so, grinning. She sat upright, astride him, and worked at it. Ferociously. Ferally. The bed springs squeaked, groaned, sang.

He put up his small, fat, white, hairless, womanish hands, and squeezed her breasts. She rode him desperately, furiously. He could feel it when she started to shudder, so he arched his thick bulk upward, thrusting. Her eyes went glassy. Her mouth came open. She threw her head back and screamed and screamed and screamed.

She collapsed on top of him. Lay there quaking, quivering, trembling.

"That, honey," he chuckled, "was mighty, mighty fine!"

"That," she grated, "was only the beginning, Lennie! You're gonna beg for mercy, before I'm through!"

He did. He had to. He wasn't even able to get up to see her to the door. She bent over him, fully dressed, getting his rank, hibernating cave-beast's stench full in her nostrils and said, mockingly:

" 'Til—this time next week, Lennie-boy!"

"Lord God! Lord God Almighty!" Lennie Colfax said.


On the way home, she was thinking:

'I have never—felt like *that,* before. Not with anybody. Not with Phil. Not with Oliver—and both of 'em are ten times the man he is. Why? He's fat and soft and sloppy and dirty and he stinks. He's a—slug. He's repulsive. The sight of him makes me want to heave. And yet—and yet—'

She stiffened suddenly. Her pale eyes were very clear.

'I've found—my match. 'Cause even Beau Dan wasn't—low enough. Not this kind of—buzzard's puke— that suits me. As low as I am. Rock bottom. Underneath that even. Down where the slime is, and all the creeping, crawling things—are blind. Vile. Like me. Utterly, utterly—vile . . .'

When she came into the house, Oliver called out to her from the parlor:

"That you, Fanny?"

"Yes!" she said breathlessly: "Just a minute, Oliver. I want to go freshen up—A—a rainstorm came up—and— and my hair's a mess!"

He came out into the hall.

"It is—" he said gravely. "Give me a kiss, hon—"

She kissed him, lightly, quickly. He frowned.

"You've—been drinking," he said.

"Just—elderberry wine," she said, with a little laugh. 'That sounds false,' he thought, 'strained—'

"Bought you a little bottle—at Miller's," she said, "but coming home I got thirsty and took a sip—and before I knew I'd drunk it all—"

" 'S all right, child," he said, amusement in his voice.

His hand rested on her shoulder. "Strange," he said: "your clothes are—dry—"

"Didn't get wet, silly!" she said, "just my *head*. Poked it out of the buggy to see where I was going. Took my hat off first so it wouldn't get wet and—"

She was lying. He knew that. 'Why is she?' he thought dismally; but then he took himself sternly in hand. 'Don't go into it, Oliver,' he told himself. 'Not now. Not yet. Not until you have to. Better—a fool's paradise than no paradise at all. So keep it—for as long as you can—'

He turned her loose. She skipped up the stairs. Went into their bedroom. Closed the door behind her. Locked it. When she took off her bolero jacket, she could smell herself. She stank like a she-goat. Her armpits were rank. She tore off her clothes, rolling her knee-length, fluffy, nainsook and lace "umbrella" drawers into a sodden ball and hurling them under the bed.

Racing to the washstand, she poured the basin full and washed herself all over, paying special attention to her armpits and her crotch. She patted perfume into the hollow of her throat, beneath her arms, onto her belly, even along her thighs. Then she dressed again in fresh linen from the skin out.

Standing there in her chemise and petticoats she went to work at the wild tangled mass of her hair.

"Honey!" Oliver's voice floated up from below, "why are you taking so damn long?"

"Just a minute, darling!" Fanny said.

When she came downstairs again, she was radiant.

"You know," he said, "when you're out of sight, I tell myself that nobody could be that beautiful. Then you come back and I see you are. A little *more* beautiful every time. You didn't have to change, though—"

"Yes, I did," Fanny said. "Tonight's—special, darling—"

He held her chair for her. She slid into it.

"Hm-m-m!" he said: "You smell so nice, hon!"

"For—you. Darling," she said, a little mischievously, "told you tonight's—special."

Then Tildy, their cook, who conformed completely to Southern tradition by being both enormously fat, and black as coal, came into the dining room with a huge roasted turkey on a platter.

"Lord God, Tildy!" Oliver said, "aren't you being a mite previous? Thanksgiving ain't 'til next month from all I ever heard tell—"

"Your missus's orders, suh!" Tildy laughed. "Turkey 'n all th' fixin's. Cranberry sauce. Candied yams. 'Tater salad. The works!"

Oliver stared at Fanny.

"What on earth—" he began.

"Later—" Fanny murmured, "after you've eaten—love!"

When the meal was over, Oliver pushed back his chair.

"Whatever's for dessert, I'll just have to skip, hon," he said. "If I eat another mouthful I'll bust a gusset, so help me!"

"Oh, Oliver!" Fanny wailed.

At the sound of her voice, Tildy came in with the birthday cake. It was ablaze with candles. Oliver stared at it, said:

"Lord God!"

Fanny slipped out of her chair knelt down beside his, rested her bright head on his arm.

"Blow 'em out, Oliver," she said gently. "Take a deep breath—and blow 'em, love!"

He did. The candles flared, gutted, went out. Then spirals of smoke rose ceilingward.

'That's supposed to be good luck,' Oliver thought, 'but—somehow, I wonder—'

"Happy birthday, suh!" Tildy said and left them there.

Fanny got up, went out into the hall, came back again. Held the tissue-wrapped package out to Oliver. He took it, broke the wrappings, opened the box, stared at the watch. And death and hell got into his eyes.

Fanny saw that. Wailed piteously, "Oh, Oliver! And I—I thought—you—you'd like it!"

"I do like it, honey," Oliver said quietly. "What I don't like—is its cost. A watch like this one—in solid gold—costs a shade over three hundred dollars. I'm sorry, Fanny; but I have to ask you: Where'd you get the money from? Even if you held back out of the household expenses, like every wife under heaven does—in the time we've been married, you couldn't have accumulated even fifty, let alone three hundred. Come on Fanny! The truth! Who gave you that much money, and for *what*?"

She stood there, staring at him. The light from the

kerosene lamps with which the house, like all farmhouses of the time, being too far from a town for either gas or electricity, was illuminated, pooled brilliantly in her pale eyes, spilled slow liquefied flame down her face. She didn't move or speak. She simply stood there like that, crying.

"Fanny, in God's name!" he got out.

"Men," she whispered. "I don't know their names—or remember their faces, Oliver. But they gave me the money—for going to bed with them. For being—a whore. But—*before* I married you, Oliver. You—you knew that. What you—didn't know—couldn't realize—was how much money I made. And—that—that I hadn't anything—to spend it on. Clothes—yes. Jewelry—a little. Never was fond of hanging junk all over myself. I used to—to *give* it away. Yes, yes—just what you're thinking—to a pimp I had on the side! But mostly to Mother Catherine's orphans' home—if you don't believe that, write and ask her—"

"Fanny—" he said, making of her name an elegy, a funeral sound.

"Because I—I hated that money, Oliver. It—reminded me of what I was—goods for sale. Dirt. Filth. And—you're right—it was an insult, wasn't it? For me to use some of it, to buy you a birthday present, I mean. Only I—I didn't think. I was—too happy to think—and—and too much—in love."

"It's all right, child," he said.

"No! No! It's not all right! Give me that damned watch, Oliver! Give it to me!"

"No, Fanny," he said sadly, "reckon I'll keep it after all. It's the thought that counts isn't it, and—"

But she flung herself upon him, snatched it from his hand. Stood there, her eyes star-blazed blind. Then she crossed to the fireplace, laid it on the hearthstone took up the poker, and slowly, ceremoniously even, smashed it into bits.

He made no move to stop her. When she had finished that, she pushed the fragments into the fire, stood watching them blacken, begin to melt.

Oliver came over to her, and put his arm around her shoulder.

"Forgive a jealous old fool, won't you, Fanny?" he said.

She whirled then, went up on tiptoe, kissed his mouth.

"Take me upstairs, Oliver!" she said, "in your arms—like the first night we came home. Then—love me to sleep. So I won't feel so rotten-low vile that—"

He bent and swept her slight form effortlessly up into his arms, went up the stairs with her, shouldered the door open, lay her down upon the bed, stood there looking at her. She had her eyes shut tight. She was trembling.

"Undress—me, darling," she said.

He did so without haste. Stood there staring at her slender fragility, and the tortured history of her life branded into her white flesh, by the surgeons' scalpels, a madman's whip, until pity was in him like a blade. It was out of that emotion rather than desire that he made love to her. He was very, very gentle. She responded in a way that was timid, shy, bridelike, almost virginal, making of her slim body one long, clinging caress whose tenderness was so achingly, exquisitely total that it brought tears to his eyes.

Later, hours later, he came awake and looked at her, lying there warm, soft, naked in his arms.

'She—is a *good* woman,' he thought. 'In spite of everything, she is! There's a vein of—of purity in her so deep that nothing has touched it, nothing ever will. Yes, I can trust her, all right. We're safe now. Very safe. We've got past the worst part. So from here on in—we're—safe . . .'

In a farmhouse six miles down the road, Lennie Colfax rubbed his aching limbs:

"Lord God!" he said. "Lord God!"


## Chapter Thirty-Four


"That's her, Isaac," Fanny said, and pointed. She had come to the Mertontown railway station in the surrey with Isaac driving, thus causing a severe case of the sulks on the part of Willie, Isaac's younger brother, who usually drove the much befringed and handsome vehicle on the rare occasions that either she or Oliver used it. But she didn't trust Willie's driving. He loved to show off and that made him reckless. Besides she was sure that Willie's sulkiness was ninety-seven percent due to the fact she was deliberately giving Isaac the chance to meet Louella first.

Isaac was not only older, he was much more steady and responsible than Willie was. And since she supposed that Louella would eventually marry one of the Negroes on the place, Fanny had decided to offer her the best from the outset.

But the real reason she had ordered Isaac to drive her into Mertontown in the surrey was that she was sure her own smart little buggy wouldn't have room in it for Louella's baggage. Louella had more fine clothes—"glad rags," she called them—than any girl in Maebelle Hartman's parlor house, most of them gifts from the girls, themselves, who, with that aggravated and exaggerated emotional instability peculiar to whores, often gave a dress away after having worn it just once.

Isaac stared at the slim black girl standing on the railway platform. His eyes quite literally bugged out in the fashion that black comics, twenty years later in the movies and forty-odd later on television, were to make a trademark of, until the rising fury of black pride shamed them out of it.

"Je-ee-ee—Zus!" he said.

Fanny laughed then, merrily.

"Over here, Lou!" she said.

Louella came swaying towards them. "Sashayin'" was the way she put it. She was a sight to see. She had on a tailored suit of the very latest mode that fitted her to perfection and beyond. It was made of burgundy red satin, and inside it her body was a midnight flame. From her shoulders to her waist, two black velvet stripes flared down her nipped-in bolero jacket; and, below it, from her waist to her hemline, two more black stripes took up where the ones on her jacket left off. Just below her slim, but shapely, hips, two horizontal stripes went three quarters of the way around her skirt to join the vertical ones, as if to emphasize what her derrière did, walking.

Isaac groaned aloud, took off his cap and put it in his lap in a vain attempt to keep Fanny from seeing what was happening to him.

Fanny's laughter rose, flutelike.

"Now that's a new way to tip your cap to a lady, Isaac!" she giggled. "Get down, you horny black scoundrel, and help her with her bags!"

Louella had had her hair straightened before starting

out, undergoing that horribly painful pulling and searing with hot irons and grease that was to cost black girls tons of hair, and years of misery, before they finally realized that imitating white women was no way to emphasize a beauty totally different from, and an antithesis to, the Caucasian version, and quit torturing themselves in the effort to accomplish an aim that not only couldn't be accomplished, but wasn't even worth attempting, based, as it was, upon a premise totally false. But Isaac would be dead and gone before that day came.

Louella wore a white, almost transparent, lingerie shirtwaist under her jacket, and beneath that, a satin corset that had her waist pulled in so tight that it hurt her to breathe and pushed her really splendid coal black breasts up so high that they were fairly poking Isaac's eyes out.

"Lord God Almighty Baby Jesus and his Sweet Mama Mary God!" he groaned.

Louella laughed, making the two bright-green stuffed birds in her red-velvet hat bob as though they were going to take off and fly.

"What ails you, cullud boy—?" she said.

What ailed Isaac could only be understood in the context of that day. In the small towns and rural districts black women still wore shapeless Mother Hubbard dresses, with an apron tucked into their draw strings, and hanging down the front. Their shirtwaists or blouses were of cheap cotton prints that faded to a uniform dirty gray after the first washing. Much of the time they went barefooted, saving their shoes for special occasions like revival meetings and church, with the result that on those occasions their unaccustomed feet underwent the tortures of the damned.

They wore "headrags"—any available piece of cloth to keep the dust out of their grease-filled, but still kinky, hair. They were ashamed of that hair, because nobody had told them that it was, in its own way, lovely. They called the curly and straight hair that the mulatto children their bosses or their bosses' sons got on them "good" hair, as opposed to their own "ol' bad nappy-headed nigger hair—"

They thought their generous, wide soft, full-lipped rounded features were ugly. Their idea of perfect beauty—an idea they'd been literally brainwashed into over several hundred years—was Fanny herself. They weren't even capable of realizing that Louella was every bit as beautiful as Fanny was, that the two of them were day and night, very nearly perfect representatives of the very best their respective races had to offer, physically, anyhow.

All of which, of course, poor Isaac couldn't say. He hadn't the words to express the obvious fact that he was wounded unto death by an emotion that in a day or two even he would begin to think of as "love."

"Nothing ma'am—I mean gal," he spluttered, and bent to pick up her bags. Then he smelt her, which wasn't hard, because Louella was fairly reeking with far-from-cheap perfume. And that, maybe, topped it all. For the first time in his life, on a weekday—Sundays, of course, were another matter, for before Sunday, Saturday night with its suds-filled stavehooped washtubs had inter-vened—he had encountered a black woman who didn't stink of honest sweat. He reeled away from her, dizzily.

"You sick, boy?" Louella said.

Fanny got down then, and the two of them kissed each other, which caused quite a sensation among the on-lookers at the station. So much of a sensation, that Sheriff Manny Gleason was moved to take a hand. He came up to where Isaac was loading Louella's bags into the surrey, pushed his hat back on his head and said:

"Miz Prescott, ma'am, 'scuse me for axin', but I kinda like to know who this here gal is—"

"My maid, Louella, Sheriff," Fanny said pleasantly, "Say hello to the sheriff, Lou—"

"Howdy, Mister Sheriff, suh," Louella said.

"Well I'll be daggumed if she look like no maid to me," Sheriff Gleason said uneasily. "Fact is, I don't rightly re-calls *ever* seein' a nigger gal like this 'un—"

"Yes, pretty, isn't she?" Fanny said.

"Daggumed right she is!" Manny Gleason said: "An' that's jist what's botherin' me, Miz Prescott. This heah gal is gonna have a mighty heap of white gentlemen aiming to change their luck, if you gits what I mean—"

"Oh Lou, can fight them off," Fanny laughed. "She's used to it. Aren't you, Lou?"

"Yes 'm," Louella said; then: "Don't you go 'n git th' Sheriff riled up, Miz Fanny ma'am. I aim to live peaceful here-abouts—"

"Look, Miz Prescott," the Sheriff said. "I don't mean no harm, but do you—do you vouch for this here gal? Mighty fancy article, if you git what I mean. And we ain't had no race trouble up here in years and—"

"Of course I vouch for Louella, Sheriff!" Fanny said; then she went on, lying with such obvious relish that Louella hugged herself in silent delight: "Her people have been in our service—*my* family's, that is; not Mr. Prescott's—for generations. My grandfather tried to send them away after the Damnyankees freed 'em, Sheriff; but they wouldn't go. Too devoted to us. I'll admit I *have* spoiled Louella rotten, giving her all my old clothes, and teaching her how to dress and fix her face; but she's a level-headed girl—You won't have any trouble out of her—"

"Nary a bit, Mister Sheriff Cap'n, suh," Louella said in a tone of voice so exaggeratedly humble that Fanny had to hold her breath to keep from literally screaming with laughter.

Then she saw Isaac's face. He was crying. His tears ploughed furrows through the gray dust on his inky face.

"Well, see that you don't, gal!" Gleason said. Then touching the brim of his Stetson, added to Fanny: "Thank you mighty kindly, Miz Prescott. Keepin' the peace is my business 'n sometimes it pays to check. Sort of head things off, if you git what I mean . . ."

"I do. Of course I do. And you're perfectly right, Sheriff," Fanny said.

Isaac was still crying.

Fanny waited until Gleason had sauntered off before hissing at him:

"Get up there and drive, you damn fool!"

"What ails you, boy?" Louella said in a gentler tone; all the mockery gone from her voice, replaced by pity, now, compassion, concern. But so habituated to her times was even she, that she couldn't see the tragedy of a man's, a big, strong, utterly masculine man's, having no other recourse but tears before blatant, casual, and unthinking insults to a woman of his race, since his life, itself, would have been the price, and on the spur of the same instant, for one rebellious word.

"Him!" Isaac wept. "Goddamn ol' white motherfucker talkin' 'bout *you* like that!"

"Isaac!" Fanny said. "You watch that filthy talk!"

" 'Scuse me, Miz Fanny," Isaac said. "You's different. You's white, but you treats us—like folks. But one o' these days whiteman like him gonna make me bust loose 'n go hawgwild. See a gal like this 'un, a nice sweet pretty plumb decent gal like this un, 'n he all but come right out 'n call her a ho'!"

Louella grinned at him, then, mischievously.

"How do you know I *ain't*, Isaac?" she said.

"Look at you, tha's how. You's a angel, Louella. Didn't know the Good Lord made *black* angels afore now, but now I does 'n that's a nach'l fact. You ain't got yo'self no man, is you? 'Cause effen you is, look out jailhouse, here I come! That there nigger damn sho' better give his soul to the Lord, 'cause his black ass is purely mine! Gonna cut him loose from under his nappy hair so damn fas' that—"

"Isaac!" Fanny said severely, but she was choking with suppressed laughter.

Louella smiled then. She was actually blushing, but she was so black that Fanny couldn't see it. Isaac was a fine-looking man, a shade under six feet tall. About thirty, Louella guessed. Which was a sight too damned old for any Louisiana Negro to be single still.

"How's about you, Big Boy?" she said. "You don' mean to tell me *all* the gals run away screamin' when you come along?"

"No 'm," Isaac said, "don' mean to tell you that, Lou. Had me a woman. Mighty good woman—th' bes'. But the good Lord called her. Her 'n my baby girl, too, at the same time. Las' summer—a year ago. Been mighty lonesome ever since—"

"That reminds me," Fanny said sharply. "You ever have yellow fever, Lou?"

"Yes 'm. When I was eight, nine year old. All my hair fell out 'n I was puking black 'n green for two weeks. But I got over it. Why, Miz Fanny?"

"Good thing. That means you're immune. You won't catch it again. I had it too—I was five, Eliza says. So we're both safe. It's awful up here. People die like flies every summer—All because Nelson Vance makes money out of muskrat skins—"

"I don't getcha, honey?" Louella said.

"Get in the surrey. I'll explain it to you," Fanny said.

And she did, repeating Hans Volker's belief that Nelson Vance had dammed up the place where the Bayou Flêche should drain off into Merry Creek, thus vastly extending the rodents' breeding grounds. She really wasn't that interested in the matter; but it was something to talk about until they got home and got rid of Isaac. Because what she wanted to talk about, she couldn't in front of Oliver's stablekeeper and groom. Isaac was too loyal to his employer for that. And much too smart not to catch her drift, no matter how she tried to disguise the matter. No, there was no alternative: She'd just have to wait until they got home before inquiring about Beau Dan.

And even then she had to wait, because Oliver himself was at home. He had come home early from supervising the very nearly scientific application of fertilizer to his fields that he did in the autumn every year, thus making his place one of the most productive in the state. He was perhaps the only diversified farmer in the parish. He planted corn, carrots, beans, potatoes, beets, radishes, oats, rye, and wheat as well as cotton. In fact, he deliberately kept his cotton acreage down. "Damn plant ruins th' land," he said. He had orchards of peach, quince, apple, crabapple, plum, and apricot as well. To anyone with an eye to appreciate it, his farm with its ancient briqueté entre poteaux farmhouse was a little paradise. Unfortunately, Fanny didn't appreciate it. Rural living bored her so bad she was looking forward to going back to Mae's.

He had come home, out of a certain worry, a certain concern, to see Louella. He had the shrewd feeling that Fanny's motives for sending for the black girl were all wrong. At the first sight of Lou he was sure of it; but then, something in her face made him less sure. There was something—well, basically open and honest in Louella's gaze. A certain defiant undercurrent of—pride.

He put out his hand to her with a smile.

"Welcome, Lou," he said. "Glad to have you here."

Louella stared at him, said, softly, sincerely:

"*Is* you, suh? 'Cause if you ain't, I won't even unpack my clo's."

"Why, Lou!" Fanny said.

"Fact, honey. Don't know whether you knows it, but you's got yo'self a man. A gentleman, too. But a man, mostly. An' I don' care how good frens you 'n me is, I can't stay here if Mr. Prescott don' 'prove of me. *Do* you, suh?"

Oliver Prescott considered that.

"Well, yes—and no, Lou," he said. "You look like an honest girl—and a good one, too, within certain limits. But you're a damned sight too pretty. And too citified. Among these country wenches you're going to stand out like a sore thumb. I don't mean to have half of my hands laid up in cuttin' scrapes over you, Missy—and that could happen. Your clothes are—a marvel. Smart as all get-out. Tell me, what do you do to your hair? It's truly lovely—"

"Oliver," Fanny said tartly, "sounds just like you're getting ready to change *your* luck, for a fact!"

"No 'm," Louella giggled, "he's your'n, ma'am. I keep outa his way!"

"All right," Oliver said with a grave smile, "I'll give you a chance, Louella. But the first trouble that breaks out among my hands over you—back you go. So you take care!"

"Thank you, suh," Louella said. "I'll do just that, me."

Then he went down the stairs, mounted Bess, touched his crop to the brim of his hat, and moved off at a brisk canter.

"Lord God!" Louella said, "is you one lucky girl, honey!"

"Oh, I don't know—" Fanny said sullenly. "C'mon, Lou! Tell me! How was Beau Dan the last time you—"

Louella bent her head, looked up again. Said, very softly:

"Sure Lord hates to tell you this, honey. But Beau Dan, him—he *daid*."

Fanny put out one hand, grasped the edge of the table, eased herself down into a chair. Her face was ghost-white. Then, silently, terribly, she started to cry.

"Now, honey," Louella said, "don' take on! You knows damn well Beau Dan wasn't worth one li'l teardrop, let alone this here flood. Now, honey—"

But Fanny sat there, shaking and shivering with what Louella didn't even know was rage, until she got it out.

"Joe! That guinea bastard! That murdering little toad frog of a wop! Just because Dan didn't have the balls to blast Angie, he—"

Sorrowfully, Louella shook her head.

"Honey," she said, "you got it all wrong. They found Angie in a drainage ditch two months after Dan was sent up. Mr. Sarcone done forgot all about that—hell, Miz Fanny, he even was pullin' wires to get Dan out—Said he owed Dan too much to get that mad at him—"

"Then?" Fanny whispered.

"Another jailbird," Louella said. "Him 'n Danny-boy was—frens. Then he found out that Dan was cheatin' on him with other fellers and—"

Fanny sat there, frozen.

"Say that again!" she whispered. "You mean to say that Dan—"

"Honey, you mean you *really* didn't know that Dan was a cocksucker? He was the sweetheart of the whole jail. Suckin' everybody off. That is except the ones what was givin' it to him up his ass. But this heah feller really fell in love with him. So when he found out Dan was doin' it for everybody, he got crazy mad 'n cut po' Danny's throat. With a razor. Hit th' jugular vein. Dan bled to death before they could get him to the prison hospital—"

Fanny sat there. Said: "Oh, Jesus!" very quietly.

By late afternoon, she had had time to think it out. What it meant. That she was trapped on this back-parish farm. That there wasn't any escape. That she was going to die, inch by inch, of boredom. Choking to death upon respectability.

So she went downstairs, just as she was, without a hat or gloves or her handbag, and ordered Isaac to hitch Danny Boy to her buggy. Then she drove away from the farm, very fast, whipping her horse into a dead run until she was past all of the various points she could conceivably have run into Oliver riding home from the fields in the dusk of evening in the last of the fading light.

But, as soon as she was sure she was safe, she slowed the poor beast down. She didn't want him blown. After all, it was still a good five miles to Lennie Colfax's farm.

Oliver waited for her as long as he could. Then, because dignity demanded it, he made Tildy bring him his supper. By an effort of will he ate it all. When he had finished it, he got up and went downstairs below the back gallerie where the house servants' quarters were.

A smell came out of the door. A smell like frying grease and burnt hair. But he knocked on it all the same. Louella opened the door. She had on a simple print dress with a wrapper over it. Cindy sat in a chair by the table. The table was covered with jars of pomade. In the fireplace the irons were heating.

Oliver smiled wearily. The room was filled to the bursting point with black women waiting their turns. But Oliver was too upset to realize what it meant: that on her own terms, Louella had a lucid, and a pragmatic mind. She knew she couldn't live here on this farm with the hand of each and every one of her racial sisters raised against her because of the threat she obviously raised to their hold over their men. So she'd set out at once to win them over. She had given a dress to every woman on the place, even though that meant reducing her own wardrobe down to five—the best five, of course, but still to do it cost her well-hidden tears. She hadn't even excluded the women, who, like Tildy, were much too fat to get into them. And she was straightening their hair, teaching them simple makeup, free of charge. That Sunday when Oliver's hands went to Church, they were going to go strutting, with the sleekest, flossiest black girls anybody in the parish ever did see on their arms. The women from the other farms were going to purely die of envy. So the Prescott plantation women waited, quietly savoring their coming triumph.

"My wife," Oliver said, "have you seen her, Lou?"

"No suh," Louella said. "Not since this evening, anyhow, suh—"

"Thank you," Oliver said grimly, and started to close the door; then a thought struck him. "Tell me, Lou," he said, "was she—upset—when you saw her last?"

Louella bowed her head.

"Yes suh," she said, "she purely was. My fault, suh. I—I brung her bad news. A feller she used to know. A—a fren o' her'n—passed on—a little after she left Nawleens, suh. She—she axed me 'bout him, 'n I had to go 'n open up my big mouf 'n—I'm purely sorry, suh, me—"

'A lover,' Oliver thought, 'one—she cared about—truly.

Lord God! That puts another face upon things! With that suicidal mania she sometimes has she just might—'

"It's all right, Lou, she had to be told sometime," he said, and got out of there.

He had Isaac saddle not Bess, but Prince Charlie, a gelding he only rode in sporting events. A jumper, and one of the fastest things on four feet. But Prince Charlie's uncertain temper made managing him too much of a chore for everyday riding. Then he set out toward Merry Creek. Toward—Deadman's Jump. He'd told her about it, about its small but steady toll of heedless riders and their mounts over the years.

But there was no sign of her there. No hoof tracks in the grassed-over path leading towards the falls. No wheel marks. He sat there, thinking about that. Then the other alternative came to him. If not—death, then consolation. But who—

He bowed his head. Pulled Prince Charlie up. Started off towards Caneville-Sainte Marie. Got there, rode on through the town without stopping. It was well after midnight by then. He went on. Came to his niece's house. Got down. Went up on the stoop. Knocked on the door.

Billie Jo opened it. She was sobbing like a demented woman. Her eyes were wild.

"He—he's left me!" she moaned. "He said he'd had enough of my stupid jealousy and—and—"

She stopped. Her mouth came open. She put both her hands over it. Said through her wide spread fingers:

"Oh, no! Oh, no! Oh, please, no; please!"

"Yes," Oliver said wearily. "Fanny, too. I suppose she must have met him somewhere by accident. Or maybe they planned it together, some time ago. Anyhow—"

His voice trailed off.

"Go to bed, child," he said.

"Oh, Uncle Oliver!" she moaned. "Uncle Oliver, please! I—I love him. I can't live without him, I—So please don't! I beg you—please—"

"Honey," Oliver Prescott said, "I haven't so much as a penknife in my pocket. And if I had, I wouldn't use it. Not in this case. Phil's a fool—and my poor Fanny is—mad. Or very nearly. If I find 'em, I'll send your boy home, unhurt. With his tail between his legs, maybe—but not a scratch on him. Now go lie down like a good girl,

Billie. I'll straighten this all out, never you fear . . ."

But he couldn't find them. He couldn't, because he didn't know where to look. His contempt for Leonard Colfax was so complete that the name of his late mistress's husband never even crossed his mind. So he didn't look in the right places. For it *was* places, plural, separate and apart. Philippe sat before the pot-bellied stove in the Mertontown Inn. He was bleary drunk. He sat there very still, not even having to resist that fat and blowsy Marie's advances any more, because she had wearied of the whole thing, given up. And Fanny—

But you know where Fanny is, what she is doing don't you? Let's skip the more than faintly nauseating details.

Oliver rode back home again when the sun was already up. But she wasn't there. She still wasn't there.

It was nearly noon when she came back again. She came into his study just the way she was. Mouth bruised, hair wild, stinking of male sweat, of her own. With semen stains dirty white on the back of the dress she hadn't even bothered to take off this time.

He sat there looking at her. She went to the mantel, took down his riding crop. Held it out to him.

"Here," she said, "take it. Beat me—to death, Oliver."

He went on looking at her.

"Take it!" she screamed at him. "Beat me bloody! Kill me!"

He went on looking at her. Sighed. Said, very gently:

"Go wash yourself, Fanny. You stink, you know."

"Yes," she said, "I stink. Only what good would washing do, Oliver? That's—my soul you smell. Rotting. 'Cause it's dead, you know. It's got—maggots in it. Buzzard's puke all over it. 'Cause not even—a buzzard could eat it—it stinks so goddamn bad . . ."

"Fanny," he said, his voice hoarse with pity. "What on earth—am I going to do with you?"

"Kill me," she said. "You'd shoot old Bess—if she broke her leg, wouldn't you? Why won't you do that much for me? Put me out of my misery. 'Cause it hurts, Oliver. All the places I'm bleeding hurt. Even though you can't see 'em. The nail holes and the spear hole, too, when they crucified me—"

"That's a blasphemy, Fanny!" he said.

"That's—a truth, Oliver. I've been crucified all my life,

because starting with Papa nobody ever really loved me or tried to understand. Only it's taking me too long to die. I can't bear it any longer. So—shoot me—Oliver. Shoot your bad-hurt mongrel bitch. Huh—please?"

"No," he said tiredly. "Reckon I'll just have to try to cure you, child."

She stood there looking at him, and her eyes were terrible.

"Oh, you fool. You poor-spirited miserable goddamn fool," she said.

## Chapter Thirty-Five

That same morning Philippe Sompayac rode slowly homeward through two simultaneously existing desolations: the rain-drenched bayou-country landscape, and that formless, featureless aching void existing in his mind, his heart.

He was trapped in a cul de sac, he realized, of his own making. His marriage, and his life, as far as any meaningful functioning as a husband and a man was concerned, were both over. He could, of course, avoid an open rupture with Billie Jo; but a relationship become in fact a carefully embalmed corpse was not, for all the chemicals pumped into veins empty of the stuff of life, any the less dead. The best one could hope for was to delay putrefaction for a while; accepting with what resignation one could muster the fact that in the end the rot, the stench, the blind crawling things would appear to work their noisome necessary ends. And if the matter finally came to a parting of their ways—as he had the despairing feeling that it would—his whole future sank away before his mind's eyes into a dismal winterscape of gray skies crisscrossed with the black naked boughs of trees—"bare ruined choirs where late the sweet birds sang . . ."

Because the possibility of taking up a new life with Fanny was not only practically nonexistent; but not even worth serious consideration if, by some miracle, it should suddenly present itself, disguised as opportunity, and ready for seizing. For, as Hans Volker had put it, being in love with a woman was no valid excuse for marrying her; conceivably it might well be the worst possible reason for doing so—especially when you knew the woman as appallingly well as he knew Fanny Turner.

Because he had found out last night, on the eve of his last, disastrous quarrel with Billie Jo—through, as usual, the Negro grapevine—that Fanny *had* in fact paid one brief call—less than an hour all told—on Leonard Colfax at his house.

'Merde!' he thought, 'the world is full of bastards made in a five-minute tumble behind the barn. As far as screwing is concerned an hour is one hell of a long time!'

But he didn't believe anything had happened—yet. What turned the little food he had been able to get down since receiving that news into a delectable stew of bats, toads, newts, lizards, snakes, polecats, and turkey buzzards, all garnished with fishhooks and broken glass, was his sick certainty that something damned well would—and soon.

'Figures,' he thought, 'Lennie is repulsive, repugnant, loathsome, nauseating—and *therefore,* he attracts her. Because in the weird depths of that little mind that Leopold von Sacher-Masoch designed for her, with some slight assistance from the Marquis de Sade, the punishment must fit the crime. Ergo: Lennie. Who merely by existing guarantees that the punishment will not only fit the crime like a second skin, but will coexist simultaneously with it, if not actually precede it!

'That's one thing. Another is—that business of the late Mrs. Colfax—of Ruth—Lennie's dead wife. Whom Oliver—took. With her own devoted assistance, of course—Sic semper mulieres mundi! But by offering Lennie vengeance, Fanny has found the very rack upon which to break Oliver. And for what? For the crime of loving her, for the sin of being good to her, for the offense of not grinding her face into the dirt—as she's sure he ought to. Bon Dieu! Quel espèce de—quoi? Madness? Worse. Madmen are sometimes—happy. And that's the final answer to Hans Volker's not-quite-rhetorical questions! Madmen are the only people who arrive at happiness, because to achieve it in this world—one must be mad—

'So, now. Back to Billie Jo—offering her the crumbs of my affection, some small portion of my vagrant heart. Along with a life of grinding poverty because I drifted into a profession that I have no talent for, slight interest in, and practice very badly indeed. Theory—all right. But get my elongated head of a Normandy âne out of a book, and I'm lost. Next to Carter and Thompson, I'm the undertaker's best friend in this parish. Nom d'un nom d'un chien, *what* am I good for, after all? Bad doctor, bad friend, miserable husband—will I even make good fertilizer after I'm dead?'

He came up to the house. Before he got there, he saw Billie Jo, dressed for travel, and surrounded by valises, standing on the stoop. Inside his guts, something pulled apart. The pain he felt then, at that moment, was the second most nearly insupportable agony he had felt in all his life; the first being, of course, the hour he'd read the cutting from the *Picayune* describing Bill Turner's death and stating its cause. Still, being who and what he was, he summoned up the bitter rod of pride to stand tall amid the bloody rags and tatters of his life, compelled himself to what even he knew was an insane and asinine show of dignity.

"Would it be too much trouble to drive me to the station?" Billie Jo said; then added, the words a whiplash, "That is, if you're not too worn out?"

"It," Philippe said, "will be a pleasure, Billie Jo. For this relief, much thanks! And don't worry your little head over whether I'm tired or not. Pleasant activites are seldom fatiguing—really—"

She stared at him, said, whispering the words:

"So—you aren't even going to deny you were with her?"

"Would you believe me if I did?" he said.

Slowly, she shook her head.

"Help me with my bags, Philippe," she said.

In the buggy, she said, quietly, another thing:

"Philippe—promise me something—"

"Now," he mocked, "that depends—"

"Promise me to stay out of Uncle Oliver's way. He—he gave me his word that he—wouldn't—take action against you or Fanny either one, but—"

Philippe turned, stared at her.

"You mean," he grated, "that you actually went to Oliver with your stupid, jealous suspicions, Billie Jo? Your utterly groundless suspicions, may I add?"

"No," Billie Jo whispered, "he—came out here. Look-

ing for her, for both of you. Since she didn't come home
all night long either, he figured—"

Then she saw his face, his eyes.

"So—" she whispered, "it—it wasn't you!"

He bent his head, stared at the hindquarters of his
horse. It seemed a singularly appropriate object to be staring at. 'Horse's ass, meet horse's ass!' he snarled inside his
mind.

"No," he said, "it wasn't me. And, for your information, just to set the record straight, since I married you, it
has never been. Now, shall I turn this creaking wreck
around and take us back to our little lovenest, there to
stay until we find or invent some other way to make each
other miserable?"

"No," she said sadly, "take me to the station, Philippe.
I'm leaving. But at least I've got—a better—no, a truer—
reason for it, now."

He whipped up his horse.

"Mind telling me what that truer reason is?" he said.

"You wouldn't understand it. You'd have to be a
woman to. Put it this way: When a man sits in a
buggy—and dies—literally dies—inside himself—behind
his eyes—because the women he *loves* has betrayed him,
he makes of any other who—shares his bed—an adulteress, even if she is his wife in the sight of God and man.
And all the solemn words and important-looking certificates don't mean a thing, against *that*. I came after you
to Paris—and led you astray—Into a marriage that was
no marriage at all. That never could have been, never
will be, 'cause you're wedded to *her*, in your mind, your
heart. I'm sorry I did it, but that's neither here nor there
now, is it?"

"No," he said bleakly, "I suppose it isn't."

They stopped talking then. There wasn't anything more
to be said between them. All the words had been used up.
Meaningful or meaningless, tender or hurtful, they all
had. There was a sense of fatality about this parting, a curious inevitablity that Fanny had nothing to do with. If,
before they had reached the Mertontown station, a rider
had brought them the news that Fanny was dead, they
very probably would not have turned back. For if the romantic assertion that this man and this woman were made
for one another is utter, blatant nonsense, its opposite is

simple truth. That this man and this woman were *not* made for one another is one of life's gratuitous cruelties, demonstrated every day.

'Along with,' Philippe thought bleakly, 'the slightly crueler one that there are quite a few men and women for whom absolutely no one is made. So—Get thee to a nunnery! Hie—away! Or to a monastery. Or to an anchorite's cell. Or—to your grave. An—appealing thought, that last. I begin to see why Fanny—so often entertained it. For right now, at this minute, I—'

They stood there on the station platform, side by side, not looking at each other. They didn't talk. The train came, even the noise it made lost in the silence between them.

Billie Jo, turned, put out her hand to him, said, gravely:

"Good-bye, Philippe."

He stood there, thinking: 'What if I were to jerk her into my arms, smother her with kisses, sweep her off her feet, bear her away by main force, what—?'

He took her hand, said, just as gravely:

"Good-bye, Billie Jo. You—you'll write me?"

She shook her head, whispering:

"No, Philippe. Halfway measures don't work. This good-bye is forever. I'm sorry, truly. But that's the way it has to be."

He didn't say anything else. He took her arm, helped her up into the train car. A passing Negro saw him do that. Stopped and watched as Philippe handed up her bags to the train porter. Then he moved on. Philippe didn't see him, wouldn't have known him if he had. Which made no difference. Helping white people wreck their lives was, at that time, one of the few instruments of vengeance that black men had.

"Miz Fanny, honey," Louella said, "I plumb don' like this! Mister Oliver find out, he—"

"Shut up!" Fanny hissed at her. "He won't find out. That's why I brought you along. You sit right here on your narrow black ass in this buggy 'til I come back. I'm going in the five and dime. In the front door and out the back. Anybody ask you, you tell 'em the truth. That I went in the Five and Ten Cents Store to buy some ribbons. And I *am* going to buy some ribbons, so the clerk will remember that. Where I'm going after I come out of the other side of the store, you *can't* tell anybody, because I'm not even going to tell *you*, understand? So if Oliver asks you, you tell the honest-God truth, that you didn't *know*. Besides, he won't be asking anybody, anything, very long—"

"Oh, Jesus!" Louella said. "Why'd I hafta go 'n open my big mouf. Shoulda known I oughtn't to a' told you that business Cindy told me about Mister Oliver and Mr. Colfax's wife! Swear to Gawd I don' see why you's taken on so over hit. That was 'fore your time 'n th' po' lady's *daid*, her. So what skin is hit off o' your nose, honey, if Mister Oliver did pleasure her a right smart bit? Knocked her up—all right. But that happens oncet in a while when menfolks drops they pants and wimmenfolks takes off they drawers 'n rolls they skirts up round they waists. Died havin' Mister Oliver's kid. Mighty sad, mighty sad. But since that happened 'fore he even knowed you was alive, it ain't no more yo' bizniss than—Oh, shit!"

"Go on," Fanny said grimly, "say it."

"Honey, I don' mean to git *you* riled, neither. But a man what can ferget his woman done spent nigh onto three years in a ho'house, his ol' lady oughta ferget that he done done a li'l cundangling in his day. Wouldn't be no man effen he didn't . . ."

"Lou, sometimes you're a goddamned fool," Fanny said.

"Knows that. Only what is I bein' a fool 'bout *now*?"

"That it even crossed the back part of your mind I give two hoots up a hollow stump what Oliver did, or what he *does* for that matter. Hell, he could bring a woman home and do it to her on the front gallerie, and I'd stand by and fan the flies off both their wiggling asses for 'em. A person doesn't have to care about a thing to *use* it, does she?"

"No 'm, honey; but what I can't figger is *why* you wants to use sumpin' 'ginst Mister Oliver in the first place. Cause if they ever was a man any gal in her right mind ought wanta keep it's—"

"Him. Only I'm not in my right mind, and I can't *stand* him. He's too *good*, Lou. Reckon it's because I'm so used to rat bastards. More my style. Now do what I say. You sit here 'til I come back, you hear?"

"Yes 'm," Lou said; then: "Oh Lord!"

One of the maddening things about small towns is that everybody knows everybody else, an accidental circumstance that results in the most effective curtailment of both liberty and privacy ever invented. So when Marie, the innkeeper's daughter let Fanny in a back door opening on a narrow blind alley and showed her those dank, interior, foul-smelling back stairs that led directly to the rooms on the second floor without passing through the tavern at all—an arrangement that was the source of a considerable part of the innkeeper's earnings, because even in small towns, human nature being what it is, fornication and adultery are not the least popular of indoor sports—she knew at once who Fanny was, just as she knew the name and a good bit of the personal history of the middle-aged gentleman farmer waiting for her in room number nine. What Marie still didn't know was that there was a certain connection—of interests say—between Mrs. Oliver Prescott, and young Dr. Philippe Sompayac; or else she would have proceeded with greater caution. But then, poor Marie was already the victim of a completely unrealistic euphoria because of the news that had just reached her ears.

For the unknown black messenger of the ribald gods had done his works well: By then, three-quarters of Mertontown knew that Philippe's wife had left him. Long before nightfall that deliciously titillating knowledge would be shared by the entire town.

"Kiss me, honey," Lennie Colfax said.

"No," Fanny said. "Your breath stinks, Lennie. Besides you disgust me, anyhow."

"Funny way you got o' showin' it if I do," Lennie said.

"You do," Fanny said, "but then, sometimes I enjoy being disgusted. That's the only thing I like about you Lennie: you don't even try to pretend you're not a filthy rat-bastard swine."

She stood there, looking at him; then she shrugged.

"Oh hell, all right," she said, and crossed over to the chair he was in and sat down on his lap. The first thing she did was to put down her hand and clutch at him, to see if he were in a state of excitement sufficient for her to risk what she had in mind.

He wasn't. Lennie's problem was not any kind of perversion, or even effeminacy. He was completely heterosexual in his inclinations. And since he had very little imagination even his vices had been more or less normal up until he had met Fanny. She had introduced him to the practice of cunnilingus out of pure abysmal malice, not because she especially enjoyed it, but because she got an obscene thrill out of degrading Lennie to that extent, and a curiously smug feeling of superiority by refusing the reciprocate in kind. Lennie's real trouble was that he was at least semi-impotent, which made having any kind of sexual relations with him trying indeed.

So now she had to submit to being pawed, fingered, mouthed over, sucked at, and otherwise abused until he was in a state of readiness. The minute she noted that he was, she jumped down from his lap, and began to put back on those items of clothing he had pulled off of her, rebutton those unbuttoned, rearrange the disarranged.

"Fanny, Lord God!" he said.

"No," she said. "I don't feel like it."

"Fan, hon, please!" he moaned.

"No," she said.

"I'll do anything you want. Go down on you. Even——"

"No," Fanny said.

"Oh Lord, Oh God, Oh Jesus, Fan!"

She peered at him, that look of idiot's cunning back in her eyes.

"If I let you," she whispered, "will you do anything I tell you to?"

"God, yes! Anything!" Lennie said.

"Even if I were to tell you to—to kill my husband?" she murmured, slowly, softly, sweetly. "Even *that*—Lennie?"

Lennie sat there. His thick lips quivered. A white slime of saliva stole out of the corners of them, dribbled down his chins. His face went whiter than its grayish bread-dough normal shade. Looking down, Fanny saw that he'd lost his erection.

She stood there, looking at him. The rage in her was absolutely bottomless. As abysmal almost as her contempt. Then her shoulders sagged. She thought: 'Should have known better. A man, in his place, would have gunned Oliver down back then—or died trying. Oh hell, I—'

"Good-bye, Lennie—forever," she said.

Coming out of that hidden back door, she walked half-way around the tavern to reach the main street of Mertontown. To go back to where she'd left Louella sitting in her buggy, she had to pass in front of the inn, itself. Since there was no help for that, she took a deep breath, and started by in a rush, giving, as she did so, a sidelong glance above its classic short swinging doors to see if there were any man in it who might recognize her and start the wave of comment that would reach Oliver's ears in days, if not in hours. And stopped dead, for standing at the bar, already glassy-eyed, was Philippe Sompayac.

'Heard that,' she thought with aching pity. 'No—Oliver told me. That Phil's turning into—a drunk. Trouble at home. And in his profession, too. Folks say he's a piss-poor doctor, bad as Dr. Carter, almost. Was trying to de-liver Sue Felthorn's twins—and couldn't. Had to send a little nigger flying for Dr. Volker to get him out of the mess he was in. Oh Lord! The poor sweet bumbling fool! And I can't even go in there to—'

It was then that Marie crossed her line of vision. Fanny didn't hesitate; she put two fingers into her mouth and whistled at the tavern wench, both the gesture and the sound being vulgar in the extreme—a thing that no lady of that slightly post-Victorian epoch would have even known how to do, much less dared attempt. But they had the desired effect: Marie whirled so fast she almost dropped the tray she had in her hands.

Fanny tossed her head in the direction of the street. Marie took the hint and came.

"Yes—ma'am?" she said; studied insolence moving through her tone.

Fanny ignored that.

"C'mon, Marie," she said, "a little further from that door. I don't want to be seen y 'know."

"Yes 'm—" Marie said.

"Here," Fanny said, and slipped a five-dollar bill into Marie's hand. "This is to exercise your memory—and your forgettery, both. Forget you've seen me today. For-get you've ever seen me—or that you know my name. All right?"

"Yes—ma'am!" Marie said.

"But remember the things I'm going to ask you now: That tall, handsome fellow in there—do you know his name?"

Marie put her hand on her hip in a gesture that was a classic of its kind.

"You mean Doc Phil Sompayac over there by the bar? *Know* him? Huh! Do I, though!" she said.

Fanny stared at her, at the small-town tavern slattern, and her fair brows crashed together above the bridge of her nose.

"What do you mean by that, Marie?" she said very, very quietly.

"Well, ma'am," Marie said, savoring her triumph, "ain't no use o' neither you nor me making like we was lilies o' the valley, if you get what I mean—"

"There, you're right, I'm afraid," Fanny said calmly; though inside her, black murder shrieked and gibbered and tore at its chains. "Go on, Marie—"

"Him 'n me," Marie simpered, "has got—well—a kind of arrangement, ma'am. Him 'n his missus don't get along. So sometimes when he's feeling real blue, he comes here, late at night—"

"And you turn him every way but loose," Fanny said.

"Right, dearie—I mean ma'am! Damn right—and is he ever the great one in th' hay!"

Fanny was trembling on the inside, but she held on to her control.

"Fact is," Marie went on, dreaming now, erecting lofty towers and battlements of her favorite castle in the clouds, "I'm pretty sure we're gonna be able to make it—permanent, him 'n me. His missus ups 'n leaves his bed 'n board this morning. Right now, he's way, way down. So's all I got to do is play my cards right 'n—"

Fanny stood there, her teeth clenched together so hard that they ground against one another until that seizure, that paroxysm of blind and blinding rage left her, turned her loose. The way she smiled at Marie then was a masterpiece of pure feline malice.

"I wish you—luck, Marie," she said. Then she moved off down the street.

One of the town's leading citizens, Brigadier General Gerald Coxsgrove, late of the C.S.A., watched her go, as he sat warming his old bones in the afternoon sun on one of the benches before the Confederate Monument. Nudging his equally ancient friend, Colonel Bill Graves, who had commanded "Graves's Raiders" in the only War there ever was or ever would be as far as Southern men were concerned, so that just to say "the War" would suffice them until the final trump of doom called the ultimate warrior home, he rasped:

"There goes Southern Womanhood, by God, Billy me Boy! A *real* Lady, that young Miz Prescott, 'pon my word, she is!"

And, who knows? In one way or another, he may even have been—right.

## Chapter Thirty-Six

Fanny pulled the buggy up before the gate. Turned to Louella.

"Get down. Go fry all your black bitch friends' hair in grease for them," she said.

"Miz Fanny, Lord God! Mister Oliver be home any minute now. What I'm gonna tell him, me?" Louella said.

"Tell him to go fuck himself. Or to change his luck with you. On the parlor rug. Or upstairs in bed. I don't give a damn either way," Fanny said.

"Honey—you's crazy, you is!" Louella wailed.

Fanny looked at her.

"You're not telling me anything I don't know, Lou," she said. "But, then, what good did being sane ever do me?"

"Miz Fanny, honey, I—"

"Get down, Lou!" Fanny said.

Slowly Louella got down. Fanny flapped the reins over Danny Boy's back. The buggy moved off.

'Can't let her do this,' Louella thought. 'Purely can't. Ruin her life this away. Ruin mine. When both of us is got a chance. Mister Oliver send me packin' sho'. Jus when I got Isaac ready to stand up 'fore the preacher 'n say "I do." Oh, Lord God Almighty, I—'

She flung herself at the horse's head, clawing at the reins.

Fanny's eyes turned gray ice, every trace of blue gone from them. She put out her hand. Took the buggy whip out of its socket.

"Turn that horse loose, Lou," she said.

"No 'm!" Louella moaned; "I won't. I can't. Lord God, Miz Fanny, you—"

Fanny brought the whip around sideways. It whistled, eerily. Bit flesh across the side of Louella's face, opening it almost to the bone.

Louella dropped the reins. Put up her hand, and felt her cheek. Her fingers came away thick with blood. But she didn't scream or cry or even moan. She stood there with blood seeping out of that whip slash and oozing down her face and watched Fanny drive away. She'd been black all her life, so she knew from experience when to quit. All black wisdom was like that, based on, and layered deep with pain.

'Wonder where she goin'?' she thought now without even anger. 'That ain't the way to ol' Mr. Colfax's house. Lord Jesus, who ever would of believed that! But Isaac swear that Colfax's nigger wasn't lyin'. Said you could tell. Lord God, was po' Isaac fit to be tied! First time I ever did see that sweet ol' long-tall black boy o' mine like that! Come home madder 'n a wet settin' hen, ready to go straight to Mister Oliver wit' hit, afore I stopped him. All set to tell that po' good-hearted, softheaded white gentleman what was fool enough to marry a ho' in the first place, what that bare-assed Colfax nigger said: "Mister Lennie sho' Lawd is gittin' even wit' Mister Oliver for po' Miz Ruth. Paying' him back th' same way—a-pleasuring that li'l yaller-headed Miz Fanny right there in th' Colfax Big House. Up in town, too. Pleasuring her right smart good, too; 'cause she sho' do sing a joyful noise unto the Lawd afore he gits through!"

'Tell Mister Oliver that—and they'll be a killin'. An' a hangin'. 'Cause ain't no jedge 'n no jury what would let Mister Oliver off for killin' Mister Lennie. They'd say Mister Oliver done done a damn sight too much to him afore now—'

She stood there, staring at Fanny's buggy as it diminished into the twin dimensions of distance, time.

'That there's th' way to Caneville-Sainte Marie. 'N Mr. Lennie live t'other way—way to Mertontown. Oh Jesus! Doc Phil live out that way! Past Caneville-Sainte Marie. Naw—don't be a Jenny-ass, Louella, gal! She wouldn't do that. Even Miz Fanny wouldn't go pay no visit on no married man in his own house with his wife to home. That's all of thirteen miles. Ten to Caneville, three to they house. Awful po li'l house. Not much better than a nigger dog-trot cabin. Be nigh onto midnight when she git there. So Miz Billie Jo be there sho'. So she won't do that. But why she go thataway for anyhow?'

Louella grinned. The gesture caused her whip-slashed cheek to hurt.

'Lord, is I ever dumb! Nachl'ly she go thataway! Go t'other, she run into Mister Oliver sho', comin' home! So she go th' wrong way, circle round wide an'—'

Louella turned, and with hand pressed to her bleeding cheek, started towards the house.

'Miz Fanny don' tell me *nothin'* no more,' she thought, sadly. 'Don' trust me, I reckon. O' scairt I tell Isaac 'n he—Shit! Don' make no never mind, nohows. Us niggers got ways o' knowin'. White folks thinks we'uns is dumb: but we ain't. We knows ever' damn thing they do almost 'fore they quit doin' it! Jesus, my face hurts. But cain't fault her now. She—crazy, th' po' li'l thing—'

Isaac went into Mertontown the next day to buy a set of harness for the twin mules who pulled the produce wagon, and were his special pride. And as always he visited the Negro quarter, had himself a shot in the black saloon. And also as always, a black messenger of mocking fate sidled up to him and said:

"Buy a feller a snort, Isaac?"

"What for, nigger?" Isaac said.

"Tell you sumpin' you oughta know—" Fate's Messenger said.

"Sumpin' worth a snort?" Isaac said.

"I tell you first, then you be th' jedge," Fate's Messenger said. "Your boss niece done left her husband flat. Took a Nawthbound train yestiddy mornin'. Po' fellow was lappin' up rotgut in th' Tavern all yestiddy evening— Now do I git my snort?"

"Hell, nigger, for that you gits *two* snorts," Isaac said.

Gentle reader, observe that timing well. For Fate has many ways of displaying her basic malice—or, if you will, demonstrating that the human condition is both absurd and tragic; that we are born of a burst-through condom, a leaky diaphragm, a forgotten pill, endure the long nausea of existence, and end in a worm's gut; motives enough to compel each generation, in its turn, to docilely reinvent God.

As in this, the almost studied cruelty of delaying for nearly twenty-four hours the information that would have let Louella know where Fanny was really going, so that when Oliver Prescott came home, bringing—in his desperation, his need of counsel—Dr. Hans Volker with him, the black girl wouldn't have misinformed him, as she actually did, out of the mistaken, but quite honest belief that she was telling the truth.

Yet—who can say? Perhaps Fate's motives were not unmixed. For, if Louella's error permitted time and to spare for sin, it also provided a slim margin for salvation. Temporary salvation, of course. For the burden of the proof lies forever upon those who insist there is any other kind.

But at the moment that concerns us here, those twenty-four hours have yet to come and go. Louella, her hand pressed to her bleeding cheek, is walking towards the house. And her knowledge of the facts, motives, circumstances, surrounding those star-crossed blighted lives is still sadly, if not fatally, incomplete, as human knowledge always is.

For, having eaten of the fruit, what did we learn but that we were naked? "Bare-assed," Louella would have put it.

Without even a fig leaf to cover our ugly hairy parts.

Oliver Prescott sat beside Hans Volker as the old doctor drove towards the farm. He had tied Bess behind the doctor's buggy so that he could go on discussing the matter on the way.

"It's like this, Doctor Hans," he said soberly. "I'm as proud as the next man—and having to tell this to anybody, even as good a friend as you, plumb makes me sick to my big gut. But it ain't—the ordinary kind of dirty linen a body can't stand to air in public. In a way this is—a professional consultation. 'Cause it seems to me—that the poor child I married is mighty sick. Hate like hell to have to commit her, but—"

Hans Volker looked at him.

"All right, Oliver," he said: "one goddamned personal question: You—don't neglect the little woman nights, do you? I ask that as your doctor, not as your friend. You're getting along—and since you always were a discreet cuss nobody's ever been able to pin anything on you, except that *one* time. So I don't know whether you're God's gift to women in the hay, or a short-fused dud. Though to judge by the poor sweet woman, you—"

"You don't *know* that, Hans!" Oliver said sharply.

"Oh don't be a horses's ass, Oliver! I can't *prove* it; but I wish I were as sure that heaven's my eventual home as I am that you were the guilty party in Ruth Colfax's case. So let's skip that part, and get down to rock bottom. You take good care of that baby girl you married nights, or don't you?"

Oliver looked away from him, looked back again.

"Damned good care, Hans," he said quietly.

"All right," Hans Volker said, "I'll buy that.    You're goddamn fit, and you're one of the Cassius types—"

"Cassius?" Oliver said.

"Shakespeare. *Julius Caesar:* 'Yond Cassius has a lean and hungry look. Such men are dangerous!' "

Oliver laughed then; but the sound of it was sad.

"Fact. Skinny fellows are better, healthier, and last longer. Besides, if a man is good at it, your age is damn near his prime. Overcome both haste and anxiety by then. All my female patients—the ones who trust me enough to talk about that aspect of life—confirm that. A seasoned swordsman is always best—"

"Thanks, Doc!" Oliver said sardonically.

"So—since you're damned sure of your abilities in that department you attribute—your wife's—cheating—to insanity?" Hans Volker said. "Lord Oliver, on that score, this parish is just full of crazy women!"

"No. Not that alone. Lord, you'd have to know her whole history to understand, and I couldn't—it wouldn' be fair to her for me to—"

"Tell me she's an ex-inmate of a Storyville parlo house. Mae Hartman's, in fact. And there's one little iten

I'll bet even *you* don't know. Mae's—her mother. Her *real* mother, Oliver. Detective Turner's *first* wife."

Oliver stared at Dr. Volker. Said: "Je-sus!" so low it almost was a variation upon the theme of silence.

"I won't tell you the original source of my information," Hans Volker said. "Can't. Call it—a professional confidence, Oliver, and let it go at that. What I will tell you is that I didn't believe it at first. Couldn't. That child has the face of an angel out of glory—"

"Which is what she acts like most of the time," Oliver said; "but the rest—she's a she-devil, or a fiend. Anyhow, I can guess who told you. My niece. It seems her husband, your fine young colleague—damned poor reputation as a sawbones he's acquiring!—is my Fanny's partner in sin."

"You don't expect me to confirm your suspicions, do you, Oliver? You should know me better than that. And I have reasons for doubting Sompayac's really guilty. Good reasons. What I'm getting at is, that seeing as how you're the best friend I've got in this world—"

"Thanks, Hans—for that," Oliver said.

"Hardly a compliment! I'm no great shakes, God knows! The point is, I made it my business to investigate. Took three days off. Went down New Orleans. Talked to everybody who ever knew the Turner family—or at least everybody I could find. Old colored woman named Eliza who used to work for them—some of the dead-game sports responsible for Fanny's first misstep, though their leader's got his, I'm told. The babes at Mae Hartman's—"

"How were they, Doc?" Oliver said with a slow grin.

"Hell, Oliver, I quit buying tail ten years ago. No—nearer fifteen. And if you want to know how they were, I'll give you one word: Horrible. Ghoulish. Painted wrecks—even the prettier ones. Don't see how little Fanny ever kept her looks—Even talked to Mae herself. Fanny's life story is one of the saddest, most dreadful, most tragic—"

"You grant her—the stature of tragedy, then?" Oliver said.

"Yes. Why yes, of course. Don't you?"

"Well—" Oliver said.

"Well, nothing! She has—a mind. And great spirit. —a certain basic fineness that none of the others have.

She's as different from the rest as day is from night. I came away convinced of the same thing that you are now: Fanny's sick—very sick. All whores are, of course. A woman who wasn't emotionally unbalanced, say, mentally retarded, too, usually, *couldn't* be a prostitute, Oliver. But because—as you know damned well—Fanny has, as a person, both depth and stature, if you get what I mean, she's even sicker than the rest. Terribly sick—even, yes, yes! I insist upon the word—tragically!"

"So?" Oliver whispered.

"So I'll do what I can, until Duncan Childers gets here. Some time after New Years, he says in his last letter. Not that even he is really an alienist. But he *has* studied it, and in Vienna, at that, so maybe—"

A silence fell between them. The house was in sight now. They could see the lamplight glowing from the windows.

"Drive around back, Hans," Oliver said. "Let Isaac take care of your nag. Water him, give him his oats. A rub-down wouldn't hurt. Poor beast looks tired—"

"This fugituve from the glue factory was *born* tired," Hans Volker snorted. "When we go inside, don't say anything, Oliver! Let me sort of ease into matters, will you?"

Isaac came out of the barn and took the reins.

"That you, Doctor Hans?" he burst out, "Oh, thank the good Lawd!"

"What's the matter, Isaac?" Oliver said. "Somebody's sick?"

"Nosuh—not sick; hurt, suh. Hit's—hit's Lou. Miz Fanny had—a kind o' fit, suh, and whupped Lou cross the face with her buggy whip. Cut her face sumpin' awful. An' an' Lou's sech a *pretty* woman, suh!"

"That she is, that she is," Oliver said. "Do you know—what caused my wife—what caused Mrs. Prescott to do such a thing, Isaac?"

"Nosuh. Not all of it, anyhow. Lou—tried to stop her from—leavin' here. From goin' someplace where she purely ain't got no business, goin', suh—beggin' you humble pardon, not seein' as how she's got herself the bes' husband any white lady could ever wish for—"

"Thank you, Isaac, Now skip the diplomacy and get to the facts. Do you *know* where Mrs. Prescott's gone?"

"*Knows* hit, suh—nosuh. But I got a mighty good idea

Only Lou *do* know. Wish you'd ax her, suh. Ain't healthy
for no nigger man to git mixed up in whitefolks business.
Ax Lou. An'—an' suh—"

"Yes, Isaac?"

"Don't be too hard on Lou. I loves her, suh. We's aiming to git hitched come Christmas time. An' 'sides, she
sho' Lawd was takin' yo' part when Miz Fanny cut her up
like that—"

"It's all right, Isaac," Oliver said. "I'll treat Louella
mighty kindly—"

He waited, all quiet patience, until Hans Volker had
finished dressing that ugly slash.

"One inch higher, and she'd have lost her left eye," the
old doctor snorted; "Lord God, Oliver—that poor child is
further along the road than even I thought—"

"You means you thinks Miz Fanny's crazy, suh?" Louella whispered. "If that what you thinks, you's right, Doctor Hans. An'—an' she been crazy a long time. Ever since
her poor Pa died, 'pears to me—"

"Louella," Oliver said, "Who was it you were trying to
stop my wife from going to see?"

Louella bowed her head. When she looked up again the
tears stood and glittered in her eyes.

"Please, suh—don' ax me that," she said. "Please, Mister Oliver, suh—please! You can't shoot him. You purely
ain't got the right—"

Oliver stood up.

"I'm not a barbarian, Lou," he said. "I have no intention of making my niece a widow, even if young Dr. Sompayac is a fool. Hardly a criminal offense, anyhow—"

"Young Dr. Sompayac!"Louella said.

Oliver stopped dead. That her surprise was genuine he
saw at once. There was nothing false in it, nothing theatrical. None of that quality that black people called so justly
'puttin' on." Louella *was* surprised. No—astonished.

He bent toward her.

"You said I couldn't shoot him. That I hadn't the
right—"

He straightened up.

"Oh!" he said; then, very softly: "Oh, my God!"

"Yassuh—*him*. You took his woman, folks say. So now
e's done gone 'n paid you back. Took your'n, suh. So,
pears to me, you ain't got no right, Mister Oliver. An'—

an' it ain't even his fault—*she* went after him—drove ou
to his place—met him in Mertontown and Lawd know.
where else—"

Oliver stared at her, and his eyes were terrible, sud
denly.

"Who told Mrs. Prescott that old story, Lou? *You?*"

"Yes, suh," Louella said, defiantly. "I told her, me.
was tryin' to prove to her that that slimy, crawly, creepy
li'l ol' fat Mr. Colfax didn't give a damn 'bout *her*, sub
that all he was tryin' to do was git even with *you* . . ."

Oliver turned to Hans Volker, looked his old friend i
the face. Opened his mouth. But no sound came out of i
No sound at all.

So Dr. Volker said it for him. Asked that question
That ultimate question. Damnable—and damning, at th
same time.

"You mean that Mrs. Prescott—and Mr. Colfa
were—were lovers—*before* you told her that scandalou
old pack of lies about the late Mrs. Colfax—and M:
Prescott, here?"

"Yassuh. She was layin' down 'n spreadin' wide for hi
afore I ever even got here," Louella said.

So, at that hour, Oliver Prescott and Hans Volker star
ed out for Lennie Colfax's farm. They went totally u
armed. There was, they both knew, a certain risk in tha
Even a cornered rat will fight. But not so great a risk :
they would face in a parish courthouse if either of the
killed him, even in self-defense. Because Lou had put t
matter very truly: Oliver couldn't afford vengeance, no
And, as his best friend and second in this matter, Ha
Volker couldn't either.

But, as it turned out, the moral issues involved had :
real bearing on the case. What did count were the blin
uncaring factors of distance, time. Leonard Colfax's far
was six miles from Oliver Prescott's. While Philippe So
payac's cottage was three miles on the other side
Caneville-Sainte Marie, which pleasant little Cajun-C
ole-German-American town was a full ten miles from C
iver's place, in the opposite direction.

So, even after Lennie—spluttering in righteous indigr
tion, and giving vent to remarks like, "You think I'm t
kind o' woman-stealin' polecat *you* are, Oliver? C'mon

both of you! Your missus ain't here, ain't been here, don't even know th' way here, and if you can't even git yours up no more so she's got to look for a little lovin' elsewhere, what skin is that off *my* nose, I ask you that?"—had allowed them to search his house, they still had to ride six miles back to the Prescott place before they could start the thirteen-mile journey to Sompayac's cottage.

And to all the generations born since 1920, say, and hence accustomed to going thirteen miles in thirteen minutes or less, it will be surely necessary to point out that fifteen miles in a horse-drawn buggy was a full day's or night's journey under the best of conditions, while Oliver Prescott and Hans Volker, leaving Lennie Colfax's farm, had to drive, starting long after midnight, a full nineteen miles behind a dead-beat horse, to even put the matter to the test.

Even so, in one way, at least, they were in time.

Going past the Prescott Place, on his way home earlier that same night, Philippe pulled up his horse and stared at the lighted windows.

'Wonder—if she knows?' he thought bleakly. 'Probably does. Even that dumb bitch Marie did, four hours after I put Billie Jo on that train! And if she does—what's she doing, now? Laughing her head off, I'll bet. Poetic justice! I deserted her—left her with child—to learn a profession at which I'm an abject failure. Got married—over there, in Paris, itself—to—Billie Jo. To the one girl on earth she could least bear my being married to. The girl she told the blackest foulest lie her warped and twisted little mind could dream up—in order to get her—get my Billie Jo—the hell out of the way . . .

'So now—Billie's gone. Your mission's accomplished, Fan! And for what? For a back-bayou pill-pusher with a fancy European education who still can't deliver a baby without killing it, or its mother, or both most of the time. Jesus! I start in to lance a boil, and my hand shakes so—

'Merde! For that. For me. The type you sent that glorious mother-naked picture to—in order to wreck his marriage. And you succeeded, Fan, baby! You've wrecked it beyond repair. Only—you don't even want me any longer, do you? Found a substitute, haven't you? For Oliver—and for me—if you even remember I'm alive these days . . .

'Tant pis! Get up, boy—take this poor tired old quack home—to his cold and empty bed! What was the word Martinez, that Cuban boy in my class at Pasteur, taught me? "Mata sanas!" Killer of the healthy. That's me, all right. Jesus, I've drunk enough rotgut to float a battleship, and I'm not even drunk. Even at drowning my sorrows, I'm a failure.'

He drove off, through the night. Got home finally—to that empty cabin, that ultimate aching desolation, just before midnight. Drove around back of it. Unhitched his horse, watered the poor beast, turned him loose in the fenced-off pasture behind the house to graze.

He came up on the stoop, yawning sleepily. Groped among all the keys in the bunch for the right one. As he did so, his elbow touched the door. It swung open, noiselessly.

He stared at it. He had locked it carefully before starting out with Billie Jo for Mertontown. He was very sure of that. He bent, peered at that lock. Searched in his pocket until he found a box of matches. Lit one. Saw the white sear of clean raw wood where someone had forced that door. Just before the match burned down to his fingers and he dropped it with a snarled curse, he looked down and saw, still lying there on the stoop, the tools the intruder had used. His own tools, taken from the toolshed next to his tiny, ramshackle barn.

He stood there peering owlishly at them through the dark. But his drink-fogged brain couldn't figure what they meant.

'A robber?' he thought. 'Petit enfant Jésus! Even a nigger wouldn't go to the trouble to break into a house like this—'

He entered, cautiously, after first having picked up the hammer to serve him as a weapon in case of need. But he really didn't expect to find the burglar there. Five minutes—no, three—would have been enough for a thief to relieve him of all his worldy goods—'And then throw 'em in Merry Creek out of pure disgust,' he thought, 'after he sees what worthless junk they are—'

But even in the dark, he could see the parlor was in perfect order. He pushed open the door to the bedroom and stopped. Lifting his head he sniffed the air. The room was redolent with perfume. That perfume reminded him of something.

'What?' he thought; then it hit him: 'Frankie Belmont's parlor house! All her bitches used to use a scent like this!'

He crossed very surely to the lamp; in his own bed-room, he knew where everything was, even in the dark. Struck a match, lit it, put it down on the mantel, turned, swept his eyes to the dress tossed over the chair, the petti-coat hanging off the corner of the armoire, the chemisette looped over the doorknob, the wide-legged lace umbrella drawers spread out grotesquely on the floor, the filmy silk stocking tossed over the chandelier, the saucy high-but-toned shoes lying, one standing up, one fallen, on the hearthstone of the fireplace, the hat on the table, the bag on the chest, then—he lifted his gaze, he looked toward the big bed where he and Billie Jo—he and Billie Jo—he and Billie Jo—

"Lord did you ever take your sweet time to get here!" Fanny said.

He hung there, fighting for breath, for voice. Found both. The first was reedy, choked, a gasp; the second was ragged, high breathless, all gone.

"You get out of there, Fanny!" he said.

"No. You get in here," Fanny said.

"Fanny, goddamn it!"

"Ah, c'mon, Phil, don't be *mean*," she said.

"Merde!" he howled. "So now I'm supposed to join the parade! Where were you *last* night, Fanny, tell me that!"

She grinned at him, made an impish face.

"Out—fuckin'," she said.

"Jesus!" he screamed. The sound of it was pure an-guish. No—agony.

"What's the odds?" she mocked him. "It doesn't wear out, Phil, darlin'. Besides, I wash. Which is more than your Marie does. Or do you like dirty stinkin' sluts? Doing it to her must be like stirring around in a can of sardines—"

"Fanny—if you don't get out of there I'll—"

"You'll what?" she taunted. "Tell me that? What can you do, you mean poor-spirited back-bayou country quack? Handling *me*—calls for a man. And a *man*—never would have let his woman leave him. He'd have beat the shit out of her first. But you—Oh, hell—Come over here

and let me cop a feel—Let's see if that little freckled
ball-whacking bitch left you anything at all. Bet she cut
'em off right up to your belly-button. Girls like her are
*born* with a gelding knife in their hands, in case you don't
know—"

He stumbled towards her like a spastic, absolutely blind
with rage. Put out his right hand, sunk his fingers into her
hair, straightened up, jerking, powerfully, hearing as he
did so, the soaring flute-note of her laughter:

"Now that's more like it, boy-baby!" Fanny said.

Then she was out of his suddenly nerveless clasp and all
over him. Her nails raked at his face, his eyes. She arched
her head sidewise and down and he felt the double semi-
circular sear of her teeth going into the flesh of his throat,
vulpine, feral, wild.

He put up his hands to break her grip; but they
wouldn't work that way. Instead they tightened around
her slender waist, and she feeling that, noting that, the anguished and agonizing tenderness of his fingers tracing
those endless, awful whipscars on her back, took both her
feet off the floor, swung her legs up around his hips, locking knee and calf behind him, and falling back back so
that his balance gone he crashed down upon her, opening
his mouth to say—to say.

Nothing. For hers was a winescald of passion covering
his, drawing him out of sense, sensibility, reason, will,
while her two hands danced down, wild at his buttons
freeing him, guiding him, arching to him impaling herself
upon him, so that there was no hope of maintaining ever
a momentary control so that powerlessly, will-lessly, but
not mindlessly, because he retained thought enough to be
ashamed of it, he surrendered to the adolescent vice of
ejaculato praecox, feeling twin claws, one of polar ice
and the other of hell's own fire, reach up through his
turned quivering-jelly carcass to the back of his tonsils
and beyond, and drag everything out of him, hollowing
him out from the roots of his hair to the nails of his
tight-curled toes, so that what throbbed burst exploded out
of him into the absolutely feral undulation, thrash boil
writhe of her, into that tight, prehensible, peristaltically
moving, live steamscalding vaginal passage to paradise to
hell, was but his life, his life.

His failure was not complete. Or rather she would neither accept nor permit his failure. She clung to him,
mouth, breasts, belly, loins, hard-gripping thighs, ferociously ripping nails, in a cataclysmic, total flagellation of
flesh upon flesh, in an interior twist and grind and scald
of engorging mucoid tissue all but flaying its erectile male
counterpart until she reached or achieved what was not so
much orgasm as a willed and willful destruction, a momentary immolation of mind, personality, reason, will
upon the penetrant blade of an ecstasy more murderously
cruel than any pain.

Her mouth tore free of his, gulped air, loosed—slow,
soft, ululant, shuddering—a wail of pure despair.

"Fanny—" he groaned.

"Love me," she said bitterly, harshly, angrily, "get out
of your things and love me. Love me to death, Phil—if
you've got the strength and the will and even the kindness,
or otherwise I'm going to have to do it myself some bad
ugly awful hurtin' way 'cause without you I can't won't
don't even want to—live—"

"Fanny!" he wept, sobbing her name.

"Don't cry," she crooned. "Kiss Mama. Here where
baby boys always kiss their mamas. Here—and here.
That's it—Ah-h-h sweet! 'Cause you never did grow up
for real, did you Phil, darlin'?"

Her hands were moving on and in his clothing, pulling,
freeing him. The coolness. Then along all his length, her
silken warmth. Her breath was a rustle in his ear, sculp-
turing words of moving air, forming a litany, a chant:

"Love me. You can. 'Cause there never was anybody
else but you and there never will be can be never. I've
been to bed with fifty thousand men and they never
reached me left me unbroke couldn't even busy my little
old cherry. So you're the only one it's ever been Phil no
man on earth ever got to me reached me made me come
through every pore in my skin just you sweet you like that
you like that slow now slow sweet—sweet slow now only
don't stop keep it up keep it up keep it up don't stop
please don't stop like that—Ah-h-h—sweet! Like that now
like that now. Ah-h-h—now! Oh, now! Oh, Christ, now!
Now, Phil! Give it to me! Give it to me Give—Oh Lord
Oh God Oh Jesus!"

"Fanny," he said, "what are we going to do?"

"Run away together. Some place up north. Or Europe. Italy. I loved Italy, Phil."

"But, Fanny, we can't!"

"Why can't we, darlin'?"

"There's Oliver—"

"Fuck Oliver."

"Fanny, be reasonable!"

"No. Don't want to. Just want you in my bed every night, doing this. Hm-m-m-m—this. M-m-m-m—more this—Now—this. Like—this—"

"Fanny!" he screamed at her.

She propped herself up on her elbow. Looked at him. Said:

"Maybe Oliver would give me a divorce."

"Lord God, Fanny—how could we even ask him that? I'm married to Billie Jo. To his niece and—"

"She left you. And this is Louisiana. Law's special down here. Based on the Napoleonic Code. Woman leaves her hubby, she's done for, Phil, honey. You can walk into any courthouse and the judge will write you out a bill of divorcement, tomorrow—"

'That,' Philippe realized wonderingly, 'is true! But how in the name of everything unholy did she, did Fanny—'

He said: "I couldn't ask Oliver that, I couldn't. He's been too good to me, Fan."

"Yes. Just the trouble with him, the bastard! So goddamned good. Makes me puking sick. All right. So don't. I'll let him catch me with Lennie and—"

He stared at her, whispered:

"Say that—again?"

"I said I'll let him catch me with Lennie. That will really burn him up. And he *can't* shoot Lennie because—of Ruth. Lennie's dead wife. You see, Phil, he—"

"I know that story," Philippe said harshly. "Billie Jo told me."

"Then you get my point. If Oliver were to blast Lennie, he's swing for it sure, and he knows it, Phil! What the hell's the matter with you—now?"

"Fanny—" he whispered, "last night—was it—Lennie?"

"Don't be silly, Phil!" she said airily, "Last night I was home in my own sweet bed—and—and—Phil!"

"Last night—or rather this morning," Philippe said

"Oliver came out here—with a gun in his pocket—looking for you. Because you hadn't been home all night long. Of course I hadn't either, but—"

She gave him a push, said:

"Get away from me! You've got crab-lice sure! If you've been poking yours into anything as filthy as that Marie, you—"

He looked at her, said, quietly:

"Come off of it, Fan! I was in the tavern 'til closing time. Getting drunk—or trying to. I can line up a whole platoon of witnesses to prove that. But you—stayed out all night long. And you have visited Lennie's farm before. A whole hour's visit. Maybe longer. So tell me: Last night—was it—Lennie?"

She looked at him. Sighed. Said:

"Yes, Phil. Doesn't mean anything. I was just getting back at Oliver and, anyhow, Lennie's awful in the hay. Can't fuck worth a good goddamn and—Phil! Don't look at me that way! I can't stand for you to look at me like that. Oh Lord, Oh God, Oh Jesus—Phil, I—"

"Get up," he said. "Get dressed. Get out."

"Phil!" she moaned.

"You heard me, Fanny!"

"But Phil I—I *love* you. You and nobody else. Don't you even understand *that*, you goddamned fool?"

"No, I don't understand it. Maybe I'm too big a god-damned fool."

"And you love *me*. You proved it just now. Nobody can do what you did just now—make me burst into ten million pieces on the inside—then melt—and—and just *flow* right out under the fuckin' doorjamb if he doesn't—"

"Love you. Merde alors! Get up from there, you abys-mal little bitch!"

"No. Come here, Phil. That's it. Closer. Love me—some more. C'mon hon—love me. Do it to me—*good*. Fuck your baby—"

He bent to her. She smiled at him, a smile of pure, tri-umphant malice, because she was sure now, very sure. She lifted her slim white arms, wrapped them about his neck, arched her breasts toward him, her nipples hard, erect, like twin, miniature phalli. He stared at her. Opened his mouth.

And spat into her face.

"*That's* how much I love you, whore," he said. "Now, will you go?"

She got up. Gathered her scattered clothing. Got into them. Stumbled towards the door. In it, she turned.

"Good-bye, Phil. See you—in hell," she said.

She had left her horse and buggy tied up in a pine grove more than a mile down the road. And she wasn't quite sure of how to get to Deadman's Jump from that direction, anyhow. She wasted two hours, all told, before she found it. Time enough for Oliver and Hans Volker to reach Philippe's house. Time for him to respond to their knocking, come padding barefooted to the door in his trousers and shirt. He was gray-faced, bleary-eyed.

"Phil," Oliver said quietly, "tell me the truth, son: Did Fanny—come here last night?"

Philippe looked at him. Said:

"Yes, Oliver." Then, cursing himself silently for a liar and a coward, added: "I put her out. Just because Billie Jo's left me, was no reason for her to think—"

"Billie Jo's—*left* you?" Oliver said.

"Yes. Yesterday. I tried every way I knew to convince her there's nothing between me and Fanny"—'Not *now* there isn't, you yellow bastard!' his mind mocked him—"but she wouldn't listen. I don't even know where she' gone. She wouldn't tell me—"

"Billie Jo's—left you. Then Fanny—came here—an you you put her out. Oh, Jesus! Hans, d'you think tha nag of yours has life enough left in him to get us t Merry Creek? To Deadman's Jump? The Falls?"

Philippe's face was old chalk, decaying plaster.

"Take—mine, Oliver; he—he's had all night to rest," h said.

So they were in time. They heard Danny Boy scream a Fanny lashed him bloody, trying to force him to go ove that blind, impossible, inevitably fatal jump that not eve a riding horse trained in steeplechasing or foxhunting ha a ghost of a chance of making, let alone a horse draggir a buggy behind him.

It was Danny Boy's stubborn refusal to kill himse along with his mistress that gave him the final minute seconds they needed to drag Fanny from that buggy. Sl screamed, fought, clawed, spat, cursed them, employir her whore's vocabulary to such effect that Hans Volker, telling Duncan Childers about it afterwards, swore: "You could smell sulphur and brimstone in the air, son; I looked up and the needles of a pine tree forty yards over-head were turning brown——"

But, after all, they saved her life.

Or perhaps not. Perhaps her private furies had other things in mind for her. Perhaps fate, destiny, God, the Devil, the Principle of Mindless Evil that rules the Universe, call it what you will, decided that getting what she wanted was forever to be denied her. Even when what she wanted was—to die.

There *are* worse things, you know.

## Chapter Thirty-Seven

"Please, suh," Louella said. "Let her come downstairs for my weddin' supper, since you won't let her come to the weddin' itself, in th' church . . ."

"Not won't, Lou; can't," Oliver Prescott said.

"But, suh—she's been so good, these here las' two weeks. You said so yo'self, suh."

"Yes," Oliver sighed, "and that's just what's bothering me, Lou. Look, you probably know her better than I do, than anybody in this miserable world——"

"Don' *nobody know* Miz Fanny, suh," Louella said. "Not for real, anyhow——"

"I'll grant you that. But in all the time you've known her, hasn't she *always* been guilty of what Dr. Childers—I took the liberty of consulting him by mail, after that Deadman's Jump business—calls alternations of behavior? Isn't she always very, very good when she's getting ready to be very, very bad, Lou?"

Louella sighed audibly.

"Well—put like that, suh, I reckon I hafta say yes. Still—I don' know. Oughta be sumpin' a body could do for her. Look how she begged 'n pleaded for me, suh, when you was all set to send me packin' 'cause Isaac wiped up half yo' plantation with Willie——"

Oliver smiled.

"I'll tell you a secret, Lou," he said. "I hadn't the faintest intention of sending you away, really. But a little discipline was in order. Isaac and Willie needed to have a little scare thrown into 'em for being a couple of burrheaded black jackasses. And you needed one, too, for disrupting the harmony of my whole plantation by exercising your feminine wiles. Besides which, you disappointed the hell out of me, anyhow—"

"I disappointed *you*, suh? How?" Louella said.

"I thought you were smarter. That trick of playing one fellow off against the other, to get the one you really want to pop the question, is the oldest one in the books."

"Yassuh," Louella giggled, "it purely is. But seein' how dumb both of 'em is, suh, I dasn't try anything *too* smart, 'cause I was scairt neither one would be able to figger it out . . ."

"But that's not the main way you weren't smart," Oliver said, deliberately making his voice sound stern. "Lou, you damn-fool you, don't you know that a fellow who isn't hungry is *always* late for supper? You could have made Isaac jump over the broomstick weeks ago if you hadn't let him sample the goods ahead of time—"

"Lawd, suh!" Louella quavered, "I never! I swear I never! I—"

"Lou—" Oliver said.

Louella bowed her head. When she looked up, she had tears in her eyes. The bright and bitter tears of honest shame.

"All right, Mister Oliver, suh, you's got me," she whispered. I pleads—guilty, suh. Human nature bein' human nature, 'n nigger nature bein' a sight randier than even that, I 'fess I slipped—once o' twice. I'm plumb downright sorry. I wouldn't have you think bad of me, for all the world—"

"I don't," Oliver sighed. "How could I? And human nature is human nature regardless of the color of the hide it wears. All right Lou, I'll let Mrs. Prescott attend your wedding supper. I'm sure she'll be on her best behavior for the event—"

"Please suh, Miz Fanny ain't—*bad*. Never was, never will be. She jus' done had so damn much happen to her that—"

"It's unbalanced her mind. I know that, Lou."

"Suh, if you could of seed her like I did, sittin' there rockin' back 'n forth with her po' dead pappy's head in her arms—"

"I understand all that, Lou. My wife's past is not the problem. I don't suppose she's ever been truly responsible for her actions, so nothing she's ever done could be truly called a sin. The problem's her future, Louella. From the letters I've had from Dr. Childers and the medical books Dr. Volker has let me read, it's evident that my poor wife is not entirely sane. But—commit her? Have you got any idea what the insane asylums are like in this state?"

"Lawd awful; I knows that, me. Couple o' the girls from the Annex—place I worked *as a maid,* suh—had to be sent up. One of 'em wouldn't take no money from the gentlemens, but when they was 'sleep she'd cut all the buttons off they pants.* And the other one—Lawdy, tha's too awful to talk about, suh! Anyhow, I usta go visit 'em— 'cause they didn't have nobody else, to. Had to quit it— made me so damn sad I was actually gittin' sick—"

"Les filles de joie!" Oliver said bitterly.

"Wha's that, suh?" Louella said. "Hit's French, ain't it?"

"Yes; it means either the girls—or the daughters—of joy. That's what the French call the members of the world's oldest profession. But then, the French call a garbage pail 'une pourbelle'—'for Beauty.' How d'you like that, Lou?"

"They's wrong on both counts then, suh," Louella said soberly. "Them po' critters is the saddest wimmen on earth. Black o' white, they is. An' not none of 'em lives to git old. Dope gits 'em. Bad sicknesses like th' clap 'n the pox, TB. O' they pimps kills 'em. O' they kills theyselves. That more'n anything else, suh. Never worked in a house what didn't have least one gal kill herself *every* month . . ."

"Which is *why* I'm keeping Mrs. Prescott locked up," Oliver sighed, "not for any other reason, Lou. All right, get out of here—I have work to do. But I'll have to admit there's one way you were smart, Lou—"

"How's that, suh?"

"Picking brothers as rivals. So now, even if you do

---

*his classic and *historic* case is part of the legend of Storyville.

present Isaac with a little bundle from heaven ahead of time, he won't be able to say it doesn't look like him. He 'n Willie are almost twins, aren't they?"

"Lord, suh!" Louella said. "I never! 'Sides, I ain't—I swear I ain't—"

"In the family way? Good. I've given my people a fairish education, so every woman on the place knows how to count. And starting from Christmas night, they'll be counting like mad, Lou. So you better make sure they get up to nine. Now get out of here, will you?"

"Yessuh, I'm a-goin', me," Louella said.

Upstairs in the small bedroom, directly above Oliver Prescott's study, Fanny got up off the floor. Then she rolled the rug back over it, covering the crack she had had her left ear pressed to in order to hear what Louella and Oliver had been talking about.

'A—a lunatic asylum!' she thought, making of the words even in her mind a wail of horror and pain. 'Just because I did it with a couple of other fellows. And one of those fellows was—Phil. He *knows* I've been in love with Phil since I was fifteen years old. he knows that. And—'

She stopped, her pale eyes very clear.

'But—the other one? Lennie? Who gives me the heaves just to look at him? So—I *am* crazy—I am. I am. I am I—

'Phil—spat on me. Hawked and spat in my face. Because of that. Because of the other one. Because of—o what's his name? Oh, Lord, I'm forgetting again! I keep on forgetting—all the time forgetting, so now—

'Papa's—going to send me away. To—to where? T school. To the—Emma Willard School—for—Young— Ladies in Troy, New York! There, you see, I remem bered!

'No—that's not right, is it? I—I've been there a ready—That was the school where I threw acid i Norma's face and Sor Giulia said—

'Oh, Jesus! I am! I am! Sor Giulia was in Italy. And wasn't Norma I threw acid on. Norma—I used to— kiss. And do things to. Filthy things. I used to put—n mouth down there between her legs—and—No! N Fanny—you didn't! You never did! It was her who d that to you—and—and you *liked* it. You liked it so much you taught—Lennie!—

'There, that's his name! That little fat sloppy man who that greasy toad frog of a guinea bastard cut all up—his toes and his fingers and his balls and—and his *thing* and put him in a trunk and shipped him to—

'To. Troy—New—York—the Emma Willard School—for Young Ladies and when Sue Beaconridge took him out she had a hemorrhage—and—and died—'

She stood there.

'Got to stop him. Got to stop Papa from sending me to the lunatic asylum. How? Kill Papa, that's how. Only Papa's already dead. He dropped down dead in a New Orleans whorehouse because he found out you were in it selling yourself to men. So if he's dead how could he say to Lou just now that he was going to have you committed? But he did, he did, did!

'So kill Papa. Kill him good this time—So he'll stay dead. With a gun. Oliver's got guns hanging all over his study. Who's—Oliver? My hubby, that's who! My ol' long-tall sweet bald-headed ancient history of hubby who—who does it to me so good! So why is he going to send me to the lunatic asylum? I—I love him. I love Oliver. At least I think I do. One of me does, anyhow, slow and sweet and quiet like music and like praying.

'And the other one of me loves—Phil—and does—awful things—like—like fuckin'—Lennie. So now Papa—No, *Oliver*; get it straight, Fanny, girl! Fat Fanny Fartbuster with pimples on your face! The boys won't dance with you 'cause you're fat and stupid and you stink. The boys won't dance the boys got you drunk and took turns doing it to you and then you somebody took a knife and Eliza said:

' "Oh Jesus!"

'I must—get—it—straight. Oliver, my husband, not my father, wants to send me to a lunatic asylum because—

'Because what?

'Because I—did it with—fifty thousand men in a New Orleans whorehouse and fell down and killed my baby—'

"Oh Lord!"

'Because I—I don't act right. He was good to me and I shamed him. I— committed adultery!—Now that's a nice sweet cultivated way of saying I went out fuckin' all over the place! With Lennie. With Phil. You see? I'm getting it straight! So Papa—No! No!—Oliver—wants to have me committed. And I've got to stop him. I've got to—kill him. Only—only—

'I don't even know how to load a gun, let alone shoot one. Isaac does. Isaac does. I—I'll fool Isaac into—

'No. Willie. Cause Isaac's gonna marry Lou and I can't leave her a widow so soon. Nigger what shoots Papa—No and No and No and No—damn it! Oliver—is going to get lynched sure and—'

She darted to her bureau, dragged the letters out. The ones from Phil. From Martha. From Billy, from Papa, from Beau Dan, from everybody who'd ever written her a line in this world. Last of all Louella. She'd kept them all—all those pitiful proofs that not everybody hated her loathed her despised her that some people a few cared about her wrote her nice sweet letters like this one from Lou.

She crossed to her secretary, sat down, wrote, with Louella's letter before her as a model, imitating very well indeed Louella's handwriting, copying her mode of expression her grammatical errors her erratic spelling, everything:

Dere Willie—

I done changed my mind. Hits you I loves not that damnfool Isaac. So jus you meet me—down by Merry Creek. You know th place folks calls dead man's jump don't you, Sugar Pie? Meet there cause its safe there don't nobody come that way. Bring all the money you got cause us going to 'lope. Cross over into Mississippi and get hitched there. Don't you show this note to nobody specially not Isaac cause he kill you sure. I be waiting. I love you, Lou.

When she had finished the note she sat there thinking about it all, what she had to do, and her mind worked very slowly and carefully and well. It wouldn't have been smart to tell Willie to bring his shotgun because men even nigger men who are eloping with their sweethearts don't ordinarily bring guns along. So she would just have to steal a gun out of the study, herself. Only that was going to take some doing because Oliver kept her locked in her

room now. He'd done that ever since the morning she'd
tried to drive Danny Boy over Deadman's Jump, buggy
and all.

At first, he had thought she had just been despondent
because of her quarrel with Phil; but then, talking to her,
he stopped and said: "Say that again!" and she realized
that she'd called him "Papa" as she often did in her mind.
Then he went on questioning her, and in five minutes flat
he found out how she forgot things and remembered
things wrong and got people and places all mixed up inside her head.

She didn't know why she confused Oliver with her dead
Papa. They didn't look anything alike. She reckoned it
was because they were both old and—and sort of stern—
and at the same time—kind. She wanted both of them to
approve of her, but they wouldn't or maybe couldn't and
anyhow Papa was dead—she had killed him she had killed
old man Jacob Fields she had killed her baby brother
Billy—no, no—not quite, she had burned that girl's
face—what *was* her name?—with acid she had killed her
baby she had killed Rod Schneider she had killed that detective fellow who had beat her with his belt buckle and
made her do that horrible disgusting filthy thing and
whose name was Buzzard she had killed Beau Dan—no!
That was somebody else.

And now she was going to kill Oliver. She really didn't
want to. But now that he'd found that she'd had these
spells of getting mixed up ever since she woke up in the
hospital with her hands and her feet tied to the bed posts,
spread eagled face down in that bed naked because they
hadn't been able to put even a hospital gown on her nor
even bandages because Joe the Whipper had used a thin
flexible steel rod on her and looking at her back had made
the doctors swear and damn and curse and one of the
younger nurses had fainted out right seeing it.

So all they had been able to put on her was salve, and
when they touched her she'd twist and moan and maybe
she would have screamed except that her tongue was so
swollen where she'd bitten it through to keep from making
even a little whimpering noise while old Joe was beating
her that she couldn't. That was when she started getting
confused, but afterwards she got better and stopped being
mixed up almost altogether, and she'd stayed all right un-

til Louella had brought her that French newspaper and Josette had translated the story about Phil's getting married to Billie Jo.

But at first her confusion had taken a different form. She had simply wanted to do bad things—like playing with herself, which was supposed to drive you crazy anyhow, and after that she'd gone out with Irene who was a womanlover like Norma and gone to bed with her and on her nights off instead of going to visit Beau Dan in jail she had picked up a little newspaper boy, a dirty ragged urchin eleven or twelve years old and took him home to Dan's flat and fed him and gave him strong drinks and played with him and made him do it to her. She who'd always bragged about being as cold as ice found that she was thinking about it all the time and dreaming about doing it with cripples and diry old men and bulldagger/dykey women like Norma and Irene and little boys and little girls and animals and even niggers. Only she still didn't enjoy herself with the clients, even though she honestly tried to now.

That was when she realized she wasn't right in her head any more. So when Oliver came and was nice and sweet and kind to her she had grabbed him as a drowning person clutches the tiniest thing that comes floating by.

And it had looked like it was going to work only there was Phil and what was more important Lennie 'cause a girl didn't have to be crazy to want Phil but any woman who even looked at Lennie sideways was stark raving out of her ever-lovin' mind cra-a-a-a-zy!

What to do next? Oliver was still downstairs in his study. Writing letters to the mail-order houses for things he needed for the farm, and sending checks out to pay bills and balancing the books, and maybe even writing a letter to Billie Jo.

Because he knew where Billie Jo was now. She was in Chicago, working as a governess for a rich Jewish family. They had hired her because she knew French and they wanted their children to grow up speaking two languages. She said she was well and happy, but Oliver had said she didn't sound like it in her letter and that she hadn't even so much as mentioned Phil's name let alone asked about him.

So now—

Fanny went back to her secretary and began to write again but in her own beautiful flowing script this time. She wrote:

> Dearest Oliver,
> When you get this I'll already be over Deadman's Jump and floating. So please come get me out and have the undertaker fix me up so I'll look natural and give me decent burial. I hate to do this but I'm just no good and not even fit to live. I reckon you don't believe I love you, but Oh, I do! I do!
>
> Fanny.

Then she got up and pinned the note to his pillow and turned the pillow upside down so that nobody would see it too soon.

She waited. In a little while he'd go out and ride all around the farm the way he did every evening before coming home to supper and to bed. That was when she would have to steal a gun and ride out to Merry Creek, to Deadman's Jump, and wait there for Willie to come out there and kill him for her when he came. She even knew how she was going to get Willie to kill Oliver but she didn't like to think about that part because it was so bad and ugly and was going to get poor Willie killed, too. She hoped the lynch mob would only shoot Willie instead of burning him the way they sometimes did when a nigger had done something really bad, but that part was out of her hands so thinking about it wouldn't do any good.

The minute she heard Oliver go out she rang the bell for Cindy, who was taking care of her these days now that Lou was too busy getting ready for her wedding to Isaac. Lou didn't have any folks so Oliver was going to give her away in the Church just like he was her father. All of the niggers thought that was just wonderful but the white people were divided. Some thought it was a nice sentimental gesture but the rest thought he was being a damn fool.

Anyhow its being Cindy made things a lot easier because Cindy was so dumb that Louella swore she had foot and mouth disease: "Open her mouf her foot jes' fly up to stick itself in it!"

So now when Cindy came and said:

"Yes 'm?" Fanny smiled at her and said:

"Take this note to Willie, Cindy. He *can* read, can't he?"

"Yes 'm," Cindy said proudly, "as we 'uns kin. Mister Oliver brung a colored gentl'm'n from up Nawth to learn us—"

"Good!" Fanny said. "It's from Lou—reckon it's a kind of a consolation letter to keep him from feeling too bad . . ."

"All right, Miz Fanny—I take it to him right now," Cindy said. And Fanny hugged herself because anybody with a spark of sense would have wondered *when* Lou had been up here to give her the note, and why the devil Lou would have given that kind of note to her mistress who was supposed to be going crazy instead of sending it directly to Willie by one of the girls. But thinking wasn't where Cindy shone. All the same, she didn't forget to lock the door behind her when she went out as Mister Oliver had told her to, so all Fanny could do was to wait for her to come back before putting into practice the second part of her plan.

Which was hideously dangerous. She climbed out of the dormer window, and stood to one side of it on the thatched roof. It had been raining and the rushes were wet and her feet kept slipping out from under her and she didn't dare look down for fear that she'd get dizzy and fall.

But it worked. Cindy came into the room saw she wasn't there saw the opened window looked out of it didn't see anything ran out of the room screaming leaving the door open. Fanny came back down the slant of roof, fell, caught the windowsill just before it was too late hauled herself into the room dashed down the stairs into Oliver's study closed the door behind her locked it.

Stood there, studying those guns. Took his favorite: The Winchester .30-30. Then she looked in the desk drawers until she found boxes of ammunition. But there were so many kinds: 12 gauge, 16 gauge, birdshot, buck-shot, .22 caliber, .44 caliber, .38 caliber, then finally one marked .30/30 so she knew that those had to be the right ones and took them.

She could hear everybody shouting and people saying to look for Mister Oliver, but in spite of that she took the long heavy rifle down from its rack and got out of the back door carrying it without anybody's seeing her mainly because they were were all running *away* from the house, looking for her. In the stable, she threw a blanket over Danny Boy's back tied a rope around his muzzle and climbed up on him. She really didn't know how to ride but the Lord looks after fools and children, so she got to Merry Creek without falling off even once.

Then she slid down off Danny Boy and waited for Willie to come.

While she was waiting she thought it all over very carefully but she didn't see any other way out. She couldn't go to an insane asylum she couldn't. So she'd just have to make Willie kill Oliver that was all. That was very bad but she couldn't help it. Then all of a sudden she remembered she had tried to get Lennie to kill him long before anybody had said anything about the bughouse, so she made an awful grimace that was meant to be a smile, and whispered.

"Reckon I can see things comin' that's all."

Then she heard Willie come clumping through the bushes, so she laid the rifle down on the ground, and put both hands on the bodice of her dress and tore it. After that she tore her chemisette, but she tore it too hard and her left breast came all the way out so that even the nipple was showing. Which was too damn bad but after all a tit was a tit, and if Willie was going to see a white one with a pale pink rosette and a hard little bud standing up in the middle for the first time in his life it wasn't going to do him any good because it was going to be the last time for him, too. Then she scratched her own face with her fingernails so hard she brought blood, and reaching down picked up some dirt and rubbed it all over her face and even into her hair.

By then Willie was very close, and she could hear him calling:

"Lou! Oh Lou, baby, here I is!"

So she said softly.

"Over here, Willie!"

He came towards her. A yard away he stopped. Opened is mouth. Said:

"Lord God!" Then: "Who done hit, Miz Fanny? Who one 'bused you that way?"

She smiled at him very sweetly; said:

"*You*, Willie. Don't you remember?"

"Me? Lordy Jesus! You *is!* Jes like Lou sez, ma'am—beggin' yo' humble pardon—you's plumb out of yo' ever-lovin' mind!"

"What difference does that make, Willie?" Fanny said. "You're still a nigger—and I'm a white wom—lady. And you know what they're going to do to you when I tell 'em what you did to me? They're going to chop off your fingers one by one. Your toes. Your ears. Your lips. And last of all they're going to cut off that long black thing you were always tryin' to shove up poor Lou and ram it down your horny throat!"

"Miz Fanny!" Willie moaned, "I never! You can't do this to me! You purely cain't!"

"Oh can't I though? I can and I will unless—"

"Unless what, ma'am?" Willie said.

"You do what I say."

"Anything, ma'am!" Willie wept, "anything you wants me to!"

"Here," Fanny said, "take this gun. Load it. Here're the bullets—"

Willie loaded the deer rifle with trembling fingers.

"Now," Fanny said. "In a little while Mister Oliver is going to come up that road. When he does—you shoot him, Willie. Dead."

"Oh, Je-e-e-zus!" Willie said. "Miz Fanny you don' know what you's axin'! I cain't! I purely cain't! Mister Oliver he th' bes' white man in th' world. Learned we 'uns how to read 'n write 'n figger. Ain't never kicked 'n cussed us. Ain't never teched a black gal on th' place. All the chilluns real *black* not yaller like on most plantations. He *good*, I tells you, good"

"You shoot him," Fanny said. "Dead. You hear me, Willie!"

Willie stared at her. Made up his mind. Made it up so completely that when he spoke, his voice was quiet.

"Yes 'm, I hears you. But you cain't make me do it Tell them Kluxers anything you wants. I be so damn fa away by t'morrow mawning they don' never ketch me 'Cause I'm a-leavin' here right *now!*"

Then Willie threw the deer rifle down and ran.

That was the first thing that went wrong.

The second was another matter.

When Oliver Prescott started homeward, he saw a rider coming towards him. When the man was close enough he saw that he was Philippe Sompayac. And Philippe was drunk. Gravely, sadly, pitifully drunk.

He put out his hand and let it rest on his nephew-in-law's shoulder.

"Phil," he said gently, "don't you think you ought to quit lappin' 'up that stuff? Never did anybody any good, you know."

Philippe grinned at him, crookedly, said:

"Me. Makes me forget I'm a butcher and a quack and the undertaker's best friend. Makes it possible for me to look in the mirror and see a liar and a coward and a cheatin' adulterer bastard lookin' back at me and not start in to puke—"

Oliver sat there.

"Why I came, lookin' for you. Couldn't stand it any-more. That morning Fanny tried to kill herself I—I put her out—just like I said. But *after*, not before. So now—you know. I've come to offer you what—what—whatever satisfaction you may—demand . . ."

Oliver looked at him. Sighed. Said:

"Phil, do you know what year this is?"

"Yep. Nineteen ought three. Why, Oliver?"

"Thought maybe you were getting it confused with 1820. People don't fight duels anymore, son. And be-sides—You and poor Fanny are hardly a killin' matter, seems to me. But I am going to demand some satisfaction of you, Phil. I've got a letter from Billie Jo right here in my pocket. From Chicago. And the satisfaction I'm de-manding of you, instead of your worthless hide, is that you come home with me right now, to my place. I'll put Tildy to sobering you up. Black coffee—mustard water to make you puke that rotgut up. And tomorrow morning I want you on a train!"

Philippe's eyes took fire. Blazed. Then they dimmed.

"But, sir," he husked, "Billie Jo doesn't want any part of me. Can't say I blame her. I'm a stinking doctor—a miserable husband and—"

"A decent enough man. A fool. But then, who isn't at your age? Get out of medicine, Phil. It's not for you. Go into your father's business. The last time I was in New

Orleans he told me that you were quite good at it. And as for Billie Jo—don't you know yet to *never* pay any attention to what a woman *says* she doesn't want? Go up there, pick her up. Paddle her fundament for her if need be. Then kiss her mouth shut every time she opens it to yell at you. That always works. Believe me, I know!"

"But, sir—about—about what I told you—you aren't—even mad?"

"Sorry, yes. Mad, no. Fanny's—not responsible, Phil. When young Childers comes up from New Orleans, I'm putting her in his care. Even so, I may have to commit her. I hope not; but I may have to. Now, damn it all, you horny young idiot, come on!"

But when they got to Oliver's farm, they found the place in an uproar. Even Louella was hysterical by then. She had gone upstairs to the bedroom to see if Fanny were hiding in the closet or under the bed and found that note. Now she stood there crying and moaning with it in her hand. Oliver took it from her, read it, said:

"Saddle Prince Charlie, for me, Isaac. Even with that delay, I'll gain time. Phil, don't wait for me. Ride on ahead. You're all right now, aren't you? Yes, I see you are. Go to Deadman's Jump. Obsessional behavior, I reckon. She's all set to try the same thing, again—"

"Right, sir!" Philippe said, and clapped spurs to his horse.

Fanny heard those hoofbeats coming on. Oliver, she thought, pulls this thing down, first. Then he aims like this and—The gun slammed into her shoulder, hard. Flame stubbed the dark. She worked the cocking lever again, smoothly, perfectly, she who'd never had a rifle before in her hands in her life. Fired. The sound was slow-rolling, definite, final. But she sighted gleefully on the dark figure reeling in the saddle going back back and put that third bullet through his head.

She threw down the rifle and ran towards where he lay in the road beside his horse. She was giggling laughing pleased with herself she wasn't going to any old insane asylum 'cause he Papa who'd always pushed her off never loved her treated her so mean was—

Then she was kneeling in the road beside him. She put her hand under his head to lift him up. It felt awful. It hadn't any back to it, because that last thirty-thirty had mushroomed going in and made an exit hole she could have shoved her two fists into, leaving all the brains that never had done him much good anyhow lying in the road like a mess of dog vomit. But even so she lifted him up and stared into that face that was staring back at her out of three awful eyes now and she, opening her mouth, said, not screaming it, not even aloud:

"Philippe—"

It was the very last word she ever said.

"It's known as a cataleptic state," Hans Volker said to Billie Jo. "Her body keeps any position its put into. She's absolutely helpless. She has to be fed, bathed—and—and changed, Billie, like a small baby. She doesn't move or speak. She hears nothing. She's shut the world out—"

"The world that was too much with her, late and soon," Oliver said.

"But why did she do it!" Billie sobbed. "She was always swearing he was the only man she ever loved and—"

"She—thought it was—me," Oliver said. "Mighty dark along that road, nights."

"Mighty dark along all life's roads," Hans Volker said, "and nary a star a-glimmering. You want to see her, child? Lou's taking care of her. Oliver had a hell of a time convincing the state parole board she'd be better off here—in his care."

"If she is," Oliver said. "You want to see her, Billie Jo?"

Billie Jo shook her head.

"No," she said. "I don't think so. What good would seeing her do, now?"

"None, I don't suppose," Hans Volker said. "Makes you—think, doesn't it?"

"Think what?" Billie Jo said. "What is there to think [abo]ut, Doctor Hans? A crazy woman—an ex-prostitute—[ruin]ed my husband. A woman who's wrecked, blighted, ru[ined], spoiled, everything she's ever touched and—"

"[T]hat, Billie," Oliver said, "that. The nature of evil, [?] The dimensions of—of tragedy. She—wanted—such [litt]le things: respect, respectability, a place in the world, [?]. And she got—nothing. Not even death when she'd [rea]ched the place she wanted that. She wasn't even al-

lowed to—die. Not all the way, anyhow. So—don't hate
her, Billie. And above all, don't scorn her. She's your sister, child. My daughter, my wife. Universal woman. The
human condition, even—Lord, what sententious rot I'm
talking! Which means I'm tired. So are we all. Too tired,
maybe. Let's go to bed."

Madrid, Spain.                              November 29, 1971.

# BEULAH LAND

by Lonnie Coleman

*the tremendously engrossing saga of a great Georgia plantation in its golden age, and of the men and women, white and black, who were born and died there, knew every pain and pleasure, virtue and vice.*

## BEULAH LAND

*where the old South as it really was is brought to intense life, in all its outward splendor and secret shame.*

## BEULAH LAND

*the novel that everybody's reading, everybody's talking about — and you will never forget.*

*"A Gone With The Wind with sex!"*—*Chicago Tribune*

### A DELL BOOK $1.95

At your local bookstore or use this handy coupon for ordering: